P9-BXX-842

THE MARK TWAIN PAPERS

THE MARK TWAIN PAPERS

Of the projected fifteen volumes of this edition of
Mark Twain's previously unpublished works
the following have been issued to date:

MARK TWAIN'S LETTERS TO HIS PUBLISHERS, 1867–1894
edited by Hamlin Hill

MARK TWAIN'S SATIRES & BURLESQUES
edited by Franklin R. Rogers

MARK TWAIN'S WHICH WAS THE DREAM?
edited by John S. Tuckey

MARK TWAIN'S HANNIBAL, HUCK & TOM
edited by Walter Blair

MARK TWAIN'S MYSTERIOUS STRANGER MANUSCRIPTS
edited by William M. Gibson

MARK TWAIN'S CORRESPONDENCE WITH HENRY HUTTLESTON ROGERS
edited by Lewis Leary

MARK TWAIN'S FABLES OF MAN
edited by John S. Tuckey

MARK TWAIN'S

FABLES

OF MAN

Edited with an Introduction by John S. Tuckey

*Text Established by Kenneth M. Sanderson
and Bernard L. Stein*

Series Editor Frederick Anderson

Mark Twain

UNIVERSITY OF CALIFORNIA PRESS
Berkeley, Los Angeles, London

CENTER FOR EDITIONS OF
AMERICAN AUTHORS

AN APPROVED TEXT

MODERN LANGUAGE
ASSOCIATION OF AMERICA

®

Editorial expenses for this volume have been
in large part supported by grants from the
National Endowment for the Humanities
administered through the Center for Editions of
American Authors of the Modern Language Association.

UNIVERSITY OF CALIFORNIA PRESS
Berkeley and Los Angeles, California

UNIVERSITY OF CALIFORNIA PRESS, LTD.
London, England

Designed by Adrian Wilson
in collaboration with James Mennick

Manufactured in the United States of America

Acknowledgments

DURING the past eight months, preparation of this volume has gone forward in the Mark Twain Papers at The Bancroft Library of the University of California, Berkeley. My thanks go first to Frederick Anderson, Editor of the Mark Twain Papers, and to those who have worked under his direction: the team for textual work that includes Kenneth M. Sanderson, Bernard L. Stein, Victor Fischer, Susan Sheffield, Linda Mullen, and Sharron Brown, and the research team of Michael B. Frank, Alan D. Gribben, Robert Hirst, and Lin Salamo.

Henry Nash Smith of the University of California gave me the benefit of his wise suggestions at the time that the volume was beginning to take shape. Matthew J. Bruccoli of the University of South Carolina provided valuable advice on textual matters. Norman S. Grabo of the University of California examined the manuscript as the representative of the Center for Editions of American Authors of the Modern Language Association and offered helpful suggestions. Howard Baetzhold of Butler University, Walter Blair of the University of Chicago, Louis J. Budd of Duke University, and Robert Regan of the University of Pennsylvania all gave me useful information and ideas.

The generous decision by Doris Webster to establish the Samuel Charles Webster Memorial Fund with a bequest to the University of California in 1968 provides continuing support for editorial costs in

v

the Mark Twain Papers. Much of the work on this volume was supported by that bequest.

The Center for Editions of American Authors generously provided funds in support of my editorial work during the summer of 1970. A sabbatical leave from Purdue University in 1967 was partly devoted to preliminary work upon the present volume, and my thanks go to Vice President C. H. Lawshe and Deans G. W. Bergren, Carl H. Elliott, and Richard J. Combs of Purdue for their assistance and their continued interest in my work. I am grateful for the assistance of the staff of the Rare Books Collection of The Bancroft Library at the University of California, Berkeley. I thank my wife, Irene, and our children, Janis and Alan, for their continued indulgence of editorial efforts that have often taken me away from home.

JOHN S. TUCKEY

January 1971

Contents

vii

Abbreviations

THE FOLLOWING abbreviations have been used for citations in the notes in this volume. Unless otherwise indicated, all manuscripts are in the Mark Twain Papers, Bancroft Library, University of California, Berkeley. Unpublished writings are identified by the number assigned to the manuscripts in the files of the Mark Twain Papers.

MS	Manuscript
MT	Mark Twain
MTP	Mark Twain Papers, Bancroft Library, University of California, Berkeley
SLC	Samuel L. Clemens
TS	Typescript

Published Works Cited

DE	*The Writings of Mark Twain,* Definitive Edition (New York: Gabriel Wells, 1922–1925)
LE	*Letters from the Earth,* ed. Bernard DeVoto (New York: Harper & Row, 1962)
MSM	*Mark Twain's Mysterious Stranger Manuscripts,* ed. William M. Gibson (Berkeley and Los Angeles: University of California Press, 1969)

MTA   *Mark Twain's Autobiography*, ed. Albert Bigelow Paine
             (New York: Harper & Brothers, 1924)

MTB   Albert Bigelow Paine, *Mark Twain: A Biography* (New
             York: Harper & Brothers, 1912)

MT&GWC   Arlin Turner, *Mark Twain and G. W. Cable* (East
             Lansing: Michigan State University Press, 1960)

MTHHR   *Mark Twain's Correspondence with Henry Huttleston
             Rogers*, ed. Lewis Leary (Berkeley and Los Angeles:
             University of California Press, 1969)

MTHL   *Mark Twain-Howells Letters*, ed. Henry Nash Smith
             and William M. Gibson (Cambridge: Harvard Uni-
             versity Press, Belknap Press, 1960)

MTSP   Louis J. Budd, *Mark Twain: Social Philosopher*
             (Bloomington: Indiana University Press, 1962)

NAR   *North American Review*

WWD   *Mark Twain's Which Was the Dream? and Other
             Symbolic Writings of the Later Years*, ed. John S.
             Tuckey (Berkeley and Los Angeles: University of Cal-
             ifornia Press, 1966)

Introduction

THIS COLLECTION offers Mark Twain's outspoken pieces on such large topics as God, providence, Christianity, and human nature, gathered from the unpublished writings in the Mark Twain Papers. Although Albert Bigelow Paine and Bernard DeVoto printed some of the works included here and various scholars have quoted excerpts in support of their arguments, none of these texts has ever appeared in an authoritative printing, and few are currently accessible. The volume includes the "Little Bessie" dialogues, in which a small girl horrifies her sanctimonious mother with probing questions about the Virgin Birth, and also a satirical tale, "The Second Advent," which places the return of the Messiah in a sleepy Arkansas village and recounts the disastrous consequences of the miracles wrought by his disciples. It also presents, in "The Secret History of Eddypus, the World-Empire," an expression of Clemens' philosophy of history and vision of the future. In a number of pieces, most notably "The Refuge of the Derelicts," it gives further disclosures, clothed in fiction, of what may have been Clemens' view of the human situation.

Such merits will be deemed slight or considerable depending upon the interests of the reader. Those who are mainly concerned with literary form will find little to value: the two principal manuscripts "Derelicts" and "Eddypus," both of which were left unfinished, are decidedly lacking in integration. Many of the shorter selections are, however, either substantially or entirely complete, and two of them, in fact, were sent by Clemens to Harper's for publication. " 'You've Been a Dam Fool, Mary. You Always Was!' " was forwarded to that house in February 1904 but failed to appear in print—probably because the mildly profane title was considered unacceptable. The letters between Clemens and his publishers concerning proposed revisions of the title are discussed in the headnote to the story. "The International Lightning Trust" was fully prepared for the press in 1909 and was in the hands of Harper & Brothers when Clemens died in 1910; it was withdrawn by his literary executor, Paine, who noted that the manuscript was not up to the author's standard. One can agree that the story is not at the level of his better work and yet suspect that it was the irreverent cast of the contents, which satirized the concept of special providences as well as shady trust operations, that caused it to be judged unsuitable for print. It is fair to add that Clemens himself interdicted publication of some of his work—especially, many sections of autobiography—until a distant future time; for some parts dealing with religion, he desired a waiting period of five hundred years. "The Second Advent," "The Holy Children," and the "Little Bessie" chapters he no doubt considered too strong for print. Even "Mock Marriage," much of which reads like a conventional romance, could have seemed offensive for the times: "Never mind what God can do; the matter on hand is what He *has* done. If He meant it for a benefaction it has miscarried, and you know it." "The Stupendous Procession," satirizing the condition of world civilization at the beginning of the twentieth century, is if possible even more controversial than the essays "To the Person Sitting in Darkness" and "To My Missionary Critics," published in 1901, and it hits at more targets close to home. It was probably withheld from print not for its stylistic defects so much as for its outspoken contents. Some plaints such as "In My Bitterness" and "The Private Secretary's Diary" may have remained unpublished because he thought of them as expressions of a private grief.

A few of the selections were written relatively early—in the 1870s and 1880s. These include "The Holy Children," "The Second Advent," "The Lost Ear-ring," "A Letter from the Comet," "The Emperor-God Satire," "Colloquy Between a Slum Child and a Moral Mentor," and "Abner L. Jackson (About to Be) Deceased." The others, comprising about four-fifths of the total contents, were composed in the 1890s or in the first decade of the new century; most were written after 1895, or after Clemens had entered his sixties. These materials do not exhaust from the Mark Twain Papers every still unpublished story, sketch, or essay; a later volume of miscellaneous writings is planned which will incorporate such remainders.

It was only after the main body of writings had been tentatively selected in terms of evident relationships that an underlying pattern emerged. It appeared that these were mostly fantasy pieces or fables: Mark Twain had let his imagination rove freely over events that he saw as representative or symbolic of the nature and condition of man, past, present, or yet to be. And it seemed that the contents might be grouped in three sections, designated as "The Myth of Providence," "The Dream of Brotherhood," and "The Nightmare of History." Generally speaking, these sections include, in the order given: (1) satirical writings on what Mark Twain saw as the outworn but still confining myths of an exploded, prescientific view of man and the universe, from which man's imagination needed to be freed; (2) representations of the dubious possibilities for a true brotherhood of man; (3) writings in which past and present conditions are seen as portending a darkened future in which a new religious myth would once more captivate and enslave man and in which still later equivalent myths, through the ages, would die and be recreated endlessly. These categories are not intended to be mutually exclusive and could not be.

Mark Twain's view of the human predicament as conveyed in the writings now published is a rather grim one, even though there are indications that he had not given himself over wholly to despair. It recognizes man as the creature of an unavailing god, a creator immensely above and remote from man—at best indifferent, at worst, vindictive. It contemplates a basely made, a destructively crafted human race that actually collaborates in its own degradation. Finally, it shows man to be on a treadmill of repeating history from which, made as he is, he is powerless to escape. What might otherwise be the unrelieved pessimism of such an outlook is mitigated by humor and irony

and by the tender-heartedness that is in contention with the works'
tough-mindedness.

The Myth of Providence

In June 1906, Clemens explained in his Autobiographical Dictation his idea of the real God. Less than consistent, he first represented
God as grandly aloof, little concerned with earthly matters, which
were only a microscopic part of his immense design; but then Clemens
worked himself up to a bitter denunciation of God for contriving
countless afflictions for the torture of man and his fellow creatures.
Both of these concepts have been given literary development in writings included in this volume. One point of "The Emperor-God Satire,"
for example, is the absurdity of God's being constantly and minutely
concerned with the affairs of a minor tribe inhabiting one tiny part of
his realm. And one lesson of both "The Holy Children" and "The
Second Advent" is that even if he were aware of people's prayers and
disposed to grant them, his interventions would be catastrophic for
human society. "In My Bitterness," "The Synod of Praise," "Little
Bessie," and "The Private Secretary's Diary" are among the works in-
dicting God for malevolence. The God these works show is one who
does nothing for the specific good of man. In time of trouble he is
unavailing, either because he is remote and indifferent or because he
is maliciously omnipresent.

Some selections even hint that the determiner of others' destiny
is the ultimate predator upon the creatures he controls. In "Goose
Fable," the geese think of man as their deity, and little goslings are
taught to expect every kindness and blessing from the human race.
The idea of "The Victims" is that all living creatures are so made that
they must feed upon other living things. The real hierarchy of existence is the order of precedence in a universal cannibalism. And in
Mark Twain's view it is God who is solely responsible for so ordering
things that none can decline this grisly banquet—and live. Moreover,
the inescapable roles of predator and victim condition many aspects
of life other than that of survival. The world and its resources are at
the disposal of cynical exploiters who know the human race and how

to trade upon its weaknesses of fear and pride and greed. Jasper Hackett and Stephen Spaulding are such characters in "The International Lightning Trust," and as the story ends they are well on their way to achieving economic, political, and religious control of the world. This fantasy resembles that of the creation of a world empire in "Eddypus": in both works great power is acquired by successful, if unwitting, charlatans who contrive to put providence on a paying basis.

The foolish readiness of the race to accept myths of providence is repeatedly satirized. In the "Little Bessie" dialogues Bessie's searching questions expose her mother's unthinking acceptance of religious fables and platitudes—an inversion of a device Clemens had used much earlier in "The Story of Mamie Grant, the Child-Missionary" in which it is the child who voices Sunday school sentiments and a blasphemous adult who opposes them.[1] "Colloquy Between a Slum Child and a Moral Mentor" not only satirizes middle-class "church" morality but also suggests that people are too ready to credit the Almighty for good deeds: a penniless waif in wintertime with nothing but a window shutter for a blanket acknowledges that God has indeed been taking special care of him when he realizes that not every child has a shutter to sleep under. In "The Lost Ear-ring" there is much concern over a young lady's loss of an earring of no real value, and providence gets full credit for restoring it to her when it is discovered that the trinket has fallen into her apron pocket.

Of the manuscripts satirizing the notion of special providences, the one of greatest interest is probably "The Second Advent." It was mentioned by Paine in his discussion of Mark Twain's earlier unpublished writings:

> Among the abandoned literary undertakings of these early years of authorship there is the beginning of what was doubtless intended to become a book, "The Second Advent," a story which opens with a very doubtful miraculous conception in Arkansas, and leads only to grotesquery and literary disorder.[2]

---

[1] *Mark Twain's Satires & Burlesques*, ed. Franklin R. Rogers (Berkeley and Los Angeles: University of California Press, 1967), p. 31.

[2] *MTB*, p. 561.

With reference to "The Second Advent," along with other pigeon-holed manuscripts, Paine wrote, "To Howells and others, when they came along, he would read the discarded yarns, and they were delightful enough for such a purpose, as delightful as the sketches which every artist has, turned face to the wall."[3] Mark Twain's mention of the year 1881 at the end of the tale appears to provide the date of composition. "The Holy Children," from which pages were appropriated for use in "The Second Advent," must have been written first. "The Holy Children" has been reconstructed here, by retrieving the pages that had been incorporated in "The Second Advent" and restoring their original text. There is necessarily, then, some duplication of content in the two selections; but it has seemed worthwhile to recover the earlier sketch, since it differs considerably from "The Second Advent." In writing "The Second Advent," Mark Twain was probably drawing on observations he had made on board the *Quaker City*, which had taken him to the Holy Land in 1867. "Imagine Christ's 30 years of life in the slow village of Nazareth,"[4] he wrote in his notebook at that time. His musings also included the idea that an unleashing of miraculous powers in such a village could cause trouble: "Recall infant Christ's pranks on his school-mates—striking boys dead—withering their hands —burning the dyer's cloth &c."[5] The idea of the direct and heavy consequences of fulfilled prayers had also come to him: "Orders executed with promptness & dispatch.—Particular attention given to thrones &c."[6] The impulse to comment on the Advent and the other miracles was not fully satisfied by what he wrote of "The Second Advent" and "The Holy Children," as later notes reveal. In May or June of 1883 he noted, "Write the Second Advent, with full details—lot of Irish disciples—Paddy Ryan for Judas & other disciples."[7] Later still, in his notebook for 1901, one finds a further evolution of the story concept:

Second Advent. Begins triumphal march around the globe at Tien Tsin preceded by Generals, Warships, cavalry, infantry, artillery, who clear

[3] *MTB*, p. 561.
[4] Notebook 8, TS p. 39.
[5] Notebook 9, TS p. 13.
[6] Ibid., pp. 13–14.
[7] Notebook 17, TS p. 8.

the road & pile the dead & ⟨the loot⟩ for "propagation of the Gospel," followed by looting mish singing "where every prospect pleases & only man is vile." Christ arrives in a vast war-fleet furnished by the Great Powers.[8]

The various elements of this satiric impulse produced "The Second Advent," "The Stupendous Procession," "To the Person Sitting in Darkness," and "To My Missionary Critics." In passages of "The Chronicle of Young Satan," the earliest manuscript of *The Mysterious Stranger*, written between 1897 and 1900, he had already expressed some of his wrath. As the nineteenth century concluded and the twentieth began, he found the world scene darkened by military actions of the so-called Christian powers; nation preyed upon nation, the strong upon the weak. "The time is grave," he wrote. "The future is blacker than has been any future which any person now living has tried to peer into."[9]

Aspects of his personal life had darkened as well: in the mid-nineties he had been overwhelmed by the death of his daughter Susy, had faced the discovery that her sister Jean was an epileptic, and had become bankrupt. In the following years his wife, Olivia, who had never been strong, continued to fail in health. Some of the writings blaming God and nature for cruelties inflicted upon human beings were obviously prompted by these family disasters; for example, "In My Bitterness," written in the summer of 1897 at about the time of the first anniversary of Susy's death, is a direct cry of the heart. "The Victims," written between 1900 and 1905 and most probably in 1902—the year in which Olivia was stricken with what proved to be her final illness—is hardly less bitter in its arraignment. "The Synod of Praise," which belongs to the same period, employs satiric indirection but arrives at the last at a sardonic jest: confronted with the proposition that God is "our loving father," the monkey does as well as he can to be dutifully thankful, "My praise is that we have not two of him."

Yet there was likely to be fun as well as fury behind even the thrusts that were at the expense of an unavailing providence. And it is worth noting that one of the "Little Bessie" chapters was written while

---

[8] Notebook 34, TS pp. 20–21. Angle brackets show Clemens' deletion.
[9] "The Missionary in World-Politics," DV 393.

Clemens was on a yachting trip with his friend and financial adviser, Henry H. Rogers. While lazing about on the commodious *Kanawha* off Bermuda, he wrote "Little Bessie Would Assist Providence." The cover sheet of his typescript copy is dated "On shipboard, Feb. 22, 1908," below which Clemens added in ink, "(It is dull, & I need wholesome excitements & distractions; so I will go lightly excursioning along the primrose path of theology.)" The circumstances under which he wrote are strikingly incongruous: we see Clemens surrounded by luxury and beauty—even dulled, sated, with these—lounging in his deck chair while writing about the persecutions of providence. Such sidelights should not be ignored if we are to have a balanced view of Mark Twain's work. And it would be perilous, especially in the present instance, to assume that he did not see and relish these contrasts.

The Dream of Brotherhood

The concern with providence carries over into this section, and indeed through the following one, but with differing emphases. Here we see Clemens primarily concerned with man's own efforts to provide for his fellow man in the absence of assistance from a higher providence. Lacking a benevolent Heavenly Father, might not the Brotherhood of Man suffice for the betterment of the human condition? Clemens was not at all sure that it could, although he was willing to look at evidence. As Louis J. Budd has noticed, in the early 1900s Clemens had much in mind the phrase "the brotherhood of man" and the ideal that it expressed.[10] Recent military action in China, South Africa, Cuba, and the Philippines had, however, deepened his skepticism, and the Russo-Japanese War of 1904/1905 gave him no basis for reviving hope. War was the antithesis of brotherhood; and so, he believed, was the kind of patriotism that was praised and demanded in times of war. In "The Lowest Animal" he observed: "For many centuries 'the common brotherhood of man' has been urged—on Sundays—and 'patriotism' on Sundays and weekdays both. Yet patriotism *contemplates the opposite of a common brotherhood.*"[11]

---

[10] *MTSP*, pp. 189–190.
[11] *LE*, p. 222.

Man would, he feared, continue to make war over lands and boundaries. And he saw that people were also denying the brotherly ideal in enforcing boundaries of race or class; this must have been the point of a brief sketch, now lost, called "The Brotherhood of Man," probably written in the spring of 1905 at about the time that he was beginning work upon "The Refuge of the Derelicts." A good deal of background information about the composition of "Derelicts" may be found in the journal of his secretary, Miss Isabel V. Lyon, who was often his listener for manuscript readings. On March 21 Miss Lyon noted:

> Tonight Mr. Clemens read a very interesting unpublishable sketch. Unpublishable because it is what an old darkey says of the universal brotherhood of man—& how it couldn't ever be, not even in heaven—for there are only white angels there & in the old darkey's vision the niggers were all sent around to the back door. It's a wonderful little sketch but it wouldn't do for the clergy. They couldn't stand it. It's too true.[12]

The particular relevance of this missing manuscript to "Derelicts" may be seen from Mark Twain's working notes for the latter, in which he wrote, "John T. Lewis is the Brotherhood Man," subsequently changing the name from the actual one of Lewis to the fictional one of 'Rastus Timson. Lewis, a Negro farmhand, had at great risk saved the lives of Mrs. Charles Langdon, her daughter, and a nursemaid in an incident like the one narrated in "Derelicts." The rescue occurred when their horse ran away near the home of Susan Crane, Mrs. Clemens' sister and owner of the farm where Lewis worked. He was handsomely rewarded with about fifteen hundred dollars, as well as other gifts, and later received, through the agency of Clemens, some pension funds from Henry H. Rogers. It appears that he accepted these tributes graciously and with gratitude and that he never claimed—as Aunty Phyllis does in the story—that he had been paid only for saving the horse and buggy, not for saving three lives. But of course Lewis, after being feted and rewarded, inescapably remained a Negro farmhand; his status had not essentially changed, though his poverty had been alleviated. Perhaps "the old darkey's vision" did apply to the situation

---

[12] Isabel V. Lyon, Journal, original in MTP.

of Lewis—and that of the fictional 'Rastus—showing how impossible it was, even in the most favorable circumstances, for the black man to have social equality. This was the darker side of the matter, even if comically treated, that obtruded itself into a story bent upon examining into the possibilities for human brotherhood—for unselfish sharing and refusal to exploit others which run counter to the doctrine of human selfishness advanced in *What Is Man?*

The strong, generous, profane, and garrulous old Admiral Stormfield maintains a home that is fitted out like a ship and is run like one. He lets this place serve as a haven for human derelicts. These are persons who are no longer contending for power, prestige, and success, who are not seeking to take advantage of others. They have declined the role of predator, or tried to, and are considered failures—and some have at length regretted not having been less altruistic and more successful. A major theme of "The Refuge of the Derelicts" is the failure of the just—a reversal of the Puritan ethic. Riches and human fulfillment are seen as the reward not of virtue but of wickedness. Or rather, of being human, for it is man's nature to feed upon and otherwise exploit others. Ironically, even the derelicts, resigned and harmless as they seem to be, are still among the devourers. They are feeding upon the Admiral's bounty, and it is fitting that on the occasion of their Plum Duff, an entertainment night with "intellectual raisins in it," they are shown in an illustrated lecture how parasites necessarily treat their host. In this last part of the manuscript a sequence of horrific motion-picture close-ups (relatively new in 1906) is projected before the assembled derelicts while a sanctimonious lecturer develops the topic of the bounty and goodness of providence (later Mark Twain substituted "Nature" in this episode wherever he had first written "Providence"). The illustrative pictures have been gathered together at the last moment, and it turns out that they are wildly out of keeping with the reassuring text of the speaker. A mother spider is shown trusting happily that food will be provided for her numerous brood of spiderlings—only to find that *she* is their food as they suddenly rush upon her and begin to devour her. A wasp then stings the mother spider to provide food for *her* young—and so on. Mark Twain's working notes envision that even the Admiral will eventually fail, and it is possible that if the story had been completed it would have shown Stormfield finally "eaten out of house and home." At any rate, the Plum Duff Night incident implies that everyone lives by destroying others, that no one can abstain from the general carnage.

Mark Twain nevertheless recognizes man's attempts to rise above the conditions of life imposed by his maker. In "Derelicts" there are several characters who display attributes of true brotherliness. There is Smith, who in reading daily newspaper accounts of tragedies suffered by strangers grieves for them as much as a person ordinarily would for his own loved ones. Smith is following the law of *his* nature, which is to be transcendently sensitive. As the bos'n, the Admiral's right-hand man, explains to the narrator George Sterling, "Smith, he can't help the way *he's* made. Land, he takes the whole suffering world into his heart. . . . Why, Mr. Sterling, that man takes into his inside enough of the human race's miseries in a day to last a real manly man thirty years!" One recalls Clemens' own sensitivity to the news, as confided to William Dean Howells: "I have been reading the morning paper. I do it every morning—well knowing that I shall find in it the usual depravities and basenesses & hypocricies & cruelties that make up Civilization, & cause me to put in the rest of the day pleading for the damnation of the human race."[13] It should not be overlooked that it was immediate sympathetic responsiveness like Smith's that would prompt Clemens' later blasphemous outbursts. There is likewise a good deal of Clemens in Sterling, who learns that there are no insignificant people and who learns to care enough about others of the brotherhood to seek out the important events, the news, of their lives. As an artist, Sterling not only makes physical portraits of the derelicts but while doing so obtains their "psychographs":

> they sit around and chat, they smoke and read, and the Admiral "pays the freight," as the slang phrase goes. And they sit to me. They take an interest in each other's portraits, and are candid with criticisms. They talk to me about themselves, and about each other. Thus I get the entire man—four-fifths of him from himself and the other fifth from the others. I find that no man discloses the completing fifth himself. Sometimes

---

[13] *MTHL*, p. 691.

that fifth is to his credit, sometimes it isn't; but let it be whichever it may, you will never get it out of the man himself. It is the make of the man that determines it. The bos'n says there are no exceptions to this law. He says every man is a moon and has a side which he turns toward nobody: you have to slip around behind if you want to see it.

Sterling finds himself in the situation of a young shipmate receiving instructions from the bos'n regarding the universal brotherhood of the human race. By such tutelage he has been learning that everyone matters. He has, for example, become aware of the tenderhearted Smith as a person worth knowing:

> Formerly if a person had said to me, "Would you like to know Smith the letter-carrier?" it would not have occurred to me to say yes. But I should say it now, believing as I now do that a man's occupation is not a mirror of his inside; and so I should want to know Smith and try to get at his interior, expecting it to be well charged with interest for me.

The disaster of Smith's life had been that, living beyond his means, he had fallen to stealing and had been caught and imprisoned. Mark Twain's progress in the composition of "Derelicts" can be measured by his use of the mail-theft incident, which was drawn from actual life. On 2 April 1905 Miss Lyon noted in her journal that she had been "searching through the multitudinous letters in the study for the one that gives the true history of 'the Postman who stole from the Mails,' and to furnish the material for the chapter in the Admiral Story." By that time the author had apparently reached page 122 of the 309-page manuscript.

The premise that every life contains an important story also underlies the other tragedies of the lowly in "Derelicts." On this subject the writing flowed easily. Miss Lyon noted on April 10, "Mr. Clemens reads to Jean & me in the evenings, his ms of the Admiral Story. . . . Mr. Clemens does probe so into understandings of humanity. He appreciates the beauty of many lives, the fearful tragedies of them, but he won't admit that they're anything but machines." The latest mention of work on the story that spring was Miss Lyon's entry of April 27: "Tonight Mr. Clemens read more of the Admiral Story."

In May of 1905 Clemens settled at Dublin, New Hampshire, for a long summer stay that was to include much literary work. He wrote "Three Thousand Years Among the Microbes" between May 20 and June 23, then composed his "Apostrophe to Death" and at the end of June continued work on the manuscript of *The Mysterious Stranger* that had occupied him in Florence during the preceding year. Discontinuing work on the latter story by about July 12, he wrote "Eve's Diary" and revised the earlier "Adam's Diary." Thereafter the pace of composition slackened, but during the remainder of the stay at Dublin, which lasted into October, he did a little more work on *What Is Man?* and wrote "Interpreting the Deity" and "A Horse's Tale." There is no indication of any more work on the "Derelicts" manuscript, however, until Clemens returned to Dublin for the summer of 1906. The latter part of the manuscript was written that June, when he was spending his mornings in autobiographical dictation and some of his afternoons in work with pen and paper. On 9 June 1906, he wrote to his daughter Clara:

> There's been no way to kill time, after my 2 hours of dictation, mornings, and I was likely to die of the boredom of it. But now I am saved. I have come across a story whose two heroes are Bambino and an old Admiral, and am enthused by it, and am going straight to work and finish it. It will take a couple of months; and so, my afternoons will not be dreary hereafter.[14]

Clemens was determined to escape the dreariness, but the battle was evidently one he had to fight daily. His morning dictation of June 11 analyzed his problem: the house he had taken for that summer stood in the middle of a "spacious paradise," but there was "the defect of loneliness. We have not a single neighbor, who is a neighbor. . . . My social life has to be limited to the friends who come to me. I can't very well go to them, because I don't like driving, and I am much too indolent to walk. The rest of the household walk and drive, daily, and thereby they survive. But I am not surviving. I am in a trance. When I have dictated a couple of hours in the forenoon I don't know what to do with myself until ten o'clock next day. Sometimes the household

---

[14] Bambino, renamed Bagheera, appears prominently in the opening pages of the story as the Admiral's cat.

are so melancholy that it ceases to be pathetic and becomes funny. Some member of it has given the house a masonic name, The Lodge of Sorrow." With a characteristic blending of irony and pathos, he added, "The Garden of Eden I now know was an unendurable solitude. I know that the advent of the serpent was a welcome change—anything for society."

It appears that the desire to work on "Derelicts" had not been strong enough to keep on filling those empty afternoons. Within the next two days, he had turned for the moment to another pigeonholed piece. Miss Lyon's journal reveals that on June 13 he "read from a ms. he wrote 30 years ago: 'Captain Stormfield's visit to Heaven'" and on June 14 "read the most readable part of the second part." It was an easy transition for Clemens' thoughts—from his story of Admiral Stormfield to that of the captain of the same name who soul-journeys through heaven. But he probably continued writing "Derelicts" at least intermittently during the middle part of June. The need that his composition was helping to meet is evident in George Sterling's insistence that life is *not* empty:

> The past few days have been like all the days I have spent in this house—full of satisfactions for me. Every day the feeling of the day before is renewed to me—the feeling of having been in a half-trance all my life before—numb, sluggish-blooded, sluggish-minded—a feeling which is followed at once by a brisk sense of being out of that syncope and awake! awake and alive; alive to my finger-ends. I realize that I am a veteran trader in shadows who has struck the substance. I have found the human race. It was all around me before, but vague and spectral; I have found it now, with the blood in it, and the bones; and am getting acquainted with it. . . . Incidentally, I am also getting acquainted with myself.

Lesser insights expressed by a creative artist about his work have passed for profundity, but Clemens seldom took the trouble to seem profound. There is something impressive and touching about this seventy-year-old man's attempt to charge the dust of an empty room with life by will and imagination; or in his ability to find the hot heart's truth of life in a dusty packet of forgotten letters—as Miss Lyon reported in her journal, "In an old sack of letters sent . . . from Keokuk about 5 years ago he unearthed a batch of 5 letters this morning which are a romance & a tragedy." These letters had apparently been turned over to him by Mollie Clemens, the widow of his brother Orion. The five selected letters unfolded the story of a pregnant young woman who had been deserted by her married lover. In his dictation of that morning of June 18 he said:

> I was never expecting to become industrious enough to overhaul that sack and examine its contents, but now that I am doing this autobiography the joys and sorrows of everybody, high and low, rich and poor, famous and obscure, are dear to me. I can take their heart affairs into my heart as I never could before. In becoming my own biographer I realize that I have become the biographer of Tom, Dick, and Harry, the voiceless. I recognize that Tom and I are intimates; that be he young or be he old, he has never felt anything that I have not felt; he has never had an emotion that I am a stranger to.

Here Clemens may be seen taking the character he projected for Smith, the sympathizer for his race, as he was its spokesman when he put into "Derelicts" little biographies of the failed and the voiceless.

There is a further parallel between his morning dictation and his afternoon writing. Beginning on the following day, June 19, he held forth for several mornings "About the Character of God, as represented in the New and the Old Testaments"; on "The defects about Bibles —Remarks about the Immaculate Conception" (June 20); on "Evil influence of the Bible upon children" (June 22); and "Concerning the Character of the real God" (June 23). These preoccupations go far to explain the abrupt shift in tone and subject when "Derelicts" reaches the episode of the Plum Duff Night. The dictation of June 23 had in part dealt with such cruelties. In it he had spoken of the spider "so contrived" that she "must catch flies and such things, and inflict a slow and horrible death upon them, unaware that her turn would come next," and of the wasp "so contrived that he also would . . . stab the spider, not conferring upon her a swift and merciful death but merely half paralyzing her, then ramming her down into the wasp den, there to live and suffer for days while the wasp babies should chew her legs off at their leisure." There is a good chance that such things in "Derelicts" were written on the same afternoon. Quite possibly he wrote on June 23 all eighteen pages of the final episode of his manuscript, for he was still capable of producing that much (about 2,000 words) when he was full of something that demanded expression. The last part of the story provides an ironic reversal that springs a tragedy-trap upon the derelicts (and also upon the reader). It is possible that he had at this point fulfilled his satiric intention and had thus satisfied one of the main impulses for composition.

The evidence regarding the chances for brotherhood was not, however, all negative. Just as in "Derelicts" there are characters who feel for others as for themselves, there are in other of these writings figures who are capable of altruism. In "Newhouse's Jew Story" and "Randall's Jew Story" a Jewish stranger risks his own life to save a worthy planter from ruin and death at the hands of a cutthroat gambler. In " 'You've Been a Dam Fool, Mary. You Always Was!' " an "honest rebel" refuses to take advantage of a former partner, a Northerner, when it would be easy and extremely profitable to do so. But these instances are minority reports; they go against the main body of testimony. They amount to lesser analogues of the exception Mark Twain had made for Joan of Arc as "that sublime personality, that spirit which in one regard has had no peer and will have none—this: its purity from all alloy of self-seeking, self-interest, personal ambition. In it no trace of these motives can be found, search as you may, and this cannot be said of any other person whose name appears in profane history."[15] Except for such rare spirits, the common condition of man was one of impurity and selfishness. Clemens saw the members of the human "brotherhood" as true children of the original Adam in their ignorance, folly, and perversity—qualities which usually proved stronger than their wistful good-heartedness. And Adam, it should be noted, figures in a secondary theme of "Derelicts"; in fact, the story has been known to scholars as the "Adam Monument Manuscript." The particular foible of George Sterling is his dream of building a monument to Adam. Clemens was here making literary capital of a proposal that he had once conceived, certainly as a hoax: in the 1880s he had persuaded the town of Elmira, New York, to request that the Congress

---

[15] Joan of Arc, DE 18:287.

of the United States grant their town the exclusive right to erect such a monument to the founder of the race. Clemens must have relished the petition as a revealing instance of human folly in which the very figure that should symbolize the united family of man, the universal brotherhood, had been made the object of a contentious local patriotism. The brotherhood of man, he believed, could not survive where there was boundary-enforcing selfishness. The point of Clemens' rueful joke is seen, finally, in the reasons for which Adam is said to deserve a monument. When Sterling tries to interest Smith in the monument scheme, the latter responds to the mention of Adam in a way worthy of Clemens himself:

> It was like Vesuvius in eruption. Lava, flame, earthquake, sulphurous smoke, volleying explosions—it was all there, and all vindictive and unappeasable hostility and aversion. I sat enchanted, dumb, astonished, glad to be there, sorry when the show was over.
>
> One would have supposed Smith was talking about an intimate enemy —an enemy of last week, of yesterday, of to-day, not of a man whom he had never seen, and who had been dust and ashes for thousands of years. The reason for all this bitter feeling? It was very simple.
>
> "*He brought life into the world*," said Smith. "But for him I should not have been born—nor Mary. Life is a swindle. I hate him."
>
> After a panting moment or two he brought forth another surprise for me. To-wit, he was unreservedly and enthusiastically in favor of the monument! In a moment he was in eruption again. This time it was praises of Adam, gratitude to Adam, exaltation of his name. The reason of *this* attitude? Smith explained it without difficulty:
>
> "*He brought death into the world. I love him for it.*"

According to the working notes, however, at least one character in "Derelicts" was not to accept the idea of the monument; the lowly 'Rastus, the hero of the runaway horse incident, was to say, "Father er de Brotherhood? Buil' a monument to *him?* No s'r!"

There was another aspect to the monument joke; man's natural selfishness resists voluntary subscriptions for such tributes—and will also resist being taxed for them. In "Concerning Martyrs' Day" Mark Twain made the tongue-in-cheek proposal that everyone "be required by Congress to contribute" a "day's earnings to an *annual Monument*" and then carried the idea to full absurdity: "I would have the government architect plan a prodigious Monument which could go on climbing toward the sky, stage by stage and year by year, for a thousand years." In the earlier of the two endings that Mark Twain wrote for "Abner L. Jackson (About to Be) Deceased," the hypocritical Jackson, whose answer to the swindle of life is an insurance swindle based upon his own death, includes in his will a sum for a monument to Adam. In his willingness to spend the money of *others* for this purpose he was acting according to his make and in Clemens' view was showing himself to be a true son of the father of the brotherhood.

The Nightmare of History

Well before the end of the last century the author had come to suspect that the brotherhood of man was unattainable; that man's desire for power was stronger than his desire for love; that selfishness, not altruism, determined human actions. In the grim finale of *A Connecticut Yankee in King Arthur's Court* Mark Twain had pictured the fatal unleashing of these aggressive tendencies. Thereafter, in the "Mysterious Stranger" manuscripts, he presented nightmare views of the pageant of human events, as well as Satan's prophecy that the race would keep on repeating its follies and depravities for the next million years. But perhaps it is in the only-now-published "Eddypus" manuscripts that he most fully discloses his historical vision. The focus here is on the sweep of human history, from the time of the original Adam to a time when he shall have turned into a myth and Mark Twain shall have become the new Adam, the earliest man on record—the Father of History. The latter venerable figure appears in "Eddypus" as the reverently quoted authority on that most ancient and fabled time, the nineteenth century—the time of a great civilization that had suddenly risen and flourished and had just as suddenly been followed by a new Age of Darkness. Clemens had come to share with Henry Adams and others a cyclical view of history. Was he not seeing in his own lifetime the whole round that would endessly repeat itself—mankind struggling out of ignorance and slavery to gain freedom and knowledge, only to be led by its own cowardice and greed into fooling away its chances and being returned to its chains? We find in "Eddypus" a dull and plodding scribe of the future nighttime of the world looking back to "the century called the Nineteenth by the Christians" as "the most remarkable century the world had ever seen" and gropingly attempting to "piece together a panorama of that ancient period out of odds and ends of history and tradition." That time, he says, "exhibits to us life in a dream, as it were, so different is it from life as we know it and live it. It is amazingly complex and wonderful, a sort of glorified and flashing and splendid nightmare, and frantic and tumultuous beyond belief." The one surviving great work of that period, he explains, that miraculously escaped the inevitable book-burnings, is "Old Comrades," by Mark Twain, Bishop of New Jersey. It becomes evident that "Old Comrades" is a fictional equivalent of Mark Twain's *Autobiography*. Also mentioned is the venerable bishop's Gospel, which corresponds to *What Is Man?* Mark Twain is thus the holy figure upon which a new faith is to be based—one which will supplant the triumphant Eddyism, the established religion of the time in which the scribe is clandestinely copying and annotating the sacred book, "Old Comrades." By this far-ranging fantasy, the hope for mankind in the future is to rest upon the example and teachings of Mark Twain. Probably there were moments when Clemens believed —or almost did—that it would all come to pass. Even allowing for humorous overstatement and mock-seriousness, the dream can be seen full-blown in his letter to Henry H. Rogers of [?17] June 1906: "Howells *thinks* the Auto will outlive the Innocents Abroad a thousand years, and I *know* it will. I would like the literary world to see (as Howells says) that the *form* of this book is one of the most memorable literary inventions of the ages."[16] He also delighted in Howells' praise of the parts of the autobiography that he had read as among "the humanest and richest pages in the history of man" and his comment, "You are nakeder than Adam and Eve put together, and truer than sin."[17] Similarly, he rejoicingly reported the judgment of George Harvey, head of Harper & Brothers: "He says it is the 'greatest book of the age,' and has in it 'the finest literature.' "[18]

Yet he could hardly have been confident that the force of even

---

[16] *MTHHR*, p. 611.

[17] William Dean Howells to SLC, 8 April 1906, *MTHL*, p. 803.

[18] SLC to Clara Clemens, 3 August 1906. TS in MTP.

his words' enduring through the ages would ever afford man a chance
to escape the doom of the historic process. It was extremely doubtful
that the chance was even there: made as he was, an inborn coward
and a lord-loving worshiper of spurious titles, the average man was
bound to be enslaved by a gilded minority who, like the providence-
trading swindlers in "The International Lightning Trust," knew how
to profit from "the assfulness of the human race." It would all keep
being repeated, without end. In "Passage from a Lecture," the "distinguished Professor of the Science of Historical Forecast" propounds
the "Law of Periodical Repetition" and conjectures:

> It is even possible that the mere *names* of things will be reproduced.
> Did not the Science of Health rise, in the old time, and did it not pass
> into oblivion, and has it not latterly come again and brought with it its
> forgotten name? Will it perish once more? Many times, I think, as the
> ages drift on; and still come again and again.

There are a good many indications that, as the new century began to
unroll, Clemens believed he had already seen it all. Like Faulkner's
Dilsey, he had seen the beginning and the end. His own times had
embraced the possibilities of human experience. He had been around
the world—and around *in* the world—and knew its peoples, its places.
And within himself he found, in some measure, all the qualities that
were present in the make-up of any member of his race. He was the
representative man, the race in singular—Adam. And the times invited
his taking the role of spokesman for humanity.

The beginning of a new century was inevitably a time for historical
survey, evaluation, and prophecy. Not surprisingly, Clemens, who had
always been interested in history, made his own try at a summation,
writing "Eddypus" in 1901 and 1902. A notebook item of 3 February
1901 reads, "Write Introduction to 100-Year book,"[19] and another of
three days later identifies this book as the "Eddypus" story: "Introduction 100-year. Gov't in hands of Xn Sci, or R. Catholic? *Whole* suffrage
introduced to save Protestantism in 1950, but too late; R C & XS^c
ahead—got the field."[20] It may be seen that he was not yet very far

---

[19] Notebook 34, TS p. 5.
[20] Ibid.

into the story, in which it is soon established that Christian Science and Roman Catholicism have long ago (as viewed from a perspective of 1,000 years hence) joined forces to form a world-dominating, absolutist church-state. The notion that the pope could seize power in America, like other "ideas seemingly hatched in cigar smoke over Twain's billiard table . . . reflected a common attitude,"[21] as Louis J. Budd has pointed out. The idea was a component of the nightmare of catastrophic expectation that ran far back in Clemens' thought. In 1883 he had noted an idea "For a play: America in 1985. The Pope here & an Inquisition. The age of darkness back again. Pope is temporal despot, *too*. A titled aristocracy & primogeniture. Europe is *republican* & full of science & invention—none allowed here."[22] The play was never written, but the concept found its way into "Eddypus" with some modifications: Mrs. Eddy and her religion were to have a large share in the envisioned despotic sway, and the new age of darkness was to overshadow not just America but all of Western civilization, leaving only China standing once again in an Age of Light.

Something must be said of Clemens' attitudes toward Mary Baker Eddy and Christian Science. He was both fascinated and exasperated by what he knew of Mrs. Eddy herself, and in criticizing her he was inclined to go to extremes, as in this passage from a letter of 21 March [1901?]:

> Mrs. Eddy the queen of frauds and hypocrites. . . . has a powerful interest for me because I think that in one or two ways she is the most extraordinary woman whom accident and circumstance have thus far vomited into the world. She is the monumental Sarcasm of the Ages and it seems to me that when we contemplate her and what she has achieved it is blasphemy to longer deny to the Supreme Being the possession of the sense of humor.[23]

In the same letter, he was careful to indicate that he was not also heaping ridicule on the religion of which Mrs. Eddy was the founder: "To me the respectibility of a religion does not depend on the religion's

---

[21] MTSP, p. 117.
[22] Notebook 17, TS p. 32.
[23] SLC to Mr. Day (Librarian of Springfield [Massachusetts] Library); TS in MTP.

authenticity but only upon the sincerity of the disciple's belief in it. These people are sincere."[24] He generally made this distinction. It is hard to escape the impression that Clemens' aversion to Mrs. Eddy had behind it something of the feeling one has toward a successful rival. He had in *What Is Man?* written his own "gospel," which he had not at the time of writing "Eddypus" had the courage to publish. *What Is Man?* was, like the record of Mark Twain the Bishop of New Jersey in "Eddypus," a *suppressed* work; Mrs. Eddy had had the needed boldness, and it was her new religion and not Clemens' that "took the field." Much too coy for the role of a messiah, Clemens, in printing a limited edition of *What Is Man?* in 1906, refused to associate his name with it. He even took the precaution of having the copyright registered in the name of an agent (his printer's superintendent). *Christian Science,* even though written as an exposé, was another work that Clemens was for a time persuaded to suppress—as he recalled it.[25] The concern with suppression that is so evident in "Eddypus" relates also to the *Autobiography*. Even as Clemens felt obliged to withhold much of the latter from publication until the remote future in order to avoid giving offense, so in "Eddypus" the Bishop Mark Twain has wanted his "Old Comrades" to remain "securely guarded" against publication of its "remorseless truth" about them while any might survive to be hurt by it.

There are other parallels. Clemens was confident that the *Autobiography* would eventually be a literary property of great value; the Bishop had thought the same of his manuscript:

At first it was his purpose to delay publication a hundred years; but he changed his mind and decided to extend the postponement to a period so remote that the histories of his day would all have perished and its life then exist in men's knowledge as a mere glimmer, vague, dim and uncer-

---

[24] Ibid.

[25] In his Autobiographical Dictation of 17 July 1906, Clemens recalled that after plans had been made to publish *Christian Science* in book form, F. A. Duneka of Harper & Brothers recommended suppression because he "was afraid of the Christian Scientists." Clemens added, "I said that my interest in a book lay in the writing of it, so it was not a matter of great consequence to me whether it was published or not. Let it be suppressed."

tain. At such an epoch his history would be valuable beyond estimate. "It will rise like a lost Atlantis out of the sea; and where for ages had been a waste of water smothered in fog, the gilded domes will flash in the sun, the rush and stir of a tumultuous life will burst upon the vision, the pomps and glories of a forgotten civilization will move like the enchantments of an Arabian tale before the grateful eyes of an astonished world."

The Bishop, wanting "his book to be readable by the common people without necessity of translation" and finding that "the English of a period 450 years back in the past was quite fairly readable [as in Malory's *Morte d'Arthur*] 'by Tom, Dick and Harry,'" had "appointed his book to be published after the lapse of five centuries." But as the scribe explains, the repository for "Old Comrades"—a vault beneath "the new Presidential palace" in Washington—has become lost and forgotten with the disappearance of the capital city long before the five hundred years have passed. So the manuscript remains buried for a thousand years before being discovered by some "shepherds digging for water"; the book, in nineteenth-century English, is "Beowulf over again. No one could spell out its meanings but our half-dozen ripest philologists." Ironically, the work is unearthed at a time when Mother Eddy's Christian Science is in control of everything. The Bishop's "Old Comrades" must remain suppressed. Only a few heretics know of it; risking their lives to correspond about it, they write in a cipher and sometimes in invisible ink.

Of course Clemens did not go to such lengths to conceal his own manuscripts, but he did store those materials that he intended only for posthumous publication. And when the 1906 edition of *What Is Man?* was printed, he advised his publisher, "Keep the 250 copies safe and secure . . . until the edition is rare and people are willing to pay $300. a copy for it. That is the price, or we hold on and wait ten years— you and my daughters."[26] Again, the life situation curiously parallels "Eddypus": the Gospel of Mark Twain is to be hidden away in a vault until after his death (he envisions being survived by his daughters and

---

[26] SLC to F. N. Doubleday, 25 May 1906. Quoted from an extract in the hand of Clemens' secretary Isabel V. Lyon, in MTP.

by the publisher F. N. Doubleday), with the expectation that it will become extremely valuable. And it is probably no mere coincidence that he makes a firm point of having this Gospel of Mark sell for three hundred dollars, exactly the price that Mrs. Eddy charged for her course of instruction in Christian Science.

After the notebook entry about planned work on the introduction to the "100-Year book," made in February 1901, he probably soon wrote much of the existing manuscript. The passage on phrenology which he brought into Book 2, Chapter 2, aids in dating the composition. This passage is not well integrated with what precedes and follows, and it appears to have been thrown into "Eddypus" for no better reason than that Clemens was interested in phrenology at the time. That time may very well have been shortly after 7 March 1901, a date on which he had a phrenological examination by the prominent firm of Fowler and Wells—the Briggs and Pollard of "Eddypus."[27] The part of the passage on phrenology that explains the basic system of ratings "on the brain-chart of the science" by numbers from 1 to 7 was taken almost verbatim from O. S. and L. N. Fowler's book, *New Illustrated Self-Instructor in Phrenology and Physiology*.[28] At the time of Clemens' death a copy of this book, signed *"Clemens, 1901,"* was in his library, as the 1911 sale catalog of Clemens' library reveals. The indication is, then, that he was well past the middle point of the existing manuscript by some time in March 1901. It is likely that in that month he also wrote through Chapter 5 of Book 2, less than four days' work at his ordinary pace of something like twelve manuscript pages a day.

It may be established that he did not, however, write the remainder of the work until the following year. On 16 February 1902 he wrote to F. A. Duneka of Harper & Brothers asking for a copy of Andrew D.

---

[27] Notebook 34, TS p. 7, records the time of his appointment on that date: "Jessie A. Fowler, 10.30." Jessie Allen Fowler was the daughter of L. N. Fowler.

[28] New York: Fowler and Wells, 1859, Preface, viii. This popular book was reissued several times during the latter part of the nineteenth century; the Library of Congress Catalog lists its publication in 1890, and it may have been reprinted even thereafter (from an essay by Alan Gribben, "Mark Twain, Phrenology, and the 'Temperaments': A Study of Pseudoscientific Influence," to be published in *American Quarterly*).

White's A *History of the Warfare of Science with Theology in Chris-tendom* and also for "any up-to-date books" he might have "on the *half-dozen great sciences*, by experts. Not *big* books, but condensations or small school-textbooks."[29] He added, "You will begin to think the large book I am writing is going to be a mine of learning. Well it *is*— a little bit distorted, a trifle out of focus, recognizably drunk. But in-teresting, and don't you forget it!" It can be deduced that he was here referring to "Eddypus," for his copy of White's book, which is in the Mark Twain Papers, shows by Clemens' marginalia and by the con-tents, from which he borrowed extensively, that he used this as a main source for his recapitulation of scientific discoveries in the final chap-ters of Book 2. He also borrowed from White—and fancifully em-bellished—the incident of the hoax in which college boys "planted" small manufactured clay animal figures which were accepted by their mentor (Martin Luther in the Mark Twain version) as the original models used for the Creation.[30] After writing the last three chapters,

---

[29] TS in MTP.

[30] See Andrew Dickson White, A *History of the Warfare of Science with The-ology in Christendom*, 2 vols. (New York: D. Appleton and Company, 1901), 1:216. Strangely enough, such a hoax seems actually to have been perpetrated. White speaks of a "farce and a tragedy. This is the work of Johann Beringer, pro-fessor in the University of Würzburg and private physician to the Prince-Bishop— the treatise bearing the title *Lithographiae Wirceburgensis Specimen Primum*." This work contained two hundred illustrations of stones and fossils. Some of Beringer's students had "prepared a collection of sham fossils in baked clay, im-itating not only plants, reptiles, and fishes of every sort that their knowledge or imagination could suggest, but even Hebrew and Syriac inscriptions, one of them the name of the Almighty; and these they buried in a place where the professor was wont to search for specimens. The joy of Beringer on unearthing these proofs of the immediate agency of the finger of God in creating fossils knew no bounds. At great cost he prepared this book, whose twenty-two elaborate plates of facsimiles were forever to settle the question in favour of theology and against science, and prefixed to the work an allegorical title page, wherein not only the glory of his own sovereign, but that of heaven itself, was pictured as based upon a pyramid of these miraculous fossils. So robust was his faith that not even a premature ex-posure of the fraud could dissuade him from the publication of his book. Dis-missing in one contemptuous chapter this exposure as a slander by his rivals, he appealed to the learned world. But the shout of laughter that welcomed the work soon convinced even its author. In vain did he try to suppress it; and, according to tradition, having wasted his fortune in vain attempts to buy up all the copies of it, and being taunted by the rivals whom he had thought to overwhelm, he died of

Mark Twain apparently abandoned "Eddypus." The chapters were not typed, and Paine filed them as a separate work under the title "On Science." They are, nevertheless, clearly a continuation of Book 2 and here have been restored to "Eddypus."

Mark Twain had spoken of making a large book, but once he had used up the ideas gleaned from White's history, he probably did not know where to go next—and followed his practice of pigeonholing. A yachting trip with Henry H. Rogers in the latter part of March and through a part of April could also have interrupted work on the book. Although composition was never resumed, he may have kept his intention of completing "Eddypus" alive for a time. At the end of July 1902 he noted that he had been asked to consider selling one of several of his books "in MS," among which he listed "the 1000 Years Hence."[31] Instead of renewing work upon "Eddypus," however, he turned within the next year to his other Eddy-inspired writings, those dealing specifically with Christian Science and with Mrs. Eddy as the founder and head of that religion and the author of *Science and Health, with Key to the Scriptures*. He published "Christian Science" serially in the *North American Review* of December 1902 and January and February 1903. For the first two parts he used materials written "Four years ago (1898–9)"; in the remaining part he presented "Eddypus"-related material in a section headed "V.—(LATER STILL.)—A THOUSAND YEARS AGO. *Passages from the Introduction to the 'Secret History of Eddypus, the World-Empire.'* "[32] In the parts written four years earlier he had credited Christian Science with certain positive values but had found fault with Mrs. Eddy's own motives and actions in establishing and maintaining her church; in the later part he summarized his historical viewpoint and the essential fable of "Eddypus." The article prompted a defense of Mrs. Eddy by W. D. McCrackan, "Mrs. Eddy's Relation

---

chagrin." Both volumes of White's book were inscribed by Clemens, but on different dates: Volume 1, on 22 February 1902, and Volume 2, "March, 1902." On the title page of Volume 2, Clemens wrote just under the title, "Being an Exposure of the most Grotesque & Trivial of all Inventions, Man."

[31] Notebook 35, TS pp. 22–23.

[32] NAR 555 (February 1903): 173–184. Published as Appendix B2 in *What Is Man? and Other Philosophical Writings*, ed. Paul Baender (Berkeley, Los Angeles, London: University of California Press, 1972).

to Christian Science," in the March issue of the *Review*. Undertaking to examine the work's arguments "with the sole object of separating fact from fiction," he implied that Mark Twain's use of both past and future viewpoints had introduced an aspect of unreality: "There are certain disadvantages about treating a present day subject either from four years back or from nine hundred and ninety-nine years ahead, which I feel certain the reader will appreciate." McCrackan charged that these writings had tended "to draw out of line the discovery and life motive of Mrs. Eddy, to swell to preposterous proportions the regular business affairs of the Christian Science denomination which she has founded, and to magnify the imperfections, while minimizing the merits, of the methods used for preserving the purity of Christian Science before the world."[33] Mark Twain replied in the following month, reaffirming his charges: in "Mrs. Eddy in Error," he asserted, "In simple truth, *she is the only absolute sovereign in all Christendom.*"[34] In the closing part of the "Later Still" section, he envisioned that her religion would eventually rule the entire world; it was to keep on "growing, ceaselessly growing. . . . When it numbered 50,000,000, it began to take a hand—quietly; when it numbered half the country's population, it lifted up its chin and began to dictate":

> its authority spread to the ends of the earth; its revenues were estimable in astronomical terms only, they went to but one place in the earth—the Treasury at Eddyflats, called "Boston" in ancient times; the Church's dominion covered every land and sea, and made all previous concentrations of Imperial force and wealth seem nursery trifles by contrast. Then the Black Night shut down, never again to lift![35]

Perhaps the publication of this projected ending for "Eddypus" satisfied or vitiated any urge toward further work on the story, and he had stolen his own thunder.

Some other pieces in this section, all relatively brief, provide alternate versions of Mark Twain's historical fantasy. "Passage from 'Glances at History' (suppressed.)" offers what is purportedly a speech "made

---

[33] NAR 556 (March 1903): 349–364.
[34] NAR 557 (April 1903): 513.
[35] NAR 555 (February 1903): 183–184.

more than 500 years ago, and which has come down to us intact," which develops the idea that the Great Republic, involved in an unjust war, had sold its honor in the name of a misguided patriotism. As Bernard DeVoto recognized, Clemens had in mind the occupation of the Philippines.[36] In "The Stupendous Procession" the view of the times is widened to include not just the Great Republic (the United States) but Western civilization. As Philip S. Foner has written, this satire is noteworthy for "linking all imperialist powers together," showing "their common brutalities and their common resort to sanctimonious hypocrisies."[37] "Flies and Russians," written at the time of the Russo-Japanese War, marks the disappointment of Clemens' hopes for a timely overthrow of the czarist regime. The piece may be read as another indication that he was still looking for positive evidence that man could somehow rise above the common weaknesses of human character —and not finding it. "The Fable of the Yellow Terror" looks beyond America and Europe to see the Far East becoming once again dominant: after the decline of the West, China is to enjoy another Age of Light, as envisioned in "Eddypus," with great economic and political power. "A Letter from the Comet" and "Ancients in Modern Dress" emphasize again the cyclical aspect of history and dwell upon Adam as the human archetype. "The Recurrent Major and Minor Compliment" relates Clemens' historical view to his personal life. In responding to the recurring comment, "I believe that at bottom you are a serious man," he must have had in mind some of his own darker times: "When was the first time you ever saw a man of fifty who had never known dread, fear, defeat, disaster, sleepless nights, the paralysis of despair and the longing for death? . . . When did you ever see *any* sane man of fifty who was not—and by awful compulsion—at bottom serious?"

One might expect Clemens to have specified sixty rather than fifty, for it was in the mid-nineties—and he reached sixty in 1895—that he had suffered failure and disaster; but he was here generalizing his own case as that of everyman and may have been taking the half-century

---

[36] *LE*, p. 107.

[37] *Mark Twain: Social Critic* (New York: International Publishers, 1958), p. 288.

point as a roundly representative one. Or had he already in his own life touched such depths by the year in which he had also reached the height of his achievement by publishing *Huckleberry Finn?* Only he could speak for the nightmare side of his own personal history. From the summit of seventy years, at the time of his birthday in 1905, he saw that history as a "foolish dream" in which he had arrived at a place of desolation: "Old Age, white-headed, the temple empty, the idols broken, the worshippers in their graves, nothing left but You, a remnant, a tradition, belated fag-end of a foolish dream, a dream that was so ingeniously dreamed that it seemed real all the time; nothing left but You, centre of a snowy desolation, perched on the ice-summit, gazing out over the stages of that long *trek* and asking Yourself 'would you do it again if you had the chance?' "

Pondering his question, one who considers Clemens' view of the human predicament and then thinks of his Stormfieldlike qualities of irascibility, compassion, and resoluteness can only imagine what, given such a chance, he would have answered.

THE MYTH OF
PROVIDENCE

Little Bessie

(1908–1909)

MARK TWAIN did not clearly designate the order that he intended for these six brief chapters. The present order has been chosen as that which seems to provide the most logical literary progression. "Little Bessie Would Assist Providence" has been chosen as Chapter 1 because it characterizes Bessie and her blasphemous mentor, Mr. Hollister, more fully than do the other chapters, which assume that these persons are already known to the reader. Chapter 2 begins with the mother's question, "You disobedient child, have you been associating with that irreligious Hollister again?" By the time of the next piece, Chapter 3, it appears that Bessie's visits to Hollister have become a habit: the mother complains, "I wish that that tiresome Hollister was in H—amburg! He is an ignorant, unreasoning, illogical ass, and I have told you over and over again to keep out of his poisonous company." In Chapter 4, which introduces the topic of the Virgin Birth, Bessie asks, "Mamma, what is a virgin?" In the next chapter she does not have to ask, and in the last one she speaks knowingly about sexual intercourse.

As noted in the Introduction, a typescript of Chapter 1 is dated 22 February 1908. The paper used in Chapters 1, 3, 4, and 6 was used extensively in 1908; "Samuel Erasmus Moffett," dated August 16, 1908 by Mark Twain, is on this paper as is Chapter 33 of "No. 44, The Mysterious Stranger."[1] Most of Chapter 1 of "Little Bessie" was printed in the appendix to Paine's biography, where Paine grouped the piece with work of June and July 1909.[2]

---

[1] See MSM, pp. 400–403, 491.
[2] See MTB, pp. 1514–1515, 1671–1673.

Little Bessie

Chapter 1

Little Bessie Would Assist Providence

L ITTLE BESSIE was nearly three years old. She was a good child, and not shallow, not frivolous, but meditative and thoughtful, and much given to thinking out the reasons of things and trying to make them harmonise with results. One day she said—

"Mamma, why is there so much pain and sorrow and suffering? What is it all for?"

It was an easy question, and mamma had no difficulty in answering it:

"It is for our good, my child. In His wisdom and mercy the Lord sends us these afflictions to discipline us and make us better."

"Is it *He* that sends them?"

"Yes."

"Does He send *all* of them, mamma?"

"Yes, dear, all of them. None of them comes by accident; He alone sends them, and always out of love for us, and to make us better."

"Isn't it strange!"

"Strange? Why, no, I have never thought of it in that way. I have not heard any one call it strange before. It has always seemed natural and right to me, and wise and most kindly and merciful."

"Who first thought of it like that, mamma? Was it you?"

"Oh, no, child, I was taught it."

34

"Who taught you so, mamma?"

"Why, really, I don't know—I can't remember. My mother, I suppose; or the preacher. But it's a thing that everybody knows."

"Well, anyway, it does seem strange. Did He give Billy Norris the typhus?"

"Yes."

"What for?"

"Why, to discipline him and make him good."

"But he died, mamma, and so it *couldn't* make him good."

"Well, then, I suppose it was for some other reason. We know it was a *good* reason, whatever it was."

"What do you think it was, mamma?"

"Oh, you ask so many questions! I think it was to discipline his parents."

"Well, then, it wasn't fair, mamma. Why should *his* life be taken away for their sake, when he wasn't doing anything?"

"Oh, *I* don't know! I only know it was for a good and wise and merciful reason."

"What reason, mamma?"

"I think—I think—well, it was a judgment; it was to punish them for some sin they had committed."

"But *he* was the one that was punished, mamma. Was that right?"

"Certainly, certainly. He does nothing that isn't right and wise and merciful. You can't understand these things now, dear, but when you are grown up you will understand them, and then you will see that they are just and wise."

After a pause:

"Did He make the roof fall in on the stranger that was trying to save the crippled old woman from the fire, mamma?"

"Yes, my child. *Wait!* Don't ask me why, because I don't know. I only know it was to discipline some one, or be a judgment upon somebody, or to show His power."

"That drunken man that stuck a pitchfork into Mrs. Welch's baby when—"

"Never mind about it, you needn't go into particulars; it was to discipline the child—*that* much is certain, anyway."

"Mamma, Mr. Burgess said in his sermon that billions of little creatures are sent into us to give us cholera, and typhoid, and lockjaw, and more than a thousand other sicknesses and—mamma, does He send them?"

"Oh, certainly, child, certainly. Of course."

"What for?"

"Oh, to *dis*cipline us! haven't I told you so, over and over again?"

"It's awful cruel, mamma! And silly! and if I—"

"Hush, oh *hush!* do you want to bring the lightning?"

"You know the lightning *did* come last week, mamma, and struck the new church, and burnt it down. Was it to discipline the church?"

(Wearily). "Oh, I suppose so."

"But it killed a hog that wasn't doing anything. Was it to discipline the hog, mamma?"

"Dear child, don't you want to run out and play a while? If you would like to—"

"Mamma, only think! Mr. Hollister says there isn't a bird or fish or reptile or any other animal that hasn't got an enemy that Providence has sent to bite it and chase it and pester it, and kill it, and suck its blood and discipline it and make it good and religious. Is that true, mother—because if it is true, why did Mr. Hollister laugh at it?"

"That Hollister is a scandalous person, and I don't want you to listen to anything he says."

"Why, mamma, he is very interesting, and *I* think he tries to be good. He says the wasps catch spiders and cram them down into their nests in the ground—*alive,* mamma!—and there they live and suffer days and days and days, and the hungry little wasps chewing their legs and gnawing into their bellies all the time, to make them good and religious and praise God for His infinite mercies. *I* think Mr. Hollister is just lovely, and ever so kind; for when I asked him if *he* would treat a spider like that, he said he hoped to be damned if he would; and then he—"

"My child! oh, do for goodness' sake—"

"And mamma, he says the spider is appointed to catch the fly, and drive her fangs into his bowels, and suck and suck and suck his blood, to discipline him and make him a Christian; and whenever the fly buzzes his wings with the pain and misery of it, you can see by the spider's grateful eye that she is thanking the Giver of All Good for— well, she's saying grace, as *he* says; and also, he—"

"Oh, aren't you *ever* going to get tired chattering! If you want to go out and play—"

"Mamma, he says himself that all troubles and pains and miseries and rotten diseases and horrors and villainies are sent to us in mercy and kindness to discipline us; and he says it is the duty of every father and mother to *help* Providence, every way they can; and says they can't do it by just scolding and whipping, for that won't answer, it is weak and no good—Providence's way is best, and it is every parent's duty and every *person's* duty to help discipline everybody, and cripple them and kill them, and starve them, and freeze them, and rot them with diseases, and lead them into murder and theft and dishonor and disgrace; and he says Providence's invention for disciplining us and the animals is the very brightest idea that ever was, and not even an idiot could get up anything shinier. Mamma, brother Eddie needs disciplining, right away; and I know where you can get the smallpox for him, and the itch, and the diphtheria, and bone-rot, and heart disease, and consumption, and—*Dear* mamma, have you fainted! I will run and bring help! Now *this* comes of staying in town this hot weather."

Chapter 2

Creation of Man

M AMMA. You disobedient child, have you been associating with that irreligious Hollister again?

Bessie. Well, mamma, he is interesting, anyway, although wicked, and I can't help loving interesting people. Here is the conversation we had:

Hollister. Bessie, suppose you should take some meat and bones and fur, and make a cat out of it, and should tell the cat, Now you are not to be unkind to any creature, on pain of punishment and death. And suppose the cat should disobey, and catch a mouse and torture it and kill it. What would you do to the cat?

Bessie. Nothing.

H. Why?

B. Because I know what the cat would say. She would say, It's my nature, I couldn't help it; I didn't make my nature, *you* made it. And so you are responsible for what I've done—I'm not. I couldn't answer that, Mr. Hollister.

H. It's just the case of Frankenstein and his Monster over again.

B. What is that?

H. Frankenstein took some flesh and bones and blood and made a man out of them; the man ran away and fell to raping and robbing and murdering everywhere, and Frankenstein was horrified and in despair, and said, *I* made him, without asking his consent, and it makes me responsible for every crime he commits. *I* am the criminal, he is innocent.

B. Of course he was right.

H. I judge so. It's just the case of God and man and you and the cat over again.

B. How is that?

H. God made man, without man's consent, and made his nature, too; made it vicious instead of angelic, and then said, Be angelic, or I will punish you and destroy you. But no matter, God is responsible for everything man does, all the same; He can't get around that fact. There is only one Criminal, and it is not man.

Mamma. This is atrocious! it is wicked, blasphemous, irreverent, horrible!

Bessie. Yes'm, but it's true. And I'm not going to make a cat. I would be above making a cat if I couldn't make a good one.

Chapter 3

M AMMA, if a person by the name of Jones kills a person by the name of Smith just for amusement, it's murder, isn't it, and Jones is a murderer?

Yes, my child.

And Jones is punishable for it?

Yes, my child.

Why, mamma?

Why? Because God has forbidden homicide in the Ten Commandments, and therefore whoever kills a person commits a crime and must suffer for it.

But mamma, suppose Jones has by birth such a violent temper that he can't control himself?

He *must* control himself. God requires it.

But he doesn't make his own temper, mamma, he is born with it, like the rabbit and the tiger; and so, why should he be held responsible?

Because God *says* he is responsible and *must* control his temper.

But he *can't*, mamma; and so, don't you think it is God that does the killing and is responsible, because it was *He* that gave him the temper which he couldn't control?

Peace, my child! He *must* control it, for God requires it, and that ends the matter. It settles it, and there is no room for argument.

(*After a thoughtful pause.*) It doesn't seem to me to settle it. Mamma, murder is murder, isn't it? and whoever commits it is a murderer? That is the plain simple fact, isn't it?

(*Suspiciously.*) What are you arriving at now, my child?

Mamma, when God designed Jones He could have given him a rabbit's temper if He had wanted to, couldn't He?

Yes.

Then Jones would not kill anybody and have to be hanged?

True.

But He chose to give Jones a temper that would *make* him kill Smith. Why, then, isn't *He* responsible?

Because He also gave Jones a Bible. The Bible gives Jones ample warning not to commit murder; and so if Jones commits it he alone is responsible.

(*Another pause.*) Mamma, did God make the house-fly?

Certainly, my darling.

What for?

For some great and good purpose, and to display His power.

What is the great and good purpose, mamma?

We do not know, my child. We only know that He makes *all* things for a great and good purpose. But this is too large a subject for a dear little Bessie like you, only a trifle over three years old.

Possibly, mamma, yet it profoundly interests me. I have been reading about the fly, in the newest science-book. In that book he is called "the most dangerous animal and the most murderous that exists upon the earth, killing hundreds of thousands of men, women and children every year, by distributing deadly diseases among them." Think of it, mamma, the *most* fatal of all the animals! by all odds the most murderous of all the living things created by God. Listen to this, from the book:

> Now, the house fly has a very keen scent for filth of any kind. Whenever there is any within a hundred yards or so, the fly goes for it to smear its mouth and all the sticky hairs of its six legs with dirt and disease germs. A second or two suffices to gather up many thousands of these disease germs, and then off goes the fly to the nearest kitchen or dining room. There the fly crawls over the meat, butter, bread, cake, anything it can find in fact, and often gets into the milk pitcher, depositing large numbers of disease germs at every step. The house fly is as disgusting as it is dangerous.

Isn't it horrible, mamma! One fly produces fifty-two billions of descendants in 60 days in June and July, and they go and crawl over sick people and wade through pus, and sputa, and foul matter exuding from sores, and gaum themselves with every kind of disease-germ, then they go to everybody's dinner-table and wipe themselves off on the butter and the other food, and many and many a painful illness and ultimate death results from this loathsome industry. Mamma, they murder seven thousand persons in New York City alone, every year—people against whom they have no quarrel. To kill without cause is murder—nobody denies that. Mamma?

Well?

Have the flies a Bible?

Of course not.

You have said it is the Bible that makes man responsible. If God didn't give him a Bible to circumvent the nature that He deliberately gave him, God would be responsible. He gave the fly his murderous nature, and sent him forth unobstructed by a Bible or any other restraint to commit murder by wholesale. And so, therefore, God is Himself responsible. God is a murderer. Mr. Hollister says so. Mr. Hollister says God can't make one moral law for man and another for Himself. He says it would be laughable.

Do shut up! I wish that that tiresome Hollister was in H—amburg! He is an ignorant, unreasoning, illogical ass, and I have told you over and over again to keep out of his poisonous company.

Chapter 4

"MAMMA, what is a virgin?"

"A maid."

"Well, what is a maid?"

"A girl or woman that isn't married."

"Uncle Jonas says that sometimes a virgin that has been having a child—"

"Nonsense! A virgin can't have a child."

"Why can't she, mamma?"

"Well, there are reasons why she can't."

"What reasons, mamma?"

"Physiological. She would have to cease to be a virgin before she could have the child."

"How do you mean, mamma?"

"Well, let me see. It's something like this: a Jew couldn't be a Jew after he had become a Christian; he couldn't be Christian and Jew at the same time. Very well, a person couldn't be mother and virgin at the same time."

"Why, mamma, Sally Brooks has had a child, and *she's* a virgin."

"Indeed? Who says so?"

"She says so herself."

"Oh, no doubt! Are there any other witnesses?"

"Yes—there's a dream. She says the governor's private secretary appeared to her in a dream and told her she was going to have a child, and it came out just so."

"I shouldn't wonder! Did he say the governor was the corespondent?"

Chapter 5

B. Mama, didn't you tell me an ex-governor, like Mr. Burlap, is a person that's been governor but isn't a governor any more?

M. Yes, dear.

B. And Mr. Williams said "ex" always stands for a Has Been, didn't he?

M. Yes, child. It is a vulgar way of putting it, but it expresses the fact.

B, (eagerly). So then Mr. Hollister was right, after all. He says the Virgin Mary isn't a virgin any more, she's a Has Been. He says—

M. It is false! Oh, it was just like that godless miscreant to try to undermine an innocent child's holy belief with his foolish lies; and if I could have my way, I—

B. But mama,—honest and true—*is* she still a virgin—a *real* virgin, you know?

M. Certainly she is; and has never been anything *but* a virgin—oh, the adorable One, the pure, the spotless, the undefiled!

B. Why, mama, Mr. Hollister says she *can't* be. That's what *he* says. He says she had five children *after* she had the One that was begotten by absent treatment and didn't break anything and he thinks such a lot of child-bearing, spread over years and years and years, would ultimately wear a virgin's virginity so thin that even Wall street would consider the stock too lavishly watered and you couldn't place it there at any discount you could name, because the Board would say it was wildcat, and wouldn't list it. That's what *he* says. And besides—

M. Go to the nursery, instantly! Go!

Chapter 6

MAMMA, is Christ God?

Yes, my child.

Mamma, how can He be Himself and Somebody Else at the same time?

He isn't, my darling. It is like the Siamese twins—two persons, one born ahead of the other, but equal in authority, equal in power.

I understand it, now, mamma, and it is quite simple. One twin has sexual intercourse with his mother, and begets himself and his brother; and next he has sexual intercourse with his grandmother and begets his mother. I should think it would be difficult, mamma, though interesting. Oh, ever so difficult. I should think that the Corespondent—

All things are possible with God, my child.

Yes, I suppose so. But not with any other Siamese twin, I suppose. *You* don't think any ordinary Siamese twin could beget himself and his brother on his mother, do you, mamma, and then go on back while his hand is in and beget *her*, too, on his grandmother?

Certainly not, my child. None but God can do these wonderful and holy miracles.

And enjoy them. For of course He enjoys them, or He wouldn't go foraging around among the family like that, *would* He, mamma?—injuring their reputations in the village and causing talk. Mr. Hollister says it was wonderful and awe-inspiring in those days, but wouldn't work now. He says that if the Virgin lived in Chicago now, and got in the family way and explained to the newspaper fellows that God was the Corespondent, she couldn't get two in ten of them to believe it. He says they are a hell of a lot!

My child!

Well, that is what he says, anyway.

Oh, I do *wish* you would keep away from that wicked, wicked man!

He doesn't *mean* to be wicked, mamma, and he doesn't blame God. No, he doesn't blame Him; he says they all do it—gods do. It's their habit, they've always been that way.

What way, dear?

Going around unvirgining the virgins. He says our God did not invent the idea—it was old and mouldy before He happened on it. Says He hasn't invented anything, but got His Bible and His Flood and His morals and all His ideas from earlier gods, and they got them from still earlier gods. He says there never was a god yet that wasn't born of a Virgin. Mr. Hollister says no virgin is safe where a god is. He says he wishes he was a god; he says he would make virgins so scarce that—

Peace, peace! *Don't* run on so, my child. If you—

—and he advised me to lock my door nights, because—

Hush, *hush*, will you!

—because although I am only three and a half years old and quite safe from *men*—

Mary Ann, come and get this child! There, now, go along with you, and don't come near me again until you can interest yourself in some subject of a lower grade and less awful than theology.

Bessie, (disappearing.) Mr. Hollister says there *ain't* any.

Little Nelly Tells a Story
Out of Her Own Head

(1907)

THIS TITLE appears on the typescript and may have been supplied by
Mark Twain; there is no title on the manuscript. In this sketch, headed
"Dictated 1907," Clemens recalls a performance by a group of children of
"a brief little drama of 'The Prince and Pauper' " as an event of "Twenty-
two-or-three years ago, in Cleveland." He and George W. Cable gave a
reading in Cleveland in December 1884, probably on the seventeenth.[1]
They would very likely have visited Mrs. Mary Mason Fairbanks, the
"Mother" Fairbanks whom Clemens had first known as a passenger on the
Quaker City cruise to the Holy Land, so the drama may have been staged
at the Fairbanks home, as Clemens recalled. The play certainly was performed in Hartford at the end of the year by a group of children as a surprise arranged by Mrs. Clemens.[2] Clemens may have mistakenly placed this
event in Cleveland.

The Little Nelly of the incident cannot be certainly identified but may
have been Helen Morton Cox, the young daughter of Cable's sister, An-

---

[1] Paul Fatout, *Mark Twain on the Lecture Circuit* (Bloomington: Indiana
University Press, 1960), p. 218; see also *MT&GWC*, p. 72.

[2] *MTA* 2:59–60. Clemens here recalls that the initial performance took place
at the home of his Hartford neighbor George Warner; there were subsequent
presentations at the Clemens residence.

toinette Cox; Clemens called Helen "Miss Nellie,"[3] and she and others of
Cable's family may have been at the Hartford house while Cable himself
was staying there.

---

[3] Clemens to "My dear Miss Nellie," 2 December 1882. See also *MT&GWC*,
p. 13.

Little Nelly Tells a Story
Out of Her Own Head

TWENTY-TWO-OR-THREE years ago, in Cleveland, a thing happened which I still remember pretty well. Out in the suburbs, it was—on the lake; the Fairbankses had bought a large house and a great place there, and were living sumptuously, after Mr. Fairbanks's long life of struggle and privation in building up the Cleveland Herald to high place and prosperity. I was there a week, and the Severances came out to dinner twice, and they and "Mother Fairbanks" and I talked over the old times we had enjoyed together in the "Quaker City," when we were "Innocents Abroad." Meantime, every day Mother Fairbanks was busy staging a brief little drama of "The Prince and Pauper" and drilling the children from town who were to play it.

One of these children was Nelly (nevermindtherestofthename) and she was a prodigy—a bright and serious and pretty little creature of nine, who was to play Lady Jane Grey. She had a large reputation as a reciter of poetry and little speeches before company in her mother's drawing-room at home; she did her work charmingly, and the sweetest charm about it was the aged gravity and sincerity and earnestness which she put into it. Latterly she had added a new laurel: she had composed a quaint little story, "out of her own head," and had de-

47

lighted a parlor-audience with it and made herself the envy of all the children around.

The Prince and Pauper play was to be given in my honor, and I had a seat in the centre of the front row; a hundred and fifty friends of the house were present in evening costume, old and young and both sexes, the great room was brilliantly lighted, the fine clothes made the aspect gay, everybody was laughing and chatting and having a good time, the curtain was about ready to rise.

A hitch occurred. Edward VI, (to be played by a girl,) had been belated, it would take a quarter of an hour to dress her for her part. This announcement was made, and Mother Fairbanks retired to attend to this function, and took Nelly's mother with her to help. Presently the audience began to call for little Nelly to come on the stage and do her little story. Nelly's twin sister brought her on, and sat down in a chair beside her and folded her pudgy hands in her lap, and beamed upon the house her joy in the ovation which Lady Jane received. Lady Jane got another round when she said she had made a new story out of her own head and would recite it—which she proceeded to do, with none of her sweet solemnities lacking. To-wit:

Once there were two ladies, and were twins, and lived together, Mary and Olivia Scott, in the house they were born in, and all alone, for Mr. and Mrs. Scott were dead, now. After a while they got lonesome and wished they could have a baby, and said God will provide.

(You could feel the walls give, the strain upon suppressed emotion was so great.)

So when the baby came they were very glad, and the neighbors surprised.

(The walls spread again, but held.)

And asked where they got it and they said by prayer, which is the only way.

(There was not a sound in the audience except the muffled volleying of bursting buttons and the drip of unrestrainable tears. With a gravity not of this world, the inspired child went on:)

But there was no way to feed it at first, because it had only gums and could not bite, then they prayed and God sent a lady which had several and showed them how, then it got fat and they were so happy you cannot think; and thought oh, if they could have some more—and prayed again and got them, because whatever you pray for in the right spirit you get it a thousand fold.

(I could feel the throes and quivers coursing up and down the body of the ripe maiden lady at my left, and she buried her face in her handkerchief and seemed to sob, but it was not sobbing. The walls were sucking in and bellying out, but they held. The two children on the stage were a dear and lovely picture to see, the face of the one so sweetly earnest, the other's face so speakingly lit up with pride in her gifted sister and with worshipping admiration.)

And God was pleased the way they were so thankful to have that child, and every prayer they made they got another one, and by the time fall came they had thirteen, and whoever will do the right way can have as many, perhaps more, for nothing is impossible with God, and whoever puts their trust in Him they will have their reward, heaped up and running over. When we think of Mary and Olivia Scott it should learn us to have confidence. End of the tale—good bye.

The dear little thing! She made her innocent bow, and retired without a suspicion that she had been an embarrassment. Nothing would have happened, now, perhaps, if quiet could have been maintained for a few minutes, so that the people could get a grip upon themselves, but the strain overpowered my old maid partner and she exploded like a bomb; a general and unrestrained crash of laughter followed, of course, the happy tears flowed like brooks, and no one was sorry of the opportunity to laugh himself out and get the blessed relief that comes of that privilege in such circumstances.

I think the Prince and Pauper went very well—I do not remember; but the other incident stays by me with great and contenting vividness —the picture and everything.

The Second Advent

(1881)

On the title page of the manuscript, A. B. Paine called this a "semi burlesque of a new Christ, born in Arkansas" and added, "Hardly usable." Probably it was again Paine who wrote at some time, "Impossible of use"— a note that was later erased. The objectionable feature was the satire leveled at conventional pieties, including belief in the Virgin Birth and in special providences. Clemens had no doubt of the absurdity of both, and he did not change his view. It was about 1905 that he wrote, "It would be difficult to construct a dog that could swallow the moon, it would be impossible to construct a virgin that could give birth to a child, but it is no trick at all to construct an ass who could swallow the whole combined menagerie and then not see the humor of criticising some other ass for being an ass."[1] It should be noted that although Clemens scoffed at the idea of a virgin birth he was a fervent defender of womanly virtue: in 1907 he spoke of seeing in the morning paper the phrase "age of consent," "that phrase which—considering its awful meaning—I think is the blackest one that exists in any language. It always unseats my self-possession."[2] He went on to contend that just as there is no age of consent to murder there should be none for a woman's seduction. He was capable of placing the Almighty in the role of seducer—thereby further ridiculing the concept of the Virgin Birth: "We

---

[1] "Comments on 'Asia and Europe'", DV 127.
[2] "Imaginary Interview with the President," DV 250. Clemens headed the typescript, "Dictated April 20, 1907."

don't *know* that Joseph didn't beget the Savior; but we do know that . . . it was much too large a contract for him. There was One, and only One, at the time, that was competent and in all ways qualified for the vast production; . . . the plausibilities favor the idea that He is the one fairly and justifiably under suspicion."[3]

The principle underlying Clemens' contempt for the notion of special providences was revealed in a notebook entry of 1886:

> Special Providence! That phrase nauseates me—with its implied importance of mankind & triviality of God. In my opinion these myriads of globes are merely the blood-corpuscles ebbing & flowing through the arteries of God, & we but animalculae that infest them, disease them, pollute them: & God does not know we are there, & would not care if He did.[4]

This perspective on the human situation was more than just a momentary conceit, for it recurs often in his writings.[5] On the basis of such a view, Clemens satirized man's self-important belief that the universe would make special exceptions for him.

In writing of "holy Talmage" in "The Second Advent," Mark Twain had in mind the Rev. T. DeWitt Talmage, a prominent clergyman and popular orator. Talmage had been a target of Mark Twain's satire in the 1870s after he had complained that the odor of the unwashed workingman was offensive to the more cultivated classes in a church congregation. Mark Twain speculated that if Talmage "had been chosen among the original Twelve Apostles he would not have associated with the rest, because he could not have stood the fishy smell of some of his comrades who came from around the Sea of Galilee."[6]

Mark Twain may have intended to develop "The Second Advent" into a novel, but it appears that he did not have enough matter and plot. His borrowing of much of another manuscript, "The Holy Children," for use as the latter part of "The Second Advent" suggests that he had already begun to improvise. Some of his later plans for continuing the story, none of which he carried out, are discussed in the Introduction.

The last line of "The Second Advent" indicates that the story was written in 1881, and the paper used for the pages written specifically for "The Second Advent" is not known to have been used before that date. However,

---

[3] Clemens to Mr. Beck, 25 April 1909.

[4] Notebook 21, TS p. 14.

[5] See, for example, *Following the Equator*, DE 20:114, and WWD, p. 454.

[6] "About Smells" in *What Is Man? and Other Philosophical Writings*, ed. Paul Baender (Berkeley, Los Angeles, London: University of California Press, 1972).

Paine noted on the title page, "Probably in 1871." He may have had other information on the date of the piece, or he may simply not have noticed the last line. But 1881 seems the more probable date for this piece.

"The Second Advent" in some ways parallels "The Man that Corrupted Hadleyburg": the events of each story prompt a reversal of religious values, and the outcomes of both are formal resolutions inverting the previous moral stances of the villagers. The citizens of Hadleyburg, after learning that untried virtue is worthless, revise their town's motto to read, "Lead Us into Temptation"; the people of Black Jack, finding that to pray for special providences is disastrous, resolve that the only allowable prayer shall be *"Lord, Thy will, not mine, be done."*

The Second Advent

BLACK JACK is a very small village lying far away back in the western wilds and solitudes of Arkansas. It is made up of a few log cabins; its lanes are deep with mud in wet weather; its fences and gates are rickety and decayed; its cornfields and gardens are weedy, slovenly, and poorly cared for; there are no newspapers, no railways, no factories, no library; ignorance, sloth and drowsiness prevail. There is a small log church, but no school. The hogs are many, and they wallow by the doors, they sun themselves in the public places.

It is a frontier village; the border of the Indian Territory is not a day's walk away, and the loafing savage is a common sight in the town. There are some other sleepy villages thereabouts: Tumblinsonville, three or four miles off; Brunner, four or five; Sugarloaf, ten or twelve. In effect, the region is a solitude, and far removed from the busy world and the interests which animate it.

A gentle and comely young girl, Nancy Hopkins, lived in Black Jack, with her parents. The Hopkinses were old residents; in fact neither they nor their forerunners for two generations had ever known any other place than Black Jack. When Nancy was just budding into womanhood, she was courted by several of the young men of the village, but she finally gave the preference to Jackson Barnes the blacksmith, and was promised to him in marriage by her parents. This was

soon known to everybody, and of course discussed freely, in village
fashion. The young couple were chaffed, joked, and congratulated in
the frank, rude, frontier way, and the discarded suitors were subjected
to abundance of fat-witted raillery.

Then came a season of quiet, the subject being exhausted; a season
wherein tongues were still, there being nothing whatever in that small
world to talk about. But by and by a change came; suddenly all tongues
were busy again. Busier, too, than they had ever been at any time before, within any one's memory; for never before had they been furnished with anything like so prodigious a topic as now offered itself:
Nancy Hopkins, the sweet young bride elect, was—

The news flew from lip to lip with almost telegraphic swiftness;
wives told it to their husbands; husbands to bachelors; servants got
hold of it and told it to the young misses; it was gossiped over in every
corner; rude gross pioneers coarsely joked about it over their whisky in
the village grocery, accompanying their witticisms with profane and
obscene words and mighty explosions of horse laughter. The unsuspecting blacksmith was called into this grocery and the crushing news
sprung upon him with a brutal frankness and directness. At first he was
bowed with grief and misery; but very soon anger took the place of
these feelings, and he went forth saying he would go and break the engagement. After he was gone, the grocery crowd organized itself into a
public meeting to consider what ought to be done with the girl. After
brief debate it was resolved—

1. That she must name her betrayer.
2. And immediately marry him.
3. Or be tarred and feathered and banished to the Indian Territory.

The proceedings were hardly ended when Jackson Barnes was seen
returning; and, to the general astonishment, his face was seen to be
calm, placid, content—even joyful. Everybody crowded around to hear
what he might say in explanation of this strange result. There was a
deep and waiting silence for some moments; then Barnes said solemnly,
and with awe in his voice and manner:

"She has explained it. She has made everything clear. I am satisfied,
and have taken her back to my love and protection. She has told me all,
and with perfect frankness, concealing nothing. She is pure and undefiled. She will give birth to a son, but no man has had to do with her.

God has honored her, God has overshadowed her, and to Him she will bear this child. A joy inexpressible is ours, for we are blessed beyond all mankind."

His face was radiant with a holy happiness while he spoke. Yet when he had finished a brutal jeer went up from the crowd, and everybody mocked at him, and he was assailed on all sides with insulting remarks and questions. One said—

"How does she know it was God?"

Barnes answered: "An angel told her."

"When did the angel tell her?"

"Several months ago."

"Before, or after the act?"

"Before."

"Told her it was going to happen?"

"Yes."

"Did she believe the angel at the time?"

"Yes."

"But didn't mention the matter to you at the time?"

"No."

"Why didn't she?"

"I do not know."

"Did she mention it to the old people?"

"No."

"Why didn't she?"

"I do not know."

"Had she any other evidence as to the facts than the angel?"

"No."

"What did the angel look like?"

"Like a man."

"Naked?"

"No—clothed."

"How?"

"In ancient times the angels came clothed in a robe, the dress of the people of the day. Naturally this one was clothed according to the fashion of our day. He wore a straw hat, a blue jeans roundabout and pants, and cowhide boots."

"How did she know he was an angel?"

"Because he said he was; and angels cannot lie."

"Did he speak English?"

"Of course; else she would not have understood him."

"Did he speak like an American, or with an accent?"

"He had no accent."

"Were there any witnesses?"

"No—she was alone."

"It might have been well to have some witnesses. Have you any evidence to convince you except her word?"

"Yes. While I talked with her, sleep came upon me for a moment, and I dreamed. In my dream I was assured by God that all she had said was true, and He also commanded me to stand by her and marry her."

"How do you know that the dream came from God and not from your dinner? How could you tell?"

"I knew because the voice of the dream distinctly said so."

"You believe, then, that Nancy Hopkins is still pure and undefiled?"

"I know it. She is still a virgin."

"Of course you may know that, and know it beyond doubt or question, if you have applied the right test. Have you done this?"

"I have not applied any test. I do not need to. I know perfectly that she is a virgin, by better evidence than a test."

"By what evidence? How can you know—how do you know—that she is still a virgin?"

"I know it because she told me so herself, with her own lips."

"Yes, and you dreamed it besides."

"I did."

"Absolutely overwhelming proof—isn't it?"

"It seems so to me."

"Isn't it possible that a girl might lie, in such circumstances, to save her good name?"

"To save her good name, yes; but to lie in this case would be to rob herself of the unspeakable honor of being made fruitful by Almighty God. It would be more than human heroism for Nancy Hopkins to lie, in this case, and deny the illustrious fatherhood of her child, and throw away the opportunity to make her name revered and renowned forever in the world. She did right to confess her relations with the Deity.

Where is there a girl in Black Jack who would not be glad to enjoy a like experience, and proud to proclaim it?"

"You suspect none but God?"

"How should I?"

"You do not suspect the angel in the straw hat?"

"He merely brought the message, that is all."

"And delivered it and left immediately?"

"I suppose so. I do not know."

"Suppose he had staid away and sent it by mail—or per dream, which is cheaper and saves paper and postage—would the result to Nancy have been the same, do you think?"

"Of course; for the angel had nothing to do but convey the prophecy; his functions ceased there."

"Possibly they did. Still, it would be helpful to hear from the angel. What shall you do with this child when it comes?"

"I shall rear it carefully, and provide for it to the best of my means."

"And call it your own?"

"I would not dare to. It is the child of the most high God. It is holy."

"What shall you call it, if it be a girl?"

"It will not be a girl."

"Then if it be a boy?"

"It shall be called Jesus Christ."

"What—is there to be another Jesus Christ?"

"No, it is the same that was born of Mary, ages ago, not another. This is merely the Second Advent; I was so informed by the Most High in my dream."

"You are in error, manifestly. He is to come the second time not humbly, but in clouds and great glory."

"Yes, but that has all been changed. It was a question if the world would believe it was Jesus if he came in that way, so the former method was reinstituted. He is to be again born of an obscure Virgin, because the world cannot help but believe and be convinced by that circumstance, since it has been convinced by it before."

"To be frank with you, we do not believe a word of this flimsy nonsense you are talking. Nancy Hopkins has gone astray; she is a disgraced girl, and she knows it and you know it and we all know it. She must not venture to show her face among our virtuous daughters; we will not allow it. If you wish to marry her and make an honest woman of her, well and good; but take her away from here, at least till the wind of this great scandal has somewhat blown over."

So the Hopkinses and the blacksmith shut themselves up in their house, and were shunned and despised by the whole village.

But the day of their sorrow was to have an end, in time. They felt it, they knew it, in truth, for their dreams said it. So they waited, and were patient. Meantime the marvelous tale spread abroad; village after village heard of the new Virgin and the new Christ, and presently the matter traveled to the regions of newspapers and telegraphs; then instantly it swept the world as upon myriad wings, and was talked of in all lands.

So at last came certain wise men from the far east, to inquire concerning the matter, and to learn for themselves whether the tale was true or false. These were editors from New York and other great cities, and presidents of Yale and Princeton and Andover and other great colleges. They saw a star shining in the east—it was Venus—and this they resolved to follow. Several astronomers said that a star could not be followed—that a person might as well try to follow a spot on the sun's disk, or any other object that was so far away it could not be seen to move. Other astronomers said that if a star should come down low enough to be valuable as a guide, it would roof the whole earth in, and make total darkness and give forth no relieving light itself—and that then it would be just as useful, as a guide, as is the eternal roof of the Mammoth Cave to the explorer of its maze of halls and chambers. And they also said that a star could not descend thus low without disorganizing the universe and hurling all the worlds together in confusion.

But the wise men were not disturbed. They answered that what had happened once could happen again. And they were right. For this talk had hardly ended when Venus did actually leave her place in the sky and come down and hang over the very building in which the sages were assembled. She gave out a good light, too, and appeared to be no larger than a full moon.

The wise men were greatly rejoiced; and they gathered together their baggage, and their editorial passes, and clerical half-rate tickets, and took the night train westward praising God. In the morning they stopped at Pittsburg and laid over till Venus was visible again in the evening. And so they journeyed on, night after night. At Louisville they got news of the child's birth. That night they resumed their journey; and so continued, by rail and horse conveyance, following the star until it came and stood over the house in Black Jack where the young child lay. Then the star retired into the sky, and they saw it go back and resume its glimmering function in the remote east.

It was about dawn, now; and immediately the whole heavens were filled with flocks of descending angels, and these were joined by a choir of drovers who were ranching in the vicinity, and all broke forth into song—the angels using a tune of their own, and the others an Arkansas tune, but all employing the same words. The wise men assisted, as well as they could, until breakfast time; then the angels returned home, the drovers resumed business, and the wise men retired to the village tavern.

After breakfast, the wise men being assembled privately, the President of Princeton made a brief speech and offered this suggestion:

1. That they all go, in a body, to see the child and hear the evidence;

2. That they all question the witnesses and assist in sifting the testimony;

3. But that the verdict be voted and rendered, not by the full body, but by a jury selected out of it by ballot.

Mr. Greeley, Mr. Bennett and Mr. Beach saw no good reason for this. They said the whole body was as good a jury as a part of it could be.

The President of Princeton replied that the proposed method would simplify matters.

A vote was then taken and the measure carried, in spite of the editorial opposition.

The President of Andover then proposed that the jury consist of six persons, and that only members of some orthodox church be eligible.

Against this the editors loudly protested, and remarked that this would make a packed jury and rule out every editor, since none of their faction would be eligible. Mr. Greeley implored the President of Andover to relinquish his proposition; and reminded him that the church had always been accused of packing juries and using other underhand methods wherever its interests seemed to be concerned; and reminded him, further, as an instance, that church trials of accused clergymen nearly always resulted in a barefaced whitewashing of the accused. He begged that the present opportunity to improve the church's reputation would not be thrown away, but that a fair jury, selected without regard to religious opinion or complexion might be chosen.

The plea failed, however, and a jury composed solely of church members was chosen, the church faction being largely in the majority and voting as a unit. The editors were grieved over the advantage which had been taken of their numerical weakness, but they could not help themselves.

Then the wise men arose and went in a body to see the Hopkinses. There they listened to the evidence offered by Nancy and Barnes; and when the testimony was all in, it was examined and discussed. The religious faction maintained that it was clear, coherent, cogent, and without flaw, discrepancy, or doubtful feature; but the editorial faction stoutly maintained the directly opposite view, and implored the jury to consider well, and not allow their judgment to be influenced by prejudice and what might seem to be ecclesiastical interest.

The jury then retired; and after a brief absence brought in a verdict, as follows:

"We can doubt no whit. We find these to be the facts: An angel informed Nancy Hopkins of what was to happen; this is shown by her unqualified declaration. She is still a virgin; we know this is so, because we have her word for it. The child is the actual child of Almighty God—a fact established by overwhelming testimony, to-wit, the testimony of the angel, of Nancy, and of God Himself, as delivered to Jackson Barnes in a dream. Our verdict, then, is that this child is truly the Christ the Son of God, that his birth is miraculous, and that his mother is still a virgin."

Then the jury and their faction fell upon their knees and worshiped the child, and laid at its feet costly presents: namely, a History of the Church's Dominion During the First Fourteen Centuries; a History of the Presbyterian Dominion in Scotland; a History of Catholic Dominion in England; a History of the Salem Witchcraft; a History of the

Holy Inquisition; in addition, certain toys for the child to play with—these being tiny models of the Inquisition's instruments of torture; and a little Holy Bible with the decent passages printed in red ink.

But the other wise men, the editors, murmured and were not satisfied. Mr. Horace Greeley delivered their opinion. He said:

"Where an individual's life is at stake, hearsay evidence is not received in courts; how, then, shall we venture to receive hearsay evidence in this case, where the eternal life of whole nations is at stake? We have hearsay evidence that an angel appeared; none has seen that angel but one individual, and she an interested person. We have hearsay evidence that the angel delivered a certain message; whether it has come to us untampered with or not, we can never know, there being none to convey it to us but a party interested in having it take a certain form. We have the evidence of dreams and other hearsay evidence—and still, as before, from interested parties—that God is the father of this child, and that its mother remains a virgin: the first a statement which never has been and never will be possible of verification, and the last a statement which could only have been verified before the child's birth, but not having been done then can never hereafter be done. Silly dreams, and the unverifiable twaddle of a family of nobodies who are interested in covering up a young girl's accident and shielding her from disgrace—such is the 'evidence!' 'Evidence' like this could not affect even a dog's case, in any court in Christendom. It is rubbish, it is foolishness. No court would listen to it; it would be an insult to judge and jury to offer it."

Then a young man of the other party, named Talmage, rose in a fury of generous enthusiasm, and denounced the last speaker as a reprobate and infidel, and said he had earned and would receive his right reward in the fulness of time in that everlasting hell created and appointed for his kind by this holy child, the God of the heavens and the earth and all that in them is. Then he sprang high in the air three times, cracking his heels together and praising God. And when he had finally alighted and become in a measure stationary, he shouted in a loud voice, saying:

"Here is divine evidence, evidence from the lips of very God Himself, and it is scoffed at! here is evidence from an angel of God, coming fresh from the fields of heaven, from the shadow of the Throne, with the odors of Eternal Land upon his raiment, and it is derided! here is evidence from God's own chosen handmaid, holy and pure, whom He has fructified without sin, and it is mocked at! here is evidence of one who has spoken face to face with the Most High in a dream, and even his evidence is called lies and foolishness! and on top of all, here is *cumulative* evidence: for the fact that all these things have happened before, in exactly the same way, establishes the genuineness of this second happening beyond shadow or possibility of doubt to all minds not senile, idiotic or given hopelessly over to the possession of hell and the devil! If men cannot believe *these* evidences, taken together, and piled, Pelion on Ossa, mountains high, what *can* they believe!"

Then the speaker flung himself down, with many contortions, and wallowed in the dirt before the child, singing praises and glorifying God.

The Holy Family remained at Black Jack, and in time the world ceased to talk about them, and they were forgotten.

But at the end of thirty years they came again into notice; for news went abroad that Jesus had begun to teach in the churches, and to do miracles. He appointed twelve disciples, and they went about proclaiming Christ's kingdom and doing good. Many of the people believed, and confessed their belief; and in time these became a multitude. Indeed there was a likelihood that by and by all the nation would come into the fold, for the miracles wrought were marvelous, and men found themselves unable to resist such evidences. But after a while there came a day when murmurings began to be heard, and dissatisfaction to show its head. And the cause of this was the very same cause which had worked the opposite effect, previously,—namely, the miracles. The first notable instance was on this wise:

One of the twelve disciples—the same being that Talmage heretofore referred to—was tarrying for a time in Tumblinsonville, healing the sick and teaching in the public places of the village. It was summer, and all the land was parched with a drouth which had lasted during three months. The usual petitions had been offered up, daily at the hearth-stone and on Sundays from the pulpit, but without result—

the rain did not come. The governor finally issued his proclamation for a season of fasting and united prayer for rain, naming a certain Sunday for the beginning. St. Talmage sat with the congregation in the Tumblinsonville church that Sunday morning. There was not a cloud in the sky; it was blistering hot; everybody was sad; the preacher said, mournfully, that it was now plain that the rain was withheld for a punishment, and it would be wisest to ask for it no more for the present. At that moment the saint rose up and rebuked the minister before the whole wondering assemblage, for his weak and faltering faith; then he put his two hands together, lifted up his face, and began to pray for rain. With his third sentence an instant darkness came, and with it a pouring deluge! Perhaps one may imagine the faces of the people—it is a thing which cannot be described. The blessed rain continued to come down in torrents all day long, and the happy people talked of nothing but the miracle. Indeed, they were so absorbed in it that it was midnight before they woke up to a sense of the fact that this rain, which began as a blessing, had gradually turned into a calamity—the country was flooded, the whole region was well nigh afloat. Everybody turned out and tried to save cattle, hogs, and bridges; and at this work they wrought despairingly and uselessly two or three hours before it occurred to anybody that *if* that disciple's prayer had brought the deluge, possibly another prayer from him might stop it. Some hurried away and called up the disciple out of his bed, and begged him to stay the flood if he could. He told them to cease from their terrors and bear witness to what was about to happen. He then knelt and offered up his petition. The answer was instantaneous; the rain stopped immediately and utterly.

There was rejoicing in all religious hearts, because the unbelieving had always scoffed at prayer and said the pulpit had claimed that it could accomplish everything, whereas none could prove that it was able to accomplish anything at all. Unbelievers had scoffed when prayers were offered up for better weather, and for the healing of the sick, and the staying of epidemics, and the averting of war—prayers which no living man had ever seen answered, they said. But the holy disciple had shown, now, that special providences were at the bidding of the prayers of the perfect. The evidence was beyond dispute.

But on the other hand there was a widespread discontent among such of the community as had had their all swept away by the flood. It was a feeling which was destined to find a place, later, in other bosoms.

When but a few days had gone by, certain believers came and touched the hem of the disciple's garment and begged that once more he would exert his miraculous powers in the name of Him whom he and they served and worshiped. They desired him to pray for cold weather, for the benefit of a poor widow who was perishing of a wasting fever. He consented; and although it was midsummer, ice formed, and there was a heavy fall of snow. The woman immediately recovered. The destruction of crops by the cold and snow was complete; in addition, a great many persons who were abroad and out of the way of help had their ears and fingers frostbitten, and six children and two old men fell by the wayside, being benumbed by the cold and confused and blinded by the snow, and were frozen to death. Wherefore, although numbers praised God for the miracle, and marveled at it, the relatives and immediate friends of the injured and the killed were secretly discontented, and some of them even gave voice to murmurs.

Now came divers of the elect, praising God, and asked for further changes of the weather, for one reason or another, and the holy disciple, glad to magnify his Lord, willingly gratified them. The calls became incessant. As a consequence, he changed the weather many times, every day. These changes were very trying to the general public, and caused much sickness and death, since alternate drenchings and freezings and scorchings were common, and none could escape colds, in consequence, neither could any ever know, upon going out, whether to wear muslin or furs. A man who dealt in matters of science and had long had a reputation as a singularly accurate weather prophet, found himself utterly baffled by this extraordinary confusion of weather; and his business being ruined, he presently lost his reason and endeavored to take the life of the holy disciple. Eventually so much complaint was made that the saint was induced, by a general petition, to desist, and leave the weather alone. Yet there were many that protested, and were not able to see why they should not be allowed to have prayers offered up for weather to suit their private interests—a thing, they said, which had been done in all ages, and been encouraged by the pulpit, too, until now, when such prayers were found to be worth something. There was a degree of reasonableness in the argument, but it plainly would not answer to listen to it.

An exceedingly sickly season followed the confused and untimely weather, and every house became a hospital. The holy Talmage was urged to interfere with prayer. He did so. The sickness immediately disappeared, and no one was unwell in the slightest degree, during three months. Then the physicians, undertakers and professional nurses of all the region round about rose in a body and made such an outcry that the saint was forced to modify the state of things. He agreed to pray in behalf of special cases, only. Now a young man presently fell sick, and when he was dying his mother begged hard for his life, and the saint yielded, and by his prayers restored him to immediate health. The next day he killed a comrade in a quarrel, and shortly was hanged for it. His mother never forgave herself for procuring the plans of God to be altered. By request of another mother, another dying son was prayed back to health, but it was not a fortunate thing; for he strangely forsook his blameless ways, and in a few months was in a felon's cell for robbing his employer, and his family were broken hearted and longing for death.

By this time the miracles of the Savior himself were beginning to fall under criticism. He had raised many poor people from the dead; and as long as he had confined himself to the poor these miracles brought large harvests of glory and converts, and nobody found fault, or even thought of finding fault. But a change came at last. A rich bachelor died in a neighboring town, leaving a will giving all his property to the Society for the Encouragement of Missions. Several days after the burial, an absent friend arrived home, and learning of the death, came to Black Jack, and prevailed with the Savior to pray him back to life and health. So the man was alive again, but found himself a beggar; the Society had possession of all his wealth and legal counsel warned the officers of the Society that if they gave it up they would be transcending their powers and the Society could come on them for damages in the full amount, and they would unquestionably be obliged to pay. The officers started to say something about Lazarus, but the lawyer said that if Lazarus left any property behind him he most certainly found himself penniless when he was raised from the dead; that if there was any dispute between him and his heirs, the law upheld the latter. Naturally, the Society decided to hold on to the man's property. There was an aggravating lawsuit; the Society proved that the man had been dead and been buried; the court dismissed the case, saying it could not consider the complaints of a corpse. The matter was appealed; the higher court sustained the lower one. It went further, and said that for a dead man to bring a suit was a thing without precedent, a violation of privilege, and hence was plainly contempt of court—whereupon it laid a heavy fine upon the transgressor. Maddened by these misfortunes, the plaintiff killed the presiding officer of the Society and then blew his own brains out, previously giving warning that if he was disturbed again he would make it a serious matter for the disturber.

The Twelve Disciples were the constant though innocent cause of trouble. Every blessing they brought down upon an individual was sure to fetch curses in its train for other people. Gradually the several communities among whom they labored grew anxious and uneasy; these prayers had unsettled everything; they had so disturbed the order of nature, that nobody could any longer guess, one day, what was likely to happen the next. So the popularity of the Twelve wasted gradually away. The people murmured against them, and said they were a pestilent incumbrance and a dangerous power to have in the State. During the time that they meddled with the weather, they made just one friend every time they changed it, and not less than a hundred enemies—a thing which was natural, and to be expected.—When they agreed to let the weather and the public health alone, their popularity seemed regained, for a while, but they soon lost it once more, through indiscretions. To accommodate a procession, they prayed that the river might be divided; this prayer was answered, and the procession passed over dry-shod. The march consumed twenty minutes, only, but twenty minutes was ample time to enable the backed-up waters to overflow all the country for more than a hundred and fifty miles up the river, on both sides; in consequence of which a vast number of farms and villages were ruined, many lives were lost, immense aggregations of live stock destroyed, and thousands of people reduced to beggary. The disciples had to be spirited away and kept concealed for two or three months, after that, so bitter was the feeling against them, and so widespread the desire to poison or hang them.

In the course of time so many restrictions came to be placed upon the disciples' prayers, by public demand, that they were at last confined to two things, raising the dead and restoring the dying to health. Yet at times even these services produced trouble, and sometimes as great in degree as in the case of the rich bachelor who was raised by the Savior. A very rich old man, with a host of needy kin, was snatched from the very jaws of death by the disciples, and given a long lease of life. The needy kin were not slow to deliver their opinions about what they termed "this outrage;" neither were they mild or measured in their abuse of the holy Twelve. Almost every time a particularly disagreeable person died, his relatives had the annoyance of seeing him walk into their midst again within a week. Often, when such a person was about to die, half the village would be in an anxious and uncomfortable state, dreading the interference of the disciples, each individual hoping they would let nature take its course but none being willing to assume the exceedingly delicate office of suggesting it.

However, a time came at last when people were forced to speak. The region had been cursed, for many years, by the presence of a brute named Marvin, who was a thief, liar, drunkard, blackguard, incendiary, a loathsome and hateful creature in every way. One day the news went about that he was dying. The public joy was hardly concealed. Everybody thought of the disciples in a moment, (for they would be sure to raise him up in the hope of reforming him,) but it was too late. A dozen men started in the direction of Marvin's house, meaning to stand guard there and keep the disciples away; but they were too late; the prayer had been offered, and they met Marvin himself, striding down the street, hale and hearty, and good for thirty years more.

An indignation meeting was called, and there was a packed attendance. It was difficult to maintain order, so excited were the people. Intemperate speeches were made, and resolutions offered in which the disciples were bitterly denounced. Among the resolutions finally adopted were these:

Resolved, That the promise "Ask and ye shall receive" shall henceforth be accepted as sound in theory, and true; but it shall stop there;

whosoever ventures to actually follow the admonition shall suffer death.

Resolved, That to pray for the restoration of the sick; for the averting of war; for the blessing of rain; and for other special providences, were things righteous and admissible whilst they were mere forms and yielded no effect; but henceforth, whosoever shall so pray shall be deemed guilty of crime and shall suffer death.

Resolved, That if the ordinary prayers of a nation were answered during a single day, the universal misery, misfortune, destruction and desolation which would ensue, would constitute a cataclysm which would take its place side by side with the deluge and so remain in history to the end of time.

Resolved, That whosoever shall utter his belief in special providences in answer to prayer, shall be adjudged insane and shall be confined.

Resolved, That the Supreme Being is able to conduct the affairs of this world without the assistance of any person in Arkansas; and whosoever shall venture to offer such assistance shall suffer death.

Resolved, That since no one can improve the Creator's plans by procuring their alteration, there shall be but one form of prayer allowed in Arkansas henceforth, and that form shall begin and end with the words, *"Lord, Thy will, not mine, be done;"* and whosoever shall add to or take from this prayer, shall perish at the stake.

During several weeks the holy disciples observed these laws, and things moved along, in nature, in a smooth and orderly way which filled the hearts of the harassed people with the deepest gratitude; but at last the Twelve made the sun and moon stand still ten or twelve hours once, to accommodate a sheriff's posse who were trying to exterminate a troublesome band of tramps. The result was frightful. The tides of the ocean being released from the moon's control, burst in one mighty assault upon the shores of all the continents and islands of the globe and swept millions of human beings to instant death. The Savior and the disciples, being warned by friends, fled to the woods, but they were hunted down, one after the other, by the maddened populace, and crucified. With the exception of St. Talmage. For services rendered the detectives, he was paid thirty pieces of silver and his life spared. Thus ended the Second Advent, A.D. 1881.

The Holy Children

(1870s–1881?)

"THE HOLY CHILDREN" satirizes the conventional Christian view of the benefits conferred upon humanity by special providences. The story was probably written during the late 1870s but certainly not later than 1881, when Mark Twain appropriated the last two-thirds of the manuscript for "The Second Advent" (as indicated in the textual commentary). That part has been restored to its original form here, eliminating the revisions made for its addition to "The Second Advent."

The demonstrations of the Holy Children, the large crowds coming from many miles away, and the mounting fervor suggest a religious camp meeting of a kind observed by Clemens in the Midwest in the 1840s, which were common for many years after—such a meeting as that in *Huckleberry Finn* at which the King trades upon the pious sentimentalism of the people in his preaching. Unlike the King, however, the Holy Children are completely virtuous; they have become "perfect and thus . . . able to bring down blessings from heaven at call." As the story progresses, enthusiasm changes to dismay: it is found that prayers that are actually answered bring not blessings but disaster to the community.

The Holy Children

THESE extraordinary beings were the wonder of our village, seventy years ago—and not of our village alone, but of a considerable section of country round about. I can remember people coming horseback or in wagons as much as two hundred miles to see them. I can remember seeing sixty-four saddle horses tied to their mother's farmfence at one time; I often saw thirty and forty tied there. Such persons as came in wagons often camped in the woods and fields near by and staid several days.—The little tavern was full, at the same time, and its overflowings had to be received into the houses of the villagers. At church and Sunday school the Holy Children sat in a pew apart, and it was adorned with evergreen wreaths. The most solemn honors were paid them by everybody; when they walked to or from church, they moved through a double row of strangers and citizens, uncovered, who bent and received their blessing; letters came from great distances begging their prayers and craving their blessing. During some months, the concerns of life were almost wholly abandoned, in our village, and none thought of anything or talked of anything but religion. It was the sweetest and happiest time I have seen in my long life, and the memory of it has been a solace and refreshment to me all my days. In all the houses there were prayers and Scripture readings at various hours during the day, whilst the main part of the night was delivered up to praise-meetings of the people in the church and the larger dwell-

70

ings. The present time seems starved indeed, religious-wise, to one who partook of the rich spiritual abundance of that period.

The Holy Children were three—Hope and Mary, sisters, the one aged ten, the other eleven—and Cecilia, their step-sister, aged a little over ten. They were pale and fragile little creatures; their bodily health was exceedingly poor, but their spiritual health was perfect. They early devoted themselves to the things of religion, and thenceforth they took no interest in other matters. They always rose at dawn, read a chapter, each, aloud, from the Bible, then prayed, each in turn. Then they joined the family, and had household worship, conducting it themselves. They asked a blessing of considerable length, at breakfast, and said grace after it. After breakfast it was their custom to devote one hour to prayer for their father, who detested religion in all its forms, and was a hardened man and singularly profane. He was kind hearted, but irascible; so, although he usually submitted, during some minutes, out of consideration for his daughters, he always lost patience sooner or later, and forsook the house, swearing horribly. He was confined to his bed a week, by and by, and then the children took turns with him, there being one or another of them on her knees in his room most part of the day or night, he blaspheming all the while, until he died, which was upon the eighth day. After the morning hour of prayer for their father, the children used to devote the day, hour by hour, to visiting and praying with the sick and the unconverted here and there about the village, and to distributing tracts, medicines, and food. From evening till midnight they studied and prayed. After their father's death they grew in grace and power with marvelous celerity. They had early taken as their motto that verse which says that faith like to a mustard seed will enable its possessor to remove mountains. The end and object of their ceaseless supplications was to acquire that puissant faith. They never doubted that they would some day succeed, and truly their prophetic hope was fulfilled. They had often said the Bible was full of instances to show that the prayers of the perfect were directly answered, in letter and spirit, no matter how extraordinary the request might be, and they were satisfied a time would come when they themselves would be perfect and thus be able to bring down blessings from heaven at call.

That time did come. It came first to Hope, and then, a little later,

to her sisters. I well remember the day Hope's power was revealed to
her. It was in church, on a Sunday, in July. All the land was parched
with a drouth which had lasted during three months. During that time
many petitions had been offered up, in churches and by firesides,
without avail—the prayers were not answered, the rain did not come.
The Governor had finally issued his proclamation, begging the combined prayers of the churches for a certain Sunday. Even this had
failed. The Sunday afterward was the one which saw Hope's first triumph. There was not a cloud in the sky; it was blistering hot; everybody was sad; the preacher said, mournfully, that it was now plain that
the rain was withheld for a punishment, and it would be wisest to
ask for it no more for the present. At that moment that pale slim child
rose up and rebuked the minister before the whole wondering assemblage, for his weak and faltering faith; then she put her two hands
together, lifted up her face, and began to pray for rain. With her third
sentence an instant darkness came, and with it a pouring deluge! Perhaps one may imagine the faces of the people—it is a matter I am not
able to describe. The blessed rain continued to come down in torrents
all day long, and the happy people talked of nothing but the miracle.
Indeed, they were so absorbed in it that it was midnight before they
woke up to a sense of the fact that this rain, which began as a blessing,
had gradually turned into a calamity—the country was flooded, the
whole region was well nigh afloat. Everybody turned out and tried to
save cattle, hogs, and bridges; and at this work they wrought despairingly and uselessly two or three hours before it occurred to anybody
that *if* that child's prayer had brought the deluge, possibly another
prayer from her might stop it. Some hurried away and called up the
child out of her bed, and begged her to stay the flood if she could. She
told them to cease from their terrors and bear witness to what was about
to happen. She then knelt and offered up her petition. The answer was
instantaneous; the rain stopped immediately and utterly.

It was soon manifest that Hope's power was permanent, and unfailing. Whatsoever prayer she uttered, it was answered, provided the
thing prayed for was a temporal and physical matter. Presently her
sisters acquired a like power. The fame of their miracles spread to long
distances, as I have already said. There was rejoicing in all religious

hearts, because the unbelieving had always scoffed at prayer and said the pulpit had claimed that it could accomplish everything, whereas none could prove that it was able to accomplish anything at all. Unbelievers had scoffed when prayers were offered up for better weather, and for the healing of the sick, and the staying of epidemics, and the averting of war—prayers which no living man had ever seen answered, they said. But the Holy Children had shown, now, that special providences were at the bidding of the prayers of the perfect. The evidences were without number and beyond dispute.

The calls for the Holy Children's services were incessant, and these services were always cheerfully granted. The results were sometimes strange and marvelous in the extreme. I remember an instance where they were asked to pray for cold weather, for the benefit of a poor widow who was perishing of a wasting fever. Although it was midsummer, ice formed, and there was a heavy fall of snow. The woman immediately recovered. The destruction of crops by the cold and snow was complete. This made the children many enemies among the farmers. The children changed the weather many times, every day, to benefit various persons, and these changes were very trying to the general public, and caused much sickness and death, since alternate drenchings and freezings and scorchings were common, and none could escape colds, in consequence, neither could any ever know, upon going out, whether to wear muslin or furs. A man who dealt in matters of science and had long had a reputation as a singularly accurate weather prophet, found himself utterly baffled by this extraordinary confusion of weather; and his business being ruined, he presently lost his reason and endeavored to take the lives of the Holy Children. Eventually so much complaint was made that the children were induced, by a general petition, to desist, and leave the weather alone. Yet there were many that protested, and were not able to see why they should not be allowed to have prayers offered up for weather to suit their private interests—a thing, they said, which had been done in all ages, and been encouraged by the pulpit, too, until such prayers were found to be worth something. There was a degree of reasonableness in the argument, but it plainly would not answer to listen to it.

An exceedingly sickly season followed the confused and untimely weather, and every house became a hospital. The Holy Children were urged to interfere with prayer. They did so. The sickness immediately disappeared, and no one was unwell in the slightest degree, during three months. Then the physicians, undertakers and professional nurses rose in a body and made such an outcry that the Holy Children were forced to modify the state of things. They agreed to pray in behalf of special cases, only. Now a young man presently fell sick, and when he was dying his mother begged hard for his life, and the Holy Children yielded, and by their prayers restored him to immediate health. The next day he killed a comrade in a quarrel, and shortly was hanged for it. His mother never forgave herself for procuring the plans of God to be altered. By request of another mother, another dying son was prayed back to health, but it was not a fortunate thing; for he strangely forsook his blameless ways, and in a few months was in a felon's cell for robbing his employer, and his family were broken hearted and longing for death. A bachelor died in a neighboring town, leaving a will giving all his property to the Society for the Encouragement of Missions. Several days after the burial, an absent friend arrived home, and learning of the death, came to our village and got the children to pray him back to life and health. He found himself a beggar; the Society had possession of all his wealth and legal counsel warned the officers of the Society that if they gave it up they would be transcending their powers and the Society could come on them for damages in the full amount, and they would unquestionably be obliged to pay. The officers started to say something about Lazarus, but the lawyer said that if Lazarus left any property behind him he most certainly found himself penniless when he was raised from the dead; that if there was any dispute between him and his heirs, the law upheld the latter. To return to my narrative. There was an aggravating lawsuit; the Society proved that the man had been dead and been buried; the court dismissed the case, saying it could not consider the complaints of a corpse. The matter was appealed; the higher court sustained the lower one. It went further, and said that for a dead man to bring a suit was a thing without precedent, a violation of privilege, and hence was plainly contempt of court—whereupon it laid a heavy fine upon the transgressor. Maddened by these misfortunes, the plaintiff killed the presiding officer of the Society and then blew his own brains out, previously warning the Holy Children that if they disturbed him again he would make it a serious matter for them.

The children were the constant though innocent cause of trouble. Every blessing they brought down upon an individual was sure to fetch curses in its train for other people. Gradually the community grew anxious and uneasy; these prayers had unsettled everything; they had so disturbed the order of nature, that nobody could any longer guess, one day, what was likely to happen the next. The popularity of the children began to waste away. The people murmured against them, and said they were a pestilent incumbrance and a dangerous power to have in the village. During the time that they meddled with the weather, they made just one friend every time they changed it, and not less than five hundred enemies—a thing which was natural, and to be expected.—When they agreed to let the weather and the public health alone, their popularity seemed regained, for a while, but they soon lost it once more, through indiscretions. To accommodate a procession, they prayed that the river might be divided; this prayer was answered, and the procession passed over dry-shod. The march consumed twenty minutes, only, but twenty minutes was ample time to enable the backed-up waters to overflow all the country for more than a hundred and fifty miles up the river, on both sides; in consequence of which a vast number of farms and villages were ruined, many lives were lost, immense aggregations of live stock destroyed, and thousands of people reduced to beggary. The children had to be spirited away and kept concealed for two or three months, after that, so bitter was the feeling against them, and so widespread the desire to poison or hang them.

In the course of time so many restrictions came to be placed upon the children's prayers, by public demand, that they were at last confined to two things, raising the dead and restoring the dying to health. Yet even these services—which at first nobody dreamed of finding fault with—began to result in serious inconveniences. A very rich old bachelor, with a host of needy kin, was snatched from the very jaws of death by the children, and given a long lease of life. The needy kin were not slow to deliver their opinions about what they termed "this outrage;" neither were they mild or measured in their abuse of the Holy

Children. Almost every time a particularly disagreeable person died, his relatives had the annoyance of seeing him walk into their midst again within a week. Often, when such a person was about to die, half the village would be in an anxious and uncomfortable state, dreading the interference of the children, each individual hoping they would let nature take its course but none being willing to assume the exceedingly delicate office of suggesting it.

However, a time came at last when people were forced to speak. The village had been cursed, for many years, by the presence of a brute named Marvin, who was a thief, liar, drunkard, blackguard, incendiary, a loathsome and hateful creature in every way. One day the news went about that he was dying. The public joy was hardly concealed. Everybody thought of the Holy Children in a moment, but it was too late. A dozen men started in the direction of Marvin's house, meaning to stand guard there and keep the children away; but they were too late; the prayer had been offered, and they met Marvin himself, striding down the street, hale and hearty, and good for thirty years more.

An indignation meeting was called, and there was a packed attendance. It was difficult to maintain order, so excited were the people. Intemperate speeches were made, and resolutions offered in which the children were bitterly denounced. Among the resolutions finally adopted were these:

Resolved, That the promise "Ask and ye shall receive" shall henceforth be accepted as sound in theory, and true; but it shall stop there; whosoever ventures to actually follow the admonition shall suffer death.

Resolved, That to pray for the restoration of the sick; for the averting of war; for the blessing of rain; and for other special providences, were things righteous and admissible whilst they were mere forms and yielded no effect; but henceforth, whosoever shall so pray shall be deemed guilty of crime and shall suffer death.

Resolved, That if the ordinary prayers of a nation were answered during a single day, the universal misery, misfortune, destruction and desolation which would ensue, would constitute a cataclysm which would take its place side by side with the deluge and so remain in history to the end of time.

Resolved, That whosoever shall utter his belief in special providences in answer to prayer, shall be adjudged insane and shall be confined.

Resolved, That the Supreme Being is able to conduct the affairs of this world without the assistance of this village; and whosoever shall venture to offer such assistance shall suffer death.

Resolved, That since no man can improve the Creator's plans by procuring their alteration, there shall be but one form of prayer allowed in this village henceforth, and that form shall begin and end with the words, *"Lord, Thy will, not mine, be done;"* and whosoever shall add to or take from this prayer, shall perish at the stake.

During several weeks the Holy Children observed these laws, and things moved along, in nature, in a smooth and orderly way which filled the hearts of the harassed people with the deepest gratitude; but at last the children made the sun and moon stand still ten or twelve hours once, to accommodate a sheriff's posse who were trying to exterminate a troublesome band of tramps. The result was frightful. The tides of the ocean being released from the moon's control, burst in one mighty assault upon the shores of all the continents and islands of the globe and swept millions of human beings to instant death. The children, being warned by friends, fled to the woods, but they were hunted down, one after the other, by the maddened populace, and shot.

The International Lightning Trust

A Kind of a Love Story

(1909)

"The International Lightning Trust," dated by Paine as 1909,[1] was intended by Mark Twain for immediate publication. The first page of his typescript bears at the top a note directing it "To Mr. Duneka" of Harper & Brothers. Paine's explanatory note on the back of the last page, "Recalled from Harpers as not usable," is elaborated by his editorial comment on a carbon copy of the typescript: "Sent to Harpers but recalled when M. T. died. Not regarded as up to his standard by C. G. [Clara Gabrilowitsch, Clemens' daughter] and A. B. P." The decision to withhold it from publication may have been based partly upon considerations other than those of literary quality. Although the satire in "The International Lightning Trust" is not as scathing as in some of Mark Twain's diatribes, it was very likely still considered too strong. Some of it is aimed not at conventional religious views but at the great business trusts that were a public concern at the time of its composition. But Clemens, who had been something of a Connecticut Yankee egalitarian and also an entrepreneur who had been saved from financial disaster by Standard Oil magnate Henry H. Rogers, was ambivalent toward the trusts. Perhaps the main satiric thrust is at the notion of special providences—a favorite target. The two schemers, erstwhile jour printers

---

[1] *MTB*, p. 1684; the manuscript closely matches "Letters from the Earth," written in 1909.

Jasper Hackett and Stephen Spaulding, profit hugely from what they pointedly call their "trust in Providence." Their lightning trust amounts to a
partnership in a divine lottery that dispenses just enough prizes to ensure
that all of the dupes will play the game. Nevertheless, there is little bitterness in the satire, but rather an almost amiable roguishness.

The idea of a lightning insurance scheme had been considered by Mark
Twain for many years. More than a hint of the idea may be seen in "Abner
L. Jackson (About to Be) Deceased," which concerns an accident insur-
ance swindle and mentions a pamphlet titled "Advice to Persons About to
be Struck by Lightning." In the working notes for "The International
Lightning Trust"[2] it may be seen that he had thought of bringing a
"Lightning-Lottery" into "Which Was It?"—a novel written between the
years 1899 and 1903.[3] It is also of interest that in "The International
Lightning Trust" Jasper claims to have gotten the idea by reading W. E. H.
Lecky's *History of European Morals*, a book that was one of Clemens' life-
time favorites.[4]

One manuscript page, evidently deleted from "Lightning Trust," was
enclosed in a volume in Mark Twain's library and sold with the book after
his death. Its text is printed in the textual note to 99.8–26.[5]

---

[2] See Appendix C.

[3] See *WWD*, pp. 20–22, 177–429.

[4] Clemens probably first read this book about 1874; see Walter Blair, *Mark
Twain & Huck Finn* (Berkeley and Los Angeles: University of California Press,
1960), pp. 134–135, 338, 401 n. 6.

[5] The book was J. G. Frazer, *Passages of the Bible chosen for their Literary
Beauty and Interest* (London, 1895). See Anderson Auction Company, catalog
no. 892—1911 ("The Library and Manuscripts of Samuel L. Clemens"), pp. 10–
11.

The International Lightning Trust
A Kind of a Love Story

Chapter 1

TWO YOUNG FELLOWS sat brooding. Jour printers out of a job: Jasper Hackett and Stephen Spaulding. Their room was a sufficiently shabby one: one frowsy bed in it for the two; three crippled chairs; a maple-grained pine table; a ditto washstand in the corner; the remains of a drugget rug in front of it; a cheap looking-glass, with a pie-slice out of it, on the wall above the stand; an old-time sheet-iron stove, cylinder-shaped; nails here and there with a scant outfit of much-worn clothes dangling from them; a mantel back of the stove with some books on it and half a dozen photographs; over the mantel a three-color God Bless Our Home. Also, two superannuated trunks, both standing open, exposing tolerably empty stomachs. Such were the aspects—and familiar enough in cheap boarding houses in the city; any city in America.

The young fellows had been smoking, but the pipes had gone out and grown cold in their unconscious fingers while they mused and sighed. Both faces, steeped in thought, were profoundly melancholy; Stephen's remained so, but by and by Jasper's lightened a little and an intense interest gradually pushed the sadness aside and took its place.

Steve got up and walked the floor miserably, a while, but got no relief for his sorrows out of it, and sat drearily down again.

"I wish I was dead," he muttered.

He waited for a comment, but none came. He said it again, a little louder. Jasper gave no sign, of either joy or regret. Steve glanced at his comrade's face; it indicated that its owner's thoughts were miles away. Steve spoke again, this time with some energy, and much bitterness.

"Lord, that I should come to this! Two weeks' board owing, and notice impending to march! You the same. Sixteen dollars due between us, and where's it to come from? God knows! I'm mortal tired! Tired of life; tired of waiting, tired of longing, tired of hoping against hope, tired of hunting for work—work that'll never, never come. Hunting for subbing, you understand! *Subbing!* I that used to have a 'case'! . . . And is this *all* the humiliation that's come? No—a thousand times no! Kitty Maloney has given me salaam aleikoom and gone over to the plumber, would that I were dead! O, damnation, why don't you *say* something!"

"Shut up! don't bother me."

"All right, I can suffer alone. We that feel, we that have hearts, we must suffer. To the ignoble is reserved happiness; to the clam repose, not to the lion, not to the eagle. . . . Ah, the bitter, bitter humiliations of these sordid days! Slice of breakfast beefsteak the size of a cat's liver. When I was going to send back my plate her mother paralysed me with a look the boarders all saw, and I desisted. That was yesterday. She served you the same. This morning, coffee without sugar—and deliberate! The boarders all noticed. It means—I know too well what it means—we are going to be fired. Fired—in the morning of life, in the bloom of youth, in the . . . ."

"For Satan's sake, *won't* you be quiet!"

"And *you* turn against me! My cup is full. It needed only this. Forsaken, at last, by the last friend I had! But I make no moan. Let me suffer, all unfriended and forlorn; I deserve it. . . . And Molly has flung *you* away, for the carpenter. Amazing creature, how can you sit there and chew your addled phantasies, and exhibit no feeling, shed not a tear, heave not a sigh over the priceless loss you have sustained? I would rather be a rock, and bay the moon, than carry in my breast a heart like—"

"By the great horn spoon, I've *got* it!" shouted young Jasper, springing up and walking the floor excitedly.

"Got what?"

"Financial salvation!"

"You don't mean it, Jasper, you *can't* mean it!"

"I do mean it. We're saved!"

"O, the dear heaven be praised—say it again, Jasper, say it again!"

"I tell you I've *got* it, Steve, I've got it, sure!"

"O blessed be this day, the clouds are vanishing, the sun illumes the sky again! Tell me, Jasper, tell me all about it."

"Not now, there isn't time; every minute is precious. We must have a hundred dollars—and right away!"

Steve moaned, and only said, despairingly—

"Alas, alas!"

"Alas your grandmother! wake up and get alive—I tell you we've got to have it! *Thousands?* No—*millions!* we are going to be submerged in cash! We can *buy* plumbers and carpenters. Buy them by the gross, by the hundred, by the ton!—on a margin, long or short, or cash down— any way you like! Clear out! leave me! go and get the hundred dollars. I've got to be alone; I want to write out the scheme."

"But where can I get it Jasper?"

"From the subs, from the comps, from anybody and everybody you can strike. Twenty of them; five dollars apiece; first half-year's income, a thousand per cent! tell them so. They'll own a tenth interest in the grand speculation. Go! march! vanish!"

"Jasper, they won't listen to me unless I tell them the scheme. They'll make fun of me. Give me an outline—just an outline, so that I—"

"Not a word. Time's precious—*do* clear out, and let me put it on paper."

Chapter 2

STEVE departed. Jasper began to write. To this effect:

LIFE INSURANCE AGAINST LIGHTNING.

We of the International Lightning Insurance Trust desire to interest the public in an enterprise which we feel has great merit and will turn out to be a boon to many of our countrymen. Every year hundreds of our people are killed by lightning. No special provision in the matter of in-surance has been made for the families of its victims. Having furnished ourselves with a cash capital ample for the purpose, we propose to rem-edy this defect. We offer to insurers what we regard as exceedingly lib-eral terms; terms so liberal, indeed, that we think it will be difficult for any to find fault with them. To wit:

$1 secures $5,000 of insurance against death by lightning.

$5 secures $35,000.

$10 secures $100,000.

The one payment covers everything, and is permanent; it insures for the client's entire life.

Our process is not complex, it is very simple, there is no red tape about it. You send us your money in a special-stamp letter, with your postoffice address, and we return to you, in the same safe way, a numbered ticket specifying the sum due your family in case of your destruction by light-ning. The said sum, in cash, in case of said destruction, will go to your family promptly, without discount.

Address: International Lightning Trust,

102 Fordham Court, New York City

Steve was gone all day. Then he arrived, tired but jaunty and well satisfied with himself, and tossed a bulky roll of bills on the table, say-ing—

"There's your money—two hundred dollars."

"*Two* hundred?"

"It's what I said."

"Why, it's astonishing! How did you ever manage it, Steve?"

"Not in the way you invented, dear-heart, I can tell you that."

"How, then? Come, you interest me."

"Well, it was like this. I didn't think there'd be much chance with the subs, poor devils, so I substituted the regulars. The first one I struck was Jim Bailey; Jim Bailey the prosperous, the practical; Bailey with a face as smooth and hard as an imposing stone. I judged I'd better get my hand in; if I could talk a scheme to *him* I could talk it to anybody. Laugh? Well, you ought to have heard him. But Jasper, that's a wise man—now he certainly is. And *he* is the reason I succeeded—what do you think of that? His heart's not hard, it's only his face. He took me

aside for a private talk; and he told me not to say another word about
that wildcat scheme—keep it to myself. He said get the money for it
another way. He said go after a comp's heart, there's no other sure road
to his pocket. Yes, that's what he said. Then he told me how, and made
up a plan for me. He said borrow the money, and don't say anything
about speculation; said the boys liked us and believed in us, and knew
we were in hard luck—where they'd been themselves, in their time. He
said to tell them we've got the chance of our lives: a chance to get a little old job office, up a back alley, dirt cheap—for a thousand dollars,
two hundred down and the rest on long time—owner of it too old and
ailing to run it any longer. And so on and so on; and he said tell the boys
we've collected a hundred and sixty-five of it and all we want is thirty-
five more to be in luck again and happy; strike them for one or two or
four or five apiece, he said, and don't raise the limit. That was the game
he charted out for me; and he put up ten himself. It worked, and
there's the money to prove it. I got it out of sixty-three of the boys—not
all paying much, of course, but all doing what they could. A wise man,
that Bailey—just a nut!"

"Shake! Why, you're a wonder, Steve—I didn't know it was in you."

"Oh, well, you'll come to know me yet, some day. Now then, what's
your grand scheme?"

For answer, Jasper read the circular aloud.

"My, but it's a daisy!"

"Well, what do you think of it?"

"Land, I don't know what to think of it. It's the wildest idea I ever
heard of."

"Why is it wild, Steve?"

"Why is it wild? Because—oh, well, I'm stunned, I'm paralysed—
you see, you've hit me unprepared. My mind's a wreck; wait and let me
pull it together a little . . . Look here, Jasper, how are we going to pay
out premiums with a shovel on a capital of two hundred dollars?"

"Oh, we'll manage that, all right, don't you be afraid."

"But hang it, Jasper, there's nothing *in* that insane scheme, absolutely nothing. There's no trade for it, don't you see—none in the
world. Consider this: did you ever know anybody that got struck by
lightning?"

"No."

"Nor I. Did you ever know anybody that knew a person that got struck by lightning?"

"No."

"Nor I. Did you ever know anybody that knew a person that knew another person that knew a person that had come pretty near knowing a person that got struck by lightning?"

"No."

"Nor I. Now, then, don't you see, yourself, that there isn't a rag of trade for this business?"

"No. Indeed I *don't* see it. I have the highest hopes. Certainties, I may say."

"Based on what?"

"Two things. One is, the *fear* of lightning."

"Sho, that isn't prevalent enough to make business for us."

"Oh, but isn't it! I'll read you a sentence or two out of Mr. Lecky's History of European Morals. Listen: 'The stroke of lightning was an augury, and its menace was directed specially against the great, who cowered in abject terror during a thunder-storm. Augustus used to guard himself against thunder by wearing the skin of a sea-calf. Tiberius had greater faith in laurel leaves. Caligula was accustomed during a thunder-storm to creep under his bed.' That's the passage that gave me my splendid idea. Here you have three Caesars afraid of lightning —miserably scared at the flash and the thunder. Now then, when Roman emperors had that fear, how is Tom, Dick and Harry to escape it? Steve, the human race is full of it. We'll have a grand trade! If fear fails, no matter, don't worry—No. 2 will make good."

"Very well, fetch out No. 2. What is it?"

"The premiums. Five thousand dollars for one! thirty-five thousand for five! a hundred thousand for ten! Show me the poor devil that can resist that temptation. Why, hang it, he doesn't exist! Don't you know *anything* about the human being? *Business?* There's not going to be any lack of it. Don't you believe so, Steve?"

"Well, it certainly does begin to look sort of plausible, I must say, now that I perceive we are going to trade on the assfulness of the human race. My, but there's plenty of *that*, for sure! Jasper, is this going to be lawful? Won't the government and the police get after us?"

"Why should they? Are we using any concealments? No. Are we cheating anybody? No. Are we making any promises we shan't fulfill? No. Are we employing a false address? No. We are all right. The first thing we want, is the spreading of this circular around, among the clergy, widows, orphans, holders of trust funds, and the other born speculators; the next thing we want is a few thousand numbered tickets—in series A ($1); series B ($5); series C ($10); and the third thing we want is a man laid out dead by lightning, with a one-dollar ticket in his vest pocket—after which, oh *see* us sail along!"

"By George, I'll get the circulars and the tickets printed right away, Monday morning! Jasper, I'm a convert, and you have my gratitude. I am almost reconciled to the plumber."

"Very good. I'll plan-out the ticket, now. For instance:

$1.   ONE DOLLAR. $1.

SERIES • **A** • NO. 21021

INTERNATIONAL LIGHTNING TRUST

PAY BEARER $5,000.

"Series A to be printed on a small red card, thick and substantial, vest-pocket size. Begin the series with No. 21021.

"Series B, good for $35,000, blue card. Begin that series with No. 21021, also.

"Series C, good for $100,000, yellow card. Begin it, too, with No. 21021 like the others."

"Why don't we begin the numbers with No. 1, Jasper?"

"The business would look too new. We want the very first customers to think it's a well-established enterprise, a going concern."

"Good idea, too. So you'd better make the circular say we are already doing business, not *proposing* to do it."

"Right you are. I'll make the correction: *There*—it's done. Another thing. We'll suppress B and C for the present and advertise A only. B and C are too costly to start with."

"That's true. Jasper, where is 102 Fordham Court?"

"It's a bill-sticker's establishment, up a back alley. Dick Adams is the bill-sticker—kind of cousin of mine, and a good sort. I'll arrange with him easy enough, and give him some stock. He receives a good lot of mail matter. We can't have ours come here; we don't want to attract too much attention, along at first. What are you looking so perplexed about?"

"Well, it's this. The circular doesn't say anything about *proof*."

"I'll fix it in two words. *There*—now it says the verdict of the inquest shall be sufficient proof that the owner or bearer of the ticket was killed by lightning."

"Oh, that's all very well, but suppose they don't hold an inquest?"

"Why, hang it, they've *got* to. Don't you know that much? It's a case of 'visitation of God,' as they call it. Well, when He calls on a person in that informal way you don't take the compliment on trust, the law makes you call an inquest and *prove* it. Go on. What else?"

"Why, this—which seems to me to be a perfectly ruinous defect—colossal, the way I look at it: the ticket doesn't contain the candidate's name, it only says Owner or Bearer. That is, Owner or somebody else—*anybody* else. Don't you see? any lightning-victim that holds the ticket can collect the money. You didn't happen to notice that, did you?"

"Oh, yes I did."

"Well then, why didn't you correct it?"

"I didn't want to."

"Oh, come—just hear yourself talk! You're not going to let it *stay* there, surely?"

"Oh, indeed yes! It's deep, it's cunning, it's gay—it's the crown jewel of the whole scheme!"

"That foolishness?"

"Yes. And it isn't foolishness; I tell you it's deep; it's fearfully and wonderfully cunning."

"Explain it, then—explain it."

"The explanation is this: it secures to us the *entire* trade; the lightning-struck trade of the whole country."

"How? Why?"

"Because the minute a person is struck dead by lightning—man, woman or child—friends will fly around and borrow a ticket, on halves, and tuck it into that person's pocket."

"Gracious! is *that* an advantage?"

"Yes, and don't you doubt it. As soon as the public find out that *we* don't care how the corpse got the ticket, everybody will buy one and lay for a chance to sell it to a cadaver. By and by we'll have a hundred million tickets out, and the money in the bank."

"Oh, but why do you *want* to pay for a corpse when he didn't own the ticket?"

"Because it's such a smashing advertisement. The watchword of modern commerce is, *Advertise! advertise! advertise!* Every time a person gets killed by lightning somebody will furnish that person a ticket before he is cold, and two or three days later the neighborhood will be electrified, transported, enraptured with the news that we have emptied a bushel of greenbacks into that bereaved family's lap and didn't ask a question. That entire community will invest in our vest-pocket lightning-rods right away and begin to take a hopeful interest in people that go loafing around under high trees in thunder-storms. People die of disease, people get killed in one way or another, and in nine hundred and ninety-nine cases out of a thousand it is regretfully discovered that they had neglected to insure their lives—which is bad for the family and bad for the insurance companies; but our case is *ever* so different! By and by not one person will be killed by lightning in America that we don't pay for. It will give us immense vogue, stunning popularity, unimaginable prosperity! . . . . Well, speak up. What's troubling you? What's on your mind? Have you struck a snag?"

"I don't quite know, but it looks so to me. We seem to be plunging into this thing helter-skelter without knowing what we are doing it on. We need to know just how much market there is. We've got to have statistics. If it was New York City surface-transportation, there you are: 200 a month killed, and 3,000 crippled. If it's U. S. railroads, there you are again: 12,000 killed per annum and 80,000 wounded; so you know how to arrange your table of rates and premiums. But when you come to lightning, we're plumb in the dark—no statistics, nothing in the world to go upon. Jasper, *we* don't know anything about this business."

"Excuse me! *I* know about it."

"Do you really, Jasper? you've got statistics?"

"I have, I give you my word."

"Oh, all right, then! I was feeling discouraged, but I'm cheerful again. How many people are killed by lightning in America in a year?"

"Twenty-eight. *There!* don't fall off your chair! What's the matter with you?"

"Matter with me? Why, you're crazy. What's the sense in an insurance company to insure 28 people?"

"There's plenty of sense in it. Besides, we are not after the 28, we are after the others."

"What others?"

"The rest of the nation. They'll all come in. Ninety millions. Most of them, anyway. They're all gamblers; everybody is. Do you think you know anybody that would throw away a chance to win five thousand dollars on a one-dollar risk? The first you know you'll be taking out a policy yourself. . . . What are you blushing about?"

"The fact is I *was* thinking of chancing a dollar on the game."

"Well, let that teach you. You're no new invention, the rest of the race is just like you. There's 100,000 clergymen in America; get a church directory, and send them a circular. Send circulars to Bryn Mawr, to Vassar, to Smith, to Wellesley. Send them to Yale, Harvard, and the other universities. Get a chambermaid's directory and send to all the chambermaids. Pull in the milliners—pull them all in. And the sales-ladies; there's a million of those, and all good for Series A. Then there's the miners, and mechanics, and laborers, and clerks, and soldiers, and sailors, and professors, and underpaid schoolmarms, and—oh, well, we'll get all the poor, the struggling, the discouraged, the unfortunate, the forlorn, the friendless, the—look here, don't you make a mistake, Steve, and underrate the value of the poor in an enterprise like this. Why, they're the very bed rock; I wish there was more of them . . . Steve!"

"Well?"

"I've got another idea!"

"What is it?"

"It's to pay ten per cent extra, where a person is killed in church. Distinctly a good idea, it seems to me. Makes us friends with the clergy right at the start—helps to fill up the pews. And there's more churches struck, you know, than any other thing except Sabbath-breakers. . . . *Come in!*"

It was the landlady, Mrs. Maloney. She stood silent a moment, accumulating gloom, then she began, austerely—

"I'll have to inform you, gentlemen—" Her glance fell upon the hatful of greasy Ones and Twos, with here and there a Five, piled up on the table, and she finished courteously and pleasantly with "Your supper's waiting, and everybody's done but you. I reckon you didn't hear the bell, but I've kept it hot for you."

"Oh, thank you, Mrs. Maloney, thank you ever so much," and the young men bowed her out.

"Steve, she came to give us notice."

"Yes, I saw it. But she changed her note with admirable art, without a break in the bar, when she saw the money. And that bell! wasn't it neat? They didn't ring the bell—I should have heard it. That bell was suppressed on our account."

"The money has saved us, Stephen. And it *is* an impressive sight. I've never had that much in my hands before. Nor you either. Steve, she was so paralysed she didn't think to call for the arrears."

"It's because we can pay; otherwise she'd have called—with a shout. It fills her with reverence. The human being's worship is divided between God and money."

"In equal proportions?"

"No, 1 to 95."

Chapter 3

PRIVATELY, each of those young men was feeling good in his heart, and deliciously anticipative. They would be waited on, at supper, by the girls, with not a boarder in the way. It might not be too late to win them back from the plumber and the carpenter, now that the sight of that money had restored the pair of delinquents to the mother's favor. She had liked them well, only a little while back, and had manifestly been pleased with their attentions to her daughters.

But they suffered a disappointment. It was mamma who presided at the table, and did the waiting. They were sad, and couldn't talk, though mamma was cheerful and friendly, and tried to make conversation. There were pauses, uncomfortable silences; silences so deep, sometimes, that you could hear the boarding-house smells; particularly that pungent pork-and-cabbage odor that pervades a boarding house from cellar to roof, and gives out a plaintive wail like the dreamy moan of the eolian harp when its chords are brushed by the wandering zephyr in the stillness of the summer night. To-night it spoke of the absent, and brought heartbreak with it, and Steve said, in the privacy of his bosom, Would it were dumb; it makes me think of her, it speaks to me of her, she carries it in her dear clothes, it haunts me like a viewless spirit—oh, my lost one! lost to me forevermore, mayhap!

They were dear girls; dear, sweet, loud, familiar, good-hearted, vulgar mechanic's-boarding-house girls, of the eternal pattern, the regulation pattern, the pattern that never changes and never fails. Pretty, too. They always are. And always young—sixteen, seventeen, eighteen—seldom above that. Innocent, cheery, full of the joy of youth, free in their ways, but clean in their souls; slangy, ungrammatical; and of such is the kingdom of heaven. As remarked by Steve when he was feeling poetic and oratorical, and wanted a happy figure, and was willing to take any that offered, just so it sounded good. Precious, precious creatures!

And now they came prancing into the sombre place and drenched it with sunshine. Clothed all in dainty summer white; short frocks, trim ancles, brown shoes, pink belts, pink ribbons bunched at the back of the comely heads—oh, just ravishing! Into the gloom comes this burst of sunshine, cackling, romping, chattering, flings out a gay greeting, "Hello, Steve! hello Jaspie! ta-ta, good-bye, so-long, be good to yourselves, dear-hearts!" and out they prance and vanish, alas! leaving sorrow and the blackness of darkness behind them.

"Stop—come back here!" shouts mamma; "where are you going?"

Out of the distance comes the answer—

"To Coney with the boys."

Then silence. They are gone. "The boys." Small words, simple words, but they sent a pain deep into two hearts there, for they stood for the plumber and the carpenter, and those hurt hearts knew it.

The girls did not come back, that night—nor yet the plumber nor the carpenter.

They all returned in the morning—*married*.

Alas!

Chapter 4

Two months later—mid-September. The International Lightning ning Trust, arrayed in new clothes, tailor-made clothes, expensive clothes, sat chatting in their little front office at 102 Fordham Court. We say front office, for already they had a back one. This shows how their business was growing. Two offices, two desks, and new clothes. Plainly the Trust was prospering.

It was afternoon; a September storm was gathering, the air was humid, close, hot, there was no breeze, the sky was steeped in a deep rich gloom, which was suddenly riven perpendicularly with a snaky ribbon of white lightning, and this was followed by a crashing thunderblast. Evidently the young men were charmed.

"My, isn't it splendid, Steve!"

"It just is!"

"I used to hate it. I wanted to get under the bed."

"Me too. I used to go down cellar. But it's all changed now. I don't feel that way any more."

"No, lightning is beautiful now. Only two weeks ago I was still dreading it. We were not ready to have it throw business into our hands yet. Steve, I didn't sleep a wink the time the papers reported that accident out in Nebraska. Remember how we watched the postmarks that week?"

"Don't mention it, pal! I thought if I should see Nebraska on an envelop I should faint."

"Just so with me. The first few that came made me sick. But they didn't bring any commands to stand and deliver, and so—"

"Oh, quite the contrary! Soon they came from out there in a flood, and they all brought dollars."

"Yes, we had a boom out there, and it's booming yet. It was a mortal pity we were not strong enough to outfit that stranger with a five thousand dollar vest-pocket lightning-rod, it would have been worth stacks of income to us. But we are strong enough to take care of the next opportunity, don't you think?"

"Sure. We could liquidate a candidate, and still have money in the bank. A fortnight from now we could easily take care of a couple, the way the receipts are increasing. Do you know, the work is getting pretty heavy for just us two? Within a week we'll need help."

"I guess so. Where shall we look, Steve?"

Steve exhibited just a touch of embarrassment, then said—

"I've already been looking."

"I just knew it! Something told me. What did she say?"

"Jumped at it! So did her mother."

"Good. How did it come about?"

"Well, it was like this. Mamma was moaning to me about that plumber and that carpenter, and seeking sympathy. She said the whole four had got enough of each other before they'd been married three weeks; then the two bridegrooms got a job out West, so they said, and departed. Going to prepare a home for their loved ones; going to send for them when it was prepared; going to write every day, and all that. Not a line, from that day to this—and there the poor old lady broke down and cried. I tell you Jasper, it was pitiful to see. Then she began to fish—and I didn't hinder her any. She said it's hard times, and difficult for her to make both ends meet; she did wish her poor deserted girls could find some kind of employment. Then she approached the subject a little nearer; she had evidently noticed our clothes and our promptness in paying board, and she had divined prosperity from those things—I could see it; and so I wasn't surprised when she asked me if we could help her find work for Kitty and Molly. Jasper, I just felt good! And I didn't waste any time. I said *we* could furnish the work; all we wanted was people that could keep our business a secret."

" 'Bless you, they'll do *that*,' she said, and called them down and I hired them both on the spot. Do you like it?"

"Don't ask me! it makes me want to gush. When did you do all this?"

"Two hours ago, right after dinner. I've ordered the desks."

"Well, isn't it luck! Steve, I reckon we'd better tidy this rookery up a little."

"All right, get at it. I'll help. It won't do any harm; *they* won't know it has been done, and they'll do it all over again. It certainly is a lucky day, now isn't it? Listen to that thunder! Jasper, it does me good to hear it. *I* think it's manufacturing business for us."

The young grass widows went to work the next day. But they were a sorrowful disappointment, in one way: they were Catholics, and they wouldn't listen to any talk about divorce—for desertion or on any other plea; neither would they allow themselves to be courted.

They held their ground straight along, day after day; then the young men laid their happy hopes aside, and Steve said he wished he was dead. Jasper said—

"Steve, you are foolish to talk like that. We are not so very bad off. You've got Kitty for society all day in the back room and I've got Molly in the front. And my, but they're lovely to look at! And they are that sweet, and chattery, and lively, and affectionate and caressing—why, to my mind, it's just the same as being in heaven."

"Yes," said Steve, bitterly, "in heaven, but nothing permanent about it. In heaven with a stop-over ticket. Those vanished mechanics can turn up, any time, and then it's a case of moving down to the other place."

"Steve, you ought not to be so despondent. Have you no trust in Providence? What are we in this world for? To do good. If we do good, Providence will make everything right for us. Aren't we doing good? Who is doing more? We are providing fortunes for the poor; fortunes for poor bereaved families; and giving every one of them a chance. I love our mission. We are Benefactors; Benefactors of the stricken, the unfortunate, the bereaved; we are the stay and support and consolation of the desolate, we heal the broken heart, we are the pauper's only friend. Providence watches over us; Providence sees what we are doing; Providence will recompense us; Providence—"

"Oh, I know it! I know all that; I know we deserve well; I know our sacrifices for the poor and the bereaved are observed by Providence; still, my conscience is not at rest, I have no peace of mind these days."

"Why, Steve?"

"Because we do so much lying. Providence is noticing *that*, too, you may be sure, and it will do us a damage."

This thought went deep, and it made Jasper tremble. He had not thought of this. It sobered him. He remembered with pain that only the last Sabbath, in instructing his Bible class he had dwelt with feeling and impressiveness upon the sinfulness of lying, and now he was himself found guilty. He realized, with shame, that every new circular he issued contained fresh lies—lies essential to prosperity and expansion in the business, it was true, but lies all the same; he realized that the size of these lies was getting bigger and bigger with every new output, and the thought of it made his cheek burn. He saw clearly that in contriving these unholy inventions he was imperiling his salvation, and he spoke up with decision, and said—

"I stop it right here! I will no longer soil my soul with it; we must hire a liar."

Steve responded with strong emotion—

"Oh, thank you for those blessed words, they heal my heart, and it was so sore, so wounded! Our sin removed, our purity restored, we are our own true selves again, dear Jasper, and I know there is rejoicing in heaven over this reform. I shall sleep again, now, as of yore, and be at peace, as knowing the approving angels are watching over me. Jasper, I am hungry to begin anew—have you thought of any one for the place?"

Several names were mentioned and discussed, experts of known ability, all of them: interviewers, fishermen, big-game hunters, and suchlike, but no decision was arrived at. In the end it was decided to call in twenty or thirty professionals and submit the prize to a competition. A man who had been trained by the inventor of the Keeley Motor got the position.

Chapter 5

Next day a thunder-storm swept northward over the city. A telegram in the evening editions said—

"A blacksmith by the name of Saugatuck J. Skidmore was struck by the lightning in the village of Dingley Crossroads, Conn., and instantly killed, leaving a wife and six children in debt and without means, the intention being to take up a subscription for them in the village church next Sabbath it is said."

Steve exclaimed—

"Oh, Jasper, how I do pity that poor widow and those destitute little ones, the thought of them wrings my heart. I do hope Providence will send some kind soul to the inquest with a ticket for that hard-working unfortunate blacksmith."

"He will! I know he will; do not doubt it. It would be ungrateful in us to fail of our trust in Providence at such a time as this, remembering how he has supported us and stood by us, Steve."

"I *do* trust in him, Jasper, I do indeed; but if there was only some way to be *sure* he would send the ticket—"

"Well, I don't doubt him. Still, maybe we better not run any risks— I'll carry it myself."

"Oh, that will be *so* much better, Jasper—it is wonderful how thoughtful you are."

"Jump for the bank and fetch me the cash; I'll take the next train."

Jasper was at the inquest, next morning, in the blacksmith shop, and tucked the ticket into the pocket of a vest that hung, with a threadbare coat, on the wall. The mourning widow and children were there, and also as many of the villagers as could get in. Three witnesses were examined. By their testimony, and that of the village doctor, it was proven that deceased came to his death by lightning, and a verdict to that effect was rendered. Then Jasper asked leave to say a word, and it was granted. He proceeded, with solemnity and deep feeling:

"I am present upon this sad occasion, this affecting occasion, by compulsion of my official character as agent for the International

Lightning Insurance Trust. Our unfortunate brother, the deceased, was insured in our company." (He paused, to let the buzz of surprise and gratification which broke from the lips of the audience run its course; also to note the half-doubting half-believing light of gratitude and hope that rose in the widow's despondent face.) "Only three days ago he sent us a dollar, to buy one of our tickets—Series A, No. 42348— and we mailed it to him the next afternoon. I have brought the money with me—five thousand dollars—" (A general and sweeping gasp of astonishment interrupted him for a moment)—"and it will be my not ungrateful duty to place it in the hands of this stricken lady—with my profound and sincere sympathy in the irreparable loss which she has sustained—upon the return, to me, of the ticket, this evidence being necessary, but quite sufficient, simple as it is." (He took a vast roll of greenbacks out of his handbag.) "Madam, if you have the ticket—"

She began to sob, and wring her hands; and said—

"Oh, he didn't think to tell me about it, he never expecting anything from it, of course, and I don't know what he did with it, and now we never *never* shall find it, O I just know it!"

Jasper spoke consolingly, and said—

"Don't despair, dear madam, I pray you. It will be found, I hope and believe. He must have had it about him. Without a doubt he received it day before yesterday in the afternoon; and if you know what clothes he was wearing then—"

"The same he is wearing now, there where he lies in his shirt-sleeves, just as he was struck. There aren't any others. Look in his pockets, Maria. Quick—oh, *do!*"

All eyes were at once centred upon Maria, intently, eagerly, expectantly. But the searching and ransacking and rummaging failed. Nothing was found, in the nature of a ticket, and something like a groan passed over the house, from lip to lip.

"Oh, dear, dear, I knew it, I just *knew* it! It'll never be found, and we haven't a penny in the world!"

"But don't give up, dear madam, maybe he had his coat on; maybe he—"

"Oh, his coat, certainly—I never thought of that! Yonder it is—do search it, some of you—and the vest, too."

Active hands snatched the things from the wall, and a cry went up—
"*Here it is!*—is this the one?"

It was swiftly passed from hand to hand, and in a minute Jasper had
it. He put on unnecessary glasses and examined it long and carefully,
while the house held its breath—he remarking, from time to time,
"we have to be careful, to guard against counterfeits." Then he put
away his glasses very deliberately; after which, without saying anything,
he stepped to the widow's side and began to lay crisp new fifty-dollar
bills in her lap, one at a time, with not a sound to disturb the deep
silence, until a hundred lay piled up there. Then the house's pent enthusiasm burst its bounds and lifted the roof!

Next day an Associated Press dispatch told the United States all
about it, and a day later the Trust began to lay in some more clerks;
some more the following day; some more every succeeding day. It took
possession of the second floor on lease, and filled it with desks; then
the third floor, then the three remaining floors, knowing they were
going to need them.

The young men were full of gratitude for these prodigious prosperities; words failed them to express all their thankfulness. But they
indulged in no self-praises, no personal boastings and braggings, no
hysterical exultations. No, they were humble. They said, "not for us
the praise; we have not done this, it comes from a higher source."

"How true that is," said Steve. "How surely, how manifestly, how
unquestionably the blacksmith was ordained for his gracious work,
his noble work, his sacrificial work—dying to save others."

"Yes, the hand of Providence was in it—how plainly I can see it
now, Steve. Can our trust in that hand ever weaken, ever waver, after
this?"

"Oh, mine never never can!" said Steve, with emotion. "And never
can I forget the humble instrument; never can I forget the consecrated
blacksmith, and what he has been to us."

"I feel the same way, Steve. I want to certify and perpetuate this
sentiment in some appropriate way. In some secondary way—but
Providence first. In the Great Seal of the Trust. I want the blacksmith,
in his shirt-sleeves and leather apron, bending over, with a horse's hind
foot between his knees and the jagged lance of lightning hitting him

back of the head, and the kneeling family in a group with faces turned thankfully aloft. Motto, 'In Providence We Trust.' "

"It's grand, Jasper, it's just grand! how did you ever come to think of it?"

"And I want to change our name a little, too, Steve. I want to call it the International Christian Lightning Trust."

"It sounds good, Jasper, it sounds noble. You have a special reason?"

"Yes. Look at Christian Science. Notice how it booms, how it spreads, how it sweeps the land. Why, you can almost *hear* it boom. What is the reason? Why, just that one word that it conjures with— Christian. It could heal without that; *did* heal, before it ever added that magic name; but did it get any business? No, sir. Not enough to pay Quimby's rent on the fourth floor. If it ever *had* a name, it couldn't get it before the public; it wasn't worth a farthing, as an advertisement; it couldn't attract attention, try as it might. But Mrs. Eddy devised that name, and hitched the business to an ancient, honored, time-tested, sound, prosperous religion—and look at the result: that religion is hauling that ambulance right along. And will keep on hauling it, too, transportation free. That word is a splendid asset—perfectly splendid!"

"It certainly looks so, Jasper."

"It *is* so. Look at Mental Science; look at Prayer-Healing; look at Faith-Cure—and a couple of dozen others, all in exactly the same business as Christian Science and using exactly the same curative force—why, you hardly ever hear of them. They don't get a start. It would be very different if they would add that name. . . . Tell me: when do you suppose we can begin to advertise the five-dollar tickets?"

"My idea is, when our income reaches a thousand dollars a day."

"Then it isn't far off."

"No. Not more than a month or so, the way things look now. In six or eight months I think we can issue the ten-dollar tickets with safety, and pull in the trade of the well to do."

"What have we arrived at with the capitalists that financed us with that $200—the 63?"

"Nothing done, as yet. Suppose we pay back the loans and a hundred per cent interest, now—"

"Agreed; and after a little we will divide up a tenth of the stock among them, pro rata."

"Yes; and by and by we will send them abroad to establish agencies around the globe."

Chapter 6

Two years later. The young men were chatting and smoking in one of their palatial private offices. The prosperity of the International Christian Lightning Trust was colossal, immeasurable, unimaginable. It was the wonder and the talk of the whole planet. It had bought the vast new Pennsylvania Railway station, and the Pennsylvania had moved up town, subways and all. The building swarmed with hurrying and rushing humanity. On one floor you would find the sign, in vast gilded letters, "GREAT BRITAIN;" on another floor, "GERMAN EMPIRE;" on other floors "CHINA;" "INDIA;" "JAPAN;" "RUSSIAN EMPIRE," and so on and so on—all countries were represented. Also, there were suits of rooms that displayed over their main doors the words "RAILROADS," "BANKS," "MINES," "MANUFACTURING INDUSTRIES," etc.; others that displayed the words "CONGRESS," "FEDERAL GOVERNMENT," "TARIFF CHAMBER," etc.; and still others that displayed the names of the several States and Territories, with the word "LEGISLATURE" added.

Daily all these departments drove a heavy trade. For the young partners bought railway systems in bulk, and sold them in bulk; they bought and sold banks and mines; now and then they bought the U. S. Steel Corporation and sold it again; now and then they bought the Standard Oil and sold it again; also they bought anything and everything that was for sale, except perhaps legislatures; and it was whispered that they were deep in a plan to buy the army and navy and start a monarchy and nobility.

In the gorgeous suite of salons that bore the sign "CORONET PARLORS" a large and increasing commerce was carried on, under the capable management of the Count and Countess Alibi. The business was planetarial in its scope. There you could get anything you wanted:

if, for the moment, it wasn't in stock, the Count would order it for you. By wireless. It would arrive by the next ship. The house dealt in everything going, from Russian and Latin princes all the way down to English viscounts—and drew the line there.

Molly had two thousand lady-clerks under her, and Kitty the same.

The vast court was full of motor-cars, the spacious roofs were full of aeroplanes.

Jasper cleared his throat, and flipped the ash from his cigar. He did it because it is always done in books, as preparation for a remark. The remark could be made just as well without it, but he was a slave to custom. Then he said—

"Steve, we have really done wonders—"

"Under Providence," Steve interrupted, austerely.

"I was going to say it, Steve, I was indeed; it would be ungrateful in me to forget. Yes—wonders! When we went into the business there was an average of only 28 death-strokes per year in America; it didn't vary more than two, either way, and was as regular and forecastable as suicide. Only two years, and already we've got it up to 280,000 per annum."

"I know; but it was our liar that did that—under Pr—*say*, Jasper! do you know that the foreign business is soaring up, now, at a most incredible rate? It certainly is. In Italy it has knocked the lottery cold, so to speak—the lottery isn't anywhere; we are getting all the business. The government is frightened, and threatens to expel us. All over the world we are doing a vast and increasing trade. Our liar has worked the several countries hard; in the most of them he has increased the lightning-stroke output away high up above the facts. Admirable genius! and so devoted to his art, and so earnest. A pity we lost him."

"Have we lost him?"

"Yes, the patent medicine Trust wanted him, and I let him go. We could spare him; I've had understudies in training, this good while. He gets three hundred thousand a year, now—a third more than we were paying him."

"Steve, what was the actual kill, this last year?"

"Thirty-one. A point above last year. Due to increase of population, you know."

"Did we get all of them?"

"Every one. Bailey has nothing to do but watch the papers and send tickets to the victims and the families. A good man, Bailey, and thoughtful. Nobody gets killed in the winter, of course, but Bailey doesn't allow *that* to keep us out of the public eye. In every winter month he pays one or two or three policies and keeps the talk going."

"How does he manage?"

"When a railroad hand gets crushed, he waits about a week to let the memory of it stale a little, then he sends five or six of his trained witnesses there, and they get up a private conspiracy to swindle our Trust and divide the swag among the confederates and a selected poor family. They send for Bailey, and he comes, looking guileless and gullible, and they convince him that the man was killed by lightning, and that the coroner's an ass. Bailey pays, and the grateful family hug him, and weep down his back, and laugh in their sleeve; and so do all the gang, including Bailey's trained witnesses. The news filters around over the country, and Bailey gets offers of all kinds of dead men, but he doesn't take them, he only takes a deceased when the business needs one."

P.S.

Our story is told. Still, a brief postscript may not be amiss. The happiness of our young men was large, but it was not complete. It could not be complete while they remained unwedded to the idols of their young hearts. The idols of their young hearts stood stedfastly upon principle, and would wed no one while the carpenter and the plumber remained undead, or, if dead, not *known* to be dead. There they sat, day after day, the beautiful ones, the worshipped—lovely, gracious, soul-intoxicating, exquisitely clothed, expensively clothed, bewitchingly clothed, from the ground up, and crowned with a pompadoured halo, a divine arrangement of their hair on the pattern of the pneumatic tyre—there they sat, day after day and smiled, sweetly smiled, tenderly smiled, longingly smiled, but remained loyal to principle, loyal to religion, loyal to their own best selves, and waited upon the will of Providence, without murmur, without complaint. They were proud, too, nobly proud. They said that even if Providence should pity them and set them free, they doubted if it would be properly self-respecting in two fortuneless young creatures to marry these billionaires and bring upon themselves the suspicion that it was their money they were marrying.

Yet the young men were bravely and unyieldingly hopeful through it all. They said Providence had never failed them yet; had they a right to doubt Providence now? No. True, the case was difficult and complex, but what of that?—nothing was impossible to Providence. No, no—all in good time Providence would find a way out. Steve said, with heroic faith,

"Give him a chance!"

This was prophetic. How seldom it is that a prophecy possesses that character. Few have noticed this, yet it is true. And how discouraging are a prophet's experiences, as a rule. Steve said prophesying was the only human art that couldn't be improved by practice. It was a most just judgment, and was admired by all who heard it.

Only thirteen days after the utterance of the prophecy just quoted, Jasper was in the Far West. He did not know why; he had no business there, and the thought thrilled him, for he recognized the hand of Providence in it. He was in the village of Arkansas Flats. It was a Sunday. In the morning. All was tranquil, peaceful, holy; the Sunday school bells were chanting, the sweet children, scoured, tidy, reverent, were wending their way, in groups and in procession, silently rehearsing their verses; the slumbering Mississippi was glassing its verdant islands in its shining surface. Such was the scene: the tragedy follows. That very evening Jasper wrote a letter, and this is what he said in it:

Far out upon the broad stream two men were fishing, in a boat. Breaking the Sabbath. Presently a vast fish, seeking nourishment, tried to climb into the boat. The frightened men sought refuge in the river, on the side opposite to the one occupied by the invasion. They could not swim. They struggled desperately, hopelessly. Kind strangers flew to their rescue. They were saved, when almost expiring. Realizing their sin, and that they had been near to death, they were now repentant, they were changed men, redeemed men, and they resolved that from that mo-

ment they would lead righteous lives. As soon as they could change their
clothes they went rejoicing to church, hosannahing their happiness out
of full hearts, and got struck by lightning. The only ones it happened to.
And who were they? *It was the plumber and the carpenter!* The hand of
Providence was in it. I now recognized, with awe and wonder, why I was
in that far region, I now recognized the source of the mysterious impulse
that had directed my wandering steps. I was in the church; I was the first
to reach the bodies; it was my pitying hands that closed the glazing eyes;
it was Providence that provided the tickets, but I helped. One apiece, of
the hundred-thousand-dollar kind—a good advertisement. You will raise
it to twenty tickets, Steve, in reporting to the bereaved the calamity
which has befallen them. Break it as gently as you can, and hand them
the money. Shall you ever doubt again, Steve? *can* you ever doubt again?

Those loving young creatures, once so poor, now so rich; once so
despised, now so courted; once so obscure, now so illustrious, are happy
to-day in holy matrimony, and are in society. By humble faith, virtue,
and brave self-sacrifice they have reached these sublime heights. They
will never doubt again.

It is a lesson for us all.

Colloquy Between a Slum Child and a Moral Mentor

(Late 1860s or late 1880s)

MARK TWAIN did not give this piece a title. "Colloquy Between a Slum Child and a Moral Mentor," a rather formal title apparently supplied by Dixon Wecter when he was Editor of the Mark Twain Papers, has been retained, since it seems in accord with the pompous gravity of the mentor's religious instruction. The only available text is a typescript made for Wecter from a manuscript once in the possession of Doris and Samuel Charles Webster. The manuscripts which formed the Webster collection were, for the most part, written either before 1870 or between 1885 and 1888, when Charles L. Webster was a partner and manager of Clemens' publishing house. "Colloquy" was probably written during one of those periods; the 1860s, when Clemens often satirized pious religious tracts and Sunday school sentimentalities, is more likely. In the event the manuscript has survived, it may, if discovered, make possible a more precise dating.

Colloquy Between a Slum Child
and a Moral Mentor

"WHO MADE the grass?"

"Chief Police."

"No, no—not the Chief of Police. God made the grass. Say it, now."

"God made the grass."

"That is right. Who takes care of the beautiful grass and makes it grow?"

"Chief Police."

"Oh, no, no, no—*not* the Chief of Police. The good God takes care of the grass and makes it grow. Say it, my boy—that's a good fellow."

"The good God takes care of the grass and makes it grow."

"How does grass grow?"

"With an iron railing around it."

"No, I do not mean that. I mean, what does it come from? It comes from little tiny seeds. The good Heavenly Father makes the grass to grow from little seeds. You won't forget that now, will you?"

"Bet your bottom dollar!"

"Ah, naughty, naughty boy. You must not use slang. Where do little boys go who use slang?"

"Dono. *I* goes to the Bowery when shining's good and I've got the lush."

106

"Tut, tut, tut! Don't talk so. You make me nervous. Little boys who talk that way go to the——bad place!"

"No—but do they? Where is it?"

"It is where there is fire and brimstone always and forever."

"Suits Crooks! *I* never ben warm enough yet, ony summer time. Wisht I'd a ben there in the winter when I hadn't any bed kiver but a shutter. That Higgins boy he busted two of the slats out, and then I couldn't keep the cold out *no* way. It had a beautiful brass knob on it, Cap., but brass knobs ain't no good, ony for style, you know. I'd like to ben in that bad place them times, by hokey!"

"Don't swear, James. It is wicked."

"What's *wicked?*"

"Why, to be wicked is to do what one ought not to do—to violate the moral ordinances provided for the regulation of our conduct in this vale of sorrows, and for the elevation and refinement of our social and intellectual natures."

"Gee—whillikins!"

"*Don't* use such words, my son—pray don't."

"Well, then I won't—but I didn't mean no harm—wish I may die if I did. But you made a 'spare,' that time, *didn't* you?"

"A 'spare?' What is a spare, my child?"

"*You* don't know what a 'spare' is? Oh, no, gov'ner, that cat won't fight, you know. Fool who, with your nigger babies whitewashed with brickdust!"

"Well, I believe it is nearly useless to try to break you of using slang, my poor, neglected boy. But truly, I do not know what a 'spare' is. What *is* a 'spare?' "

"Well, if *you* ain't ignorant, I'm blowed! Why a spare is where you fetch all the pins with two balls—and when you make a ten-strike, you've got two spares, you know. Well, when you got off all of them jaw-breakers, I judged the pins was all down on *your* alley, anyway."

"I stand rebuked, James. Egotism will betray the best of us to humiliation."

"Spare! I tell you them winders of yours snakes the head pin every time, gov'ner."

"Conquered again!—Well, James, we will go back to the old lesson. I am out of my element in this. James, what is grass for?"

"To make parks out of,—like the City Hall."

"Is that all? Isn't it to make the pretty fields, and lawns, and meadows?"

"Don't know nothing about them things—never seen 'em."

"Ah, pity. What does our Heavenly Father do with the grass when He makes it?"

"Puts it in the Hall park and puts up a sign, 'Keep off'n the grass—dogs ain't allowed.' "

"Poor boy! And what does He put it there for?"

"To look at, through the railings."

"Well, it really does seem so. What would you do with the beautiful grass that God has made, if you had it?"

"Roll in it! Oh, gay!"

"Well, I wish in my heart the City Fathers would let you—so that you might have *one* pleasure that God intended for all childhood, even the children of poverty!—yea, that He intended even for vagrant dogs, that shun the tax and gain precarious livelihoods by devious ways and questionable practices."

"Set 'em up again, gov'ner!"

"I was partly talking to myself, James—that is why I used the long words. James, who made you?"

"Chief Police, I guess."

"Mercy! I wish I could get that all-powerful potentate out of your head. No, James, God made you."

"Did he, though?"

"Yes—God made you, as well as the grass."

"Honest injun? That's bully. But I wish he'd fence me in and take care of me, same as he does the grass."

"He does take care of you James. You ought to be very thankful to Him. He gives you the clothes you wear—"

"Gov'ner, I got them pants from Mike the ragman, myself."

"But they came from above, James—they came from your Heavenly Father. He gave them to you."

"I pass. But I reckon I had to pay for 'em, though. Mike never told me. He never said nothing about parties giving 'em to me."

"Why, James! But then you do not know any better. And He gives you your food—"

" 'Spensary soup! I wisht I had a cag of it!"

"And the bed that you sleep in—"

"Cellar door and a shutter with a brass knob on it. Now look-a-here gov'ner, you're a guying me. You never tried a shutter. *I* ain't thankful for no such a bed as that."

"But you ought to be, James, you ought to be. Think how many boys are worse off than you are."

"I give in, I do. There's that-there Peanut Jim—his parents is awful poor. He ain't got no shutter. I was always sorry for that poor cuss."*

---

* Founded on absolute fact. A little girl sleeping in an upper room of a New York tenement house on a cold night, with a dilapidated window-shutter for a coverlet, said: "Mother, I am so sorry for poor little girls that haven't got any window-shutter! I ought to be very thankful." (Respectfully recommended for the Sunday School books.) [Mark Twain's note]

Thoughts of God

(Early 1900s)

FOR CLEMENS the fly was a symbol of divine malevolence. In his 1903 notebook he wrote:

> The morals of a God ought to be minutely perfect. I would not worship a God that made the fly.[1]
>
> If God invented the fly, that is enough. It gives us the measure of His character. If a man had invented the fly, we should curse his name forever. And he would deserve it.[2]

The content of "Thoughts of God" places the composition of the manuscript in the same period as the notebook entry, a judgment confirmed by the evidence of the paper Mark Twain used for the work. It is "unthinkable," he says in "Thoughts of God," that there could be "a Man of a sort willing to invent the fly." But the existence of the fly is taken as proof that there is a god of such a kind—one who has "cunningly designed" the fly to make every creature's life a misery. The idea that living beings have been fashioned by and are at the disposal of a god that does not wish them well is possibly the most unsettling one that can be entertained—and it would be useless to pretend that Clemens was merely joking when he expressed such a view. It appears that he meant it when he charged:

> The real God, the Supreme One is not a God of pity or mercy—not as we recognize these qualities. Think of a God of mercy who would create the typhus

---

[1] Notebook 36, TS p. 11.
[2] Ibid., p. 16.

germ, or the house-fly, or the centipede, or the rattlesnake, yet these are all His handiwork. They are a part of the Infinite plan. The minister is careful to explain that all these tribulations are sent for a good purpose; but he hires a doctor to destroy the fever germ, and he kills the rattlesnake when he doesn't run from it, and he sets paper with molasses on it for the house-fly.

Two things are quite certain: one is that God, the limitless God, manufactured those things, for no man could have done it. The man has never lived who could create even the humblest of God's creatures. The other conclusion is that God has no special consideration for man's welfare or comfort, or He wouldn't have created those things to disturb and destroy him. The human conception of pity and morality must be entirely unknown to that Infinite God, as much unknown as the conceptions of a microbe to man, or at least as little regarded.[3]

[3] *MTB*, p. 1356.

Thoughts of God

How often we are moved to admit the intelligence exhibited in both the designing and the execution of some of His works. Take the fly, for instance. The planning of the fly was an application of pure intelligence, morals not being concerned. Not one of us could have planned the fly, not one of us could have constructed him; and no one would have considered it wise to try, except under an assumed name. It is believed by some that the fly was introduced to meet a long-felt want. In the course of ages, for some reason or other, there have been millions of these persons, but out of this vast multitude there has not been one who has been willing to explain what the want was. At least satisfactorily. A few have explained that there was need of a creature to remove disease-breeding garbage; but these being then asked to explain what long-felt want the disease-breeding garbage was introduced to supply, they have not been willing to undertake the contract.

There is much inconsistency concerning the fly. In all the ages he has not had a friend, there has never been a person in the earth who could have been persuaded to intervene between him and extermination; yet billions of persons have excused the Hand that made him—and this without a blush. Would they have excused a Man in the same circumstances, a man positively known to have invented the fly? On the contrary. For the credit of the race let us believe it would have

112

been all day with that man. Would these persons consider it just to reprobate in a child, with its undeveloped morals, a scandal which they would overlook in the Pope?

When we reflect that the fly was not invented for pastime, but in the way of business; that he was not flung off in a heedless moment and with no object in view but to pass the time, but was the fruit of long and pains-taking labor and calculation, and with a definite and far-reaching purpose in view; that his character and conduct were planned out with cold deliberation; that his career was foreseen and fore-ordered, and that there was no want which he could supply, we are hopelessly puzzled, we cannot understand the moral lapse that was able to render possible the conceiving and the consummation of this squalid and malevolent creature.

Let us try to think the unthinkable; let us try to imagine a Man of a sort willing to invent the fly; that is to say, a man destitute of feeling; a man willing to wantonly torture and harass and persecute myriads of creatures who had never done him any harm and could not if they wanted to, and—the majority of them—poor dumb things not even aware of his existence. In a word, let us try to imagine a man with so singular and so lumbering a code of morals as this: that it is fair and right to send afflictions upon the *just*—upon the unoffending as well as upon the offending, without discrimination.

If we can imagine such a man, that is the man that could invent the fly, and send him out on his mission and furnish him his orders: "Depart into the uttermost corners of the earth, and diligently do your appointed work. Persecute the sick child; settle upon its eyes, its face, its hands, and gnaw and pester and sting; worry and fret and madden the worn and tired mother who watches by the child, and who humbly prays for mercy and relief with the pathetic faith of the deceived and the unteachable. Settle upon the soldier's festering wounds in field and hospital and drive him frantic while he also prays, and betweentimes curses, with none to listen but you, Fly, who get all the petting and all the protection, without even praying for it. Harry and persecute the forlorn and forsaken wretch who is perishing of the plague, and in his terror and despair praying; bite, sting, feed upon his ulcers, dabble your feet in his rotten blood, gum them thick with plague-germs—

feet cunningly designed and perfected for this function ages ago in the beginning—carry this freight to a hundred tables, among the just and the unjust, the high and the low, and walk over the food and gaum it with filth and death. Visit all; allow no man peace till he get it in the grave; visit and afflict the hard-worked and unoffending horse, mule, ox, ass, pester the patient cow, and all the kindly animals that labor without fair reward here and perish without hope of it hereafter; spare no creature, wild or tame; but wheresoever you find one, make his life a misery, treat him as the innocent deserve; and so please Me and increase My glory Who made the fly."

We hear much about His patience and forbearance and long-suffering; we hear nothing about our own, which much exceeds it. We hear much about His mercy and kindness and goodness—in words—the words of His Book and of His pulpit—and the meek multitude is content with this evidence, such as it is, seeking no further; but whoso searcheth after a concreted sample of it will in time acquire fatigue. There being no instances of it. For what are gilded as mercies are not in any recorded case more than mere common justices, and *due*—due without thanks or compliment. To rescue without personal risk a cripple from a burning house is not a mercy, it is a mere commonplace duty; anybody would do it that could. And not by proxy, either—delegating the work but confiscating the credit for it. If men neglected "God's poor" and "God's stricken and helpless ones" as He does, what would become of them? The answer is to be found in those dark lands where man follows His example and turns his indifferent back upon them: they get no help at all; they cry, and plead and pray in vain, they linger and suffer, and miserably die. If you will look at the matter rationally and without prejudice, the proper place to hunt for the *facts* of His mercy, is not where man does the mercies and He collects the praise, but in those regions where He has the field to Himself.

It is plain that there is one moral law for heaven and another for the earth. The pulpit assures us that wherever we see suffering and sorrow which we can relieve and do not do it, we sin, heavily. *There was never yet a case of suffering or sorrow which God could not relieve.* Does He sin, then? If He is the Source of Morals He does—certainly nothing can be plainer than that, you will admit. Surely the Source of law cannot violate law and stand unsmirched; surely the judge upon the bench cannot forbid crime and then revel in it himself unreproached. Nevertheless we have this curious spectacle: daily the trained parrot in the pulpit gravely delivers himself of these ironies, which he has acquired at second-hand and adopted without examination, to a trained congregation which accepts them without examination, and neither the speaker nor the hearer laughs at himself. It does seem as if we ought to be humble when we are at a bench-show, and not put on airs of intellectual superiority there.

The Emperor-God Satire

(1870s)

In this satiric fable the Emperor-God displays toward the Unyumians the qualities Clemens had in the 1870s associated with the "God of the Bible." At the same time, this deity also exhibits toward other peoples some of the attributes of the real God, as Clemens had envisioned him:

> Its [the Bible's] God was strictly proportioned to its dimensions. His sole solicitude was about a handful of truculent nomads. He worried and fretted over them in a peculiarly and distractingly human way. One day he coaxed and petted them beyond their due, the next he harried and lashed them beyond their deserts. . . .
>
> To trust the God of the Bible is to trust an irascible, vindictive, fierce and ever fickle and changeful master; to trust the true God is to trust a Being who has uttered no promises, but whose beneficent, exact, and changeless ordering of the machinery of his colossal universe is proof that he is at least steadfast to his purposes; whose unwritten laws, so far as they affect man, being equal and impartial, show that he is just and fair. . . .[1]

Much of what is here expressed remained Clemens' view throughout his life. In one important regard, however, he modified his outlook: he came to doubt the justice and fairness of the real God. In his Autobiographical Dictation of 23 June 1906 the actual God is seen to be as intolerable as the biblical one: he does not answer prayers or otherwise relieve human miseries. Instead, "He made it an unchanging law that that creature should

---

[1] *MTB*, p. 412.

suffer wanton and unnecessary pains and miseries every day of its life—that by that law these pains and miseries could not be avoided. . . ."[2] Clemens concluded:

> the genuine God, the Maker of the mighty universe is just like all the other gods in the list. He proves every day that He takes no interest in man, nor in the other animals, further than to torture them, slay them and get out of this pastime such entertainment as it may afford—and do what He can not to get weary of the eternal and changeless monotony of it.[3]

In "The Emperor-God Satire" it may be seen that for Clemens the distinction between the God of the Bible and the real God was in the 1870s already becoming blurred—and that neither kind of deity was beyond the range of his satire.

"The Emperor-God Satire" is a descriptive title applied to the manuscript at the time Bernard DeVoto was the Editor of the Mark Twain Papers. The sketch is written on the same paper as that used for the essay "The Proportions of God," which Paine indicates was written in the 1870s. This piece may be conjecturally assigned to the same period.

---

[2] "Reflections on Religion," *Hudson Review* 16 (Autumn 1963): 346.
[3] Ibid., pp. 348–349.

The Emperor-God Satire

THE EMPEROR is not merely honored by his subjects, but actually worshiped. His hair and beard are as white as snow, but his countenance is gloomy and forbidding. He is said to be more than a hundred years old, and certainly he looks it. He says—and the people believe—that he has always reigned there, and never died. When his spirit is tired of occupying one body, it enters into another, (always that of a priest,—a priest of the highest rank,) and the former is embalmed and placed with its innumerable predecessors in a vast and ancient mausoleum. This immortal Emperor visits the mausoleum, at long intervals, and contemplates himself in the twelve hundred and forty-six varying forms which he has worn during eleven thousand years. The embalming has been perfectly done; a stranger could not tell the oldest mummies from the newest but by the dates marked upon them. The Emperor has had preferences among these forms. He will point to one and say, "I enjoyed that body, it had a youthful spring in its muscles; also the one in yonder alcove—in the five thousand years that have passed since I occupied it, my spirit has not been clothed in such comely flesh."

The great cities and civilized nations are all in the interior; none are close to the sea. The belt which borders the sea, all around, is occupied by savages entirely, and always has been. The Emperor lives in a remote little valley called Unyumi, whose half-score of meagre tribes are mere savages, and by nature childish, troublesome, and vicious. Nevertheless

118

they have been the object of the Emperor's sole solicitude, from the beginning. He is only the spiritual head of the rest of the land, a sort of Pope, and has never had anything to do with its civil government nor had any desires in that direction. In all the lagging ages that have drifted over his head he has never once visited the civilized regions. The priests in the civilized regions sacrifice to him in their temples before congregations more or less devout, but made up mainly of women. The men show no great zeal except in time of sore private or public distress. Prayers, for help, temporal and spiritual—in the form of written petitions,—are offered in the temples by the people, accompanied by more or less costly gifts. At stated intervals deputations of priests gather the prayers together and convey them across the plains and mountains and deposit them, with a small per centage of the gifts, in an empty temple situated just outside the limits of the Unyumi valley, and then return home. They have seen no one. Priests of the Emperor remove the deposits by night. The gifts, coming as they do from so many communities, make a great revenue for the Emperor and his Unyumi temples. The prayers are laid before the throne with the unvarying formula, "The petitions read as always—will your Sacredness examine them?" The answer is always the same: "My laws are equable and permanent, I cannot interrupt their wide and beneficent ebb and flow to accommodate ephemeral caprice—burn the prayers."

The Emperor's relations with his handful of ignorant and brutish Unyumi tribes is wholly different. His interest in them and fondness for them amount to infatuation.—While he will not trouble himself in the least degree with the governmental affairs of the island at large, he gives constant and tireless attention to the state affairs of the Unyumians. He sets up their petty tribal kings, he suspends them, chastises them, pulls them down, slaughters them, alters the succession, reinstates the former line—all according to his moods and caprices. So long as one of these shabby princes pleases him he heaps favors and benefits upon him with a frantic and spendthrift lavishness; but any petty offense will instantly turn the Emperor's love to hate and he will straightway launch death and desolation upon that prince and all his belongings.

The Emperor not only fills and empties the inconsequent thrones of Unyumi, he descends lower, and writes the tribal laws with his own hand; lower still: he orders the details of priestly service in the temples, appoints this underling and that, for this and that office, and even tells how the sacrificial animal shall be baked, and which portions of it shall be eaten by the priest and which discarded; and yet lower: he concerns himself with the small domestic matters of the Unyumi families, even exposing in plain words and compacting into inflexible laws, things pertaining to the married relation which are considered of too private a nature for such handling in other countries.

He looks at no prayer that comes from beyond the limits of Unyumi, nor interrupts the operation of any law in answer to such; but no prayer of an Unyumian, howsoever base his estate, goes unconsidered, even though it propose to arrest the movement of the most important of his edicts. Tradition says that some centuries ago the most enlightened and exalted of the great nations of the interior implored him to send rains upon their parched fields. This time his priests read the petition to him, because of its extreme importance, that nation being threatened with the horrors of famine; but he answered that the law of rains and drouths was general, and he would not alter it for the momentary benefit of a community. Yet at the same time he interrupted a great general law, upon quite trifling grounds, in behalf of an Unyumi priest. He had sent this priest to command a neighboring tribe of pagans to retire into banishment and give up their lands to some families of Unyumians who needed them as a grazing ground for their flocks and herds. The pagans mocked at the priest and scouted his credentials, saying these were forged. So the priest petitioned the Emperor for a sign that would convince the insulters, and in answer the Emperor caused the moon to turn back upon its path in the sky and re-traverse the arch from horizon to horizon. This wonder wrought the purpose it was designed to work,—and much more beside; for it so disordered the tides that they did not recover their regular ebb and flow for many months, and during that interval the turbulent waters leaped their bounds and destroyed untold thousands of people in all the seacoasts of the island—yet these were people who were remote from the scene of the eviction, were not connected with the stubborn and doubting tribe, nor even aware of its existence, but imagined that they had brought these fatal invasions of the seas upon themselves through some unwitting neglect of theirs toward the Emperor.

The Ten Commandments

(1905 or 1906)

IN HIS Autobiographical Dictation of 25 June 1906 Clemens said:

> Man is not to blame for what he is. He didn't make himself. He has no control over himself. All the control is vested in his temperament—which he did not create—and in the circumstances which hedge him round, from the cradle to the grave, and which he did not devise and cannot change . . . He is a subject for pity, not blame—and not contempt.

This view is in accord with the contention of "The Ten Commandments" that man is no more blamable than the animals for acting according to his temperament and that to punish man for violating laws is unjust, though politic. On another occasion, Clemens took a somewhat different view—that man requires commandments in order to have the pleasure of breaking them. Isabel V. Lyon, Clemens' secretary, noted in one of her journals on 26 March 1905:

> This morning when I went into Mr. Clemens's room he asked me something about Moses & the 10 Commandments, and that lead up to making Mr. Clemens say "If those ten Commandments had never been written, man would be making some for himself. He has to have a code—he'd be saying—Thou shalt not sit up all night. Thou shalt not drink coffee at midnight. Thou shalt not eat cabbage & beans." "They would all be Commandments that he is in need of and he wouldn't be happy if he wasn't making them to break."

The character Slade, who like the Chicago murderer Holmes, is presented in the essay as an example of the "man-tiger," is discussed at greater length in Chapters 9 through 11 of *Roughing It*.

"The Ten Commandments" is Paine's title.

121

The Ten Commandments

THE TEN Commandments were made for man alone. We should think it strange if they had been made for *all* the animals.

We should say "Thou shalt not kill" is too general, too sweeping. It includes the field mouse and the butterfly. They *can't* kill. And it includes the tiger, which can't *help* it.

It is a case of Temperament and Circumstance again. You can arrange no circumstances that can move the field mouse and the butterfly to kill; their temperaments will keep them unaffected by temptations to kill, they can avoid that crime without an effort. But it isn't so with the tiger. Throw a lamb in his way when he is hungry, and his temperament will compel him to kill it.

Butterflies and field mice are common among men; they can't kill, their temperaments make it impossible. There are tigers among men, also. Their temperaments move them to violence, and when Circumstance furnishes the opportunity and the powerful motive, they kill. They can't help it.

No penal law can deal out *justice*; it must deal out injustice in every instance. Penal laws have a high value, in that they protect—in a considerable measure—the multitude of the gentle-natured from the violent minority.

For a penal law is a Circumstance. It is a warning which intrudes and stays a would-be murderer's hand—sometimes. Not always, but in many and many a case. It can't stop the *real* man-tiger; nothing can do that. Slade had 26 deliberate murders on his soul when he finally went to his death on the scaffold. He would kill a man for a trifle; or for nothing. He loved to kill. It was his temperament. He did not make his temperament, God gave it him at his birth. Gave it him and said Thou shalt not kill. It was like saying Thou shalt not eat. Both appetites were given him at birth. He could be obedient and starve both up to a certain point, but that was as far as he could go. Another man could go further; but not Slade.

Holmes, the Chicago monster, inveigled some dozens of men and women into his obscure quarters and privately butchered them. Holmes's inborn nature was such that whenever he had what seemed a reasonably safe opportunity to kill a stranger he couldn't successfully resist the temptation to do it.

Justice was finally meted out to Slade and to Holmes. That is what the newspapers said. It is a common phrase, and a very old one. But it probably isn't true. When a man is hanged for slaying *one* man that phrase comes into service and we learn that justice was meted out to the slayer. But Holmes slew sixty. There seems to be a discrepancy in this distribution of justice. If Holmes got justice, the other man got 59 times more than justice.

But the phrase is wrong, anyway. The *word* is the wrong word. Criminal courts do not dispense "justice"—they *can't*; they only dispense protections to the community. It is all they can do.

The Private Secretary's Diary

(June 1907)

THE CHARGE that the punishments inflicted by God through nature were likely to be incredibly cruel and severe was often made by Clemens in his later writings, perhaps most pointedly in his Autobiographical Dictation of 23 June 1906:

> The ten-thousandfold law of punishment is rigorously enforced against every creature, man included. The debt, whether made innocently or guiltily, is promptly collected by Nature—and in this world, without waiting for the ten-billionfold additional penalty appointed—in the case of man—for collection in the next.[1]

The ordeal of seeing a loved one undergo successive periods of extreme suffering, with intervening periods of relief that restored hope just to have it mocked again, was only too familiar to Clemens. The letter that he wrote on 12/13 May 1904, several weeks before the death of his wife, Olivia, describes one of these distressing sequences:

> For two entire days, now, we have not been anxious about Mrs. Clemens (unberufen). After 20 months of bed-ridden solitude and bodily misery she all of a sudden ceases to be a pallid shrunken shadow, and looks bright and young and pretty. She remains what she always was, the most wonderful creature of fortitude, patience, endurance and recuperative power that ever was. But ah, dear, it won't last; this fiendish malady will play new treacheries upon her, and I shall go

---

[1] "Reflections on Religion," *Hudson Review* 16 (Autumn 1963): 347.

back to my prayers again—unutterable from any pulpit! . . . May 13 10 A. M. I have just paid one of my pair of permitted 2 minutes visits per day to the sick room. And found what I have learned to expect—retrogression, and that pathetic something in the eye which betrays the secret of a waning hope.[2]

During the years that followed, Jean Clemens suffered recurrent epileptic seizures, prolonging Clemens' ordeal. Miss Lyon recorded his reactions to adverse news of Jean's condition on 2 February 1906, noting in her journal that Jean had attacks at 9 A.M., 6 P.M., and 10 P.M.:

> I had a very plain talk with Mr. Clemens this morning about Jean's condition & told him how on Tuesday I had talked with Dr. Quintard. The dreadfulness of it all swept over him as I knew it would and with that fiercest of all his looks in his face, he blazed out against the swindle of life & the treachery of a God that can create disease & misery & crime—create things that men would be condemned for creating.

Clemens' expression of relief after the death of Jean had come on 24 December 1909 is a further indication of what he had been enduring:

> And so I am already rejoicing that she has been set free. . . . For sixteen years Jean suffered unspeakably, under the dominion of her cruel malady, and we were always dreading that some frightful accident would happen to her that would stretch her mutilated upon her bed for the rest of her life—or, worse—that her mind would become affected; but now she is free, and harm can never come to her more.[3]

The "R. C." who reads the history of Mrs. Fannie Griscom's case in "The Private Secretary's Diary" is probably a recording clerk, one of the "official sleuths in the employ of the Recording Angel." The cabinet members "F., S., and H. G." are of course the Father, the Son, and the Holy Ghost. The date of composition is established by Mark Twain's reference in the text to June 1907.

---

[2] *Mark Twain's Letters*, ed. Albert Bigelow Paine (New York: Harper & Brothers, 1917), pp. 755–756.

[3] SLC to Mrs. [William R.] Coe, 27 December 1909.

The Private Secretary's Diary

MONDAY. The Cabinet met at the usual hour. Present, F., S., and H. G.

The case of Mrs. Fannie Griscom was taken up.

The R. C. read the history of it, beginning with the record of Sunday, June 17, 1858, forty-nine years ago, when the said Fannie was 4 years old. She and her little brother and sister were playing circus in the spare chamber, and were discovered by their papa, who severely scolded them for breaking the Sabbath; then prayed for them; after which he ordered them to sit still for an hour and reflect upon the enormity of their conduct; after which, he left them, closing the door behind him.

At the end of half an hour the remembrance of a funny incident of the previous week came suddenly into the mind of the said Fannie, and she, being taken unawares, broke out in a shriek of joyous laughter.

Georgie and Hattie promised not to tell, and kept their pledge.

These facts being conveyed to heaven by official sleuths in the employ of the Recording Angel, the Cabinet was convened in extra session to discuss them and award the penalties.

Penalties were pronounced against Georgie and Hattie for concealing their sister's sin from their papa. See Auxiliary Record of that date.

The crime of the said Fannie was then taken up. After various penalties had been suggested by S. and H. G., the Father, disallowing them, said—

F. Let her be wasted by scarlet fever—preliminarily. Let the after-effects begin to appear four years later, and continue at intervals of several years during the rest of her life.

Accordingly it is of record that—

The next day, Monday, June 18, 1858, the child was taken very ill with scarlet fever. In agony the father and mother prayed night and day begging the Lord to reveal to them wherein *they* had sinned and brought this retribution. By command of the Cabinet this prayer was not answered.

At the end of three weeks of great peril the disease began to modify, and the child's health was presently restored. In broken voices, and with tears of happiness the parents poured out their praises and their gratitude to the All-Merciful, who in His infinite kindness had spared their undeserving child.

These encomiums were registered, and June 18, 1861 was appointed for the beginning of the after-effects.

On that date the child, being then 8 years of age, caught a severe cold, which settled in her ear and produced exceeding great pain, and her life was threatened. In agony the parents prayed to the Lord, beseeching Him to acquaint them with the sin which had brought upon them this heavy judgment.

By command of the Cabinet this prayer was not answered.

A tumor formed in the child's head, and became a running sore, and in time it burst, and rent the drum of the ear, causing semi-deafness. During four years the sufferer's misery was very great, the flux of fetid matter meantime continuing.

A cure was then effected by a foreign physician; and the child, now 12 years of age, entered upon a long season of rest.

These facts being reported to the Cabinet by the R. C., God the Father spoke, saying—

F. Let her have peace until she is 37 years old, then let her punishment be resumed.

Accordingly, on the 18th of June, 1890, the said Fannie, being now mother of a family, was seized with a desolating pain at the back of the diseased ear, and surgeons were summoned. They said an operation might kill her, but without it death must quickly come. Therefore they cut a hole in her skull, back of the ear, and some relief was afforded;

she gradually mended, during 8 weeks, when the pains returned.

The operation was re-performed, and a larger hole cut in the skull.

After four months the operation was again performed, the patient begging the surgeons to kill her and end her sufferings.

But she now grew steadily better, and in two years became strong and well, but with the side of her face drawn down by the operations, and her speech affected.

Thenceforth until now (June 1907) she has had intervals of comfort, with longer intervals of distressing pain between, and the matter was now taken up once more by the Cabinet and its further needs discussed.

After careful examination of the Record, it appearing that the said Fannie had now suffered 45 years for the flagrant sin committed by her when she was 4 years old, it was decreed (only the H. G. dissenting) that she should not be punished further in her own person for her misconduct, but that she should now be forgiven and the punishment continued in the person of her eldest son, in the form of softening of the brain, and in *his* son, (when he should have one) in the form of idiotcy.

In My Bitterness

(Summer 1897)

THE DEATH of his daughter Olivia Susan—Susy—of meningitis on 18 August 1896 was felt by Clemens as an "unspeakable disaster."[1] Susy had died in the Hartford home before Clemens could return from Europe, where he had just concluded his global lecture tour of 1895/1896. "To me our loss is bitter, bitter, bitter," he wrote to W. D. Howells. "What a ghastly tragedy it was; how cruel it was; how exactly & precisely it was planned; & how remorselessly every detail of the dispensation was carried out."[2] Clemens had idolized Susy, and he never fully overcame his grief and resentment. In the following August, which brought the first anniversary of Susy's death, he was still sorrowing. He was then summering at the Swiss village of Weggis, beside Lake Lucerne, and there on August 18 he composed the poem "In Memoriam Olivia Susan Clemens." In it he represented Susy as a spirit "all of light" dwelling within a temple attended by "adoring priests":

> And then when they
> Were nothing fearing, and God's peace was in the air,
> And none was prophesying harm—
> The vast disaster fell:
> Where stood the temple when the sun went down,
> Was vacant desert when it rose again![3]

---

[1] *MTHHR*, p. 235.
[2] *MTHL*, p. 663.
[3] *DE*, 22:386.

129

In all likelihood it was during the stay at Weggis, which lasted from mid-July to the last week of September, that he wrote "In My Bitterness." (The piece is written on a paper which Clemens used only at Weggis and shortly thereafter.) This anguished complaint may also have been written on August 18. It expresses what he managed to keep out of the memorial poem—his deep anger and sense of Nemesis, his idea that a malevolent deity had laid a trap and sprung it upon him. A few months later he wrote to Howells, who had also lost a daughter, "It is my quarrel—that traps like that are set. Susy & Winnie given us, in miserable sport, & then taken away."[4] Clemens probably saw it as a particular irony of his situation that, having long derided the notion of a special providence, he was now forced to consider himself the personal victim of a scheme of providential retribution.

In the first sentence of "In My Bitterness" Clemens left a blank space in the phrase "in the   years that you have lived" (thus). He may have intended to fill in Susy's exact age. Born 19 March 1872, Susy died at the age of twenty-four.

The title has been supplied for this edition.

---

[4] *MTHL*, p. 669.

In My Bitterness

IN MY bitterness I said, blaspheming, "Ah, my darling there you lie, rescued from life; fortunate for the first time in the   years that you have lived; there you lie dumb and thankless, in this the first moment that ever you had anything to thank God for; there you lie, poor abused slave, set free from the unspeakable insult of life, and by the same Hand that flung it in your face in the beginning. But I lie: you have still nothing to be thankful for; for you have not been freed out of pity for you, but to drive one more knife into my heart.

"There—that is something which I have noticed before: He never does a kindness. When He seems to do one, it is a trap which He is setting; you will walk into it some day, then you will understand, and be ashamed to remember how stupidly grateful you had been. No, He gives you riches, merely as a trap; it is to quadruple the bitterness of the poverty which He has planned for you. He gives you a healthy body and you are tricked into thanking Him for it; some day, when He has rotted it with disease and made it a hell of pains, you will know why He did it. He gives you a wife and children whom you adore, only that through the spectacle of the wanton shames and miseries which He will inflict upon them He may tear the palpitating heart out of your breast and slap you in the face with it. Ah yes, you are at peace, my pride, my joy, my solace, He has played the last and highest stake in His sorry game, and is defeated: for, for your sake, I will be glad—and am glad. You are out of His reach forever; and I too; He can never hurt me any more."

The Victims

(Early 1900s)

Paine's title is apt: at all levels of being, creatures are seen preying upon their inferiors—and in their turn being so served by their superiors. Predation is represented to be the universal condition of life. Mark Twain expressed the same view in "Three Thousand Years Among the Microbes," in which even the microbes are found to be victims of submicroscopic germs. Each of the latter "is similarly infested, too," and "below that infester there is yet another infester that infests *him*—and so on down and down and down till you strike the bottomest bottom of created life—if there is one, which is extremely doubtful."[1]

The final sentence of "The Victims" points the moral of the fable: Mamma Molecule sees only that "The good spirit has deserted [her] Willie, who trusted him," but the reader understands that the controlling spirit has betrayed the trust of all the members of his predatory chain. Mark Twain here approaches a demonic or even a Satanic point of view. A master and maker who has so ordered things that each creature must live by murdering a fellow creature can be regarded as an evil deity, one against whose tyrannies the brave may justifiably, if futilely, rebel.

His lifetime friend the Reverend Joseph H. Twichell understood Clemens' despair: "He was ever profoundly affected with the feeling of the pathos of life. Contemplating its heritage of inevitable pain and tears, he would question if to any one it was a good gift. 'Would you,' he demanded

---

[1] WWD, p. 527.

133

of me once—'would you, as a kind-hearted man, start the human race? Would you, now?' "[2]

Mark Twain probably worked very rapidly in making this skeletal draft, which is nevertheless sufficient to suggest what the fully written version would have been. Paine dated the manuscript 1902; Mark Twain used the paper between 1900 and 1905, and the ink and handwriting, as well as the bitter irony, make the early 1900s a probable date for this piece.

---

[2] Quoted in "Mark Twain, In Memoriam: Interesting Passages From The Tributes Paid To The Great Humorist At The Memorial Meeting In Carnegie Hall, New York," *Harper's Weekly* 54 (17 December 1910): 10.

The Victims

LITTLE Johnny Microbe begged and begged his mother to let him go to the picnic and said all the nicest creatures were going to be there, and went on saying and saying and saying *Please*, ma, can't I? *please*, ma, let me, till at last she said he might, and he must be good, and behave, and be sure and be home before sundown, and put his faith in the good spirit and no harm would come to him, and oh, do be careful, she said, it would break mamma's heart if any harm came to her darling. And she promised to have something nice for his supper when he got home.

So Johnny went to the picnic, and mamma Microbe went over to a white corpuscle to hunt the kind of game he preferred for supper. And by and by her microscopic eye discovered little Willie Molecule going along on his way to the picnic, and grabbed him and bit the back of his head off and took him home and knelt down and prayed, giving thanks to the good spirit for that he watches tenderly over them that love him and trust him, allowing none to go hungry from his door.

Little Peter Anthrax begged and begged

So little Peter went to the picnic, and mamma Anthrax went out to hunt the kind of game he preferred for supper. And by and by her quick eye discovered little Johnny Microbe going along on his way to the picnic, and grabbed him and bit his face off.

Little Robbie Typhus Germ begged

So little Robbie went to the picnic and mamma Typhus Germ went out to hunt

little Peter Anthrax going along
and bit his chest off

Little Davy Itch Germ begged

So little Davy went to the picnic and mamma Itch Germ went out to hunt

little Robbie Typhus Germ going along
and bit his bowels out

Little Tommy Red-Speck Spider begged

So little Tommy went to the picnic and mamma Red-Speck Spider went out to

little Davy Itch-Germ going along
and bit his buttocks off

Little Fanny Ant begged

So little Fanny went to the picnic and mamma Ant went out to hunt

little Tommy Red-Speck Spider going
and bit his spine out

Little Phoebe Gray-Spider begged

So little Phoebe went to the picnic and mamma Gray Spider went
out to hunt

little Fanny Ant going along
and bit her forequarters off

Little Sammy Pinch-Bug begged

So little Sammy went to the picnic and mamma Pinch-Bug went out
to hunt

little Phoebe Gray Spider
and pierced her through the body from both sides

Little Dora Sparrow begged

So little Dora went to the picnic and mamma Sparrow went out to hunt

little Sammy Pinch-Bug and harpooned him with her beak

Little Harry Weasel begged

So little Harry went to the picnic, and mamma Weasel went out to hunt

and joined her teeth together in the person of little Dora Sparrow

Little Jacky Fox begged

So little Jacky went to the picnic and mamma Fox went out to hunt

and bit little Harry Weasel in two

Little Sophy Wildcat begged

So little Sophy went to the picnic and mamma Wildcat went out to hunt and broke little Jacky Fox's back with a bite

Little Caleb Sierra Lion begged

So little Caleb went to the picnic, and mamma Sierra Lion went out to hunt

and removed little Sophy Wildcat's interiors

Little Sissy Bengal Tiger begged

So little Sissy went to the picnic and mamma Bengal Tiger went out to hunt

and caved-in the west side of little Caleb Sierra Lion with a pat of her paw

Little Jumbo Jackson Elephantus Ichthyosaurus Megatherium begged

So little Jumbo Jackson went to the picnic, and mamma Elephantus Ichthyosaurus Megatherium went out to hunt

and fetched little Sissy Bengal Tiger a wipe with her 60-foot tail, and a rap with her 19-foot trunk, and observing that she did not respond but

seemed satisfied with things as they were, carried her home, cradled on
her pair of curled-up 22-foot tusks and

Little Jimmy Gem-of-the-Creation Man begged

So little Jimmy went to the picnic and papa Gem-of-the Creation
went out to hunt for—for—anything that might contain life and be
helpless—

and hid behind a rock and shot little Jumbo Jackson dead with a magazine rifle and took his tusks and traded them to an Arab land-pirate for
a cargo of captive black women and children and sold them to a good
Christian planter who promised to give them religious instruction and
considerable to do, and blest the planter and shook hands good-bye,
and said "By cracky this is the way to extend our noble civilization,"
and loaded up again and Went for More.

The sun went down, and it was night.
Then mamma Molecule's heart broke and she gave it up, weeping
and saying The good spirit has deserted my Willie, who trusted him,
and he is dead and will come no more.

The Synod of Praise

(Early 1900s)

THIS PIECE is more nearly a set of working notes than a finished composition. The idea that God was not moral was to be proved by his persecutions of the creatures he had made to suffer without any hope of future reward: "*Brutes*. They cannot enter heaven. Their sufferings are merely to punish their present sins and discipline them." The satire on the conventional religious idea of disciplinary affliction resembles that in the "Little Bessie" chapters.

In designating the title, Mark Twain noted "Synod" as a possible alternate for "(Concert?)"; since he let "Synod" stand without parentheses or question mark, the present title has been used as the form he may have preferred. Paine dated this satire "1900s" on the first page of the manuscript. The paper was used between 1900 and 1905; the ink is a variety much used by Mark Twain between 1900 and 1903.

The Synod of Praise

Animals and Insects

Moderator, the Cow,

    1st Vice—the Giraffe (spectacles)
    2d   ″ —the Rabbit (″   )
    3d   ″ —the Goat   (″   )

Gᴏᴅ—*the Elephant.* Knocks an innocent over now and then or steps on him—this comes out in the speeches—it is always either for His "glory" or to teach some kind of saving lesson, or to over-adequately punish an unknown offence.

Monkey has a disease inherited from his grandfather—is *this* a punishment? Then for what? For a lesson? then how? Evidently God is not moral (sensation). Dull—no perception of justice. No generosity, courtesy, magnanimity.

Invites me to his house, I am his guest. He insults me, maltreats me, cripples me, diseases me, kicks me out when he is tired of me. No gentleman.

Expects me to worship him. A guest worship his host? A guest owes no worship to his host. When hospitably treated he owes acknowledgments, worded in dignified and self-respecting phrase, but no servility, no bending of the knee.

But he has a right to require worship?

Then I his guest am also his slave.

142

The slave says "I belong to my master, he has a right to do what he pleases with me." Which is a lie. The master has no rights at all over his slave. Unless force creates rights. If compulsion over the helpless creates rights, God has rights—he has no other. If the exercise of lawless force is moral, God is moral.

Blame. It is word applicable to God only. Unrequested, he made man, and is responsible for all man's words and deeds. The vote of a continent of Gods could not absolve him from his responsibility nor wash him clean of the stain of any harm that may befal his creature.

Brutes. They cannot enter heaven. Their sufferings are merely to punish their present sins and discipline them.

Grasshopper. Spider fast to his body and sucking its juices.

Caterpillar the same.

Fish with parasites on eye. Etc.

All humbly praise God for these deserved afflictions.

The parasites have parasites and these have others. They all praise.

Cow: He is our loving father.

Monkey. My praise is that we have not two of him.

The Lost Ear-ring

(June 1878)

THIS rather charming, ironic sketch can hardly be called a satire, but it nevertheless arrives at the point also made in the more overtly satirical "About Asa Hoover"—the Almighty is not blamed when things go wrong ("We are born to suffer—God's will be done!") but receives much gratuitous credit for favors he has not dispensed. The tale begins with the date 6 June 1878, and the verso of manuscript page 13 bears the heading "Schloss Hotel Heidelberg, June 5." One finds in "The Lost Ear-ring" a viewpoint that Mark Twain often expressed more strongly in his later years.

The title was supplied at the time Bernard DeVoto was the Editor of the Mark Twain Papers.

The Lost Ear-ring

J UNE 6, 1878. I reached the little house on the peak of the Königs-
stuhl this morning, about 11. As I stepped into the small living-room,
Fräulein Marie stepped into the same room from the kitchen. Her
head was down. She raised it and showed such a heart-broken face! Her
eyes were dim with tears which she was trying hard to keep from flowing. The mother, the two sisters, the good old stocking-knitter and I all
sprung forward with one impulse and one exclamation of distress and
sympathy: "O, child, what has happened!" She could not speak; but
she touched one of her ear-rings with one fore-finger, and laid her other
fore-finger eloquently upon the remains of the other, and her tale was
told.—Two-thirds of the pendant was broken off and lost. They were
simple jewels, these ear-rings, and had not cost what a lady pays for a
pair of kid gloves in America, but they were precious to the owner, for
she was not rich in such things. Now from all lips burst a simultaneous
torrent of mingled consternation, grief, pity, and attempted consolation. All crowded about Marie and touched and examined the remnant
of the trinket which remained in her ear, and out of the confusion of
exclamations I caught odds and ends here and there: like this, from the
mother: "Ach Gott, my child! Gott be with thee in thy misfortune!"
and this from the good old stocking-knitter: "Ach Gott, it is a blow!
try thou to bear it, child—we will help thee!" The sisters offered to go

145

and ransack the house, the wood, the road—please God it might be found yet. I put in my word; and grateful I was that I had one German phrase which I could depend on to convey something of what I felt and wanted to say in this time of trouble: "Ah, Fräulein, *es thut mir* SEHR *leid!*"—("Ah, Fräulein, I am *so* sorry!") Then I fell into irregular grammar, and tried to cheer her up with the suggestion that a jeweler could mate the remaining ear-ring by making another just like it; but she shook her head, uncomforted, and said, Ah, it would cost so much money—as much, indeed, as a new pair. The mother and the others said the same, and I easily saw, myself, that they were right, and that my solution of the difficulty was no solution at all. Then I said, it was too early to give up hope—without a doubt the lost part would be found again. I said that this ear-drop was different from some other things: if one lets a perfectly round grape fall on the floor, it does not roll away, but places itself carefully right where you are bound to step on it the moment you start to hunt for it; but if you drop a perfectly square piece of billiard chalk, it will roll to the other end of the house, avoiding all chair-legs and things, and hide where you will never find it again; now this ear-drop is light, and thin, and flat—it cannot roll, it lies at this moment right where it fell; it will be found again, without the slightest question in the world. But the Fräulein shook her head as hopelessly as before, and said, if she lost it when she walked out yesterday noon, God help us, think where it is now!—there was the heavy rain in the afternoon, then the people, then the wagons—ah, it is trampled deep in the mud, and none will ever see it again! This thought so wrung her heart that for once the tears got the better of her resistance, and a crystal drop or two stole over the lids. The mother and the sisters agreed with what the Fräulein had said; so also did the kindly old stocking-knitter, interlarding her speech with many an Ach Gott! and Gott abide with us in our sorrow! and so on. However, they were all getting ready to go out and begin the search.

My work was urgent, so I went up stairs and set myself at it; but I could get no life into it; this house was a house of mourning, and there was no getting away from the sense of it. To argue that nothing was the matter except that an almost costless trifle had been lost, was an easy thing to do, but it did no good after it was done. There was no arguing away the fact that the only real thing about affliction is the affliction itself—the cause of it is not a thing to be considered; the loss of a king's crown and a young girl's trinket weigh just the same in the scales of the Angel of Calamity.

At the end of three hours I judged that I had worked enough; so I went down stairs and struck into the road which leads through the beech wood. The old stocking-knitter was in her usual nook among the trees, plying her needles. The face bent over the work was sorrowful, so I knew that the season of mourning still continued. When I had almost reached her, she heard my step, looked up, then glanced at my white canvas walking shoes; the next moment she was on her feet and running toward me, her face ablaze and her ball of yarn tumbling and tangling after her on the ground. "O, the beautiful shoes! O, the lovely shoes! O, the strange white foreign things, and *so* beautiful!" Then down she plunged, clasped my ancle, thrust up my pantaloons to see how high the shoes came, then stroked the instep and the toe and broke forth again: "O, in God's name, *cloth!*—all cloth!—can one believe the wonder of it!—and so *wunderschön!*"

I explained that I was rather a starchy person and accustomed to wearing just such princely things as these dollar-and-a-half shoes, and then I inquired about the ear-ring. The shadow of mourning fell upon the old dame's face again, and she gathered up her trail of yarn and sat down to her work again, with a dreary shake of the head. Then she told how the house had been searched, and re-searched, and searched again; and how Marie had sadly traced out every step she had taken in the road and the forest the day before, the family following in procession behind her, all stooping and turning over every leaf and clod and peering around every root and bowlder—all in vain; and how the procession had gone searching back and forth over the same ground, time and time again, still patiently searching—and all in vain; and how all had given up hope at last, and gone once more about their usual avocations, with sad faces and heavy hearts: "We are born to suffer—God's will be done!"

I left her in the vale of sorrow, and moved on—not cheerfully, and light of step, but otherwise—and unconsciously scanning the ground for the lost trifle, too. By and by I turned back; when I was nearly to my old dame, I stopped, and stood there watching her; I could see the side of her grieving face over an intervening leafy bough, and was near enough to hear her deep sighs and broken ejaculations. Presently I caught the flutter of a dress beyond, and the next moment Fräulein Marie, with radiant face, stood before the old soul, and held up a glittering object, uttering never a word! Down went stocking, ball and all, up went the clasped old hands, and out came an indescribably eloquent "'GOTT *sei dank!*"

Then followed a rattling volley of questions: Where was it? How did she find it? When did she find it? How did it come about? The Fräulein's rapture was as mastering, now, as her grief had been in the morning—she could not speak; but she did what answered just as well: with a pretty grace she spread open a little pocket in her apron with one hand, placed the recovered trinket at her ear with the other, bent her head to one side, like a bird, and let the jewel drop. Yes—that had been the way of it; when the ear-drop broke, she had had the luck to be in such a position that the dismembered part fell into her apron pocket. Up went the devout hands again, and out came a fervent, "The ways of God are wonderful!"

My friend the reader is privileged to imagine for himself what the rejoicing in the homestead was like when we all ran thither—it is beyond my art to paint it.

Goose Fable

(1899–1900)

IN WRITING of the foolish trust of the geese in their "gods," the human race, Mark Twain evidently meant to suggest that man also was too trusting toward his own gods. He made the same point more directly in his Autobiographical Dictation of 25 June 1906: "It is to these celestial bandits that the naïve and confiding and illogical human rabbit looks for a Heaven of eternal bliss, which is to be his reward for patiently enduring the want and sufferings inflicted upon him here below." The expectation of wise guidance from the cow in "Goose Fable" is a further instance of misplaced trust.

"Goose Fable" is written on a paper which Mark Twain used only in 1899 and 1900, most notably for the last part of "The Chronicle of Young Satan"[1] and the essay "Dollis Hill House, London, 1900." Paine dated the piece 1900.

---

[1] See *MSM*, p. 488, and John S. Tuckey, *Mark Twain and Little Satan* (West Lafayette: Purdue University Studies, 1963), pp. 48–51, 76.

Goose Fable

THE Wild Geese were flying northwards in a branching long procession shaped like a harrow. At the end of one of the lines was young Snowflake and her mother, and the mother was instructing her child about the gods.

"I have a presentiment that I am not long for this world, my daughter," she said, "and I wish to impress upon you some solemn truths for your guidance when I shall be no more. And first I will ask you the usual questions of the daily lesson, for it is not permitted to neglect this necessary office. Who created us and gave us all we have, my child?"

"The gods, mamma."

"Who are the gods?"

"They are called the Human Race, mamma."

"What is their character, my child?"

"They are righteous, good, perfect in all ways, and without spot or blemish."

"And merciful?"

"Their mercy has no bounds."

"All that they do is right?"

"All. The Human Race can do no wrong."

"If acts of theirs shall seem wrong?"

150

"We must not regard it—knowing that the act, however unjust it may seem to us in our blindness and ignorance, is done only for our good."

"If the gods should seem cruel?"

"We must bear the pain, and still adore the hand that inflicts it, for we know that the hidden spirit of it is merciful."

"What, then, is our duty toward the gods?"

"To accept what they give, whether of pain or pleasure, with humble and thankful hearts, loving them always, and worshiping them to the end."

"It is well, my child. Do not forget the lesson, but carry it in your heart and study it every day, remembering, when I am gone, that it was your mother, who loves you so, that begged this of you."

Snowflake was weeping, for her mother's words filled her with dread, but she promised. Then the mother continued—

"I will now speak of a matter which is near my heart. You are pure, and you are good, and have been trained from the egg in high and righteous ways; but you are very young, you are gentle, and winning, and innocent, and beautiful—oh, so beautiful! And so, you will be hedged about with temptations, and I not by to watch over you and save you. Remember my words, and be careful—do not trust all comers. The cow is our friend, and is old and wise; go to her in time of trouble and she will advise and help you."

About Asa Hoover

(1908 or 1909)

THE Old Walters who recalls the "village scoundrel," Hoover, may possibly have been William Thompson Walters (1820–1894), a railroad executive, an art collector, and a breeder of fine horses whom Clemens had known in the 1880s.[1] The handwriting on the manuscript and the paper, the same used in four chapters of "Little Bessie," suggest that "About Asa Hoover" was not written until 1908 or 1909; however, Clemens could have been recalling an earlier visit with Walters. The date, September 6, with which the manuscript begins could mark the time either of composition or of Walters' visit. John Tolliver is not mentioned in "Villagers of 1840–3," in which Mark Twain listed people he had known in Hannibal, Missouri, during his early years.[2] Asa Hoover cannot now be identified, and the name may be a fictitious one. The title has been supplied here by the editor.

---

[1] *Mark Twain, Business Man*, ed. Samuel C. Webster (Boston: Little, Brown and Co., 1946), pp. 374–375.

[2] *Hannibal, Huck & Tom*, ed. Walter Blair (Berkeley and Los Angeles: University of California Press, 1969), pp. 23–40.

About Asa Hoover

SEPTEMBER 6. Old Walters came. We talked of old times in the West. I drifted into the history of John Tolliver, of our village on the Mississippi, whom I had often seen when I was a boy. Then Walters told about the village scoundrel of his own juvenile days. His name was Asa Hoover, and this is in substance what Walters said about him:

He was the only rich man in the town. Just how rich he was, nobody knew; it was only known that there seemed to be no bottom to his purse. Everybody looked up to him, bowed down to him, flattered him, and everybody stood in mortal fear of him, and would go any length to keep from getting his ill will, for he was malignant and vengeful, and spent much of his time imagining slights and injuries and inventing oversized punishments for them.

The people were so afraid of him that they always shut their eyes to his cruelties and injustices when they could; and when they couldn't they said the victims were in the wrong and deserved what they got. On the other hand, whenever any villager came forward and helped a neighbor out of trouble everybody said Hoover was privately at the back of the act, so they loudly and gratefully praised him for it; and so also did the very villager who had done the good deed. As a result, you have this curious condition of things: whenever a villager did a generous thing, Hoover got the credit for it, and whenever Hoover in-

153

flicted a cruelty upon a villager the blame was always put upon the villager, and everybody was agreed that he had earned what he got, and richly deserved it.

Hoover had a large family, and everybody said that he loved all his children equally. If any one noticed that his conduct toward them did not bear out this statement, the person noticing it kept discreetly still about it. One of the children, aged four years, fell in the fire, and when its small brothers and sisters begged him to save it he made no reply, and looked on unmoved. Then two of the older children saved it at risk of their lives. Both were badly burned, and one of them lost the use of a hand. Hoover got the credit of saving the child, because the savers of it did their brave work by his mute permission, which was the same as doing it himself.

THE DREAM OF
BROTHERHOOD

The Refuge of the Derelicts

(1905–1906)

MARK TWAIN began writing "The Refuge of the Derelicts" in March 1905, while he was living at 21 Fifth Avenue in New York City. The winter of that year had been for him a time of great social consciousness. In January and February he had produced "The Czar's Soliloquy" and "King Leopold's Soliloquy," satirizing both the cynical exploitation practiced by monarchs and the cowardly self-abasement of their subjects. During the last week of February he was writing still another soliloquy, as the journal of his secretary Isabel V. Lyon shows: "Thursday evening—Feb. 23—Mr. Clemens said he was now on 'Adam's Soliloquy'." In the latter Adam is a visitor in New York City who enjoys the private joke that everyone is his relative. But Clemens had been finding in the Russo-Japanese War fresh proof of the tragic failure of the human family to get along together, and early in the following month he crystallized his view in a small satiric masterpiece. Miss Lyon noted in her journal on March 10, "Mr. Clemens read his 'War Prayer' after dinner." During this period Clemens often read to the household, usually in the evening, the result of his day's work at the writing desk. Miss Lyon's description of his beginning of "The Refuge of the Derelicts" is in her note of March 17:

> Tonight after dinner Mr. Clemens read us a new story that he is writing. Two chapters he read. I don't know what he calls it, but "The Admiral's Cat" will do here. It is a story of the poet who had a marvellous idea of erecting a statue to Adam, & he tells a friend of his project. He had no money & so would have to interest other people in the idea. The first person he goes to is an old Admiral

whose weak point is his beautiful black cat—& Mr. Clemens's description of the
cat through the old Admiral's comments upon it is a master stroke. He calls it
Bagheera & draws upon a word or more of Kipling's when he describes that glorious black panther of his. It is a beautiful story. The old Admiral is drawn from
two old whaling captains—Capt. Ed. Wakeman & Commodore Smith. The
former was born on a whaler, & when he retired after 70 years of sea life he used
to cruise as a passenger up & down the Pacific coast from San Francisco to
Panama. Mr. Clemens paced up & down the living room as he described the two
old sailors—& he grew more & more interesting every moment.

This enthusiastic commentary reveals some of the elements of the story
but necessarily leaves untouched many aspects that were yet to be disclosed as Mark Twain proceeded with the writing. In a disarmingly amiable way, he was easing into a work that was to range from comedy to
tragedy, from gentle humor to bitter satire. For example, the notion of
building a monument to Adam, a casually humorous idea as presented
early in the manuscript, later receives a cynically ironic twist. The idea had
originated as a joke, as Clemens recalled in "A Monument to Adam," a
short essay written after he had begun "The Refuge of the Derelicts":

> It is long ago—thirty years. Mr. Darwin's *Descent of Man* had been in print
> five or six years, and the storm of indignation raised by it was still raging in pul-
> pits and periodicals. In tracing the genesis of the human race back to its sources,
> Mr. Darwin had left Adam out altogether. We had monkeys, and "missing
> links," and plenty of other kinds of ancestors, but no Adam. Jesting with Mr.
> Beecher and other friends in Elmira, I said there seemed to be a likelihood that
> the world would discard Adam and accept the monkey, and that in the course of
> time Adam's very name would be forgotten in the earth; therefore this calamity
> ought to be averted; a monument would accomplish this, and Elmira ought not
> to waste this honorable opportunity to do Adam a favor and herself a credit.
>
> Then the unexpected happened. Two bankers came forward and took hold of
> the matter—not for fun, not for sentiment, but because they saw in the monu-
> ment certain commercial advantages for the town. The project had seemed gently
> humorous before—it was more than that now, with this stern business gravity in-
> jected into it.[1]

Here were practical men seriously proposing the "insane oddity of a monument set up in a village to preserve a name that would outlast the hills
and the rocks without any such help. . . ."[2] Clemens had done his best
to keep the jest going:

---

[1] In *The $30,000 Bequest and Other Stories*, DE, 24:296–297.
[2] Ibid., p. 297.

In the beginning—as a detail of the project when it was as yet a joke—I had framed a humble and beseeching and pervervid petition to Congress begging the government to build the monument. . . . It seemed to me that this petition ought to be presented, now—it would be widely and feelingly abused and ridiculed and cursed, and would advertise our scheme and make our ground-floor stock go off briskly. So I sent it to General Joseph R. Hawley, who was then in the House, and he said he would present it. But he did not do it. I think he explained that when he came to read it he was afraid of it: it was too serious, too gushy, too sentimental—the House might take it for earnest.[3]

The project had then languished until some time in the early 1900s when Clemens, having heard of the refusal of applications for places in the ministry to two young men who believed Adam to be a myth, drafted a new proposal as pervervid as the original. Adam, he contended, should have "a costly and noble monument to mark our recognition of his intellectual greatness," which vastly exceeded that of such "intellectual giants" as Socrates, Aristotle, Shakespeare, and Darwin: "These great men knew all that men can know—it was their limit; but Adam knew more. He knew all things, and more than all."[4] In bringing the Adam monument scheme into "The Refuge of the Derelicts," Clemens was returning to an idea that he had at least twice before developed as a hoax; his use of this scheme in a story is enough in itself to alert the reader to possible authorial duplicity.

There is reason enough to suspect that Mark Twain may have meant to spring a kind of trap upon the reader, misleading him with an amiably chatty narrative that included a number of comic elements only to bring him finally to a tragic outcome. For "The Refuge of the Derelicts" is at least distantly related to the Great Dark Manuscripts, including the story "The Great Dark," itself, of which Clemens had written to Howells in 1898, "I feel sure that all of the first half of the story—& I hope three-fourths—will be comedy . . . I think I can carry the reader a long way before he suspects that I am laying a tragedy-trap."[5] One of the comic elements of "The Great Dark"[6] is also presented in "The Refuge of the Derelicts"—that of three years of tortured abstinence by a grog-loving shipmaster who thinks he has joined a temperance society, only to find out after all that he was blackballed and never had been a member. This

---

[3] Ibid., pp. 297–298. See Appendix B; also *MTB*, pp. 1648–1650.
[4] See "Proposal for Renewal of the Adam Monument Petition" in Appendix B.
[5] *MTHL*, pp. 675–676.
[6] *WWD*, pp. 115–117.

anecdote is the "disaster" (comically treated) in Admiral Stormfield's life that has taught him to live with failure and that has established in him a bond of sympathy with all of life's defeated people. His home has become a haven for these—a refuge for human derelicts. The earliest of the Great Dark writings, "The Enchanted Sea-Wilderness," broke off after a description of a vessel in a graveyard of ships, a Sargasso-like trap called the Everlasting Sunday.[7] The crewmen, who sit thinking of their pasts and of the hopelessness of their present condition, have no prospect but starvation and death. "The Great Dark" was to end in a similar despair, as Mark Twain's notes for that story show.[8] In the early part of "The Refuge of the Derelicts," the strong and generous-hearted old Admiral, true to the image of the admirable Wakeman and of Clemens' yachting friend "Admiral" Henry H. Rogers, nourishes and sustains the derelicts. His home is a social Sargasso:

> Life's failures. Shipwrecks. Derelicts, old and battered and broken, that wander the ocean of life lonely and forlorn. They all drift to him; and are made welcome.

> Privately his friends have a name or two for his house,—half a dozen, in fact—founded on his special compassion for life's failures—ironical names, but there's no sting in them: "Haven of the Derelict," "Refuge of the Broken Reed"—that's a couple of them.

These hopeless figures sit around and rehearse the past events that led to their ruin: "Lord, those pathetic figures! Here, and there and yonder they hung limp upon their chairs, lost to the present, busy with the past, the unreturning past—there, brooding, they hung, the defeated, the derelicts!"

> [They] dream their great days over again, and count up the money they used to have, and mourn over this and that and the other disastrous investment, and reason out, for the thousandth time, just how each mistake came to be made, and how each and all of them could have been so easily avoided if they had *only* done so and so. Then they sigh and sorrow over those dreary "onlies" . . . . and take up the tale again, and go wearying over it, and over it, and over it, in the same old weather-worn and goalless track, poor old fellows!

The phrasing here suggests the plight of the crew in "The Enchanted Sea-Wilderness," caught "in the whirl and suck of the Devil's Race-

---

[7] *WWD*, pp. 82, 86.

[8] See Bernard DeVoto, *Mark Twain at Work* (Cambridge: Harvard University Press, 1942), illustration following p. 122, and *WWD*, pp. 19, 100–101.

Track," the region of endlessly circling storm in the center of which there is perpetual calm—and stagnation and eventual death. "The Refuge of the Derelicts" has its own "tragedy-trap" aspects, including the view of the human situation that is portrayed in the final episode of Plum Duff Night. The story culminates in a dramatic presentation of the indictment of the "real God" that Clemens had been voicing in very similar terms in his Autobiographical Dictation. To illustrate his assertion that God had so ordered the conditions of life that each creature's "way, from birth to death, should be beset by traps, pitfalls and gins, ingeniously planned and ingeniously concealed," he spoke of the spider "so contrived that she . . . must catch flies" and of the wasp "so contrived that he . . . [would] stab the spider. . . . In turn, there was a murderer provided for the wasp, and another murderer for the wasp's murderer, and so on throughout the whole scheme of living creatures in the earth."⁹ The effect he was probably striving for in bringing such things into "The Refuge of the Derelicts" was that of making the reader share his own sense of entrapment and the shock that he had expressed in his Autobiographical Dictation: "We stand astonished at the all-comprehensive malice which could patiently descend to the contriving of elaborate tortures for the meanest and pitifulest of the countless kinds of creatures that were to inhabit the earth."¹⁰ Mark Twain had finally contrived and sprung his own literary tragedy-trap. Once he had done so, he evidently lost interest in the story. Recalling a number of abandoned books in his Autobiographical Dictation of 30 August 1906, he spoke of one "which I should probably entitle 'The Refuge of the Derelicts' "—one that began with a "pretty brusque remark by an ancient admiral, who is Captain Ned Wakefield under a borrowed name"; he added, "It is half finished, and will remain so."¹¹

---

⁹ Autobiographical Dictation, 23 June 1906; published as "Reflections on Religion" in *Hudson Review* 16 (Autumn 1963): 347.

¹⁰ Ibid.

¹¹ Published in part in *Mark Twain in Eruption*, ed. Bernard DeVoto (New York: Harper & Brothers, 1940), p. 200.

The Refuge of the Derelicts

Chapter 1

"TELL HIM to go to hell!"

"So *that* was the message the footman brought you from the Admiral!" said Shipman, keeping as straight a face as he could, for he saw that his friend the young poet-artist was deeply wounded, therefore this was not a proper time for levity. He loved the poet-artist better than he loved any other creature; loved him as a mother loves her child; loved to touch him, pat him, look into his eyes, loved to listen to his voice, knew his footstep from any other, and thrilled to it. And so, for him, this was not a time to laugh, this was not a time to add a pang to that smarting wound. He made him sit down on the sofa by him, laid a caressing hand upon his knee, and said, "You have been so excited, George, that you haven't been altogether clear in your narrative. You called at the Admiral's house—that much is clear—you sent in your request for a ten-minute interview—that is clear, too—the footman came back with an invitation—"

"Yes"—bitterly—"invitation to go to hell!"

"Clear again. But the rest of it is confused. You *think* you have explained to me how you came to go there without an introduction, and you also think you have made me understand what your project was, but it's a mistake; I didn't get it. You are calmer, now, George; tell me the whole thing; maybe I can help you."

"No," said George, "You are mistaken as to the project, I only said I had a project, I didn't tell you what it was. I was coming to that. It is great and fine and will be costly; it may be a dream, but it is a noble dream—that I know." The thought of it lit the poet's deep eyes as with a sunbeam. "I went there to ask him to subscribe to it."

"What is the project?"

"A monument."

"A monument?"

"Yes."

"To whom?"

"Adam."

Shipman was caught unprepared, and he burst out with—

"Gr-reat Scott!"

He was almost startled from his base, but he immediately followed his give-away exclamation with a remark intended to express pure admiration, and "save his face," which it did. The poet was visibly pleased, and said—

"I'm so glad you like the idea, David."

"Why, I couldn't help but like it, George. I think it's one of the greatest and most unusual ideas I have ever heard of. I wonder it has never been thought of before."

"So do I. But I am glad it wasn't."

"You may well be. It is an august idea, there's nothing to compare with it, nothing that approaches it. None but a poet's mind could ever have conceived it!" and he seized the dreamer's hand and crushed into it the rest of the enthusiasm he was persuading himself to feel.

"It *is* wonderful, isn't it, David?" said George, flushing with pleasure.

"Boy, it's *great!* And you will succeed, too."

"Do you really think so, David?"

"Think it? I *know* it! Another couldn't, but you will. Because your heart is in it; and when your heart is in a thing, George, you've got the words to match, words that persuade, words that convince. Is that a list of people you hope to round-up? Give it to me."

He ran his eye down it.

"Do you know any of these, George?"

"Well, no—I don't."

"It's no matter, I know them, and I'll steer you. It's a large thing, and will take us both. I'll furnish the bait, and you'll land the fish. Tell me—what was your plan? As regards the Admiral, for instance."

"Plan, David? Why—I hadn't any."

"Hadn't any *plan!* How did you mean to go at him?"

"I was only going to tell him the idea, and ask him to subscribe. That was all."

"And you a perfect stranger! Why, George, *that* was no way to do. How could you be so innocent? Don't you know that in all cases where you are interested and the other person isn't, there are four thousand wrong ways to go at him, and only one right one?"

"Why, no, I didn't know it. It wouldn't ever have occurred to me, David. Do you mean that the one right way to go at one person is the *same* way to go at all the others?"

"Broadly speaking, yes. You must apply the same persuader in all the cases."

"David, you surely can't mean *all?*"

"Yes, all. The whole human race."

"David, if you are not joking, what is the one right way?"

"*Purchase.* Bribery. Bribery and corruption."

The poet was dumb for a minute—paralysed. Then he said, gravely—

"I was in earnest, David. It isn't kind to treat it like this."

Shipman laid an affectionate hand upon his shoulder, and said—

"Forgive me, lad, I meant no harm, I wouldn't hurt you for the world—you know that. I was too abrupt, that was all. It misled you. I was not joking, I meant what I said, and what I said is true—I give you my word it is. Now, as soon as I come to expl—"

"But David! Look at that list. Think what you are saying. The purest people, the noblest people, the—some of them not rich, but there isn't gold enough in Klondike to—"

"*Money?* Dear me, I didn't say anything about money—I wasn't thinking of it. I—"

"Why, David, you *said*—"

"*Buy? Bribe?* So I did, but I didn't say buy with money."

"Oh, well, goodness knows I don't know what you are driving at. If you think you know, yourself, I do wish you—"

"I do know, George, I do indeed. What I was meaning was, that every human being has his price, every human being can be bought—"

"Now you are saying it again! yet you said, only a minute ago—"

"Hush! Let me talk. You interrupt me so, I can't arrive anywhere. Now then, the thing is perfectly simple. Listen. Every human being has a weak place in him, a soft spot. In one it is avarice—you buy him with money; in another it is vanity—you beguile him through that; in another it is a compassionate heart—you work him to your will through that; in another—a mother, for instance—it is adoration of a child, perhaps a crippled one, an idiot—she sells a politician her husband's vote for a judas-kiss bestowed upon her bratling; she doesn't know she is being bribed, but she is; the others don't suspect that they are selling themselves, but they are. It is as I tell you: every person has his price, every person can be bought, if you know where his weak spot is. Do you get the idea now?"

There was no answer; the poet was lost in thought. The burden of his thought was: "How true it is, no doubt . . . . poor human nature! . . . . what children we are—and don't know it, don't suspect it . . . . the proudest of us, the biggest of us, purchasable! . . . . purchasable with a toy! . . . . Even the old Admiral, too?—bronzed by the storms of all the seas, old, white-headed, beloved of his friends as Arthur was by his knights, brave as Launcelot, pure as Galahad . . . . what might *his* price be!"

Meantime Shipman had retired to his den with the list, and was making skeleton notes. He finished them, then sat musing a moment. His thoughts ran something like this:

"God knows it's the insanest idea that ever . . . . but it's colossal, there's no denying that . . . . and new—oh, yes indeed, there's nothing stale about it! . . . . How *can* he be so serious over it? But he is. He sees only the dignity of it, the grandeur of it; to him it has no frivolous side, to him there is no glimmer of the humorous about it. My, but he is innocent!—poet to the marrow, dreamer, enthusiast . . . . conceive of his selecting *these* people to place such a project before, and strike them for contributions! No matter, they are bribable—for this queer project or any other, if he follows my instructions—borrowed from Lord Bacon—and concentrates his forces upon their weak spots."

A minute or two later he was saying to his pupil:

"Now then, here we have the campaign planned out. Take these notes, and think them over at your leisure—they point out the weak spots of each person in your list—come whenever you like, and we will elaborate the matter with talk. To each in turn I will certify you before your visit—then you will be expected, and your road will be smooth."

"Oh, it's ever so lovable in you, David!"

"I know it. First,—and right away—you will assault the Admiral again. I will telephone him. As you didn't give your name before, he won't know it was you he sent that invitation to." The poet colored, and shifted his body nervously, but said nothing. "Now I will post you about the Admiral. He is a fine and bluff old sailor, honest, unworldly, simple, innocent as a child—but doesn't know it, of course—knows not a thing outside of his profession, but *thinks* he knows a lot—you must humor that superstition of course—and he *does* know his Bible, (just well enough to misquote it with confidence,) and frankly thinks he can beat the band at explaining it, whereas his explanations simply make the listener dizzy, they are so astronomically wide of the mark; he is profoundly religious, sincerely religious, but swears a good deal, and competently—you mustn't notice that; drinks like a fish, but is a fervent and honest advocate and supporter of the temperance cause, and does what he can to reclaim the fallen by taking the pledge every now and then as an example, with the idea that it is a great encourage-ment to them; he can't sing, but he doesn't know it—you must ask him to sing; is a composer—good land!—and believes he is a musician; he thinks he is deep, and worldly-wise, and sharp, and sly, and cunning, and underhanded, and furtive, and not to be seen through by any art, whereas he is just glass, for transparency—and lovable? he is the most lovable old thing in the universe."

"My word, what a person! David, is he insane?"

"He? If he is, he has never suspected it. And the man that suggests it to him will do well to take a basket along to carry what's left of him home in. Do you want a basket? There's one in the other room."

"No. I am not going to need it. David, he seems to have quite a lot of vulnerable points—bribable points—"

"No he hasn't. He has only one. I haven't spoken of it yet. These others are to show you what to talk about, when you get started, and *how* to talk—they are aids, helpers, and very useful—but the one I haven't mentioned is the one that opens the door to his heart and puts him up for sale. That one, properly handled, will thaw him out and start his talking-mill—then you've got him!"

"I see! It's his magnificent achievements, his illustrious record, his great deeds in the war, his—"

"No, it isn't; it's his cat."

The poet was paralysed again, for a moment; then he regained his voice—

"His *cat?*"

"That's it. You get at him through his cat. He is bribable through his cat, but in no other way. In all other ways, his probity is adamant, he is as chaste as the driven snow, he is unpurchasable. But don't forget the cat. Work the cat; work him for all he is worth. Go along, now; I will telephone the Admiral you are on the way."

Chapter 2

The Admiral

H E W A S eighty years old. Tall; large; all brawn, muscle and health; powerful bass voice, deep and resonant. He was born at sea, in the family's home, which was a Fairhaven whaleship, owned and commanded by his father. He was never at school; such education as he had, he had picked up by odds and ends, and it was rather a junk-shop than a treasury; though that was not his idea of it. He had very decided opinions upon most matters, and he had architected them himself. Sometimes they were not sound, but what they lacked in soundness they generally made up in originality.

He spent seventy years at sea, and then retired. He had now been retired ten years. He had never served in a warship, and did not get his title from the government; it was a token of love and homage, and was conferred upon him by the captains of the whaling fleet.

He was sitting in an arm-chair when George entered, and close at hand were various objects which were necessary to his comfort: grog, a

Bible, a Dibdin, a compass, a barometer, a chronometer, pipes, tobacco, matches, and so on. His ancient face was mottled with pinks, reds, purples and intermediate tints, and wrinkled on the plan of a railroad map; his head was wonderfully bald and slick and shiny and dome-like, and stood up out of a fence of silky white hair in a way to remind one of a watermelon in a bucket. Friends who liked to pester him said —not in his hearing, but to get it reported to him—that the flies used to slip, on his baldness, and fall and cripple themselves, and that in his native good-heartedness he rigged shrouds, made of thread, so that they could go aloft and return without risk.

He motioned George to a chair, then snuggled back into his own, with a contented grunt, and began to examine his guest with a calm and unblinking and prejudiced eye. This silent inquest was a little em-barrassing for the guest; an effect which was distinctly enhanced when the Admiral presently began to reinforce it with audible comments— under the impression that he was thinking to himself:

"Pale . . . . slim . . . . anemic . . . . half-fed . . . . timid. Lawyer? . . . . doctor? . . . . school-teacher? No. Not those. Hard to make him out. . . . . Good enough face, all but the eye. Has a malignant eye. What's his game, should you say? Has a game, of course; they all have. . . . . Wants my influence, I reckon—most of them do. Wants to get a billet in the navy. They all think I've been in the navy. . . . . . Job where he'll have a salary and nothing to do . . . . it's the usual thing. Well, to come down to business, what does this one want, do you reckon? Paymaster? no. Captain's secretary? no. Those require work. Not in this one's line. . . . . Ah, ten to one he wants to be chaplain. Yes, that's it. Well, I'll beat his game." Without taking his eye from the uncomfortable poet the Admiral reached for a pipe, lit it, and resumed. "That chair makes him squirm. They all squirm when they sit in that chair. They think I put them in it by accident. . . . . Chaplain—*him!* Probably couldn't expound a miracle to save his life. But that's nothing, I've never seen one that could. No—and when I show them the trick they are jealous, and resent it; and they feel their ambition stirring in them, and they pipe to quarters and clear for action, and start in all cocky and conceited and do their idiotic damdest to put me in the wrong; and when I break in and tell them to go to—

I say!—" (this in a trumpet-blast that made the poet jump), "can you expound the miracles?"

"Can I, sir?"

"Yes, you. Can you do it?"

"Really, I am afraid not, sir."

The Admiral stared at him with astonishment, the sternness in his face perceptibly relaxing a little, and muttered to himself—audibly —"a *modest* one, at last!—I never expected to see it." Then to the poet, with the eager light of controversy rising in his eyes—

"Try it, young man, try it! Let's see what you can do; take any in the lot—pick your own miracle, and make sail. Try an easy one, first-off."

George found himself feeling relieved and measurably comfortable all at once. The Admiral's soliloquy and David's instructions had furnished him a safe cue, and he knew how to proceed. He said, with judicious humility—

"Anywhere but here, Admiral Stormfield. But here, if you will excuse me—"

"And why not here?"

"Because David Shipman warned me. He said 'Keep out of that subject if you don't want to come to grief, you would only expose yourself; Admiral Stormfield could give any man of your calibre ninety in the game and win out with one hand tied behind him."

"Did he say that? Did he?" The old gentleman was profoundly pleased.

"Yes, that is what he said. And he—"

The cat came loafing in—just at the right time, the fortunate time. George forgot all about the Admiral, and cut his sentence off in the middle; for by birth and heredity he was a worshiper of cats, and when a fine animal of that species strays into the cat-lover's field of vision it is the one and only object the cat-lover is conscious of for one while; he can't take his eyes off it, nor his mind. The Admiral noted the admiration and the welcome in George's face, and was a proud man; his own face relaxed, softened, sweetened, and became as the face of a mother whose child is being praised. George made a swift step, gathered the cat up in his arms, gave him a hug or two, then sat down and spread him out across his lap, and began to caress his silken body with lingering long strokes, murmuring, "Beautiful creature . . . . wonderful creature!" and such things as that, the Admiral watching him with grateful eyes and a conquered heart. Watching him, and talking to himself—aloud:

"Good face—full of intelligence . . . . good eye, too—honest, kind, couldn't be a better one . . . . a rare person, and superior—superior all around—very different from the run of lubbers that come here legging for influence—tadpoles that think they are goldfish—"

And so on and so on. What was become of the poet's "malignant eye" all of a sudden? If the question entered the Admiral's head at all, it created no disturbance there, aroused no concern; the Admiral's latest view of a thing was the only one he cared for; he had never been a slave to consistency.

The caressing of the purring cat went on, its flexile body hanging over at both ends, its amber eyes blinking slowly and contentedly, its strong claws working in and out of the gloved paws in unutterable satisfaction, the pearl-lined ears taking in the murmured ecstasies of the stranger and understanding them perfectly, and deeply approving them, the Admiral looking on enchanted, moist-eyed, soaked to the bone with happiness.

By and by he sprang up abruptly and shook himself together with the air and look of one who is pulling himself out of a dream, and began to move briskly about, muttering, "Manners? What the hell have I been thinking about?—and him a guest?"

He got a feather-duster and zealously dusted off a leathern arm-chair that had no dust on it, handling the duster not like a housemaid who is purifying furniture but like a chief of police who is dispersing a mob with a club; then he polished the leather with his silk handkerchief until it was as shiny as his own head; finally he stood aside and said, with a wave of his hand—

"Do me the honor. I'm ashamed. I don't know how I came to give you that chair, it's not fitting for the likes of you."

George began a polite protest, and got as far as that he was "quite comfortably seated, and—" The Admiral interrupted, with a burst as of thunder—

"Do as I *tell* you!" and the poet had accomplished the change before the curtains had stopped quaking.

The Admiral was pacified, and muttered to himself, "he don't mean any harm, all he wants is discipline—has been brought up loose and harum-scarum, the way they do on land." Meantime he was busy stuffing a pipe. He handed it to George, lifted a leg, gave a strenuous forward-rake upon its under-half with a match—successfully; in fact that kind of a rake would have lit a nail. He held the match to the pipe, while he worded another apology—

"You mustn't mind—I never meant any unpoliteness, but just as I was going to reach for a pipe for you, Bags came a-loafing in, and when a cat comes my way I forget myself for a minute."

"So do I!" responded the poet, eagerly. "Why, I shouldn't ever be able to keep my head, with a cat like *this* one anywhere between me and the horizon."

The emphasis on that word fell with a most pleasant thrill upon the Admiral's ear, and he said, with affectionate pride in his tone—

"Now he *is* a daisy, ain't he?"

The response to this was up to standard. The Admiral, chatting comfortably about his cat, and weaving into the meshes of his theme another apology as he went along, got a little table and placed it between his chair and George's, set bottle and glasses on it, seated himself, brewed a couple of punches, remarked, "now we'll take a bit of comfort," then got some photographs of the cat out of his pocket and spread them out on the table for inspection. The cat was interested at once. He leaped upon the table, sniffed at the bottle and at each punch in turn, then arched his neck, curved a paw, and flirted the photographs off the table one at a time, the Admiral observing the performance admiringly, and remarking, "graceful? it ain't any *name* for it!" The cat bent down over the edge, inspecting the fallen cards longingly and turning his lively head this way and that, then he cast an eloquent glance at the Admiral, who said, "he's asking me to get them for him, you see?" and proceeded to pick them up and replace them, saying "notice that thankfulness in his eye and the way he acts? *talk* ain't any plainer;" the cat eagerly flirted them off as fast as they were restored, the Admiral remarking "notice that? You'll see he'll keep it up as long as it int'rests him—always does." The patient picking-up and the cheerful flirting-off continued for a minute or two, then the cat sat up and began to lick his paws and use them to rake forward his ears and scrub his cheeks, paying no further attention to the re-placing of the cards. "You notice?" said the Admiral, with a successful prophet's satisfaction, "didn't I tell you he would? oh, I know *him*, I reckon! now I'll show you the pictures."

But he was disappointed. The cat lay down and stretched himself out lengthwise of the table, which was only about two and a half feet long—stretched himself to his utmost length, with each end of him projecting a trifle beyond the edge. His body covered the cards and left but scant room for the bottle and glasses. The Admiral sighed, and said—

"Well, I wanted to show them to you, but it ain't any matter; there's plenty of time, and maybe he'll think of something else he wants to do, pretty soon. Often he does. Every night when we play cards on this little table—me and my grand-niece or her Aunt Martha—he comes and spreads out all over it the way he's doing now, and is most uncom-monly in the way; you have to play *on* him, you know, because there isn't any other place, he flats out so; and if he gets a chance he flirts off the tricks with his paw; and if he lays down on a trick, the game's up; you can't get at it, because he don't like to be disturbed. . . . Well, we can talk, anyway, whilst he's thinking up something fresh to do—*say!* now the light's coming just right—look at him! *ain't* he the very blackest object that ever cast a gloom in the daytime? Do you know, he's just solid midnight-black all over, from cutwater to tip-end of spanker-boom. Except that he's got a faint and delicate little fringe of white hairs on his breast, which you can't find at all except when the light strikes them just right and you know where to look. Black? why, you know, Satan looks faded alongside of Bags."

"Is that his n—"

"Look at him *now!* Velvet—satin—sealskin; can't you pick them out on him? Notice that brilliant sheen all down his forrard starboard paw, and a flash of it in the hollow of his side, and another one on his flank: is it satin, or *ain't* it?—just you answer me that!"

"It *is* satin, it's exactly the name for it!"

"Right you are. Now then, look at that port shoulder, where the light don't strike direct—sort of twilight as you may say: does it just pre-cisely counterfeit imperial Lyons velvet, forty dollars a yard, or *don't* it: come!"

"It does, I take my oath!"

"Right, again. The thickest fur and the softest you ever s— there! catch it in the shadow! in the deep shadow, under his chin—ain't it sealskin, *ain't* it? ain't it the very richest sealskin you—*say!* look at him now. He's just perfect now; wait till he gets through with that comfortable long summer-Sunday-afternoon stretch and curls his paw around his nose, then you'll see something. You'll *never* know how black he is, nor how big and splendid and trim-built he is till he puts on his *accent.* . . . . . Th—there it is—just the wee tip of his pink tongue showing between his lips—now he's *all* there!—sheen and gloom and twilight—satin, sealskin, velvet—and the tip of his tongue like a firecoal to accent him, *just* the blackest black outlay this side of the subcellars of perdition,—now I ask you honest, *ain't* he?"

The poet granted it, and poured out praise upon praise, rapture upon rapture, from his sincere soul, closing with—

"He *is* the last possibility of the beautiful! But oh, Admiral! how did you ever come to name him—"

"Bags? Sho, *that's* not his name, it's only his nom de plume. His name's Bagheera."

"Bagheera! Admiral, I could hug you for that! And he's worthy of it, too. If anybody can add anything to that praise, all right, let him try."

"You forgive me, don't you?" said the Admiral, oozing gratification from every pore; "I reckon I knew what I was about when I promoted him to that." He rose and moved toward his book-shelves. He took out a volume and patted its brown back. "Here she is," he said. "Kipling. Volume VII, Collected Works. Jungle Book. Immortal?"

"It's the right word, Admiral, in my opinion."

"You bet you! It'll outlast the rocks. Now I'm going to read to you out of this book. You look at the cat, and listen: 'A black shadow dropped down into the circle. It was Bagheera the Black Panther, inky black all over,'—*now notice, keep your eye on the cat*—'inky black all over, but with the panther markings showing up in certain lights like the pattern of watered silk.' There—don't he fill the bill? ain't he watered silk? look at his high-lights—look at his twilights—look at his deep glooms! Now you listen again: 'He had a voice as soft as wild honey dripping from a tree, and a skin softer than down.' *Bags!*"

The cat raised a sleepy head, and delivered an inquiring look from a blinking eye.

"Speak!"

The cat uttered a quivery-silvery mew.

"You hear that? is it soft as wild honey dripping from a tree? fills the bill don't it? Times, it is that rich and soft and pathetic and musical you wouldn't think it was a cat at all, but a spirit—spirit of a cat that's gone before, as the saying is. You ought to hear him when he's lonesome and goes mourning around empty rooms hunting for us; why, it just breaks your heart. And he's full of talent; full of tricks and oddities that don't belong in a cat's line, which he invented out of his own head."

"Could I see him do some of them?"

"—*sh!*" said the Admiral, putting his finger to his lips. "Change the subject. He *seems* to be asleep, this last half-a-minute, but that ain't any proof; it's just as likely he's awake, and listening. In that case you couldn't get him to do a thing. He's just like a child about that; the more you want him to show off, the more he won't do it to save your life."

"Admiral, is he so bright that he—"

"Understands? Every word!"

"I think, myself," George began, doubtfully, "that some animals understand a good deal of what we say—"

The Admiral stepped over and whispered at the poet's ear—

"*Every word!* Wasn't *that* what I said?"

"Yes, but—"

"I *said* it, didn't I? Well, it means par. He understands every word. Now I'll prove it"—still whispering. "It's a fad of his, to play with fire, and—"

"What, a cat play with fire?"

"Not so loud! Yes; it's because he found out that other cats don't. That's the way he's made—originality's his long suit; he don't give a damn for routine; you show him a thing that's old and settled and orthodox, and you can't get him to take any int'rest in it, but he'll trade his liver for anything that's fresh and showy. Now I'll light a little alcohol lamp and set it over yonder on the floor, and if he hasn't overheard us he'll put it out with his paw when he gets up; but if he is shamming and listening, now, he'll put up a disappointment on us, sure: he'll go over and give it an indifferent look and pass by on the other side, like the Good Samaritan."

The little lamp was duly lighted and placed, and the experimenters waited, in a solemn silence, for the result. Pretty soon—

"Watch him!" said the Admiral. "He's turning on his back to—look at that! when he gets that stretch completed and everything taut, he'll be twice as long as you think he is. There—how is that? as long and stiff as a deer-carcass that's frozen for transportation, ain't it? Notice the flash of that sheen on his garboard strake, port side of his keelson, just forrard of the mizzen channels—ain't that a gloss for you! Now then—stand by for a surge, he's going to gape. When he gets his mouth full-spread, look in, and see how pink he is inside, and what a contrast it is to his thunder-black head. There you are! ain't it pretty? ain't it like a slice out of a watermelon? . . . . Now—stand by again—he's going to break out his spinnaker."

The cat rose, added some fancy touches to his luxurious stretch, then he skipped to the floor and started across the room, making long final stretch-strides which extended first one hind leg and then the other far to the rear—then he discovered the lamp, and made straight for it with strong interest. The Admiral whispered, in high gratification—

"I bet you he didn't hear a word we said! Come, this is luck!"

The cat approached to within a foot of the lamp, then began to circle warily around it and sniff at it.

"It's the way he always does," whispered the Admiral, "he'll attack it in a minute."

The cat presently stopped, stood high, raised a paw—

"You see that? ain't it a pretty curve? he'll hold that paw that way as much as a half-a-minute, measuring his distance—sometimes he'll hold it out as straight as a stunsl-boom and—there, see him strike? Didn't fetch it this time, but you'll see he'll never let up till he does."

"Admiral, he burnt his fur; I smell it."

"That's nothing, he always does; he don't care. Another whack! ain't it graceful? ain't it resolute, ain't it determined? He's going to try with the other paw, now. He was left-handed when he was born, but

I learnt him ambidexterousness when he was little. . . . . There!—that was a good spat, you could hear it! That's four—about next time he'll fetch it. . . . . There! what'd I tell you?—he's done it."

The cat gave his paws a lick or two, then loafed off to a corner and stretched himself out on the floor. George said he could not have believed in this extraordinary performance if he hadn't seen it; that he had never heard of a cat before that would attack fire. He wanted to know who taught him.

"Nobody. It was his own idea. Took it up when he was a kitten. But never mind that—that ain't the thing that's before the house." The Admiral gave his head a prideful toss, and added, "the thing that is before the house is, did I *prove* it? That's the thing for you to answer: did I, or didn't I?"

"Prove what?"

The Admiral was a little nettled.

"Come! what did I start *out* to prove?"

"Well, I don't qui—I—"

"You've *forgot*, by gracious!—that's it—forgot it a'ready! Didn't I say he understood every word? Didn't I say I would prove it? Well, then—have I, or *haven't* I?"

George began to stammer and hesitate, showing that the proof had missed him; that he didn't know what it consisted in, and was fighting for time and revelation. The Admiral was surprised at his stupidity, and said with severity—

"Didn't I *tell* you, that if he was actually awake and overhearing us he would understand every word and wouldn't do a thing? Well, didn't he put out the lamp? Now then, what does it prove? It proves that he *didn't* overhear us, don't it? And *that* proves that he understands every word when he *does* overhear, don't it? I knew perfectly well I could prove it, I told you so before."

The Admiral had him under his severe and unrelenting eye, and so he was obliged to confess the "proof," for diplomacy's sake, though deep down in his heart he couldn't seem to see any convincing connection between the evidence and the alleged fact. However, he had wit enough to throw out a nicely buttered remark which beguiled the Admiral away from the danger-line and saved the situation: he said it

was perfectly wonderful the way the Admiral could "argue." The old
gentleman melted to that rather gross contribution; he was pleased to
the midriff, and said complacently—

"Well, they all say the old man can do a tidy thing in that line now
and then, but I don't know—I don't know."

The poet followed up his advantage with more butter, and still more
butter, until all possible peril was overpassed, and quite new and safe
ground reached. To-wit, music. The poet was fond of it, the Admiral
was fond of it—here was a new tie; the two men were already friends,
through the ministrations of the cat, their mutual passion for music
added several degrees of Fahrenheit to the friendship; by this time the
Admiral had dropped all formalities and was calling the poet by his
first name. Also, he was requiring George to come often—"the oftener
the better." George was more delighted than he could tell in words. It
seemed a good time to bring forward his great project, and he did it.
His delivery accomplished, he watched the Admiral's face with anxious solicitude. That patch-quilt remained calm. No lights, no shadows,
no changes of any kind moved across its surface. The Admiral was
thinking. Thought he was thinking. He was often calm and expression-
less, like that, when he thought he was thinking. After a silence so
extended that the poet was beginning to lose heart and wish he had not
ventured so soon, the Admiral lifted his glass and said gravely—

"I have examined it, I have looked it all over in my mind, carefully. I
see the grandeur of it. Drink!—then we will talk."

The poet was profoundly relieved; his spirits revived, and he cried—

"Thank you, thank you, Admiral, for being willing to discuss it!"

"Willing, yes, and glad to. Discussion throws light. I always want to
discuss a thing, no matter how well I am disposed to it; it's best to feel
your way on a strange coast, so I always take soundings."

"It's the wise course—I know it. I wish I did it more myself."

"You'll come to it—you're young, yet, and we don't learn such
things early." He disposed himself comfortably, and took a pipe, and
passed one to George; then he resumed. "A monument to Adam, says
you. Very well, let's look at the case. Now then, I'm going to admit, to
start with, that of all the minor sacred characters, I think the most of
Adam. Except Satan."

"Satan?"

"Yes. Jimmy differs. That's all right, it's her privilege."

"Her?"

"Yes—*her*. What of it? She's an orphaness. Also, Aunt Martha differs. That's all right, too, it's her privilege—although she's only a second cousin, and not an aunt at all. It's what we call her—aunt. Yet she's no more an aunt than you be, although she's a Prisbyterian. It's only a formality—her being an aunt is. It's only her being it through being a second cousin to some of our ancestors, I don't know which ones. But she's gold!—and don't you forget it. She's been with me twenty years; ten at sea, and ten here on land. She has mothered Jimmy ever since she was a baby."

"Ever since—since—*she* was a baby?"

"Certainly. Didn't I just say it?"

"I know; but I mean, *which* she?"

"*Which* she? What are you talking about with your *which* she?"

"I—well, I don't quite know. I mean the one that was a baby. Was *she* the one?"

The Admiral nearly choked with vexation; his face turned storm-blue, its railroad-lines turned fire-red and quivered over it like lightnings; then he did the thundering himself:

"By God, if you say it again I'll scalp you! you've got me so tangled up that I—*say!* can you understand *this?* Aunt Martha—SHE—understand?—mothered Jimmy ever since she was a baby—ever since SHE was a baby! SHE—get it?"

The poet—still uncertain—gave up, and falsely indicated comprehension with a strenuous nod, to pacify the Admiral and avert war. Things quieted down, then, and the Admiral growled his satisfaction:

"I'm glad. Glad I've succeeded. It's been admitted before this, that I can state a thing pretty limpid when I try. . . . . Very well, then. As I was saying, she did the thing I said. And nobody could have done it better—I'll say that, too. Jimmy's twenty-one, now. Baby on shore, first; then all of a sudden an orphaness, and so remains to this day, although at sea ten years, as I told you before. Aboard my ship. Along with Aunt Martha, who fetched her. I've been her father, Martha's been her mother; mother, old maid, and a Prisbyterian, all at the same time, a combination to beat the band. Heart of gold, too, as I told you before. Sixty years old, and sound as a nut. As for the name, I thought of it myself. I gave it to her."

"Martha is a good name," suggested the poet, in order to say something, it being his turn.

"Martha? Who said anything about Martha? Can't you keep the run of the ordinariest conversation?—say, can't you?"

"Oh, I—you see—well I understood you to say that she—"

"Hang it, what you understand a person to say hasn't got anything to do with what the person says, don't you know that? I was talking about Jimmy—my grand-niece."

"Oh, I see, now. I quite misunderstood, before, for I thought you said she was only twenty-one, and—"

"I *did* say it! George, take something; damned if you don't need it; your mind is failing. Now then, listen, and I'll try to put it so that even you can understand it. Aunt Martha is sixty—second cousin out of sources of antiquity—old maid, Prisbyterian from cat-heads to counter —get it? Very well. Jimmy is twenty-one—grand-niece—ex-fathered by me, ex-mothered by Martha—orphaness to this day—orphaness to this *day*—get it? Very well. Now we come to the place where you stuck: it was *her* I named, not Martha—get it? Named her James Fletcher Stormfield; named her for her little brother that had gone before, as the saying is. It broke my heart when he went—the dearest little fellow! but I saved the name, and there's comfort in that, I can tell you. As long as I've got Jimmy and the name, the world ain't going to get blacker than I can stand, although she's nothing but an orphaness when all's said and done, poor little thing. *But*—gold, all gold, like our Aunt Martha out of the geological period. Got it *all*, now, haven't you George?"

"All, and a thousand thanks, Admiral—you're ever so good."

He stopped with that, and thought he would economise words whenever he could, now, so as to keep out of trouble, and also trick the Admiral into sticking to his subject. The Admiral resumed:

"Now that we've got that settled, we'll return back to Adam and see if we can pull *him* off. I wish Aunt Martha was on deck, but it's her watch below. You see, she— *Bags!*" In the midst of the black velvet mask two disks of fire appeared—gleamed intensely for a moment, then the mask closed upon them and blotted them out. "He heard me, you see. Bags! turn out and tell your Aunt Martha to report in the chart room." The Admiral waited a moment, the fires did not reappear; then he explained, regretfully: "That's the way with a cat, you know—any cat; they don't give a damn for discipline. And they can't help it, they're made so. But it ain't really insubordination, when you come to look at it right and fair—it's a word that don't apply to a cat. A cat ain't ever anybody's slave or serf or servant, and *can't* be—it ain't *in* him to be. And so, he don't have to obey anybody. He is the only creature in heaven or earth or anywhere that don't have to obey *somebody* or other, including the angels. It sets him above the whole ruck, it puts him in a class by himself. He is independent. You understand the size of it? He is the only independent person there is. In heaven or anywhere else. There's always somebody a king has to obey—a trollop, or a priest, or a ring, or a nation, or a deity or what not—but it ain't so with a cat. A cat ain't servant nor slave to anybody at all. He's got all the independence there is, in heaven or anywhere else, there ain't any left over for anybody else. He's your friend, if you like, but that's the limit—equal terms, too, be you king or be you cobbler; you can't play any I'm-better-than-you on a cat—*no*, sir! Yes, he's your friend, if you like, but you've got to treat him like a gentleman, there ain't any other terms. The minute you don't, he pulls his freight. And he—*say!* you get that new tint?—on the curve of his counter—see it? delicate coppery mist, faint as dream-stuff—just like you catch it for a second in a mesh of the purple-black hair of a girl when the slant of the sun is right, ain't it so? Gone, now. Aunt Martha says—George, you'll like Aunt Martha."

"I'll be glad to, Admiral, and I'm sure I shall."

"Oh, yes, you will, there's no doubt about it." After a moment, he added, casually, "she has a ferocious temper."

"Is that so?"

"The worst there is. I wouldn't blame her, for she didn't make her temper, it was born in her; I wouldn't blame her if she didn't *hide* it; but I have to blame her for that, because it's deception."

George tried to say the kindly and modifying thing—

"Maybe she is only trying to keep it *down*, Admiral, instead of concealing it—and there should be merit in that."

"No, I know her—she just hides it, lets on it ain't there; she don't let a sign of it slip. She's deep, Martha is; you could be with her years and years and never find out she had it if I hadn't told you." A silence ensued; George could not think of any appropriate thing to say. The Admiral added, "she swears a good deal." George started, but ventured nothing. "You can't break her now," continued the Admiral, "it's too late; she's sixty, you see, and she's been at it twenty years. Picked it up from the sailors."

George thought of saying, "and from you, perhaps?" but concluded to stay on safe ground, now that he was doing well. He had been wanting to know Aunt Martha, on account of her heart of gold, but he hoped for better luck, now. He was afraid of her. The Admiral drifted tranquilly along with his treasonable revelations.

"Well, she's been through a lot, poor thing, and it's only right to make allowances. You see, she got a blight."

Pause.

"A blight?"

"That's it." (Pause.) "Got a blight."

This conversation was difficult.

"Got—er—got a—"

"That's it. Blight." (Pause.) "Early."

"How—er—how sor—unfortunate."

"Right again. She wasn't quite seventeen, he was just the same age."

"Oh—I see: unhappy love-passage."

"Yes, that was the trouble. Reefing a gasket in a gale, and fell off the foretogallantstunslboom. No-o—come to think, that was another one —the first one. This one's boat was smashed by a bull whale after he was struck, and a wave washed him down his throat—unhurt. He was never seen again."

"How dreadful!"

"Yes. You don't want to speak of it to her, she can't bear it."

"I can easily believe it, poor lady."

"No, she can't. It blighted her. Blighted yet. They were to 've been married as soon as he got to be mate, and he was already boat-steerer. It's the uncertainty that makes her life so mournful."

"Un— What uncertainty?"

"About his fate, you know."

"Why—I thought he went down the whale's throat?"

"Yes, that's it; that's what happened to him, poor boy."

"Yes, I understand that, but what I meant was, what was the uncertainty?"

"Why—well, as to what went with him after that, you know."

"Why, Admiral, there *couldn't* be any uncertainty as to that, could there?"

"I don't rightly know. At bottom, as between you and me, I don't think him likely to turn up again, but I don't *say* it, of course, and—"

"Does *anybody* think it likely that he—"

"*She* does; yes, she can't give up the hope that he'll fetch around yet, poor thing. She's to be pitied, I think."

"Indeed with all my heart I pity her. It is one of the saddest things I have ever heard of. But surely, after all these many many unrevealing years she—"

"No, nothing can convince her. You see, she's a Prisbyterian, and it makes her feel near to Job in the whale's belly—nearer than you and me can ever feel, not being situated like her—and she can't help feeling that what's happened once can happen again."

"True—but in that other case it was only three days, whereas in this one it is a whole generation and more. The cases are very different."

"I know it, but she holds to it that Job was old, and maybe, being superannuated, that way, he would have struck the limit before this, but her Eddy being young and hardy it could be different with him. But I know you wouldn't ever find any way to comfort her anyhow, because he was the only one the whale got. The others escaped, you see, and got drowned."

George struggled with this proposition, but could not work his way through the fog of it. He finally said—

"I don't quite see how his being the only one the whale got affected his unhappy case either one way or the other."

"That's what *I* think; but she keeps brooding over his being in there so long without any company. So lonesome, you see."

"I—yes—yes, I seem to see it, but I should not have thought of that," said George, bewildered.

"Well, it troubles her, every time she thinks of it. So dark in there, you see, and nothing doing. Night all the time, you know, and such a sameness and so dull. She longs to be with him."

George was not able to drum up a comment.

"Yes, it's a hard life for her, George; hard for her, hard for him, if he's there yet, which is far from likely, in my opinion, and I've thought it over a good deal. She always sees him the same way."

"How do you mean, Admiral?"

"Young, you know—not seventeen. Sees him the same way: young, fresh, rosy, brim full of life and the joy of it; always sees him the way he was when she saw him last, swinging down the road after his kiss, with his white ducks, and his tarpaulin with a dangling ribbon, and his blue neck-scarf, and his blue-bordered broad collar spreading upon his shoulders; sees him like that, with the sunset painting him all red and gold and glorious—the last sight of him she was ever going to see, George."

"How pitiful, how pathetic!"

"Yes, that is what I say. Sees him always just so—blooming, boyish, beautiful. Always the same—never adds a day; stands still in his youth, and she gets old and older, and gray and grayer, and—"

"*That's* pitiful, too!"

"It's the right name for it, George. Well, for ten years it was sweetheart and sweetheart; then she reconnized that she was outgrowing him—twenty-seven too old for seventeen—so she had to make a change; so she gradually got to regarding him as her son."

"How curious!"

"Yes. Well, that was all right and satisfactory till she drifted away from him wider and wider till last year she reconnized that the whole gap between them was forty-two years; then she shifted him to grandson. And there he is now. If she lives, he's good for a twenty-year rest. Then she'll promote him again. George, she's had a bitter hard time, and I want you to try to overlook her defect and feel the best and charitablest you can towards her, considering everything."

"O, God knows I would not add a pain to her sorrows for anything this world has to give!"

"I'm glad to hear you say that, George, it shows you've got a good heart. Jimmy's always kind and gentle to her. She's got the devil's own temper, too, but never shows it. I want you to know Jimmy."

"I shall be g—glad to, I'm sure."

It didn't sound quite like it.

"She'll play the penola for you. She's musical, like the rest of the breed. When she's a little further along I'm going to learn her to work the squawkestrelle. *Say!* look at him! look at his eyes!—locomotive head-lights, ain't it? Look at his attitude: whole body advanced and rigid; one front paw lifted and curved and motionless—looks so, but it ain't; he's putting it down, but you can't detect any motion to it; he's letting on that I'm a bird and he's creeping up on me and I don't know it; see him whimper and whicker with his lips and not make anything but just barely a little flicker of sound—a cat never does that but when it's slipping up on a bird and lusting after it; starboard paw's down at last—lifting the port one, now, but you can't perceive it; see him glare at me—never budges his eyes from me nor winks; six feet to come, and it'll take him five minutes; see him droop his belly, now, most to the floor, and whimper with his mouth and quiver his tail; I'll turn my face away, now and let on I don't know there's any danger around—it's part of the game—he expects it."

By and by the cat completed his imperceptible journey; then squatted close to the floor, worked his haunches and twitched his lithe tail a moment, then launched himself like a missile from a catapult and landed with a smashing impact upon the Admiral's shoulder. Before he could be seized he was away again. The Admiral was as vain of the performance as if it was the world's last wonder and he the proprietor of the sole miracle-monger that could achieve it.

"Does it every day!" said he. "Often he—*come in!*"

It was Aunt Martha. Seeing the stranger, she was going to retreat, but the Admiral gripped her by the hand and led her in, saying cordially—

"Don't you mind, it's nobody but George. Here she is, her own self, George—Martha Fletcher, heart of gold, chief mate, brains of the house—there! ain't she a daisy?" He swept her figure with an admiring look, gave a wave of his hand as if to say, "what did I tell you?—up to sample, ain't she?" then he bustled her into a chair and finished the introduction.

The poet had been expecting to be afraid of her if chance should some day bring him face to face with her, but he was pleasantly disappointed. There was nothing formidable about her, nothing to frighten any one; on the contrary, she was charming. Her hair was white and wavy and silky, she had a soft voice, her face was beautiful with the beauty of kindliness, human sympathy and the grace of peace, and upon her sat a gentle dignity which any could see belonged to her by right of birth. The Admiral beamed affection and admiration upon her, and the poet could not help doing the same—tempered, in some degree, by the remembrance of what he had heard about her profanities and her temper. His interest in her grew by swift stages, and in no long time he found himself condoning those defects, and even trying to believe they were not really defects at all, but only eccentricities, and not important. By and by she arrived at the errand she had come about: she wanted to advertise for a lodger. George pricked up his ears.

The Admiral said there was no occasion—there was money enough, and to spare. Aunt Martha said, no matter, the empty rooms were a reproach—some one ought to be enjoying them; even a charity-lodger who paid nothing would answer; she was not particular, as to that, but it was on her conscience that those good rooms were going to waste— and so she gently stuck to her point. The Admiral wavered, then surrendered, saying—

"All right, Aunt Martha, you would have it your own way sooner or later, anyhow, you are so obstinate when you are set. Go ahead and advertise."

She thanked him sweetly, and rose to go. George thought that now was his chance or never; so he made bold to say—

"If the Admiral would be willing, Miss Fletcher, do you think you could try *me* for a month and see if I would do? I am leaving my lodgings to-day." Which was not true.

"The very thing!" This from the Admiral. "Get your kit aboard and begin right away. I'll not let her overcharge you."

"Abner, I was not going to do it,—you know that," said the aunt in gentle reproach.

"Yes, you had it in your mind, I saw it. Go and fetch your things, George, you can look to me for protection. Another plate for supper, Martha—you hear?"

George brought his belongings and delivered them to the old sailor who did duty as the Admiral's butler, bos'n, second mate and one thing or another, then he called on his friend David and reported his great luck in securing lodgings in the Admiral's house. David asked why he had needed to do that, and George explained:

"It took me two hours to get him down *to* Adam and the monument, and that is as far as I've got, he scatters so. I hope to land him, but it will take time. He's worth it, though; he's worth no end of effort, I think. So I call it good luck that I got the lodgings. And there's another reason: I was lonesome where I was."

"Well, *that's* at an end, now, sure!" said David. "Sure—whether you like each other or not."

"I'll tell you our talk, David, then you can judge which it is."

When he had finished, David conceded that the new relationship did not seem to have anything cold about it. Then he added:

"You have done well, George, you have indeed. Well and judiciously. You've gone far with the Admiral. It is good diplomacy and a creditable performance. I hope you will land him, and I also believe you will."

"I am glad to hear you say it, David. It will take time, as I've said, but that's nothing; it's not going to be dull."

"Oh, on the contrary. Inasmuch as you want society, you are in even better luck than you think for, George."

"How is that? Are you thinking of Aunt Martha?"

"No—outsiders. Protégés of the Admiral."

"Protégés?"

"Yes. Life's failures. Shipwrecks. Derelicts, old and battered and broken, that wander the ocean of life lonely and forlorn. They all drift to him; and are made welcome."

"David, it is beautiful! He didn't mention this."

"He? No, he wouldn't be likely."

"Then it's all the more beautiful!"

"So it is. They drop in on him, whenever they please, and he comforts them. A poor old pathetic lot."

"I want to see them, David; I'd like to know them."

"Well, you will, if the Admiral sees that sort of spirit in you. Otherwise not. It is thought that he helps them with his purse as well as with his sympathies; in fact, between you and me, I know he does, but you will keep this knowledge to yourself. He's a man, George—he's a whole man. There's delicacies in him that you wouldn't suspect, he seems so rough."

"I suspected them, the minute the cat came in, David!" said George, proud of his penetration. "Delicacies are of the heart; and the minute the cat came in, his heart was exposed. He was not much better than a pirate when he was talking to himself before that; but afterwards it was very different. And a good deal of a relief to me, too. Once he started to reveal to me how Bags stands in the matter of morals, but changed the subject when Bags let an eye fall open, showing that he wasn't asleep. I recognized, then, that what he had been going to let out was something shady, or partially so, and he didn't want to hurt Bags's feelings."

"It was like the Admiral. Privately his friends have a name or two for his house,—half a dozen, in fact—founded on his special compassion for life's failures—ironical names, but there's no sting in them: 'Haven of the Derelict,' 'Refuge of the Broken Reed'—that's a couple of them."

"Why, they're lovely, David! It's the lead of irony transmuted into the gold of homage. Do you—"

"Wait—I want to give you a point, while I think of it. Talk temperance—*general* temperance—with the Admiral, if you want to—he likes the subject—but don't go into the history of it; at least don't go away back; don't go back as far as Father Matthew. Because mention of that name is a thing he can't stand. It has been tried. By an ignorant person. Ignorant and innocent. He was fooled into doing it by a friend of the Admiral's who knew a secret and tender spot in the old mariner's history and wanted to get some effects out of it without taking the risk of putting his own finger on it. They say that the eruption of profanity that ensued lasted several hours and has not been equaled since Vesuvius buried Herculaneum. Do as I tell you: leave Father Matthew alone—let the Admiral's volcano sleep."

"All right, I will, but tell me about it. Why should the name rouse him so?"

"Because it reminds him of an incident of his early life which he hates the memory of. It was like this. Away back, fifty or sixty years ago, when the Admiral was about twenty-five, he came back from a three-year voyage to find a melancholy change at home in New Bedford and Fairhaven: Father Matthew, the great apostle of temperance, had been sweeping New England like a prairie-fire, and everybody had joined the Father Matthew Societies and stopped drinking. When Stormfield realized the situation, his heart almost broke. Not a comrade would drink with him, he had to drink all alone, and you know what that means to a sociable soul. He wandered the streets disconsolate, bereft, forsaken; nobody wanted his company, the girls cut him, he was not asked to the parties and the dances.

"And he had come home so triumphant, so joyful! For he had been promoted from mate to captain, and was full of the glory of it, and now there was nobody interested in his honors, no one cared to hear about them. He endured his sufferings as long as he could, then he broke his jug and surrendered, and sent in his name to be balloted for at the Father Matthew Society's next meeting. That same night his crew arrived—Portuguese and Kanakas from the Azores—and at daybreak in the morning he sailed.

"He was gone three years. He was firm; he drank not a drop the whole time, but it was a bitter hard battle, from the first day to the last—with the grog circulating among those brown men every few hours, and his mouth watering for it unspeakably! For he had begun to repent of what he had done before he was out of sight of land; he repented every day and all the days, for three years—and most deeply of all on the last one, which was fearfully cold, with a driving storm of wind and snow, and he had to plow the fleecy deck and face the gale, *dry*—oh, so dry! and those brown people comforting themselves with hot grog every little while and he getting the whiff of it; and so, the minute he made port he bought a jug and rushed to the Society and hit the secretary's desk with his fist and shouted—

" 'Take my name off your cussed books, I'm dying of a three-years' thirst!'

"The secretary said, tranquilly—

" 'Hasn't ever been on—*you were black-balled.*'

"Those are the facts, George." That far in his talk David was serious; possibly he was serious in the rest of it; most people would have doubted it; George might have doubted it himself if he had been differently made. "You would think, George, that after the incident had had a year's wear, the soreness would have passed out of it and left nothing behind but a text for the Admiral to joke about; it is what would have happened if anybody else had been in the Admiral's place, but in his case it did not happen. With him it has remained a serious matter, and when you consider the make of him you can understand why. To him the thing stands for one thing only: bitter *loss*, irreparable loss. Suppose a happy bridegroom should lie in a trance three years: would not he recognize that he could never catch up, in this life? Well, that is the way the Admiral feels."

There was a sigh, and George said—

"I am glad you have shown me this aspect of it, David. At first I saw only one side, and so it seemed funny, but I see now that it is not. It would pain me to laugh at it now; I think it would pain any one who has any heart."

"Yes, I am sure it would. George, he has borne this sorrow for fifty years, without outward complaint; borne it with dignity, borne it with a certain composure. One cannot reflect upon this and not revere him."

"You could not say a truer thing than that, David. I feel just as you do about it."

"In a large sense it is a blighted life. Yet it has been blest to him, and richly blest to others, for it has borne precious fruit. It has made him the friend and brother of all upon whom disaster and blight have fallen; out of it has grown the 'Haven of the Derelict,' the 'Refuge of the Broken Reed.'"

"David," said George, deeply touched, and awed, "that incident of the long ago was not an accident, it was *meant*, and it had a purpose. The hand of Providence was in it—I know it, I see it. It was no earthly hand that black-balled him."

"I have never doubted it," said David, impressively; "there are no accidents, all things have a deep and calculated purpose; sometimes the methods employed by Providence seem strange and incongruous, but we have only to be patient and wait for the result: then we recognize that no others would have answered the purpose, and we are rebuked and humbled."

Chapter 3

From George's Diary

I WAS in time for supper. The Admiral sat at the head of the table, Aunt Martha at the foot; I and the cat (the latter on a high baby-chair) sat on one side, and Jimmy and a middle-aged lady in rather loud and aggressive young-girl dress on the other. The Admiral made the introductions. He called the elderly girl the Mar*cheeza* di Bianca —"otherwise White," he added, "Eyetalian for White." The marchesa corrected his pronunciation—

"Mar*kayza*," she said, unpleasantly.

The Admiral was not troubled. He nodded at me and said, tranquilly—

"In a way, she's right; they say it that way over there, they being backward in their spelling, but over here it's not right, because the Constitution don't allow it. The Constitution says we've got to pronounce words the way they are spelt." Jimmy and the aunt glanced up at him doubtfully, (or maybe it was reproachfully,) and the marchesa opened her mouth—"Close it!" said the Admiral fiercely, and was obeyed. "It's spelt the same as cheese, and when I heave it out, cheese it *is*." He glared around, from face to face. "Any objections?"

None were offered. The ancient sailor-butler was serving. He was tall, grave, grizzled, muscular, he wore sailor-clothes, was stiff-legged on the near side, and had the gait of a carpenter's compass when it is semi-circling its course across a ground-plan; for one of his legs was made of wood, or iron, or some other rigid material. The Admiral and his family called him Bos'n, and he always answered "aye-aye, s'r," regardless of sex. George noticed that he skipped the cat. The Admiral noticed that George noticed. He explained:

"Bags don't eat with the rest of the family, he waits, and eats by himself. It's his own idea. But he most always comes and looks on, because he likes company, and wants to hear the talk. Often he takes a hand in it himself."

Jimmy and the aunt cast that mystic glance at him again. It seemed to me that it might mean "Remember, there is a stranger present; he is not used to you, and will misunderstand." If that was the look's message, there was nothing to show that it reached port; the Admiral went on talking about the cat's interest in dinner-conversations and participation in them, and pretty soon he was enlarging. It did not take him long to enlarge to where he was giving samples of what the cat had actually *said* on one or another occasion. Then the ladies seemed to give it up. They looked resigned; and I did not see them employ that glance any more. I felt sorry for them, but there was nothing I could do; at least nothing but try to relieve the situation by changing the subject. I did that a couple of times, but it did no good, the Admiral changed it back as soon as it suited him. He got to reporting political and theological views—of the cat's—which were manifestly beyond and above a cat's reach, and although I could easily see that this distressed his ladies and made them bend their heads and look at their plates, he did not seem to be aware of it himself. He quoted remarks—of the cat's —which were often discreditable and sometimes profane, and then made the matter worse by approving and defending them. It was a sufficiently embarrassing situation. Now and then he would throw out a remark of the cat's that was really and extravagantly outrageous; then he would look aggressively around upon the company, as if he were expecting a revolt, and wishing for it. But it never happened, and he had to put up with his disappointment the best he could. He realized that there was doubt in the air, and it annoyed him, and made him want to remove it. Instead of reasoning the matter with *us*, he sought refuge in a transparent absurdity; he asked the *cat* if he had quoted him correctly. The cat always said something back; then the Admiral would cast a lurid look of triumph upon the company and say, "I reckon that settles it!" whereas it settled nothing, for we could not understand the cat. But we had to leave it his way, there was no other course. By help of our silence, which he translated into assent, he was able to establish all his points. This pleased him, and made him periodically happy, and saved us from getting flung out of the window.

When the dinner was ended, with its procession of alternating storms and calms, fearful perils and blessed rescues, I realized that I had had an interesting time, and said so. The Admiral was perceptibly flattered and gratified, and confessed, on his part, that he had seldom participated in a more informing and satisfying "discussion." That was his word. If he had searched the dictionary through, he could not have found a more fiendishly inappropriate one. It was the kind of discussion a saw has with a saw-log. My indignation rose, for a moment, for it was very trying to have him empty that offensive word upon me in that bland way, but I held my peace and put my feelings away, and it was better so. To have challenged the word would merely have brought on another discussion—of his kind—with no profit to any one.

He was feeling good and sociable, now, and we all went to his parlor in a promisingly comfortable condition of mind. Under the pleasant influences of punch and pipe the Admiral presently broke ground on the monument scheme of his own volition, and explained it to the ladies. It produced effects—one could see it in their faces. The Admiral then proceeded, without waiting for comments:

"When you come to consider the minor sacred characters, it seems to me that Satan and Adam—"

"Abner!" This from Aunt Martha, with gentle surprise.

"Now then, what's the matter with *you?*"

"Abner, Satan is not one of the sacred characters."

"The h—alifax he ain't!"

"Why, no, he isn't. But don't lose your temper, dear heart."

The mild admonition and the affectionate epithet modified the Admiral, and he dropped into what I suspected was his favorite argumentative plan of hunting an objection down:

"Martha, ain't he in the Book?"

"Yes."

"Martha, is it a holy Book?"

"Yes."

"*All* holy?"

"Yes, it is all holy."

"Is there another word for it?"

Aunt Martha hesitated; as one might who is becoming uncertain of his ground. The Admiral took notice, gave a complacent nod, and furnished the word himself:

"*Sacred* Scriptures, ain't it?"

"Ye-s."

"*The*, ain't it?"

"I—I know; yes."

"What does *the* stand for? The *only* one that's sacred, ain't it?"

Aunt Martha's gun was silent.

"Well, then!" and he began to tally-off the conceded points on his fingers, point by point: "One, it's in the Book—you give in to that. Two, the Book's *holy*. Three, it's *all* holy, says you. Four, it's the *sacred* Scriptures. Five, it's *the* sacred Scriptures. Grand total: holy, all holy, sacred, *the* sacred. Very well, then; when a thing is so utterly and altogether and absolutely and uncompromisingly and all-solitary-and-alone sacred, without any competition in the business, how are you going to make out that there's anything in it that *ain't* sacred? You just answer me that, if you think you can!"

This burst of remorseless logic seemed to wither Martha. One might imagine her a rumpled and collapsed flag that has been hauled down; whereas the Admiral looked as pleased as a mine might that has done its job well and blown up an assaulting party. Smiling benignantly upon the wreckage, he was about to start his talk again, when the marchesa sniffed and dropped a comment:

"Putting buttons in the contribution-plate don't make them holy."

Martha and Jimmy glanced at her. As to what the glances meant I could not be sure, but to me they seemed to mean, "*Don't* do that!" Then, before the Admiral could open up on the marchesa—which he was evidently going to do—Jimmy said, persuasively—

"Please begin over again, Uncle Abner, I want to hear all I can about the monument before bedtime, and no one can make it so interesting as you."

The storm-cloud flitted out of his face and he went at his work at once, quite evidently gratified by that just remark.

"As concerns Satan and Adam, I was going to say I rank them about on a par among the minor prophets, and—"

"Prophets!" scoffed the marchesa, and was going to enlarge, when the Admiral turned a warning eye upon her and put the ends of his thumbs and of his middle fingers together in the form of an open mouth—for a moment, then impressively brought the parts together, thus closing that mouth. The marchesa closed hers. The Admiral resumed:

"I rank them about on a par, as regards intelligence. And yet Satan was one of the oldest of the sacred characters, and therefore—"

He stopped and glanced around, apparently to see if that word was going to be attacked again. It didn't happen.

"The idea that he ain't a sacred character! Suppose you handle him in a humorous lightsome way just once,—only just once—in a magazine, if you want to know! You'll have all the pulpits and deacons and congregations on your back in a minute, in the correspondence-columns, for trifling in that unsolemn way about a person that's in the Bible. Haven't you seen it? Don't you know it's so?"

Nobody ventured dissent.

"You know mighty well it is. That's the reason you don't try to call the hand. Very well then. As I was saying, Satan was very old and experienced, yet he didn't outrank Adam in intelligence, which was only a child, as you may say, though grown up. How do I make it out? I will tell you. Satan offered all the kingdoms to our Savior if he would fall down and worship him. Did he own them? No. Could he give title? No. Could he deliver the goods? No. Now I'll ask you a question. If a slave was to go to a king and offer to trade him his own kingdom for a dollar and a half, how would we rank him for intelligence? Way, way, *way* down! ain't it so?"

He polled the company; there was not an opposition vote.

"Carried. Now then, I'll ask you another question. Can you find anything anywhere in Satan's history that's above that mark, for intelligence? No. In the Middle Ages he was always building bridges for monks in a single night, on a contract—and getting left. Ain't it so? And always finishing cathedrals for bishops in a single night, on a contract—and getting left. Ain't it so? And always buying Christian souls, on contracts signed with red Christian blood—and getting left. Every time. Can you find a case where they didn't *do* him, as the saying is? There isn't one. Did he ever learn anything? No. Experience was wasted on him. Look at his trades; he was as inadequate in the last one as he was when he first started. Finally—I'll ask your attention to this: didn't he start in to convert this whole world to sin and pull in everybody and range them under his banner? Certainly. Hasn't he been hard at it for centuries and centuries? Certainly. Well, how does the thing stand now—is it his world? No, sir! if he has converted nine-tenths of it it's the most you can say. *There!* Now then, you answer me this: is he one of life's failures?" He paused, took a drink, wiped his lips thoughtfully, and added: "*One* of them? why, he's *It!*"

Then the idea of Satan's being a life's failure seemed to touch him, and he said with a little quiver in his voice:

"Well, he's out of luck—like so many—like so many—and a body has to pity him, you can't help it."

I was not expecting to be moved by any gentle word said about Satan, but the Admiral surprised me into it. It was ridiculous, but at the moment it seemed a natural thing and a matter-of-course. Well, I suppose that it isn't so much *what* a man says that affects us as the *way* he says it. I will make a note of it.

The Admiral began—

"We will now examine Adam. As far as—"

The soft rich note of a Japanese temple-bell interrupted: "plung-plung—plung-plung—plung-plung—plung-plung!" Then the bos'n's deep voice pealed through the house—

"E-i-g-h-t bells—starboard watch turn out!"

"Divine service," said the Admiral, and rose and took his place behind a stand that had some religious books on it. The young girl Jimmy seated herself at the piano, which was equipped with a pianola attachment. Footsteps were heard approaching, and a rustling of gowns, and several servants entered softly and stood against the wall. The Admiral read a prayer from the Episcopal prayer-book, and did it nobly. To me it seemed a marvelous performance. Where did he get that great art, that rare art? David says there are only a hundred and thirteen people in the world who know how to read. When he hears the Admiral he will add one to his list.

Then the Admiral read a familiar hymn. This was the first time that the deeps and graces and sublimities of that hymn were ever revealed to me. The congregation—save the Admiral—sang the piece, Jimmy playing it with the pianola-thing which the renowned musical profes-sionals puff so much. Then the Admiral prayed a prayer of his own make. With a word or two it invoked a blessing upon the national government. Next, it implored salvation for the "anchor watch"—

apparently a brevity-title for his college of derelicts; then he implored salvation for his mother and father, dead a generation ago; then for the household, servants and all; then for me. He paused, now, and there was silence for some seconds. Then he bowed his head, and added in a low voice—

"And humbly I beseech, O Lord, salvation for one other . . . . not named."

It startled me. Who was the unnamed one? Ah—Satan? No. I put that out of my mind. The sentiment for Satan had of course been an accidental thing born of his discourse about him, and not permanent. Then—why, it must have been himself! I was sorry. It suggested theatrical humility—show-off humility, for people to admire—and he so finely and faultlessly genuine, so worshipfully genuine, up to that moment! It was as if the robes of an image of gold had blown aside and exposed legs of clay. I was sorrier than I can tell. I went to bed depressed.

Chapter 4

From George's Diary, a Week Later

THIS is not a dull house. The human interest is pervasive here, pervasive and constant. I did not know, before, how interesting our race can be; I only knew how uninteresting it can be. I see, now, that it was uninteresting merely because I had no close contact with it, and not because the people of my acquaintanceship were commonplace. In a single week I have come to doubt if there *are* any uninteresting people. Certainly most people are commonplace,—a word which, taken apart and examined, merely means that their tastes, ideals, sympathies and mental capacities are below your standard—a word which contains and conveys the fact that those people are dull to you—but when you get *on the inside of them*—well, I begin to think that that is quite another country. If to be interesting is to be uncommonplace, it is becoming a question, with me, if there *are* any commonplace people.

Broadly speaking, my previous contacts have been with persons whose ways and standards did not tally with mine, and I thought that that was the reason their company was a weariness to me. But I see that that could have been a mistake. If I had happened to get at their insides I think I should have found interesting things hidden there. Books? Yes, books. So the bos'n says. He says a man's experiences of life are a book, and there was never yet an uninteresting life. Such a thing is an impossibility. Inside of the dullest exterior there is a drama, a comedy, and a tragedy. The bos'n says there is no exception to the rule. But how difficult it is to get at those poems!

My life was dull before luck got me into this house; I had only outsides to contemplate, but here it is the other way. Here I have opportunity to penetrate beyond the skin. The contacts with the household are frequent, and the same is the case with the derelicts and their intimates. As a rule I have not had friends before, but only acquaintances; they talked the news and gossip of the day—which was natural—and hid their hurts and their intimate joys—which was also natural—and so I took them for light-weights and commonplace, and was not glad of their society. Lord, they all had their tragedies!—every one of them, but how could I suspect it?

Formerly if a person had said to me, "Would you like to know Smith the letter-carrier?" it would not have occurred to me to say yes. But I should say it now, believing as I now do that a man's occupation is not a mirror of his inside; and so I should want to know Smith and try to get at his interior, expecting it to be well charged with interest for me.

The fact is, I do know Smith the (ex-)letter-carrier, though it is only by accident that I have used him as an illustration. He is a derelict. I asked him to sit, and am painting his portrait. He is from a distant State and city. His young wife is there. He is silent and abstracted, and usually sits apart, with his head bent, and thinks his thoughts, and does not smile. When he supposed I was meaning to charge him for the portrait he looked up, pulled his wandering mind home with an effort, and said no, he had no money; I explained that it was not a matter of money, I only wanted to paint it for practice and he could have it when it was done. The idea did not seem to take hold.

I could see that he was vaguely wondering what use it could be to him; he looked up vacantly—the problem had baffled him; I said "for your wife"—then his eyes filled.

The first sitting thawed him a little; before the second one was ended he was telling me how he was occupying himself and how the Admiral came to run across him and add him to his accumulation of human wreckage; in the third sitting the thawing reached still further into his mass and he talked about his boyhood and his parents, his playmates and his brothers and sisters; in the fourth the melting was nearly complete and he talked freely and trustingly of some of the things hidden away in the deeps of his heart—such as the happinesses of his married life, and how Mary looked, and how she talked, and what her opinions were, on this and that and the other matter of moment, and how sterling she was, and how sane, and how good-heart-ed, and all that; and in the fifth—in the fifth the last ice-shield broke away and out came the tragedy! There is always one, if you can get at it. Often it looks trivial on paper, but never is trivial when it trickles out before you tinged with heart's blood.

This tragedy will look trivial to an outsider. It cannot be put in words that could save it from that. The conventions are in the way; they blur our vision, and keep us from perceiving that the sole tragic thing about a hurt is the hurt itself and its effect upon the sufferer, not the noble or ignoble factors and conditions involved in the infliction of it. The present tragedy is a brief story. This is what happened.

Smith was nineteen years old, and was already a journeyman ma-chinist, with a year's savings laid up. He had a good reputation as a workman, a good wage, a permanent job, and a sweetheart to his taste. He had reached the very top of his ambition, his dearest dream was realized; he was grateful, proud, satisfied, happy, to a degree be-yond any words of his to express. His family were proud of him, his friends were proud of him; this was the best and the most that a duke or a king could have, and so he believed he felt just as kings feel. What could he want more? Nothing.

He lived, moved, and had his being in this delicious incense, the approval, amounting to deference, of his family and friends. He and they were all of humble estate—mechanics and laborers. His father was a day laborer and unschooled; his mother took in washing; his

Mary's people were conditioned in like way; her father was a pavior, her mother a washerwoman, Mary was a helper. The two families lived high up in mean tenement houses.

Young Smith had given himself a pretty fair education, by sitting up nights, and was fond of study. He and Mary spent their evenings in study together. They married—he nineteen and she a year younger. They went on with their studies, and were perfectly happy. For a year. Smith repeated that. "For a year."

I noted it; it foretold disaster. There was a competitive examination, for the office of letter-carrier. Smith entered the competition—"just to see what he could do," he said; he did not need the place, and did not want it. To his and Mary's astonishment—and joy—he came out on top and got it! With something near to a moan he added, "that was where our ruin began—lord, if I had only lost it!"

The pride and exultation of the two families and the friends exceeded all bounds. Smith's and Mary's happiness soared to the limit of human endurance; they thought they felt as kings feel when accident promotes them to emperorship. When Smith appeared for the first time in his uniform the families and the friends did not stop with admiration, they were *awed*; so awed that they acted more like strangers than friends; they were constrained, their tongues were crippled, they talked disjointedly, they were embarrassed, and they embarrassed him. He was an officer of the government of the United States, and they were —what they were; they could not bridge the chasm. It took the old-time easy familiarity all out of them.

That was the beginning of the tragedy. Next, the uniform introduced certain compulsions. Among other things, it—I can't recal his precise words, I wish I could, for they were beyond all art for innocent quaintness; but the sense of them was this: it raised them to a higher and more exacting social plane than they had been occupying before and they had to live up to the change, which was costly. I risked a delicate question and asked him who these exclusives might be— though of course I did not use that word. The inquiry did not disturb him; he was quite simple and frank about it, and said—

"Shop-clerks, sales-ladies, and such. And there was a steamboat mate and a type-writer."

Mary had to get some suitable clothes. Smith had to take to cigarettes—he had not smoked at all, before. Also, he had to rise above five-cent drinks, which made treating a noticeable burden. He paused, at this point, reflected, then recalled another detail—collars; he had to wear white ones.

The next step was inevitable: they had to move into better quarters, they must live up to the uniform, and to the new social altitude. Slight as the added rent was, it was a burden. They visited their new associates, and were visited by them. This had a foreseeable result: it presently broke off intercourse with the old friends, for between these and the new people were several inharmonies—discords in the matter of clothes and manners, furniture, upholstery, ideals, interests, and so on. When the two classes met at Smith's there were embarrassments and a frost. Intercourse between the Smiths and their ancient and cordial friends ceased, by and by, and the couple were left to the new people and a frivolous and empty and cheerless life.

Next stage. The added expenses were infinitely trifling,—would have seemed so to the reader's ear, at any rate—but no matter, they strained Smith's purse beyond its strength. He could not bear to reveal this to Mary, and he didn't. When he was depressed and sore and she put her arms about his neck and begged him to tell her what was the matter, he said it was headache and made him feel a little down. Then, with a loving desire to cheer him up, she would take the worst way she could have found: she would invite their fashionables to cake and tea, and make another expense. When at last he was at his wits' end—

"What do you reckon I did?" he asked, looking at me out of what one might have mistaken for the face of a dead man, so wan and white it was. "Lord God forgive me, I began to rob the letters!"

Mary did not know, nor suspect—until the black day when the officers came, and tore him from her clinging arms and his heart almost broke under the misery of hearing her despairing shrieks and moans and sobs.

He was in prison two years. When he got out, not even his light fashionables would associate with him, and they had cut Mary long before. The brand was upon him, the machinists' union rejected him, he could get no work. For three years he "has been in hell." The words are his. He has drifted hither and thither, and earned bread when he could. But for the Admiral, who happened upon him when he was at his lowest, death by starvation would have been his fate, he thinks. It is seven months since he last saw Mary; and then she did not know him. A fall on the ice injured her spine, and she is a helpless invalid. Her mind has failed. She is in the tenement again, with her old father and mother.

Chapter 5

From George's Diary—the Same Day

AT THIS point I shifted the subject, for it was bearing too hard upon the young fellow's spirits—and upon mine too. I tried a reference to the monument, hoping that the change would change his mood. It did. At the mere mention of Adam's name his temper rose with a flash, and it was wonderful to see what a customarily reserved man can do with his tongue when an inspiring theme comes its way. It was like Vesuvius in eruption. Lava, flame, earthquake, sulphurous smoke, volleying explosions—it was all there, and all vindictive and unappeasable hostility and aversion. I sat enchanted, dumb, astonished, glad to be there, sorry when the show was over.

One would have supposed Smith was talking about an intimate enemy—an enemy of last week, of yesterday, of to-day, not of a man whom he had never seen, and who had been dust and ashes for thousands of years. The reason for all this bitter feeling? It was very simple.

"*He brought life into the world,*" said Smith. "But for him I should not have been born—nor Mary. Life is a swindle. I hate him."

After a panting moment or two he brought forth another surprise for me. To-wit, he was unreservedly and enthusiastically in favor of the monument! In a moment he was in eruption again. This time it was praises of Adam, gratitude to Adam, exaltation of his name. The reason of *this* attitude? Smith explained it without difficulty:

"*He brought death into the world.* I love him for it." After a little he muttered, like one in a reverie, "death the compassionate . . . . the healer of hurts . . . . man's only friend . . . ." He was interrupted, there —the bos'n came in for a sitting.

The bos'n didn't think much of me the first day or two, because there was an impression around (emanating from David,) that I was a poet; but when he found that my trade was artist in paints the atmosphere changed at once and he apologised quite handsomely. He had a great opinion of artists, and said the Admiral was one. I said I was glad, and would like to see his pictures, and the bos'n said—introducing a caution—

"That's all right, but don't let on. When you want anything that's private out of the Admiral, don't let on. He might be in the mood, and he mightn't. As soon as the mood takes him he'll open up on it himself—you'll see—but not any sooner. There ain't anybody that can unlock him on a private lay till he's ready. Not even Miss Jimmy, not even Aunt Martha."

I said I should remember, and be careful. I repeated that I was glad the Admiral was an artist. The bos'n responded, with feeling and emphasis.

"An artist he *is*—I can tell you that. Born to it, *I* think. And he ain't only *just* an artist, he's a hell of an artist!"

The form of a compliment has nothing to do with its value—it is the spirit that is in it that makes it gold or dross. This one was gold. This one was out of the heart, and I have found that an ignorant hot one out of the heart tastes just as good as does a calm, judicial, reasoned one out of an educated head. I hope to be a hell of an artist myself some day, and hear the bos'n concede it.

As I was saying, the bos'n arrived. The ex-postman went away. I settled myself for a stage-wait. The bos'n was just from the looking-glass, but no matter, he would prink again; his first sitting had taught me this. But it was no matter, he couldn't well be uninteresting, no matter what he might be doing, for he was good to look at; besides, he was generally talking, and his talk was not borous. He was past sixty, but looked considerably younger, and had a fine and tall figure and an athletic body—a most shapely man when standing before the glass, with his artificial leg quiet. He had a handsome face and an iron jaw, and that tranquil and business-like eye which men and tigers have so much respect for. He is very likeable. We chatted while he prinked. Mainly about Smith. Presently I said I was sorry to see that Smith was a pessimist.

"A whichimist?" inquired the bos'n, turning a glance of interest at me over his shoulder, while rearranging for the fourth time the sailor-knot in his flowing neckerchief.

"Pessimist."

"Good word. As good as they make. What's a pessimist?"

"The opposite of an optimist."

"Another one. What are they both?"

"An optimist is cheery and hopeful—looks on the bright side of things. A pessimist is just the other way. Smith has no business to be a pessimist, he is too young."

"Is—is he? What's your age, Mr. Sterling?"

"Twenty-six."

"What's his?"

"About the same."

He came and took his seat and arranged his pose.

"He oughtn't to be a pes—pes—"

"Pessimist. No, he oughtn't. He has had trouble, he is in trouble, but at his age he oughtn't to give himself up body and soul to his sorrows. He ought to be more of a man. Shutting himself up to selfishly brood over his troubles and pet them and magnify them is a poor business, and foolish. He ought to look on the bright side of life."

"Now then," said the bos'n, "I'll set you right. Aunt Martha set me right when I was thinking the same as you, and I'll pass it along—then you'll see the rights of it, too. Smith's made on another pattern from you. Well, he can't help that. He didn't make his pattern, it was born to him, the same as yours was born to you. Smith *don't* brood mainly over his troubles; he's built so's 't he's got to suffer and sweat over everybody else's. You read the papers, don't you?"

"Yes."

"So does Smith. Do you read the telegraph news—all of it?"

"Yes, all of it."

"This morning, as usual?"

"Yes."

"How did you feel, after it—cheerful?"

"Yes. Why?"

"Comfortable?"

"I—well, I don't remember that I didn't."

"All right. It's the difference between you and Smith. *He* can't read the paper and not break his heart. Other people's troubles near kill him. It's because he was born tender, you see—not indifferent." I winced a little. He took up the paper and began a search, turning it this way and that, and still talking along. "You see, if a person shuts himself up inside of himself and don't worry about anybody's troubles but his own, he . . . . I can't seem to find the telegraphs . . . . he can get to be considerable of an octopus—"

"Optimist."

—"optimist, by and by, you know; and manly, and all that . . . . oh, now I'm striking the telegraphs . . . . and can look on the bright side of life and . . . . here they are! . . . . admire himself."

He uttered that vicious sarcasm so absently and so colorlessly that for a quarter of a second I hardly felt its teeth go in; then the bite took hold. I tried to look unaware, but I probably merely looked ashamed, and sorry I had exposed my self-complacency so brashly. He began to read the head-lines; not with energy and emphasis, but with a studied seeming of indifference and lack of interest which I took for a hint that perhaps that was my way of reading and feeling such things:

"Child crushed by mobile before its mother's eyes."

"Factory burned, 14 young work-girls roasted alive; thousands looking on, powerless to help."

"Little Mary Walker not found yet; search relaxing; no hope left; father prostrate, mother demented."

"Aged couple turned out in the snow with their small effects by landlord for lack of rent-money; found at midnight by police, unconscious; rent-money due, $1.75."

I recognized all these items; I had already read them, but only with my eyes, my feelings had not been interested, the sufferers being strangers; but the effect was different, now. The words were the same, but each of them left a blister where it struck. I was ashamed, and begged the bos'n to stop, and said I was a dog, and willing and even anxious to confess it. And so he softened, and put away the paper and said—

"Oh, I beg pardon; but as you said you'd already read them, I
thought it wouldn't be any harm to—to—why, Smith was up at day-
light reading them. And b'god he was near to *crying* over them!"

"Hang it, so am I, *now*, but—but—well, I never took the thing *in*,
before."

"Oh, *that's* all right," said the bos'n, soothingly, "you ain't to blame,
you can't help the way you're made. And Smith, he can't help the way
he's made. Land, he takes the whole suffering world into his heart, and
it gives him hell's-bells, I can tell you! Why, Mr. Sterling, that man
takes into his inside enough of the human race's miseries in a day to
last a real manly man thirty years!"

"Oh, rub it in, I'm down, rub it in!"

"No,"—appealingly—"*don't* talk like that, Mr. Sterling, *I'm* not
saying anything, I'm only trying to *show* you that a person ain't to
blame that's made—made—well, that's made the way you be. So's 't
you'll feel good."

"Oh, thanks, it's ever so kind of you! I haven't felt so good in a year."

"Now I'm right down glad of that. Say—Mr. Sterling, Smith ain't
twenty-six, he's sixty."

"Lord, I understand, I understand!"

"Yes, that breed—people that's made that way—people that have to
bear the world's miseries on top of their own—why, it makes them old
long before their time; *they* can't find any bright side of life. Lord, yes,
it makes them old, long, *long* before their time. But it's different with
your make, you know; *you* might live a thou—"

"Oh, let up, and change the subject! Haven't I *said* I'm a dog? Well,
then, have some pity!"

Chapter 6

George's Diary—Continued

THE PAST few days have been like all the days I have spent in this
house—full of satisfactions for me. Every day the feeling of the day before is renewed to me—the feeling of having been in a half-trance all

my life before—numb, sluggish-blooded, sluggish-minded—a feeling
which is followed at once by a brisk sense of being out of that syncope
and awake! awake and alive; alive to my finger-ends. I realize that I am
a veteran trader in shadows who has struck the substance. I have found
the human race. It was all around me before, but vague and spectral; I
have found it now, with the blood in it, and the bones; and am getting
acquainted with it. That is, with the facts of it; I had the theories before. It is pleasant, charming, engrossing. Incidentally, I am also getting acquainted with myself. But it is no matter, it could not well be
helped, the bos'n is around so much. I do not really care.

I have not lost my interest in the monument—that will stay alive,
there is no fear as to that—but the human race has pushed it to second
place.

The Admiral, of his own motion, is allowing me to use what he calls
the ward-room as a studio. It is spacious and airy, and has plenty of
light. The derelicts and the friends of the derelicts have the freedom of
it, night and day. They come when they please, they sit around and
chat, they smoke and read, and the Admiral "pays the freight," as the
slang phrase goes. And they sit to me. They take an interest in each
other's portraits, and are candid with criticisms. They talk to me about
themselves, and about each other. Thus I get the entire man—four-
fifths of him from himself and the other fifth from the others. I find
that no man discloses the completing fifth himself. Sometimes that
fifth is to his credit, sometimes it isn't; but let it be whichever it may,
you will never get it out of the man himself. It is the make of the man
that determines it. The bos'n says there are no exceptions to this law.
He says every man is a moon and has a side which he turns toward nobody: you have to slip around behind if you want to see it.

I began on the Admiral's portrait this morning. Every derelict that
happened in was at once interested. They sat around and kept one eye
on the brush, the other on the sitter, and talked. It was very pleasant.
"Uncle 'Rastus" was one of the group—'Rastus Timson. He is a colored man; 70 years old; large, compact, all big bone and muscle, *very*
broad-shouldered, prodigiously strong—can take up a barrel of beer
and drink from the bung; shrewd, good-natured, has a sense of humor;
gets up his opinions for himself, and is courageous enough to change

them when he thinks he has found something better; is plain, sincere, and honest; is ready and willing to debate deep questions, and gets along pretty well at it; has a pronounced Atlas-stoop, from carrying mighty burdens upon his shoulders; wears what is left of a once hat—a soft ruin which slumps to a shapeless rumple like a collapsed toy balloon when he drops it on the floor; the remains of his once clothes hang in fringed rags and rotting shreds from his booms and yard-arms, and give him the sorrowfully picturesque look of a ship that has been through a Cape Horn hurricane—not recently, but in Columbus's time. He lives by such now-and-then whitewashing jobs as he can pick up; was a Maryland slave before the War. In those distant times he was a Dunker Baptist; later, a modified Methodist; later still, a Unitarian, with reservations; he is a freethinker now, and unattached—"goes in a procession by himself, like Jackson's hog," as the bos'n phrases it. A good man and a cheerful spirit; the other derelicts like him; his is a welcome face here.

He lives at "Aunty Phyllis's" humble boarding house, where the derelicts Jacobs and Cully put up—"the Twins," as the bos'n calls them. Aunty Phyllis was born and brought up in Maryland—Eastern Shore. She was a slave, before the War. She is toward seventy, stands six feet one in her stockings, is as straight as a grenadier, and has the grit and the stride and the warlike bearing of one. But, being black, she is good-natured, to the bone. It is the born privilege and prerogative of her adorable race. She is cheerful, indestructibly cheerful and lively; and what a refreshment she is! Her laugh—her breezy laugh, her inspiring and uplifting laugh—is always ready, always on tap, and comes pealing out, peal upon peal, right from her heart, let the occasion for it be big or little; and it is so cordial and so catching that derelict after derelict has to forget his troubles and join in—even the ex-postman.

She is a Methodist, and as profoundly and strenuously religious as Uncle 'Rastus isn't. The pair are close friends in other things, but in the greater matter of religion—well, they debate that. Pretty much all the time; at least Aunty Phyllis debates it and 'Rastus listens; he does not get much chance to air his side. There is apparently but one text: are there such things as special providences, or aren't there? Aunty Phyllis "knows" there are, 'Rastus denies it. It is going to take time to

settle this. Both belligerents were on hand to-day, and of course there
was a debate; but when I began on the Admiral's portrait the new interest suspended it.

After some general chat the Admiral drifted into the matter of the
monument, and I was glad of that, for his views regarding Adam had
only been hinted, as yet, not developed.

"As concerns Adam in general," said the Admiral, "I have been
thinking him over, several days, and I have to stand where I stood before; I have to rank him with the minor sacred characters, like Satan.
But I want to be fair to Adam, and I make allowances; he hadn't had
Satan's experiences, he hadn't Satan's age; if he *had* have had, I don't
say but what it might have been different. But we have to judge by the
facts we have, we can't go behind the record; we have to look at what
he did, not at his might-have-dones. Adam was only a child, when you
do him square justice, and so I don't hold him down to the mark the
way I do Satan—I make allowances. Now then, you want to put Adam
out of your minds, and take *another* child—it's the only way to get a
right focus on the situation and understand it, because you've always
been bred up to the fact that Adam was a full grown *man*, and so you
forget to remember that he could be a man and a child both at the
same time, and *was*. Well, put another child in his place. You say to
that child, 'let this orange alone.' The child understands that—ain't it
so? Ain't it so, Aunty Phyllis?"

"Yes, marse Stormfield, de child un'stan'."

"Next, you say to the child, 'if you disobey, arrested development
and ultimate extinction shall be your portion.' What does that mean,
Aunty Phyllis?"

"Umhh! Bless yo' soul, honey, if I was to die for it I couldn't tell
you!"

Of course those long words compelled her wonder and admiration
and brought out of her a powerful laugh—it was her way of expressing
applause.

"What does it mean, 'Rastus?"

"Deed'n'deed, I don't know, marse Stormfield."

"*Why* don't you know?"

"Becaze I hain't ever struck dem words befo'."

"Very well, that was the case with Adam. How was he going to know what 'surely die' meant? *Die!* He hadn't ever struck that word before; he hadn't ever seen a dead creature, there hadn't ever been a dead creature for him to see; there hadn't ever been any talk about dead things, because there hadn't ever *been* any dead things to talk about."

He paused, and waited for the new idea to take hold. Presently Aunty Phyllis said—

"Well, dat do beat me! But it's so—I never see it befo'. It's so, sure as you bawn. Po' thing, it didn't mean nothin' to him, no mo'n de 'rested distinction mean to me when I hain't ever hearn 'bout it befo'."

The other derelicts granted that this was a new view, and sound. Sound and surprising. The Admiral was charmed. He resumed.

"Now then, Adam didn't understand. Why didn't he come out and *say* so? Why didn't he ask what 'surely die' meant? Wouldn't he, if he had felt scared? If he had understood those awful words he would have been scared deaf and dumb and paralysed, wouldn't he? Aunty Phyllis, if they had been said to you, you would have left the apple alone, wouldn't you?"

"Yes, marse Stormfield, I mos' sholy would."

"*I* wouldn't tetched it if it was de las' act," said Uncle 'Rastus, fervently.

"Very well, it shows that he didn't suppose it was anything serious. The same with Eve. Just two heedless children, you see. They supposed it was some little ordinary punishment—they hadn't ever had any other kind; they didn't know there was any other kind. And so it was easy for Satan to get around them and persuade them to disobey."

The mother-heart of Aunt Phyllis was touched, and she said—

"Po' little Adam—po' little Eve! It was de same like my little Henry: if I say, 'dah you is, a-snoopin' 'roun' dat sugar agin; you dast to tetch it once, I lay I'll skin you!' 'Cose de minute my back's turned he's got de sugar; 'caze *he* don't k'yer nothin' for de skinnin', de way *I* skun him. Yes-suh, I kin see it all, now—*dey* didn't k'yer nothin' for de skinnin', de way de good Lord allays skun 'em befo'."

Uncle 'Rastus highly admired this speech, and admitted it, which greatly pleased Aunt Phyllis. 'Rastus added—

"It's plain to me, dey warn't fa'rly treated. If de' *was* a Adam—which people says nowadays de' wasn't. But dat ain't nothin', justice is justice, en I want him to have de monument."

"Me too!" from Aunt Phyllis.

Two new converts. I was prospering. The Admiral proceeded with his examination of Adam.

"As far as I can see, he showed up best in naming animals. Considering that he hadn't ever seen any animals before, I am of the opinion that he did it very well indeed, as far as he got. He had a sure touch, on the common ones—named them with insight and judacity, and the names stick, to this day, after all the wear and tear they've been through; it was when he struck the big ones and the long ones that he couldn't cash-in. Take the ornithorhyncus, for instance."

The music of it and the majestic outlandishness of it broke Aunty Phyllis up again, and it took her a while to laugh out her admiring astonishment.

"Ornithorhyncus." The Admiral paid out the great word lingeringly; it tasted good to him. "As we know, he skipped the ornithorhyncus. Left him out of the invoice. Why?"

He looked blandly around for answers. The others showed diffidence about entering the field, but Aunty Phyllis ventured—

" 'Fraid of him, *I* bet you! I wouldn't gone anear him, not for pie!"

'Rastus turned upon her and said argumentatively—

"You old fool, what does *you* know about him?"

"You mine yo' manners, 'Rastus Timson, er I lay I'll take 'n wipe de flo' wid you! What does *I* know 'bout him! I reckon I knows dis much: dey never gin him no name like dat less'n he *deserve* it. So dah, now!"

'Rastus—with the grateful air of one who has received new light—

"Well, it—yas, it sutt'nly do look reasonable. When a body git a name like dat, a body deserve it." (Thoughtful pause.) "Same like *Phyllis*."

The Admiral lifted his hand, and Phyllis quenched the battle-light in her eye, and reserved her retort. The dipsomaniac Strother, a dreamy and melancholy wreck, muttered absently, with a sigh—

"Ornitho . . . tho . . . rhyncus. Sounds like . . . like . . . well, I know I've *had* it."

The Admiral resumed—

"In my judgment the alphabet was just beginning to accumulate, in that early day, and there wasn't much of it yet, and so it seems reasonable that he had to skip it because he couldn't spell it." The company did not need to speak out their praise of this striking and happy solution, their faces did the office of their tongues, and did it with an eloquence beyond the arts of speech. After a little, Jimson Flinders—young colored gentleman—stenographer, sub-editor of his race's paper—visitor—dressy—thinker, in a way—somewhat educated —said, with honest admiration—

"Why, it's so simple and plain and dead-sure, that what makes me wonder, is, that there didn't somebody hit on it long and long ago."

This brought emphatic nods of agreement and approval, and the Admiral could not entirely conceal his pleasure. He took up his theme again.

"Adam skipped a lot of the creatures. This has been the astonishment of the world for—well, from away back. Ages, as you may say. But you can see, now, how it was. He didn't want to skip, he wanted to do his honest duty, but there he *was*—he hadn't the ammunition. He was equipped for short names, but not the others. If a bear came along —all right, he was loaded for bear. There was no embarrassment. The same if a cow came along; or a cat, or a horse, or a lion, or a tiger, or a hog, or a frog, or a worm, or a bat, or a snipe, or an ant, or a bee, or a trout, or a shark, or a whale, or a tadpole—anything that didn't strain his alphabet, you know: they would find him on post and tranquil; he would register them and they would pass on, discussing their names, most of them pleased—such as leopards and scarlet tanagers and such, some of them pained—such as buzzards, and alligators, and so on, the others ashamed—such as squids, and polecats, and that kind; but all resigned, in a way, and reconciled, reconnizing that he was new to the business and doing the best he could. Plain sailing, and satisfactory, you see. But in the course of trade, along comes the pterodactyl—"

There was a general gasp.

"Could he spell that? *No*, sir. Solomon couldn't. Nor no other early Christian—not in *that* early time. It was very different from now, in those days. Anybody can spell pterodactyl *now*, but—"

The eager and the ignorant interrupted the Admiral and asked him to instruct them in that formidable orthography, but he shivered slightly and hastened on, without seeming to hear—

—"but in those old early geological times the alphabet hadn't even got up to the Old Red Sandstone period yet, and it was worse in Adam's time, of course; so, as he didn't want to let on that he couldn't spell it, he just said, 'Call again, office hours over for to-day,' and pulled down the shades and locked up and went home, the same as if nothing had happened.

"It was natural, I think, and right enough, too. I would have done it; most people would. Well, he had a difficult time, limited the way he was, and it is only fair for us to take that into account. Every few days along would come an animal as big as a house—grazing along, eating elephants and pulling down the synagogues and things: 'Dinosaurium-iguanodon,' says Adam; 'tell him to come Sunday;' and would close up and take a walk. And the very next day, like enough, along comes a creation a mile long, chewing rocks and scraping the hills away with its tail, and lightening and thundering with its eyes and its lungs, and Eve scoops up her hair over her arm and takes to the woods, and Adam says 'Megatheriomylodonticoplesiosauriasticum—give him his first syllable and get him to take the rest on the instalment plan,' which it seems to me was one of the best ideas Adam ever had, and in every way creditable to him. He had to save *some* of the alphabet, he couldn't let one animal have it all, it would not have been fair, anyway.

"I will say it again, I think Adam was at his level best when he was naming the creatures, and most to be praised. If you look up your fossiliferous paleontology, I acknowledge you will have to admit that where he registered one creature he skipped three hundred and fifty, but that is not his fault, it was the fault of his alphabet-plant. You can't build a battleship out of a scrap-heap. Necessarily he couldn't take the whole of one of those thirteen-syllabers and pay spot cash; the most he could do was to put up a margin. Well, you know what happens to that kind of financing."

Chapter 7

George's Diary—Continued

AT THIS point the marchesa came tripping girlishly forward from the other end of the ward-room, the bos'n half-spiraling along after her, pivoting on his game leg—with a corky squeak—and fetching a curve with his good one, in accordance with the requirements of his loco-motion-plant. The poor old girl was girlishly indignant about some-thing—one could see it in her eyes and in her manner. She came straight to the Admiral and broke into his discourse with a complaint against the bos'n. Another man would have been annoyed; the Admiral was not. He is frequently a little sharp with the marchesa, but as a rule he soon softens and looks remorseful and begins to betray his discomfort and repentance in ways which beg forgiveness without humbling him to the spoken prayer. It is a mystery; I don't understand it. She is fretful, offensive, ungracious, disagreeable, ungrateful, impossible to please, and I can't see why these people don't fly out at her every day and give her what she deserves. But they don't. They put up with it, they are mistakenly gentle with her, and of course she goes right on. Every time I think the bos'n is going to let her have it, he most strangely doesn't. He says irritating things to her whenever he can think of any to say, but there is no viciousness in them, no temper; often they are merely idiotic, yet *he* is not idiotic. He doesn't seem to know they are idiotic; they seem to drop out of him without inten-tion and without consciousness. But they irritate the marchesa, and then he doesn't seem to understand why they should. If he would give her a dressing-down once, it would do her good. And he is quite competent. But no, she can't seem to exasperate him into a harshness. The same with Jimmy and Aunt Martha: they are persistently and devilishly kind to her, in spite of all she can do. They even strain the human possibilities to be benevolent to her: for they go with her daily on her long and objectless tramps about the streets, and she in that outrage that she wears—tricked out in a gay and girly costume which is all of twenty years too young for her; and stared at, and she and her escort laughed at, by everybody that comes along, of course. What can the mystery be? Every time I think the bos'n is going to explain it, he doesn't. The same with Jimmy and Aunt Martha. And they are all like what the bos'n said about the Admiral: if you want to get at his privacies, wait till it suits him to start the subject himself—you will get nothing by trying to start it. Every night the Admiral prays for the salvation of that unnamed person again, and I would like to know if it is himself, but I suppose I must wait until some member of the family starts the subject. This only keeps my curiosity fretting, and does no good. I have to assume that it is the Admiral, and it is not pleasant—a bluff and open self-appreciation is more in his line.

The marchesa's temper was pretty well up; she was flushed, and her lips quivered nervously. The Admiral listened patiently to her charges; respectfully, too, though there was nothing in them. It turned out that she and the bos'n had been having a scrap over the Rev. Caleb Parsons—again. This was a visitor—not a derelict. He is what we call a "regular," as distinguished from casual visitors to the Anchor Watch. He is disliked. That is enough for the marchesa: she always manages to like—or think she likes—whoever or whatever is disliked by the rest of us. So she is championing Mr. Parsons in these days—just as she had championed Satan until the Admiral took him under his wing that night, then she turned against him, horns, hoofs and all, and was so bitter that she said she wouldn't lend him a shovel of coal if he was freezing to death. That is what the bos'n said she said, but she denied it and was in a great fury about it, and said she never said coal at all, she said brimstone. As if that made any great difference! And she complained to the Admiral and said the bos'n was always distorting her words and making them seem worse than they were, and she wanted him punished; whereas the bos'n complained that she was always distorting *his* words. And he was right. So was she. Both of them were persistently guilty of that same offence.

As I have said, the Watch did not like Rev. Mr. Parsons; it was not because he wasn't a good enough man, and well-meaning, but because he hadn't any talent and was over-sentimental. He was always getting thunderstruck over the commonest every-day things the Creator did, and saying "Lo, what God hath wrought!" The bos'n called him Lo, for short, the Anchor Watch adopted it, and this aggravated the marchesa, and she added it to her list of grudges against the bos'n, and between them they made it do good service in their debates. It was upon trifles like this that the marchesa lived and throve.

As usual, the present charges were of no consequence, and not worth coming to the Admiral about, but he listened, good man, without fret. She wanted the bos'n put in irons—a thing she was always longing to accomplish, but she never could. She had two or three of these little charges this time. To begin with, she said she was remarking upon Mr. Parsons's early history and how good he was, and at last had his reward and heard God call him to His ministry; and she said the bos'n interrupted her and said it was probably an *echo*, the call was from the other direction—

And she was going on to give the bos'n down the banks, when the Admiral put up his hand for silence. Then he sat there and thought it out. Thought it out, and gave his verdict. To this effect: that the *sky* can't produce an echo, for the sky is made of air and emptiness; a call coming from below would have to have something hard and solid to hit against and rebound from, otherwise it would keep on going and never be heard of again: so, as this call *was* heard, it is proof that it did not come from below; not coming from below, it could not be an echo, and wasn't; not being an echo, it *had* to come down from above, and did; therefore, the bos'n was "in the wrong, and is decided against. But there is no punishment, no harm being intended. We will pass to the next charge if you please, madam."

The marchesa blazed out and denounced the verdict as being "rotten with nepotism;" and on top of that she shook her little nubbin of a fist in the Admiral's face and called him plainly and squarely a "hardened and shameless old nepot."

The Admiral winced, but made no retort. Everybody was shocked and offended, and Aunty Phyllis spoke out without reserve and said it warn't to nobody's credit to live on the Admiral's goodness and hostility and then call him a teapot. The marchesa would have resented this, and Aunty Phyllis cleared for action and invited her to come on, but the Admiral interfered. Then once more he asked for the next charge, and the marchesa furnished it:

"He said I was so deaf I couldn't read fine print."

The Admiral's face clouded up and he gave the bos'n a severe look and said—

"Tom Larkin, what do you say to this charge?"

The bos'n answered, without bitterness, but in a wounded tone—

"I give you the honest truth, sir, I never said it. She is always distorting my words. All I said was, that she was so near-sighted she couldn't hear it thunder."

The Admiral went away down down into this difficult thing with a patience and a judicial calm that were beyond belief. He reasoned it out, detail by detail, and decided that both parties were in the wrong—because:

"Deafness has nothing to do with reading fine print—it is a matter of vision, not auricularity. Therefore the charge has no legal standing, no basis; it falls to the ground of its own weight. The defendant was in the wrong to make it, it not being true; but the plaintiff cannot claim that it is a slander, because, true or untrue, it is merely an infirmity, and innocent of criminality, all infirmities being visitations of God and visitations of God being not actionable, by reason of lack of jurisdiction. The other charge is of the same nature, substantially. Whether true or false, the act of not being able to hear it thunder on the part of a near-sighted person is not reprehensible, because not intentional, not dependent the one upon the other, and both coming under the head of infirmities—hence properly recognizable as visitations of God and not actionable, therefore not slanderous, by reason of lack of jurisdiction. And so it is manifest that both parties to these charges are guilty: the defendant for making them with probable intent to slander, and the plaintiff for claiming them as slanders when they are not slanders because based upon infirmities and not avoidable. And both parties are innocent, of a necessity, considering the circumstances; the defendant being innocent of accomplishing his probable design, and the plaintiff through not being able to convict him of it, although such was her intention. The cases are dismissed."

Sometimes he makes my head ache, it is so difficult to understand him. And I can't see how he understands himself, when he strips and goes floundering out into these tumbling seas of complexities, but he probably does; thinks he does, I know; and certainly he always gets through, and wades ashore looking refreshed and all right.

Chapter 8

George's Diary—Continued

I HAD the hope that we were going to get back to Adam, now, but it failed. The marchesa was not in any degree satisfied with the way things had gone with her, and she could not reconcile herself to the idea of leaving them so; and so she begged for one more chance. The Admiral sighed, and told her to go ahead; go ahead, and try to let this be the last, for the present. Whereupon she accused the bos'n to this effect:

"He said I said the lack of money is the root of all evil. I never said it. I was quoting, and said the *love* of money is the root of all evil."

The Admiral's eyes flashed angrily and he burst out with—

"*Another* of your damned trivialities! Now look here, marcheesa—"

He stopped there. His lips remained parted, the fire in his eyes sank down to a smoulder. He sat like that—thinking—and he had that faraway look which comes upon him when something has hit his thought a blow and stunned it, or sent it wandering in other fields. In the stillness he loomed there on his raised platform like that, looking like a bronze image, he was so motionless. We sat looking at him, and waiting. You could hear the faint wailing of the winds outside, rising and falling, rising and falling, you could catch the rumble and murmur of the distant traffic. Presently he muttered, as to himself—

"The lack of money . . . . the *lack* . . . . is the root of all evil. The . . . ."

He fell silent again. There was no passion in his face, now; the harshness had passed out of it and left only gentleness. As one in a reverie, his eyes began to drift to this figure and that and the other, and dwell a little space upon each—dreamily, and no words uttered. Naturally my gaze journeyed with his.

Lord, those pathetic figures! Here, and there and yonder they hung

limp upon their chairs, lost to the present, busy with the past, the unreturning past—there, brooding, they hung, the defeated, the derelicts!
They all had a droop; each a droop of his own, and each telling its
own story, without need of speech. How eloquent is an attitude—how
much it can say! When a silence falls, we who are alive start out of
our thoughts and look about us, but it descends upon these dead-in-
hope like the benediction of night, and conveys them gently out of this
workaday world and the consciousness of it.

There sat Strother the dipsomaniac, his graying head drooped, gazing at the floor—and not seeing it. He was awake only a moment ago,
he is dreaming now, already. A flabby ruin, his flesh colorless and puffy
with drink, his nerves lax, his hands uncertain and quivery. You would
not think it, but he was a man, once; and held up his head with the
best; and had money to waste—and wasted it; and had a wife who lived
in the light of his eyes; and four children who loved him with a love
that made him proud, and paid him a homage that made him humble,
so innocent and honest and exaggerated it was. Well, his money is
gone, the respect of men is gone, his self-respect is gone, his life is
bankrupt; of all his possessions nothing is left but five accusing graves,
and memories that tear his heart!

Near by, droop "the Twins." They are always together. In a bygone
time Jacobs was rich, and his money made him happy—happier than
anything else could have made him. Cully was his coachman. Speculation impoverished Jacobs; sudden and great wealth came to Cully
from a departed Australian uncle, and Jacobs became Cully's coachman. By and by, speculation made a pauper of Cully. Now in their
gray age they are derelicts. The Admiral finds odd jobs for them when
he can, their brother derelicts helping in this when opportunity offers.
They board cheaply with Aunty Phyllis's humble colored waifs and
hand-to-mouths, and come here to dream their great days over again,
and count up the money they used to have, and mourn over this and
that and the other disastrous investment, and reason out, for the thou-
sandth time, just how each mistake came to be made, and how each
and all of them could have been so easily avoided if they had *only* done
so and so. Then they sigh and sorrow over those dreary "onlies" . . . .
and take up the tale again, and go wearying over it, and over it, and

over it, in the same old weather-worn and goalless track, poor old fellows!

Other derelicts sit drooping, here and there—the forgotten ex-Senator, once so illustrious and so powerful; the ragged General, once so great, once so honored—long ago; the Poet, once so popular and so prosperous, until he took a stand for straight talk and principle, and lost his place on the magazine and never could get another start. And so on and so on, derelict after derelict—a melancholy landscape to cast your eye over. And beyond them, walking wearily to and fro, to and fro, to and fro, like a tired animal in a cage, is Peters the inventor. He is always doing that. I wonder when he rests? If you speak to him he gives you a dazed look and a wan smile, and takes up his dreary tramp again. He scraped and scraped, spent and spent, and was always going to get his great invention launched—next month—the month after, sure—*then*, oh, then the roses would come back to his young wife's cheeks, and she would have silks to her back, only just wait a little while! And he saw her youth pass, and age come, and the patient face fade toward the inevitable—and *that* came, and left him forlorn, to fight his fight alone. Always the vision was rising before him of a capitalist—a capitalist who would give his great invention to the world and add another splendid factor to its advancing civilization and its fabulous forces. There was nothing needed but that capitalist—who never came. In his desperation, Peters committed a forgery, and sat in a prison five years, eating his heart out. Now he walks the floor, and dreams of what might have been—what might have been—what might have been! if only the capitalist had come!

The ex-postman haunts his neighborhood—out of a natural fellow-feeling for him, perhaps; and droops his head and dreams of his ruined life, and of how it came about.

The Admiral was still gazing, lost in thought. He came to himself, now, and said, very quietly—

"The lack of . . . . *both* are true! The case is dismissed."

I thought it a good verdict, but the marchesa was of another opinion —mainly because she was disappointed again, most likely—and she began to rail against it fiercely. Nobody interrupted her, and she kept it up until she ran out of vitriol. But it did good service. Its electricity cleared the air; drove away the gloom, and let in some cheerfulness. We all felt better, the Admiral chirked up and was himself again. I think he was grateful to the marchesa; he looked so, and he said to her, in almost a petting way, as it seemed to me—

"Let it go, marcheesa, put it behind you and let's go about and try a slant up to wind'ard, so to speak, and forget about it—change the subject, you understand, if we can find one. It's wholesome—a change is —if a person hits it right."

Two or three suggested a return to Adam, and wanted to hear the rest about him, in case there was anything lacking to make his rehabilitation complete. It flattered the Admiral, and he looked nearly as gratified as he was.

"Well," he said, reflectively, "let me see. Since you want it, I think there's a word more that I would like to say. Only just a word, in palliation of his simpleness and unworldliness, as you may say. Eve's, too. I think it was beautiful, the amount they didn't know about common ordinary things. Take the matter of clothes, for instance. It is perfectly astonishing, the way they would go about like—like that. And perfectly unconcerned, too. But I am not reproaching them for it—no, just the contrary. They are to be praised. They had the right kind of modesty, to my mind—the kind that ain't aware of itself. I think it's a much better sort than these statutes that stand around in parks with a fig-leaf on to set a good example. I believe it's a mistake. Who ever follows it? Nobody. Adam and Eve didn't think about their modesty, didn't fuss about it, didn't even know they had it; and so it was sound modesty, real modesty; whereas some people would have gone blustering around. The more I think of those beautiful lives of theirs, the more I lean to the idea of the monument.

"And there's other reasons. Adam is fading out. It is on account of Darwin and that crowd. I can see that he is not going to last much longer. There's a plenty of signs. He is getting belittled to a germ— a little bit of a speck that you can't see without a microscope powerful enough to raise a gnat to the size of a church. They take that speck and breed from it: first a flea, then a fly, then a bug, then cross these and get a fish, then a raft of fishes, all kinds, then cross the whole lot and get a reptile, then work up the reptiles till you've got a supply of lizards and spiders and toads and alligators and Congressmen and so on, then cross the entire lot again and get a plant of amphibiums, which are half-breeds and do business both wet and dry, such as turtles and frogs and ornithorhyncuses and so on, and cross-up again and get a mongrel bird, sired by a snake and dam'd by a bat, resulting in a pterodactyl, then they develop *him,* and water his stock till they've got the air filled with a million things that wear feathers, then they cross-up all the accumulated animal life to date and fetch out a mammal, and start-in diluting again till there's cows and tigers and rats and elephants and monkeys and everything you want down to the Missing Link, and out of him and a mermaid they propagate Man, and there you are! Everything ship-shape and finished-up, and nothing to do but lay low and wait and see if it was worth the time and expense.

"Well, then, was it? To my mind, it don't stand to reason. They say it took a hundred million years. Suppose you ordered a Man at the start, and had a chance to look over the plans and specifications—which would you take, Adam or the germ? Naturally you would say Adam is business, the germ ain't; one is immediate and sure, the other is speculative and uncertain. Well, I have thought these things all over, and my sympathies are with Adam. Adam was like *us,* and so he seems near to us, and dear. He is kin, blood kin, and my heart goes out to him in affection. But I don't feel that way about that germ. The germ is too far away—and not only that, but such a wilderness of reptiles between. You can't skip the reptiles and set your love on the germ; no, if they are ancestors, it is your duty to include them and love them. Well, you can't do that. You would come up against the dinosaur and your affections would cool off. You couldn't love a dinosaur the way you would another relative. There would always be a gap. Nothing could ever bridge it. Why, it gives a person the dry gripes just to look at him!

"Very well, then, where do we arrive? Where do we arrive with our respect, our homage, our filial affection? At Adam! At Adam, every time. We can't build a monument to a germ, but we can build one to Adam, who is in the way to turn myth in fifty years and be entirely forgotten in two hundred. We can build a monument and save his name to the world forever, and we'll do it! What do you say?"

It was carried, with a fine enthusiasm; and it was beautiful to see the pleasure beam out all over the Admiral when that tribute burst forth. My own pleasure was no less than his; for with his favor enlisted in my enterprise, it was recognizable that a great step had been made toward the accomplishment of the grandest dream of my life.

Chapter 9

The Diary Continued

TEN DAYS LATER. The derelicts get a certain easment by talking to me about their sorrows. I can see it. I thought it was because my sympathy was honest and prompt. That is true, it is a part of it, the bos'n says, but not all of it. The rest of it, he says, is, that I am new. They have told their stories to each other many times, for grief is repetitious; and this kind of wear eventually blunts a listener's interest and discourages the teller, then both parties retire within their shells and feed upon that slow-starving diet, Introspection. But a new ear, an untired ear, a fresh and willing and sympathetic ear—they like that!

About a week ago the bos'n said another thing:

"They've all one burden to their song, haven't they?"

"Yes. Sorrow."

"Right enough, but there's more than one kind of sorrow. There's the kind that you haven't helped to bring about—family bereavements, and such; and then there's the kind that comes of things you did, your own self, and would do so different if it was to do over again."

"Yes, I get the idea. That kind is repentance. It's when you have done a wrong thing."

"You've got the name right—repentance. But you don't cover enough ground with it. Repentance ain't confined to doing wrong, sometimes you catch it just as sharp for doing right."

I doubted that, and said it was against experience.

"No—against teaching," the bos'n retorted. "You get taught, right along up, that if you always do the rightest you can, your conscience will pat you on the back and be satisfied; but experience learns a person that there's exceptions to the rule. We've got both kinds here."

We couldn't argue it any further, because there was an interruption. Aunt Martha of the welcome face and the lovely spirit shone in upon us like another sunbeam, for a moment, to say the Admiral wanted the large Atlas and couldn't find it, and did the bos'n know where it was? Yes, and said he would go and send for it right away, adding, "it got left behind at Hell's Delight when we broke camp there—I forgot it."

That was a private summer resort, instituted by the Admiral for the derelicts. Hell's Delight was not its official name; in fact it never had one. In the beginning the Rev. Lo-what-God-hath-Wrought had called it "The Isles of the Blest," and every one liked it, but when the bos'n got to referring to it by that other name it was soon adopted because it was short and unpretentious, and the pretty one fell into disuse and was forgotten.

I began to take note, and presently found that the bos'n was right about the conflicting sources of repentance. The revealments of my sitters showed that several of them were penitents of the class that regret and grieve over righteous things done. It cost me a pang to have to register these exceptions to the fairer and pleasanter law of my teaching and training, but it had to be done, the hard facts of experience put in their claim and stood by it and made it good.

For instance, there was the case of Henry Clarkson, Poet: the derelict with the deep eyes, the melancholy eyes, the haunting eyes, the hollow face, the thin hands, the frail figure—draped in that kind of clothes that hang, droop, shift about the person in unstable folds and wrinkles with every movement, take a grip nowhere, and seem to have nothing in them. He is old, yet is not gray, and that unpleasant incongruity makes him seem older than he really is; his hair is long and black, and hangs lank and straight down beside his face and reminds one of Louis Stevenson.

The first stage of his life went well enough. He struggled up, poor and unaware of it, his heart full of the joy of life and the dance-music of hope, his head full of dreams. He climbed and climbed, diligently, laboriously, up through mean employments, toward a high and distant goal, and there was pleasure in it. He kept his eye fixed steadily on that goal, expecting to make it, determined to make it, and he did make it; and stood on that high place exultant, and looked out over the world he had conquered with his two hands. Far down on the earth stood the memory of him, the vision of him—shop-boy, errand-boy, anything you please; and here he stood, now, on this dizzy alp, at twenty-eight, his utmost ambition attained: literary person, rising poet, first assistant editor of a magazine!

It was a wonderful thing to see, how the old dead fires flamed up in his eyes when he got to that proud climax and stood again in fancy upon that great summit and surveyed his vanquished world! And he lingered there lovingly, and told me all about the sublimities of the position, and the honors and attentions it brought him; told me how the greatest in the region round about fellowed him with themselves, and familiarly chatted and laughed with him, and consulted him on large affairs; and how there was a seat for him at the dais-table of every banquet, and his name on the program for a stirring poem; and how satisfied with him the aging editor-in-chief was, and how it was well understood and accepted that he was to be that great functionary's successor, all in good time . . . .

He was so eager, so earnest, so inspired, so happy, so proud, in the pouring forth of these moving memories, that he made me lose myself! I was no longer I, he was no longer the mouldering derelict: he lived his sumptuous and coruscating romance over again under my eyes, and it was all as if I was in it and living it with him! How real it was!

Then all of a sudden we crumbled to ashes, as it were! For his tale turned down-hill on the sunset side; his voice and his face lost their animation; the pet of fortune, the courted of men, was gone, the faded derelict was back again—all in a moment. It seemed to make a chill in the air.

He told me how his ruin came about, and how little he was expecting it, how poorly prepared for it. Everything was going well with him. He had recently seen one of his grandest dreams come to fruit: he had issued his poems in a volume; a fine large step for a person who had been of the ephemerals before; he felt that permanent fame, real fame, even national fame, was close ahead of him, now. The poems wouldn't bring money, but that was nothing, poems are not written for that. And he had made still another large step—his idol had appointed the wedding day. The pair had been waiting until the editorial salary should reach a figure that would support two in a fairly adequate way. It had reached it, now, and would by and by double with the impending chief-editorship. Well, it was at this time of all times, when the poet's sun was blazing at high noon, that the disaster fell.

He made a discovery one morning, while reading proof. It was an article in praise of an enterprise which some unusually good people were getting up for the profit of the working girl, the mechanic, the day laborer, the widow, the orphan—for all, indeed, who might have poor little hoards earning mere pennies in savings banks. These could get into the enterprise on the instalment plan, and on terms so easy that the poorest could not feel the burden. For the first year the dividend would be ten per cent—not a mere possible or probable ten per cent, but "guaranteed." In the second year this would certainly be increased by fifty per cent, and in all probability doubled. Parties proposing to subscribe for the stock must lose no time. It could be had at par during thirty days; after that, for thirty days, the price would be 1.25; after which the price would be augmented by another 25.

The discoverer was as happy as Columbus. He had saved the magazine! But for the accident that he had happened to be reading proof that morning, to relieve the proof-reader of a part of his burden and hasten the "make-up," this vile masked advertisement would almost certainly have gone into the forms, escaping detection until too late. He carried the poisonous thing to the sanctum, and laid it before the chief editor. Without a word; for he did not want to betray his joy and pride in his lucky achievement. The chief ran his eye over the opening paragraph, then looked blandly up and said—

"Well?"

That was all. No astonishment, no outraged feelings, no—well, no nothing. Just tranquillity. Not even a compliment to the discoverer. Young Clarkson was very much surprised—not to say stunned. It took him a little while to find some words to say. Then, said he—

"Please read a little more of it, and you will see that it is really a masked advertisement—smuggled past the staff by the advertising agent, without doubt."

"Umm. You think so, do you?"

"I feel sure of it, sir. It came near getting into the forms; I stopped it just in time."

"You did, did you?"

"Yes, sir."

The chief's manner was very calm, very placid, almost uncomfortably so.

"Mr. Clarkson, have you been officially authorized to stop articles?" A faint red tinge appeared in the chief's cheek and a just perceptible glimmer as of summer lightnings in his eye when he said this.

"Oh, no, sir, certainly not! I only thought—"

"Then will you be kind enough to tell me why you took it upon yourself to stop this one?"

"I—I—why, I hardly know what to say, I am so—so unpre—I thought I was doing the magazine a great service to stop it—and time was precious."

"Umm. What was your objection to the article?"

"If you would only read it, Mr. Haskell! then you would see what it is, and you would approve what I did. I meant no harm, I was only— If you will read it, you will see that it is just the old wrecked "Prize-Guess" swindle hidden under a new name. It robbed hundreds of thousands of poor people of their savings before, and is starting out now to do the like again. The magazine's moral character and reputation are without spot, and this article could heavily damage these great assets; and so I at once—"

"Yes, you did. . . . . Well, well, let it go, I think you meant well. Sit down; I will throw some light."

Henry took a seat, wondering what kind of light he was going to get. The chief said—

"I do not wish to mince matters, and I will be perfectly frank. This is a great and prosperous periodical; to continue so, it must sail with the times. The times are changing—we must change with them, or drop behind in the race. Very well, this *is* immoral advertising and iniquitous, but the others are engaging in it, and we've got to fall into line. Our board of directors have so decided. It pays quintuple rates, you see; that hits them where they live. It is odious, it is infamous, it kept me awake several nights, thinking of the shame of it—that this should come upon my gray head after an honorable life! . . . . But it is bread and butter; I have a family; I am old, I could not get another place at my time of life if I should lose this one; I must stick to it while my strength lasts. I have had principles, and have never dishonored them— you will grant me that?"

"Indeed I do—oh, out of my heart!"

"Well, they are gone, I have turned them out of doors—I could not afford them. Ah, you *stung* me so, when you brought this accusing thing here! I was getting wonted to my chains, my slavery, by keeping them out of sight. I wanted to strike you for reminding me."

"Forgive me! I did not know what I was doing."

"Oh, it wasn't you—it was myself, slapping my own face over your shoulder, so to speak. I have succumbed, Benson has succumbed. He wrote that article—by command of the directors. Henry, you have a good place here. In time you will step into my shoes, Benson into yours. I will not advise you—that is, urge you—I cannot venture such a re- sponsibility as that—but if you are willing to stay with us under the new conditions, I shall be glad—more glad than I can say. Will you stay?"

"It is hard to part with you, sir, for you have been a good friend to me, but I feel I must not stay. Indeed I could not. I could not bear it."

"How right you are, my boy, how absolutely right! I am grown so uncertain of my species of late that I was afraid—half afraid, at any rate—that you would stay. You are young, you can get another place— this world is for the young, they are its kings."

Henry went to the counting-room, got his money, left his resigna- tion, and went forth into the world a clean man and free.

Then, proud and light of step, he went to his bride-elect, and told her his news. . . .

Those dots are to indicate that a blank in Henry's tale occurred at that point.

I felt that blank. The derelicts are always leaving such. They skip a great episode—maybe the greatest in their lives—and pass, without dropping so much as a crumb of that feast, to their next stage. You get not a trace of that episode except what your imagination can furnish you.

Henry supposed he could get a new berth right away. He was mistaken; it did not happen. He went seeking, from town to town. For a while he was merely surprised at his non-success; but by and by he was dismayed. Terror succeeded dismay. They turned him out of his last boarding house; his money was all gone. He wandered everywhither—further and still further away, subsisting as he could, doing what he could find to do, in whatever corner of the earth he chanced to be—shoveling sand, scouring pavements, sawing wood, selling papers, finally doing clog dances and general utility in a "nigger" show.

After three years of this, he surrendered; from Australia he wrote Mr. Haskell and begged for his place again, saying he was done with virtue and its rewards, and wanted to eat dirt the rest of his days.

After a month or two the answer came—from Benson: Haskell was dead, Benson was chief, now, and sorry there was no vacancy on the staff.

It is thirty-three years since Henry resigned, on that proud day, that unforgettable day; he has never had another literary situation since. He has wandered and wandered, regretting, lamenting, and at last he is here, member of the Anchor Watch, a forlorn and cheerless derelict—with all hope of better things gone out of him long ago.

So ends his tale. Now then, he is one of those people the bos'n classified to me: people who do a thing they know to be clearly right, absolutely right and clean and honorable, and later come to grieve over it and repent it. Henry has been miserably grieving over that good and righteous act of his for thirty years. Benson is well off, influential, important, honored, stands high in his guild from one ocean to the other, is a deacon or a church committee or something, and has children and a grandchild. It makes me wretched to see this poor derelict clasp his head with his hands and impotently cry out in his anguish—

"Oh, to think *I* could be in his place, if only I had not been such a fool—oh, *such* a fool, such a vain, stupid, conceited fool! Oh, why did I ever do that insane thing!"

It seems a tragic tale to me. I think it *is* tragic. When he finished it my mind ran back over it and again I saw him make his eager climb, a hopeful and happy boy; and I climbed with him, and felt for him, hoped for him; when he stood on his great summit a victor, I was there, and seemed to be in the sky, we were so far aloft and the spread of plain and mountain stretched so wide and dwindled to such dreams in the fading distances; and I turned with him when his trouble came; I was with him when he reached the abyss, his life ruined, his hopes all dead —and behind us that stately summit still glittering in the blue!

How could it affect me like that? how could it seem a tragedy to me? Because it contained a disappointed life, and the woe of a human heart—that was all. Apparently that is all that is necessary to make tragedy; apparently conditions and altitudes have nothing to do with the size and the reality of the disaster—they are conventions, their measurements are without a determining standard.

If I had gone into particulars about that "summit," the conventions would have belittled the tragedy and made it seem to you inconsequential. But I will furnish the particulars now. The summit was a summit to the boy who made the fight for it, and to the man who conquered it and lost it; but it would not have been a summit to you who are reading this. The magazine was a religious periodical in an interior city; as important as any other religious magazine, but a place on its staff or at the staff's head would not have been considered a Matterhorn by the average budding hero.

Yet—toward it this poor defeated poet has looked for thirty years, and seen it coldly glinting in the sky, and wished he had thrown away his fatal honor and stayed there—there where would be with him now, in his loveless age, those children and that grandchild, destined for him, lost to him by his own act, whose faces he has never seen and will never see. To him this is tragedy.

Chapter 10

Diary—Continued

THERE IS a new face or two every day—gone the next, perhaps. When they are derelicts, they are usually members of the Watch who have been off wandering in the world for refreshment. Some are gone a week, or a month or two, some are gone half a year. Then they come back eager to see the old stay-at-homes and tell their adventures; they bring fresh new blood, you see, and are very welcome. There are perhaps thirty stay-at-homes. These lodge not far away, and they drift to the house at one time or another every day and every night when the weather will let them. Their desultory occupations are not much of a hindrance. They use the ward-room as a club; they loaf in and out at their pleasure; from breakfast till midnight some of them are always on hand, weather or no weather; on pleasant nights, and at the Admiral's two Sunday services, they gather in force. Members only, and the household, are allowed at those services. A good while ago chance visitors used to come, some out of general curiosity, some to stare at the derelicts, some to hear the Admiral read, and get the thrill of his organ-voice and his expression. He would not have that; so no visitors get in, now, not even the "regulars," with the exception of Lo and two or three other clergymen. Some of the aged derelicts who had a religion once, haven't any now, but they all come. It is their tribute of reverence to the Admiral, and does them credit. Once, in the days when outsiders were admitted, one of the strangers smiled superciliously when the Admiral mispronounced a word; Bates, the infidel, who sat near, leaned over and whispered to him, "Straighten your face—if you want any of it left when you leave this place!" He was obeyed; he was a man-o'-warsman before his derelict days, and can still furnish to an offender the kind of look that carries persuasion with it. The bos'n says all the derelicts are loyal to the Admiral.

The flitters—Members that come and go—are very numerous. They

bring tales and tidings from all over the continent and from all about
the globe. It is astonishing, the miles they cover, and the things they
see and hear and experience. My days here seem rather a brisk dream
than a flesh-and-blood reality. I believe I have not had a dull day yet,
nor one that hadn't part of a romance in it somewhere.

The bos'n claims that there isn't an entirely bad person in the whole
Membership, flitters and all. He says there is a good spot in each one;
that in a lot of cases many people can't find it and don't, but that the
Admiral can and does—every time; and Martha too. He says it isn't
smartness, it's instinct, sympathy, fellow-feeling—which is to say, it is
a gift, and has to be born in a person, can't be manufactured. He says
it can be trained, and developed, away up—but you have to have the
gift to start with, there's no other terms.

I said it would probably puzzle a person to find the good spot in the
marchesa.

"No," he said, "she's got it. She loves children; she'll do anything for
a child—anybody's."

"Give it candy, perhaps. Is that it?"

"More than that—go through fire for it."

"Bos'n, aren't you romancing, now?"

"No—there's those that saw her do it. It was a tenement house. She
went in and helped, just like a fireman—she did indeed. A woman with
a child in her arms slumped down on a hall floor, smothered by the
smoke. A fireman saved her, but the marcheesa saved the child. She
gathered it up and fetched it down three iron fire-escape ladders,
through black smoke that hid her half the time, the crowd cheering;
and that mother was laying for her at the bottom and nearly hugged
the life out of her when she got down, being one of those Irish mothers
with a heart in her the size of a watermelon, and the crowd cheered her
over and over again, and the firemen said she was a brick; and she's
honorary member of No. 29 ever since, and can wear the badge and go
in the procession and ride the engine if she wants to—yes, sir, and
welcome."

"My word!"

"Good spot, ain't it?"

"I should say so! Who could ever have believed it?"

"Well, she's so full of ginger and general hellishness a person naturally wouldn't—but there 't is, you see. You can't ever tell what's in a person till you find out. Look at Satan, for instance."

"Satan?"

"Oh, helm-a-lee—hard-a-port! Of course I don't mean the sacred one, I mean the derelict that *thinks* he's it. Now to look at his wild eye and hear him talk, you'd think there's nothing in him but everlasting schemes for hogging money—hogging it by the cart load, the ship load, the train load, though dern seldom it is he sees a cent that's his own—yet he's got his good spot, Martha will tell you so. Why, the very reason he's so unfamiliar with a cent is that the minute he's got it he gives it away to any poor devil that comes along. It's the way he's made, you see; it's his good spot; they've all got it. Including you."

"Thanks, awfully! What is my good spot?"

"Damned if *I* know. But you've got it—everybody has. You know a cat's passion is fish. Particularly somebody else's fish. There's an awful lot to a cat—anybody knows that. Now then, you can train a cat up, in an ecclesiastical way, till it is that sunk in righteousness you couldn't any more get him to break the Sabbath than you could get a cowboy to keep it; but all the same, you lay a fish down and turn your back and there ain't real religion enough in that whole ornithological species to save that cat from falling. Especially a tomcat. For they're the limit, you know. Look at Bags. He don't miss the services, does he? No; you couldn't get him to. And as for self-sacrifice, why, in the coldest weather he'll quit a warming-pan to sleep on a sermon. It shows you how earnest he is; it shows you how anxious he is to do just right. But all the same, although he *looks* purified, he ain't transmuted all through, and when the time of stress comes you'll find there's hunks of unconverted cat in him yet. Now you lay out a fish handy, and you'll see. He would hog that fish if it was his last act. Well, what fish is to a cat, cigars are to Satan—just a wild unmeasurable passion. So you know by that, that for him to give away his last cigar is to give away his blood —ain't it so? Well, I've seen him *do* it! It's just as I told you—there's a good spot tucked away somewhere in everybody. You'll be a long time finding it, sometimes, if you ain't born to it, like the Admiral and Martha, but I haven't spent twenty years with that pair, and ten of it here and in Hell's Delight, not to get convinced it's so."

I said I felt bound to believe him, "but who is this Satan—and where is he?"

"Oh, there's no telling. He's a flitter. But he'll turn up; he's never gone for very long. I was thinking he was here when you came, but I remember, now, he was just gone. He's a busy cuss—as busy as the other one."

"Why do they call him by that name?"

"They? Because it's what he calls himself. He thinks he *is* Satan."

"Oh—I understand it, now."

"Understand what?"

"Why, the reason of it. He's crazy."

The bos'n gave me a solemnly inquisitive look, and then translated the look into words:

"Well . . . . are you acquainted with anybody that ain't?"

"That ain't? What do you mean?"

"Oh, when you come down to it fine, there's some that ain't as crazy as others, but as far as I've come along the road I haven't run across any yet that was perfectly straight in their minds. You see, everybody is a *little* crazy—some about one fool thing, some about another, and nearly all of them harmless—but as for a person that ain't any way crazy *at all*, damn'd if there's any such!"

"Oh, come!"

"Well, now, honor bright, do you know anybody that's right down sane—to the bottom?"

"Very well, then, honor bright, I am quite sure *I* am, myself."

"Oh, you—with your Adam monument!"

I thought that this was carrying jesting a little too far; so I made a stiff bow whose meaning could not be easily misunderstood, and strode away pretty haughtily.

Chapter 11

Diary Continued

PERHAPS it was natural enough and human enough for the Poet
to feed daily for thirty years upon the memory of a disaster which
wrecked his life, and for the General, the ex-Senator, the inventor and
others of our derelicts to do the same. But is it natural and human for
a couple of persons to keep up a mere dispute that long?—a dispute
that can never be settled?—a dispute about a matter of not the least
consequence?

Well, natural or unnatural, we have a case of it here. Thirty years
ago Uncle 'Rastus hired himself out to work on a farm on top of a high
hill in a New England State, and there he found Aunt Phyllis, who
was the farmer's cook. They at once began to dispute about the question of special providences, and from that day to this they have continued the debate whenever there was opportunity.

Two years later, luck added another matter to argue about. They
discussed it a few weeks; dropped it, took it up again a year later; and
again after two or three years; once more after a longer interval; then
gave it a rest—apparently for good and all. But not so. After a quiescent
interval of as much as half a decade, they got out that hoary mossback
once more, to-day, and gave it a final overhauling. This aged contention had its origin in a heroic act performed by 'Rastus twenty-eight
years ago. These are the details.

One summer afternoon a pair of visitors drove up from the town
down below in the valley—the charming and beautiful young wife of a
wealthy citizen, and her child, aged two years. Toward sunset the lady
started homeward. The horse was young and nervous, and unac-
quainted with hill-work. The farmer and his family stood on the porch
and watched the start with some uneasiness. There was a straight
stretch of slanting road for a third of a mile, downward from the house,
and the first half of it was visible from the porch, but at that point a
curtain of trees intervened and hid the rest.

The buggy made the first two or three hundred yards at a safe gait, then it began to move faster—faster—still faster; soon it began to fly; then the dust rose up in a cloud and hid it, just as it was reaching those intervening trees. It was a narrow road; at the end of the straight slant there was a very sharp turn and an unfenced precipice.

The farmer said, "Oh, my God, there is no hope for them—no power on earth can save their lives!" and he and his family sprang from the porch and went racing down the hill through the dust-cloud—not to help, but to mourn; not to save, but to seek the dead and do such reverent service as they might. When they reached that sharp elbow, —right there, right at that deadly spot—they saw, dim and spectral in the settling dust, the horse standing at ease, with 'Rastus at its head, and nobody hurt!

It was unbelievable—clearly unbelievable—yet it was so. 'Rastus had been coming up from town with his farm-team, and had halted at the turn to rest. He heard a noise, and looked up the road and saw the dust-cloud sweeping down upon him. When the interval between him and it had diminished to fifty steps, he got a vague glimpse of the horse's head, and understood. With an undisturbed head, and all his wits about him, he stepped to the right spot and braced himself; and the next second he grabbed the flying horse and stood him up on his hind legs!

The news sped to the town, but was not believed. Every one said the feat was impossible; that it was beyond the strength of the strongest man on the continent. But no matter, it had actually been performed, the proofs of it were unassailable, and had to be accepted. The newspapers applauded it; for several days people climbed up from the town to look at the spot, and wonder how the incredible thing was done; 'Rastus was a hero; there was not a white man nor a white woman in the region round about who was ashamed to shake hands with him; wherever he appeared the people took him by his horny black hand and gave it a good grip, and many said, "I'm proud to do it!" Last happiness of all, the rich man handed 'Rastus his check for a thousand dollars—the first time in his life that 'Rastus had ever owned above thirty dollars at one time.

Then that dispute began. Aunt Phyllis charged 'Rastus with cheating. He was indignant, and said—

"It's a lie. Who has I cheated?"

"Dat gen'lman. De idea o' you takin' a thousan' dollars! De hoss en harness en buggy warn't wuth it, en you knows it mighty well."

"Woman, what's de matter wid yo' brains? What is you talkin' 'bout?"

"Nemmine 'bout my brains, you stick to de pint, dat's all. You ain't gwyneter dodge it whah I is. You cheated, en I ain't gwyneter let you fo'git it, mind *I* tell you!"

"I didn't!"

"You did!"

"I didn't!"

"You did! Dey warn't wuth mo'n eight hund'd dollars—anybody'll tell you so. Now look at dat. You save' eight hund'd dollars for de gen'lman, en take a thousan'. It's cheatin', dat's what it is. No Christian wouldn't 'a' done it, nobody but a low-down inf'del would. S'pose you was to die—right now? Dat's it—s'pose you was to die?"

"Well, s'pose I *was* to? *Den* what?"

"Ain't you got no shame, 'Rastus? How'd you like to 'pear up dah, wid dem two hund'd dollars stickin' to yo' han's?"

"I'd hole my head up, dat's what I'd do. Hain't you got no sense, can't you git nothin' thoo yo' head? You's got de whole thing hindside fust—can't you see dat?"

"Who? me? How has I got it hindside fust?"

"Becaze you keep arguin' dat de gen'lman gimme de thousan' dollars for savin' de hoss en de buggy, but if you had any sense you'd know he didn't gimme it for *dat*, at all."

"De nation he didn't!"

"No, he didn't."

"Well den, you 'splain to me what he did give it to you for, if you think you kin."

"Why, for savin' his *fambly*."

"For savin' his *fambly*, you puddn'head!"

"Yes, for savin' his fambly. Anybody'll tell you so."

"In my bawn days I never see sich a numskull. 'Rastus, don't you know it don't stan' to reason? Now you pay 'tention—I's gwyneter show you. It's a new hoss en a good one, ain't it?"

"Yas."

"Cost five hund'd en fifty dollars, didn't it?"

"Yas."

"New buggy, ain't it?"

"Yas."

"Cost two hund'd en fifty, didn't it?"

"Yas."

"Dat make eight hund'd widout de harness, don't it?"

"Yas."

"You save' de whole outfit, didn't you?"

"Yas."

"Dat's eight hund'd dollars wuth ain't it?"

"Yas."

"Now den, we's got down to de fambly. How much is de lady's clo'es wuth?"

"How's I gwyneter know?"

"Well, I knows. Dey's spang-bang new, en dey cost a hund'd en sebenty-fo' dollars. How much is de chile's clo'es wuth?"

"I don't know nothin' 'bout de chile's clo'es."

"Well, I does. Dey cost twenty-five dollars. So, den, all de clo'es cost a hund'd en ninety-nine, ain't it?"

"Oh, yas, yas, yas, I reckin so. Git done wid de business!"

"Now den, what's de *lady* wuth?"

"Lan', you make me tired wid dis foolishness! How's I gwyneter know what she's wuth?"

"What's de *chile* wuth?"

"I don't k'yer nothin' 'bout it, en I ain't gwyneter *say* nothin' 'bout it."

"Now den, I's gwyneter come back to de harness. I knows what de harness cost, and so does you, en I's gwyneter c'rect you if you tries to fo'git en make a mistake 'bout it. What did de harness cost, 'Rastus?"

"It cost—cost—"

"I has my eye on you, 'Rastus."

"Cost fifteen dollars. . . . *Damn* de harness!"

"Now den, 'Rastus, de fac's is all in. All de thousan' dollars is 'counted for. You been 'cusin' me o' gittin' de matter hindside fust, en it hurt me to hear you say dat, 'caze it make it seem like I ain't got good sense; but 'Rastus, de figgers *shows* you was in de wrong en I was in de right. Dey shows you he didn't give you de thousan' dollars for savin' de fambly, he give it to you for savin' de *truck*. En he didn't pay full up, nuther, 'caze *he owes you fo'teen dollars on de harness!*"

. . . . It all happened twenty-eight years ago, when these dear old things were young—only forty. 'Rastus bought a farm for sixteen hundred dollars, paid a thousand down and borrowed the six hundred on mortgage. During eighteen years, by working sixteen hours a day and watching the pennies and economising on clothes and tobacco, he made enough to pay the interest each year and reduce the mortgage-debt ten dollars per annum; then the rheumatism claimed him for her own and he gave the property to a nephew and wandered out into the world. He turned up here, in the course of time, and has been free of the ward-room ever since, and has had the Anchor Watch's privileges here and in Hell's Delight—as good a man and as contented a soul as I know. The nephew still runs the farm, pays the interest, and in ten years has reduced the mortgage by thirty dollars. The child that survived the runaway through 'Rastus's once famous miracle has a prosperous husband and a family, is beautiful in character and in person, is happy, and to this day does not know that any one ever saved her life.

As I have said, that long-neglected dispute was resurrected to-day. At the close of it Aunty Phyllis had a happy idea, and fetched it out with glee, and confidence, and vast expectations. But 'Rastus was loaded, *that* time! Phyllis said—

"You is de man dat's allays sayin' de' ain't no sich thing as special providence. If 'twarn't for special providence, what would 'a' went wid dat buggy en harness? Who put you in dat road, right exackly in de right spot, right exackly at de right half-a-second?—you answer me dat, if you kin!"

"Who de nation sent de *hoss* down dah in sich a blame' fool fashion?"

Chapter 12

From Intermittent Diary

I HAVE skipped a week. Trifles of interest got in the way, and it was easier to skip than to write. One of the trifles was a "regular"—Stanchfield Garvey, called "Governor." The title dates from away back, years and years ago. He served four years as Secretary of a territory, and meantime as Acting Governor twice or thrice, during brief absences of the actual Governor. Once "Governor" Garvey, always Governor Garvey; once General on a Governor's staff, always General; once justice of the peace for a year, always "Judge" thenceforth to the grave—such is our American system. We have a thoroughly human passion for titles; turning us into democrats doesn't dislodge that passion, nor even modify it. A title is a title, and we value it; if it chance to be pinchbeck, no matter, we are glad to have it anyway, and proud to wear it, and hear people utter it. It is music to us.

Governor Garvey is eighty years old, but does not look nearly so old. He is a good six feet high, and very slender; he has the bearing of a gentleman; his hair is short and thick, and is silver-white; his face is Emersonian, and he has intellect, but as it is of an ill-ordered and capricious and unstable sort, his face mis-states and over-states its character and bulk. However, his eyes correct these errors. They are kind and beautiful and unsteady, and they tell you he is weak and a visionary. He is not a derelict, but that is because the Admiral saved him from it several years ago by getting him a job as rough-proof reader on an evening paper—an easy berth which pays him ten dollars a week and supports him. He has a bed and an oil stove in a small room in a tenement house, and is his own chambermaid and cook.

He began life as a printer's apprentice in a western city. He was sixteen or seventeen, then, and had a common-school education of a meagre sort, which he tried to enlarge by studying, nights. Without serious success; for he was shavings, not anthracite. That is to say, that whatsoever thing he undertook, he went at it in a blaze of eagerness and enthusiasm and burnt the interest all out of it in forty-eight hours, then dropped it and went at something else in another consuming blaze. During the four years of his apprenticeship he carried his conflagrations into the first chapter of every useful book in the Mechanic's Library, but never any further than that in any instance. And so, whereas he picked up a slight smattering of many breeds of knowledge, his accumulation was valueless and unusable, it was a mere helter-skelter scrap-heap.

For a week or two, in the beginning, he had a burning ambition to be a Franklin; so he lived strictly on bread and water, studied by the firelight instead of using candles, and practised swimming on the floor. Then he discarded Franklin, and imitated somebody else a while. This time an orator; and went around orating to his furniture with pebbles in his mouth. Next, he proposed to be a great lawyer, and with this idea he read Blackstone a couple of weeks. Next, with an earnest desire to make men better and save them from the pains of that fierce hell which all believed in in those days, he studied for the ministry for a while. But his path was beset with difficulties. Not his path, his wash; for he washed from one religion to another faster than he could keep count, and never landed on the shore of any one of them long enough to dry his feet. He has kept up these excursions all his life. He has sampled all the religions, he has been an infidel, he is a Christian Scientist, now. I mean, this week.

Nobody could ever tell what he would do next. His friends and family expected much of him, for he was bright above the average, but he disappointed every hope of theirs as fast as it was born. He was always dreaming—of doing good to his fellow-man, as he supposed—whereas at bottom his longing was for distinction, though he didn't suspect it. When he was studying to be a Franklin, he copied Franklin's brief and pregnant rules of conduct and stuck them in the frame of his mirror. He lived by them until he recovered from the Franklin disease, then he lived by the next model's rules, and the next and the next. When a model hadn't a set of rules, he supplied him with one. In his time he has lived by more different kinds of rules than has any other experimenter in right and rigid conduct. He has a set now, drawn from "Science and Health," and thinks he understands what they mean.

When he was twenty years old, he resolved upon a visit to his people. They lived in a village a hundred miles away. It was in the winter time. He gave no notice that he was coming. He thought it would be romantic to arrive at midnight, and surprise them in the morning. This was not well conceived, for the family had moved to another house, and the one which they had been occupying was now occupied by an old doctor who hadn't any romance in him, and by his two maiden sisters who had long ago outlived their romantic days. Stanchfield slipped into the house the back way, and up stairs with his boots in his hands. He undressed in the dark in his room, and got into bed with the old maids, whom he supposed were his brothers. Presently one of them said, drowsily—

"Mary, don't crowd so!"

Stanchfield began to scramble out, and he was feeling very sick and scared, and much ashamed. He had been nurturing a beard, and one result of this was that the other maid cried out "There's a man in the bed!" and both maids began to scream. Stanchfield fled, just as he was, and met the doctor on the stairs, with a candle in one hand and a butcher knife in the other. An explanation followed, and the doctor brought the clothes.

Two or three nights afterward, Stanchfield sat in his room at home, reading, also dreaming. At four in the morning he started out to call on a young lady—without looking at the clock. He hammered on her door a good while, then her father appeared, shivering in his dressing-gown, learned his business, admitted him to a freezing parlor, and sat there silent and lowering for an hour—waiting for an opportunity to say something cruel. At last Stanchfield timidly asked when Miss Louise would be down.

"As soon as she's done dressing for breakfast! Won't you wait?— oh, do!"

Stanchfield was in the town a fortnight. In that time he joined the Sons of Temperance, agreed to make a speech at a temperance mass meeting, and meantime he furnished the mottoes for the torchlight procession; but when the time came he was on the other side and made an impassioned plea for unlimited whisky.

When he was twenty-three and had been a journeyman printer a year, he returned to his village home, bought the weekly paper for five

hundred dollars, borrowing the money at ten per cent, and at once reduced the subscription price one half. He made a clean paper, and
worked hard; but he got but a meagre subsistence out of it for his
widowed mother and her young family. He paid his interest every year,
but was never able to pay any of the principal. At the end of six years
he gave the paper to his creditor and moved to another town. There he
bought a part of a paper on credit, and fell in love with a girl in a neighboring town and engaged himself to her. A few weeks afterward he engaged himself to a girl in his new home-town. He found himself in a
difficulty, now, and did not quite know how to get out of it. It seemed
to him that the right way, the honorable way, would be for him to go
and explain to girl No. 1 and abide by her decision as to what he should
do. He told his project to girl No. 2, who remarked that he would
marry *her*—and now—and he could afterward go and explain to No. 1
at his leisure, if he wanted to.

So said, so done. No. 2 was a good and patient and valuable wife to
him—as far as any wife could be valuable to such a weather-vane. After
three years he gave his share of the paper to his creditor and moved to
another town, where he bought a wee little business, on credit, and at
once cut prices till there was no profit in it. He scrambled along for
four years, meantime making and losing friends continually by changing his religion and his politics every three months; then he chanced
upon a new opening. In his apprenticeship-days, eighteen years before,
a great lawyer had taken an interest in him, and this acquaintanceship
came good, now. The lawyer got him appointed Secretary of one of the
new territories.

He made a good Secretary, for he performed his duties well and
faithfully, and was a strictly honest man where honest men were scarce.
He was very popular, he had the confidence and the friendship of the
whole territory, and for four years he and his wife knew to the full what
comfort and happiness were. Then the territory was elevated to State-
hood. There was much fussing at slates for other State officers in his
party, but none about the Secretaryship: no one thought of giving that
post to anybody but him.

But he had to have a freak on nomination-night—he wouldn't have
been himself if he had failed of that. He would not go to the conven-

tion. For two reasons: he thought candidates ought to keep away from conventions—they ought to leave the delegates unembarrassed to choose the candidates. Also, the convention was to meet in a liquor saloon, and he could not conscientiously enter there, for his turn to be a prohibitionist had come around again, lately. His friends could not persuade him, his wife could not persuade him. Very well, the thing happened which all expected except himself: he was left off the ticket.

A few months later the State assumed command, the territory went out of business, and he with it. There was nothing for him to do; he could find no employment. By and by he and his wife gave up and went home—expensively; so recklessly expensively that they spent all their savings on the road. Poor creatures, they had never had a real holiday in their lives, before, and knew they might never have another one. It turned their heads and abolished their prudence. For thirty years Garvey's friends stood by him, for he was good at heart, and without stain, and well beloved. During all that time they found place after place for him, but he lost them all. Lost them by throwing them away to hunt for something better. He always gave satisfaction to others, but could never be satisfied himself.

Eight years ago his wife died. After that, he had nothing to care for, nothing to live for, and he went wandering. Her devotion had been his stay and support; such courage as ever he had had she gave him; after each of his thousand failures she lifted him out of his abysses of despondency and found for him a new hope. For three years he drifted in a starless gloom, rudderless; then the Admiral found that proof-reading job for him, and he holds it yet; his old hankering to throw away good things to hunt for better ones is dead in him. He spends all his evening with the Anchor Watch, and has, for company and sympathisers, the General, the ex-Senator, the Poet, and one or two other derelicts who look back upon a special disaster which ruined their lives, and which they only live to regret and repent and mourn over. From the day that the Governor stood stanchly by his principles and lost the Secretaryship he has lamented that righteous act, and cursed it and bitterly grieved over it. It has wrung his heart for forty years. If he could only get back there and have that chance again! That is the dirge he sings. That, and how much of sorrow and privation and humiliation he could

have saved his patient and faithful wife if he had not been such a fool,
"oh, *such* a fool!" And who knows? she might be with him now and
blessing him! Ah, yes; and what would he not give to see that dear face
once more! And so he murmurs along, and it is pitiful to hear.

Chapter 13

Intermittent Diary—Continued

INTERRUPTING myself to gossip about the Governor has made a
blank where the Plum Duff occurred. By help of Jimson Flinders the
colored stenographer and sub-editor, I can fill it now. The bos'n says
plum duff is the sailor's luxury-dish in whaleships, and is a dough pudding with raisins in it, as distinguished from dough pudding plain. It
is served once a week—usually on Sundays. Duff is probably the fo'-
castle way of pronouncing *dough*; and a good enough way, too, if it be
righteous to pronounce tough *tuff*. Plum Duff, here in the Haven of
the Derelicts, is the Anchor Watch's name for Entertainment-Night.
And well named, too. It is the night that has the intellectual raisins in
it, and is as welcome here as is plum duff at sea.

The weather was bad, but no matter, we had a full house. All the
derelicts were present, all the "regulars," and all the "casuals"—in
fact, everybody possessing the high privilege of assisting at Plum Duffs.
We had as many as fifty people on hand. This time the feature of the
evening was to be a lecture, in the form of a story, illustrated by "living
pictures" thrown upon a screen. Subject, "The Benevolence of Nature." Lecturer, Rev. Lo-what-God-hath-Wrought. Edgar Billings, am-
ateur naturalist, was to manage the picture-machinery. He stood at one
end of the great room with his apparatus, and the lecturer stood by the
vast white screen at the other.

The idea of illustrating the story was a late thought; so late that
there was no time for lecturer and illustrator to go over the ground in
detail together, but apparently this kind of particularity was not going
to be needed. Lo gave Billings a synopsis of the story, and Billings said

it was a plenty; said he had just the pictures for it, and could flash the right one onto the canvas every time, sure, and fit every incident of the tale to a dot as it went along. Billings is an earnest and sincere and good-hearted creature, but hasn't much judgment.

First we had some music, as usual, Jimmy doing the pianola-business and the Admiral the orchestrelle, then the lecturer began. He said it was most wonderful, most touching and beautiful, our dear old Mother Nature's love for her creatures—for *all* of them, from the highest all the way down the long procession of humbler animated nature to the very worms and insects. He dwelt at some length upon her unfailing goodness to her wards, and said he wished especially to note one feature of it, her intricate and marvelous system of providing food for the animal world; her selection of just the right and best food for each creature, and placing each creature where its particular kind of food could never fail it. Her tender protection, he said, was over all—the humble spider, the wasp, the worm, all the myriads of tiny and helpless life, were under her watchful eye, and partakers of her loving care. By Mr. Billings's help he would exhibit this love as exercised toward two or three of the lowliest of these creatures, and would ask the house to remember that the same love and the same protection were exercised in the same way toward the unspecified myriads and millions that creep and fly about the earth. Should these little creatures be grateful? Yes. If we understood their language we should hear them express that gratitude, should we not? Without a doubt, yes, without a doubt. Might he try to put himself in their place and speak for them? He would make the effort, putting it in the form of a little story.

The room was then darkened; an intensely bright great circle appeared upon the white screen; the lecturer began to read:

The Story

Once there was a dear little spider, who lived in a web pleasantly situated, and was expecting a family; and she was very happy—happy, and tenderly grateful to the dear Mother Nature that gave her so lovely a world to live in, and surrounded her with so many comforts, and made her little life so sweet and beautiful—

Instantly a wide-spreading web appeared upon the screen, and in the middle of it a hairy fat spider as big as a watermelon, with bunches of crumpled legs which seemed to be all elbows. It made the audience start, it was so alive, and sharp-eyed and real. The lecturer glanced at it, looked uncomfortable, and moved a little away. After a pause to recover his serenity, he resumed his reading.

She was lonely, and sweetly sad, for her dearest, her heart's own, her young husband, was absent, and she was fondly dreaming of him and longing for his return—

A smaller devil of the spider species—evidently the husband—appeared on the frontier of the web, took a hesitating step or two toward his wife, then changed his mind and began to crawl slowly and almost imperceptibly backward toward foreign parts.

She was very hungry, for she had been without food for a whole day; but did she lose faith? did she complain, as we too often do? No; dropping her eyes meekly, she murmured, "Our dear Mother Nature will provide—"

A sudden commotion on the screen attracted all eyes. With a rush which broke the smooth web into waves the big wife swept down upon the poor cowering little husband, and as she sunk her fangs into him and began to suck he struggled and squirmed in so pitiful a way that many of the audience turned away their eyes, not being able to bear the sight of it. There were some subdued and scarcely audible chucklings here and there, but they lasted only a moment. The lecturer took one glance, and looked embarrassed—as one could see, for his face came within the circle of light—also he looked as if he was not comfortable in his stomach. Soon he went on with his reading. He had to stick to his text; he was not a person who could change it to meet an emergency.

Now came an event which filled her mother-heart with joy—the birth of the expected family. Out from the silken bag attached to her body poured a flood of little darlings, dainty little spiderlings, hundreds and hundreds of them, and she gathered them to her maternal breast in a rapture of gratitude and joy—

And in an instant there it was, on the screen!—a mighty swarm of frisky little spiders the size of horseflies—just a tumultuous confusion of ten thousand legs all squirming at once. They attacked their mother.

She tried to get away, but they overflowed her, overwhelmed her, and began to chew her legs and her body—a horrible sight! The lecturer did not take a look this time. No, he made a half-motion to do it, but changed his mind and went on reading.

Her first thought, poor little mother, was, how should she find food for her nine hundred little darlings; but her second was, "Nature will provide." What a lesson for us it is! Ah, my friends, when the larder is empty and in our despair we know not where to turn, let us remember the faith of this humble insect and imitate it and be strengthened by it; let us be brave, and believe, with her, that nourishment will be provided for our little ones.

At this moment, dear friends, arrived a wasp. In a sunny meadow she had digged a hole and prepared a cosy home for the dear offspring she was expecting. Now she was abroad to secure food for that offspring. Her happy heart was singing, and the burden of that grateful song was, "Nature will provide." She hovered over our mother-spider, then descended upon her—

Instantly it was on the screen! A wasp the size of a calf swooped down upon wide-spreading wings, gripped the struggling mother-spider, and slowly drove a sting as long as a sword, deep into her body. The audience gasped with horror to see that hideous weapon sink in like that and the spider strain and quiver and rumple its legs in its agony, but the lecturer ventured no look; he went right on with his reading.

The spider was not killed, my friends, it was only rendered helpless. That was the intention. It was to serve as food for the wasp's child, and would live a week or two—until half eaten up, in fact. She deposited an egg on the spider's body, carried her prey to her dark home in the ground, crammed the prisoner in there and went for more, radiant with that spiritual joy which is the reward of duty done. In two days the wasp's child was born, and was hungry; and there at hand was its food, the melancholy spider, faintly struggling and weary. With a deep hymn of gratitude to kind and ever-watchful Nature, who allows none of her children to suffer, the larva gnawed a hole in the spider's abdomen, and began to suck her juices while she moaned and wept—

Straightway the revolting banquet was pictured upon the screen, the larva munching its way, most comfortable and content, into the spider's vitals, and the helpless spider feebly working its legs and probably trying to think of a grateful sentiment to utter that would not sound too grossly insincere.

Has the spider been forgotten? is the spider forsaken in its time of sorrow and distress? Ah, no, my friends, neither she nor any other creature is ever forgotten or ever forsaken. Soon the spider will have the reward of its patience, its faith, its loving trust. In six days the half of it will have been eaten up, then it will die, and pass forever to that sweet peace, that painless repose which is provided for all, howsoever humble and undeserving, who keep a contented spirit and cheerfully do the duties allotted to them in their sphere. I will now show you, with Mr. Billings's help, how wonderfully we have been provided with yellow fever and malaria by the ministrations of a humble little mosquito which—

And so on, and so on. It would take me too long to write down the rest of it, but it was very interesting. Everybody was pleased, and many said they shouldn't want to eat anything for a week. It seemed to me that it was a most charming and elevating entertainment, and others thought the same, and said it was ennobling. They said they never should have thought of such ways to feed animals, and regarded it as most intelligent and grand. I think the Rev. Mr. Lo will stand on a higher plane with us hereafter than he did before. Many shook hands with him and congratulated him, and he was greatly pleased and thankful. Bates the unbeliever conceded that the lecture had given him a new view of the benevolence of Nature.

"You've Been a Dam Fool, Mary. You Always Was!"

(December 1903)

IN 1895 Clemens recorded in his notebook:

> Man on the steamer abusing southern honesty. Told him about Mr. Hand, northerner who went to S. C. 2 or 3 years before the war; came north & couldn't return. Southerner went to another part of the south & speculated in cotton with the mutual money, $20,000. Tried for years to find out where Hand was; 20 years after the war found out his whereabouts—he was working for wages—& sent him a check for $600,000, his half of the avails.[1]

Some eight and one-half years later Mark Twain wrote the story based upon this incident. He was then in Florence where the Clemenses had moved in the fall of 1903 for the sake of Olivia's health. On December 30 he reported to F. A. Duneka of Harper & Brothers, "Yes, I've written the Midsummer Story ('You've Been a Dam Fool, Mary. You Always Was,') and the next-Xmas Story ('The $30,000 Bequest'), and Mrs. Clemens is editing the hellfire out of them. The typewriter will take hold, next."[2] There is no indication that his wife actually edited the story; instead, Mark Twain continued to work on the manuscript, for the note that comprises its final three pages was dated "Villa di Quarto, Florence, January, 1904." A Paine note on the manuscript indicates that a typescript, now missing,

---

[1] Notebook 28, TS p. 11. This entry is undated; the preceding one is dated 26 May 1895.
[2] TS in MTP.

249

was sent to Harper & Brothers on 19 February 1904. However, the story was not published—perhaps in part because the title was considered objectionable. On 14 March 1904 Clemens' secretary, Isabel V. Lyon, wrote to Duneka, "Mr. Clemens wishes me to add a postscript to his letter saying that if there would better be a change in the title of 'You're a damfool Mary'—and he gathers that you desire one—the change which he would prefer is this; use the word *Jackass* instead of *Damfool* in both title and closing remark."[3] But this modification did not satisfy Duneka; more than a year later the title was still being revised. Duneka wrote to Clemens on 19 July 1905, "I have Miss Lyon's note granting permission to strike out the word 'Damn' from 'You're a Fool Mary—you always was'; and that will be done." Clemens may have been willing to accept this weakened form of his title, but there is no reason to think he preferred it. His original title has been restored here.

---

[3] Miss Lyon's copy in MTP.

"You've Been a Dam Fool, Mary.
You Always Was!"

Chapter 1

IT WAS seventeen miles from Charleston, South Carolina, at a place where the roads crossed. There were half a dozen houses; one of them was the store, another was the smithy. These two industries were just beginning their career in the hands of a couple of young experimenters, strangers to each other and to their neighbors. The storekeeper, James Marsh, was a Georgian, twenty-three years of age; Thomas Hill, the blacksmith, was a Connecticut Yankee, fresh from the North; his age, also, was twenty-three.

It took Marsh and Hill only a day to size each other up favorably, and only a week to become close friends. Then Marsh made a business proposal.

"Let's pool interests," he said. "This place commands the custom of all the planters and all the negroes for five miles around, and is going to be a good stand for both of us. You've got eight hundred dollars of newly-inherited cash; you don't need it, and I do. Give it to me, and become a full partner with me. It's a lot of money, and I can get a heavy credit and long time on that kind of backing."

Many a Hill would have hesitated, and felt that this was rather sudden, in the circumstances. Many a Hill would have said to himself, "It won't do—I don't know anything about this young fellow yet." Many

251

a Hill would have exhibited some shade of natural caution, and asked for time to think the matter over. But this Hill did none of these things. His character was of a simple sort; it was not in his nature to wrong any one, nor to suspect any one of being willing to wrong him; in his village at home he had had no experiences calculated to damage his confidence in the honesty of his fellow men; therefore he handed over his little hoard without hesitation and became his new friend's partner.

Time drifted along, the business prospered, the friendship held, the young fellows were inseparable comrades. They "Tom'd" and "Jimmy'd" each other, and were deeply affectionate, each in his own way. The Southerner was demonstrative, the Northerner less so; the one flamed, the other smouldered, but both were warm enough. The Southerner was full of energy and business shrewdness, the Northerner was untiringly industrious, faithful, and valuable, but he had no faculty for business, nor for planning and pushing, and was not of the kind that get rich. The Southerner was all life, activity, breeziness, and he had a fine large romantic streak in him, the Northerner was quiet, gentle, plodding; to him life was a pleasant enough journey, but only a journey, not an excursion, not a procession with banners and music.

At the end of three years the clouds of the Civil War closed down, and business came to a stand-still. The partners realized that their prosperity had undergone a collapse. They sat sadly considering the situation. Marsh said—

"I am to blame, Tom. I have carried sail too long. I ought to have seen what was coming, and begun to collect the outstanding bills and close up the business. It's too late, now—we are caught. Ruined is the word."

"I reckon it's so, Jimmy, but don't you blame yourself—I can't allow it. If you ought to have seen it, I ought to have seen it too, but I didn't, and so nobody's to blame. It's your brains that built the business—I never should have arrived anywhere with it. If you've made a miscalculation, there's nothing to blame about it. Don't you worry, and I shan't."

"It's good of you to say it, Tom, and it's like you, you old good-hearted frog, but I can't help it, I've ruined us both, and it's all my fault —I ought to have been looking out for what was coming. Ah, by

George, just think of it! If we had begun to close up six months ago we'd be out and safe, now, with four or five thousand dollars in our pockets. But *now*—oh, Great Scott, who's going to pay up!"

The men were patriots—each from his own point of view. It was time for Hill to go; in a little while it would be too late; the region was already becoming uncomfortable for Union men. The parting was not gay, but it was not sad. Marsh said—what everybody thought—

"It's only a little flurry; it'll be over in three months, then you'll be back again. Meantime I'll do my level best; I'll save such dollars as I can out of the wreckage, and then we'll make a fresh start and build the business up again as good as new. Good-bye and good luck! Sun gwyne shine t'morrer, as the niggers say."

Hill bent his way northward, and presently the gigantic "little flurry" opened up behind him, and for four years and more the great world stood open-mouthed and gazed at the vast tragedy.

Chapter 2

THEY WERE long years, but the finish came at last. Peace was declared, the war was over. About the end of April, 1865, a letter addressed to Hill and bearing the Charleston postmark arrived at the blacksmith's late home in Connecticut. It went back to Marsh, the sender, marked "Address not known." A month later Marsh arrived in the village in person. The postmaster could tell him nothing about Hill's whereabouts, but said Henry Addicks would be more likely than another to know his address. Addicks kept the boarding house. Addicks was quite ready to talk, and said—

"Did I know him? Knowed him from the cradle! And good friends always, him and me. Now as to finding him—let me see. Um—well, I'll think of the name of the place in a minute. When he moved away from here he wasn't expecting any letters, you see, and so—"

"Not any from the South?"

"Along at first, yes, I think he was, but not after the war got a good start. Might you be from the South?"

"Yes, I knew him there. I knew his partner, too."

"No—is that so? Name was—name was—"

"Marsh."

"That's it! Is he alive yet?"

"I think so; yes, I believe he is."

"Well, he set great store by Marsh. Believed in him. The boys didn't, but *he* did. They laughed at him, and said Southerners didn't pay Northern debts, but they couldn't shake him. He always said he knowed *one* Southerner that would pay if he could. There was a money-account betwixt them, I forget now, just what it was. But my! he'd believe in *anybody*—born so, you know. Oh, I knowed him from the cradle. Good cuss, dreadful slow, but stiddy as an island."

"How did he come to leave here?"

"Well, first-off, he was going into the army, but got knocked out with typhoid for six weeks; then he started up his shop and run it about a half a year, I sh'd say, but he didn't prosper. He can *make* money, for he's a hard worker; but he can't collect it—so there 'tis, you see. So then, as I was telling you, he got sort of discouraged, and struck for the West. Told me he was going to make a try at a little place in Indiana, by the name of—name of—no, sir, I can't 'call it. Now if you were going to be here a couple of days—"

"I'll be here that long, maybe longer."

"All right; my wife's down east, and I'll write her; she'll remember that name, and if you'll look in here about day after to-morrow in the evening, I'll let you have it."

Marsh got the name at the time promised, and left for Indiana the next day. He found the village, but not Hill. Hill had stayed there until along in the spring of '62, and had then gone away—whither, no one was now able to say. Abel Smith would probably remember, for he and Hill were together a good deal. Good; and where might Smith be found? Nowhere, just now; he was down South-west somewhere, but "liable" to come back any minute.

And it happened according to the conjecture; Smith came back in about a month. He said Hill had gone to the village of Freeman's Flats in northern Ohio. Marsh went to Freeman's Flats. Everybody there remembered him, everybody spoke well of him; but they spoke as of one absent. Marsh asked—

"Is he gone?"

"Yes. He was here a good deal over a year—till October, '63."

"Then he went away? Where to?"

The villager studied a moment or two, then answered hesitatingly—and conscientiously—

"Well, I don't rightly know. He got burnt up in a boarding house."

"Burnt up?"

"It's what happened. Anybody can tell you about it. Billy Samson buried him—what was left."

Marsh hunted up Billy Samson. His address was "the s'loons—any of them." There were but three; Samson was easily found. He was not interested, at first, but after Marsh had treated a couple of times, the spirit of accommodation came upon him and he offered to show the grave and tell all about the tragedy.

They went to the forlorn little graveyard, and the "town loafer"—which was Samson's village title—pointed out the resting place of Thomas Hill. Marsh noticed that the grave had a tidier look than was the case with the most of the others, and that at the head of it was a bunch of wild flowers in a tin can. He said—

"I am glad to see that somebody remembers him kindly."

"Yes. It's me."

"You liked him, then?"

"Like a dog."

"Well, he was a good man."

"Many's the good turn he done *me*, I can tell you that. You know a poor devil like me ain't lousy with friends, and so—*say*, there was a bully here that used to put upon me and lick me every time he got a chance, but he started in on that lay once too often. Tom Hill happened along and advised him to leggo me, and got some sass, and he took him up—just so—and slammed him down and broke him in two—"

"Good for Hill!"

"—and he's a cripple from that day to this, and can't scare a cat, now, let alone a human. *I* keep that grave looking thataway. *Say*—you know he ought to prospered, but somehow he couldn't seem to. Why, he worked like a nigger, but he hadn't the heart to crowd a man that let on to be hard up, and when these hellions found that out they took advantage of him and didn't pay him. He got to running behind-hand,

and was two hundred dollars in debt when he got burnt up. It was the only thing that saved him. Creditors going to sell him out the very next day, tools and all. Lord, he was low-spirited that evening! We set and talked about it, and he said they couldn't sell him out for enough to pay his debts, and he wouldn't be allowed to go away and try another start somewhere, and was plumb discouraged and wished he was dead; said if he was fifty dollars in debt after the sale he was going to kill himself. Well, he was in earnest, you know; so maybe he was willing enough for the fire to take him, poor fellow."

Marsh heaved a deep sigh and said—

"I wish I had been here, I would have scraped that two hundred dollars together for him if it took my shirt."

"No!" exclaimed the town loafer, "would you though? Where did you know him? What is your name?"

"James Marsh."

"No! *Jimmy?*"

"Yes—Jimmy."

"From down South! Land, he believed in *you!* They all chaffed him, and said down there they didn't pay Northern debts, but it never phazed him—said he knowed *one* Southerner that was different. It was you, you know; he told all about that business down there." He cast a swift glance at Marsh's face, and said, "Ah, by Jackson, if he was only alive now! You *would* rake together that two hundred for him, wouldn't you?"

"If it took my last shirt I would."

Samson flung a searching and excited look around the place, then put his mouth close to Marsh's ear, and said—

"B' god, he ain't dead!"

He did not wait for expressions of astonishment from Marsh, but plunged eagerly into the history of the case.

"Hold still and lemme tell you. I've held onto that secret two years, and it a-swelling and a-swelling all the time and phizzing and sizzling to get out, and now that it's safe to uncork, if I don't pull it I'll bust. You see, it was like this. It was a rickety old shack, a played-out boarding house, and Tom was the only boarder left; he was the only man poor enough to stand the 'commodations. Old Sam White and his wife kept it, and he went on crutches and was cook and chambermaid, and she was close to death with consumption, and due to cash-in in about a week. The fire was in their end of the house and got both of them early. I was the first man there, and Tom Hill busted out of the window with his hair afire and come rushing past, breaking for the river, and I reconnized him. He says 'Don't gimme away,' and I understood, and says 'You bet!' He run down the bank and into the river, and shoved out and grabbed a drift-log, and that's the last I've seen of him. And he was pretty dim, then, because his head wasn't afire any more, by that time.

"Well, next, the town arrived—a whole crowd, as many as a hundred and fifty, I reckon—and watched the fire down to the last ember, and I explained to them in a way cal'lated to crowd the actual facts a little, how I'd seen old *White* rush out with his hair afire and take to the river, and was under water and gone before I could get to him. When I got that far I was hit with a terrible uneasiness."

"Why?"

"The crutches, you know. They'd properly expect to find them on the bank or down the shore somewheres, and I knowed they wouldn't. But—well, you know, humans are just cattle, *they* don't think. I never had any trouble about the crutches. They warn't mentioned.

"Nobody bothered about old Sam and his wife, they only just talked and talked and talked about Tom Hill and how blame' good he was, and how pitiful it was to have him go thataway. I said I done what I could to save him, but was too late, and said it was awful to see him scrambling around in the fire like a lawyer in hell, so they was satisfied and felt resigned about it, and said His ways ain't like ourn, but generly better in the long run, and I told them a lot of other int'resting things—mostly made up, you know—and kep' them from suspicioning the true facts of the business.

"When it was dawn we raked the two bodies out of the embers. They were just black hunks, you know, and hadn't any shape, but I selected the best one and put it in a candle-box and buried it here where you see the grave, and they buried the other one. They don't take any care of theirn, but mine's going to continue up-to-date whilst I'm on top of the ground, for Tom Hill was a good friend to me."

"But dear me, since it isn't Tom at all that's under there—"

"That's all right, that hunk's *representing* him, it's his debbuty, and

as long as I'm on deck that hunk is going to be respected. *Say*—I know
where Tom is, and I'll tell you."

He took out of his pocket a handful of soiled envelops. They bore
his name and address—not written in an adult hand, but disguised in
a child's roman capitals. He took a slip of paper from one of them,
and showed it to Marsh. It had an address on it, and the word
"*Thanks.*"

"This is not disguised," said Marsh, "it's his hand; I recognize it."

"Well, the others have got just that in them. They're from the places
he's lived in since he got burnt up and slid out. Here's the last two.
They're from the same place, a year apart. Rocky Hill, Wisconsin.
The last one ain't a month old, yet. You notice he's been there a year
and more, now."

"Yes."

"What would you argue out of that?"

"Well, I don't know. What?"

"Time for him to be busted again, don't you reckon?"

"I didn't think of that, but certainly it's well reasoned."

"Mr. Marsh, you remember about your last shirt? If he was busted,
now, and a hundred dollars would pull him through, you would raise
that hundred if it took—"

"My last shirt? I give you my word I would."

"All right, then, you can look at *this* one. I got it day before
yesterday."

He took a small, badly printed handbill out of an envelop and passed
it to Marsh, who read it.

"*Public Vendue.* The smithy of Thomas Hill will be sold at public
vendue on Tuesday the 28th inst., to satisfy an expired note of hand
for $100."

"Poor old chap!" Marsh began to walk slowly up and down, musing,
planning, lost in reverie. As his plannings gathered form, his pace
quickened and his face began to light up and his eyes to show excitement. Presently he stopped short, and said—

"I've got it! And plenty of time—a week to spare. Billy Samson, are
you theatrical, romantic, and all that? Because—look here, can you
spare a week from your—from your—"

"Engagements? Likely that's the word that's got mislaid. None this

year; never mind about next—the Lord'll provide. Play ball—I'm
a-listening."

"All right, we'll be at that vendue! You'll go with me? I pay the
freight. You'll go?"

"Will a duck swim? Will I travel, and see the world—free gratis for
nothing? I bet you! Why, I've never been thirty mile from this town!"

Then he remembered his clothes—his rags—and was ashamed, and
glanced down at them, and up at Marsh—a pantomime which said,
"But these block the game, you see."

"They're all right," said Marsh, "you'll see. Billy, we'll have the
stunningest theatrical time you ever saw. I'll dress up like that, myself,
and we'll play a game on Tom Hill that'll beat the band. Look at this."
He got a great roll of greenbacks out of his pocket. "Count it."

"Land, but it's a pile!" said Samson.

He counted the bills, slowly, lingeringly, lovingly, then drew a deep
and reverent breath.

"Eight hundred dollars—by jimminy but it's a pile!"

"Half of it's mine, Samson, half of it's Tom's."

"Shake! By God, he *said* you was white, and it's so!"

"But that's not all. In the bank there's four thousand more, and half
of that's Tom's, too."

"Shake again—shake! Tom's rich and out of his troubles, goodness
knows I'm glad I've lived to see this day. He's just a love, Tom is"—
the tears came, his voice trembled with affectionate emotion—"and
he broke that son of a bitch's back, you know. Go on, I'm a-worshiping;
go on, White Man, tell me the rest of the scheme."

"It'll be great, Billy, great—you'll see. I'll dress up as a tramp and
we'll ride in emigrant cars; and when we get there we'll say we've been
out of luck, and strike him for a loan—"

"By George, it'll lay over the circus! We'll fool him down to the
ground. I can see him now. He'll be that sorry for us he'll clear forget
his own troubles, and if *he's* got a last shirt—"

"That's it—he'll sell it on the sly and we'll get the money—"

"And *take* it, too. And then—"

"Then we'll be at the vendue, Billy—"

"I know! My, it'll be grand when the surprise comes!"

The pair spent two or three days in Chicago, on the way, and then left for Rocky Hill—to all appearance tramps of old experience and squalid degree. For baggage Samson had a soiled bundle on the end of a stick, and Marsh a travel-worn large valise of the kind that is made of linen, in halves that telescope together and are held so by leather straps.

Chapter 3

ABOUT this time Hill was making a last effort to save himself, being moved to this by worry concerning his sweetheart, Mary Lester, niece and heir of Jacob Lester, the man to whom Hill owed the hundred dollars. Lester was proprietor of the sawmill, and was reported to be worth twenty thousand dollars. He was middle-aged, a childless widower, and rather a hard man. Of late years he had become a lender of money, and in that field was prospering to his satisfaction. He did not admire unsuccessful people, and his niece's engagement to the blacksmith was not to his taste. He spent much time planning underhand ways to break it off; the rest of his leisure he spent in trying to persuade Mary to retire from it. Mary was weakening, and he could see it. He began to intimate vaguely, now, that he was thinking of changing his will. He was able to notice that this had an effect. Mary, poor thing, had known nothing but poverty and hard work; in her private dreams she was always consoling herself with pictures of a gilded future in which her uncle's fortune would release her from labor, clothe her in a way proper to her blooming youth and beauty, and raise her several degrees in the respect and esteem of the village. The hints about the altering of the will blew cold upon these prospects, and cost her much and serious reflection, and some sleep.

Uncle Jacob, wily strategist, had another card up his sleeve, and was waiting. At this stage he played it. This card was young Charley Hall, son of the chief storekeeper in the next village, and full partner in his father's prosperous business. Charley Hall was invited, and came, and was deeply smitten. He came in his own buggy, which was new and shiny, and the aspect of it was not without influence upon Mary Lester. That buggy kept on coming, kept augmenting its influence, too. Mary presently recognized that her interest in her blacksmith was losing fervency. She wished he would notice it, too, for she had a kind enough heart, though it was a weak one in places; but he did not see it, he was serenely unaware that anything was happening. He was born loyal and steadfast, and was never expecting other people to be otherwise.

He was now come to the house on the errand heretofore mentioned. Mary admitted him, showed him to the parlor—where her uncle was waiting—and was turning from the door to go away, but he said appealingly,

"Don't go, Mary—stand by me."

Uncle Jacob, also, said,

"Set down, Mary, like enough it might int'rest you." So she remained.

There was an embarrassing silence; then after some halting and dry-swallowing, Hill got a start. He rambled along in a confused and humble and ineffectual way for a while, then the capitalist cut him short.

"It don't need so many words," he said, acidly, "the upshot of it is, you want the vandue put off, you want more time on the debt. Now then, it stands to reason you wouldn't come on such a business, without you've got grounds. What's the grounds? What you got to offer?"

It was a cold place for Hill's "grounds." He realized it; and the offer which he had come to make, and which had seemed rational, suddenly lost much of its sanity, and he found himself ashamed to put it into words. But those intense old eyes were on him and waiting; silence was less endurable than speech; he had nothing in stock to make words out of but that forlorn offer, so perforce he began upon it and blundered miserably along until the capitalist broke in once more with an interruption.

"Oh, I reckon that'll do!" he said, with a touch of sarcasm in tone and manner. "I git the idea. Gosh, what a layout! I'm to take the smithy, and give you time to work out the debt. I'm to collect what you earn, you having no gift to do it yourself. When the debt's paid, me and you to be partners in the business, and I to go on collecting. It's a noble layout, jest so; then on top of it you pile a gold mine, so to speak: I'm to have half of whatever's coming to you from South Carlina, *if* your partner ain't dead, *if* he collected anything, *if* the State didn't hog it—Great Scott, half partner in a basketful of *ifs*—is that it? And the main one left out, to-wit, namely, *if* your pard's gone back on his section's religion and going to play honest with a Yank!" He snapped his fingers, adding, "I wouldn't give *that* for the half nor the whole of that swag—understand *that?* No, sir, I decline—surprising as it may look!"

He got up and moved to the door. There he turned, and finished with this:

"Just a last word, now—with the bark on it. *The vandue goes on, to-morrow.* You're a well enough meaning young man, but you ain't ever going to make a living, you ain't ever going to see the day that you can feed a wife. But there's Mary; she can marry you if she wants to, but she'll never get a cent of *my* money!"

Then he disappeared. So did the color from Mary's face. The dreaded blow had fallen. She began to sob, hysterically. Hill flew to her side and took her hand, saying—

"Never mind his money, dear, I never loved you for that—"

She put him from her, still sobbing, and said—

"But *I* want the money; I'm so poor and dependent—just a slave, and I don't *want* to be a slave any more. I've loved you, but you can't *ask* me to—to—"

The young fellow was stunned. He stood aside, and looked down upon her, bewildered.

"Mary—Mary," he said, "do you mean that if I had money it would make a difference?"

She went on sobbing, but made no reply. Presently Hill moved toward the door; in it he turned and said, in an unsteady voice—

"Good-bye, Mary. I loved you dearly. This is a hard day for me."

When Mary heard the front door close, she said to herself, mournfully, "I am not very happy, now that it's done and ended, but—well, I have done the wise thing."

From the ambush of the window-shade she watched him drifting out of her life, and the melancholy droop of his figure smote her, made her heart sore, and she said, trying to forgive herself, trying to justify herself—

"Oh, dear, I *had* to!—I had to, or I wouldn't ever done it! Why *didn't* he have something put away—just enough for us to get along decently on, and hold our heads up. But—but—oh, well, I've done right, there wasn't any other way."

All the same, ten minutes later she was not so certain about it. She was beginning to waver. In another ten minutes she was saying—

"If Charley Hall doesn't come this very minute—"

But he did come. And she gave him her promise with a suddenness which greatly gratified him; for he could not know she was afraid that if she did not say yes on the instant she wouldn't ever say it.

Uncle Jacob came in presently and gave the pair his blessing, and was very happy. So was Charley Hall.

Then uncle Jacob retired, saying he would intrude again in a few minutes, and bring something nice. He kept his word. He brought three hundred dollars in bank bills, and gave the money to his niece and said it was his betrothal-gift and she could squander it in any way she liked—there would be "another hunk for the trosso."

It was many times more wealth than the girl had ever possessed before, and she could hardly cramp her thanks into words. The proud old gentleman took his leave again, and left her caressing the notes. Then her thoughts turned remorsefully to her debt-enslaved late sweetheart and a solacing thought came to her: she would make a vast sacrifice which might maybe appease and pacify her troubled conscience and bring it peace. There would be women and girls at the vendue—they always went to auctions, for the sake of the stir and excitement—she would go, too. And she would bid. She would spend her whole three hundred there, so that Tom Hill would be out of debt and have two hundred dollars to start again with. And her new sweetheart must be there, too—but not with her and not near her— they must not seem to be acting in concert. She frankly explained her idea and its purpose, and said he must bid against her and help run the things up. The young fellow was charmed with this mark of attention, this distinction; and he praised her generous spirit and said he would "blow in" three hundred on the scheme on his own account and "make a dandy thing of it."

Chapter 4

DURING THAT same afternoon the pair of tramps drifted into the village and spent two or three sociable hours in the company of the outcasts and loafers of the place—gathering information. They located the smithy, and when they rapped on the door of the humble dwelling-end of it at early candle-light they were not strangers to Hill's recent history but were well posted. They found Hill sitting with bowed head, forlorn and despondent. Without rising or speaking, he took up the bottle that held his candle, shaded his eyes with his hand, gave the visitors a searching and unwelcoming look—for only a moment—then sprang up, with their names on his lips, and threw his arms around their necks. It was a warm embrace and warmly returned, the candle taking part and setting fire to Samson's hair. But this was only a detail, and no one minded it.

"Now then," said Hill, "sit down—sit down, both of you, and let me look at you. Lord, it's so good to see you!"

"You knew me!" said Marsh, with dancing eyes; "I knew you would —I *said* it!"

"Knew you? *Knew* you?—and I've ached so to see you all this long time? Well, I should say so! And you knew me, too, didn't you, Jimmy? How could you?—I must be so changed."

"Tom, I'd know you stark naked and *painted!*" said Marsh; "I said so—said it to-day—didn't I, Billy?"

"Your very words; if it ain't so, I hope to go to—*say*, is that a heavenly side of bacon hanging up there?"

"It is, my child, and there's corn meal in the barrel, and coffee in the pot. Fire up on the stove, Billy, and put on the pot and the pan while I mix a pone. I've got an appetite myself, but I didn't know it a little while ago."

Supper was soon cooked and ready. It was dispatched with cordial relish, and seasoned with good talk over old times. In due course Hill said—

"Things have gone hard with me, Jimmy, and I can see that they've gone hard with you, too; but it's only because we weren't together. When we're together we're a team, but one of us is no good without the other."

"It's so, Tommy, and from this out we'll stick together, won't we?"

"That we will; and Billy with us. We'll tramp off somewhere and get credit and start a shop, and I'll make the money and you'll collect it; and Billy—"

"Billy can't go with us."

"Why can't he?"

"He has to go back home and take care of your grave. And then—"

"Say—do I smell something a person might make a hot whisky out of?"

"No, you don't Billy, but you will, pretty soon. Fire up on the pipes and make yourselves comfortable; I'll be back in a minute."

Hill went out, and the two tramps slapped each other on back and thigh in exultation, and Samson said it was all "just immense—makes the circus pale!"

Marsh agreed. "Splendid," he said, "it's splendidly romantic and dramatic."

"Well, *ain't* it, Brer Marsh! He's worth upwards of two thousand dollars—"

—"and thinks he hasn't a cent—"

—"letting on to go out and *buy* whisky! *Say*—what do you reckon he's going to put up the spout? Hat? Shirt? Which do you sup—"

" 'sh! he's coming."

It was his coat that was lacking. But he brought the whisky. He said—

"Now for a night!"

"So say we all of us!—hey, Marsh?"

"Indeed we do, Billy. We'll wet down the new firm—Hill, Marsh and Samson. One, two, three—"

"Drink!"

"Bumpers!"

The wassail proceeded, the common joy deepened and mellowed, there were old-time songs, there was laughter. When the whisky ran low, Marsh disappeared, and returned minus hat and coat,—hidden in a convenient place—but with a fresh bottle. Samson brought the next one, leaving his bundle outside with Marsh's discards. Hill protested, but his guests said they would not allow him to bear any but his proper share in wetting down the firm. Then he confided a secret to them, to explain and justify his not pawning his blacksmithing plant to further and properly boom and celebrate the formation of this promising new Trust; he said the plant wasn't his, now, he was to be sold out next day for a hundred dollars.

This revelation fell like a blight upon the hilarity of the tramps. It had that look, at any rate. They seemed so stunned by the disaster that Hill was sorry he had spoken of the matter; there was no hurry, it could have waited; now he had gone and spoiled the night, and all to no useful purpose. He started to say something of the sort, but Marsh put up his hand, as who should say, "keep still—let me think." A long and oppressive silence followed, then Marsh said, gravely—

"No more whisky to-night; put it away; this thing is serious." He walked the floor a while, thinking; then he said—

"I believe I see the way out. Wherever we go, we've got to have a plant. We'll bid this one in. How does that strike you?"

"We-ll," said Hill, hesitatingly, "it—why, it's a good idea, of course, but how are we going to bid it in without any money?"

"I'm coming to that. What are the terms of the sale?"

"Twenty dollars cash, the rest in three and six months."

"Good enough. All we want is that twenty dollars, the rest will take care of itself."

The hopefulness that had for a moment dawned in Hill's face passed out of it and he sighed and said—

"You see, the twenty dollars being an impossibility—"

"No, wait a minute; we'll see about that. What is the business worth, Tom?"

"A hundred and fifty dollars a month—if I could collect."

"Let me see your liabilities."

"A hundred and ninety-six dollars—here is the list."

"Goodness!" said Samson, despairingly; "Marsh, the Trust can't stand a load like that."

"It's heavy, certainly, but what of it? You wait a minute. Now the assets, Tom."

Hill smiled a dim smile and said—

"Bad debts! That's all; there's nothing else. Here is the list."

Marsh rapidly summed up the figures, and said—

"Why, man, it's nobby, it's noble! Nine hundred and forty-two dollars! I'll collect every cent of it. I tell you, this Trust is going to go!"

Hill's face lit up again, and he exclaimed—

"Jimmy, so help me I never thought of that! Of course the assets are as good as gold, with you to do the collecting—with me to do it they are only trash."

Then his face sobered again. Marsh noticed it.

"Is it the twenty dollars, Tom?"

"You've guessed it. The impossible twenty. It's a sixty-foot wall, Jimmy, with the promised land on the other side. We can't climb over it, nor tunnel under it, nor get around it. We are stuck—that's the amount of it."

"I don't believe it. We'll get to bed, now, and between this and morning I pledge you I'll hit on a plan."

Hill cheered up again. He said he regarded a pledge from that source as worth par. He turned in with the remark that he should have a sound sleep this time, and it would be the first for many nights. His lost sweetheart came and troubled his thoughts and grieved his heart for a little while, then she faded away and he began to snore with power.

"Brer Marsh?"

"Yes, Billy."

"It's panning out elegant, ain't it?"

"A1."

"What are you going to pretend about the twenty dollars? Going to turn out early and come back and pretend you've squeezed it out of them blatherskites that's been bilking him?"

"It's a good idea. I'll do it. Billy?"

"Go ahead."

"Who do you reckon are the noblest friends poor people have, and the best?"

Billy—after a careful spell of thinking—

"Billionaires?"

"Sho!"

"Who then?"

"Why, *other* poor people."

"No—do you mean it?"

"There's nothing truer in the world. *They* know how to feel for the unfortunate—they've *been* there. Look at the widow's mite; it tells the whole story. Billy, there's more money goes out in coppers every day from the poor *to* the poor, than is spent on them by the rich, twice over."

"B' George I never thought of it, but I reckon it's so."

"It's so, for certain. Look at Hill. Always poor, always in debt. And I know one of the reasons is, that he helps the other poor. And I know another thing—at least I think I do."

"What is it, Marsh?"

"That in their turn they help *him*. There are signs about that unprotected ninety-six dollars of indebtedness that indicate to me that those creditors are poor folk—widows, niggers, and that sort. Billy?"

"Here, and a-listening."

"When we get through with him he'll cash-in on that 96 right promptly, don't you think?"

"I go bail he will."

"Billy, what is going to be the gaudiest theatricality of the whole game?"

"I—well, I don't know, it's all so gilt-edged and red-hot and nobby. Tell me."

"You know the town talk: about his Mary; and about her rich uncle working all he knows how to break off the match because Tom's poor, and worry her into marrying that young Hall, who is worth thirty thousand dollars; and how she has stood her ground and is going to marry Tom, poverty and all, and get disinherited that very day?"

"Yes, I know, and it's splendid of her, and all that—but where does the dramatics come in?"

"Why, it's at the grand climax, of course—where Tom heaves his fortune into her lap before the whole crowd, and she is astonished, and grateful, and triumphant and gratified to death. Don't you see?"

There was silence—which indicated that Samson was disappointed. After a little he reluctantly brought out his criticism—

"Marsh, when you come to look at it from the stage-side, you know, trading off thirty thousand and a buggy for two thousand-odd and a blacksmith shop ain't a good place to turn on the lime-light. Get it?"

There was no response. Samson waited and listened. Gradually a fine and experienced treble snore rose out of the darkness and reinforced Hill's bass. Then Samson joined the band.

Chapter 5

SAMSON and Hill woke a little late in the morning. Marsh was up and gone. Samson explained: Marsh had planned a scheme for raising the twenty dollars, and had said, the last thing before going to sleep, that breakfast must not be delayed for him. What was the scheme? Samson did not know. At least he said he did not know.

Hill cooked, Samson set the table. They waited a reasonable time, then began on the meal. By and by Marsh came, but he was looking troubled and worried, and said he could not eat, he had no appetite. The remark meant disaster, and it took away what was left of the appetites of the two other members of the Trust. Marsh said—

"I see you have divined what has happened, boys, but don't give up yet; I will succeed, I certainly will, I give you my word. At least—at least I have hopes," he added, less fervently.

Hill gave him a grateful hand-shake, and tried to say the encouraging word, but he was not able to find a sincere one, and so forbore to venture a counterfeit. Samson sighed heavily, and rose and walked to the window and seemed to be crying. Marsh continued—

"Here is what I have raised—twelve dollars. I am awfully disappointed; I would have bet any amount on that scheme. But don't give up, I'll invent another. Let me walk the floor and think; don't disturb me."

He walked back and forth, and back and forth, for an hour, muttering, shaking his head, and clawing his hair, while the others sat still and suffered—Samson to keep from laughing, Hill to keep his heart from breaking, for it was frightfully precious time that was being expended on this difficult scheme. At last there was an interruption—a knock, and a wrinkled woman of sixty or seventy, with a kind face and an anxious mien came in. Without seeming to see the guests, she hastened to Hill and said, eagerly and anxiously—

"I have been away, I have just come back. I did not know about this. How much do you need, to save you; I will run about among our friends, and try to get it—I hope it is not too late."

Hill's eyes filled, and he said aloud—

"Only eight dollars; and I would take it from you in a minute, you unfailing friend, for I know, now, that I could pay it back soon, and all that I owe you besides."

"I am so thankful. I have brought six; two of it is from old Mat, and two from Irish Dennis—I met them on the way. There is time yet; I will find the rest. I will hurry, and—"

Marsh broke in with—

"Oh, generous soul, oh benefactor of a despairing man, fly! get one more dollar and bring it—I've struck the scheme that will fetch the other one!"

Both flew.

Hill was trembling with excitement. Samson ran and fell upon his neck, murmuring—

"Saved—the Trust is saved!"

"I do believe it, with all my heart I do," said Hill, gently unhitching from the embrace. "That good soul is a widow, and poor—the widow Foster; Mat is an old negro that whitewashes for a living; Dennis does odd jobs—when he can get them. Among them I owe twenty-eight dollars—this addition raises it to thirty-four. A body never had better friends, Billy."

"I reckon it's so. The poor we have with us always. Lucky, too. It's so's we can pull through when we're in a tight place, ain't it? I wish there was more of them; we could capitalise this Trust away up. *Say* —do you know, this is going to be one of the biggest things in the market?"

"Do you really believe it?"

"You wait till we launch it into Wall street—you'll see. Squat, and

I'll show you. Gimme that rag of wrapping paper—I've got a pencil."
He began to cipher, and Hill tried to show interest; but there were
noises from the smithy which indicated that an audience was beginning to assemble, and his nerves began to strain and flutter. He couldn't
keep from watching the door and praying for Marsh and the widow to
come with his fate. Minute after minute, Samson, absorbed in his
work, went ciphering eagerly on. Finally he looked up satisfied, and
said—

"Now then, there you are—all figured out! A hundred and fifty a
month is eighteen hundred a year. It's the interest on a capital of eighteen thousand, at ten per cent. Sell out half for nine thousand cash,
water the rest—barrels and barrels of it, you know—get up a combine
of all the smithies in the State—add water, more water, lakes of it,
rivers of it—set her afloat in Wall street, and she'll breed greenbacks
like—"

The door burst open and Marsh flung in a half dollar and was gone
again, saying he was hot on the trail of its mate.

The noises in the smithy were increasing. Hill got up and walked the
floor, pale and breathing hard; he could no longer listen to Samson,
who went enthusiastically on with his ever-growing greenback-factory.

But at the last moment, just as the first cries of the auctioneer rose
on the air, Marsh and the widow arrived, breathless, panting, and triumphant. The next moment the happy four were in the smithy.

The place was packed. Among the women sat Mary, looking dis-
traught and downcast; among the men sat young Hall. Everybody
glanced at Mary when Thomas Hill entered, and all noticed, with approval, and without surprise, that she gave him no welcome with her
eyes. It was custom for engaged girls to let on that they did not know
when a sweetheart was around.

The two tramps created great attention, also amusement. They were
immediately recognized, for the village had had glimpses of them the
day before, and been refreshed and delighted with their costumes, particularly with Marsh's, whose chaos of rags, patches, and quarrelsome
and implacable colors was a work of art which had been designed by
himself, and which fed to satisfaction his passion for startling and impressive effects. It had been his intention that whoso saw it should admire it and remember it. He was gratified to see, now, that part of this

intention had materialized. His face was beamy with smiling comradeship and good nature, and it suited his dramatic side to pretend that
he was just a trifle under the influence of gracious and benevolent stim-
ulants. This grieved Hill a little, and seemed an impolitic addition to
his friend's effects, in the circumstances, but he was too loyal to let any
see that he had noticed it. Marsh whispered to Samson—

"Find a place at a distance from me. Don't bid till I bid; then follow
me and raise me, every time, till we get the anvil. The anvil's the main
thing, you know."

Plenty of room was made for the tramps; the people squeezed apart
and gave them more than they needed, but not in sign of welcome; indeed they made it plain that their proximity was not wanted. Marsh
had brought his uncanny telescope-valise with him, and kept it in his
lap when he seated himself. The widow found a seat beside Mary, who
whispered to her—

"I am so glad. I want to bid it in for him, and I haven't the courage
before so many. You must bid for me."

The auctioneer had been praising the anvil humorously, but had
stopped to admire Marsh's outfit; he resumed, now—

"As I was saying, this anvil's a daisy. The only one of the kind. Make
me an offer, gentlemen. Hair-spring steel—came over with Columbus
—no sign of decay, pure as bell-metal, sweet as a flute—listen!" He gave
it a bang with the sledge. "Do you hear that? Gimme a bid. How much
am I offered, gentlemen? How—"

"Five dollars."

It was Harvey, the cross-roads smith.

"Five I'm offered. Five—five—going at five; six, do I hear?"

"Six!"

It was Jenkins, the Roopville smith.

"Six—six—going at six—this noble anvil, I'm ashamed!—going at—"

"Seven!"

From Collins, the Bloomfield smith.

For a time, these were the only bidders. A dollar at a bid they ran the
offers up to nine dollars; then at half a dollar they carried the rise up
to thirteen. That seemed to end the matter. The auctioneer turned on
more steam, and tried hard for a further raise, but presently gave it up
as a waste of time, and began on the familiar winding-up formula—

"Going! Once—twice—three times and—"

"Fifteen dollars!"

It was Charley Hall. It made a splendid surprise, and the house said to itself, "Why, what's the matter *now*? Does he want to help the winning rival out of his trouble?" The auctioneer's spirits revived.

"*Thank* you, sir, thank you—nobly done, sir, nobly! Fifteen—fifteen —going at fifteen—speak up, gentlemen, it's the chance of your life. Going at fif—"

"Raise him ten," whispered Mary.

—"teen—going at—"

"Twenty-five!"

It was another surprise. The house said to itself, "*Now* what's happened? is the widow going into the business?" The auctioneer shouted compliments, banged the anvil, played all the tricks of his trade for adding heat to a growing excitement—and meantime Mary whispered to the widow, "Go on—double his bids right along, until he stops."

"Going—going—twenty-five, twenty-five—it's a great day!—give us another lift!—twen-ty five, twen—"

In her excitement, the widow doubled her own bid, crying out— "Fifty!"

The house sent up a roar, long-drawn and powerful, and through the fog of it broke Charley Hall's clear voice—

"A hundred!"

"Im-mense! It's a wonderful day! Going—going—one hundred dol—"

"*Two* hundred!" from the widow.

"Three!" from Hall, who rose in his place, excited—

"*Six* hundred!" and the widow rose, and the house with her, storming its applause. It never occurred to anybody that this bid would bankrupt the widow, the house thought of nothing but the grand time it was having. Slowly it sank panting into its seat, and out of the expiring din the auctioneer's submerged voice began to rise to a hearing once more—

"Six—hundred—dollars! for the imperialest anvil that ever electrified the world—and worth every cent of it! Six hundred—going, going—do I hear seven? Seven am I bid? Going, going, at six—do I hear fifty? Six hundred, ladies and gentlemen—*one* more lift, just one more, *only* one

—do I hear twenty-five? Going—going—last call! One—two—three—
and g—"

"*Nine* hundred, b' George!"

It was Marsh; who sat, finely dramatic, with head up and arms folded
across his breast above his valise. The house and the auctioneer gazed
a moment, then an avalanche of derisive laughter swept the place.
Presently the noise died down, and the auctioneer began a little speech,
in his best vein—

"My friends and fellow-citizens, I need hardly say that this is the
proudest moment of my life, and the most memorable. In concluding
my duties, and in turning over this henceforth forever-renowned anvil
to its fair purchaser, I—"

"I have outbid her," observed Marsh, politely; "go on with the
auction."

The auctioneer withdrew his professional smile, and said with chill
severity—

"Young man, you are not quite at yourself, and your behavior is
unbecoming. Do not carry your joke further; the time is not suitable, it
cannot be permitted."

Many were sorry for Marsh, and this was a gratification to him—it
made him a centre of attraction. He was happy, and he answered gall
with sweetness:

"Go on with the show," he said, blandly. "The other gentleman
yonder" (Samson—the audience tittered) "and I are here for business;
it isn't for fun. He thinks he wants this anvil, I think I want it. Now
then, I can tell him one thing" (reaching into his valise) "if he gets it
he'll *grub* for it, and don't you forget it!" He pulled out a thousand-
dollar government bond, and passed it along. "Didn't I bid nine hundred? Charge it up to that piece of government paper, and go on with
the show!"

In awe and silence the villagers passed the imposing document from
hand to hand, reverently gazing upon it and lingering over it as it
moved upon its course. The auctioneer received it, opened it, verified
its genuineness, stared wonderingly upon it a while, then laid it tenderly down and said—

"Well—this whole occasion is more like a dream than anything I've
ever struck in the daytime since I was born. It's all just astonishers and

surprises straight along from the start, and you never know where the lightning's going to hit next. I apologise sir—and *honest.*"

"All right, and no harm done, auctioneer—go right ahead."

"With the greatest pleasure in the world. Nine hundred—nine, going at nine, do I hear ten?—*going* at nine, do I hear ten—nine, do I hear the—"

"Thousand!" and Samson pulled a bond from his bosom and held it up.

"Five hundred!" from Marsh, before the auctioneer could speak.

"See it and raise you five!"

"*Three* thousand!" shouted Marsh. "Come on—now is your time, if you want the anvil!"

"But I'm out of bonds; I only had two, and so are you!" cried Samson.

"Nothing of the kind, I was fooling! Go on, auctioneer, I raise it to five thousand!"

"Five thousand—five, five—man, are you in earnest?"

"Go on, I tell you, I'm only just getting started. Make it ten!"

"Ten thousand dollars for the anvil—going, going, at ten thous—"

Marsh was on his feet, now, excited, gesticulating, bidding against himself with all his might, the auctioneer was going mad, the house was following suit.

"Ten thousand, ladies and gentlemen—going, going—will the gentleman say—"

"Yes! Fifty thousand—go it, auctioneer, turn yourself loose!"

"Fifty, fifty—it's a wonderful day!—going, going at fif—"

"Hundred thousand!"

"Hundred! going at a hundred, the great High-yu-muckamuck-and-Whoopjamboree of all the anvils!—going, going at a hun—"

"Two hundred thousand!"

"Two hun—"

"Three! Four! Five! *Six* hundred thousand, and last bid—knock her down, auctioneer, and here's your mud!"

He unscooped his valise and emptied the bonds in a pile on the floor, then broke into a speech, and the audience hushed its clamorings to listen:

"It has all the look of a joke and a burlesque," he said, "but at bot-

tom it is quite sober earnest, as you shall see. The other gentleman
yonder" (Samson—but the reference provoked no smile) "will pass to
me the two bonds I lent him for the occasion—there, now they are
where they belong, with the others. Let me tell you a little tale. My
name is James Marsh. Ah—I see by your faces that you have heard it
before. That indicates that Thomas Hill has told you the first half of
the tale already; very well, I will cut short and tell only the sequel—
the half which neither you nor he knows about.

"When he left for the North, I went to work collecting, and had
very good luck indeed, all things considered. As fast as I scraped the
money in, I put it to work earning its living, in this and that and the
other speculative way; and if I do say it myself, I made things hum.
By and by came the blockade, and I was on hand and ready. Only in a
small way, true, but I was *there* just the same. It was just a gamble—
that's all it was—but I didn't like it any the less on that account.

"Sometimes I lost, sometimes I won, but I won oftener than I lost.
Every now and then I got a scare, on Tom Hill's account, and had a
bad night and a good deal of floor-walking, these being occasions when
I was putting up the firm's whole capital on a single throw; but at last
I found a way to shut down on those worries and have peace. It was a
pretty thin device, but it worked. That device was, to get my partner's
consent, *first*, when I was proposing to bet the whole capital. How did
I manage it—and him away up North? By flipping up a copper: heads,
Tom is willing, tails he isn't. (*Laughter.*) It makes you laugh, and certainly it *was* pretty thin, but it worked. And I will say this for myself:
whenever it went tails I was loyal to the arrangement; I said, to myself,
'I think Tom's judgment is wrong, this time, but it's his right, and I'll
not bet'—and I didn't. (*Applause.*) I didn't care what the temptation
was, I always played square with him, every time. Here is that old copper; I saved it for him, and I can pass it along to him, now, without a
blush, for it's like himself—there isn't a stain on it. (*Great applause.*)

"Cotton was pretty kind to us. But by and by I concluded to go out
of business, and I did. I've been out ever since, but I've kept the firm's
capital well and safely placed. A month or two ago the mails resumed,
and I wrote Tom Hill and reported results, but my letter came back to
South Carolina—his address wasn't known. So I came North to hunt
him up, and I've found him.

"I found out, before I got here, that he was going to be sold out to-day and hadn't a cent. So for fun I came as a tramp, and said to myself, 'I know him; he'll not go back on me on account of my clothes; if I let on to be thirsty he'll pawn his coat for a bottle'—and that is what he did, last night! (*Great applause.*)

"The tale is done. This anvil belongs to him. I've bought it for him with his own half of the money—six hundred thousand dollars in government bonds, gold 7 per cents—and here they lie!"

The applause burst upon him, wave after wave, and he uncovered and stood bowing, smiling, and entirely happy, for that was the kind of bath his dramatic soul delighted in. By and by when the tumult was dying down, cries arose, of—

"Hill! Hill! Speech, speech!"

Hill got up, enthusiastically welcomed, and stood a while, embarrassed, and strongly moved; then he got partial command of his voice, and said:

"I am not a speaker. I can't make a speech, but I ask you to say I was always loyal to him. You will bear me out in it—I always said I knew *one* Southerner that would pay his debts if he could, and now you see for yourselves. And I've known others, and said so, but you wouldn't believe me; but now you will."

The response to his simple little speech was prompt and cordial, and he sat down a successful orator.

There was one other speech, but it was made later in the day, and in private. Uncle Jacob made it to Mary. He said:

"You've been a dam fool. You always was!"

NOTE. Sober history hardly contains a more beautiful incident than the gracious and enduring friendship which is the basis of this little tale. A few persons—a very few, for the episode is not widely known—will recognize in *Thomas Hill*, Daniel Hand of New England, and in *James Marsh*, George W. Williams of South Carolina. I could have followed history, but have preferred to follow, instead, tradition, because of certain effective little details which it has gathered and added to the actualities in the course of its travels from mouth to mouth in New England in the past thirty-nine years. Tradition makes Hand a wandering and unlucky blacksmith who keeps pure in his heart and

loyally upon his tongue his faith in his Southern friend, defending his
probity against all scoffers and doubters; it makes Williams come
North after the five years of separation caused by the war, and track
Hand from village to village, month after month, until he finds him
at last bankrupt in a remote hamlet and about to be sold out for a
trifling debt; it makes him appear at the auction just at the right moment with a certified check for $600,000, drawn to Hand's order, which
he shows to him and says, "It's all yours, old man—now watch me
raise them out!"

Twenty-three years afterward (this is history) Mr. Hand established
the "Daniel Hand Educational Fund for Colored People," and endowed it with interest-bearing securities to nearly the amount of eleven
hundred thousand dollars. He has been dead many years, but his fund
still lives, and its good work goes on. Its income for 1902 was $66,636,
and in the same year it spent upon the cause in the South $66,577.
(From the Official Report.)

Since writing the above tale a friend in America has procured for me
a "Sketch of the Life of Daniel Hand," prepared by Mr. George A.
Wilcox, of Detroit, for the *Magazine of American History*, and from
it I quote this eloquent passage:

"Rarely is there an instance of more implicit mutual commercial
faith and confidence than is shown in these transactions; a faith preceding, living through and surviving a war that swept men and fortunes
away like chaff, yet in this instance survived to point the moral that
honesty and honor are not sectional but national American traits."

Newhouse's Jew Story

(Late 1890s)

CLEMENS saw many gamblers during his Mississippi piloting years, from 1857 to 1861, and must also have heard many stories about them. This tale is offered as one he had "heard . . . first in 1860." In Chapter 36 of *Life on the Mississippi* he wrote of an attempt of riverboat gamblers to cheat a wealthy cattleman. In that version of the incident, the supposed rancher proved to be another gambler who turned the tables on his would-be victimizers; thus the moral responsibility of the observer—Clemens—was not put to the test as is that of the Jew in "Newhouse's Jew Story." The courage, humanity, and general superiority shown by the Jew, only briefly treated in this narrative, are more fully presented in "Randall's Jew Story."

The manuscript pages are numbered 10–19, and the story may be a discarded portion of *Following the Equator*, which was written between October 1896 and May 1897. The paper is the same as that used in "The Enchanted Sea-Wilderness" (1897).

Newhouse's Jew Story

THERE WAS nothing funny about the story, but that is no matter, it had value, nevertheless. I heard it first in 1860.

I belonged on board the *Alonzo Child* at that time, and one trip we had an ancient pilot along—George Newhouse—who had been out of employment a year or two, because of his age and infirmities, and he was allowing himself a pleasure trip to New Orleans. He used to stand part of a watch at the wheel every day for recreation and practice. When he was taking his trick one day, a passenger came into the pilot house and began to be sociable, and presently made a scurrilous general remark about Jews. Mr. Newhouse turned him out of the place. I asked him what he did it for, and he said it had been fifteen years since he would allow Jews to be abused where he was. This, he said, was for the sake of one Jew, in memory of one Jew. And then his story came out.

The date of it was 1845—that old time of much poker and high gambling on the boats. The professional card-sharp was always in evidence; he was always on hand to fleece the green passenger. Every officer on the boat knew the members of the tribe by sight, and knew their histories. The boat was glad to have these people—at least the quiet and peaceable ones—for gamblers were good bar-customers. There were two or three desperadoes among the gamblers, and their presence was tolerated because the captain and his officers preferred not to get

into trouble with them. The worst of these desperadoes was a gentle-
manlike man named Jackson. He was cruel by nature, and unforgiving.
The average professional did not mind being abused a little by the beg-
gared loser in the game; but not so, Jackson. Jackson's preference was
settlement by duel; no fisticuffs, no vulgar row, but a duel. And not a
duel where he was the challenger, but where he could force that office
upon the other man and so be able to name the weapons himself. He
always named bowie-knives. As a rule, that settled it; the meeting was
declined; a particularly abject apology was then required; and it was
furnished, before all the on-lookers. Few men like to face a bowie-knife.
Now and then at long intervals, a man accepted the terms. And got
killed.

One day, coming off watch, Mr. Newhouse met the mud-clerk on
the boiler-deck, and the mud-clerk told him that Jackson was aboard,
and was in a game with old Mr. Mason, the rich Louisiana planter, and
was robbing him. A young Jew stood near, and he asked if this was the
notorious Jackson of the bowie-knife—the man who forced challenges
out of dissatisfied people by getting a deadly insult in, himself, before
the other man had time to do it. Yes, this was the one, the mud-clerk
answered, and the young Jew turned away and said he would go in the
social hall and have a look at him. The mud-clerk told Mr. Newhouse
that Jackson had won all of Mr. Mason's ready money and two slaves,
man-servant and maid-servant, and was gambling his daughter's maid
away, now. This latter maid was almost white, and was young and
beautiful. She had been reared in the house with her young mistress,
and had been her playmate and companion as well as servant, from
the beginning.

Mr. Newhouse went into the social hall, and found the passengers
packed together around the gaming table, holding their breath for interest. The maid was standing there crying. The gambler had just won
her, and was chewing his toothpick nonchalantly and gazing across the
table in an amused way at the white-headed planter, who was begging
him to let him have the girl back and take his cheque for her value.
The gambler went on chewing his toothpick contentedly, and made no
reply. Then there was a stir in the crowd, and the young mistress came
flying down the long cabin with her hair down her back and her tears
flowing, a young thing not above eighteen or maybe twenty; and as the

crowd fell apart she swept through and stopped before the gambler and
began to plead wildly and pathetically for the maid, saying she was the
same to her as a sister, and she could not live without her, she could not
bear to part with her, they had never been separated in their lives, and
he *must* have pity, God would bless him forever, and she would too,
and he should have twice her value in money, and wouldn't he please,
oh, *please*—

The gambler cut her prayer short and said, rudely—

"The wench is mine and money can't buy her."

The girl's face flushed at the affront, and she said—

"Coward! to insult me, who cannot defend myself."

An ugly light came into Jackson's eyes, and he spoke across to old
Mr. Mason and said, "I can't punish a child for that, but I will slap
your face for it," and was just going to do it when that young Jew
jumped for him and hit him on the mouth with the back of his hand,
and the crowd gave him cheer. Jackson's voice shook with anger when
he said—

"Do you know the price of that? What did you do it for?"

"Because I know your game. You wanted to make him challenge
you, and then apologize before everybody when you named the weapons, or go ashore and get himself butchered. What are you going to
do about it?"

"I know what *you* are going to do about it. You are going to fight
me."

"Good. It is pistols this time. Will somebody ask the captain to
land the boat?"

Twenty people rushed to do it; one would have been enough. The
duellists chose a second apiece and went ashore, and disappeared in the
woods. Pistol shots were heard, presently. "Then," said Mr. Newhouse,
"three of the men came aboard again, and we backed out and went on
down the river."

He stopped there, and began to hum a tune to himself. I waited a
little, then asked—

"Which one did you leave ashore?"

He finished the tune, then winked a satisfied wink, and said—

"Well, it wasn't the Jew."

Randall's Jew Story

(1890s)

THE JEWS had appealed to Clemens' imagination from the time that he had attended Dawson's school in Hannibal. He later recalled, "In that school were the first Jews I had ever seen. It took me a good while to get over the awe of it. To my fancy they were clothed invisibly in the damp and cobwebby mold of antiquity. They carried me back to Egypt, and in imagination I moved among the Pharaohs and all the shadowy celebrities of that remote age."[1] He credited the Jews for generosity to others: "The Jew has always been benevolent. Suffering can always move a Jew's heart and tax his pocket to the limit."[2] In "To the Editor of the American Hebrew" (written in 1889 or 1890; see Appendix A), Clemens examined the basis of anti-Jewish prejudice and stressed the Jew's great qualities, as he did again in his essay "Concerning the Jews" (1898). This story largely avoids the patronizing tone, the didacticism, and the simplistic analysis of social attitudes that reduce the effectiveness of Clemens' essays on the topic.

Clemens used the paper of the manuscript in his correspondence in 1894, but he continued to use the ink until 1898, when, moreover, his interest in Jews was still strong. Thus, the work cannot be dated more precisely than Paine's "90's." Mark Twain left the manuscript untitled.

---

[1] MTA 2:218.
[2] MTA 2:294.

Randall's Jew Story

Hath not a Jew eyes? hath not a Jew hands, organs, dimensions, senses, affections, passions? fed with the same food, hurt with the same weapons, subject to the same diseases, healed by the same means, warmed and cooled by the same winter and summer as a Christian is? If you prick us do we not bleed? if you tickle us do we not laugh? if you poison us do we not die?
—*Merchant of Venice.*

It was a group of elderly gentlemen. The talk had been running along in an intemperate way for some little time. The subject was a heating one—the Jews. Clearly the Jew was well hated there. Finally old Mr. Randall, president of the Farmers' Bank, began to speak.

You have all known me a great many years, he said, but none of you has ever heard me say an ill word about the Jews when I could think of a good one in place of it—and I always could. I have said the good word and suppressed the ill one for forty-four years, now; and I've done it for the sake of a Jew that I knew once, and for the sake of a thing which he did. I want to tell you about that thing. Before it happened I wasn't able to see any good thing in the Jews and didn't believe there was any good thing in them to see.

284

It was in 1850. I was a brisk young man then, flying around trying to get a start in the world. I was a Marylander, and naturally full of variegated southern prides and self-complacencies and aristocratic notions, and all that sort of thing, and I was feeling fine and ambitious and romantic, for I was on my first trip out into the big world. I was a long way from home, now—away down the Mississippi, passenger on a steamboat bound for New Orleans.

Among the passengers was a nigger-trader, who was also a professional gambler in his off hours, and a desperado when occasion offered. I avoided his society of course. Then there was a young Jew—Rosenthal —handsome, courteous, intelligent, alert, good-hearted, but a Jew; so, naturally I kept away from him, too. Then there was a courtly old Virginian planter—Fairfax—plenty good enough to associate with me, but as he didn't offer any advances we remained apart. He had a beautiful daughter, a lovely young thing, sweet and winning. And she had a maid,—Judith—who was almost as white and pretty as she was herself. These two girls had been reared together from the cradle; and although Judith had always been a servant and a slave, she and her mistress were about as affectionate toward each other as sisters.

By and by the nigger-trader—Hackett—got old Mr. Fairfax into a game of poker one night, to the surprise and distress of such of the passengers as were still up. This was about eleven o'clock. Luck favored the trader, straight along; but the more money the simple old planter lost the more eager and excited and infatuated he became. The bystanders looked on absorbed but saying nothing. Their sympathies were with the planter, but they did not know how to interfere, or maybe did not want to risk it. Finally that young Jew asked Mr. Fairfax to let him take his place "until the luck should turn." Hackett gave him a vicious look and said:

"Look here, young fellow, I'll thank you to keep yourself to yourself, and not meddle where you hain't got any business."

"Excuse me, but it *is* my business."

"It is, is it? *How* is it?"

"It's my business and it's anybody's business to interfere when an honest man is being robbed."

The trader's face flushed, and he said, angrily:

"Leave the place! I'll give you just half a minute to take yourself out of danger."

The Jew said, mockingly:

"Thanks—many thanks. With your permission I will remain and sample the danger."

The group of onlookers applauded, and the trader looked uncomfortable. He muttered a curse or two, and said:

"Stay as long as you want to. The thing'll keep. You'll settle with me in the morning"—and he went on with the game.

The bystanders ventured a derisive laugh, but the Jew merely nodded his satisfaction with the trader's proposal.

About half past three o'clock there was a scene. Each player drew one card, and the betting began—with serene confidence on the part of the trader; with confidence but not serenity on the part of the planter, whose tones were hoarse and low, and whose breath came and went in gasps:

"Fifty."

"I see it and go you a hundred better."

"Two hundred better."

"Three hundred better."

And so on, the dozen spectators pressing around the players, all of them tense and excited, but no one speaking. Finally the planter pushed a bundle of notes to the pile on the table and said wearily:

"It's the last I've got."

The trader's face lit victoriously, as he said:

"I raise you twelve hundred!"

The planter slumped back in his chair with a sort of groan. The trader smiled a smile of deep contentment, and reached for the stakes.

"Wait! Give me one more chance, for God's sake. Let me put up my girl Judith at twelve hundred and call you."

"Done! What have you got?"

"Four kings."

The trader laid down four aces and gathered in his spoil; then he said:

"The girl must be delivered now—on the spot."

The old planter struggled feebly to his feet, moaning, and muttering

"Ah, my God, what have I done, what have I done!" and wandered away. All stood mute; no one thought of anything to say, but all pitied that old man. Presently he brought the slave girl, and she was crying and sobbing; and she looked timidly from face to face, as if hoping she might in her extremity find a friend and savior there. It was a pitiful thing to see. The trader took her by the wrist, saying "You will come with me, wench—you have a new master, now"—and tried to drag her away, she holding back and crying. The Jew said, as if to himself:

"It is inhuman. By God it is fiendish. The man has no heart in his body."

At this moment that young white girl burst among us like an angel out of heaven, and flung herself upon the other girl, crying passionately and winding her arms about her in a clinging embrace, and pouring out endearing names upon her, and saying she should *not* be taken away, she should *not* be torn from her home, she should *not* suffer this shame, this indignity; and oh, oh, oh, was there *nobody* to help, was there *nobody* to do anything?—and then *she* looked around, begging and pleading, just as the other had done.

Then the Jew said again, as if to himself, "It is enough to break a person's heart—it is a shame that such a thing can be." Then he said to the poor old distressed planter:

"It is a bad business, but do not trouble about it. It can be made all right. I will buy the girl back and you can pay me another time, when it is convenient."

Then they raised a cheer, the bystanders! And the young lady turned her thankful eyes upon him and was going to put her thankfulness into words, but before she could begin the trader fired up and shouted:

"Oh, you had your turn a while back, young man, and you thought you came out of it in great style, didn't you! But it's my turn, this time. Let's *see* you buy her back."

The lights burned dim, now; the day was breaking. The Jew was pale; well, he looked gray in that light; pale and gray; and it was from good wholesome anger, as it seemed to me. But he was a self-contained fellow. He didn't raise his voice or make any gestures. What he said he said in a persuasive way:

"Yes, it was my turn, and perhaps I didn't make the best use of it;

but that was between you and me and can be settled in another way—
you won't let it prejudice the case of these others, who have not done
you any harm or wanted to. Come, be fair; let the girl stay where she
belongs; I will pay you the twelve hundred dollars."

"N-*no*, sir!"—and the trader laughed at the young fellow. But the
Jew was not disturbed. He kept his temper down, and said:

"I will give you fifteen hundred."

The crowd cheered—it was a crowd by this time, for the passengers
were flocking to the spot from everywhere down the long cabin, some
of the male part of it putting their last things on as they came.

"Come—say you'll take fifteen hundred."

"No, I *won't*. And that's the word with the bark on it."

Then the Jew took a couple of steps and stood in front of the trader,
and said:

"I've started in to get the girl back, and I will not fail. I've offered
money twice, now I will offer something else. You shall have choice of
arms, by virtue of—this!"

And he hit the trader a sounding blow on the mouth with the back
of his hand. Then he turned, and said:

"Gentlemen, who of you will be my second?"

They all jumped for the chance, but I was in ahead. And they
cheered that young Jew, and kept on cheering him till you would have
thought it would raise the roof. The boat was landed straight off, and
we four went ashore and entered the woods—the principals and their
two seconds. It was a brief matter. There was a couple of sharp reports,
then silence.

When the boat backed out and started away, we were all aboard
again—except the nigger-trader. The slave girl was all right, now, and
safe; for there was no bill of sale to tell tales; and the dead trader's
heirs, if there were any, would not get any information out of our
passengers.

Now there are two or three things about that transaction which are
fine, as I look at it. All those men present there, felt a deep pity for that
young slave girl and a sincere desire to save her; but the Jew went further—he *materialized* his pity—put up his money to try to save her; he
had a bigger heart than those others. There was one other way left, to

save the girl, but only the Jew was bright enough to think of it—he had the better head, you see. To kill the trader would leave everything as it was before the poker-game; so it was a neat idea to spring a duel on that fellow. If the others had thought of that plan, would they have materialized it? Would they have risked their lives on it? Well, the Jew did it. So he held over those others in pluck you see. If he had killed his man in a mere fight, the courts would have taken the matter up; but in those days he could kill him in a duel and go free. He was smart—smart all around—perfectly level-headed and in his right mind all the time, you see—a very superior man. And the finest thing of all was his risking his life out of pure humanity on such unequal terms: his life—a man's life—against a mere animal's life, a mere brute's life—for nobody in the South considered a nigger-trader a man.

In my opinion—said Mr. Randall in conclusion—he was a man; an all-around man; a man cast in a large mould; and for his sake, and in memory of that thing which he did, I have weighed his people ever since in scales which are not loaded.

Mock Marriage

(Early 1900s)

THE IDEA behind this unfinished, lightly satirical romance is one that is more somberly presented in some of the other selections in this volume: people cannot rely on an unavailing providence but must help themselves and each other. The practical Minna labels as "twaddle!" the pious notion that a "seeming calamity may be good fortune in disguise" and initiates action to avert disaster and ensure a happy result. The last paragraph brings in as a kind of afterthought another human force that is seen to be working to the advantage of the young lovers—the telepathic power of their unconscious minds. Mental telegraphy, as he called it, had long been of particular interest to Clemens. The title has been supplied in this edition; Paine wrote "Mock Marriage Story" on the typescript and dated the piece 1903. Mark Twain was using the paper of the manuscript between 1900 and 1905 and the typescript paper by 1902.

Mock Marriage

I T WAS the most ingenious scheme the Four Hundred had ever
invented. It was so original, indeed, that no one outside that Reservation believed it *was* an invention of the Four Hundred. The office of
the scheme was, to raise $2,000 for one of the F. H.'s numerous chari-
ties, the Decayed Ladies' Retreat. The tickets—as usual—were limited
to 400. The price—as usual—was $50 per ticket. The cash result would
be—as usual—$20,000. The ball and supper, and certain other neces-
saries would cost—as usual—$18,000. Thus—as usual—the $2,000 for
the charity was safe and certain the moment the Reservation heard of
the project.

The ingenious new scheme had an attractive title—"the Multiplex
Mock Marriage"—and was booked for the 17th of the month; scene of
it, the state drawingroom of the Vanastordam palace. All unmarried
ticket-holders, male and female, were to come in mask and domino.
Out of these, 13 grooms and 13 brides would be chosen by lot, for the
mock marriages. The men would draw lots from a vase containing the
first 13 letters of the alphabet, and a number of blanks; the girls would
draw from a vase containing the rest of the alphabet, (beginning with
N), and a lot of blanks. The man drawing A would be married to the
girl drawing N; B to the girl drawing O; C to the girl drawing P, and so
on. The losing lots were gold rings set with a single diamond, the win-

291

ning ones were gold rings bearing a letter of the alphabet formed of small emeralds set in a crust of diamonds.

Being masked, the marrying couples would not know each other. After the first dance, the fun would begin. The man with the A ring would be called, and must stand forth; his bride with the N ring would be called, and must step out and stand by him and be married; then they would separate at once and mingle with the crowd. This procedure would be followed, couple by couple till the thirteen lots were all wedded and tallied off. A dance would follow, then the married couples would form in line, and at the word of command remove their masks. It was certain that there would be a sufficiency of grotesque mismatings revealed to furnish a quality of fun that would come handsomely within the limitations of the Four Hundred's sense of humor. The second dance would be a waltz, and only the 13 couples would perform in it. After that, the ball would proceed upon the usual terms.

It was a great scheme, and raised the dead. For once the Reservation was excited. During several weeks it could talk of nothing but the coming event. It even forgot its French, and did its talking in English. When the memorable night arrived there was a crush at the Vanastordam palace, and the scene under the mellow moonlight of the veiled electrics was spectacular and beautiful, and it had a touch of novelty besides; for, drifting in and out and hither and thither through the sea of rich color and flashing jewels, were masked black forms to the number of nearly a hundred—candidates for mock matrimony.

By and by the music struck up "Let each now choose," etc., and this was a signal. The masked persons formed up in two lines—the males on one side, the other sex on the other—and down between were borne the vases. In a few minutes the lots had been drawn—twenty-six winners, and sixty or seventy blanks. Next, to an accompaniment of gay music the mock clergyman entered, with his acolytes and stalactites, and uttered the order—

"Let A advance to the altar."

A stepped forward and stood waiting.

"Let N, his bride, advance."

She stepped forward and stood by A. The usual marriage service followed. At the words "With this ring I thee wed," A put his ring upon N's finger, and N placed hers upon his finger. The couple were duly pronounced man and wife; then they went apart and were swallowed up in the crowd.

B and O were called; then C and P; then D and Q; and so on. In due course the 13 couples were disposed of and distributed among the throng. Then came the command—

"Form for the waltz! After which, the 13 happy couples will form up in line and unmask."

"Wait!" cried a voice. "Now is the time for the cream of the joke. And do you know what the cream of the joke is? The cream of the joke is, that by the laws of the State of New York these thirteen mock marriages are not mock ones at all, but the genuine simon-pure thing, and sound as a nut!"

It made an immense sensation. The house stood dumb and pale for as much as half a minute; then broke out a buzz of whispered inquiries that swept the place like a breeze—inquiries which always brought the answer, "It's perfectly true—why didn't the managers think of that?" Within five minutes every mock-married person had fled the palace and left no sign; within another five the rest of the assemblage had begun to stream in a panic from the doors. The collapse was complete; the memory of it survives unto this day.

Chapter 2

THE AFTER-FORTUNES of twelve of the married couples we shall not at present inquire into, but will limit ourselves to a consideration of those of the remaining couple—young Schuyler van Bleecker and his sweet and beautiful little wife Edith Depuyster-Brevoort.

At midnight Edith's parents were still up, and still talking. It was storming outside but they were not conscious of it in their luxurious surroundings, and besides, the matter in hand was of profound interest to them. Also it was a very private matter; so private, indeed, that Colonel Depuyster-Brevoort chunked up the wood fire and replenished his toddy himself, instead of ringing for a servant to do these things for him. A fine old gentleman he was; tall, slender, handsome, with a bearing part courtly, part military, a shapely head, intellectual face, silver moustache and hair, and a pronounced air of distinction. His wife was a proper match for him; beautiful with the beauty of age, aristocratic in mien and carriage, a Dowager Duchess to all appearance. The Colonel was finishing a remark—

"And so I think there could not be a better match."

"Perhaps so. It is good blood, the van Bleecker strain."

"Good on both sides. His mother was a Schuyler."

"Yes, that is true. As concerns religion—"

"That is satisfactory also. Dutch Reformed. And he lives it. Lives it as his forefathers lived it. His five years abroad have not weakened his principles; he is sternly truthful and conscientious, and nothing can swerve him a hair's breadth from a duty, whether it be a large one or a small one."

"It is as if you were describing Edith, Derrick."

"You may well say it, Louise; he is exactly like her in these regards."

The old madame reflected a while, then said—

"In his family, religion and character I find no blemish, and I realize that these are three of the main things. But without the fourth he is not complete, and not the husband for our child, Derrick."

"Means?"

The Dowager nodded assent.

"I—I will not deceive you, Louise. There he is deficient."

"I was afraid of it, and am sorry, for I do find myself leaning toward him, after what you have said—I confess it. For in the other ways he is perfect—ideally perfect. I wish—"

She did not finish, but dropped into a reverie, and sat unconsciously clasping and unclasping the white hand which lay upon her knee. The Colonel rose and made a few turns up and down the room, silent and thinking, then sighed and resumed his seat. Presently he said with a note of appeal in his voice—

"But Louise, could we ever hope to find so many of the essentials in another? Surely we cannot. Is not this a case where, for once, poverty—"

"Ah, you have voiced the very thought that was in my mind, Derrick. We ought, we *must* find a way to—to— Tell me—what is his income? I can bear it."

The Colonel hesitated, and for a moment hope brightened his eye; then he shook his head and said—

"If I must confess it, the truth is, he has none."

"None, Derrick?—none? Oh, don't say that."

"Indeed, it is next to that. It is not more than a quarter of a million a year."

A deep silence of some minutes followed; then the Dowager lifted a troubled face and said, laying her hand gently upon her husband's arm—

"Derrick, they could not live upon it, but—"

"Ah, I was afraid you would say it, dear wife, but you are right, you are right, I know it, I feel it. It was a dream, a beautiful dream, and it was near my heart, but I realize that we can never—"

"Wait, dear, let me finish. All my life it has been my dearest privilege to make your dreams come true when the power in me lay, not thwart them; and it shall be now as always. You shall bring them together; we will support them. Does that please you, dear?"

For all answer he pressed her to his bosom, in a strong embrace which uttered his loving gratitude more eloquently than could any words have done it, even if his emotion had allowed him to command them.

Hark—footsteps! The door flew open and Edith was before them. She stood for a moment as one dazed; then with a swift movement or two she stripped away her mask and domino and sank white and trembling to her knees and buried her face in her mother's lap, sobbing bitterly.

"My child, oh my child, what is it!"

"Oh, mother, take me to the refuge of your arms and let me cry out my heart, for I—"

"My darling! There—clasp me close—now, rest in peace, tell your poor mother all. What is it, dear?"

"Oh, mother, God help me—I—I am married!"

"Married!"

"Married?" echoed the father, springing to his feet with the force and suddenness of the shock.

"Married? To whom?"

"Alas, I do not know! Oh, let me die, let me die!"

The mother gathered her suffering child to her heart, murmuring, "Ah, my God, what a tragedy is this, and what a strange mystery! Oh, it is a dream, my darling, it is a delusion—it will pass. The doctor, Derrick, the doctor—hurry!"

"No, papa, don't! Oh, not for the world! I could not bear another presence; let us shut up in our own bosoms the secret of this awful disaster."

Then, sobbing and mourning, she told the pitiful tale, the parents listening in tense and wordless silence. Closing, she said—

"Here on my hand is his ring, on his hand is mine." She looked up sadly through her tears and murmured, with quivering lip, "Think—bride of an hour, and already a widow! for it is beyond hope that in this life I shall ever see my husband again."

The thought struck a chill to the hearts of the parents, for they realized that upon this fair young creature, this fresh and dewy blossom, lay indeed the withering blight of a hopeless widowhood. Then came another thought, another sharp pain: how lovely and how gracious was that dream of an hour ago, and what a ruin is it now! At bottom and secretly, how questionably valuable had seemed marriage with that high-born pauper youth—how inestimably precious were it now, now that the chance of it was forever lost!

Chapter 3

A LITTLE LATER the Colonel was sitting by the fire alone, absorbed in unhappy thinkings. Presently his wife joined him and sank into her chair, troubled and weary.

"She is asleep, Louise?"

"Yes; and steeped in the peace of forgetfulness; let us be thankful for it."

After a pause the Colonel said, drearily—

"I have tortured my mind for a way out of this deep misfortune, but it is of no use—I find none."

The mother wiped her eyes and said—

"No—there is no hope. She is married; she does not know what it is to be false to her word; she will stand by it till death releases her."

"Thank God for such a child! It breaks our hearts, Louise, but we would not have her act otherwise."

"Oh, I know it, I know it. It wrings my heartstrings, but all our heredities and the training of our lives from childhood up require fidelity to our engagements, at all cost, even of life itself, and there is no way out. She must stand by her duty, and we must support her in it."

The Colonel was proud of his wife, and his eyes showed it.

"How right you always are, Louise! When a principle is at stake, one always knows where to find you; not Gibraltar itself is more steadfastly based. Edith is our own child. When that is said, all is said. She will stand to her word."

"Yes. Oh, Derrick, there is something heartbreaking about her humble and uncomplaining resignation to this miserable stroke—just as if she deserved it, poor dear little pious creature."

"She is right, Louise; you and I know that, and feel it. In her heart she knows that this seeming calamity may be good fortune in disguise, for good fortune is often sent in these mysterious ways, and—"

"Brother, don't twaddle!"

This was from the Colonel's maiden sister, Minna, who had noise-lessly entered the room at that moment. She was tall, and gray, a little angular, and not sentimental. She came and sat down, and again requested her brother not to twaddle. Then she went on, with decision, like the practical person that she was. "Good fortune in disguise! To my mind it is a little too damned well disguised. Some people are always finding in a thing what they want to find in it, not the thing that is plainly there—and that is your way, Derrick. Why can't you look an occurrence frankly in the face, and accept it for what it plainly is? This poor child is married to a shadow. Moreover, she can't locate the shadow. It is her shadow if she can get it, but how is she going to get it? There is no way to deliver the goods—*you* know that."

"Minna, God can—"

"Never mind what God can do; the matter on hand is what He *has* done. If He meant it for a benefaction it has miscarried, and you know it." She lit a cigar, and resumed. "That poor thing—do you know, she is set upon sticking to that silly marriage. She said so in the carriage, coming home, and she said it again a while ago."

"Has she been awake?"

"For a minute or two, yes—a little after you left. She has been praying for that shadow; that is what she woke up for. She forgot it before, and only prayed for herself and the rest of the family. Neglected the shadow. Prayed that it might be watched over and protected from harm and sin, and all that. All this for a shadow. I couldn't believe my ears. It's as uncanny as praying for a clothes-pin. She calls it husband —think of it—and the word falls as pat from her mouth as if she had been used to it a year. Is this foolishness to be allowed to go on? There is only one common-sense thing to do, and she won't listen to it."

"What is that, sister?"

"Advertise for the shadow."

The parents were struck by that.

"Why, that is an excellent idea, Minna," said the Colonel; "and easily and secretly managed, too."

"Certainly. Put it in the agony column. Something like this: 'The holder of the E ring desires to communicate with the holder of the R ring, with a view to permanent matrimony, if satisfactory to both. Confidential. Address box X, General Postoffice. *Send photograph.*'"

"Oh, Minna, it is beautiful—how did you ever think of it?"

"Thank you for the compliment, Louise; but to fail to think of it would have required a more remarkable mind. However, if you wait for Edith's consent, you will not get it."

"Indeed, she cannot object, for she will not appear in it and cannot be discovered."

"But she did object, for I proposed it."

"Why did she?"

"She said she would have to take that husband, no matter what his photograph might look like, her conscience would require it of her; and so she would not run the risk. She has a strong instinct that he is old, and bald, and worldly."

"Why, that is a foolish fancy, and may be wholly wrong."

"Of course. But you know your daughter. She has said she will not run the risk."

The parents sighed, and said in a breath, "That settles it."

"So it does, as far as you and she are concerned."

That was all that Minna said, but the parents understood, and gave her a grateful look. To herself she added, "I will attend to the advertising. I will land that damned shadow, and see what he is like." She drained the Colonel's glass, and departed to her bedchamber. There she wrote her advertisement; reflected a while, then added these words: "Please furnish address for a return-photograph." This seemed a good idea, and likely to hasten matters. If R should send a satisfactory picture, well and good; if he sent an unsatisfactory one he would get none in return, and the thing could be dropped at that point without compromising any one.

Chapter 4

MEANTIME young Schuyler van Bleecker, holder of the R ring, was having a sorrowful time at home. He had arrived stunned with the disaster which had befallen him, and longing for privacy and seclusion, for he wanted to think it over undisturbed, and plan a course of action; but it was as he had been expecting—his good old mother was waiting up for him.

"Did you see her?" she asked, eagerly. "Why, how ghastly you look! what has happened?"

Fortunately his horses had been running away with him and had flung the footman from the box and crippled him. He made the most of the accident, and did not have to tell about his marriage. Since he had suffered no hurt himself, his mother was satisfied and grateful, and she soon returned with interest to her original question—

"Did you see her?"

"No, mother; if she was there I did not recognise her."

"Oh, I am so disappointed."

"She was only fourteen and I nineteen when I went abroad, mother; we could have met and not known each other."

"Hardly, and you such old playmates. And besides, you were the

handsomest and manliest young fellow there—*that* I know—and she
would have heard people exclaiming about you by name, everywhere
you moved, and you would have heard people saying 'There she is—
that's Edith!' for she is the loveliest thing alive and can't appear anywhere without stirring up that kind of a hubbub. So she wasn't there;
and it is a pity, for I have set my heart on this match, as I wrote you,
and I wanted no time lost. Schuyler!"

"What, mother!"

"You don't take any interest. And yet you were so full of it, and so
fine and alive and sparkling when you stepped ashore yesterday. Her
father and I spoke of it afterwards, when we were planning together.
He was ever so much pleased with you—but now! why, now you are
lifeless—even flabby. What *is* the matter with you, Schuyler? You
never cared for a runaway before. I'm ashamed of you!"

With a wan look, the young man said—

"Bear with me, mother—I am sorry to grieve you, but I have changed
my mind—"

"What do you mean?"

"Mother, I shall never marry."

The mother was not able to speak, for astonishment. When she presently got command of her tongue again she urged, besought, implored
him to explain, but in vain. He said he might tell her his reasons some
day in the future, but he could do nothing now but repeat his resolve,
which was irrevocable—he should never marry. He hoped she would
be patient with him, pity him, bear with him—and not urge him to say
more upon the subject, since it could only distress him and do no good.

She cried bitterly, for her disappointment was deep; then mother-
like, she put away her own troubles and did all that in her lay to soothe
his mysterious hurt and make him forget it for the time. She was not
utterly cast down, for in her secret heart she believed that she and
Colonel Depuyster-Brevoort would know how to bring about a re-
change of his mind and banish the clouds that were brooding over
him now.

When she had left him he began his thinkings. There in the fore-
front stood the odious fact that he was married—hard and fast. To
whom? Oh, without shadow of doubt, to some stale old back number!

—a thought which made him sick with anguish. He reminded himself that those poor old relics were always the first to come forward when they could have the chance to frolic in the shelter of a disguise; and now—why now, without question he had annexed the oldest and dryest one for life.

And so he went on, thinking, thinking, suffering, despairing. But finally a happy thought flashed upon him: he would advertise. Yes, this promised something. E might be endurable—why, she really might; he need not despair yet. With a great hope rising in his heart, he sat down with his pen—unconscious that Minna was at the same moment doing the same thing—and then mental telegraphy did the rest. The two ads. were almost word for word alike.

Concerning "Martyrs' Day"

(19 September 1902)

CLEMENS WROTE to F. A. Duneka of Harper & Brothers on 19 September 1902, "To-day I have written a little short dab of sarcasm—'Concerning Martyrs' Day'—and shall mail it when it is type-wrote. Tomorrow or next day I reckon." He added a postscript: "It is for the *Weekly*."[1] It is interesting that Paine was able to note the year of composition correctly on the manuscript although he did not have this letter to consult.

It is not clear whether Mark Twain or his publisher decided to withhold the piece from print. Since the typescript survives in the Mark Twain Papers, the author may have changed his mind about submitting it; or, it may have been sent to Harper's and later returned. The "sarcasm" is directed at peoples' unwillingness to mourn for their fellow man with their pocketbooks as well as their hearts.

---

[1] Roy J. Friedman Collection, copy in MTP.

Concerning "Martyrs' Day"

I HAVE READ in the newspapers the suggestion that we institute a Martyrs' Day, and make it a national holiday. I recognize here an admirable idea. I hope the President will give this matter a conspicuous place in his Message next December, and that the Congress will take hold of it with promptness and pass the proper bill without any avoidable delay.

If I may have the privilege, I will offer a suggestion or two as to the form which it seems to me the bill ought to take.

In the first place I would slightly alter the plan of the contemplated homage—merely the plan, and only slightly. I would give the Day a double name and a double object, instead of limiting it to a single name and a single object. I would call it Martyrs' Day and also Monument Day. As a further amendment, I would not make it a public holiday, but would allow the industries of the nation to go on as usual. I will explain.

By the records of the Bureau of Statistics we are aware that last year wages were earned by 52,264,534 of our people—men, women, youths and children—and that the average earned per day per person, was $1.24¼. Thus the workers of the Republic earned an aggregate of $64,000,000-odd per day. This year the daily aggregate will be a little above $70,000,000, by estimate based on natural increase of popula-

303

tion. Ten years hence the aggregate will have reached $100,000,000 per day; and three times that splendid sum fifty or sixty years hence—that is to say $300,000,000 a day.

Now if we merely compel the nation to knock off work on Martyrs' Day, what do we accomplish? Nothing, in particular. The nation will voluntarily mourn without that. The bulk of the nation, I mean. The others will mourn by statute. Mourning by statute is not objectionable, it is the customary thing in all countries. More mourning is done by statute than in any other way. New York mourned bitterly for General Grant, but was not able to raise the money for his tomb, though it would have cost the grieving people only 16 cents apiece. I speak of the time before the scare came—the time when the friends were about to remove the body to the Soldiers' Home in Washington, so that the lamented soldier might find rest. The people were like all other peoples, they would mourn with their hearts, but not with their pockets, if they could avoid it.

There was the Washington Monument. It was estimated that it would cost $250,000. It took Edward Everett and a host of hard-working Associations years and years to raise it. And after all, the legislatures had to contribute all the principal rocks. The nation mourned for Washington all it knew how with their hearts, but you couldn't get its pocket to shed a tear—I mean, a proffered one, a volunteer.

It is this hoary and international and universal aversion to mourning by voluntary contribution that ages ago invented the idea of mourning by statute. It was found impossible to get any creditable mourning done in any other way. It has always been a heroic and dare-devil job in all countries to carry around a voluntary-subscription-paper; and the dare-devils have seldom been able to stand the discomforts and humiliations of the work long enough to raise the required amount of money. The remains of these brave efforts are sad little monuments, in themselves. In every town and village and city in the civilized world little dabs of money lie mouldering which were tomahawked from voluntary contributors at one time or another to build a monument with. Only ten per cent was ever raised, then the enterprise died; the monuments were never built.

Necessity, then, was the mother of Mourning by Statute. It is the best way, it is the honestest way, it is the kindliest way. In every case, without exception, the voluntary-subscription-by-tomahawk produces a grudged memorial—when it produces one at all—and it dishonors the person it professes to honor. But with the contribution-by-compulsion-of-law it is different. Congress appropriates the liberal and proper sum, nobody's pocket feels it, everybody is proud and gratified. Another point: the money comes out of the tax-payers, the well-to-do, and *the poor escape*. You get it?

However—I believe I am going too fast. Ought the poor to escape—when it is a great national matter? Is it fair? Is it right? No, it must be conceded that it is not. The poor are in the mighty majority, they are almost the nation: a National Monument to which they do not contribute nine-tenths of the cost is not national—far from it.

Then an *appropriation* made by Congress is not the right way, for it leaves them out.

I now arrive at my reason for approving the idea of a universal cash-levy in the form of a national holiday: it takes the nine-tenths out of the wage-earner, and this makes it properly and genuinely national. Congress will pass the bill about the 9th of December, and next year the wage-earners will each contribute a day's wages apiece toward attracting attention to Martyrs' Day and keeping it from getting overlooked. This will aggregate $70,000,000, and will cause the day to be remembered for weeks in many households. In every succeeding year for ten centuries it will grow steadily larger and more satisfactory—for a national holiday is a permanent asset.

I now arrive at the amendment which I have already vaguely referred to. It is this. Let the bill provide for a Martyrs' Day, but not make a *holiday* of it. Let the people go on working, just the same, but be required by Congress to contribute that day's earnings to an *annual Monument*. The result to the worker is the same, in any case. In the one case he doesn't get the money, in the other he doesn't keep it.

Now, then, I would not really build a fresh Monument every year—no, I have a better idea. I would have the government architect plan a prodigious Monument which could go on climbing toward the sky, stage by stage and year by year, for a thousand years. With next year's $70,000,000 I would mark out the foundations; with the following year's $75,000,000 I would set up a piece of the wall; the year after, I would set up another piece with that year's $80,000,000—and so on and so on. I would build it of massive and indestructible masonry, and I would have it circular, and rising into the sky on a noble and gradual taper. It would be a hundred miles in diameter, and when it was finished, in a thousand years, it would be nine miles high and you could see it from Europe on a clear day. This would annoy the English, for they would be celebrating Alfred's bi-millenial then—and on a sufficiently small scale, by comparison. Centuries before that time our annual one-day's-wage levy would have reached a billion dollars, and the completed Monument would represent an approximate aggregate cost of Seven Hundred Billions—that is to say $700,000,000,000-worth of good commercial mourning bought and paid for. Ten billions would pay all the National Debts that exist in Christendom to-day. This gives us an idea of the majesty of the Monument. It will be the grandest monument in the earth; contrasted with it snow-capped Mont Blanc would be but a circus tent to a sky-scraper. I would have it so situated that the nation's capital city and the capitol and the Washington Monument could stand in the front door, on the left-hand side as you go in, and not be in the way.

In this way we should have a Martyrs' Day and a Monument Day in one, and everything satisfactory to everybody. We could put up posters to explain to the poor that it was not called Martyrs' Day on their account, but quite different.

It may be that you will hear some complaint, but not much, I think. Widows with four children and a 20-cent wage in a sweat-shop to starve them on will say another national holiday will be the last straw, and things like that; that it takes the children a week, seven times a year, to get over the famine of Lincoln's Day, and Washington's Day, and Labor Day, and Decoration Day, and Fourth of July, and Thanksgiving, and Christmas; and hard-pressed Jews in the tenement-regions of the cities will say they have 52 holidays of their own, by compulsion of their religion, and 52 contributed by Christian compulsion—111, with the above seven—and that an added one will break their backs; and still others will say that if Latin Europe could have foreseen what a blighting thing, by and by, the occasional sticking on of a fresh holi-

day would turn out to be, they would never have allowed the burden
to grow to such proportions as it has reached now, when in Italy they
have 227 public holidays, at an expense of nineteen million dollars a
day and can't get work-time enough to support their cats. Even in those
brand-new countries, Australia and New Zealand, they have a national
holiday three times a week, and would like to sell us an assorted lot on
easy terms and long credit.

But all that is nothing. Mourning by Statute is the right way;
mourning by Universal Squeeze is the holy thing; it doesn't cost the
rich anything, and what is one day's added hunger in the year to the
poor? Nothing; we can easily stand it. On the 9th of December Congress will pass the bill, on the 10th the 52,264,534 Contributors by
Compulsion will return thanks, and the very next day we can start
the Monument.

We must remember that this is not only the best way and the right
way, but is also the only way. Experience warns us that the Voluntary
Subscription would not be safe, even if we wanted only a mere million.
We could not place it, even if we had all mankind to draw upon. Men
dread it; nothing embarrasses them like a Voluntary-Subscription-
Paper. If it were 10,000 miles square and we should paste it on the sky
where all the globe could see, the human race would disappear.

Abner L. Jackson
(About to Be) Deceased

(1880–1881)

THIS PIECE takes the form of a letter to "Rodney Dennis." Geer's 1882 *Hartford City Directory* lists Rodney Dennis as the secretary of The Travelers Insurance Company—the company from which Jackson has bought his policy in this satiric obituary notice. The Reverend Abner Jackson, President of Trinity College in Hartford, was a member of the Monday Evening Club from 1869 until his death in 1874. None of the statements made in this sketch coincide with the facts of his life.

Mark Twain left the work untitled and included two endings in the manuscript. It is possible, with the work in an unfinished state, that he wished to retain alternative possibilities. Probably, however, he simply failed to discard his original draft when he supplanted it with the later and longer ending. The earlier ending, on a single manuscript page, was to follow "dollars' " at 311.32 of the present text. It reads:

[dol]lars' worth of Traveler's Accident tickets. His will sets apart $90,000 for his family; the residue goes to the Adam Monument Association, he being the originator of the noble enterprise which that society was instituted to achieve.

Very Truly Yours

S. L. Clemens

P. S. He takes passage in the boat at 4 p.m. to-day. I am his chief executor. Are any formalities necessary?—or do I simply draw on you?

S. L. C.[1]

The reference to the Adam Monument Association in the superseded ending helps date the work. Clemens first seems to have entertained the idea of a monument to Adam in October 1879;[2] from then until the summer of 1881, but seldom thereafter, he was concerned with promoting such a project. The paper which Mark Twain used through the first ending was, according to Walter Blair, used by the author only between September 1879 and June 1881.[3] Finally, Mark Twain wrote "Hartford June 1880" on the verso of one of the manuscript pages, apparently while testing his pen.

In expanding the list of Jackson's bequests to pious-seeming organizations and their ridiculous projects, Mark Twain did not include the reference to the Adam Monument Association, which appears only in the superseded passage quoted above. The new ending reveals instead that Jackson has specified a "Monument for Self" but has provided no funds for it. Possibly we are to understand that Jackson was expecting his family, including the "1 gross distant relatives" valued "@ $1 per sample," to pay for the monument—and also for the funeral expenses and the prize for a biography, which he also left unfunded. Or perhaps Clemens simply did not bother to complete his intended draft: it will be noticed that the total amount of the bequests falls $2,338 short of the one hundred thousand dollars that the insurance is to provide. It is also possible that Clemens' intention stopped short of the labor of arithmetic.

---

[1] In the postscript "takes" and "to-day" replace canceled "took" and "yesterday," and the question mark following "you" replaces canceled "for."

[2] *MTB*, p. 708.

[3] "When Was *Huckleberry Finn* Written?," *American Literature* 30 (March 1958): 8.

Abner L. Jackson
(About to Be) Deceased

R ODNEY DENNIS, Esq.

Dear Sir:

This town has just sustained a heavy blow, in the loss of Mr. Abner
L. Jackson, an old and greatly respected citizen. Mr. Jackson was born
in Farmington, Conn., June 13, 1810, where he attended the school
kept by the Misses Wright all through his boyhood, and was noted for
his diligence, his capacity, and the simplicity and purity of his character,—these latter qualities being inherited from his mother, who was a
lineal descendant of Jabez Parks, a prominent member of the little
colony which settled Hartford in 1635.

Young Jackson lost his father in 1823; and in the spring of 1824 his
mother passed away, also, and he found himself alone in the world and
without other resources than his own strong hands and willing heart.
He entered Yale, supporting himself by teaching school during vaca-
tions, but was not able to finish his term, and therefore did not gradu-
ate. He studied law, during four years, in the office of the late Abel
Thompson, of New Haven, and then entered the ministry of the Presbyterian church in the town of Glastonbury, but after two years of excellent service his views concerning future punishment underwent a
change and he considered it his duty to retire from that communion.

He became a citizen of Elmira in 1840, and in 1846 he raised a company and started to Mexico, but when he arrived the war was over. The rest of his life was embittered by unavailing efforts to obtain a pension. In the memorable canvass of 1854 he was elected to the legislature, after months of unremitting labor in the cause, but an informality in the returns made a new election necessary, and this time his opponent was elected by a majority of one.

When the rebellion broke out he was one of the first men in this town to offer his services and experience to the government; he received a lieutenantcy at once, with promise of early promotion, but on his way to headquarters to get his commission signed, he was struck a violent blow in the back by an elephant belonging to a passing menagerie, and disabled from further service. He was forced to lie on his back during several years. He felt sure of getting a pension this time, but was again disappointed; this second repulse wounded him deeply, and he was never the same man afterward.

He employed the last ten years of his life, and won golden opinions from all, as sexton to the Presbyterian church, his former views about future punishment having returned to him in consequence of his misfortunes.

He will be greatly missed, here, and sincerely mourned, by the whole community.—It was noticed by many, last week, that something was wrong with him; and as it was known that he was hopelessly in debt for the past year's household expenses and had only a hundred and thirty dollars in the world, the worst was feared—and but too justly. Yesterday morning he called his family together, and confessed that he was tired of life; then bade them farewell, begging them to try to forgive him for what he was about to do, and went to New York to take a trip on an excursion steamer.

He leaves a wife and seven children. His thoughts were with them to the last; for his latest act was to invest all his little hoard of savings in a hundred thousand dollars' worth of Travelers Accident tickets. His will sets apart $90,000 for his family; the residue goes to the following objects:

6 first cousins, @ $25 . . . . $150.00
3 uncles, @ $15 . . . . 45.00
2 aunts, @ $10 . . . . 20.00

1 brother and 1 half-brother, @ $100 .   .   .   .   . 150.00
1 gross distant relatives, @ $1 per sample   .   .   . 144.00
Society for the Propagation of the Gospel
    among the Inhabitants of Lands Within
    the Open Polar Sea, When Found 22.00
American Board of Commissioners for Foreign
    Missions 11.00
National Sunday School Union 4.00
Society for the Prevention of Cats 465.00
American Tract Society 7.00
Ladies' Union for Providing Aprons for the Female
    Residents of Dahomey 359.00
Fund for Providing Policy in Hereafter Fire
    Insurance Co. for Robert G. Ingersoll .   .   . 135.00
Society for Extending the Suffrage to Non-resident
    Foreigners 586.00
Fund for Providing Flowers, Music, Tears,
    Lamentations, and the usual Religious
    Hurrah over Assassins about to ship
    for Abraham's Bosom from the Gallows   .   . 748.00
Society for the Discouraging of Profanity among
    Parrots 116.00
To print my work entitled "Reminiscences of my
    Career in the Military Service of the
    United States" 3,000.00
To print my medical pamphlet entitled "Advice
    to Persons About to be Struck by
    Lightning" 1,700.00
Prize for best Biography of Self .   .   .   .   .
Funeral Expenses for Self .   .   .   .   .   .
Monument for Self   .   .   .   .   .   .
    Such are his bequests.

Very Truly Yours
Nathaniel E. Harrison.

P.S. He takes passage in the boat at 4 p.m. to-day. I am his chief executor. Are any formalities necessary?—or do I simply draw on you?

N. E. H.

THE NIGHTMARE
OF HISTORY

The Secret History of Eddypus, the World-Empire

(February–March 1901; February–March 1902)

"IT IS NOT worth while to try to keep history from repeating itself, for man's character will always make the preventing of the repetitions impossible," Clemens observed in his Autobiographical Dictation of 15 January 1907. On that date he expressed a personal view of history that is essentially the same one he had fantasized five or six years earlier in "Eddypus." Civilization, he believed, was due to perish and be followed by a new Dark Age: "Riches and education are not a permanent possession; they will pass away, as in the case of Rome, and Greece, and Egypt, and Babylon; and a moral and mental midnight will follow—with a dull long sleep and a slow re-awakening." Central to his concept of such a cycle of history was the idea of an inevitable return to monarchy:

> For twenty-five or thirty years I have squandered a deal of my time—too much of it perhaps—in trying to guess what is going to be the process which will turn our republic into a monarchy, and how far off that event might be. Every man is a master and also a servant, a vassal. There is always some one who looks up to him and admires and envies him; there is always some one to whom he looks up and admires and envies. This is his nature; this is his character; and it is unchangeable, indestructible; therefore republics and democracies are not for such as he; they cannot satisfy the requirements of his nature. . . .
> Republics have lived long, but monarchy lives forever. By our teaching, we

315

learn that vast material prosperity always brings in its train conditions which debase the morals and enervate the manhood of a nation—then the country's liberties come into the market and are bought, sold, squandered, thrown away, and a popular idol is carried to the throne upon the shields or shoulders of the worshiping people, and planted there in permanency.

He found parallels between the conditions before the fall of Rome and those of his own time:

> We have the two Roman conditions: stupendous wealth, with its inevitable corruptions and moral blight, and . . . pensions—that is to say, vote-bribes, which have taken away the pride of thousands of tempted men and turned them into willing alms-receivers and unashamed.

In the preceding year he had enlarged upon his view that religions were also cyclical:

> There had been millions of gods before ours was invented. Swarms of them are dead and forgotten long ago. . . . I think that Christianity, and its God, must follow the rule. They must pass on, in their turn, and make room for another God and a stupider religion. A better than this? No. That is not likely. History shows that in the matter of religions, we progress backward. . . . At this very day there are thousands upon thousands of Americans of average intelligence who fully believe in "Science and Health," although they can't understand a line of it, and who also worship the sordid and ignorant old purloiner of that gospel—Mrs. Mary Baker G. Eddy, whom they do absolutely believe to be a member, by adoption, of the Holy Family, and on the way to push the Savior to third place and assume occupancy of His present place, and continue that occupancy during the rest of eternity.[1]

"Eddypus" is a fictional presentation of these views, a nightmare vision of a future in which the religion of Mrs. Eddy has become all-powerful as a world empire whose leader is both pope and monarch. The story is also a fantasy of Clemens' own historical role. As the most ancient authority on record, the revered Mark Twain, Bishop of New Jersey, he is the prophet whose sacred writings will keep the truth alive through the coming dark period, whose gospel may eventually supplant the long-dominant Eddyism, whose personality may be impressed upon the future ages when all others of his own times have been forgotten. "Eddypus" is in part the story of Clemens' attainment, through his writings, of a kind of immortality. But so garbled has the record of this "Bishop" become that the reader may think the lamentations of his future translator over the perishable renown

---

[1] Autobiographical Dictation, 22 June 1906.

of "Tom, Dick and Harry" might as well apply to the Father of History himself: "Ah, the pathos of a finite immortality!" These words echo an observation Clemens had set down in his 1867 notebook, when he was in his early thirties: "Fame is a vapor—popularity an accident—the only earthly certainty oblivion."[2]

It was probably inevitable that Mark Twain would leave "Eddypus" incomplete. In the latter part of Book 2 it is especially evident that he was improvising in an attempt to keep the story going. He fell back upon a favorite device—that of treating a succession of historical figures in a fanciful, burlesque fashion.

Considerations relating to the dating of "Eddypus" are discussed in the Introduction. The evidence presented there indicates that Mark Twain began writing this manuscript about February 1901 and probably continued until some time in March 1901; that work was then suspended after he had written through Chapter 5 of Book 2; that he resumed work some time after 16 February 1902, or after he had acquired the copy of Andrew D. White's *A History of the Warfare of Science with Theology in Christendom*. White's book was a major source for the remaining thirty-five manuscript pages of his "history." After composing this small amount, probably in February or March 1902, he left "Eddypus" incomplete.

Mark Twain provided no title on the manuscript or typescript, but referred to the work by its present title in the portion of "Eddypus" which he published with chapters from *Christian Science* in 1903.[3] That part, headed "(LATER STILL.)—A THOUSAND YEARS AGO.," was subtitled *"Passages from the Introduction of 'The Secret History of Eddypus, the World-Empire.'"* Since "LATER STILL." postdates the author's last work on the "Eddypus" manuscript, it seems to embody his final thoughts concerning the title.

---

[2] Notebook 9, TS p. 30.
[3] NAR 555 (February 1903): 173–184.

The Secret History of Eddypus, the World-Empire

Book I
A Private Letter
Date, A.M. 1001*

Dear X. I have sent you a new cipher by the usual conveyance. There is danger in clinging long to one form of a cipher in times like ours.

You have made a mistake. The tenth word in my ninth paragraph was not 888, but 889, hence your confusion of mind. You perceive now, that I said "arbitrary," not "independent." Read it with this new light and you will see that I have not "contradicted" myself.

Warn your friend that he is getting Christian Science history mixed up with *history*. There is a difference between the two. If you are sure he is a safe person and not in the clandestine service of the Holy Office, you may whisper to him certain of the facts—but on your life put nothing on paper! Tell him these:

The so-called "Fourth Person of the Godhead and Second Person in Rank—Our Mother,"—was born a thousand and odd years ago, *not* twelve hundred, as claimed in the Bull *Jubus Jorum Acquilorum*. There is (forbidden) documentary evidence of this. To-wit: in a paper by one Mark Twain, (A.D. 1898 = A.M. 30) a revered priest of the

---

* Equivalent to A.D. 2901. Note by translator.

earlier faith, sometime Bishop of New Jersey, hanged in A.D. 1912 = A.M. 47. Also in the Introduction to the first edition (A.D. 1865 = A.M. 1) of Science and Health. Although the sole remaining copy of this Bible is locked behind heavy iron gratings in the Vatican at Eddyflats, (anciently called Boston,) with a perpetual lamp burning before it and has_been under the guard, both night and day, of fifty papal soldiers for many centuries and none allowed to touch it, not even the Pope, *it has been examined* within this present decade, and by a *heretic*, who carried away that Introduction in his memory and delivered it to three other heretics, one of whom I know and have conversed with; and I assure you that the contents are as I have indicated. Do you remember the burning of one F. Hopkinson Smith, a philologist, two or three years ago on suspicion of having a familiar? That was the charge the Holy Office chose to bring against him, but it was false. He was the man who stole the secrets of the Introduction, and the Church pleases itself with the belief that it consumed the secrets with him. Let the Church go on thinking so, if it likes.

The Bull *Jubus Jorum Acquilorum* to the contrary notwithstanding, Our Mother was born in the usual and natural way. There is in safe hiding an ancient paper which clearly reveals to us that the statue of the Immaculate Conception which was dug up at Eddyburg, (where Rome once stood,) was not cast in honor of Her, but *antedates* Her. That paper is a chapter of travel. It was written in the declining days of the Ages of Light by one Uncle Remus, celebrated as a daring voyager and explorer in his time. He was with Columbus in the Mayflower and assisted him in discovering America and Livingston. Livingston was an island. It is not now known where it was situated, nor what became of it. Since it was not worth keeping track of, the most intelligent historians think it was one of the Filopines.

The Bull *Jubus* to the contrary notwithstanding, the Popes do *not* wear female apparel solely in honor of Our Mother the first Pope; they do *not* call themselves "She" solely in honor of Her; they do *not* bear Her name and no other solely in honor of Her. These are all falsehoods and evasions. A thoughtful and unprejudiced reading of section 3 of the "Final Revelation for the Government of My Church" will prove this. For instance, examine two or three of the commands, and consider how very suggestive they are:

a. "Every Pope, immediately after her election, shall be consecrated with My Name and shall bear no other afterward."

b. "She shall be distinguished from the others her predecessors and successors by a *number* solely, and in no other way. As thus: Her Divine Grace Pope Mary Baker G. Eddy II; Her Divine Grace Pope Mary Baker G. Eddy III; Her Divine Grace Pope Mary Baker G. Eddy IV, etc.; to the end that My Name and the worship of It shall abide in the earth until the Last Day."

c. "She shall not depart from the fashion of My garments while the centuries shall endure."

Are not those laws plain enough? Do they not mean that She never had in Her mind any but a female Pope? Do not they mean that She was deliberately and purposely closing the august function against the other sex in perpetuity? None can doubt it. How did the ancients understand those laws? I think that this question is convincingly answered in the fact that *not a single male* Pope was elected to the Christian Science Throne during the first two centuries Anno Matris.

Was not the change to male Popes an evasion? Was it not a usurpation? I think so. Indeed I know it was so regarded at the time. Do you know that the so-called Conquest of the Roman Catholic Church was not a conquest at all but a pure matter of trade? That is what it was—that and nothing more. The secret history of it is quite simple and business-like. Deadly, too; do not be indiscreet with it. The last female Christian Science Pope that ever reigned was Her Divine Grace Pope Mary Baker G. Eddy XXIV (A.M. 219–226). Her contemporary of Rome, His Holiness Pius XII, was the last Pope that ever reigned over the Roman Church. Throughout the world, with the exception of the Roman Catholic power, Christian Science had abolished Christianity. That is, by substituting itself for it. The Roman power was failing—Rome had to perish. This was plain. Her chiefs were as they had always been—bold and brilliant—and they set themselves the task of trading off their diminished powers at an inflated figure. With a strong Pope on the Science Throne they would have gotten nothing at all for them—which would be just their value after no very long time,—and the Scientists were in a safe position to tranquilly wait and assuredly win. But Mary Baker G. XXIV was a weak woman and over-anxious to end the wearisome rivalry of the two Churches, therefore she favored a merger. Her hierarchy were bitterly opposed to this, and fought it the best they could; but what could they do? Really nothing. They could advise and implore; she could *command*. Her authority was from heaven; and had no limits. She alone, of all the world, possessed the divine prerogative of "demonstrating over" things. When she had demonstrated over a thing, heaven had spoken, and that settled it. She listened to the proposition of the other Pope's envoys. She retired to her sanctum sanctorum, and there in sacred privacy she demonstrated over it, assisting herself with the consecrated formula, "Liver, Lights, Blood, Bones—Good, All-Good, Too-Good—Mortal Mind, Immortal Mind, Syrup, Sawdust, Keno—ante and pass the Buck!"—and then she saw how it all was, and what was heaven's will concerning the Trade. She returned to the Hall of Audience and accepted the offered terms of half-and-half; whereat the envoys smiled up their sleeves and were glad, for they were expecting her to pare their share down to as much as a shade or two below its immediate value, say twenty per cent of the whole.

By those strange terms the two Papacies were to consolidate their properties and powers; until the death of one of the Popes, both should reign; after that, the survivor should reign alone until death; after that, there should be but one Pope thenceforth.

Her Divine Grace Mary Baker G. Eddy XXIV died first; *it had been supposed she would*. Then Pius XII relinquished his title, abolished his Papacy and his Church, put on the late Pope's clothes, and became Mistress of the World and of Christian Sciencedom, under the name and style of Her Divine Grace Mary Baker G. Eddy XXV, and went to demonstrating over things like an Old Hand. She (that is, he) was English, and in his boyhood her name was Thomas Atkins.

She (that is, he) reigned sixteen years; and when she died she left the cards most competently stacked, and secure in the hands of such as knew the Game. It is eight hundred years ago, or nearly that at any rate, and since that day Her Divine Grace Mary Baker G. Eddy, Pope, has reigned 103 times, but has never been a woman in a single instance—nor a Christian.

That is the secret history of the "Conquest" you hear so much about, and it is authentic.

Another Private Letter

Write a history? A private one, for you and your friend? You mean a real history, of course? not the ruck of pious romances which the Government calls history and compels the nations to buy—every family a set, along with Science and Health, at a price so exorbitant that in a multitude of cases it costs a man of slender resources a year's earnings to meet the tax. I shall be glad to do it, and will set about it this day or at furthest to-morrow; for in my clandestine trade of antiquary and student of history I am like an artist who paints beautiful pictures and hungers for the happiness of showing them, but lives among the blind. I will show my pictures to you. It will refresh my life and fill it with satisfactions. There is peril in it, but even in that there should be and must be an element of pleasure. I will protect myself the best I can; and you also, at the same time. There is more or less danger in a cipher, but sympathetic ink is a secure vehicle—at least the kind I shall use is. It is an invention of my own. Go to the Church bargain-counter and buy a bottle or two of sacramental wine,—the white kind used to commemorate Our Mother's First Inspiration. When you receive a packet of blank paper by and by, wet it with that, and my writing will appear. It will fade out and disappear in the course of a few hours, but it will come back as often as you like if you heat the paper.

History of Holy Eddypus

Chapter 1

The World-Empire of Holy Eddypus covers and governs all the globe except the spacious region which has for countless ages borne the name of China, and which is the only country where an enlightened civilization now exists.

"Holy" is a word which in ancient times,—if our best scholars are right—referred to personages and things worthy of homage, reverence, and worship. The word is still so applied, though with caution.

"Eddypus" is a combination; the first half of it preserves the family name of the Founder of the only religion now permitted in the World-Empire; "pus" is an ancient word meaning (as asserted and settled by Papal decree seven centuries ago) a precious exudation, a sanctifying ointment. Hence *pustule,* an Eddymanian priest, a person full of pus; that is to say, holiness.

A number of other words in our language have their source in the Founder's name. In the third century of our era the Only True Religion displaced and abolished a religion of considerable antiquity called Christianity, and began to reign in its stead under the name it now bears, Eddymania.

From this word is derived the designation of the individual subject of the Papacy—Eddymaniac—and also the word which classifies its peoples in mass—Eddymanians, Eddymaniacs.

Also the word which has replaced the obsolete word Religion—Eddygush.

Also the one which gives name to Our Mother's natal day—Eddymas—in ancient times called Christmas.

Also the one which gives name to the sacred formulas, from Science and Health, chanted by the clergy before the altar during the Prostrations and other solemn ceremonies accompanying the Adoration of Our Mother—Eddymush.

Also the word indicative of such of the Sacred Writings as are in the prose form—Eddygraphs—the principal of these being Science and Health, the minor ones being the Sermons, Essays, Letters, Addresses, and the Advertisements soliciting investments in the Memorial Spoon.

Also the word which gives name to such of the Eddygraphs as are in verse-form—Eddyslush.

Also, we have these:

Eddygas, the spiritual intoxicant which rises to the brain from the Eddygraphs and entrances the mind in a delirium of uplifting and rapturous confusions, giving a foretaste of

Eddyville—formerly called heaven, in the ages preceding our era.

Eddycation—culture, enlightenment, wisdom, drawn from the Eddygraphs, the only intellectual nourishment permitted in the Em-

pire. At the time of the destruction of the secret libraries, in the beginning of our sixth century, the Papal command was, to burn all books
and writings except the Eddygraphs, it being held that all knowledge
not contained in these was valueless, also hurtful. Some books of the
day, and one ancient one, escaped, and a few of us know where they
are and how to get access to them. The ancient one is worth more than
all the others together, and indeed is inestimably precious, it being the
sole record of the ancient life and times which can be regarded as his-
torically accurate and trustworthy. This treasure, this mine of truth
and virtue, is chiefly a record of its author's own life and experiences,
and was ten centuries old when it was discovered twenty years ago. It
is called "Old Comradeships," and I shall frequently draw upon its
stores of fact in this History. This immortal benefaction we owe to the
pen of the revered and scholarly Mark Twain, Bishop of New Jersey,
hanged A.M. 12.

Eddycant—the Scientific Statement of Being; the formula "Blood,
Bones, Hash—Mortal Mind, Immortal Mind, Vacant Mind—God,
Good, All-Good, Good-God—Ante-up, Play Ball, Keno!" In its several forms this is the most august of the Sacred Incantations, and is
uttered five times a day, with genuflexions and with the face turned
toward Bostonflats, in whatsoever quarter of the globe the supplicant
may be. For failure the penalty is the Penalty of Penalties—Excom-
munication, with forfeiture of goods and of civil rights, degradation
of the family, burial in unconsecrated ground at the cross-roads at
midnight, with a stake through the breast, as if the man were a suicide.
In all times of danger or of sickness the Eddycant is recited, to save the
supplicant by keeping him reminded that there is no such thing as
danger or sickness.

Eddyfication—the processes which go to the building up of the
Faith.

Eddyolatry—special worship of the Founder.

Eddycal—formerly medical. Relating to treatment for removing
imaginary fractures and illnesses, and raising the dead.

Eddyplunk—the Dollar.

Eddyphone—lightning-rod down which revelations and prophecies
are transmitted from Eddyville to the Pope.

Eddycash—formerly ready-cash. Derived from Chapter I, verse i, Scientific Statement of Being: "On this Rock I have built My Church." And so on—there are many others.

Chapter 2

I T APPEARS that there was a destruction of libraries when our era was only a century old—a prodigious destruction, and nearly complete. During the following fifty years some books were privately made, and kept in concealment; then the most of these were discovered and burned. Fifty years later—shortly after the Papal Consolidation—all the seats of liberal or profane learning were destroyed; also, collections called museums. Then, intellectual Night followed, everywhere but in China. It is believed that no more book-making was ventured for nearly four hundred years, and that then a number of ventures were made, in the way of histories—histories founded largely upon tradition. These were swallowed up in the final raid—beginning of our sixth century—with the few exceptions already noted. No first century work of wholly unassailable historical veracity escaped that final raid except "Old Comrades." This great work was not found until twenty years ago. Its author had taken measures to have it lie hidden five hundred years; fate decided that it should not be seen by men for a thousand. Book-writing absolutely ceased with the final raid. (So the Government thinks; there are those who know better.)

Of the books which survived that raid, the bulk are histories. They are precious, but in the nature of things they cannot be infallibly accurate, for their facts must in many instances have been handed down the centuries by word of mouth; still, there is internal evidence that their narratives are substantially correct. From their stories we are enabled to at least outline the history of our world with reasonable correctness, even if we have to leave patches of the skeleton unfilled, here and there, and the bones showing. I will make an outline such as I have mentioned.

In the earliest times there was a Christian Empire, and its seat was at Rome, (now Eddyburg.) Then Columbus and Uncle Remus followed, and discovered America and Livingston. There was a Greek Empire, too, but we do not know when, nor just where it was located. Its capital was called Dublin, or Dubling. We only know that it flourished some time, then was overthrown by Louis XIV, King of England, who was beheaded by his own subjects for marrying the Lady Mary Ann Bullion when he already had other wives sufficient.

He was succeeded by his son, William the Conqueror, called the Young Pretender, who became embroiled in the Wars of the Roses, and fell gallantly fighting for his crown at Bunker Hill.

He was succeeded by his nephew Saxton Heptarky, so called on account of the color of his hair, and with him real history may be said to begin. The historic atmosphere clears, the clouds pass, and we move out of a mist of conjecture into the sunlight of fact. Comparatively. Doubtless a good deal of it is *not* fact, but it is near enough, and for this we should be grateful and refrain from wanton fault-finding.

This King laid the foundations of England's greatness. He encouraged literature, he exalted the arts, he fostered agriculture and extended commerce. He learned languages, he codified the laws, he granted Magna Charta and collected ship-money; and under his patronage Sir Francis Shakspeare translated the philosophies of William Bacon into tragic verse. From his lips we have the great saying, "Let me make the tax-rates of a country and I care not who makes its songs." He had many romantic and perilous experiences, and after a career unexampled for brilliant exploits and hair-breadth escapes, was drowned by accident in a butt of Malmsey while hunting in the New Forest.

He was succeeded by his son, George III, who fell in the crusades. The crusades are frequently mentioned in the surviving histories; but what they were, and what their object was, is not explained. Constantly and always people fell in them, that is all we know. They are supposed to have been a kind of holy wars, undertaken for the introduction and enforcement of what was known as the Golden Rule, and it is thought by some authorities that the word Crusades, changed by the erosions of time, survives in our word Eddyraids. Flinders (vol. iv, ch. 14, "Glimpses of Antiquity,") thinks there is reason to believe that about the beginning of our era the Golden Rule was being introduced with vigor into China by chartered propagators sent thither from America and Europe, and he states that the spirit of the Rule was identical with that of our so-called Brazen Rule, and the practice also. Our attempts to propagate it in China, during our early Eddyraids, resulted in disaster, and in the expulsion of all foreigners from the land. Few aliens have been admitted there since; none, indeed, that were suspected of having a religion, or of being in sympathy with Civilization.

Civilization is an elusive and baffling term. It is not easy to get at the precise meaning attached to it in those far distant times. In America and Europe it seems to have meant benevolence, gentleness, godliness, justice, magnanimity, purity, love, and we gather that men considered it a duty to confer it as a blessing upon all lowly and harmless peoples of remote regions; but as soon as it was transplanted it became a blight, a pestilence, an awful terror, and they whom it was sent to benefit fled from its presence imploring their pagan gods with tears and lamentations to save them from it. The strength of such evidence as has come down to us seems to indicate that it was a sham at home and only laid off its disguise when abroad.

George III was succeeded by his grandson, Peter the Hermit, called the Black Prince from the color of his armor. He was of a noble nature, broad, liberal, and incandescent in his views. Under his beneficent patronage science and the mechanic arts flourished as they had never flourished before. It is one of the abiding glories of his reign that it was while he was occupying the throne that yellow journalism was invented by Ralph Waldo Edison. What that was we have no means of knowing, we only know that it was one of the abiding glories of his reign. We also know that he made numerous attempts to colonize America, and that several of them succeeded, in some degree. Sir Walter Raleigh settled Plymouth Rock, but was driven away by the Puritans and other Indians; after which he discarded armed force, and honorably bought a great tract of land and named it Pennsylvania, after himself. He prospered exceedingly, and after a few years was able to buy the legislature. As we learn from a chapter of "Old Comrades," this custom continued in his family down to the time of Mark Twain, Bishop of New Jersey,* who was himself present at an auction of this property, when one Quay was the purchaser.

---

* Hanged, A.M. 47.

To the initiated few there is a most interesting fact associated with Peter the Hermit's reign—the translation of the Bible into English. Not many have heard of that book; therefore I will go into some particulars. Bible is its ancient name. It is that part of the Sacred Eddygraphs which follows next after Science and Health, and is sometimes called the "Annex," sometimes the "Apochrypha," and in the day of its prosperity was the Book of the Christians. It is in two parts; one part was anciently called the Old Testament, the other the New Testament. The earliest editions of Science and Health made constant reference to it, and reverently and pains-takingly endeavored to explain what it was about—this is known to be a fact—but that was all changed five centuries ago. At that day our language had so radically changed, by the mutations of time, that the Sacred Writings were no longer intelligible to the bulk of the people, and they murmured. Her Divine Grace Mary Baker G. Eddy LII called the princes of the Church together in conclave from the ends of the earth to consider the question of a new translation, up-to-date, and with him they searchingly canvassed the arguments that were offered for and against the proposition. It was finally decided not to translate Science and Health, but to re-write it altogether and expunge the most of the references to the Bible and medicate the others. The Revised Version was furnished by a revelation dictated to the Pope through the Eddyphone, he being the only person qualified to receive revelations and demonstrate over them; he, in turn, repeated the words to his secretaries, and they wrote them down. The Bible of the Christians was left untouched, and soon none but philological experts could read it. Since it could not be read it was not an embarrassment, therefore it was suffered to retain its place as an Annex, and still retains it; which is wise, for it doubles the price of the book and at the same time cannot limit the sale, that being compulsory.

Parcelsius (vol. 2, ch. 2) has this remark: "From odds and ends of history which have wandered to us down the centuries we infer that in allowing the book called the Bible to sink to oblivion in an unreadable language the Church of Our Mother had warrant in the policy of the abolished Roman Christian Church itself, which kept its Bible in a dead language in order that the common people might not be able to read it."

The successor of Peter the Hermit was Charles the Bald, called the Unready. His conduct toward the American colonies incensed the patriot George Wishington, who hewed down a cherry tree, the emblem of British tyranny, and brought on the Declaration of Independence. Who this person was, originally, we cannot now know; we only know that his destruction of the cherry tree was regarded as a patriotic act, and that it brought him at once into prominence and popularity by precipitating the Declaration. He did not write the Declaration, as some historians erroneously believe, but excused himself on the plea that he could not tell a lie. It was the intention of the Americans to erect a stately Democracy in their land, upon a basis of freedom and equality before the law for all; this Democracy was to be the friend of all oppressed weak peoples, never their oppressor; it was never to steal a weak land nor its liberties; it was never to crush or betray struggling republics, but aid and encourage them with its sympathy. The Americans required that these noble principles be embodied in their Declaration of Independence and made the rock upon which their government should forever rest. But George Wishington strenuously objected. He said that such a Declaration would prove a lie; that human nature was human nature, and that such a Declaration could not long survive in purity; that as soon as the Democracy was strong enough it would wipe its feet upon the Declaration and look around for something to steal—something weak, or something unwatched—and would find it; if it happened to be a republic, no matter, it would steal anything it could get.

Still the Declaration was put forth upon the desired plan, and the Republic did really set up fair temple upon that lofty height. Wishington did not live to see his prophecy come true, but in time it did come true, and the government thenceforth made the sly and treacherous betrayal of weak republics its amusement, and the stealing of their lands and the assassination of their liberties its trade. This endeared it to the monarchies and despotisms, and admitted it to their society as a World Power. It lost its self-respect, but after a little ceased to be troubled by this detail.

George Wishington fought bravely both by land and sea in the Revolution which emancipated his country from the dominion of England, and was drowned at Waterloo, so called on account of the looness or lowness (shallowness?) of the sea at that point, a word whose exact meaning is now lost to us in the mists of antiquity.

Many legends cluster around his name. It is related of him that once in the wilds of Wessex, while wandering in the disguise of a journalist to pick up information concerning the enemy, a peasant woman who did not suspect that he was the Admiral of the Fleet, set him to turn the cakes and he fell asleep and ate them, wherefor she cuffed his ears. And once when he was a hunted refugee and almost in despair of his country's cause, he saw a spider, and from that moment took courage and went boldly on with his great purposes and succeeded. The point of this legend seems to have been lost in the lapse of time.

Wishington had a younger brother by the name of Napoolyun Bonyprat, but of him we know nothing.

Chapter 3

I N T H E century which elapsed after the Separation of America and England, both countries grew by leaps and bounds in power and population, in mechanics, manufactures, commerce, and all forms of material prosperity. This was the century called the Nineteenth by the Christians. There are many indications that it was the most remarkable century the world had ever seen; that the change from previous times was prodigious; that by comparison with its lightning advancement, all previous ages might be said to have stood still.

That century was sown thick with mechanical and scientific miracles and wonders, and it was these that had changed the face of the world. Also, in it occurred two stupendous events—unnoticed at the time— which were to totally change the face of the world *again*: the birth of Our Mother and of Her Church. The second of these happened at the very close of that extraordinary century; with the opening of the so-called Twentieth century the new religion entered with vigor upon its memorable career.

We are able to piece together a panorama of that ancient period out of odds and ends of history and tradition which is absorbingly interesting, though vague and dim in places and sometimes marred by details of a doubtful sort. It exhibits to us life in a dream, as it were, so different is it from life as we know it and live it. It is amazingly complex and wonderful, a sort of glorified and flashing and splendid nightmare, and frantic and tumultuous beyond belief.

It would seem that in the earliest days, time was reckoned from the date of the Creation, and was expressed by the formula *Anno Mundi,* the Year of the World—abbreviated form, A.M.

Then came the Christians, and instituted Time-Series No. 2, expressing it by the formula *Anno Domini,* the Year of Our Lord—abbreviated form, A.D.

Series No. 3 replaced this with the formula of our own era, *Anno Matris,* the Year of Our Mother—abbreviated form, A.M.—a return to Series No. 1, as far as initials go.

It took the Christians three or four centuries to become powerful enough to abolish A.M. and institute A.D.; it is claimed that we moved so much faster that we extinguished A.D. in America in 1960 and replaced it with our A.M.; in England in 1998; in many other countries within fifty years later; and everywhere except China in A.M. 226; then redated all time on a basis of B.M.B.G. and A.M.B.G., (before and after Mary Baker G.).

When our era begins, we know. It begins A.D. 1865. The Church says it marks the birth of Our Mother; some of us privately believe She was born earlier, and that 1865 marks the birth of the first edition of Her Book. There were early historians (discredited now by command of the Church), who asserted that She did not invent Christian Science, but "lifted" it from a man named Quim, or Quimber, or Quimby. In the ancient tongue "lifted" was an expression confined to poetry, and seems to have been in some sort the equivalent of our words *took, conveyed, ravished.* Other early historians (similarly discredited) asserted that Our Mother did Herself put Her Book together—albeit in a notably crude form—and that a salaried polisher labored it into literary shape for Her and introduced examples of grammar. Still other discredited historians asserted that Our Mother's claim that Her Book was the veritable Word of God was necessarily true, because none but

He could understand it. Still other suppressed historians combatted this opinion, on ground of conviction that not even He could tell what it was about.

The Church to the contrary notwithstanding, we do not know the year of Our Mother's birth, nor how long She lived before—according to the Sacred Eddygraphs—She was caught up into heaven in a chariot of fire. That She passed alive to heaven may be true, but there is reason to believe that for a time it was forgotten, since the first mention of it occurs in an Encyclical of Her Divine Grace Mary Baker G. Eddy LIII, as much as five centuries after Our Mother's (probable) translation. No, we do not know how long She lived in the earth, we only know that She never grew old. She was always young and beautiful. The ancient coins, medals, great seals, images, also portraits by the Old Masters, preserved in the Papal treasury at Bostonflats all testify to this. In none of these is She above 18. In all of them She is ethereal and girlish. It is so in the last portrait made of Her, which was painted from life by Dontchutellim only a month before the Ascension, and hangs before the great Altar of Adoration in the First Mosque—called the First Church, in Her lifetime. Admission one dollar, children and slaves half price. Certain early historians asserted that as soon as She became renowned She withdrew Her contemporaneous portraits from sale on the sacred bargain-counter, replaced them with pictures made of Her "when She was a bud," and never suffered Herself to be limned again. Those historians have been placed upon the Index. "Bud" is an ancient term whose meaning cannot now be ascertained with certainty, but philologists think we have a descendant of it in our word *brick*—young, sweet, lovely, gracious, arch, sparkling, companionable, up-to-date, larky, unconventional, ready-for-anything, so it be innocent. This word brick—differently clothed, as to significance—existed in the ancient language, and commonly meant a kind of building material, but it had also another meaning, not now determinable, but believed to represent a specialty of the clergy and a part of their state equipment when conducting solemn spiritual functions, for Mark Twain, Bishop of New Jersey, observes (ch. 7, vol. II, "Old Comrades,") that on two occasions when he was the celebrant in charge of the ceremonies of the High Jinks Night of the Order of the Scroll and Key, he carried one in his hat. This Scroll and Key was evidently an order of monks, and had its seat at a place called Yale. Later—or perhaps previously—a university had its seat there. All present on the named occasions had bricks in their hats; therefore it is inferable that all present were ecclesiastics. What the nature of the function was, we have now no means of determining, and the Bishop throws no light upon it, further than to say it differed from Sunday-school.

Chapter 4

We ARE IN the habit of speaking of the "dawn" of our era. It is a misleading expression inherited from the ancients. It conveys a false impression, for it places before the mind's vision a picture of brooding darkness, with a pearly light rising soft and rich in the east to dispel it and conquer it. In the interest of fact let us seek a more truthful figure wherewith to picture the advent of Christian Science (as it was originally called) as a political force.

At noonday we have seen the sun blazing in the zenith and lighting up every detail of the visible world with an intense and rejoicing brightness. Presently a thin black line shows like a mourning-border upon one edge of the shining disk, and begins to spread slowly inward, blotting out the light as it goes; while we watch, holding our breath, the blackness moves onward and still onward; a dimness gathers over the earth, next a solemn twilight; the twilight deepens, night settles steadily down, a chill dampness invades the air, there is a mouldy smell, the winds moan and sigh, the fowls go to roost—the eclipse is accomplished, the sun's face is ink-black, all things are swallowed up and lost to sight in a rayless gloom.

Christian Science did not create this eclipse unaided; it had abundant help—from natural and unavoidable evolutionary developments of the disease called Civilization. Within certain strict bounds and limits Civilization was a blessing; but the very forces which had brought it to that point were bound to carry it over the frontier sooner or later, and that is what happened. The law of its being was Progress,

Advancement, and there was no power that could stop its march, or even slacken its pace. With its own hands it opened the road and prepared the way for its destroyer.

It was a strange and mad and wonderful world that lay shining under the skies when the thin and scarcely-noticed border-line of the Christian Science eclipse appeared upon the edge of the Sun of Civilization. The old writers call that world's brief period by a majestic name, a beautiful name—the *Age of Light*. We are moved to uncover when it falls upon our ear, as in some way vaguely realizing that we are standing in an august presence. When we look athwart the sombre centuries which lie between us and that fair time, it is as if we saw on the edge of the far horizon the white flash of a hidden sun across the fields of night.

From the old writers we catch many informing glimpses of that strange and enticing and drunken world; we have only to put them orderly together and we have it before our eyes and perceive what it was. The government of our section of the globe was a Republic, and was called the United States of America. There were many Provinces, or States—some think as many as fifty, some think a hundred. Each of these had a government of its own—governor, law-making body, army, etc.,—and was itself a subordinate republic. The provincial law-making body was sometimes called Legislature, sometimes Asylum; the law-making body of the central or supreme government was called Congress, or Head Asylum. All grown-up men were eligible to these bodies, particularly idiots. Why this preference was shown is not now ascertainable. Indeed the preference is not anywhere stated in so many words, the fact is merely deduced from circumstantial evidence.

Every grown-up man had a vote, and highly valued it, though it was seldom worth more than two dollars. This is shown by an election-record of a legislature called Tammany, preserved in the Appendix to "Old Comrades." The Tammany was a private property belonging to one Richard Croker, and it governed a vast city whose remains are believed to lie under the extensive group of forest-clad hills and hillocks called the Great Mounds. It is thought that interesting revelations of the ancient life could be unearthed there if the Popes would allow excavations to be made. There are antiquaries who (privately) contend that the colossal copper statue of Her Divine Grace Mary Baker G. Eddy Enlightening the World (now in Holy Square, Bostonflats), once stood upon the sea-verge near the Great Mounds, and was not there to represent Our Mother at all. This is unquestionably true, for Mark Twain, Bishop of New Jersey, ("Old Comrades," vol. II, ch. 5) makes a reference to that very statue, and calls it "Charley's Aunt." We search the old writers in vain to find out who she was, or by what noble service she won this splendid homage, we only know that she was Charley's Aunt, and that Mark Twain paid for the statue and presented it to "the city," for he says so. There is evidence elsewhere that she had a nephew named Charles Frohman, or Fromton, and that he wrote a book, presumably upon architecture, called "The House of the Seven Gables," and another one called "The House that Jack Built," but this is all we know of him with certainty. It is the irony of history that it so often tells us much about an illustrious person's inconsequential relatives, and gives us not a word about the illustrious person himself. That stately copper colossus can have but one meaning: Charley's Aunt once filled the ancient world with her fame; and where is it now? Thus perishable are the mightiest deeds of our fleeting race! It is a pathetic thought. We struggle, we rise, we tower in the zenith a brief and gorgeous moment, with the adoring eyes of the nations upon us, then the lights go out, oblivion closes around us, our glory fades and vanishes, a few generations drift by, and naught remains but a mystery and a name—Charley's Aunt! Ah, was it worth the hard fight, the weary days, the broken sleep, the discouragements of friends, the insults of enemies, the brief triumph at last, so bitterly won, at such desolating cost—was it worth it, poor lass? But you shall not have served in vain. There is one who loves you, one who mourns you, one who pities you and praises you; one who, ignorant of what you did, yet knows it was noble and beautiful; and banishing time and ignoring space, drops a worshiping tear upon that lost grave of yours made for you by friendly hands a thousand years ago, dear idol of the perished Great Republic, Charley's Aunt!

You have seen what the Government of the United States was. Take your stand, now, upon that resting-place for your feet—and look abroad over the land. You shall see what you shall see.

Figure to yourself—for the moment—that the aspects before you are those of the First Year of the century called by the ancients the Nineteenth. Next we will vault you over decade after decade until you stand in the First Year of the century called by the ancients the Twentieth. There will be contrasts.

Book II

Chapter 1

Inasmuch as the authority most frequently drawn upon in Book Second will be his Grace Mark Twain, Bishop of New Jersey in the noonday glory of the Great Civilization, a witness of its gracious and beautiful and all-daring youth, witness of its middle-time of giant power, sordid splendor and mean ambitions, and witness also of its declining vigor and the first stages of its hopeless retreat before the resistless forces which itself had created and which were to destroy it, it seems wise and well to halt here a moment, and say one or two words about this author and many about his invaluable book and how we became possessed of it.

Mark Twain is the most ancient writer known to us by his works. They have come to us exactly as they were when they left his hands— complete, undoctored by meddling scholars of later days, no word missing, no word added. All other literary remains of the early ages are fragmentary and disjointed, and in all cases have suffered from the impertinent so-called "emendations" and "explanations" of well-meaning archaeologists who may have been competent but may have been otherwise. Mark Twain antedates all these shreds and fragments; hence his title, The Father of History.

From his hand we have the great historical work, in several volumes, called "Old Comrades;" also a philosophical work, in one miniature volume, called "The Gospel of Self," with chapters treating of the "Real Character of Conscience," "Personal Merit," "The Machinery of the Mind," "The Arbitrary and Irresistible Power of Circumstance and Environment," etc. Against advice, he ventured to publish this little book during his lifetime. From hints dropped here and there in the fragmentary histories above mentioned we gather that it cost him dear. We infer that many persons adopted his philosophy and proposed to mould their lives upon it; and that by and by, when Christian Science was become strong, it extinguished both the philosopher and his disciples. There is abundant reason to believe that he was hanged. The date is uncertain; some authorities fix it at A.D. 1912 = A.M. 47; others distribute it forward, stage by stage, up to A.D. 1935 = A.M. 70. It could easily have been later, even, than A.M. 70, for men lived to far greater ages then than they do now. Mark Twain was himself acquainted with an English peasant called "Old Parr," who lived to be 152.

The Father of History does not say when nor where he was born, he only states that he was of high and ancient lineage. There is constructive confirmation of this in the fact that by his own showing he was several times the guest of kings and emperors, who called him in to ask his counsel concerning matters of international politics.

He had a wife and family; indeed, random drippings from his gossipy pen rather clearly indicate that he had more than one family; for he often mentions by name "children" of his who must have been illegitimate, since he nowhere gives them the family surname. Among these are two sons whom he is so weakly fond of that he parades them literally without discretion or shame—Huck Finn and Tom Sawyer. In unguarded moments he quotes remarks of theirs which expose the fact that their mothers were of low origin and illiterate. From these revelations we get a flood of light upon the manners and morals of the clergy of the Bishop's time. Those people were as loose as are their successors of our own day. If anything, they were even more brazen in their immoralities than are our consecrated official Readers of the Sacred Eddygraphs, and less concerned to throw an ostensible veil over their irregularities. Of the Bishop's accumulation of children we are able to classify twenty-six who did not bear his surname, and were manifestly born out of wedlock. If it had been unusual for a Bishop to have twenty-six children of this sort, this one would have covered up his record, not advertised it; therefore we know, and may state with confidence, that in his day the high clergy kept harems, and that nothing was thought of it. One of the most admirable things about history is, that almost as a rule we get as much information out of what it does not say as we get out of what it does say. And so, one may truly and axiomatically aver this, to-wit: that history consists of two equal parts; one of these halves is statements of fact, the other half is inference, drawn from the facts. To the experienced student of history there are no difficulties about this; to him the half which is unwritten is as clearly and surely visible, by the help of scientific inference, as if it flashed and flamed in letters of fire before his eyes. When the practised eye of the simple peasant sees the half of a frog projecting above the water, he unerringly infers the half of the frog which he does not see. To the expert student in our great science, history is a frog; half of it is submerged, but he knows it is there, and he knows the shape of it. Our Bishop had twenty-six children not born in wedlock, and took no pains to conceal it. In the vacancy beyond, we infer a harem, and we know it is there. In the place of a statement that the rest of the high clergy had harems we have a vacancy; by inference we insert a harem in that place, and we know it was there. It was a loose age, like our own.

The Father of History was a great reader; but like all lovers of literature, he had a small and choice list of books which were his favorites, and it is plain, although he does not say so, that he read these nearly all the time and deeply admired them. We do not know what their character was, for he does not say, and no shred of one of them now remains, not even a paragraph—an immeasurable loss, the mere thought of which gives us a sharp pang, a sense of bereavement. We have nothing but the names; and they move our curiosity and our longing as do the names upon ancient monuments to the unknown great, whose informing epitaphs have been obliterated by the storms of time. No, we have only the names: Innocents Abroad; Roughing It; Tramp Abroad; Puddnhead Wilson; Joan of Arc; Prince and Pauper—and so on; there are many. Who wrote these great books we shall never know; but that they *were* great we do know, for the Bishop says so.

The Father of History had many gifts, but it is as a philosopher that he shows best. But he had a defect which much crippled all his varied mental industries, and impaired the force and lucidity of his philosophical product most of all. This was his lack of the sense of humor. The sense of humor may be called the mind's measuring-rod, also its focussing-adjustment. Without it, even the finest mind can make mistakes as to the *proportions* of things; also, as to the *relations* of things to each other; without it, images which for right and best effect should be absolutely perfect, are often a little out of focus, and by consequence are blurred and indistinct; also, they are sometimes so considerably out of focus as to present the image in a highly distorted form —indeed in a form which is actually grotesque. An illustration or two will make my meaning clear. An Appendix to the Bishop's Essay "On Veracity and How to Attain to It" consists of "Maxims for the Instruction of Youth." There are several hundred of them. Examine this one:

"No real gentleman will tell the naked truth in the presence of ladies."

Through the absence of the protecting faculty of humor he has been betrayed into a crass confusion of ideas. The "naked" truth is not always and necessarily indecent; and if he had possessed the sense of humor he would have perceived that his maxim, worded as he has worded it, was in the first place but half true, and that in the second place—owing to the labored solemnity of its form—was an absurdity. He had an idea, and it was a good enough one, but in his attempt to express it he failed to say what he thought he was saying. What he meant to convey, and what he should have said, was this:

"No real gentleman will utter obscenities in the presence of ladies."

Again:

"We should never do wrong when people are looking."

The first five words are true, and admirably stated; the rest of the maxim is idiotic. Idiotic because it almost as good as conveys the idea that when people are *not* looking we are privileged to do wrong!!! He would have seen this himself, but for his defect.

Again:

"Truth is the most precious thing we have. Let us economise it."

His misapprehension of the true meaning of "economise" renders the maxim almost ridiculous, for it as good as advises the young to *save up* the truth—not *tell* it!! What he supposed he was saying will appear when we word it thus:

"The truth is precious; do not be careless with it."

That is sufficient. In this form it is compact and valuable; to add words to it would only impair its compactness without increasing its value.

Again:

"We invariably feel sad in the presence of music without words; and often more than that in the presence of music without music."

The first clause of that is true, and there is a recognizable pathos in it; but there is no sense in the other clause, because there is no such thing as music without music. Music consists of sounds; when there are no sounds, there is no music. It seems almost a pity that some sarcastic person did not say to him, "There is something very impressive about a vacuum without vacancy!!" It would have been a hard hit, but deserved. If he had written his first clause and stopped there, there would be no fault to find; adding the other merely spoiled the whole thing. Many people do not know when to stop. It is a talent, and few possess it.

Finally:

"Let us save the to-morrows for work."

The *to-morrows!!!* Then what shall we do with the to-days? Play? It is amazing that a person of this Bishop's fine intelligence could set that down, and not perceive its obvious defect. Its defect is this: it makes *all* days play-days, because the moment a to-morrow arrives *it* becomes in that very moment a *to-day*,—hence, of course, a play-day. To-morrows are a pure abstraction, an unconcreted and unconcretable thing of the *future*; no man has ever stood in the actual *presence* of a to-morrow, a *present* to-morrow is an impossibility. Now then, how is a person to *work* in a day *which can never have an existence?* Do you not see that the maxim is an absurdity? Do you not perceive that it says, in effect, "Play *all* days—never work at all!!!" Instead of benefiting the young, this heedless and ill-considered admonition could do them inestimable damage. For—read by the unthinking—it could be, and as a rule would be, supposed to advise *perennial idleness!!* Lacking the saving gift of humor, this good Bishop was betrayed into saying the very opposite of what he wanted to convey—which was this:

"Let us work, to-day, *in order that we may play to-morrow.*"

In this form the maxim becomes at once clarified of confusion, and valuable both to young and old alike.

Of the several hundred maxims set down in the Appendix not *one* lacked blunders, irrelevancies and incongruities as laughable as those cited and corrected above. I have edited these deformities out of them all. It has cost me heavy labor, but I think it will be conceived, upon a careful consideration of the maxims which I have quoted, and of the corrective work which I have put upon them, that the little book has merit, and that my labors in relieving that merit of its obscuring and obstructing cloud of defects were worth the fatigue those labors imposed upon me.

Our venerable historian was a man of great learning and large activities, in the several realms of science, invention, politics and philosophy. He was the founder of the Smithsonian Institute, and inventor of several notable aids to verbal communication—among them the electric telegraph, the phonograph, the telephone, and wireless telegraphy. For these and other contributions to science he received many decorations—among them the Black Eagle of Germany, the Double Eagle of Austria, the French Legion of Honor, the Golden Fleece, the Garter, the Victoria Cross, etc. For his "Veracity, and How to Attain It," a system which was adopted as a text-book in all the schools and seats of learning, he "got the chromo." The meaning of the word is lost, but the chromo was no doubt a prize of great cost and distinction awarded by the Government for moral teachings of an eminent character.

It is but seldom that the Father of History mentions a date, but we have one for the completion of "The Gospel of Self" and for the beginning of "Old Comrades"—A.D. 1898 = A.M. 33. When he began "Old Comrades," in Vienna (now Eddyburg), he intended to make it a record, of the most searching and intimate sort, of the life of every person whom he had known—not persons of illustrious position only, or of renown springing from high achievement, but interesting persons of all sorts and ranks, whether known outside their own dooryards or not. He carried out this intention faithfully. His idea was, that to write a minute history of *persons*, of all grades and callings, is the surest way to convey an intelligible history of the *time;* that it is

not the illustrious only who illustrate history, *all* grades have a hand
in it. He also believed that the sole and only history-*makers* are *circumstance and environment*; that these are not within the control of
men, but that men are in *their* control, and are helpless pawns who
must move as they command.

He believed that while he wrote his personal histories, *general* history would flow in a stream from his pen, of necessity. His book con-
firms his theory. In it are intimate biographies of his multitude of
friends, from emperors down through every walk of life to the cobbler and the sheeny—whatever that may be—and the result is as he
had expected: his book reveals to us the wide history of his time, spread
upon pages luminous with its combined and individual life and stirring and picturesque ways and customs.

He believed that no man could write the remorseless truth about his
friend, except under this condition: that the publishing of it be securely guarded against while any one of that friend's name and blood
survived to read it and be hurt by it. He believed that nothing but the
uncompromising truth could be supremely informing, and accurately
convey the history of a period. And so, to enable himself to put away
all embarrassment and be absolutely truthful, the Father of History
resolved to write his book for a distant posterity who could not be
hurt in their feelings by it; and to take sure precautions against the
publishing of the work before that distant day should have arrived.

This made his pen the freest that ever wrote. As a result, his friends
stand before us absolutely naked. They had not a grace that does not
appear, they had not a deformity that is not present to the eye. There
is not an entire angel among them, nor yet an entire devil. Evidently
he was intending to wear clothes himself, and as constantly as he could
he did; but many and many is the time that they slipped and fell in a
pile on the floor when he was not noticing. It would surprise his shade
and grieve it, to find that we know him naked as intimately as we know
him clad. Indeed, we know him better than he knew himself; for he
thought his main feature was an absence of vanity amounting to poverty, even destitution, whereas we are aware that in this matter he was
a person with a close approach to independent means. We could point
out other defects, other blemishes, but he has done us noble service,
and for that he shall go unexposed.

At first it was his purpose to delay publication a hundred years; but he changed his mind and decided to extend the postponement to a period so remote that the histories of his day would all have perished and its life then exist in men's knowledge as a mere glimmer, vague, dim and uncertain. At such an epoch his history would be valuable beyond estimate. "It will rise like a lost Atlantis out of the sea; and where for ages had been a waste of water smothered in fog, the gilded domes will flash in the sun, the rush and stir of a tumultuous life will burst upon the vision, the pomps and glories of a forgotten civilization will move like the enchantments of an Arabian tale before the grateful eyes of an astonished world."

He often takes on like that. In these moods he *invents* things—in accordance with his needs—like that word Atlantis. But we may allow him this small privilege, since he swerves from stern fact only when he has some fine words in his head and wants to spread them out on something and see them glitter.

He thought he would put off the publication a thousand years, but he gave up that idea because he wanted his book to be readable by the common people without necessity of translation. "The epic of Beowulf is twelve hundred years old," he says; "it is English, but I cannot read a line of it, so great is the change our tongue has undergone." He examined, and found that the English of a period 450 years back in the past was quite fairly readable "by Tom, Dick and Harry." Such is his expression. Since he does not explain about these people it is inferable that they were persons of note in his day; and indeed so much so that their names fall from his lips unconsciously, he quite forgetting that he was writing for a far future which might have no source of information concerning the renowned of his time but himself. Again and again, as we dream over this ancient book and see its satisfied and self-important spectres go swaggering by, the thought rises in our minds, how perishable is human glory! Oh, Tom, Dick and Harry, so noted once, so remarked as ye passed along, so happy in the words caught in whispers from the vagrant airs, "Look—there they are!" where now is your fame? Ah, the pathos of a finite immortality!

It was in a book called *Morte d'Arthur* that he found an English still readable by Tom, Dick and Harry after a lapse of 450 years of verbal wear and waste and change, and he copies several passages from that book in order that he may contrast their English with his own and critically note and measure the difference.

He was satisfied, and appointed his book to be published after the lapse of five centuries. In calculating that the man who could read the *Morte d'Arthur* passages without a glossary would be able to read his own book upon the same terms, he was quite within the likelihoods; but his book got delayed so many centuries beyond the date appointed, that when it finally reached the light it was Beowulf over again. No one could spell out its meanings but our half-dozen ripest philologists.

The material of his book is vellum. Its pages were secretly printed by a member of his family on a machine called a type-writer. He bound the volumes himself, then destroyed the original manuscript. The book was privately given into the hands of the President of the United States, and it was sealed up in a vault constructed especially for it below the foundations of the new Presidential palace, and a record made of the matter in the public archives, with a note appended authorizing the Government that should be in power five centuries later to take the book out and publish it at the rates current at said remote time, the proceeds of the sales to be applied to the education of a corps of specialists who should in the fulness of time be required to contrive a copyright law recognizable by sane persons as not being the work of an idiot.

The Father of History believed that a million sets a year would be sold thenceforth so long as governments and civilizations should last, producing an annual revenue of several millions of dollars, and that in the course of ages a copyright law without ass's ears on it—might result.

The Presidential palace was in the capital city, whose name was Washington. It is not doubted that this spelling is a corruption of *Wishington*, the early patriot heretofore mentioned by me; there is much history to show that few names escape misspelling as the wearing centuries roll over them. Washington disappeared long ago, and its place was lost until the finding of the Bishop's great book revealed it. Shepherds digging for water came upon the vault after piercing through a depth of thirty feet of ancient rubbish, and they broke into it and brought up the relic, all the volumes complete, and all sound, after an interment of ten centuries. This was three years ago. My uncle, who was passing by on a horseback journey, bought the find for three eddyplunks, and kept the dangerous property concealed until he found an opportunity to convey it safely to me. I keep it in a sufficiently secure place, and to me the learned come, ostensibly upon other errands, and thus the translation has been patiently worked out, and was completed forty-three days ago.

Here following I give a faithful translation of the Author's Introduction to his venerable work.

To the First Opener of this Book

I SEE this page now for the last time; you will be the next to see it—and there will be an interval between! There is a tie between us, you perceive: where your hand rests now, mine rested last—you shall imagine you feel some faint remnant of the warmth my hand's contact is communicating to the page as I write—for I am *writing* this word of greeting and salutation, not *type*-writing it. You notice that this draws us together, you and me? that it removes the barriers of strangership, and makes us want to be friendly and sociable, and cosy and gossipy? Draw the table to the hearthstone; freshen up the fire with another log or two; trim the candles; set out the wine and the glasses.

So there—you on your side, I on mine, we reach across and clink our goblets. I am come from my grave, where I have mouldered five hundred years—look me in the eye! There—clink again. Drink—to the faces that were dear to my youth—dream-faces these many centuries; to the songs I loved to hear—gone silent so long ago; to the lips that I have pressed in their bloom!

Don't shiver so—don't look crawly, like that; I am only a dead person, there is no harm in me; let us be friendly, let us dissipate together; there is but little time—you hear that clock striking?—when it strikes again I must go back to my grave. You will soon follow.

You shudder again! don't do that; death is nothing—it is peace; the grave is nothing—it is rest. Look kindly upon me; be friendly—I am only a poor dead person, and harmless. And once I was like you: try to see me as I was then; then I shall not seem unpleasant. Once I had hair; there is a little shred of it still hanging from this corner, above and back of where my left ear was—hold the candle—now you see. Like a rusty cobweb? Yes, but you should have seen it when I was alive; you should have seen it then! Lord, how it was admired! Not like Howells's, not like Aldrich's—much handsomer, every one said. And I had eyes then, too; handsome, liquid, full of flash and fire!—and very dear to some, *that* I know; yes, some that looked into them as into mirrors, and saw their own love reflected there, and doubled. Put your finger in, and you can feel where they once were. You don't like to? Why? I would do as much for you. Will, some day. There, you shiver again! don't do that; I don't act so when *you* speak. Clink again. Drink—to the eyes that looked their happiness into mine out of glad hearts that held it a privilege; drink—to the eyes that shone, now dimmed and gone, the happy hearts now broken!

That is from a song. I knew it all, once; but the grave and the ages rot the memory. And this—put your finger on it—you see, it is only a thin column of bony knots, now, but once it was a neck—yes, and fair and round and comely; not like Howells's, not like Aldrich's, which were yellow and scrawny. And it had collars on it, in those days —white, polished, a fresh one every week, sometimes—I speak of my brisk young pre-ecclesiastical days. And over these time-stained and rusty ribs, that stick out, now, and look like the remains of a wrecked ship projecting out of the sands of the shore, I used to wear a snow-white shirt, and a low-cut vest, and as trim and natty a coat as ever you saw—called swallow-tail; it was for evenings, when I went to state banquets, and stood in the flooding light before the applauding aristocracy of learning and literature, and made great and moving speeches —for in my young days I was the national mouthpiece of poesy and science. I notice you are peering through my ribs to see my wine trickle down my spine—and your expression has aversion in it. Do not let it distress you, I am used to it and do not greatly mind it; I am always leaking, like that. A handkerchief? Thanks. Just pass it up and down the front surface of my back-bone, please. Not quite agreeable?

Let me, then . . . . Now it is better. I hate to be wet. As for myself, I can stand it, but it is not pleasant for company—live company, I mean. My own kind do not care. Do you see this aged umbrella? It is the only wearing apparel I have, yet I seldom raise it. I carry it rather for show than use; my neighbors haven't any. This one is a keepsake; it was given me by Howells. After he was done with it. To remember him by. It is not as good now as it was. I have to be careful with it, it is sensitive to weather. I have not exposed it for centuries. And I do not care for rain, anyhow; it passes right through, and I soon dry off. Howells and Aldrich were the dearest friends I ever had. But Howells was the most thoughtful. It was Howells that gave me the umbrella. After he was done with it. Clink again. Drink to them! Aldrich was dear, both were dear. But Howells was the most thoughtful.

Do you notice these arms? Only bones, now, and singularly long and thin. But they have clasped beloved forms, and known the joy of it. Wife—children—think of it! Clasp yours—every time you can—for there is a time coming, when— Drink—drink—and no more of this!

Do you see these hands? these jointed bones? these talons? these things that look like a stripped fan? Shake! *Don't* skringe like that! Look at them. Once they were fair and slender, eloquent with graceful motion, a dream of beauty, everybody said. Howells had no such hands. Nor Aldrich. But mine are no better than theirs, now. Look at them. They have been shaken by all the grades of the human race, in every quarter of the globe, and shaken cordially, too; and now—why now, they disgust you, I can see it in your eye! Clink! Drink—to all good hands that did their best, such as it was, and have finished their work and earned their rest, and gone to it!

Oh, and these legs and these feet—bamboo stems rising out of a splay of polished joints that look like broiled gizzards on skewers. And once they were shapely, and fine-clothed and patent-leathered, and could weave, and wave, and swing and swim in the dreamy waltz! I will show you. Look at this! Do you like it—except the click-clack, and the screeching of the joints? Oil—give me oil! . . . . Now it goes better. The wine is in my head. Join me! *Don't* hold back like that! My arm around your waist. There—now we go! Oh, the days that will come no more! oh, my lost youth!

x x x x Ah—the clock!

! ... ! ... ! ... ! ... ! ... ! ... ! ... ! ... ! ... ! ... ! ... ! ... !

Midnight! Read my book. Read it in a charitable spirit, in a gentle spirit; for we have drunk together and are friends. Shake these poor bones that were once a hand! x x x I thank you. Goodbye, till we foregather again—yonder, with the worms!

Chapter 2

A CHARACTER-SKETCH—INCOMPLETE

I N THE third chapter of his first volume there is a curious character-sketch of the Father of History which is sufficiently puzzling. The first division of it breaks off in the midst, and has no ending.

One perceives that a poet had paid the historian a majestic compliment; that it had produced a physical change in his skull, in the nature of an enlargement; that he had hopes that this might mean a corresponding enlargement of his mental equipment, and also additions to the graces of his character. To satisfy himself as to these matters he went to a magician to get enlightenment. He calls this person a "phrenologist." He nowhere explains, except figuratively, who or what the phrenologists were, and it seems probable that he was not able to classify them quite definitely; for whereas in the beginning of his third chapter he twice speaks of them as "those unerring diviners of the human mind and the human character," in later chapters he always refers to them briefly and without ornament as "those damned asses."

In this place I will insert the first division of the fragmentary character-sketch; and, with diffidence, I will add a suggestion: Might not the historian have been mistaken concerning the poem? It does not mention him by name; may it not have been an apostrophe to his country, instead of to him?

It was in London—April 1st, 1900. In the morning mail came a Harper's Weekly, and on one of its pages I found a noble and beautiful poem, fenced around with a broad blue-pencil stripe. I copy it here.

THE PARTING OF THE WAYS

Untrammelled Giant of the West,
　With all of Nature's gifts endowed,
With all of Heaven's mercies blessed,
　Nor of thy power unduly proud—
Peerless in courage, force, and skill,
And godlike in thy strength of will,—

Before thy feet the ways divide:
　One path leads up to heights sublime;
Downward the other slopes, where bide
　The refuse and the wrecks of Time.
Choose then, nor falter at the start,
O choose the nobler path and part!

Be thou the guardian of the weak,
　Of the unfriended, thou the friend;
No guerdon for thy valor seek,
　No end beyond the avowèd end.
Wouldst thou thy godlike power preserve,
Be godlike in the will to serve!

　　　　　　　　　　　　　Joseph B. Gilder.

It made me blush to the eyes. But I resolved that I would do it, let it cost what it might. I believe I was never so happy before.

My head began to swell. I could feel it swell. This was a surprise to me, for I had always taken the common phrase about swell-head as being merely a figurative expression with no foundation in physical fact. But it had been a mistake; my head was really swelling. Already —say within an hour—the sutures had come apart to such a degree that there was a ditch running from my forehead back over to my neck, and another one running over from ear to ear, and my hair was sagging into these ditches and tickling my brains.

I wondered if this enlargement would enlarge my mental capacities and make a corresponding aggrandizement in my character. I thought it must surely have that effect, and indeed I hoped it would. There was a way to find out. I knew what my mental calibre had been before the change, and I also knew what my disposition and character had been: I could go to a phrenologist, and if his diagnosis showed a change, I could detect it. So I made ready for this errand. I had no hat that would go on, but I made a turban, after a plan which I had learned in India, and shut myself up in a four-wheeler and drove down Piccadilly, watching out for a sign which I had several times noticed in the neighborhood of New Bond street. I found it without trouble—

"Briggs and Pollard, American Phrenologists."

What I desired was the exact truth. If I gave my real name and quality, these people would know all about me: might that not influence their diagnosis? might they not be afraid to be frank with me? might they not conceal my defects, in case such seemed to be found, and exaggerate what some call the great features of my mind and character? in a word, might they not dishonorably try to curry favor with me in their own selfish interest instead of doing their simple and honest duty by me? Indeed this might all happen; therefore I resolved to take measures to hide my identity; I would protect myself from possible deception, and at the same time protect these poor people from sin.

Briggs and Pollard were on hand up stairs. There were bald-headed busts all around, checkered off like township maps, and printed heads on the walls, marked in the same way. Briggs and Pollard had been drinking, but I judged that the difference between a phrenologist drunk and a phrenologist sober was probably too small to materially influence results. I unwound the turban and took a seat, and Briggs stood up behind me and began to squeeze my head between his hands, paw it here and there, and thump it in spots—all in impressive silence. Pollard got his note-book and pencil, and made ready to take down Briggs's observations in short-hand. Briggs asked my name; I told him it was Johnson. Age? I told him another one. Occupation? Broker, I said—in Wall street—when at home. How long a broker? Five feet eight and a half. Question misunderstood, said Briggs: how long in the broking *business?* Always. Politics? Answer reserved. He got other information out of me, but nothing valuable. I was standing to my purpose to get an estimate straight from the bat and the bumps, not a fancy scheme guessed out of the facts of my career. Briggs used a tape-measure on me, and Pollard wrote down the figures:

"Circumference, 46 inches. Scott! this ain't a human head, it's a prize pumpkin, escaped out of the county fair."

It seemed an unkind remark, but I did not say anything, for allowances must be made for a man when his beverages are working.

"Most remarkable craniological development, this is," mumbled Briggs, still fumbling; "has valleys in it." He drifted into what sounded like a lecture; not something fresh, I thought, but a flux of flatulent phrases staled by use and age. "Seven is high-water mark on the brain-chart of the science; the bump that reaches that altitude can no further go. Seven stands for A1, *ultima thule*—that is to say, very large; organ marked 7 is sovereign in its influence over character and conduct, and, combining with organs marked 6 (called large), direct and control feeling and action; 5 (called full) plays a subordinate part; it and 6 and 7 press the smaller ones into their service; 4 (called average) have only a medium influence; 3 (called moderate) below *par*; medium influence, more potential than apparent; 2 (called deficient) leaves the possessor weak and faulty in character and should be assiduously cultivated; while organs marked 1 are very small, and render their possessor almost idiotic in the region where they predominate.

"In the present subject we find some interesting combinations. Combativeness 7, Destructiveness 7, Cautiousness 7, Calculation 7, Firmness 0. Thus he has stupendous courage and destructiveness, and at first glance would seem to be the most daring and formidable fighter of modern times; but at a second glance we perceive that these desperate qualities are kept from breaking loose by those two guardians which hold them in their iron grip day and night,—Cautiousness and Calculation. Whenever this bloody-minded fiend would carve and slash and destroy, he stops to calculate the consequences; then he quits frothing at the mouth and puts up his gun; at this point his total destitution of Firmness surges to the front and he gets down in the dirt and apologizes. This is the low-downest poltroon I've ever struck."

This ungracious speech hurt me deeply, and I came near to striking him dead before I could restrain myself; but I reflected that on account of drink he was not properly responsible for his acts, and also was probably the sole support of his family, if he had one, so I thought better of it and spared him for their sake; in case he had one. Pollard had a hatchet by him; I was not armed.

"Amativeness, 6. Probably keeps a harem. No; spirituality, 7. That knocks it out. A broker with spirituality! oh, call me early, mother, call me early, mother dear! Veneration, 7. My! can that be a mistake? No—7 it is. Oh, I see—here's the solution: self-esteem, 7. Worships himself! Acquisitiveness, 7; secretiveness, 7; conscientiousness, 0. A fine combination, sir, a noble combination." I heard him mutter to himself, "Born for a thief."

"Veracity? Good land, a *socket* where the bump ought to be! And as for—

There the first division breaks off. The Bishop makes no comment, but leaves it so. This silence is to me full of pathos; it is eloquent of a hurt heart, I think; I feel it, and am moved by it, after the lapse of ten centuries; centuries which have swept away thrones, obliterated dynasties and the very names they bore, turned cities to dust, made the destruction of all grandeurs their province, and have not suffered defeat till now, when this little, little thing rises up and mocks them with its immortality—the unvoiced cry of a wounded spirit!

The Bishop did not rest there. He had come to believe that the phrenologists were merely guessers, nothing more, and that they could rightly guess a man only when they knew his history. He resolved to test this theory. He waited several months, then went back to those experts clothed in his ecclesiastical splendors, with his chaplain and servants preceding and announcing him, and submitted his mentalities and his character to examination once more. His "regimentals," as he calls them, disguised him, and the magicians were not aware that they had seen him before. This is all set down in the seventh chapter of volume IV and forms the first paragraph of the second division of the fragmentary character-sketch. The Bishop then summarises the results of his two visits, under the head of "Remarks of the Charlatan Briggs—with Verdicts." Thus:

OBSCURE STRANGER.	RENOWNED BISHOP.
"Not a head—a prize pumpkin."	"A noble head—sublime!"
"Low-down poltroon."	"Lion of the tribe of Judah!"
"Bloody-minded fiend."	"Heart of an angel!"

"Probably keeps a harem."

"Worships himself."

"Born for a thief."

"Veracity? Good land!"

"Others are dirt in presence of this purity!"

"Here we have a divine humility!"

"This is the very temple of honor!"

"This soul is the golden palace of truth!"

The fragment closes with this acrid comment:
"Phrenology is the 'science' which extracts character from clothes."

Chapter 3

N ow THEN, with your feet planted in the First Year of the Nineteenth century, cast your eyes about you, and what do you see? Science had not been born, the Great Civilization had not been born, the land was dully dozing there, not dreaming of what was about to happen! Look. What do you see? Substantially, what you see to-day, eleven centuries later. The aspects are familiar. Twice in the week a stagecoach jogs along, over ill-kept roads, and carries its weary passengers a hundred miles in fourteen hours. The driver is a negro slave. Oxwagons, few and far between, go creaking along these roads, dragging freight from distant great marts to towns and villages, at a pace of a hundred miles in the week. The driver is a negro slave. Mainly, the farms along the road are small, with rickety poor dwellings built of logs—a double-cabin for the white family, a cramped small one for the half-dozen slaves. The slaves sleep indiscriminately on the dirt floor, the married, the single, the children; they work eighteen hours a day; a rag or two is their clothing, their food is a peck of corn apiece per week; for sole entertainment they are allowed to attend church service on Sunday, and sit in the gallery, where they sleep off some part of the week's fatigue and praise God for the privilege. Sunday was the Christian holy day, or day of rest. It is the equivalent of our Motherday, which supplanted it and occurs on Monday.

The white family are lazy and ignorant slatterns, and bear themselves as princes toward the slaves. I must note one little difference, here. These slaves were not the Church's property, as with us; all over the Union of States, from end to end, the families owned them; and owned them as absolutely as does our Church to-day throughout the globe—save China, of course, where slavery does not exist. The farm produced almost all the requirements of the family. The wooden plow, the wooden rake, the wooden harrow, the wooden flail—none of them in repair—were the implements of husbandry, and they differed in no respect from our own. The farm-sheep furnished wool; it was woven into rude fabrics on the premises on primitive looms; from the farm-flax was made a coarse linen; thus the clothing for white and black was furnished, and it was put together on the premises. Sometimes a little cotton was raised, and dyed with homely art, and made up into gala-dress for the women. Cotton was sometimes raised in considerable quantities on the larger farms, with an eye to sale and profit, but this was a trade which could not flourish, because of the expense; for the slave then, as now, could gin only four pounds of cotton in a day, and profit was hardly achievable on those terms. The food was raised on the farm—meat and vegetables. The drink was produced on the farm—cider, beer, and several kinds of strong beverages. Also, two drinks which are but names to us—tea and coffee. It is believed that they still exist in distant regions of the earth, but it is many generations since any wanderer of ours has come back to tell us whether this is true or not. Also, we know that the white family had constructions called pies; and tradition avers that they were only the projectiles which in the modern tongue are called "I would not live alway, I ask not to stay."

There was a church, a whipping-post, stocks, a jail, a gallows, in every town and village; and in the public square was a fenced slave-pen, and near it an auction-block for the sale of slaves and vagrants. They were sold in perpetuity, whereas our Church sells them for terms of years only. Do we miss something? Yes, the Inquisition. There was no Holy Office, neither was there a stake and chain in the square for the burning of heretics and suspected free-thinkers. Otherwise, as you see, this square is a familiar picture to us.

There were canals; and along them poked sleepy barges, drawn by animals and conveying freight and passengers at the gait of the present day.

Now we come to things which are unfamiliar.

In three or four of the large cities a journal was printed every week, for the distribution of intelligence among the people. It contained essays on morals, advertisements of cheese, slaves and dried fish for sale, political news of a former month from the seat of government, and European news of the previous century.

There was an ocean commerce, carried on in sailing ships of a burden ranging from 100 to 350 tons, and there is reference to several of a tonnage reaching even five and six hundred. There were war ships of a thousand tons. All ships were built of wood. The average speed of a sailing vessel was under 150 miles a day. The war ships carried cannon capable of accurate and destructive fire at two hundred yards; also capable of heavily damaging wooden hulks and fortress walls at a quarter of a mile when they could hit them.

There was an army—in all countries. It had cannon; also muskets, which could kill at seventy yards, and sometimes did it. In great European battles it often happened that 5,000 dead were left upon the field, and 15,000 wounded. Of the wounded, four-fifths presently died of their hurts. In the track of war followed broken hearts, poverty, famine, pestilence and death. These miseries continued for thirty years after the war was forgotten. *They* were the important disasters of the war; the killed and wounded were a matter of small consequence.

This talk of war and ships will mean little or nothing to you, but you will recognize the *domestic* features, for they are not novelties to you. That is, the outside aspects, the things visible to the eye, are not. There are inside aspects which you do not see, and which are foreign to your experience.

For instance, in time of peace the people were comfortable and happy—the whites, I mean. They were free. They governed themselves. There were no religious persecutions, no burnings, no torturings. The Roman Catholics were on the other side of the water, working their mischiefs on the continent; the Americans were all Protestants—seventy-five kinds, but living kindly toward each other, and each

willing to let the others save themselves according to their own notions. In this multitudinosity of sects was safety, though they did not
know that. They policed each other, they kept each other out of
mischief. Their disunion was union, but they did not know it. It was
a priceless possession for them and for their country, but they did not
suspect it. They were always and sincerely and earnestly praying that
God would gather His people together in one united whole—over-
looking the fact that that was the very thing which had happened in
Catholic Europe with miserable consequences. We do not now know
what they were, but we know they were of a character to breed fear
and detestation in the breasts of the Protestants. The Americans
hated Catholicism with a deep and strong hatred, and it was their
hope and prayer that it would never grow to a position of strength and
influence in their Republic. Alas for that gentle dream!

There. You have now looked out over fair America reposing in peace
and contentment in the shelter and protection of liberal and wholesome laws honestly administered by men chosen for their proved ability, education and purity, under Chief Magistrates illustrious for
statesmanship, patriotism, high principle, unassailable integrity and
dauntless moral courage—and you have seen what you have seen.

There is not a whisper in the air, not an omen in the sky—yet the
Great Civilization is about to burst upon the drowsing world!

But whether from hell or from heaven, is matter for this history to
determine.

Chapter 4

ALONG through the early months of the first year of the Nineteenth century a host of extraordinary men were born—the future
supreme lords and masters of science, invention and finance, *creators
of the Great Civilization*. At the time, and for years afterward, no man
suspected that these mighty births had happened, and the drowsing
world drowsed on undisturbed.

Then, twenty-five and thirty years later, these wonderful men rose up in a body, and began their miracles; at the same time, another crop of their like appeared in the cradles; another crop was born a generation later; thenceforth to the end of the century and beyond, these relays wrought day and night at the Great Civilization and perfected it.

In the first band we have Priestley, Newton, Lyell, Daguerre, Vanderbilt, Watts, Arkwright, Whitney, Herschel, Galileo, Bruno, Lavoisier, Laplace, Goethe, Fulton, a number of others; and in the second and third we have Adams, Hoe, Darwin, Lister, Thompson, Spencer, Morse, Field, Graham Bell, Bunsen, Kirchhoff, Edison, Marconi, Ericson, McCormick, Kinski, Krupp, Maxim, Cramp, Carnegie, Rockefeller, Morgan, Franklin, Lubbock, Pasteur, Wells, and many, many others.

We are on firm ground, now; and we stand, not in a shredding and shifting fog of conjecture, with glimpses of clear history showing through the rifts, but in a flood of light. I shall draw mainly from the stores of fact garnered up in "Old Comrades," and subordinately from histories saved from the raids of later centuries; but in this latter case I shall use no fact until I have closely examined it and satisfied myself of its authenticity.

The first of the mighty revolutionizers to step forth with his miracle was Sir Izaac Walton. He discovered the law of the Attraction of Gravitation, or the Gravitation of Attraction, which is the same thing. He had noticed that whenever he let a thing go, it fell. He was surprised, and could not think why it should do that, the air being unobstructed and nothing to hinder it from falling up the other way, if it liked. Then the question arose in his mind, *Does* it always fall in the one direction? He was a professional scientist, and a rule of the guild was, that nothing must be taken on trust; therefore he did not announce his discovery but kept it secret and began a series of experiments to prove his hypothenuse. Hypothenuse, in the ancient tongue, was scientific and technical, and meant theory. He made and recorded more than two thousand experiments with all manner of ponderable bodies, and in no instance did one of them fall in any direction but straight down.

He then publicly announced his discovery, and found to his chagrin that others had noticed it before. He was coldly received, now, and many turned from him and sought other excitements. For a time he was sad and discouraged, having now no way to earn his living. But one day when he was in the orchard he saw an apple fall, and at once this great thought burst into his mind: The fact that it falls downward always is not the important question at all, but what *makes* it do it?

It was the turning point of his fortunes. It afforded him business; he began to think it out, and soon had all he could do. The result of his grand meditations was, the conviction that the core at the centre of the earth was of the nature of a magnet, and irresistibly attracted all weighable bodies, whether light or heavy. Thus was discovered the stupendous law of the Attraction of Gravitation; and from the hour of its announcement the name of Izaac Walton was immortal. He received the Victoria Cross, and was made a director of the Bank of England and Superintendent of the Mint.

At first there was no particular use for the law, except as regards apples; but as the years rolled on, zealous experimenters applied it with constant success to wider and still wider and ever widening fields, until at last it became the supreme law of the land, and many wondered how they had ever done without it.

Next, it bridged the seas and became international; and next it bridged space and became inter-stellar. Tycho Bruno presently announced the discovery that the world was turning over. Why this was so, he was not able to discover. Then John Calvin Galileo applied the law of Izaac Walton and found it was because the moon was attracting it, and the sun standing still and helping. His great-great-grandson was afterward burnt at the stake for this, when Our Mother's Church came into power, because it conflicted with the Eddygraphs, which maintain that the world stands still and the sun and moon revolve around it.

Presently astronomers began to think that since the law had the sun and the moon for subjects, maybe its authority extended to the stars as well. To many conservative persons this seemed to be carrying speculation to an extravagance, and they scoffed. Ah, they little dreamed of what was about to happen!

About this time a man by the name of Herschel was examining

some spectacle-glasses one day, with an eye to buying, and by accident he held one glass a few inches above another one and caught a glimpse of a fly through the two. He noticed that the fly looked as big as a dog. He had made a wonderful and revolutionizing discovery, without knowing the name of it. It was the telescope. He constructed a number of these—some of them forty feet long and of great power—and they were distributed among the observatories. With his telescope he discovered the moons of Jupiter and Saturn, and a planet named Uranus—supposed to be, at any rate, though it was too far away for him to determine its name with certainty. These were the first heavenly bodies, floating in remotenesses beyond the reach of the naked eye, that a human being had ever seen since the creation of the world. The event made a gigantic sensation in the earth. One of the telescopes came into the hands of an astronomer named Leverrier, and he turned it upon one of his favorite stars, which was away off on the frontier of the heavens, and immediately saw that it was disturbed about something, for its motions were jerky and irregular—even scandalous, as *he* said. What could be the reason of this? At once he thought of Izaac Walton's law, and said to himself, It is another case of the attraction of gravitation; the star is being pulled and hauled this way and that by the powerful attraction of an invisible orb which is heavier and stronger than itself—an orb which the eye of man has never yet seen. With no guide but the uneasy star's perturbations he weighed the invisible orb, calculated its orbit, found out its name—which was Neptune—determined its period and its gait, and ciphered out whereabouts it would be at 10.40 p.m., Monday three weeks; then he wrote another professional, who was in Germany and nearer the place and had a stronger telescope than his own, to point his barrel at the indicated spot on the indicated night at the specified hour, and he would find a new planet there! It turned out exactly so, and that prodigious fact—the inter-stellar jurisdiction of Izaac Walton's law—was established on foundations as firm as Gibraltar's!

Gibraltar. We cannot now know what Gibraltar was, but we easily perceive from the nature of the sentence that to the ancients it conveyed the idea of a peculiar steadiness and solidity.

Before the world had had time to get its breath it was shaken to its marrow with another amazing thing. The distance of a star had never been measured; to do it had always been considered a thing not possible. All of a sudden, now, this feat was accomplished, by a man named Bessel. He found that the stars were billions and billions of miles away, and that the light from some of them was centuries on its flight before it reached the earth.

The world was dazed by this stunning and swift series of surprises, shocks, assaults; before it could recover from one and get its bearings, another was upon it. And the massed result—what was it? A strange thing, indeed. From the beginning of time the earth had been the one large and important and dignified and stationary thing in the universe, and a little way beyond gunshot, just overhead, there was a sun the size of a barrel-head, a moon the size of a plate, and a sprinkle of mustard-seed stars—the whole to furnish light and ornament; and now, in the twinkling of an eye there had been a mighty stampede and the proud globe was shrunk to a potato lost in limitless vacancy, the sun was a colossus and millions of miles removed, the stars, now worlds of measureless size, were motes on the verge of shoreless space.

That is what had happened. The lid had been taken off the universe, so to speak, there was vastness, emptiness, vacancy all around and everywhere, the snug cosiness was gone, the world was a homeless little vagrant, a bewildered little orphan left out in the cold, a long way from any place and nowhere to go.

A change? A surprise? It is next to unimaginable. What should you say would happen if prisoners born and reared in the stench and gloom of a dungeon suddenly found their den shaken down by an earthquake some day, and themselves spilt out into a far-stretching paradise of brilliant flowers, and limpid streams, and summer-clad forests, set in a frame of mountains steeped in a dreamy haze,—a paradise which is a wonder and a miracle to their eager and ignorant eyes, a paradise whose spiced airs bring refreshment and delight to their astonished nostrils, and whose prodigal sunlight pours balm and healing upon their sick souls, so long shut up in a smother of darkness?

No doubt they would say, They who told us there was nothing but the dungeon deceived us; we perceive that there was more than that and better than that; if there is still more to see and enjoy, beyond these wide horizons, point the way—lead on, and we will follow.

The guides were ready, and each in his turn they fell in at the head of the column and led it a day's march toward the shining far summits of the Great Civilization.

Chapter 5

FIRST came Priestley. He discovered oxygen. By diligent and patient prying and experiment he found out that a fifth part of the air was oxygen; that half of the earth's crust and of pretty much everything on it was oxygen; and that eight-ninths of the ocean's weight was oxygen. He proved that if we remove the oxygen from the air, nothing is left but poison. First he proved it upon insects, then upon mice, then upon rats, then upon cats, then upon dogs and calves, and on up and up to the ignanodon, the giant saurians and the megatherium—for this was the scientific method. The scientist never allowed himself to be sure he could kill a man with a demonstration until he had followed the life-procession all the way up to that summit without an accident; he was then ready for man, and confident. When Priestley finally arrived at the summit, with his chain of dead behind him and not a link missing, he offered to persuade man. Every facility was furnished him, and the world of science looked on with profound interest. The experiment was conducted under the auspices of the Smithsonian Institute, one of the foremost scientific bodies of the time. One hundred and forty-five men and one woman were confined in a room eighteen feet square called the Black Hole of Calcutta, with the air passages stopped up. Priestley said that in seven hours their breathing would exhaust the oxygen in the air, and that then they would all die. He was right, and thus the fact was established that the life-principle of atmospheric air was oxygen. The results were incalculably beneficent. From that date the law commanded that every man should have 144 cubic feet of air to sleep in, even if he must reside on a bench in the park to get it, anything short of 144 being unwholesome and a peril to the man's health and the public's; from that date, by compulsion of the law, the herding of human beings together in deadly little coops and cells ceased, except among the poor.

To prove that oxygen constitutes one half of the earth's crust, Priestley extracted the oxygen from a ten-acre lot and reduced it to five. The land belonged to another person. This person reproached Priestley for not having chosen property of his own for the costly experiment, but Priestley defended his act upon the argument that to choose his own would have been against nature, whereas to choose another man's was quite natural; indeed, inevitable. Thus dimly, gropingly, almost unconsciously, was delivered to an unperceiving and unsuspecting world the rudimentary idea of a mighty law—the law of Natural Selection! By and by it was to be re-discovered and patiently worked out by another man, whose labors would make it a benefaction to men, and upon whose name it would confer immortality.

But for the Bishop—who was present at the time—poor Priestley's connection with that illustrious law would have been unrecorded, and would presently have passed out of man's memory and been forgotten.

Yet Priestley could have suffered that loss and still have remained rich in achievement. Perhaps the most far-reaching and revolutionary of all his contributions to science was his discovery that without oxygen there is no combustion. He proved that you cannot set fire to anything unless oxygen be present with its help. This revelation created a world-wide excitement and apprehension, and this was natural, for it compelled the inference that the earth's life was in danger. The presence of oxygen being universal, in combination with the rocks, the plants, the earths, the air, the ocean, necessarily the opportunity for conflagration and annihilation was also always present. Priestley was assailed from all sides by the terrified human race, and required to give security for the globe or stop meddling with it. He was in great danger for a time, but got out of it by explaining—at least asserting—that the consuming of the globe was *already* going on, and had been going on from the beginning; not by visible fire, but by the slow processes of decay and disintegration—fire, just the same, but not quick fire. He assured the people that there was no immediate danger. The world breathed freer, but was still disturbed. People said that these processes must gradually and ruinously shrink the world's bulk, in time reducing empires to small States, States to counties, counties to townships, and by and by there would be standing room only, and not enough of that. Priestley was asked if this was so, and he was obliged to concede that in his opinion it was. He was now the object of universal execration, and the enraged people resolved that the inventor of combustion should feel in his own person the consequences of his crime— as they regarded it. In this spirit they burned his house. They then drove him into exile.

It was now that Lavoisier moved to the head of the column and saved the earth. He had long been meditating upon the vexed subject of Lost Particles, and endeavoring to find out what became of them. When a boy he had gone North with the Geodetic Survey, and had helped to measure a meridian of longitude. He still had the figures by him, and now a fortunate idea was born to him. Without revealing his purpose, he now, in his age, went North and measured the same meridian again. To his unspeakable joy it measured the same length as before, to a quarter of an inch!

This could mean but one thing—in sixty years the globe had not lost a dust-particle of its bulk. The fact stood proved that Matter was eternal and indestructible; it could change its position, it could change its form, but it could not perish; every atom that was in the world at the Creation was still in it, not a new one had been added nor an old one lost. The globe was saved!

But he kept his secret; for he was a true scientist, and the true scientist proves his hypothenuse down to the last minute detail concerned in it or affected by it, before he is utterly convinced; and not until then can he be moved to proclaim his discovery. Lavoisier now introduced the *scales* into the workshop of science—an epoch-making departure from the old methods, and big with memorable results! That little, little man, with his matchbox and his scales—ah, he was a portent! He went stealthily about, burning and weighing, weighing and burning, and always he kept his secret and bided his time. If anyone left a pair of socks in his way he weighed them, then burnt them, then weighed the ashes and set down the figures in his book; the same with a chair, the same with a hat, the same with an umbrella, the same with a loaf, with a ham, with a picture, a bone, a note of hand, a government bond; whatever he found unwatched, he weighed it, burnt it, weighed it again, and set down the figures. And so he proved at last, and beyond cavil, that the difference between the weight of a thing before it is burnt and the weight of what remains of it after the burning exactly represents the weight of the oxygen that has been set free. Set free, but not lost. It entered into the growing corn, the flower, the child, the passing dog, and became a part of it and a renewer of its decaying fibre and substance. Nothing deterred him in his mad zeal for science; when he could not find other people's things to burn, he burnt his own; though this did not degenerate into a habit. He was often invited to leave localities, he being regarded in some sense as a burden; and this he did, without complaint or show of resentment, but only taking such things as were handy and necessary, and moving on.

He proved that the rains, the dews, the fogs, the hail, the snow, come from the ocean, the lakes and the rivers by evaporation, and that they are condensed in the upper air and returned whence they came, their bulk undiminished, their weight uncurtailed, and that they keep up this industry throughout the ages, gaining nothing, losing nothing. He proved that solids repeated the same history year after year, age after age: decaying, perishing, disappearing, only to return again in other forms—the vanished sheep as part of a hog, part of a tree, part of a deer, part of a cat, part of a fish, part of a king, part of a million things and creatures—but never an atom lost. He maintained that a heretic burnt was but a heretic distributed, and that every time Rome burnt one his released particles went to the making of a hundred Christians. Rome was willing to try it, but he escaped back to America, which was his native land.

It had always been supposed, up to Herschel's time, that the stars were golden nails in the floor of heaven, and were there primarily to hold the floor together, and incidentally to help the sun and moon light-up the earth, and thus save expense; but the telescope showed that those shining bodies were not nails but prodigious worlds, and their obedience to the law of Gravitation proved that they were not of the furniture of heaven but of the family and kinship of the earth. A finer quality of creature, no doubt, but still kinsmen, in some subtle spiritual way, of the humble globe. The announcement gave universal satisfaction, and was indeed epoch-marking in its effect upon man's self-esteem, which it raised by many degrees, banishing from his character such remnants of humility as lingered in it, and causing him to carry himself with the air and aspect of a godling. He felt as a peasant feels who has found out that he belongs to the royal family.

At this pregnant moment appeared Kirchhoff and Bunsen and completed his contentment; for they proved that some of the materials employed in the construction of those grand orbs were identical with certain of the materials which form a part of our world's body, thus establishing actual blood-kinship between them and us, on top of the spiritual relationship already discovered through the operation of Sir Izaac Walton's law. In honor of this event, salutes were fired in all the principal cities, followed by fireworks at night. Bunsen and Kirchhoff's achievement was the outcome of an invention of theirs called the spectroscope, which resolved rays of light into the several colors of which they were originally composed. It was found that these colors got their tints from metals and earths existent in the bodies from whence the rays proceeded. These men could snare a ray from any star, take it apart, analyse it by chemical methods, and tell what the star was made of. They found familiar minerals and gases in the stars, also things new and unfamiliar: hydrogen in Sirius and the nebula of Orion; in the sun, sodium and potassium, calcium and iron; also a quite new mineral which they called helium. This very mineral was afterwards found in the earth. It proved to be valuable. A company was then formed, called the Heavenly Trust, for the exploring of the skies for new products, and placed in the hands of an experienced explorer, Henry M. Stanley. It was granted monopolistic powers: whenever it discovered a new product in the skies it could claim and hold the like product when found in the earth, no matter who found it nor upon whose premises it was discovered. The parent company worked the Milky Way personally, but sublet the outlying constellations to minor companies on a royalty. The profits were prodigious, and in ten years the small group of original incorporators came to be described by a word which was as new as anything they had found in the stars—billionaires.

Thus was launched upon the world the first of the great Trusts. The idea was to be imitated later and distributed far and wide—with memorable consequences to the human race.

Spectrum analysis enabled the astronomer to tell when a star was

advancing head on, and when it was going the other way. This was regarded as very precious. Why the astronomer wanted to know, is not
stated; nor what he could sell out for, when he did know. An astronomer's notions about preciousness were loose. They were not much regarded by practical men, and seldom excited a broker.

The great services of Kirchhoff and Bunsen were frankly recognized,
and they were elected to the legislature.

Meantime an obscure worker by the name of Dagger, or Dugger, or
Daguerre, a citizen of Salem, Massachusetts, had been for some time
privately developing a new and startling idea—the sun-picture—destined to be another revolutionizer. One day he was looking at himself
in a bright square of tin-plate, and he noticed that the portrait displayed in it was exact, and beautifully soft and rich. He was charmed
with his discovery, and sent and had the plate framed at once. But
when it came back the portrait was gone. He was profoundly astonished, also troubled and frightened. As was natural in those days, he
attributed the strange disappearance of the portrait to witchcraft. It
was a carpenter who had made the frame, a man whose reputation had
been under a cloud for some years, because of a suspicion that he had
dealings with a familiar spirit in the form of a black cat. The suspicion
was not without foundation, for he did possess a cat of that complexion, and many had seen it.

Dagger acted honorably in the matter, and with much charity. He
did not denounce him to the authorities at once, but gave him twenty-
four hours in which to restore the portrait, then he told the neighbors
what he had done, and they told the Rev. Cotton Mather. A widespread consternation was the result and all the village clamored for the
carpenter's life. He was put upon his trial the next day—a memorable
episode, for it was the first of that series of Witch Trials which was to
cause the hair of Europe to stand up with horror and its mouth to dis-
charge Vesuvian eruptions of execration and malediction upon the
American name—a natural thing, for Europe had been burning witches
by the million for eight hundred years and knew how to feel about it
when another country got itself tarred with that stick.

On the trial the carpenter proclaimed his innocence humbly and
with seeming sincerity, and his old wife sat at his side with her with-

ered hand in his and pleaded for the court's mercy with moving tears and lamentations. The carpenter offered to prove that the tin plate would produce anyone's portrait without a wizard's help, and that without a wizard's help it would vanish again; and he begged the court and the people to make the test; whereat they all shuddered and refused, and reviled him for the horrid suggestion. He begged Dagger to be merciful and make the trial, but Dagger also was afraid and turned pale at the idea. Then, in his despair the prisoner made the test himself. He looked in the plate—there was his portrait; he removed the plate from before his face, and it was blank.

This was fatal. His jugglery stood proved. Many fled from the place in a frenzy of fright; and the court, with quaking voice and in great excitement, condemned the accused to immediate death by the awful torture called the peine fort et dure.

The sentence was carried out; from that moment Salem was mad. Trial after trial followed; children, servants, idiots became accusers and witnesses; one frail old creature after another was charged with witchcraft, and under the piteous spell of confusion and terror cast by the desertion of family and friends and the curses and black looks of the community their poor intellects went to ruin and they confessed whatever fatal thing they were told to confess; and so, went to the scaffold and perished there, glad of the refuge and peace of the friendly grave. To the number of nineteen poor souls.

But when the accusers began to hale the rich and the high and the influential to court, along with *their* black cats—ah, that was another matter! It was time to call a halt, and the halt was promptly called, and effectually. The Witch Madness was at an end, to be revived no more.

When Dagger's mind got straightened out and adjusted by and by, he began on his idea once more. By setting up tin plates in his back yard, and watching them from points out of range, he saw dogs and chickens produce their portraits and retire in safety, leaving no image behind. This went near to convincing him that the appearances and disappearances were in some mysterious way natural, and that they were also harmless. He then boldly made the test upon his wife's mother, whom he did not need, and who was not aware of what he was doing, she being asleep, and the result was both disappointing and gratifying. After this he proceeded with the development of his great idea with confidence and courage. In the course of his experiments he discovered that by coating his plates with nitrate of silver the mirrored images would stay if he subjected them to a Turkish bath and then covered them with a protecting skin of collodion.

He took out a patent, went on the road, and soon made his tin-types lucrative and famous. He made canvas screens, and painted palatial balustrades on them, with flowering vines clambering about them; also lake scenes, with a sure-enough boat for farmers to sit in in sailor clothes and hold the tiller; also military parade grounds, with a fluted short pillar for the militia-man to stand by in his soldier clothes, or the village fireman to stand by and rest his helmet upon, with trumpet in one hand and spanner in the other; also Niagara Falls, for groups to pose against and look pleasant ten minutes while the camera labored. For balustrade scene he charged two dollars; for sailor in boat, and for militia or fireman, two and a half; for Niagara groups, five; for family, with poppa and momma in the middle and arms about waists,—three dollars; with gold chains and rings manufactured out of brass-dust stuck on with white of an egg, three and a half; for sweethearts holding hands and looking sick and happy—plain, three dollars; with painted clothes and red cheeks, and conferred jewelry, price raised to the limit of probable competence.

Next came the grand development—paper photographs, printed by the thousand from the one form; next, the still grander development— the electrical instantaneous picture, which produced the surprising discovery that when a horse is in motion his limbs jumble themselves ungracefully up as do the legs of a spider who is frizzling in a candle-flame; next, the most amazing development of all—the living picture: all life, all motion exactly and vividly reproduced on a screen before the spectator's eyes. All natural forces being now expended, Dugger invaded the domain of the supernatural, now, and scored an actual miracle: by help of the telescope he photographed stars which were so far away in the fathomless deeps of space that even the telescope could not see them!

He was now requested to resign. This was just and proper, for he had already privately gone yet one other step beyond the jurisdiction of international law and was beginning to photograph the wandering spirits of the departed and trying to collect from them.

Chapter 6

THE EFFECTS of these giant discoveries were in evidence everywhere; the atmosphere of the whole world was electric with them, the Nineteenth century was full of growing-pains, its every nerve was tingling with strange new sensations, all its muscles were straining under the tug of new and resistless forces. The nations reeled and staggered under the enthusing wine of new and noble ideas and ideals in philosophy, politics and religion conveyed to their thirsting lips by great men with great missions who rose up in every land and flooded the dark places with gracious light far-flung from their luminous minds.

With a clarion cry for liberty, equality and fraternity the French Revolution burst out and swept away the regal tyrannies of a thousand years and replaced them with the austere tranquillities of the Bartholomew Massacre and the Reign of Terror; the Huguenots and the emigrés were hunted to their lairs and slaughtered, and piteous were the tales written down of treacheries, privations, and dangers experienced by diarists who escaped. Rank was not a protection, but a peril; Henri IV was stabbed to death by Coligni on the altar-steps of Canterbury Cathedral; Coligni was shot by Charles IX from a window of the Louvre; Charles was guillotined by Louis XVI; Louis was assassinated by the Duke de Guise; the Duke was beheaded by Marat; Marat was butchered in the bath-tub the first time he was ever there, by Charlotte Corday, who was his own mother, but was deceived by his resemblance to Mirabeau; Charlotte Corday was burned at the stake for delivering France, but was afterwards canonized by the Pope for raising the siege of Orleans in the Hundred Years' War. Thus ended the French Revolution, but the turmoil continued in other oppressed countries until they also, like France, had conquered their liberties and turned the sword of war into the pruning hook of peace.

The expression is the Bishop's, and he does not explain it. A pruning hook was probably an implement of agriculture, and may have been the same which in another place he calls a shepherd's hook and says it was to catch sheep with.

Meantime Martin Luther had appeared upon the horizon—a stately figure, a mighty personality, and destined to begin a great work. He reformed religion and for this his name became an honored one and illustrious in all lands; but he was the beginner of a still greater work, although he died ignorant of the importance which that work was to attain to in the world. He was the Father of Geology. One day he found a fossil animal; it was sticking out of a precipice. He brought it home and studied it. He could not make out how it had come to be where he had found it. It could not have entered the rock precipice by any force of its own weak body; therefore a supernatural force must have put it there. He reasoned that that force was God—no other was competent. Why did God put it there? There must have been a purpose; what was that purpose? Luther reasoned that it could have been a model, used in creating the animals of its kind, then concealed in the rock in order that it might be used again in case of need. If this theory was the right one, there would be other models in the cliff, stored there after they had served as patterns to make the various other creatures by. He looked—and found them. The correctness of his theory was thus established to his satisfaction.

With devout joy and gratitude he proclaimed his great discovery, and it aroused the interest of all; particularly that of the undergraduates of the University. They neglected their studies to help him find models. They never found any when he was by, but they found many when he was absent; and theirs were better than his. His were often only skeletons, often merely portions of such; whereas theirs were the animal complete: plump and shapely and beautiful cows no more than three inches high; little elephants, dogs, cats, monkeys, alligators, horses, chickens, crows, eagles, trout, salmon, turtles, all drawn to scale, all in the proper proportions according to the scale, all made out of well baked clay, with a vitreous glaze to protect them from the tooth of time.

The world was excited and entranced, Luther no less. He made beautiful drawings of the animals as fast as they arrived, and had them engraved on steel to illustrate the great book he was writing about the matter. He issued the first volume, with steel reproductions of two hundred breeds of creatures, and was beginning on the next volume, when the zeal of the undergraduates carried them over the frontiers of discretion and they made a mistake. Their grandest discovery—which was Man—had made such a stupendous sensation in the world that it tempted them beyond their strength and they went ahead and discovered *Woman*.

A damp chill fell suddenly upon Luther's enthusiasm. Out of six hundred models captured and classified, this was the first female one. The fact was sodden with solemnity, pregnant with grave suggestion. There was no blinking the seriousness of the situation. The mathematics of the case figured thus—and they did not whisper, but shouted: the chances stood 600 to 1 that female models had never been employed at all. The almost unavoidable inference deducible from these formidable figures was, that the females of the animal world had not been built from special models, but generalized from the male models—a procedure eminently calculated to render them liable to those strange and multifarious defects of construction which had been observable in them from the beginning of time but which had persistently remained unaccounted for until now. This argument was strongly reinforced by the fact that the females of all species are not only physically but mentally inferior to the males, a truth conceded by every masculine person, and by the Bibles of all nations and creeds, without exception. Moreover several of the Bibles of best repute stated that the First Woman was made out of a *bone* extracted from the First Man—with no mention of a model: fair presumptive evidence that none was used; whereas the Man *was* made from a model, a model of baked clay, and moreover—this was a crusher, a demolisher!—when the Man was finished his model had ceased to exist as a model, for *it* was Man, with the breath of life blown into it.

Now, therefore, whence came this baked miniature model of the First Man, fetched by the undergraduates, and reverently employed as a paper-weight by Luther these many weeks?

The students were in evil case, their situation was fraught with danger; for they had fallen under grave suspicion, a suspicion which gathered force and currency day by day, bringing them cold looks at first, then more or less frank avoidance, then "not at homes" where they called, then open snubs on the street, then cessation of invitations to balls and parties, then curt notes from daughtered fathers and mothers desiring a discontinuance of their calls; then utter ostracism from all society, high and low, with insolence and insult from mechanics and servants, sometimes accompanied by blows. Then at last the beer cellars were closed against them.

So young they were, poor lads, to know the anguish of death in life—to be flesh-clothed wandering spectres—to move among the living, yet be not of them! When the court assembled for their trial, it had been long months since they had amused their play-hours with planning gay and humorous ingenuities of defence—oh, that bright time seemed ages in the past! They had no smiles, now, no heart for anything, no care for what might befal.

The charge was read out to them: Profane conspiracy to improve on the plans of God. Without any word of defence, or plea of extenuating circumstances, they confessed their guilt. In answer to questions, their story came out. In brief, it was to the following effect.

In the beginning they had acted quite innocently. They were stirred and interested by Luther's enthusiasm and by the marvelous and imagination-kindling nature of his theories concerning the origin of the strangely-placed bones, and they were eager and anxious to help him in his sublime work and be in a humble way sharers in the glory which would come of it for him and for the Fatherland, they believing unquestioningly in his wisdom and knowledge and not doubting that the results would prove their trust well placed. They found bones and brought them to him; he praised their zeal, and these praises from the great man made them proud and happy, and intoxicated them with desire to win to higher and still higher places in his favor and regard.

But presently the bones began to fail, and next they gave out. He was saddened by this. They were touched, and wished they could do something that might bring back his smile again and the vanished gladness to his heart. And so, with the best intentions, they tried to manufacture bones. But this failed; it was an art above their ignorance; the things they made lacked many of the aspects of nature. Their patron grew more and more despondent. They could not bear to see his sorrow; they could not sleep for trying to think of ways to relieve it.

Then, one day, among the toys in a shop window they came upon a small brown-painted and black-spotted clay dog, of accurate shape and just proportions, exceedingly life-like and natural, the head cunningly canted to one side, one ear hanging, the other archly cocked, the eyes alight with mischief. They felt a hope, and one said—

"Would he accept it? Would he, do you think?"

But another said—and sighed—

"Ah, if it were bones!"

They realized that it was not up to standard; still they tarried—thinking, thinking. They could not tear themselves away. Finally one said—

"We might try. Might we not try?"

Another said, reluctantly—

"I believe he would not take a whole dog. He has not had the whole of anything, yet."

They still remained, and still gazed, lost in thinkings. At length one said—

"If we broke it?—If we brought him part of it?—"

They considered. Then gave it up, saying—

"No, the new break would show."

After a little, one had a fortunate idea, and said—

"*We* need not find it. Let him find it himself, and then if doubts and questionings arise in his—"

"That is the thing! that is the very thing!" they cried out in one voice, and were going to race in and buy the dog; but one put out a hand and stayed them, saying—

"Wait, it will not do. How long must this dog have lain since he was created?"

"Six thousand years."

"He is painted. Paint would not last so long."

That was true, as they all perceived. And one said—

"Even if he were washed he would not do. He would not last six thousand years without a hard strong protecting glaze."

It was then that the clouds passed and they knew what to do. They got the address of the house and place where the dog was made, and one of their number traveled that long journey to a far country, the others sparing of their scant means to provide the cost, and making the sacrifice without murmur or repining, out of the loyal love they bore their patron and the pity they had for him in his grief over his suspended triumphs and his diminished prosperities.

When the glazed dog was come they sought a good hole in the precipice and banked it in there with dry earth, with only the tip of its nose exposed. Then they joined their patron daily in his search, and led him by the place, then back again, then forward again, trying always by furtive devices to get him to see the dog, yet without avail. But at last he found the creature, just as they in their despair were thinking of advertising it, a cost which they could ill afford. They had noble reward for all their hard work and kindly pains, for he burst into raptures and tears of joy, which moved them so that they were resolved that he should not suffer again as he had suffered before, if any sacrifice of time and labor and money on their part could save him from it. And they had a right to be proud and happy, for he said this dog was worth a thousand skeletons, for it was the original model of the primal dog of Creation and beyond estimation precious.

They then arranged with the factory and imported models as needed, ordering them by letter, and having the animals properly sized-up to a standard and built to agree with it, a horse longer than a cow, a cow longer than a bear, and so on. Thus were made and furnished all the animals of the earth, the air and the water that they were acquainted with or could find pictures of. Then they were troubled as to what to do now. In talks with their patron they threw out cautious feelers, and when he mentioned a fresh animal and wished he had it, they showed such a flattering interest that he found high pleasure in telling them all about it and in drawing a picture of it. In two or three weeks they always found it for him and fetched it.

By and by *he* ran out. Ran out of creatures he actually knew about; so then he began to tell about dragons and sea serpents and various kinds of devil-animals and hideous monsters which lived in far countries and were known to him by report and tradition only; but as he did not know their sizes nor shapes nor indeed any definite thing about them, they offered no difficulties for the undergraduates and were not an embarrassment; more, they were an inspiration and a joy. The boys threw all their talents, all their young and flaming energies and ambitions into these things, and loaded up the museum with a fiendish menagerie of grinning, rearing, wild-eyed, beclawed and spike-tailed horrors that gave everybody the dry gripes that even so much as glanced at them—except the patron, who adored them, and labeled them with names to lock the jaw and break the ten commandments.

And still there was no rest for the weary. In the fulness of time the boys had bankrupted invention, their imaginations had gone dry, not another fiend could they contrive. The professor was a-hunger for more, he put on the pressure, put it on heavier and heavier; they did not know what to do nor where to turn.

It was then that they hit upon the great idea of finding the original working model of Man. That mighty find filled the whole world with thunders of jubilation and applause. Luther walked on the clouds, in the worshiping sight of the universe, his boys became illustrious in a day, so to speak. They lost their heads, and did that fatal, fatal thing —they found Woman. And through her they fell.

Such was their story; and some there were in that hard assemblage that were touched by it; touched by its heedless and boyish but prodigal and whole-hearted generosities and untrumpeted sacrifices, and sorry for the poor lads as they sat there friendless and forsaken. But Judge Jeffries was not of these. As sternly as in other days he had gloomed above the Bloody Assize, distributing death among Wat Tyler's ragged ruck and rabble, so gloomed he now above these erring youths; and in tones wherein was no accent of compassion or regret he pronounced their doom—

"Death by the hand of the common headsman, confiscation of your goods, banishment of all whom you hold dear through ties of blood, obliteration of the family name from the registry of the church and of the commune!"

Companioned with Martin Luther's great soul was as great a heart, made all of gentleness and compassion. What he so finely said of Goethe he could with truth have said of himself: "His heart, which his friends knew, was as great as his intellect, which all the world knew." He was far away, at Rome, defending John Calvin from the wanton charge of nonconformity, but as soon as he heard of the sentence he left Servetus to protect Calvin and hastened to Canossa, where the Emperor Henry IV was visiting the Pope on a matter of urgency; the Emperor yielded to the enchantments of an eloquence which had never been voiced in a bad cause and had never failed in a good one, and Luther carried with him thence pardon for the lads and rehabilitation of their fortunes and their names.

But he suppressed his book.

Chapter 7

THE "model" theory fell with the book. But no matter, the first step in Geology had been taken, notwithstanding; for, with the models gone, the fossil skeletons found by Luther still remained, and these could not be flung out of court. They were demonstrably genuine. They must be accounted for. Of one thing there was no doubt, no question, to-wit: all the animals were created in a single day, and all the rocks were created in another single day of the same week. Also, the rocks were made before the animals; then how did the animals get into the rocks? The creatures were too soft, they could not bore their way into the rocks—yet there they were. And not only there, but turned to stone. In a single day?

For a time the problem was difficult. But the science of the day presently solved it. It decided that "these fossils were created already dead and petrified."

That settled it. For a while; indeed for a good while. Then the question came up, What was that *for?* This question was a natural product of a well known fact, to-wit: that in the world nothing was made in vain that was made. Therefore the petrified fossils had been made for a purpose, there was a business reason for their invention. What was that reason; what useful function were they intended to perform? There was worry again, and unrest. Many teeth were injured in trying to crack the new nut. No one was able to furnish a tranquillizing answer. Then the Church did it. She burnt an inquirer or two, and invited further and free investigation into "reasons and purposes which were no man's affair." There were no takers.

By and by, after a sleep, the matter was to stir again, when some inquiries into other things, not at first supposed to be related to it, should prepare the way. People had always believed that the world had been made right in the first place and had never been altered, except now and then by explosions and earthquakes sent as judgments upon people for misconduct, or as warnings to them to behave; and they believed that the oyster shells on the mountain tops had been left there by the Deluge. But by and by Lyell pointed out that the world was undergoing slow and steady and hardly noticeable changes all the time; and he claimed that while some of the changes were certainly and manifestly prodigious, none were unachievable by the slow processes observed and proven, if a sufficiency of time for their work be conceded them—say some millions of years instead of six thousand.

It was then that the fossils got a new chance. It was found that the earth's crust consisted of distinct layers, one on top of another; that in the bottom layers were no fossils; that in the next layers above, were the fossils of primitive and poorly contrived and inconsequential animals and plants; that in the succeeding layers, these developed improvements; and so on, up and up, each layer improving the breeds, and now and then dropping one out of the scheme and leaving it extinct, like the dodo and the moa, the pterodactyl and the mastodon; until finally the surface is reached and we have an immense and highly organized fauna and flora; and then, belated Man appears.

That arrangement was lucid and satisfactory, and Geology had come to stay.

It was not recognized at first that the plants and animals of each layer were descendants of those of the preceding layers; that was noticed later. It made immediate trouble, for it threatened the doctrine of "special creations." Then Darwin studied the matter all out and found that there hadn't *been* any special creations. He found that the original investment had been only a microscopic germ, and that that had developed into a gnat, the gnat into a mosquito, the mosquito into a housefly, the housefly into a horsefly, the horsefly into a bug, the bug into a rat, the rat into a cat, the cat into a dog, the dog into a raccoon, the raccoon into a kangaroo, the kangaroo into a monkey, the monkey into a man, who in time would develop into an angel and go up and wear a halo.

He was asked to resign. But no matter, he had settled the business, and it had to be accepted, there being no way to get around it.

All this happened just in time to powerfully reinforce Herbert Spencer, who was introducing his wonderful all-clarifying law of Evolution, a law which he claimed was in force throughout the universe, and proved that the never-resting operation of its authority was exhibited in the history of the plants, the animals, the mountains, the seas, the constellations, the rise and development of systems of morals, religions, government, policies, principles, civilizations: the all-supreme and resistless law which decrees slow, sure, implacable, persistent, unresting change, change, change, in all things, mental, moral, physical, out of one form into another, out of one quality and condition into another, shade by shade, step by step, never halting, never tiring, all the universe ranked and battalioned in the march, and the march eternal!

Oh, then they saw! even the stupidest perceived and understood. Evolution is a blind giant who rolls a snowball down a hill. The ball is made of flakes—*circumstances*. They contribute to the mass without knowing it. They adhere without intention, and without foreseeing what is to result. When they see the result they marvel at the monster ball and wonder how the contriving of it came to be originally thought out and planned. Whereas there was *no such planning*, there was only a law: the ball once started, all the circumstances that happened to lie in its path would help to build it, in spite of themselves.

The ball of the Great Civilization was well under way, in these days, and plowing along; and flake by flake it grew in bulk and majesty. Priestley contributed oxygen, Sir Izaac contributed Gravitation, Lavoisier contributed the Indestructibility of Matter, Herschel removed the speckled tent-roof from the world and exposed the immeasurable deeps of space, dim-flecked with fleets of colossal suns sailing their billion-leagued remotenesses, Kirchhoff and Bunsen contributed Stellar Chemistry, Luther and Buffon, Cuvier and Linnaeus contributed the

Origins of Life, Lyell contributed Geology and spread the six days of Creation into shoreless aeons of time comparable to Herschel's limitless oceans of space, Darwin abolished special creations, contributed the Origin of Species and hitched all life together in one unbroken procession of Siamese Twins, the whole evolved by natural and orderly processes from one microscopic parent germ, Herbert Spencer contributed the climaxing mighty law of Evolution, binding all the universe's inertnesses and vitalities together under its sole sway and command—and the History of Things and the Meanings of them stood revealed!

Each of these contributions was a *circumstance*; every circumstance begets another one; every new thing that is done moves many many minds to take up that thing and examine it, expand it, improve it, add to it, exploit it, perfect it. Each result of each effort breeds other efforts of other minds, and the original idea goes on growing, spreading, ramifying, and by small and hardly noticed degrees changing *conditions*. And so the snowball adds circumstance after circumstance to its bulk and importance; no contributor is much concerned about anybody's labors and purposes but his own, none of them is intending a snowball, but a snowball will result in spite of individual indifference, and the outcome will be a changed and quite unforeseen condition of things. The tallow candle may remain the universal and satisfactory light for a thousand years; but the first man who invents and introduces a small improvement on that light has made the first step on a long, long road, though he doesn't suspect it—the road to the electric. Many will follow, each with his small contribution; the electric may be three centuries away, but the law of Evolution is at work, and it will be reached.

Individuals do not project events, individuals do not make events; it is massed *circumstances* that make them. Men cannot order circumstances, men cannot foresee the form their accumulation will take nor forecast its magnitude and force. But often a bright man has at the right moment detected the bigness and power of an accumulation, and has mounted it and ridden to distinction and prosperity on its back and gotten the credit of creating it.

Chapter 8

THE vast discoveries which have been listed above created an intellectual upheaval in the world such as had never been experienced in it before from the beginning of time, nor indeed anything even remotely resembling it. The effects resulting were wholly new. Men's minds were free, now; the chains of thought lay broken; for the first time in the history of the race, men were free to think their own thoughts instead of other people's, and utter their conclusions without peril to body or estate. This marked an epoch and a revolution; a revolution which was the first of its kind, a revolution which emancipated the mind and the soul.

It opened the gates and threw wide the road to a gigantic material revolution—also the first of its kind. The factors of it followed upon each other's heels with bewildering energy and swiftness, each a surprise and a marvel, and each in its turn breeding other surprises, other marvels, by the natural law of Evolution, automatically directed and executed by the forces inherent in massed circumstances.

The fell way in which the plans and foreordainings of men go down before the change-making orderly march of the serried battalions of blind Circumstance is impressively exhibited in the history of some of these things. For. instance, at a certain time wise men were prophesying the early extinction of slavery in America, and were forecasting the very date, with confidence. And they had their reasons, which were logically sound and mathematically sure: for slavery had ceased to pay, in some States, and had disappeared; it had now ceased to pay in the other States and was disappearing; its death was manifestly close at hand. But a very small circumstance can damage plans and prophecies, and can follow this up by breeding a posterity of quite natural and inevitable assistant circumstances, family by family, each an added force, each a damager; and in time the accumulation bowls down all resistance, and plan and prophecy are routed and swept away.

In the case of American slavery, the first circumstance that got in the way of the plan and the prophecy was a small thing, and not noticed by any one. But it was a breeder, as time would show. It was Arkwright's spinning-frames, an English invention. Its function was to make clothing-fabrics out of cotton. But there was no business for it, because it could not make a profit upon its work, for two reasons: its driving-power was too expensive and raw cotton too scarce and costly.

Another circumstance intervened now: Watt improved the steam engine, greatly increasing its effectiveness and correspondingly diminishing the cost of its output of force. This saved Arkwright's machine, and it began to turn out its cloth at a profit and call for increasingly large invoices of raw material—which raised the price of American cotton.

That raise was a circumstance which bred another. America had long ago been turning her cotton fields into cornfields because cotton was unprofitable; it was profitable, now, and she resumed its culture. Slavery had long ago ceased to be profitable and was disappearing; it was profitable, now, and the disappearing process stopped. But raw cotton was still too expensive, both for Arkwright's best prosperity and the planter's, because a slave could pick the seeds of only four pounds of cotton in a day.

Then the next circumstance arrived. Eli Whitney tried to invent a machine which would gin the cotton. He made one which would do fifty men's work, then a hundred, then the double of that, and Arkwright and the planter experienced a boom. Slavery got a new impulse; the slave's price rose higher and higher, the demand for him grew more and more pressing; men began to *breed* him for the market, other men (pirates under the law) began to kidnap him in Africa and smuggle him into the country. Whitney went on improving his machine and—

So many people stole his invention and manufactured it that another circumstance resulted—the enactment of a *rational patent law* —the first that had ever existed anywhere; and out of this grew a colossal thing, the stupendous material prosperity of the Nineteenth century!

At last Whitney pushed his machine up to such a degree of effectiveness that it could do the work of 2,000 men and—

Slavery was gratefully recognized by press, pulpit and people, all over the land, as God's best gift to man, and the Prophecy which had once been so logically sound and mathematically sure drew the frayed remnants of its drapery about it and in sorrow lay down and died.

Defeated, not by thought-out plan and purpose, but by natural and logical and blind Evolution, each stage a circumstance whose part in a vast revolution was unforeseen and unpremeditated, the linked march a progress which no man planned nor was able to plan, the resulting compact and connected achievement the work of the miracle-accomplishing unintelligent forces that lay hidden from sight in the little drops that made up that irresistible tidal-wave of accumulated accidents.

Eddypus Fragment

(1901–1902)

MARK TWAIN probably intended to insert this untitled fragment in his
"Eddypus" manuscript; however he failed to indicate where it should be
placed, and the writing materials are so common that it cannot be determined whether the fragment was written during the composition of Book 1
or Book 2.

This brief section is interesting for its quotation of "one S. L. Clemens"
by the Bishop (who in "Eddypus" is "Mark Twain," as remembered a
thousand years later). Clemens himself thus appears as the ultimate authority on that time of most ancient record, the nineteenth century. In
"Eddypus" the future historian relies heavily on the writings of the Bishop;
here it is disclosed that the Bishop quotes Clemens "with . . . much frequency and confidence."

Eddypus Fragment

Elsewhere in his book the Bishop quotes this remark from one S. L. Clemens:

"While Herschel's mighty discoveries were new to the astonished world it was the privilege of Andrew Jackson to point out their destructive bearing upon the ancient and accepted theory that the stars had been devised and created for the sole purpose and function of furnishing light at night to an earth only six thousand years old. It being now known and proved that some of these lamps were so far away that it took their light two million years to reach the earth and do their office, the unbusiness-like anomaly was presented of a lamp made and set going at great expense two million years before its light could become valuable. Andrew Jackson believed there was an improbability lurking here somewhere, and said so. He believed he knew where that improbability was ambushed. He said it was distinctly improbable that the stars were created for the purpose claimed. He was a hard-headed, commercial-minded person, and he lit up his objection with this striking common-sense suggestion: 'If you had a gas contract to light a thousand cities in the Sahara,' said he, 'would you put in the whole plant and start up the whole business now, or would you wait till some of the cities were built?' The world recognized the simple strength of the argument, and the venerable notion that the stars

384

were created to give light to the earth went down with a crash, never more to rise from its ruins. In recognition of this important service to science he was chosen President in the ensuing election."

Such is the version of Clemens. We do not know who he was, since the Bishop does not explain; but he must have known things which the Bishop was not certain about or he would not have quoted him with so much frequency and confidence.

History 1,000 Years from Now

(January 1901)

THIS "translation" (the title is Paine's) may well have been the germ of "Eddypus." The second paragraph reads almost like a prospectus: the "flood of history" prompted by the end of a century is to be condensed into "a bare sketch," "a mere synopsis." The idea that the sketch is to be the work of some benighted scribe of a new Dark Age is implicit in the reference to the "destruction of historical records which occurred during the long and bloody struggle which released us from the cruel grip of democracy."

Paine dated the piece 1900. It is quite likely that Mark Twain wrote it only a short time before "Eddypus," which he began in February 1901. Internal evidence tends to support the later date. During the last days of December 1899 the pages of the New York *Herald* were enlivened by a debate over whether the nineteenth century would end on 31 December 1899 or 31 December 1900. "History 1,000 Years from Now" refers to an identical controversy "a couple of years ago . . . as to whether the dying century closed with the 31st of December 2899, or whether it would close with the last day of last year." In the time scheme of the narrative, then, "the last day of last year" would be the end of December 2900 and the imagined date of the work's composition some time in 2901. If, as the implied reference to the newspaper debate seems to indicate, the narrative's time scheme is an extrapolation from the actual time of composition, Mark Twain must have written the work after December 1900.

History 1,000 Years from Now

A translation

THE COMPLETION of the twenty-ninth century has had at least one effect which was no doubt common to the completion of all the centuries which have preceded it: it has suddenly concentrated the thoughts of the whole thinking and dreaming world upon the past. To-day no subject but the one—the past—can get much attention. We began, a couple of years ago, with a quarrel as to whether the dying century closed with the 31st of December 2899, or whether it would close with the last day of last year, and it took the entire world the best part of a year to settle it; then the past was taken hold of with interest, and that interest has increased in strength and in fascination ever since. To-day men are reading histories who never cared for them before, and men are writing them who had found no call to work such veins previously. Every day brings forth a new history—or shall we say a dozen new ones? Indeed we are floundering in a flood of history.

It will be difficult to condense these narratives into a sketch, but the effort is worthwhile; at least it seems so to the present writer. This sketch must be drawn, fact by fact, trifle by trifle, from the great general mass, therefore it will not be possible to quote the authorities, the number of names and books would be too great for that. And we must make a bare sketch answer, we cannot expand much; we must content ourselves with a mere synopsis.

387

It is now a thousand years since the happy accident—or series of accidents—occurred which after many years rescued our nation from democracy and gave it the blessed refuge and shelter of a crown. We say a thousand years, and it was in effect that, though the histories are not agreed as to the dates. Some of them place the initial events at nine centuries ago, some at ten, others at eleven. As to the events themselves, however, there is less disagreement.

It is conceded that the first of these incidents was the seizure, by the government in power at the time, of the group of islands now called the Vashington Archipelago. Vashington—some say George, some say Archibald—was the reigning President, hence the name. What the group was called before is not now known with certainty, but there is a tradition that our vast Empire was not always called Filipino, and there are those who believe that this was once the name of that archipelago, and that our forefathers adopted it in celebration of the conquest, and out of pride in it. The universal destruction of historical records which occurred during the long and bloody struggle which released us from the cruel grip of democracy makes our history guess-work mainly—alas that it should be so!—still, enough of apparently trustworthy information has survived to enable us to properly esti-mate the grandeur of that conquest and to sketch the principal details of it with a close approach to exactness.

It appears, then, that somewhere about a thousand years ago the Filipino group—if we may use the legendary name—had a population of 260,000,000—Hawkshaw places it at more than this, as does also Dawes—a population higher in civilization and in the arts of war and manufacture than any other in existence.

Passage from "Glances
at History" (suppressed.)

Date, 9th century

(Early 1900s)

THIS ESSAY on the duty of righteous dissent is as timeless as it is plain-spoken. Mark Twain had in view, as the immediate target of his criticism, American military actions in the Philippines and the reactions of the American public to those events. The Lincoln of our literature—as Howells once called Clemens—speaks with the force and vision and high resolve of a true leader—but also recognizes that the "citizens of the Great Republic" could be stampeded into an unjust war and into treating men of honor and principle as traitors by "a silly phrase."

Bernard DeVoto implied that 1906 was the date of composition of both "Glances at History" and "Outlines of History" and published both as part of the "Papers of the Adam Family."[1] Examination of the manuscript paper, however, suggests a somewhat earlier date; Mark Twain used such paper between 1900 and early 1905. His concern over the country's involvement in a dishonorable war would be likely during the first years of the new century, when the question of American intervention in the Philippines was an important issue. The manuscript is, moreover, thematically related

---

[1] LE, pp. 107-111.

to "Eddypus," which also deals in part with the decline and fall of the Great Republic. The most likely time of composition may be between 1900 and 1902, when Mark Twain was attempting other historical essays on very similar topics.

Passage from "Glances at History" (suppressed.)

Date, 9th century

X X X In a speech which he made more than 500 years ago, and which has come down to us intact, he said:

We, free citizens of the Great Republic, feel an honest pride in her greatness, her strength, her just and gentle government, her wide liberties, her honored name, her stainless history, her unsmirched flag, her hands clean from oppression of the weak and from malicious conquest, her hospitable door that stands open to the hunted and the persecuted of all nations; we are proud of the judicious respect in which she is held by the monarchies which hem her in on every side, and proudest of all of that lofty patriotism which we inherited from our fathers, which we have kept pure, and which won our liberties in the beginning and has preserved them unto this day. While that patriotism endures the Republic is safe, her greatness is secure, and against them the powers of the earth cannot prevail.

I pray you to pause and consider. Against our traditions we are now entering upon an unjust and trivial war, a war against a helpless people, and for a base object—robbery. At first our citizens spoke out against this thing, by an impulse natural to their training. To-day they have turned, and their voice is the other way. What caused the change? Merely a politician's trick—a high-sounding phrase, a blood-stirring phrase which turned their uncritical heads: *Our Country, right or wrong!* An empty phrase, a silly phrase. It was shouted by every newspaper, it was thundered from the pulpit, the Superintendent of Public Instruction placarded it in every school-house in the land, the War Department inscribed it upon the flag. And every man who failed to shout it or who was silent, was proclaimed a traitor—none but those others were patriots. To be a patriot, one had to say, and keep on saying, "Our Country, right or wrong," and urge on the little war. Have you not perceived that that phrase is an insult to the nation?

For in a republic, who *is* "the country?" Is it the Government which is for the moment in the saddle? Why, the Government is merely a *servant*—merely a temporary servant; it cannot be its prerogative to determine what is right and what is wrong, and decide who is a patriot and who isn't. Its function is to obey orders, not originate them. Who, then, is "the country?" Is it the newspaper? is it the pulpit? is it the school-superintendent? Why, these are mere parts of the country, not the whole of it; they have not command, they have only their little share in the command. They are but one in the thousand; it is in the thousand that command is lodged; *they* must determine what is right and what is wrong; they must decide who is a patriot and who isn't.

Who are the thousand—that is to say, who are "the country?" In a monarchy, the king and his family are the country; in a republic it is the common voice of the people. Each of you, for himself, by himself and on his own responsibility, must speak. And it is a solemn and weighty responsibility, and not lightly to be flung aside at the bullying of pulpit, press, government, or the empty catch-phrases of politicians. Each must for himself alone decide what is right and what is wrong, and which course is patriotic and which isn't. You cannot shirk this and be a man. To decide it against your convictions is to be an unqualified and inexcusable traitor, both to yourself and to your country, let men label you as they may. If you alone of all the nation shall decide one way, and that way be the right way according to your convictions of the right, you have done your duty by yourself and by your country—hold up your head! you have nothing to be ashamed of.

Only when a republic's *life* is in danger should a man uphold his government when it is in the wrong. There is no other time.

This republic's life is not in peril. The nation has sold its honor for a phrase. It has swung itself loose from its safe anchorage and is drifting, its helm is in pirate hands. The stupid phrase needed help, and it got another one: "Even if the war be wrong we are in it and must fight it out: *we cannot retire from it without dishonor.*" Why, not even a burglar could have said it better. We cannot withdraw from this sordid raid because to grant peace to those little people upon their terms—independence—would dishonor us. You have flung away Adam's phrase—you should take it up and examine it again. He said, "*An inglorious peace is better than a dishonorable war.*"

You have planted a seed, and it will grow.

Passage from "Outlines of History" (suppressed.)

Date, 9th century

(Early 1900s)

LIKE "Glances at History," this essay is intended to be understood as a fragment of suppressed history. With "Glances at History," it was published as part of the "Papers of the Adam Family"[1] and was also apparently written between 1900 and 1905, probably between 1900 and 1902. Not a part of "Eddypus," it offers an alternate fantasy of the collapse of the Great Republic and the rise of a form of monarchical tyranny. In his Autobiographical Dictation of 15 January 1907 Clemens commented further on the inevitability of monarchy:

> Republics have lived long, but monarchy lives forever. By our teaching, we learn that vast material prosperity always brings in its train conditions which debase the morals and enervate the manhood of a nation—then the country's liberties come into the market and are bought, sold, squandered, thrown away, and a popular idol is carried to the throne upon the shields or shoulders of the worshiping people, and planted there in permanency.

In prophesying a new version of monarchy, Clemens may have had in mind what the twentieth century learned to call a dictatorship—as the rise to power of the shoemaker and the militaristic basis of that power may suggest.

---

[1] LE, pp. 107–111.

Passage from "Outlines of History" (suppressed.)

Date, 9th century

B

x x x ᴜᴛ ɪᴛ ᴡᴀѕ impossible to save the Great Republic. She was rotten to the heart. Lust of conquest had long ago done its work; trampling upon the helpless abroad had taught her, by a natural process, to endure with apathy the like at home; multitudes who had applauded the crushing of other people's liberties, lived to suffer for their mistake in their own persons. The government was irrevocably in the hands of the prodigiously rich and their hangers-on, the suffrage was become a mere machine, which they used as they chose. There was no principle but commercialism, no patriotism but of the pocket. From showily and sumptuously entertaining neighboring titled aristocracies, and from trading their daughters to them, the plutocrats came in the course of time to hunger for titles and heredities themselves. The drift toward monarchy, in some form or other, began; it was spoken of in whispers at first, later in a bolder voice.

It was now that that portent called "The Prodigy" rose in the far South. Army after army, sovereignty after sovereignty went down under the mighty tread of the shoemaker, and still he held his conquering way—North, always North. The sleeping republic awoke at last, but too late. It drove the money-changers from the temple, and put the government into clean hands—but all to no purpose. To keep the

power in their own hands, the money-changers had long before bought
up half the country with soldier-pensions and turned a measure which
had originally been a righteous one into a machine for the manufacture of bond-slaves—a machine which was at the same time an ir-
removable instrument of tyranny—for every pensioner had a vote, and
every man and woman who had ever been acquainted with a soldier was
a pensioner; pensions were dated back to the Fall, and hordes of men
who had never handled a weapon in their lives came forward and drew
three hundred years' back-pay. The country's conquests, so far from
being profitable to the Treasury, had been an intolerable burden from
the beginning. The pensions, the conquests, and corruption together,
had brought bankruptcy in spite of the maddest taxation, the government's credit was gone, the arsenals were empty, the country unprepared for war. The military and naval schools, and all commissioned
offices in the army and navy, were the preserve of the money-changers;
and the standing army—the creation of the conquest-days—was their
property.

The army and navy refused to serve the new Congress and the
new Administration, and said ironically, "What are you going to do
about it?" A difficult question to answer. Landsmen manned such
ships as were not abroad watching the conquests—and sunk them all,
in honest attempts to do their duty. A civilian army, officered by ci-
vilians, rose brimming with the patriotism of an old forgotten day and
rushed multitudinously to the front, armed with sporting-guns and
pitchforks—and the standing army swept it into space. For the
money-changers had privately sold out to the shoemaker. He conferred
titles of nobility upon the money-changers, and mounted the republic's
throne without firing a shot.

It was thus that Popoatahualpacatapetl became our master; whose
mastership descended in a little while to the Second of that name, who
still holds it by his Viceroy this day.

Passage from a Lecture

(Early 1900s)

"PASSAGE from a Lecture" asks, "Will this wonderful civilization of to-day perish?" and answers that it will. This essay is thematically related to "Eddypus" and also to the two other "passages" in this volume—those represented to be from two suppressed works. "Glances at History" looks at the Great Republic at a time of moral and political crisis; "Outlines of History" explains that "it was impossible to save the Great Republic" and records the establishing of a totalitarian regime; "Eddypus" more elaborately chronicles the flowering of the great civilization and the rise of the Great Republic and the subsequent decline into a religious despotism in a new Dark Age. "Passage from a Lecture," asserting the Law of Periodical Repetition, forecasts the recurrent popularity of the Science of Health (first called "Christian Science" in the manuscript); "Eddypus" is purportedly the history of one of its periods of ascendancy. "Passage from a Lecture" also bears some relation to Mark Twain's sequence of biblical writings, with which it was published by Bernard DeVoto in *Letters from the Earth* as part of the "Papers of the Adam Family."[1] One of these pieces, "From the Diary of a Lady of the Blood, Third Grade," ends with the Mad Philosopher "just beginning to speak about his 'Law of Periodical Repetition'—or ... about his 'Law of the Permanency of the Intellectual Average' ";[2] in "Passage from a Lecture" the Professor of the Science of Historical Fore-

---

[1] *LE*, pp. 98–101.
[2] *LE*, p. 97.

cast discusses these laws. The latter manuscript seems to have been written as a continuation of the "Lady of the Blood" fragment; however, Mark Twain later designated "Passage from a Lecture" as either a separate manuscript or as a section of some other projected sequence: he repaginated it 1Cc–8Cc. In a somewhat similar fashion he numbered "Glances at History" 1x–5x and "Outlines of History" 1xx–4xx. Conjecturally, he was finding it difficult to integrate his fantasies of current and future history with those of biblical history and was separating the divergent materials. For a time he probably thought of carrying his Adam and Eve sequence on into the future, showing the rise of Christian Science and the decline of civilization, and he may have intended to erect a module of history that would eventually comprise part of an endlessly repeated cycle. At least, it may be seen in Group C-1 of the working notes for "Eddypus" that he was trying to bring biblical history into a cycle that would include Christian Science: "Religion become perfunctory—x_n Science & Health—hence a flood. x_n S. will come again & in 300 yrs will be supreme—then another flood. . . . Adam died 930. Discov. of America, yr 314[.] Eve dies 972. Decay of civiliza[tio]n begins then: spread of X^n Sci. Religious wars produced. By 1200 civ. is dead, & X^n S with it. Savagery till ressurec of X^n S—flood results." In the same group of notes he also wrote the name of the despot who assumes "mastership" in "Outlines of History," Popoatahualpacatapetl. Probably the brief "passage" pieces, including "Passage from a Lecture," represent some intermediate stage of composition between Mark Twain's work on the Adam and Eve sequence and his work on the "Eddypus" sequence.

Passage from a Lecture

T HE MONTHLY meeting of the Imperial Institute took place on
the 18th. With but two exceptions the seats of the Forty Immortals
were occupied. The lecturer of the evening was the distinguished Professor of the Science of Historical Forecast. A part of his subject concerned two of the Laws of Angina Pectoris, commonly called the Mad
Philosopher; namely, the "Law of Intellectual Averages" and the "Law
of Periodical Repetition." After a consideration, at some length, of
cognate matters, he said:

I regard these Laws as established. By the terms of the Law of
Periodical Repetition nothing whatever can happen a single time only;
everything happens again, and yet again, and still again—monotonously. Nature has no originality—I mean, no large ability in the
matter of inventing new things, new ideas, new stage-effects. She has
a superb and amazing and infinitely varied equipment of old ones, but
she never adds to them. She repeats—repeats—repeats—repeats. Examine your memory and your experience, you will find it is true. When
she puts together a man, and is satisfied with him, she is loyal to him,
she stands by him through thick and thin forevermore, she repeats
him by billions and billions of examples; and physically and mentally
the *average* remains exactly the same, it doesn't vary a hair between the
first batch, the middle batch and the last batch. If you ask—

"But really—do you think all men are alike?" I reply—

"I said the *average* does not vary."

"But you will have to admit that some individuals do far overtop the average—intellectually, at least."

Yes, I answer, and Nature repeats *those*. There is nothing that she doesn't repeat. If I may use a figure, she has established the general intellectual level of the race at say, six feet. Take any billion men and stand them in a mass, and their head-tops will make a floor—a floor as level as a table. That floor represents the intellectual altitude of the masses—and it never changes. Here and there, miles apart, a head will project above it a matter of one intellectual inch, so to speak—men of mark in science, law, war, commerce, etc.; in a spread of five thousand miles you will find three heads that project still an inch higher,—men of national fame—and *one* that is higher than *those* by two inches, maybe three—a man of (temporarily) world-wide renown; and finally, somewhere around the circumference of the globe, you will find, once in five centuries of waiting, one majestic head which overtops the highest of all the others—an author, a teacher, an artist, a martyr, a conqueror, whose fame towers to the stars, and whose name will never perish, never fade, while time shall last; some colossus supreme above all the human herd, some unmated and unmateable prodigy like him who, by magic of the forces born in him, turned his shoe-hammer into the sceptre of universal dominion. Now in that view you have the ordinary man of all nations; you have the here-and-there man that is larger-brained and becomes distinguished; you have the still rarer man of still wider and more lasting distinction; and in that final head rising solitary out of the stretch of the ages, you have the limit of Nature's output.

Will she change this program? Not while time lasts. Will she repeat it forever? Yes. Forever and ever she will do those grades over and over again, always in the same proportions, and always with the regularity of a machine. In each million of people, just so many inch-superiorities; in each billion, just so many 2 inch superiorities—and so on; and always that recurrent solitary star once in an age, never oftener, never two of them at a time.

Nature, when pleased with an idea, never tires of applying it. She

makes plains; she makes hills; she makes mountains; raises a conspicuous peak at wide intervals; then loftier and rarer ones, continents
apart; and finally a supreme one six miles high. She uses this grading
process in horses: she turns out myriads of them that are all of one
common dull gait; with here and there a faster one; at enormous intervals a conspicuously faster one; and once in a half century a celebrity
that does a mile in two minutes. She will repeat that horse every fifty
years to the end of time.

By the Law of Periodical Repetition, everything which has happened
once must happen again and again and again—and not capriciously,
but at regular periods, and each thing in its own period, not another's,
and each obeying its own law. The eclipse of the sun, the occultation of
Venus, the arrival and departure of the comets, the annual shower of
stars—all these things hint to us that the same Nature which delights
in periodical repetition in the skies is the Nature which orders the affairs of the earth. Let us not underrate the value of that hint.

Are there any ingenuities whereby you can discredit the law of suicide? No. It is established. If there was such and such a number in
such and such a town last year, that number, substantially, will be repeated this year. That number will keep step, arbitrarily, with the increase of population, year after year. Given the population a century
hence, you can determine the crop of suicides that will be harvested in
that distant year.

Will this wonderful civilization of to-day perish? Yes, everything
perishes. Will it rise and exist again? It will—for nothing can happen
that will not happen again. And again, and still again, forever. It took
more than eight centuries to prepare this civilization—then it suddenly
began to grow, and in less than a century it is become a bewildering
marvel. In time, it will pass away and be forgotten. Ages will elapse,
then it will come again; and not incomplete, but complete; not an invention nor discovery nor any smallest detail of it missing. Again it will
pass away, and after ages will rise and dazzle the world again as it
dazzles it now—perfect in all its parts once more. It is the Law of
Periodical Repetition.

It is even possible that the mere *names* of things will be reproduced.
Did not the Science of Health rise, in the old time, and did it not pass

into oblivion, and has it not latterly come again and brought with it its forgotten name? Will it perish once more? Many times, I think, as the ages drift on; and still come again and again. And the forgotten book, Science and Health, With Key to the Scriptures—is it not with us once more, revised, corrected, and its orgies of style and construction tamed by an educated disciple? Will it not yet die, once, twice, a dozen times, and still at vast intervals rise again and successfully challenge the mind of man to understand it? We may not doubt it. By the Law of Periodical Repetition it must happen.

The Stupendous Procession

(Early 1901)

INTERNAL and external evidence suggests that "The Stupendous Procession" was probably written in January or February 1901, shortly after Mark Twain had, in 1900, written "A salutation-speech from the Nineteenth Century to the Twentieth."[1] It was at the beginning of 1901 that Mark Twain also wrote "To the Person Sitting in Darkness," which he published in the February *North American Review*. The latter article includes two quotations also used in "The Stupendous Procession": the casualty list at 415.18–20 and the statement about bayonetting the wounded at 415.23–25. Many of the events which figure in "The Stupendous Procession" were apparently taken from reports in the New York newspapers from mid-January 1901 to the end of that month. For example, the battle between Lieutenant Steele's men and the Filipinos was described in the New York *Herald* on January 25 in language almost identical to that used by Clemens. A close reading of the author's references to months, weeks, and years in his reckoning of the number of pensioners produced by the war in the Philippines also supports the deduction that he was writing at about the end of January 1901.

At the top of the first page of his typescript Mark Twain wrote in pencil: "Motto—Indemnity and 'one-third extra—to be used in church expenses.' As per statement of Rev. Dr. Ament, Dec. 24, 1900."[2] He was referring to

---

[1] "New Century Greeting Which Twain Recalled," New York *Herald*, 30 December 1900, Section 1, p. 7.

[2] Mark Twain added "church expenses" to replace canceled "propagating the Gospel."

403

actions of the American Board of Foreign Missions which he had satirized
in "To the Person Sitting in Darkness" and which he would attack again in
"To My Missionary Critics" which was to appear in the April 1901 *North
American Review*. In the second of these articles Mark Twain quotes a
cable from Ament in China in which the words "one-third" and "church
expenses" are used in the same sense as in the marginal note. Since the
cable was first published on 20 February, the note cannot have been written
before that date, although it seems probable that it was added not long
afterward, while the information was fresh in Mark Twain's mind and before he had made full use of it in "To My Missionary Critics."

"THE GOOD QUEEN, borne in state, mourned by the world," mentioned in "The Stupendous Procession," is presumably Queen Victoria,
who died on 22 January 1901 and whose funeral procession took place on
4 February 1901. Clemens had witnessed the great procession of Victoria's
Diamond Jubilee in London in June 1897 and had been tremendously impressed; it is likely that in writing "The Stupendous Procession," which is
in part Victoria's funeral procession, he was making a sardonic comparison
of that earlier proud event and the debased condition of the world some
three and one-half years later.

The Stupendous Procession

At the appointed hour it moved across the world in the
following order:

THE TWENTIETH CENTURY,

a fair young creature, drunk and disorderly, borne in the arms of *Satan*.
Banner with motto, *"Get what you can, keep what you get."*

Guard of Honor—Monarchs, Presidents, Tammany Bosses, Burglars,
Land-Thieves, Convicts, etc., appropriately clothed and bearing the
Symbols of their several Trades.

CHRISTENDOM,

a majestic matron, in flowing robes drenched with blood. On her head,
a golden crown of thorns; impaled on its spines, the bleeding heads of
patriots who died for their countries—Boers, Boxers, Filipinos; in one
hand a slung-shot, in the other a Bible, open at the text, "Do unto
others," etc. Protruding from pocket, bottle labeled "We bring you
the Blessings of Civilization." Necklace—handcuffs and a burglar's
jimmy.

405

Supporters. At the one elbow *Slaughter,* at the other *Hypocrisy.*
Banner with motto—"Love your Neighbor's Goods as Yourself."
Ensign—the Black Flag.
Guard of Honor—Missionaries, and German, French, Russian and
British soldiers laden with loot.

MUSIC
Of the Spheres (of Influence.)

Groups of Christendom's Favorite Children—with their Purchases
and Other Acquisitions:

ENGLAND.

Supporters, Mr. Chamberlain and Mr. Cecil Rhodes. Followed by
Mutilated Figure in Chains, labeled "Transvaal Republic;" and
Mutilated Figure in Chains, labeled "Orange Free State."
Ensign—The Black Flag; in its union, a Gold Brick.

THE GOOD QUEEN,

borne in state, mourned by the world. Embroidered on the trappings
of the catafalque, *"These broke her heart."*

SPAIN,

A haughty dame, crowned and sceptred. Naked and not ashamed.
Attended by the Head of the Holy Office and subordinates bearing the
broken and rusty torture-tools of the Inquisition. Also, Bull and Bull-
Fighters.
Banner, with motto—"We have these left—life is not all dark."

RUSSIA,

A crowned and mitred Polar Bear, Sacred and Supreme Pontiff of the Great Church, head piously a-droop, paws clasped in prayer. Followed by
    Weary Column of Exiles—Women, Children, Students, Statesmen, Patriots, stumbling along in the snow;
    Mutilated Figure in Chains, labeled "Finland."
    Floats piled with Bloated Corpses—Massacred Manchurian peasants.
    Ensign—The Black Flag.
    Banner, with motto—"In His Name."

FRANCE,

In gay and scant ballet costume and worn-out liberty cap—riding on a Float. Attended by Meline, Esterhazy, the Shade of Henry, and the rest of the beloved—laureled. *Guillotine*. Zola under the axe; France's eleven other patriots—gagged, and awaiting their turn.
    On foot—
    Mutilated Figure, labeled "Dreyfus;"
    Mutilated Figure in Chains, labeled "Madagascar;"
    Mutilated Figure in Chains, labeled "Tonquin;"
    Guard of Honor—Detachment of French Army, bearing Chinese "heads" and loot.
    Ensign—The Black Flag.
    Banner, with motto—"France, the Light of the World."

GERMANIA,

A Helmeted Figure with Mailed Fist holding Bible aloft—followed by
    Mutilated Figure in Chains, labeled "Shantung;"

Property on a Float, labeled "A Province, three tons of Gold Coin, a Monument, and a Memorial Church—price of two slain missionaries."

Guard of Honor—Column of German missionaries bearing their exacted tribute—famous, now, in the world—of "680 Chinese heads." As per unrepudiated statement of Rev. Mr. Ament.

Ensign—the Black Flag.

Banner, with motto—"For God and Swag."

Standing upon a Float—

AMERICA,

a noble dame in Grecian costume, crying. Her head bare, her wrists manacled. At her feet her Cap of Liberty.

Supporters. On the one hand *Greed*; on the other, *Treason*.

Followed by

Mutilated Figure in Chains, labeled "Filipino Independence," and an allegorical Figure of the Administration caressing it with one hand, and stabbing it in the back with the other.

Banner, with motto—"Help us take Manila and you shall be free—in a horn."

On a Float—

Fat Spanish Friar wrapped in the Treaty of Paris—labeled "This is Nuts for Us." Grouped about him, 16 recent children, with wet-nurses.

Banner, inscribed—"Under the Treaty-protection we can start our population-factories again."

1. *Banner*, inscribed—"And autocratically govern the country again, in spite of the Yankees—if they let us return."

2. *Banner*, inscribed—"And sell Tammany-indulgences and salvation at the old rates."

3. *Banner*, inscribed—"And keep the estates we have annexed, and annex more."

4. The Friar supports his back against a miniature mountain labeled with several placards: "Our Property, protected by Treaty: Millions to

lend, at good interest; fat places for 1200 monks; 403,000 acres richest
land in the Archipelago; much real estate in Manila."

5. On the summit sits

THE AMERICAN EAGLE,

Ashamed, bedraggled, moulting; one foot chained.

Placard, hanging from his tail: "Washington revered me, the great
hand of Lincoln caressed me: and now I am become policeman over
this carrion!"

The Immortals—12,000 Filipino recruits, labeled "Some of us may
seem to die, as time drags on, but it will be an illusion—there will always be just 12,000 of us."

Adjutant General—remarking "It was a good idea to persuade these
hungry poor devils to turn traitor to their country and become American citizens—no, not quite that—American serfs, and murder their
fathers and brothers and neighbors, and burn the humble homes that
sheltered them as children, and which now shelter the mothers that
bore them in pain and the sisters that were the pets and playmates of
their youth; and there is warrant for it, for the Scripture says '*You shall
seethe the kid in its mother's milk.*' And besides, England does it in
India and in China; and what Christian England does, cannot we—as
usual—imitate? Moreover, we did it in the Civil War—made soldiers
of the negroes—"

A *Frivolous Stranger.* "But *they* didn't fight their own race and
blood, they fought only their hated white enslavers and oppressors."

Adjutant General. "Please leave the procession—you are in the way."

Master of Ceremonies. "And damned irrelevant, besides."

6. *Body of American Volunteers*—three hundred in number, the
patriotic product of a week's arduous recruiting among 75,000,000 of
patriotic Americans who ardently approve of the Government's desire
to confer Our Civilization upon the Filipinos with the bayonet.

7. Roll call: the Three Hundred answer, "O'Shaunessy; Joblokoff;
Allessandro; Villeneuve; Sancho Panza; Bjjwskp; Tcherniejoosky;
Mahomet Osmanlie; Jokai Borowackovitch; Denis O'Hooligan; Dun-

can MacGregor; Arthur Wellesley Wellington; Kanaka Okahana; Otto Allerheiligenpotstausenddonnerwetter," etc.

Adjutant General—to the Three Hundred. "Stop reeling, will you! Straighten up and let out some enthusiasm for the Cause. Sing, you sons of . . . . . America!"

The Three Hundred American Volunteers—singing, in 298 languages: "We are coming, Father Corbin, a scant three hundred more!"

The Frivolous Stranger—privately. "Thank God, there isn't an American in the lot."

Another Stranger—jubilantly singing:

> "Up in the fields where the daisies bloom,
> Down in the city's dingiest room,
> Out on the plains, or in the hills,
> Deep in the mines, or in the mills,
> From everywhere they're rising, then,
> Ten thousand regiments of men—
>   *And every man is ready!*"

Adjutant General, suspiciously: "Look here, young man, who are you?"

The Stranger. "A humble poet, sir—W. J. Lampton by name."

"Are you singing about my enlistments?"

"Oh, bless you, no! I was thinking of Cuba—thinking of how the boys came with a rush when there was a chance to set an oppressed little nation free. A body could pronounce *their* names without warping his jaw—oh, yes!"

"Get out of the procession! Stop—what have you been figuring at, there?"

"Only ciphering up how long it will take."

"Take to what?"

"Raise the army to the 104,000 officers and foreigners allowed by the Military Bill. It promises to be a long and giddy entertainment, sir."

"What do you mean by that?"

"Well, it is like this, sir. Although you have judiciously so modified the standard as to admit cripples, consumptives and dwarfs, it is still going to be long, I think. Consider, sir: 70,000 men now in the Philippines—mainly in the hospitals on account of the climate; 50,000 of them finish their time the 1st of July and come home in the invalid fleet, leaving 20,000 behind in the cemetery or the hospital, or around somewhere—anyway they are *there,* and each one and his relations due to pull 43 pensions for four centuries—do you follow me, sir?"

"I am preparing to follow you—and with violence. Continue—and cut it short."

"I hear and obey. From now till July, 22 weeks. At 300 recruits a week, it figures up 6,600. We shall then begin to run a little short of standard cripples, consumptives and dwarfs of foreign origin—unless we import. That will be cruelly expensive. We can't get any to enlist but paupers—can't *now,* I reckon—and the duty on them at Castle Garden is $50 a head."

"*Will* you hurry?"

"I hear and obey. From July till next January we can squeeze out 800 a month, I reckon—4,800 for the 6 months. Next 12 months, 400 a month—call it 5000 in round numbers. End of 1902. For 1903, say 2,500; for 1904, say 1200. Thereafter, say 600 a year, right along—for if they won't enlist, we can tell them it is a pleasure excursion, and they won't know any better, as they won't understand our tongue if we catch them while they are fresh."

"Is the procession to wait all day? Hurry!"

"I hear and obey. Recapitulation: 6,600 and 4,800 for this year—11,400; 5,000 for 1902; 2,500 for 1903; 1200 for 1904; for 1905, say 600 —and thereafter. Total to end of 1905, say 21,000, without counting the dead—for most of those poor old things will die, of course. What we shall then need, to chock up the army full, will be, let us say, somewhere about 80,000 men, for naturally the 20,000 we left in the Archipelago will all be in the cemetery and collecting their pensions long before that day. At 600 a year—no, say 500, for those foreign tramps are bound to grow steadily scarcer unless we import—we shall get the army full-up in a little over 40 years, almost sure, which brings us to A. D. 1946, let us say . . . . . oh, blazes, we've *got* to import! Don't you see it yourself?"

"No, sir! We can put on the draft."

"What—on Americans? To go—now that they have found out the
Government's game—and grab a weak little people's country and give
it *our* liberties for theirs, without their asking,—just as we should like
Germany to do by us, perhaps? You don't know your countrymen, dear
sir, I assure you you don't. They wouldn't stand it a minute. There
would be a riot—a riot like Waterloo! Why, dear sir—"

Master of Ceremonies. "There—that is sufficient, sir."

A *Float*—piled high with barrels. Label: "Report of Philippine Commission. The value of the Archipelago is daily more and more apparent. In one year the war has cost but $200,000,000. To offset this, we
have imports from America, this year, amounting to $1,200,000, one-
third of it whisky for the army; in time, as the natives gradually relinquish their habits of sobriety, we are confident that this detail of the
imports will vastly increase."

A *Large Float.* Upon it a house of a peculiar sort, with the American
flag floating over it and running some risk of "pollution."

A *Figure*—representing Lieutenant Brewer buried alive by the La-
drones.

Spectre of Jefferson Davis. "The North said that as I manufactured
the Civil War, I was personally responsible for every man that was
killed in it. Then who is responsible for this awful Brewer tragedy?
The Administration?"

The Frivolous Stranger,—trying to be sarcastic. "Oh, no, the La-
drones, of course!"

The Spectre. "Excuse me—they had nothing to do with starting the
war; they, nor any one else except the Administration. If it was logic
to accuse me as I was accused, the same logic is good now, and
Brewer was slain by the Administration."

Band of Filipino Prisoners—for deportation to Guam. Labeled,
"Governor General's Report: The native has no fear of death when
fighting for his country's independence—he despises bullets, the bayonet and starvation. It is found that separation from the land of his
birth, which he adores, is the only thing he dreads. It unmans him, it
breaks his heart, he pines under it and dies. *We have adopted
deportation.*"

Head of the Spanish Inquisition,—with envy. "We thought we were past-masters in inventing human miseries—these American Christians can teach us our trade."

THE CONSTITUTION, a giant figure, clothed in a ragged blanket full of holes, marked "Declaration of Independence," a caved-in cap of liberty on its head, its shirt-tail hanging out, labeled *"Fourteenth Amendment."*

CONGRESS follows after, pelting it with mud.

THE GETTYSBURG SPEECH—a noble figure, and mournful. Broken sentences, embroidered upon its robe, are vaguely legible: "Our fathers brought forth a new nation, conceived in liberty and dedicated to the proposition that all men are created equal. . . . . Now we are . . . . . testing whether this nation, or any nation, so conceived and so dedicated, can long endure."

SULTAN OF SULU, wrapped in the Star Spangled Banner. Attended by 2000 slaves and 800 concubines—being his property and the property of the United States. The Sultan lights his pipe with a copy of the Fourteenth Amendment.

Band of Filipinos, marked "Rebels."

Shade of Washington. "Why that name?"

The Frivolous Stranger. "Because they resisted an authority to which they had not promised allegiance."

"Is it not a new meaning to an old word?"

"August shade, it is."

Band of Filipinos—marked "Unclassifiable."

Band of Porto Ricans—marked "Subjects."

Shade of Washington. To the Frivolous Stranger. "Why are those brown people marked 'Unclassifiable?' "

The Stranger. "They do not resist our Government, therefore they are not rebels; they do not acknowledge the authority of our Government, therefore in a sense they are not subjects; they are not saleable, therefore in a sense they are not slaves; they are a part of the population of the United States, but they are not citizens; they belong to America, but are not Americans. Politically they are mongrels—the only ones on the planet, Sir."

Shade of Washington. "And those others?"

The Frivolous Stranger. "The Porto Ricans, Sir? They are a part of our population, their country is a part of America, but they are not citizens, not Americans, not rebels, not slaves. They willingly acknowledge our authority, hence they are subjects."

Shade of Washington—not pleased. "A degrading term, and apes monarchy."

CUBA,

a stately dark maiden, with the light of an unhoped-for freedom glowing in her uplifted face. Necklace of broken chains worn as jewels. Motto—*"Forever free, by the pledge of Congress."*

Supporters—a Congressman at each elbow, the one carrying a set of new handcuffs, the other a set of new leg-irons.

A *Pulpit*, mounted upon a Float. In it, two Preachers, the one bitterly protesting against the Philippine business, the other discreetly silent. Each carries a banner.

1. *Banner* with motto—"Strike for the right—the earned obloquy is praise."

2. *Banner*, with motto—"When your country's honor is breached, think of your bread and butter before you speak."

PATRIOTISM.

On a float, two majestic female figures struggling over the Star Spangled Banner; the one is trying to pour a pail of Administration sewage upon it, the other is trying to prevent it.

Banner, with motto—"It is a free country, take your choice."

PARIS COMMISSION

Grouped upon a Float, with Spain and a pair of Spectres representing "Spanish Sovereignty and Ownership of the Philippines." Market value of the Spectres, ten farthings each; price paid, Twenty Million Dollars for the lot.

Placard, inscribed—"We couldn't buy them of the real owners, who wouldn't sell; we *had* to buy them of somebody, to try to cover up the obtrusive fact that the Administration's seizure of them was theft. Let Europe sneer at the juvenility of the trick if she likes, it is nothing to us; it is not Europe that we are hired to deceive."

Banner, with motto—"It buys us a back seat in the Family of Nations, anyway, and Poor Relation is better than nothing."

Procession of Floats. Upon them are piled 6,000 sick, wounded, and dead American soldiers. The flag at half-mast above them.

Banner, inscribed—"We honestly believed it a patriot's duty to follow his flag, even when its mission was to seize by force a feeble people's country and rob it of its independence. Perhaps it might have been a better quality of patriotism to use our strength in keeping our flag at home—and clean."

Float—with group upon it representing a victorious battle, and our methods. Soldiers armed with guns and bayonets, naked Filipinos armed with bolos and brickbats.

Placard—bearing the Commanding General's report: "Our losses for ten months, 268 killed, 750 wounded; Filipino losses, *three thousand two hundred and twenty-seven killed,* and 694 wounded."

Star Spangled Banner, with motto—"Massacre pacifies quickest."

Float, with another victorious group upon it. Waving over it—

Star Spangled Banner, inscribed with extract from letter of an Iowa soldier-lad to his mother:—"*We never left one alive. If one was wounded we would run our bayonets through him.*"

Banner, inscribed—"The White Man's Burden has been sung. Who will sing the Brown Man's?"

Float, with still another victorious group performing upon it.

Star-Spangled Banner, inscribed: "January 9 Lieut. Steele, with ten men and seven *native* soldiers fought fierce engagement with large force of Filipinos, *more than one hundred* of whom were *killed.* Our loss, *private Edward McGugie killed.*"

Star-Spangled Banner, inscribed—"Filipinos *wounded,* o."

Star-Spangled Banner, inscribed—"A Christian Government's highest duty is to persuade these ignorant brown creatures to massacre their friends and neighbors—and call it 'patriotism.' "

TAMMANY HALL

Disposed in groups upon floats.

1st Group. Mr. Croker with his arms in the city treasury up to the elbows.

2d Group. Tammany agent collecting blackmail from public officials and from a multitude of incorporated companies.

3d Group. Chief of police organizing riot to influence election.

4th Group. Policeman insulting a clergyman.

5th Group. Cabman swindling a fare; policeman standing by, not interested.

6th Group. Stranger trying to find his way in the only world-metropolis on the planet where street-designations do not exist.

7th Group. Cable-car with 1800 people mashed into a solidified mass in it—and all hands submitting to it without complaint. *Banner*, inscribed—"When smitten on the one cheek, give thanks and turn the other."

8th Group. Parlor car in winter; temperature 280 in the shade. No one complaining. Thirsty cat lapping up the perspiration. Roasting passenger, muttering piously—"The best way of employing this life is in fortifying for the next." *Banner*, inscribed with a now famous utterance—"Damn the public."

9th Group. Hospital attendants breaking the ribs and legs of insane patients.

10th Group. Tammany agent collecting blackmail from gambling hells.

11th Group. Tammany agent collecting blackmail from prostitutes.

12th Group. Tammany-licensed children of 5 to 8 years old soliciting in the streets for prostitutes.

13th Group. Tammany-protected prostitutes gathered on stoops, summer evenings, soliciting, chattering obscenities, and shouting indecent remarks at honest women and their husbands, passing by. Policeman listening, undisturbed.

14th Group. Scene in a tenement house owned by a Tammany leader, in the Red Light District. Not describable in print.

15th Group. Youths and young men employed by Tammany people to recruit for their brothels; $25 apiece for each girl seduced—if a city girl; $50 if a country girl, hunted down and brought from the innocent farming regions of New England.

16th Group. Kidnapped country girl—naked—her clothes carried off—screaming for help at a window of a Tammany brothel. Tammany policeman listening, but not hearing.

17th Group. A dispensary under Tammany authority—and profit. Company of children, both sexes, 9 to 13 years of age, *undergoing treatment by the physicians for unnameable diseases.*

Banner, with Tammany's famous sarcastic motto—"What're you going to do about it?"

PHILIPPINE COMMISSION

Grouped upon a Float.

Banner inscribed

"IN OUR OPINION THE FILIPINOS ARE INCAPABLE OF SELF-GOVERNMENT."

The Frivolous Stranger. "What a hell of a sarcasm!"

Master of the Ceremonies. "I told you to leave the ranks; you are getting irrelevant again."

THE AMERICAN FLAG

Waving from a Float piled high with property—the whole marked *Boodle.* To wit:

1200 Islands—when we get them.

Filipino Independence.

Crowd of deported patriots—called "rebels."

Crowd of slaughtered patriots—called "rebels."

Filipino Republic—annihilated.

A Crowned Sultan—in business with the United States and officially-recognized Member of the Firm.

2,000 slaves—joint property of the Firm.

800 concubines—joint property of the Firm.

Motto on the Flag—"*To what base uses have I come at last. But am I polluted?*"

THE PIRATE FLAG.

Inscribed, "Oh, you will get used to it, Brother. I had sentimental scruples at first, myself."

Banners—scattered at intervals down the long procession, and glinting distantly in the sunlight; some of them bearing inscriptions of this sort:

"ALL WHITE MEN ARE BORN FREE AND EQUAL." *Declaration of Independence.*

"ALL WHITE MEN ARE AND OF RIGHT OUGHT TO BE FREE AND INDEPENDENT." *Ibid.*

14th AMENDMENT: "WHITE SLAVERY SHALL NO LONGER EXIST WHERE THE AMERICAN FLAG FLOATS."

> "Christ died to make men holy,
> *He* died to make white men free."
> (Battle Hymn of the Republic. "He" is Abraham Lincoln.)

"GOVERNMENTS DERIVE THEIR JUST POWERS FROM THE CONSENT OF THE GOVERNED WHITE MEN." *Declaration of Independence.*

STATUE OF LIBERTY

Enlightening the World. Torch extinguished and reversed. Followed by

THE AMERICAN FLAG,

furled, and draped with crêpe.

SHADE OF LINCOLN,

towering vast and dim toward the sky, brooding with pained aspect over the far-reaching pageant.

Flies and Russians

(1904 or 1905)

PROBABLY written between November 1904 and February 1905 while Clemens was following the events of the Russo-Japanese War with the hope that the czarist regime would be ended, "Flies and Russians" superimposes Mark Twain's philosophical viewpoint and fantasy upon contemporary history. The satire is not primarily directed at the Russian subjects who are seen as too foolish and too cowardly to achieve their independence; rather, it is aimed at nature and by implication at the Creator for having apparently made these people (and flies) for no good purpose. Mark Twain sometimes represented the whole of humanity to be as useless and degraded as he here shows the Russians, who had been merely the latest to disappoint his hopes for human liberty and brotherhood.

"Flies and Russians" was written at about the same time as "The Czar's Soliloquy." The twelve pages of the manuscript were originally numbered 1–12 and later renumbered 14–25. There is a possibility that, as renumbered, the manuscript may have been part of a draft of "The Czar's Soliloquy," which ends as the czar, standing naked before a mirror, is about to dress. In "Flies and Russians," as the manuscript now begins (the original opening and a "Postscript" were canceled), "his Majesty"—presumably the Czar of Russia—is reading, undershirt in hand. Published in the March 1905 *North American Review*, "The Czar's Soliloquy" was there dated "February 2, 1905." "Flies and Russians" may have been written about then or as much as two months earlier—the date "November 29" was written and canceled on the last page of the typescript. The title is Paine's, who dated the work, "about 1904 or 5."

420

Flies and Russians

(A PAUSE *and a grimace—then his Majesty continues to read.*
Takes up his undershirt but forgets it and stands with it dangling from
his hand while he reads on, spell-bound, unconscious, fascinated.)

There are a number of ways of justifying the existence of the human
race, some of them quite plausible. There are also approximately
plausible ways of justifying and excusing the continuance of several
nations which apparently ought to have been discontinued many
centuries ago. Among these the Russian nation may be instanced as an
example. When we look down the ages and examine the history of that
people we are puzzled and keep asking, What are the Russians *for*?
How did the Russians happen? Were they intentional, or were they
an accident? If they were intentional, what was the intention?

In my opinion,—after months of considering and examining—they
were intentional. I think this because I am sure their history shows
indications of intelligent design—at least design—in the invention
and creation of those people. It is my belief that they were created
for an object; I think there was a purpose in view. I think this is evi-
denced in the fact that century after century, from the beginning of
Russian time, they have clung, without wavering, to a single ideal, a
single ambition, a single industry, and have cared for nothing else,
labored for nothing else, been indifferent to all things else.

Examine the proposition for yourself, by the light of analogy. How

421

do we know what a rabbit is for? The rabbit's history tells us what the rabbit is for. How do we know what a mollusk is for? The mollusk's history tells us what the mollusk is for. How do we know what an idiot is for? The idiot's history tells us what the idiot is for. If we combine these three and add the bee, what do we get? A Russian. How do we know that we have got a Russian? The Russian's history tells us we have got him; and at the same time reveals to us what he is for.

The captive rabbit spends its whole life in meek submission to whatever master is over it; the mollusk spends its whole life asleep, drunk, content; the idiot lives his days in a dull and cloudy dream, and reasons not; the bee slaves from dawn to dark storing up honey for a robber to live on.

Since history shows us that through all the ages from its birth the Russian nation has devoted all its strength and mind and soul to coddling, aggrandizing, adoring and enriching a single robber family, a single family of bloody and heartless oppressors, it seems proven and established that that is what the Russian nation is for. It seems proven and established that the creation of that nation was intentional. Coldly intentional. Why a nation should be created for such a function, is another matter. We have no way of finding out. We only know that nothing was to be gained by it; that nothing has been gained by it; that nothing is ever going to be gained by it. It is an enigma, a miscarriage—like the founding of the fly.

It is possible that at the time the idea of creating the Russian nation was first conceived, the grotesque nature of the result was not clearly foreseen. I think that this is the honorable view to take of it. It was so with the fly. It would not be right for us to allow ourselves to believe that the fly would have been created if the way he was going to act had been fully known beforehand. I think we may not doubt that the fly was a disappointment. I think we have reason to believe that he did not come up to expectations. This argument justifies us in surmising that it is the same with the Russians. The making of flies and Russians—just as they are, I mean—could not have been intentional. Necessarily the idea was to supply a long-felt want; we know this because that was always the idea whenever anything was made. Very well, where was the long-felt want? We all know there wasn't any.

And suppose there had been a long-felt want,—do you reckon you could supply it with flies and Russians? Certainly not. Then what do these reasonings force upon us? They force upon us the conviction that while they were of course intended to supply a long-felt want, they presently developed unforeseen novelties and abnormalities which disqualified them. Nobody is to blame, but there are the facts. We have the flies and the Russians, we cannot help it, let us not moan about it, but manfully accept the dispensation and do the best we can with it. Time will bring relief, this we know, for we have history for it. Nature had made many and many a mistake before she added flies and Russians, and always she corrected them as soon as she could. She will correct this one too—in time. Geological time. For she is a slow worker, and not to be hurried by any one's complaints or persuasions, nor by the skippy activities of her own frivolous intellect.

She made a mistake in the megatherium. It turned out to be absolutely useless. It took her a million years to find it out; then she abolished the megatherium. By and by she tried saurians; she made saurians ninety feet long, and what to do with them after she made them, she did not know. They were long enough to supply any long-felt want that merely required inches and plenty of them; but there was no such want. Others found it out early; it took Nature a million years to perceive it; then she abolished the brood. Next she tried to make a reptile that could fly. We know the result. The less said about the pterodactyl the better. It was a spectacle, that beast! a mixture of buzzard and alligator, a sarcasm, an affront to all animated nature, a butt for the ribald jests of an unfeeling world. After some ages Nature perceived that to put feathers on a reptile does not ennoble it, does not make it a bird, but only a sham, a joke, a grotesque curiosity, a monster; also that there was no useful thing for the pterodactyl to do, and nothing likely to turn up in the future that could furnish it employment. And so she abolished it.

Nature made thousands and thousands of now extinct species in her apprentice-days which turned out to be pure failures, like the flies and the Russians, and she devoted millions of years to trying to hunt up long-felt wants for them to supply, but there were none, and a museum never occurred to her. So she abolished them all, and scat-

tered their bones in myriads in the eternal rocks, and there they rest
to this day, a solemn reminder for us that for every animal-success
achieved by her she has scored fifteen hundred failures. And this without including the flies and the Russians.

Herein we find our hope. We shall not live to see the happy day,
but it will come. It will take her a million years to find out that there
is no use for flies and Russians, then she will act with her accustomed
promptness.

There is also another hope, and a pleasanter one. The first time
Nature tried to make a horse, the result was pathetic. A stranger would
have supposed it was a dog. But she worked at it a million years and
enlarged it to the dimensions of a calf, removed a toe or two from its
feet, and in other ways improved it. She worked at it another million,
then another and another and still another million, and at last after
nine or ten million years of thought and labor and worry and cussing
she turned out for the grateful and cordial admiration of the world
the horse as we see him to-day, that noble creature, that beautiful
creature, that matchless darling of our love and worship. Ten million
years are soon passed: what may not the fly and the Russian become?

And yet, when we reflect! Even in our own day Russians could be
made useful if only a way could be found to inject some intelligence
into them. How magnificently they fight in Manchuria! with what indestructible pluck they rise up after the daily defeat, and sternly strike,
and strike again! how gallant they are, how devoted, how superbly unconquerable! If they would only reflect! if they could only reflect! if
they only had something to reflect with! Then these humble and lovable slaves would perceive that the splendid fighting-energy which
they are wasting to keep their chipmunk on the throne would abolish
both him and it if intelligently applied.

The Fable of the Yellow Terror

(1904–1905)

In "The Mysterious Stranger" Mark Twain had written, "the pagan world will go to school to the Christian: not to acquire his religion, but his guns. The Turk and the Chinaman will buy those, to kill missionaries and converts with."[1] This fable offers a similar prophecy: the "Butterflies" (the Western powers) "have taught one tribe of Bees how to use its sting, it will teach its brother-tribe. The two together will be able to banish all the Butterflies some day." Mark Twain proclaims as well the coming commercialization and industrialization of the Far East: "Also, you have given the Bees the honey-appetite—forced it upon them—and now the frenzy of it will never leave them."

Paine dated the manuscript "About 1905—on the Russo-Jap. War." The paper is the same as that used for "Flies and Russians," and, like that work, this tale was probably written in late 1904 or early 1905.

---

[1] *MSM*, p. 137.

The Fable of the Yellow Terror

A LONG, long time ago the Butterflies held a vast territory which was flowery and fragrant and beautiful. The Butterflies were of many kinds, but all the kinds were richly clothed and all had a fine and cultivated taste in colors and were highly trained in etiquette, and de-portment and in the other graces and accomplishments which make the charm of life in an advanced and elegant civilization. There was not another civilization among the animals that approached that of the Butterflies. They were very proud of it, insufferably proud of it, and always anxious to spread it around the planet and cram it down other people's throats and improve them.

They had an idea that they were the only people that knew the true way to be happy and how to lam happiness into other people and make them good. So they sent missionaries to all the pagan insects to teach them how to be tranquil and unafraid on a deathbed, and then sent trader-bugs to make them long for the deathbed, and then followed up the trader-bugs with diplomat-bugs and undertaker-bugs to perfect the blessings of the conferred civilization and furnish the deathbed, and charge for the funeral. There was hardly a single But-terfly of all the millions that did not boast of this civilization with his mouth, and laugh at it in private. For truly it was a whitewashed hum-bug, and few there were that prayed for it. Except with the mouth.

The Butterflies had what is called a cinch on a great and profitable art. This was the art of making honey. Also a cinch on another great and profitable art. This was the art of killing. For in those days the Butterfly had a sting. He not only had a sting but he was the only bird in the world that had studied out how to use it scientifically and devastatingly. It made him Boss. There was not a weak and ignorant nation that could stand against him. Multitudes were nothing to him —nothing at all. If they had a property he wanted, he went there and took it, and gave them his civilization in the place of it, and was pleased with himself, and praised his Maker for being always on his side, which was quite true, and for giving him such a chance to be noble and do good.

His whole time was taken up in shoving his civilization and his honey. His whole ambition was to widen and ever widen the market for his honey, and get richer and richer and richer and holier and holier and holier all the time.

At last he had covered all the ground but one. That was the vast empire of the Bees. He tried to get in there, but was warned away. He kept trying, but the Bees kept discouraging him. Courteously, but firmly. The Bees were a simple and peaceable folk, poor and hard-working and honest, and they did not want any civilization. They begged to be let alone; they held out against all persuasions. They wanted no honey, and said so. They did not know how to make it themselves, and did not wish to learn. They still held out. Courteously and kindly, but firmly.

At last the Butterflies were tired of this. They said that a nation that had a chance to get civilization and buy honey and didn't take it was a block in the way of progress and enlightenment and the yearning desires of God, and must be *made* to accept the boon and bless the booner; so they set about working up a moral-plated pretext, and soon they found a good one, and advertised it. They said that those fat and diligent and contented Bees, munching grass and cabbage, ignorant of honey, ignorant of civilization and rapacity and treachery and robbery and murder and prayer and one thing and another, and joying in their eventless life and in the sumptuous beauty of their golden jackets, were a Yellow Peril.

It took. It went like wildfire. It was a splendid phrase. It didn't seem to have any meaning, as applied to a far-away and unoffending mighty multitude that hadn't a desire in the world but to stay by themselves and be let alone, but that did not signify: a Yellow Peril is a Yellow Peril, and a shuddery and awful thing to think of, and has to be crushed, mashed, obliterated, whether there is any such thing or not.

So each of the different tribes of Butterflies sent in a two-hundred-dollar missionary with the private purpose of getting him massacred and collecting a million dollars cash damages on him, along with a couple of provinces and such other things as might be lying around; and when the Bees resisted, civilization had its chance! When it got through, there wasn't a Bee that wasn't bruised and battered and sore, and most humble and apologetic and submissive.

The enlightened world of Butterflydom rejoiced and gave thanks. And properly; for wasn't the Yellow Peril over and done with, for good and all?

It looked so. Then there was a great peace, and a holy tranquillity, and the Finger of God was visible in it all, as usual. When a paying job is finished and rounded up, he is a cross-eyed short-sighted person indeed who can't find the Finger of God in it.

Things went on handsomely. And handsomer and handsomer all the time. The Bees began to like honey and buy it. And they liked it better and better, and bought more and more of it, and civilization was happy to the marrow. One clever tribe of Bees even began to learn how to make honey itself—which made civilization proud, and it said "They are rising out of their darkness—we have lifted them up—how noble we are, and how good." Next that tribe wanted to learn the other great art, the sacred monopoly of the loftiest of civilizations—the art of how to kill and cripple and mutilate, scientifically. And they did learn it, and with astonishing quickness and brilliancy. Whereupon civilization rejoiced yet more, and was prouder of its nobleness and beneficence than ever.

For a time. Then there was an episode. This progressive tribe of Bees had picked up another specialty of all high civilizations, ancient and modern—land-grabbing; and presently, while working this specialty it came into collision with a vast tribe of Butterflies who were likewise out grabbing territory, and a fight resulted. The Bees showed that they had learned to be remarkably prompt and handy with their stings, those little weapons which had been so harmless until education taught them what God had intended the weapons for.

There was a market for wise observations, now, and a grave gray Grasshopper supplied it. He said to a prominent Butterfly—

"You have taught one tribe of Bees how to use its sting, it will teach its brother-tribe. The two together will be able to banish all the Butterflies some day, and keep them out; for they are uncountable in numbers and will be unconquerable when educated. Also, you have given the Bees the honey-appetite—forced it upon them—and now the frenzy of it will never leave them. Also, you have taught the brilliant tribe how to make it, and you will see results. They will make as prime an article of honey as any Butterfly can turn out; they will make it cheaper than any Butterfly can make it; they are here on the spot, you are the other side of the world, transportation will cost them nothing—you can't compete. They will get this vast market, and starve you out, and make you stay at home, where they used to beg you to stay, and you wouldn't listen. That will happen, no matter how this present scuffle may turn out. Whether Bee or Butterfly win, it is all the same, the Butterfly will have lost the market. There are five hundred million Bees; it is not likely that you can whip them without combining, and there is nothing in your history to indicate that your tribes can combine, even when conferring enlightenment and annexing swag are the prize. Yet if you do not subdue them now, before they get well trained and civilized, they may break over the frontiers some day and go land-grabbing in Europe, to do honor to your teaching. It may be that you will lose your stings and your honey-art by and by, from lack of practice, and be and remain merely elegant and ornamental. Maybe you ought to have let the Yellow Peril alone, as long as there wasn't any. Yet you ought to be proud, for in creating a something out of a nothing, you have done what was never done before, save by the Creator of all things."

The Butterfly gave thanks, coldly, and the Grasshopper asked for his passports.

The Recurrent
Major and Minor Compliment

(Early 1900s)

"WHAT IS the difference between an optimist of 50 & a fool? Do not know of any,"[1] Clemens wrote in 1901. Here he maintains that "any sane man of fifty" must have had enough dreadful experiences to make him "by awful compulsion—at bottom serious." Mark Twain's list of the sorrows and tragedies that are the common lot of all who have lived for half a century is a comprehensive one. "The Recurrent Major and Minor Compliment" conveys his sense of his own representative experience of the nightmare of human history.

Paine wrote "About 1903." on the first page of the manuscript; the paper used is characteristic of the period between 1900 and 1905. The piece could have been written at any time during the early 1900s.

---

1 Notebook 34, TS pp. 17–18.

430

The Recurrent
Major and Minor Compliment

A BEAUTIFUL girl realizes, in the course of time, that in her case the recurrent major compliment—I mean, the compliment she oftenest gets from people's tongues and eyes—is one which is called out by her beauty. In Daniel Webster's case the major recurrent compliment was of course paid to his oratory; in Sandow's case, it is paid to his physical strength; in Hobson's, to his splendid daring; in Funston's, to the excess of dirt in him over that employed in the construction of Adam—even in that early day, when dirt was cheaper than it is now.

Now, as regards the minor recurrent compliment. It *does* recur, but that is the most you can say under that head. It recurs three or four times in a lifetime. But its value to you is so great, that by comparison the major compliment is a cheap thing. The major compliment comes to you every day of your life, and it always brings you a pleasure—but, after its youth is past, seldom a thrill. But the Minor Compliment—ah, that seldom guest, that gracious guest, that welcome guest! its period is a comet's, and you may grow gray and die ere its glow shall have appeared in your sky three times; but *when* it appears, then you seem to hear the music of the spheres!

You have a dozen qualities, like everybody else. You have one which

431

is so prominent and so apparent that everybody recognizes it, nobody overlooks it. That one daily bags the Major Compliment. Now and then, at considerable intervals, some one detects and compliments one or another of ten of the other eleven—causing a mild pleasure in you, but nothing more—hardly a response, indeed. Meantime nobody stumbles upon that tenth quality—yet, mind you, that one is your secret darling, your treasure of treasures, your joy! At last some noble creature strikes that hidden string, and then—why then your whole being is deluged with a rich harmony, a celestial ecstasy!

Nearly twenty-five years ago an illustrious European—poet, sage, thinker—spent a week in my house as my guest. At parting, he said to me privately—impressively, too, after the manner of one who has made an almost unbelievable discovery—

"I believe that at bottom you are a serious man."

That is my Minor Recurrent Compliment. It comes to me about once in every three years. The complimenter always shows by his manner that he thinks he is the first; that he takes for granted that there has been no other Columbus there ahead of him. He also plainly takes for granted that his discovery is going to astonish me, too; that he is far from imagining it could ever have occurred to me that at bottom I was a serious person.

I am always courteous to this discoverer. I always show gratitude for being thus admitted to the human race, I always exhibit as much surprise as I can, in no case do I ever sit down and explain to the discoverer that he is an idiot; not even when he is a poet, a sage, and a "thinker" of international renown.

"I believe that at bottom you are a serious man."

That is what the Thinker said—Thinker and Discoverer. It was about as sane as if he had said, solemnly and with profound conviction—

"I believe a cat is a quadruped."

One might imagine a dialogue something like this:

I. When was the first time you ever saw a man of fifty who had had no acquaintance with physical pain?

He. I have not met such a person at all. If you will reflect a moment, it will be borne in upon you that such a person is not possible.

I. When was the first time you ever saw a man of fifty who had not had a large and rememberable and remembered share of such pain?

He. Again, if you will reflect, it will occur to you that *that* kind of a person is not possible.

I. When was the first time you ever saw a man of fifty whose happy hopes had all been fulfilled?

He. Dear sir, such a person has never existed, and cannot exist; is it possible you have never thought of that?

I. When was the first time you ever saw a man of fifty, one-third of whose happy dreams had come to pass, and only the other two-thirds had gone down in ruin and the bitterness of disappointment?

He. Dear, dear, if you knew even the rudiments and commonplaces of human life, you would know that *that* person is also impossible!

I. When was the first time you ever saw a man of fifty who had never known dread, fear, defeat, disaster, sleepless nights, the paralysis of despair and the longing for death?

He. Can't you understand that that is the common lot and that no person of fifty has escaped it?

I. When was the first time you ever saw a man of fifty who had never known shame, insult, self-contempt for guilty conduct, and the scorching humiliation of exposure?

He. Why, there never *was* a man that—

I. When was the first time you ever saw a man of fifty who had not grown old in the comradeship of grief and tears, whose heart had not been bruised with sorrows, whose memory did not wander away at some hour of every day and every night to worship at a grave? When did you ever see *any* sane man of fifty who was not—and by awful compulsion—at bottom serious? Even a poet, "thinker," or any other kind of an ass ought to know that such a man is impossible and has never existed.

Ancients in Modern Dress

(1896–1897)

IT IS HARDLY surprising that the "ancient" whom Clemens is particularly interested in seeing in modern clothes is Adam, for no other figure appealed more strongly and persistently to his imagination—unless it was Satan. The Mark Twain whose eyes become moist as he looks at the portrait of Adam (modernized) recalls the Mark Twain who in *The Innocents Abroad* weeps before the tomb of Adam, lamenting, "Noble old man—he did not live to see me—he did not live to see his child. And I—I—alas, I did not live to see *him*."[1] There is also a hint of Clemens' view that the present is a repetition of some time long past, since history is cyclical; once the difference of clothes has been removed, modern man is seen to be Adam all over again.

The title and dating are Paine's. His assignment of date of composition is supported by the fact that the paper used is the same as that in the manuscript of *Following the Equator*.

---

[1] DE 2:307.

Ancients in Modern Dress

A FEW MONTHS ago an interesting find was made in London—some old letters of Gainsborough's which had not seen the light before. In one of these letters there was a revelation—a revelation which struck me forcibly. It exposed the fact that when a lady of quality sat for her portrait in that day, she invented a costume for the occasion; and she made it as fine and showy and beautiful and outlandish and theatrical as she could. The letter referred to is from Gainsborough to a titled lady who is dissatisfied with her portrait—her friends think it does not look like her. The artist complains that an unusual dress is a disguise, and that a lady can not look much like herself in it; and that this condemned portrait of her ladyship would be recognizable by her friends as a good one if it were clothed as they have been used to seeing her clothed.

The artist was clearly right; an unaccustomed dress makes a very great change in a person. You have noticed this in private theatricals. We have great difficulty in recognizing our young friends when they are dressed up in the bloomy costumes of Henry VIII's time or Marie Antoinette's.

And so at last we have found out why it is that our English ancestors of a century or so ago all look like foreigners. It is their clothes. We are not used to those clothes, and so the people in them do not look as they ought to look—they are misrepresented to us. If those people could appear before us dressed as we ourselves are dressed, we should see them truly for the first time; they would then have a native and natural look, a friendly look, and we should see at once that they are blood kin to us, and not strangers and foreigners. Shakspeare, dressed as he ought to be dressed, would *look* Shakspeare, and cease to be a melon-headed and characterless Italian frump.

After thinking these things over, it occurred to me that it would be a benefaction to the world if I could enable it to see its historic idols undistorted, unfalsified, for once, see them looking their true selves, and *natural*; and I perceived that this desirable thing could be done by dressing them down to date, clothing them as they would be clothed if they were now with us and moving about in the society which would be theirs—that of the Queen, and the President, and Mr. Gladstone, and Prince Bismarck, and Ibsen, and the poet laureate and the rest. So I copied several of the authentic great portraits—copied them exactly, in all details of face, form, feature, expression, attitude, but abolished their misinforming costumes and put upon them the truth-conveying familiar clothes of our own day. The result was surprising. Even to me, who expected much.

To me Adam had never appealed—at least never to my heart; never in any warm and sympathetic way; never as his fatherhood should appeal to his child; for I was not used to his skins and his fig-leaves, and they made him a stranger to me, and cold. But as soon as I had put upon his portrait the clothes which he would wear to-day in the street or in the park, he was a different man, and I loved him. My whole heart went out to him. I saw the real Adam for the first time, and the long dormant feeling of kinship rose powerfully in me, and I could not look upon the portrait with dry eyes.

The portrait from which I made my copy is the one in the collection of his Holiness the Armenian Patriarch of Jerusalem, and is the only one now in existence which was taken from life. The one in the Vatican, held during many ages to be authentic, has within our time been discovered to be only a copy of the original above referred to.

A Letter from the Comet

(1880s)

IN WRITING "A Letter from the Comet" Mark Twain at first made a false start. He began with the comet's disdainful comments on its supposed discoverer, after whom it had lately been named:

> SIR: So it appears I am "the Brooks Comet." Is it because one Brooks "discovered" me? I beg pardon; if any discovering has been done, the shoe is on the other foot: for I discovered Brooks; he[1] was in his cradle at the time. At any rate I could have discovered him, if I had considered the thing important enough to make it worth my while to leave business some billions of miles removed, and come here and do it. I was elderly before Mr. Brooks was born; I was discovered before Mr. Brooks was thought of; I shall still be an

The paragraph breaks off in midsentence; the manuscript then starts anew along somewhat different lines.

This piece might have been prompted by news of any one of the several comets discovered by William Robert Brooks which drew public attention in the 1880s. The manuscript is on a paper that Mark Twain was using during that decade.

---

[1] Clemens canceled "at least" before writing "he."

A Letter from the Comet

Sir: There are several things I would like to inquire about if I
may. I come here every seventy-one years, and look about me a while,
and get acquainted with names, faces, and events of the day; then
comes my long absence of seventy-one years, and next time I arrive the
people I knew have either disappeared or have changed so much that I
cannot recognize them. This is strange and annoying. And it was not always so. It is only a peculiarity of recent times. Did you know a man by
the name of Adam?—fine well-made fellow dressed in skins, who used
to live near you in a garden which he called Eden? And did you know
his wife—she that was—but I forget now what her name was before she
was married. What ever became of him?—and her? I used to see him
every time I came. During thirteen of my visits to this part of the universe I saw him every time. Consequently he came to be a very familiar
object to me, and in time I got to looking forward with pleasure to my
customary visit because I should see Adam again. He was a person who
was always adding to himself new interests, too. When I first knew
him, he was farming by himself, and had no neighbors; but after that,
his family began to come on, and the last time I saw him they numbered many thousands. But when I came the fourteenth time, he had
moved. Since then I have always kept a lookout for him, but have never
discovered a trace of him. I do not know how to account for this. This

is such a little bit of a world, that I cannot understand how I am always managing to overlook him. Large as Sirius is, I do not overlook anybody there. I always see my friends there, every time I go. I have not missed a friendly face there in thirty million years. Yet here is Adam, whom I used to run across every little while until the other day—then he suddenly disappears, and permanently. If you know his address, I shall be under many obligations if you will give it to me. I would also like to have the addresses of a couple of other men whom you may possibly know—Methuselah and Noah; I do not remember their first names. I have the impression that I saw the latter quite recently—I should say five or seven hundred years ago—and no doubt I did; but I am quite sure I have not met him since.

Old Age

(December 1905)

SHORTLY AFTER 30 November 1905, his seventieth birthday, Clemens wrote this retrospective essay outlining the stages of his long climb from infancy to old age, a progression that he described more elaborately in the speech which he delivered at the anniversary dinner given in his honor.[1] A part of the last paragraph of "Old Age," in which the author addresses himself as the "belated fag-end of a foolish dream" of which there is "nothing left but You, centre of a snowy desolation," echoes the conclusion that he had written in 1904 for "No. 44, The Mysterious Stranger": "It is all a Dream, a grotesque and foolish dream. Nothing exists but You. And You are but a *Thought*—a vagrant Thought, a useless Thought, a homeless Thought, wandering forlorn among the empty eternities!"[2]

---

[1] *Mark Twain's Speeches*, ed. Albert Bigelow Paine (New York: Harper & Brothers, 1923), pp. 254–262.

[2] *MSM*, p. 405.

Old Age

I THINK it likely that people who have not been here will be interested to know what it is like. I arrived on the thirtieth of November, fresh from care-free and frivolous 69, and was disappointed.

There is nothing novel about it, nothing striking, nothing to thrill you and make your eye glitter and your tongue cry out, "Oh, but it *is* wonderful, perfectly wonderful!" Yes, it is disappointing. You say, "Is *this* it?—*this*? after all this talk and fuss of a thousand generations of travelers who have crossed this frontier and looked about them and told what they saw and felt? why, it looks just like 69."

And that is true. Also it is natural; for you have not come by the fast express, you have been lagging and dragging across the world's continents behind oxen; when that is your pace one country melts into the next one so gradually that you are not able to notice the change: 70 looks like 69; 69 looked like 68; 68 looked like 67—and so on, back, and back, to the beginning. If you climb to a summit and look back—ah, then you see!

Down that far-reaching perspective you can make out each country and climate that you crossed, all the way up from the hot equator to the ice-summit where you are perched. You can make out where Infancy merged into Boyhood; Boyhood into down-lipped Youth; Youth into indefinite Young-Manhood; indefinite Young-Manhood into

441

definite Manhood; definite Manhood with aggressive ambitions into sobered and heedful Husbandhood and Fatherhood; these into troubled and foreboding Age, with graying hair; this into Old Age, white-headed, the temple empty, the idols broken, the worshippers in their graves, nothing left but You, a remnant, a tradition, belated fag-end of a foolish dream, a dream that was so ingeniously dreamed that it seemed real all the time; nothing left but You, centre of a snowy desolation, perched on the ice-summit, gazing out over the stages of that long *trek* and asking Yourself "would you do it again if you had the chance?"

APPENDIXES

APPENDIX A

To the Editor of the American Hebrew

FOR ITS 1890 Passover issue, *The American Hebrew*, a New York journal, solicited opinions from prominent Christian clergymen and intellectuals on the reasons and remedies for anti-Semitism. They were asked to consider the following four questions:

I. Can you, of your own personal experience find any justification whatever for the entertainment of prejudice towards individuals solely because they are Jews?

II. Is this prejudice not due largely to the religious instruction that is given by the Church and Sunday-school:—for instance, the teachings that the Jews crucified Jesus; that they rejected him and can only secure salvation by a belief in him, and similar matters that are calculated to excite in the impressionable mind of the child an adversion, if not a loathing, for members of "the despised race?"

III. Have you observed in the social or business life of the Jew, so far as your personal experience has gone, any different standard of conduct than prevails among Christians of the same social status?

IV. Can you suggest what should be done to dispel the existing prejudice?[1]

---

[1] *Prejudice Against the Jew*, ed. Philip Cowen (New York: Philip Cowen, 1928), p. 31. A reprint of "A Symposium By Foremost Christians" published in *The American Hebrew*, 4 April 1890.

Mark Twain's reply was not published in the symposium. No record remains which would indicate why it did not appear, or whether or not it was,
in fact, submitted to the editor.

To the Editor of the American Hebrew

Private. Please suppress my nom de plume. I use it only when joking.

SLC

To the Editor of the American Hebrew:

I read your questions hurriedly, a week or two ago, and then lost them;
but I have the impression that they were ground-plots upon which you were
inviting a number of people to build such explanations as they were able, of
the Christian world's antipathy to the Israelite.

My guess may not be valuable, but it is offered in good faith, and with
the conviction that it is near the mark. If you have a list of illustrious Jews
—of any century or of all centuries—will you please append it to this article? My other instanced facts are well enough known to need no confirmation by statistics.

If Christ's fellow-Jews numbered a million persons, and a hundred out
of this mass procured his death, the guilt of the hundred would outweigh
the innocence of the rest of the million for all time—among bigoted and
unthinking people. That would be but human and natural. But one might
expect to find ten considerate and fair-minded persons among every hundred thousand men and women in our age—and in previous ages—who
would not allow the act of that handful of the guilty to bring and keep the
innocent vast body of that nation under condemnation and obloquy. Has
this ten in the hundred thousand ever existed? It is questionable; any one
will say this who reads history either for study or for amusement, or who is
in friendly and familiar intercourse with the best and most cultivated
minds in his community.

But do I seriously believe that the almost universal antipathy to the Jew
issues from the daily and deliberately pondered fact that the Jews crucified
Christ? No. It is impossible to believe such a thing. It is irrational, it is opposed to common sense. Manifestly the fact of the crucifying was reason
enough in former ages, cruder ages, but certainly the world has outlived
that. Outlived all of it but the dry husk—a prejudice, which our minds in-

herit as our male breasts inherit and accept the rudimentary nipple without much troubling ourselves about the why or the wherefore of it.

Do I wish to intimate that this inherited prejudice is a factor of small dimensions in this baffling and stubborn problem of the Christian's antipathy to the Jew? No—quite the contrary. I think it must constitute, all by itself, nine-tenths of the why and the wherefore. I think that if it were absent, the Christian antipathy to the Jew would not be more pronounced than the slight antipathy which individuals of any nation feel toward all foreigners, or which the people of one part of a country often feel to the people of another part of it: the comically superior and compassionate attitude of the far-western miner or cow-boy toward the "tender-foot" from the east, for instance.

When one, in our day, tries to array light-giving facts, figures and reasons in explanation, support and justification of the world's contempt and hatred of the Jew, a sort of light-giving facts, figures and reasons do certainly respond to his call—but as a rule they are defective, disappointing, not usable. He finds himself considering, weighing and analyzing propositions like the following:

If an International Intellectual Fair should be held three times per century, its prizes to go to the race furnishing the largest number of persons illustrious for intellectual achievement according to population, what race would carry away those prizes, regularly, persistently, monotonously? The Israelites. Was there ever a race that would consent to work with its hands if it could get its living with its brains? We know of none. Was there ever a race that did not have to get its living with its hands? Only one—the Israelites. Was there ever a race that contributed no beggars to the world? Only one—the Israelites. Is there a race which takes care of all its poor, and suffers none to perish for want of food and shelter? Only one—the Israelites. The love of the members of an Israelitish family for each other is so strong that it amounts to devotion. Social intercourse among the Israelites is notably warm and affectionate, and but little obstructed by chilling conventions and formalities.

These striking facts show the presence in those people of the sort of qualities which civilized folk customarily admire and approve. Then if our inherited prejudice were removed, how would the Israelite stand with us? As a fellow American? No, as a foreigner, I think, temporarily. He would still be kept off a little. As long as an Englishman is an Englishman, we feel a slight reserve toward him. We retain this until he has by and by changed into an American.

I think that if our inherited prejudice against the Israelite were removed, he would presently be seen to be as American as anybody, and that would end the ciphering over this puzzle by abolishing the puzzle.

Do I think that that day will ever come? I do not know the trick of prophecy. But I do know, or think I know, that an antipathy with a reason back of it has no advantage in lasting qualities over an inherited antipathy whose origin has been forgotten. I hope, and think, and even believe, that the useless and ridiculous mammals will disappear from the male human being's breast by and by, and I try to believe that the rudimental Christian antipathy to the Jew will disappear during the same week; but my confidence is pretty rocky.

Hartford, March.

S. L. Clemens

APPENDIX B

Adam Monument Proposal—Documents

1. Petition to the Honorable Senate and House

THE PETITION is written in ornate calligraphy on two sheets of legal paper and is attached with brads to a legal-style folder, on which is written "Petition of F. G. Hall and others of Elmira N.Y. relating to the proposed monument to Adam." Since the petition is not in Mark Twain's hand, errors in spelling and punctuation have been silently corrected. The list of the 94 signatures it bears is not included here but may be found in Paine's biography.[1]

PETITION TO THE HONORABLE SENATE AND HOUSE

To the Honorable Senate and
House of Representatives
of the United States in
Congress Assembled:

Whereas A number of citizens of the City of Elmira in the State of New York, having covenanted among themselves to erect in that city a monument in memory of Adam the father of mankind, being moved thereto by a sentiment of love and duty, and these having appointed the undersigned to communicate with your honorable body, we beg leave to lay before you the following facts and append to the same our humble petition

---

[1] MTB, Appendix P, pp. 1648–1650.

1. As far as is known, no monument has ever been raised in any part of the world, to commemorate the services rendered to our race by this great man, whilst many men of far less note and worship have been rendered immortal by means of stately and indestructible memorials.

2. The common father of mankind has been suffered to lie in entire neglect, although even the Father of our Country has now and has had for many years, a monument in course of construction.

3. No right feeling human being can desire to see this neglect continued, but all just men, even to the farthest regions of the globe, should and will rejoice to know that he to whom we owe existence is about to have reverent and fitting recognition of his works at the hands of the people of Elmira. His labors were not in behalf of one locality but for the extension of humanity at large and the blessings which go therewith; hence all races and all colors and all religions are interested in seeing that his name and fame shall be placed beyond the reach of the blight of oblivion by a permanent and suitable monument.

4. It will be to the imperishable credit of the United States if this monument shall be set up within her borders, moreover, it will be a peculiar grace to the beneficiary, if this testimonial of affection and gratitude shall be the gift of the youngest of the nations that have sprung from his loins, after 6000 years of unappreciation on the part of its elders.

5. The idea of this sacred enterprise having originated in the City of Elmira, she will be always grateful if the general government shall encourage her in the good work by securing to her a certain advantage through the exercise of its great authority.

Therefore, your petitioners beg that your honorable body will be pleased to issue a decree restricting to Elmira the right to build a monument to Adam, and inflicting a heavy penalty upon any other community within the United States that shall propose or attempt to erect a monument or other memorial to the said Adam, and to this end we will ever pray.

[The petition bears 94 signatures, some of which are identifiable as those of Elmira residents.]

2. Letter, Harriet W. Hawley to Clemens, 25 June 1880

Mrs. Hawley's letter was enclosed with the returned petition in an official House of Representatives envelope addressed to Clemens in Elmira, N.Y.

LETTER, HARRIET W. HAWLEY TO CLEMENS, 25 JUNE 1880

Guilford, Conn.

June 25th, 80

Dear Sir —

Just as he was leaving for England, my husband gave me this petition, requesting me to return it to you. He said he was sorry not to present it to Congress, but, on showing it to several of the Members both of the House and Senate, they unanimously advised against it, saying that they thought "it would not do"—and at last he decided to return it to you. I may be permitted to beg for myself, that I am very sorry, for I really think it would have been a good thing for Congress in various ways! However, I suppose it can go into the papers just as well, and perhaps be just as much of an advertisement.—

I was sorry not to see Mrs Clemens when I was in Hartford last week, but I hope she is "cool and comfortable" in Elmira, which is much better than Hartford in such weather as this. Please give my love to her, and believe me

Sincerely your friend

Harriet W. Hawley.

3. Proposal for Renewal of the Adam Monument Petition

Mark Twain rejected the manuscript by tearing it in two lengthwise.

PROPOSAL FOR RENEWAL OF THE ADAM MONUMENT PETITION

Now that the Presbytery has turned down a pair of young applicants for places in the ministry because they believed Adam to be a myth, I feel encouraged to resume my effort of twenty years ago and try once more to get justice done to our common ancestor—justice in the form of a monument. We have raised monuments to less worthy men, and it is no credit to us that we have so long neglected this one, to whom we owe so much. Putting aside his other merits and distinctions, we should build him a costly and noble monument to mark our recognition of his intellectual greatness. We cannot blind ourselves to the plain fact that his was incomparably the greatest brain the world has ever produced. We pay a due and willing homage to certain splendid names: Socrates, Aristotle, Homer, Alexander, Caesar, Cicero, Shakspeare, Napoleon, Humboldt, Darwin, Herbert Spencer—intellectual giants we call them, and rightly; yet in mental stature the best of them was but a dwarf by contrast with Adam.

These great men knew all that men can know—it was their limit; but Adam knew more. He knew all things, and more than all.

APPENDIX C

Mark Twain's Working Notes

MARK TWAIN'S notes are often chaotic or obscure, yet they provide glimpses of his imagination at work, of the germ of his finished work and of the ideas and insights which proved unmanageable and were discarded. Because their relationship to one another and to the finished work is so frequently a matter of interpretation, these notes have been presented with as little editorial mediation as the rendering of handwriting into type permits.

They have been grouped on the basis of physical characteristics, comparisons with the manuscript, the matter treated within each set, internal cohesion, and topical references. When Mark Twain numbered his pages, his numbers have been printed. In addition, a number has been given to each manuscript leaf within a sequence.

No emendations have been made in Mark Twain's holograph notes. His ampersand has been retained. Single underlinings are presented as italics; double underlinings are rendered in small capital letters. Cancellations are included and marked by angle brackets, thus, ⟨⟩; substitutions by vertical arrows, thus, ↑↓, though context usually makes substitutions clear without the arrows; added words or phrases, by carets, thus, ʌ ʌ; additions at some later date in pencil or ink different from the original by boldface, thus, **Eddymania**; and editorial explanation by square brackets, thus, [ ]. Mark Twain's alternate readings are separated by virgules, thus, long/irresistible.

453

The International Lightning Trust

These working notes were written in pencil on a sheet of tablet paper of a kind often used by Mark Twain between 1900 and 1904. The page is very tattered; a piece at the top has been lost and, with it, much of a note which appears to read "pages of Which was It?" There is no apparent connection between this note and Mark Twain's story "Which Was It?"[1]

[top of page torn]
Which was It?

Pop. 30,000,000
    Consisting of 300,000 persons of each age from 1 year to 100.
30,000,000 tickets in series of 300,000 for each age, at $100 each.
Any person killed at say 1 yr of age, 300,000 ticket-holders got a prize.
Prize should be $2,000, & require $6,000,000 to pay it.
12 persons killed in ⟨the year⟩ ∧8 months∧ (for the tickets carry no
    further require a paymen[t] [page torn] of $72,000,000
Lightning-Lottery

---

[1] *WWD*, pp. 179–449.

Refuge of the Derelicts

Group A

This group of working notes consists of a "Par Value" tablet cover, ten sheets of "Par Value" paper, and an extra cardboard back from another tablet, arranged in the order given here. The tablet cover, A-1, is still hinged to its original back, which is blank; the inscription on the cover's verso, A-2, appears at the bottom of the page, so that when the cover is open the writing is just above the top line of the tablet page. Pages A-3 to A-11 apparently were originally part of the tablet; A-12 is a page from a different tablet. On the extra cardboard back, A-13, the inscription runs along the length of the page; on all others, across the breadth.

A–1

Notes.

Adam

The House of Tragedies.

Bos'n is a Bob Howland (looks Jack Perry.
So is the Admiral.

A–2

CHARLEY ROSS
Marchesa wears girl-costume so he will know her—thinks he is ⟨w⟩ held in town here—she goes out every day & looks (& attracts laughter) & jimmy go with her

A–3

1

ʌYou can date him by these—they were in use in his boyhood.ʌ

"God called him." Bosn' thinks it was an echo—call came from the other
direction.

So deaf he can't read fine print.

So near-sighted he can't hear good.

> author of his being
> accomplished his hellish purpose
> laconic
> cast a gloom
> rejoiced in the euphonious Cognomen
> ⟨I am sorr⟩ I regret to say
> tresses (raven)
> locks (his)
> poor but honest parents
> To have a "strain" of Indian blood was
>   romantic & swell.

Going all alone to Burlington from K in hope of a glimpse of
   Dʳ· Gwin after a lapse of ⟨5⟩68 years.

risibles
regardless of expense
upon whose head the frosts of 60 winters
a girl of 20 summers—didn't ⟨s⟩estimate them by any other table

A–4

2

virginette

Man that started dog-bite & lightning insurance Co

History of story of man blown up (Stingy Co)—Paul Blouet ruined
it in Aus.

lips (cherry)   visage rubicund
teeth (pearl)   could no longer conceal the evidences of
chin (dimpled)   her shame.
ears (shells)   betrayed

hair { golden, auburn, raven   accomplished her ruin
     (obese)

maiden, not girl

A–5

3

ᴧAunty Phillips (Cord)ᴧ

The Twins

Derelicts

Jacobs & Cully

Man once wealthy; had a coachman; became poor; became coachman to his
former coachman; now both serve the present occupant of the ⟨house,⟩
ᴧformer home,ᴧ which is a negro boarding-house, ᴧnow,ᴧ kept by the
once ladysmaid—they follow her around the market & carry two baskets
each ᴧ& clean sidewalk, winter & summerᴧ. In her kindness she pays
them ⟨25 ↑40ᶜ↓⟩ ᴧ50ᶜᴧ a day each & their grub in kitchen—which is
overpay; she could get it cheaper. But one relic is left these men—the
coupon-scissors. ᴧRastus boards there.ᴧ
They feel with Smith—death-Adam is the real benefactor of the race.

⟨John T. Lewis⟩ ᴧ'Rastus Timsonᴧ is the Brotherhood Man.

"Father er de Brotherhood? ⟨Sho!"⟩ Buil' a monument to *him?* No s'r!"
Aunty Cord a derelict. Special Prov'dence.
She tells the "True Story."
He saved the Langdons, 28 yrs ago.
He was a Dunker—is freethinker now.

The Ungentlemanly Nation.

A–6

⟨2⟩4

"Storm at Sea—insurrection in hell."

Born with false teeth.

Anchor Watch.

Smith wants monument to Adam not because he brought life—he hates him unforgivably for that—but because he brought the valuable boon —Death.

Jimmy wants it because he brought life.

Opinions of Anchor Watch.

Admiral is a Bob Howland—brave.

Ned Wakeman's Dream of heaven.

His capture of the murderer of his mate.

His 2-yr absence "practising" swearing.

ʌVerses—"The Derelict." & that other one.ʌ

A–7

5

ʌRev. ⟨Paxton⟩ ↑Caleb Parsons.↓ʌ ʌ(Tom Beecher)ʌ   Enthusiast on "What god hath wrought." (nick-name)
ʌ"People say, if he only *could* look out for his own damnation & let other people's alone.ʌ [may have been intended to follow "Washburn."]
ʌIngersollʌ [circled] ʌWashburn.ʌ   Despiser of the human race,ʌ's high & unwarranted opinion of itself,ʌ—enthusiast. Curious? he has been most fortunate (in the world's view) all his life & people can't understand his attitude—whereas it is the massed suffering⟨s⟩ of the race that em-

bitters him, not his *personal*—(though theirs are his, & *hence* his suf-ferings).

(*Pityer* of the race, too.) The above.

Calls man a machine, & irresponsi[ble] [page torn]

Moved by (primarily) selfishness.

Does kindly things—takes them apart [&] [page torn] explains the selfish motive.

Wants to keep Smith at his job & away from whisky temptation—

Also wants to send him home on a visit to Mary.

His father a pres. minister, himself another one a while—Vol. brigadier in war—good record—is infidel, now—Sunday lectures big crowds—splen-didly hated—comes to che[er] [page torn] & help the Watch.

A–8

6

B

> ∧"Ad. don't care so much for poets, but does for artists;" is one himself.∧

Bos'n.

He's more'n that—he's a *hell* of an artist.

He furnished the name, Anchor Watch—because they've knocked off regular duty & are on deck to take care of the ship. Suppose it's only a couple—no matter, it's a good time for songs & yarns, & so in a good climate you'll find the rest there that are not on liberty—

How—on liberty?

Yes—ashore.

> ∧They go out with the Marchesa.∧ [written diagonally above "Martha."]

Call her∧s∧ ∧Miss∧ Jimmy & aunt Martha.

Was aboard at Jimmy's advent. Ad. rescued him in the Chinchas; shot in a few places & leg smashed—(knock from ⟨poop-deck⟩ ∧porch∧— Ad. stood over him there⟨)⟩, took him aboard, ∧& he & Martha∧ nursed him 4 weeks; then carried the lantern when Ad. arrested the man who killed his mate; also helped in the hanging.

Ad? Hasn't any particular religion. They're all grog to him. ∧Sterilized X^n∧

How?

Thinks if ⟨you've⟩ ∧they've∧ got the right basis

A–9

7

B [half-circled]
they'll all do. Mix 'em as much as you want to, they'll still be grog, & there
ain't any bad grog.
Don't you know about his *dream?*
    No.
    Then don't ask him—he might be in the mood, & he mightn't. But
he'll just naturally drop into it some time or other. When he *is.*
    Has been with Ad nearly as long as Jimmy. He does not mention Ad's
wife—*he never saw her.*
    Considers Martha plum duff
    Plum duff?
    Yes—with extra raisins in it.
    Describes plum duff. ⟨H⟩
    Have a "gam" with her when you can.
    Ad always allowed a "20th lay."
    And didn't swindle on "slops."
    Jimmy is plum duff, too.
    "That leg was ∧a∧ compound ⟨∧multiplex∧⟩ constipated fract⟨ion⟩ure
—bones sticking up through, in a circle all around—as many as a dozen—
like umbrellas in a stand.
    Martha helps run the midnight mission.

A–10

8

∧Uncle Jim & the dissecting room∧   ∧Strother, dipsomaniac∧

    The Admiral? Well, he's a ⟨kind of a⟩ sterilized X^n. ∧So that old chem-
ist says.∧
    How do you mean.
    Well, ∧one time & another∧ he had all the germs ⟨in him⟩ of the
132 X^n sects⟨,⟩ ∧in him,∧ but they are all killed out ∧now∧ & nothing left
in him but the Golden Rule.
    His dream.

Maj. Gen. D^r· Wood⟨'s⟩ᴧ? Well, hisᴧ war record don't *begin* with his peace record, when it comes to killed & wounded.

Yes, we educate them at West Point & when war breaks out we officer the army with tailors & doctors—cousins of Congress you know.

Bos'n makes all the sarcasms—they are reported by hearers. When there is opportunity for one, put i⟨n⟩t in his mouth "as the bos'n says"

Explain Pessimist—Whichimist?

A–11

2

let the brontosaur go anonymous, we had to name it ourselves. The real truth is there was lots that he was not equal to naming & gave it up—like the dinotherium, the pterodactyl, the ornithorhyncus & all that family of ᴧprotoplasmicᴧ plantigrade⟨s⟩ invertebrates.

He lived to be 920 & died poor. It shows that he hadn't any gift for business. ⟨No more than Satan. I put them on a level.⟩ If Jay Gould had been Adam he would have owned the planet. He would have got the apple, too, & no punishment, because he would have worked out a way to beat the judgment.

A–12

4

These patriots are never plenty in any country. They do not allow ⟨ass-⟩Congresses ⟨& cabin⟩ & newspapers to dictate to them. They are at all times in a minority in the beginning.

The thing called P has 3 seeds.

Moral Courage

To what degree does it exist?

A–13

ᴧ[page torn] *Adullam.* ⟨Hospi⟩ Asylum of the Ruined. Hospital of the Broken Reed.ᴧ [page torn] *Comforter* self. ∧says no man to blame—no sin.∧ *The Pension-er.* Came out of the war Br. Gen of Vols a manly man. Sent to Con-gress several years—rising ever in fame & value; supported the first pen-sion bills—for the disabled, & ∧later∧ the widows & orphans of the killed —with enthusiasm. Violently attacked the later ones as being bribes for votes; was promptly turned down; deserted by friends & fortune, ruin⟨ed⟩ followed. Is old, now & sorry he did it. Tried for years to get a pension; at last let in at 70 because 60 yr old. Is demoralized & pauperized—dreams only of further pensions.

[in margin next to "*Comforter* . . . pensions."]
∧Author of a Philosoph[page torn]
faield. Classed with Ro[page torn]
& ruined. *John Fillens.* [or "*Fillmo*"] [page torn]∧

The Senator (H.). Same history, but finely successful, because he threw away his honor & supported Blaine; never recovered it, remained a slave to the party; tremendously zealous; outwardly not regretting; his furious speech on Philippine petition, showed that his mind was gone as well as his principles; kept in Senate as party reward, when old & imbecile. Envied by the Pensioner, who wished *he* had been wise. In almost all cases life is a *failure,* & regretable, no matter which way you do.

Rev. Twichell & Rev. Smyth. Bulkley Senator. Former got his lesson & was saved by Hubbard. ∧& accident.∧ Latter got his lesson, but there was no accident to save him. Young then, old now; does hack-word for Foreign Board, is a despised & humble slave—wishes he had another chance, he would be wise this time, but his trespass is remembered & he can't get another pulpit.

Admiral the only optimist. Presently *he* is ruined.

[on verso]
incandescent
transubstantiation.

Group B

This group of working notes consists of six pages of tablet paper, num-bered consecutively. Pages B-4 and B-5 are slightly narrower than the others, so they apparently were not part of the original tablet. The last half of page B-6 is canceled with a wavy line down the center of the page, sometimes used by Mark Twain to indicate that he had made use of the material.

B–1

Talk

Thinks he's Satan. (Charley Clark) ∧perfectly beautiful if not worn & lean. Intellectual. Beautiful eyes—in repose, sweet.∧

Bos'n. It could be that the A had ∧partly∧ in his mind the other Satan, without knowing it. ⟨At⟩

Is he crazy?

Of course. Do you know anybody that ain't? This one is crazier than you or me—maybe—which isn't saying much. He is crazy on moral laws. Thinks he gets a commission ⟨of⟩ on tainted (legal) money, but wants to get it extended to fractured moral laws, so as to bring in Ament & Reed, & Order 78 & all other pensions *after* the first one. All are soiled, now, by the *motive* back of them, which is the same as the motive back of high tariffs—the one to buy the votes of the poor, the other those of the rich (factor) *and* the poor (his workmen, whom he can influence—& *force.*—

B–2

2

Moral law—under it he could collect from half-rate clergymen. He collects on shirkings of personal tax; on 9 out of $10 that go to Amer. Board—

(does a vast business—converts 3 Chinamen a day—only 33,000 born per day—will catch up by & by.

What drove him crazy?

He was a captain of police, & collected 15 ∧pr∧ cent on the business of the w h's in his district & on the cadets. It was discovered that he was not dividing with Croker—so he was "disgraced" & dismissed. He was already getting crazy through money-lust, & that finished him. They first noticed it on the 30 pieces. He had the idea that more than 18 centuries'

B–3

3

interest was due, & he kept calculating & compounding it & laying before lawyers to help him collect it or tell him where to apply. He is *always* calculating it & worrying over it.

Nobody is more pitied than he. He was a fine & honorable man before he got on the police & fell under the money-lust influence—at a good time, for he had lost all but his little daughter, he was bound up in her, & no way to save her but send her to Davos; he sent her, with a woman who kept wanting more & more money; & finally when he was disgraced & was going to her for comfort, came a cable she was dead—from the commune, then a letter explaining she was deserted in her extremity by the woman, who had gone off with a courier. Buried by the commune. Always saying if he had had his % on 30 pcs he would have been rich, & been with her himself.

"It seems curious, but money-lust

B–4

4

ᴧPension-crank, Corporal Plunkett.ᴧ

ᴧoftenᴧ originates in the heart, ⟨about as often as⟩ ᴧnotᴧ in the head.

Likes the monument-pension scheme—he can collect on that. It fires him.

First offered American Board 5% to ⟨use its⟩ help him collect on 30 pc.—then 10—then a point at a time—is up to 20 now.

Wants to go on, with Congress & the Party, raking ⟨violating⟩ the graveyards to get more pensioners.

⟨P⟩

Thinks he is entitled to 10% on the monument-pensions, & disputes with the crazy Pension-Crank, who recognizes the value of his influence with Congress, but wants to beat him down to 2%

"I'll agree, if you'll get Congress to assume the 30 pc interest. Is willing to throw off the principal.

Pension-Crank is ancient ⟨bounty-jumper.⟩

B–5

5

C. W. veteran with a good war record who was debauched by pensions & turned into a ravenous beggar for them & made crazy. He has pensions for

1. Being a soldier
2. Wounded in battle
3. Sick in hospital
4. Permanently disabled by falling down stairs at pension office.— (broke 3ᵈ finger of left hand.)

∧4½ For being 60 yrs old—& a voter.∧

5. Father   a   sutler   in   Mex.   war
6. ⟨Grand⟩"   "   "   " Seminole war.
10   two uncles helping in both
14   Some grandfathers in '12.
18   "   "   " Revoluⁿ.
22   "   "   Boston Massacre
26   "   "   died in the Mayflower
16 Assortment of grandmother connected with above.
17 They lost a cat, previously.

Has children, grand-ch & 1 gr-gr, already pensioned.

Hopes to have a widow soon.

Thinks he is descended from one of the Roman soldiers at Xⁿ & is willing to pool interests with 30 p.c of equal date—maybe one day's difference (in *his* favor.)

B–6

6

60-year pensions to all who were not in the war, but who can prove that they have voted right—

or

will vote right in the future.

ʌThese to descend to posterity. G. A R
of 300,000,000, all ravenous for pensions. It will then be no longer a discredit to belong to it.ʌ

Rockefeller's $100,000.

⟨Shall we receive tainted money for the monument? Yes, there being no
other kind.

If Satan should offer ʌmoney forʌ bread ⟨to⟩for my starving child I would
take it & thank him—

but if offered for the saving of ⟨another⟩ ʌtheʌ child's soul, that would
be another matter. ⟨In that case⟩

1. In the first case I should know that his motive was, to advertise his
benevolence & soften people's acrimony—a permissible thing⟩

The Secret History of Eddypus, the World-Empire

Group A

This short group of working notes is written on the front and back covers of a "Par Value" tablet. Most of the notes on the front cover, A–1, were written in pencil; a few notes on it and most of those on the back cover are in faded blue ink.

A–1

liquefies on Eddymas

mas, Xmas

⟨Holy Edd⟨i⟩ypus = ∧from∧ *Eddy*, name; *pus*, ⟨meaning now lost⟩
—together mean World-Empire
—*pus*, ∧2∧ a healing ointment, ∧1∧ precious exudation⟩: [canceled in ink]
the sacred phial of it is liquefied by miracle on the Eddybirthday—Xmas
—every year, & millions come to see—$5 a ticket—& worship.

Eddymania.   Eddymush, the language

Coat of arms—Golden Calf   625 titled Amer girls in Europe?
Great Seal—the dollar.

Old Comradeships.

Get a history of the Saints

Show an Excommunicaⁿ

Science forbidden & Education
All necessary science is Eddygush (religion) ∧the only true∧
  " needful education is in Science & Health
Education is by decree called Eddycation   150/00
Eddygas = inspiration   100/00
Eddydrivel
    China alone keeps her name & is not part of Holy Eddypus. Drove out all foreigners & missionaries.
    The "Golden Rule"—what could it have been. Supposed to have been, "Intrude where are not wanted; stay where not welcome.
Or, "Intrude upon these as we would not allow them to intrude upon us."

A–2

ʌ√ masʌ
ʌ√ mush—the language—Adoration of Our Mʌ
ʌ√ʌ Eddygush   ʌ"   sacred to the priestly orderʌ
        ʌ√ʌ slush ʌ—poetical portions of the Eddygraphʌ
        ʌ√ʌ gas—Scientific Statement of Being   *The Spoon.*
        bank
        bunk
        blend
ʌ√ʌ cation
        cant [a line drawn to "Scientific," above]
The   ʌblink—ʌ
        fication, ʌthe building up of the Faithʌ
        olatry worship of the Founder
        cal (medical)
        plunk (dollar)
ʌgas—incenseʌ
        quack
        ring (cabinet) P⟨ope⟩apal
        rist (reader & ⟨pro⟩ʌexʌpounder of Sci & H
        phone (for receiving revelations
        graph (things she wrote—ʌtheʌ sacred writings
        cash (rom ready cash—basis of Xⁿ Cc
        slug, teacher, Expounder [a line drawn in margin to "rist," above]
        cat, one who cates—teacher, catechiser
        tor—who mends the grammar &c of S & H
        torial, the Great Eulogy on the birth-day
        made
        mule, one immovable in the faith
        milk, little holy tales of her for children
        vine, formerly divine—sacred to priest
        water, holy water
        wax for candle-vows
        whopper, private name for E. miracles

                [in margin]
ʌBoston, ⟨Eddybunk⟩ Eddyflatsʌ

Group B

These working notes, written on both sides of a "Par Value" tablet cover, are written in two inks. Most of the notes on the recto are in the same faded black ink used for the manuscripts of Book 1 and parts of Book 2; apparently they were written after Mark Twain began Book 1, since the title "Old Comrades," mentioned in the notes, is "Old Comradeships" early in Book 1. The remainder of the notes are in a bright blue ink not used in the manuscript of "Eddypus."

B–1

Last C. S. Pope was XXIV, AM 219–226—7 years.   24
First male, *was* R. C. Pope (Pius XII) till *full* Pope XXV, 226   7
C. S. supremacy dates from 226—*then* A.M assumed,   ‾‾‾‾
  ∧everywhere∧ & dated back to 1865; it had been in   20
use⟨d⟩ by C. S. ⟨m⟩ since about 100, but not recog-   3,360
nized by others, who still used A.D.
"Old Comrades discovered 981—20 years ago (I helped translate it.)

All slaves are Church property,
& ⟨leased.⟩ saleable for life—but
not the future children

Motherday—sunday

B–2

Buffon dis. quad. have 4 legs.   Cuvier dis. that mammals do not
  proved it on rats, &c. & was   lay eggs. Ornotho- had not been
  made Mem. Institute. (Head.)   disc. then. Whale not a fish

Sherlock Holmes.

Bunsen

Martin Luther said fossils were artificial. He built a cathedral out of worms.

The poor built Chs & Monuments, no protection-fed M contrib to McKin mon.

∧Gould—first to get r. by theft.—he followed Cal∧
Stanton $20M
Rocke   10 ″ Chic.
Carnegie, 100 lib & 10M in Scot.
∧Vand. nigger college.∧
German's loving-cup

Wedding⟨:⟩ Xmas pres.
  & birthday.

Lincoln
  Grant
  Sherm—Sher^{n}.

Bessemer

Cal. gold & Australia—
This *starts* the materialising ball—word came back of sudden riches. This had never previously occurred save in fairy tales.

[perpendicular to previous entries]

The Start
====

Benton—Pac. RR.—only 3 rich men then, of very humble origin: Astor⟨ia⟩, skins, Girard. (college—stolen) Vand. boating—1 in Cin (Longworth)—1 in N.O., Jew., not another in Amer. Vand. first to consolidate a trust. Gould followed the ∧CIVIL WAR &∧ California sudden-riches disease with a *worse* one, s. r. by swindling & buying courts. Cal. & Gould were the beginners of the moral rot, they were the worst things that ever befel Amer; they created the hunger for wealth when the Gr. Civ. had just completed its youth ∧& its ennobling WAR∧—strong, pure, clean, ambitious, impressionable—ready to make choice of a life-course & move with a rush; *they & circumstances* determined the choice. Remark of ∧young∧ broker about Gould in Lotos billiard. Circumst. after Vand. wrought railways into systems; then Standard Oil; Steel Trust.; & Carnegie. CALIF—causes Pac. R.R. ∧UNCLE TOM∧ WAR ∧TELEGRAPH.∧ to *restrict* slavery—Circum. *abolished* it. GOULD, R. by theft.—R.R. wrecker & buyer of courts. ∧CABLE.∧ CONSOLIDATION invented by Vander. Other RRs follow. STAND. O. begins CON of *Manufac.* ∧FILIPINE & S. A.–CHINA∧ MORGAN consolidates, steel, copper, cables, ships, the WORLD's commerce—Europe began to decline. ∧Alliance with Rome—FRIARS.—Protestant distress.∧ Consol. NEWSP. Editorials (40,000 w. an hour—sent to *all* journals from Morgan's office. ∧The new Morgan a *Catholic*. WORRY. That Ch growing.∧ All politicians in his pay (a national Tammany). Conventions, both State & National, a form-⟨ula⟩. Candidates named, & *ordered* to be elected. ⟨P⟩Ohio *ordered* to be Democratic. Army & Navy under Morgan—officers at his command. Cath. strong; Prot. weak; X^n spreading. X^n welcome, as the only possible Savior from Cath. The struggle is now *on*. Morgan meditates a monarchy—800 Amer. duchesses &c abroad. It is found out, & *all* the common people go over to X^n—common soldiers & sailors too, by command of *second*(?) X^n Pope.

Group C

Most of these working notes, written on the recto of a "Par Value" tablet cover, are in the faded blue ink used for parts of the manuscript of Book 2 and revisions in Book 1; the notes in ink were canceled; the rest are written in pencil. "SUSY" was printed in a large uneven hand. "The Czar's Soliloquy," written at the bottom of the page, may indicate that the tablet once contained that piece. It was published in March 1905 in the *North American Review*, and the manuscript is not known to have survived. Paine's note "About 1905 or later" which appears at the top of the cover probably refers to that piece rather than to the "Eddypus" working notes.

C–1

Clover. Be another flood & others. Average of life 1000 yr. Geology shows 1,000,000 years—fossils to tell its age by. Webster, Snakspeer, Apollyon Prodigy, Pitt

General average of pulpit &c raised, but no supremacies any more— no great book or statesman.

Religion become perfunctory—x_n Science & Health—hence a flood. x_n S. will come again & in ⟨2⟩300 yrs will be supreme—then another flood.

Gospel of Selfishness.

Adam died 930.

Discov. of America, yr 314
Eve dies ⟨1032?⟩ 972.
Decay of civiliza^n begins then: spread of X^n Sci. Religious wars pro-
duced. By 1200 civ. is dead, & X^n S with it. Savagery till ressurec of X^n
S—flood results.

No trade for life ins. except insuring the Ins. Companies.

Ruined monument to Adam. A savage discourses upon it.

SUSY

Condemned
The Czar's Soliloquy [written over "Condemned"]

[in margin]

Popoatahual⟨l⟩pacatapetl I
II
pronounced pie-crust
⟨**necess** [unrecovered words]⟩

TEXTUAL APPARATUS

Textual Introduction

PERHAPS no major American author has left so large and varied an archive of literary remains as Mark Twain. If he seems at times to have thrown nothing away, his preservation of so much unachieved writing stems as much from his method of composition as from his well-known inability to distinguish his good work from his bad. It was his habit to compose several works at the same time; to pigeonhole projects when his interest or invention waned, then resurrect them when it was rekindled; and to extract passages from one work and introduce them in another. Moreover, a substantial portion of this labor, especially in his later years, was performed as therapy or experiment, with no thought of publication; or it recorded ideas Mark Twain considered so controversial that he believed they could only be published posthumously. Thus few, if any, of these stories and essays can be considered to have been finally abandoned. His unpublished writing is unfinished in every sense—not only is much of it fragmentary or unstructured, but it was always in a state of flux, subject while its author lived to constant change. It formed a store of raw material whose contents he might drastically alter, rearrange, or cannibalize.

Although the works in this volume are unified in theme, they are disparate in character and completeness. "The Victims" is scarcely more than a set of preliminary notes; "The International Lightning Trust" is a finished story which was in the hands of a publisher when Mark Twain died. The volume includes autobiography ("Little Nelly Tells a Story Out of Her Own Head"); expressions of personal pain ("In My Bitterness") and political conviction ("The Stupendous Procession"); and exercises written, according to the author, to while away the time (the "Little Bessie" sequence). Manuscript originally written for "The Secret History of Eddypus, the World-Empire" found its way instead into the periodical publication of chapters from *Christian Science*, though "Eddypus" itself is among the stories shelved without an ending. "Abner L. Jackson (About to Be) Deceased" has two endings; "A Letter from the Comet," two beginnings. "The Refuge of the Derelicts" lacks structural coherence; "The Stupendous Procession," formal consistency. "Newhouse's Jew Story" and "Randall's Jew Story" are two drafts recounting the same episode, while in his two efforts to satirize special providences by showering disastrous miracles on an Arkansas village, "The Holy Children" and "The Second Advent," Mark Twain incorporates pages from the earlier version in the later one. "Flies and Russians" and "Passage from a Lecture" appear to be attempts to transform passages deleted from other works into independent essays.

The editor of works so varied in character and completeness cannot claim, as the editor of published writing may, that he is fulfilling the author's intentions. To put such work into print is itself to exceed the author's intentions, not only in the broad sense that he did not publish it, but because printing fixes its form. What is lost is the sense of manifold possibility which these works held for the author and which can still be discerned by surveying the manuscripts. In a number of intangible ways, a printed text cannot be quite the same as a manuscript: type is inevitably reductive, transforming the physical association of lines on the written page; calling attention to what is there rather than what is nascent; conveying a sense of permanence instead of fluidity. Moreover, in his unfinished writing, Mark Twain often had no settled intent, or failed to make his intentions clear. Thus, the goal of this edition is a modest one: to present texts at once readable, and, within the limits of type, true to each work as Mark Twain left it.

Copy-Text

Modern editorial theory stipulates that in order to produce a definitive text an editor must place before his readers not only the text itself, but all of the reasoning and evidence by which he reached his conclusions. Whenever the editor must make a choice, he is obligated to report and defend it. As the first step toward fulfilling this obligation, the editor designates a "copy-text"—the basis for his own text, which he must follow in all particulars except where emendation is required. The choice of a copy-text determines the form in which the evidence for establishing the final text and recording its history is organized; and it informs the reader of the source of every reading in the edited text, for each reading must either originate in the copy-text or be listed with its source as an emendation. From the evidence presented in the textual apparatus, the reader must be able to reconstruct the copy-text and to judge the reasonableness of each decision to incorporate a variant reading in the edited text or to exclude it.

Thus two standards guide the choice of copy-text: the text chosen must permit the editor to marshal all the significant information about his text with the least possible confusion or distraction; and it must be the least corrupt text available to him, the text which is nearest the author's holograph. Although in practice the copy-text usually coincides with a single document—it is generally identical to a manuscript, typescript, or copy of an impression—"copy-text" is a conceptual tool; it "signifies an arrangement of words, abstracted from their physical embodiment."[1]

This distinction between the abstract copy-text and the actual text or texts before the editor is crucial to the establishment of five of the texts in this volume.[2] These texts survive both in manuscript and in typescripts bearing Mark Twain's holograph revisions. Because Mark Twain never typed his own literary work, the introduction of the typewriter caused the functions of creating a text and producing legible copy to be divided between author and typist. Typists make mistakes and authors revise their typescripts without noticing many of the new readings produced by typing errors and sophistications. On the typescript of "The Refuge of the Derelicts," for example, Mark Twain altered the manuscript reading "then the roses would come back to his young wife's cheeks" to "*then*, oh, then the roses would come back to his young wife's cheeks." On the same line of the typescript (219.14 in this volume) he missed the obvious typographical error "monyh" for manuscript "month," and a few lines later (219.19) overlooked a typist's eye skip (she omitted "—a capitalist")

---

[1] G. Thomas Tanselle, "The Meaning of Copy-Text," *Studies in Bibliography* 23 (1970):192.

[2] The works are "Little Bessie," "The Refuge of the Derelicts," "The International Lightning Trust," "The Secret History of Eddypus, the World-Empire," and "The Stupendous Procession."

which seriously affected the rhythm and sense of his prose. Thus neither manuscript nor typescript is both complete and completely authorial: the manuscript lacks the revisions made by the author on the typescript; the typescript bears the author's readings side by side with transcription errors he overlooked. In order to represent accurately the course of composition and the editorial choices made for these works, it is necessary to distinguish firmly between concept and object in choosing a copy-text—to disembody the editorial basis of the text from the particular documents with which the editor is confronted.

In practice, the choice is simple. Because the typescripts were made directly from the manuscript, typing errors can be detected by collating the typescript against the copy from which it was prepared. Any typed reading which is not identical to a manuscript reading can only have been introduced by the typist without authority.[3] Only the author's inscription, in the manuscript or as an alteration on one of the typescripts, can be authoritative. Therefore, the copy-text chosen for these five works is Mark Twain's inscription, abstracted from the documents in which it is imbedded.[4]

The choice of copy-text for the remaining thirty-one works in the volume is unambiguous: only one authoritative text exists for each, and the copy-text naturally coincides with these unique documents.[5] Mark Twain had eleven of these works typed, but did not revise the typescripts, so that they are without textual significance.

---

[3] Typed readings can have no authority so long as the typescript is a direct transcription of the manuscript, made without the intervention of verbal instructions from the author or a lost copy. The textual commentary for "Little Nelly Tells a Story Out of Her Own Head" considers the possibility that such intervention took place in the transmission of that text.

[4] One could arrive at the same edited text by designating either the manuscript or the typescript as copy-text. What would be sacrificed would be the clarity of the textual apparatus. If the manuscript were copy-text, each revision in the typescript would have to be listed as an emendation instead of appearing in the record of the work's course of composition where it belongs. If the typescript were copy-text, a list of emended typing errors—cruxes which can be detected and eliminated without editorial inference or judgment—would be intermingled with emendations that do call for editorial decision.

[5] With one exception, the copy-text for these works is Mark Twain's manuscript. Dixon Wecter's typescript of "Colloquy Between a Slum Child and a Moral Mentor" is the source for the text in this volume because it is the only accessible copy of the work. Apart from "Colloquy," unrevised or modern typescripts and modern printings have only been used as an occasional aid to editorial correction of the author's errors and for conjectural reconstruction of readings in damaged manuscripts.

Principles of Emendation

A conservative policy of emendation has been adopted. The texts are unmodernized—spellings, usages, and forms authorized by nineteenth-century dictionaries and grammar books are retained. Thus, old-fashioned spellings, like "ancle" and "recal," and obsolete punctuation, like commas before opening and closing parentheses or semicolons inside closing quotation marks, have not been altered. Mark Twain was meticulous about his punctuation and resented any interference with it. Most emendations of punctuation correct mechanical errors—the use of a period in an interrogative sentence where a question mark is clearly needed, for instance, or the inadvertent omission of quotation marks in dialogue. Mark Twain's nonmechanical punctuation—especially the commas, semicolons, and dashes which serve his style or establish his meaning—was largely oral. It often appears to be idiosyncratic, but it has been respected even in its inconsistencies unless it is glaringly defective. He was less careful about spelling, capitalization, and hyphenation, however, and was often pointlessly inconsistent even when he was correct. His work contains outright errors, such as his habitual misspelling "sieze"; lapses stemming from haste or carelessness, like the omission of a letter in "superanuated" ("Lightning Trust," 80.10); and miswriting, like the fusion of strokes in "mechanc's" for "mechanic's" ("Lightning Trust," 91.19). Frequently the need for emendation arises from revision: Mark Twain often forgot to reduce an initial capital after adding new material to the beginning of a sentence, for instance. Obvious mistakes of this kind have been emended; speculative emendation, largely on literary grounds, has been necessary only when the editor has had to choose between alternative readings left unresolved by Mark Twain.

The correction of inconsistencies is more problematic, and a more flexible policy has been adopted toward it. Mark Twain found the chore of hunting down and changing his inconsistent forms distasteful and expected it to be performed by the editors and compositors of his published work. Because he expected others to smooth the formal texture of his work and because inconsistencies can be distracting to a reader, emendations for consistency have been adopted when the work as it stands is complete or nearly so, when retaining the inconsistency serves no conceivable purpose, and when Mark Twain's preference is discernible. As a rule, the resolution of inconsistencies is guided by the preponderant usage in the work itself. The consistent appearance of a form in the later part of a work may indicate that it was the author's latest preference even if it is not numerically preponderant, however. The capital and lower-case forms of "Aunt" and "Aunty" appear in about equal number in "The Refuge of the Derelicts," for instance, but because they are always capitalized in the last hundred pages of manuscript, the upper-case form has been adopted. Occasionally, when frequency of occurrence within a work is inconclusive, reference has been made to other writings of the same period. And in a few instances, as with the spellings "recognize/recognise," Mark Twain appears to have been utterly indifferent, and the choice is essentially arbitrary. Emendations for consistency have only been made within each work, not imposed on one work from another. Since Mark Twain's practice varied from time to time, the form rejected in one work may be the one adopted in another. In every case, however, the form chosen has the warrant of the author's usage.

Inconsistent readings have not been changed if there is any possibility that Mark Twain may have intended them to remain. The alternative spellings "suit" and "suite" have been allowed to stand in "Lightning Trust," for example, because Mark Twain may have felt that the latter spelling was a pompous one and used it for satirical reasons (see the textual note to 100.29). Sometimes the unfinished character of a work dictates the retention of inconsistencies. Their presence may be a sign of the author's indecision; or, although a problem may stem from lapse of memory, the manuscript may provide no indication of how to resolve it. In "Eddypus," for instance, the Christian Science empire is said in one passage to have renamed Boston "Bostonflats" and in another "Eddy-flats." The inconsistency may have arisen from error or from uncertainty about which name to settle on. But in either case, to resolve it through emendation would distort the text by obscuring Mark Twain's indecision or by imposing a subjective editorial preference on an indifferent variant. Finally, a work may be so far from completion that a polished texture would clash with the rough state of the work as a whole. In order to preserve the flavor of a preliminary sketch in "The Victims," its inconsistencies have been retained; in "The Stupendous Procession" the variations in format and style are not only consonant with the incomplete state of the work, but with the evidently experimental character of the essay. Mark Twain apparently tried to convey a sense of the line of march in the placement and type style he assigned to floats, banners, and participants; to impose consistency on those features he left inconsistent would be to foreclose options he left open. By the same token, to leave these features of the work inconsistent but to style spelling and hyphenation consistently would produce a hybrid of editorial and authorial forms.

A few mechanical changes have been made throughout the volume without being listed in the tables of emendations. Forms peculiar to the written page have not been transferred to the printed page. Ampersands have been expanded to "and," "&c." to "etc." Superscript letters have been lowered to the line. Eccentricities of Mark Twain's handwriting have not been noted unless they produce an ambiguity that requires an editorial decision. Mark Twain used both square brackets and parentheses where a modern author would use parentheses; square brackets are here reserved for editorial insertions; Mark Twain's square brackets appear here as parentheses. He designated chapter headings with a variety of abbreviations, in upper or in lower case, or with blank spaces. Sometimes he numbered his chapters; sometimes he lost track and left the numbers for others to fill in. Chapter headings in this volume have been standardized as "Chapter" followed by an arabic numeral. The typography of chapter headings and titles is editorial; periods and flourishes following headings and titles have been dropped. Mark Twain's signature, which appears at the end of some manuscripts, has also been omitted. The opening words of each chapter appear in small capitals with an ornamental initial letter. This convention is only noted in the emendations list if the words styled are italic in the copy-text.

Two forms of authorial revision in the typescript require editorial decision. Mark Twain frequently instructed his typist to omit manuscript underlinings because he wanted to rehear the work and add fresh emphasis marks. On the first page of the "Eddypus" manuscript, for instance, he wrote "Pay no attention to italics, Jean." When he came to read a typescript, however, he sometimes carried out his intention of supplying new italics, but sometimes marked only part of it for emphasis, and sometimes none at all. When the typescript has been fully revised in this respect, it becomes the sole authority for italics in this edition; when it is not marked at all, the manuscript emphasis has been restored; partially marked typescripts have been considered individually. The textual commentary on each work for which revised typescript survives sets forth the authority for the italics in the edited text.

Sometimes, Mark Twain's revisions are occasioned by a typing error. Working without reference to the manuscript, he revised on the basis of the corrupted reading instead of restoring the manuscript reading. In "The Refuge of the Derelicts," for instance, the typist skipped the word "pride";

Mark Twain caught the error and supplied "endorsement," without consulting the manuscript. Such changes produce two independent authorial variants, in effect, alternative readings. The conflict can only be resolved by emendation on literary grounds. A textual note identifies and discusses each of these choices.

Guide to the Textual Apparatus

The textual apparatus strives for completeness and clarity, so that interested readers can judge editorial decisions in the broadest context and have the evidence to reconstruct the full history of each text.

Depending on the complexity of the work, the apparatus may be divided into as many as five sections: "Textual Commentary," "Textual Notes," "Emendations of the Copy-Text," "Word Division in the Copy-Text," and "Mark Twain's Revisions." Two special listings, for "The Second Advent" and "Little Nelly Tells a Story Out of Her Own Head," also appear.

An objective designation of ink color is impossible because of variation in chemical reaction to age, light, and paper, and differences in shading caused by a change in pens or angle and pressure of writing. Therefore, ink colors, when noted, are designated only for purposes of comparison within each work. An ink may be called light blue in "Eddypus" to distinguish it from a darker blue in that work, but it is not necessarily the same color as the ink called light blue in "The Second Advent."

Line numbers in cues and citations do not count titles and chapter headings. Alternative readings are separated by a slash; a vertical rule indicates the end of a line in the text under discussion.

Textual Commentary identifies the copy-text for each work and specifies those sections of apparatus which are omitted as irrelevant. Whenever a text presents unusual features which require expansion or modification of the general editorial principles set forth in the textual introduction, the commentary describes the problems and notes the new procedures.

Textual Notes specify those features of the text discussed generally in the commentary, record all of Mark Twain's marginalia, and discuss emendations, refusals to emend, or aspects of Mark Twain's revision which require fuller explanation.

Emendations of the Copy-Text lists every departure from the copy-text with the exception of the normalizations set forth in the textual introduction. The adopted reading as it appears in the text of this edition is in the left-hand column, the rejected copy-text reading in the right-hand column. When Mark Twain's typist supplied a needed correction accepted by the editors, the symbol "TS" follows the adopted reading, but does not imply any "secondary authority" in the document cited. Emendations made by the editors without such aid appear without ascription. Starred emendations are discussed in textual notes. When an error was occasioned by a revision, a dagger appears at the entry to refer the reader to "Mark Twain's Revisions."

Word Division in the Copy-Text presents the readings adopted when a compound which could be rendered as a solid or hyphenated word is hyphenated at the end of a line in the copy-text. These ambiguities are resolved in the same manner as Mark Twain's inconsistencies: by other appearances of the word or by parallels within the manuscript when possible, or by his practice in other works of the period when it is not. The table lists the words as they appear in the present text.

Mark Twain's Revisions records every change made by the author in manuscript and typescript. The only exceptions are essential corrections that Mark Twain made as he wrote or reread his work. These fall into six categories: (1) letters or words that have been mended, traced over, or canceled and rewritten for clarity; (2) false starts and slips of the pen; (3) corrected eye skips; (4) words or phrases that have been inadvertently repeated, then canceled; (5) corrected misspellings; and (6) inadvertent additions of letters or punctuation that have been subsequently canceled, for instance, an incorrect "they" or "then" altered to "the," or superfluous quotation marks canceled at the end of a narrative passage.

When more than one ink color appears in a manuscript, the color of ink used for the initial inscription of each section of manuscript is given in centered headings; the ink color of a revision is mentioned only when it differs from that of the original inscription. All revisions appear in the manuscript unless their origin in a typescript is noted.

"Above" in the description signifies "interlined," and "over" signifies "in the same space." "Follows" and "followed by" are physical, not temporal, descriptions.

Following the textual apparatus, a list of ambiguous compounds hyphenated in the copy-texts and at the end of a line in this volume provides the correct form for quotation.

Little Bessie

Textual Commentary

The first chapter survives both in manuscript and in a typescript containing a few holograph revisions; the remaining chapters survive only in manuscript. Mark Twain's typist transcribed his manuscript italics; accordingly, they are retained in the present version, along with the emphasis added on the typescript.

Because the chapters were written at various times and Mark Twain made no effort to integrate them, no consistency has been imposed on the author's usage from one chapter to the next. The spelling "mama" in Chapter 5 is retained, for instance, although it varies from "mamma" in the preceding chapters. When Mark Twain is inconsistent within a chapter, however, his variant usages are emended.

Textual Notes

34.title   Little Bessie Would Assist Providence] Typed on the title page of the typescript is "On shipboard, Feb. 22, 1908." Below the chapter title, Mark Twain wrote "(It is dull, & I need wholesome excitements & distractions; so I will go lightly excursioning along the primrose path of theology.)" The title page is followed by two numbered but blank pages.

40.13–21   Now . . . dangerous.] The quoted passage, clipped from an unidentified periodical, is pinned to the manuscript.

41.title   Chapter 4] In the upper right-hand corner of the manuscript page, Mark Twain wrote and canceled the cue words "bastard" and "corespondent."

Emendations of the Copy-Text

	MTP READING	COPY-TEXT READING
†34.18	heard	heard of
36.11	burnt TS	burn't
36.19	its TS	it's
36.21	it?" TS	it?
37.22	MAMMA	*Mamma*
38.20	*H.*	H.
39.23	He	he
39.28	him	Him
39.33	*pause.*)	*pause*).
†40.35	it	It
41.5	Himself	himself
41.20	Physiological	Phisiological
41.22	mamma?	mamma.
44.5	His	his

Word Division in the Copy-Text

43.24	newspaper

Mark Twain's Revisions

34.title	Little . . . Providence] *originally* 'Little Bessie Assists Providence'; 'Would' *interlined with a caret; the final* 's' *of* 'Assists' *canceled.*
34.1	Little . . . old] *interlined with a caret.*

34.4   One day] *interlined with a caret above canceled* 'More than once'.

34.9   for] *interlined with a caret.*

34.15   always] *mended from* 'all'.

34.18   call] *follows canceled* 'think'; *originally* 'calling'; *the* 'ing' *canceled.*

34.19   and merciful."] *added following a canceled period.*

35.15   his] *mended from* 'he'; *the italics added on the TS.*

35.20   a judgment] *follows canceled* 'to pun'.

35.30   *Wait!*] *the italics added on the TS.*

35.32   His] *the* 'H' *mended from* 'h'.

36.8   mamma] *interlined with a caret following a comma added on the line.*

36.17   or fish] 'or' *interlined with a caret above canceled* 'and'.

36.18   other] *interlined with a caret.*

36.21   Mr. Hollister . . . it?] *originally* 'he laugh?'; 'Mr. Hollister' *interlined with a caret above canceled* 'he'; 'at it?' *added following wiped-out question mark.*

36.27   hungry] *interlined with a caret.*

36.35   her] *interlined with a caret above canceled* 'his'.

37.2   grateful] *interlined with a caret in black ink on the TS.*

37.3   she's] *interlined with a caret in black ink on the TS.*

37.9   Providence,] *interlined with a caret above a canceled comma.*

37.10   that won't answer] *originally* 'if that would answer,'; 'if' *canceled;* 'won't' *interlined with a caret following canceled* 'would'.

37.11   duty and] *follows canceled* 'way to'.

37.20   *Dear*] *follows canceled quotation marks.*

37.21	*this] roman in the MS.*
38.7–8	I . . . Hollister.] *squeezed in.*
38.11	took] *follows canceled* 'g'.
38.12	the man] *interlined with a caret above canceled* 'and forgot to put in the Moral Sense; so the Monster'.
38.17	and you . . . cat] *interlined with a caret.*
38.24	Criminal] *the* 'C' *mended from* 'c'.
39.14	and so,] *followed by an unrecovered cancellation; the comma appears to have been added.*
39.16	which] *interlined with a caret.*
39.33	house-fly] 'house-' *interlined with a caret.*
40.2	He] *the* 'H' *mended from* 'h'.
40.13–21	Now . . . dangerous.] *the text of a newspaper clipping pinned to the MS.*
40.22	fifty-two billions of] *interlined with a caret above canceled* 'thirteen million'.
40.23	in 60 days] *interlined with a caret.*
40.35	You have said] *interlined with a caret; the* 'I' *of MS* 'It' *not reduced to* 'i'.
41.1	He] *interlined with a caret above canceled* 'God'.
41.3	commit] *follows wiped-out and canceled unrecovered letters.*
41.3	therefore,] *interlined with a caret.*
41.23	let] *written over wiped-out* 'it's'.
42.12	B,] *originally* 'B,'; *the italics canceled.*
42.18	you know?] *followed by canceled* 'because Mr'.
42.19–20	oh, the] *originally* 'in the'; 'in' *mended to* 'oh'; *the comma added.*
42.20	One] *the* 'O' *mended from* 'o'.

42.21   she] *originally 'she'; the italics canceled.*

42.22–23   was begotten . . . anything] *interlined with a caret above canceled* 'made so much trouble in the world,'.

42.28   and wouldn't] *originally* 'and you couldn't'; 'you' *canceled; the* 'c' *mended to* 'w'.

42.29   instantly!] *the exclamation point appears to have been mended from a period.*

43.1   Mamma,] *follows canceled* 'Little Bessie.'

43.8   sexual] *interlined with a caret above canceled* 'adulterous'.

43.9   sexual] *interlined with a caret above canceled* 'adulterous'.

43.14   You] *the italics appear to be added.*

43.19–20   He wouldn't . . . He] *the* 'H' *of* 'He' *mended from* 'h' (*twice*).

43.23–24   and got . . . way] *interlined with a caret.*

43.25   get] *interlined with a caret.*

43.29   do] *interlined with a caret.*

43.30–31   God. . . . Him;] *the* 'G' *mended from* 'g'; *the* 'H' *mended from* 'h'.

43.32   way.] *the period added preceding a canceled question mark.*

44.4   got] *the* 'g' *written over wiped-out* 'G'.

44.4–5   and His Flood . . . morals] *interlined with a caret; the* 'H' *of* 'His' *preceding* 'Flood' *mended from* 'h'.

44.5   ideas] *originally* 'idea'; *the* 's' *added.*

44.15–16   some subject] *originally* 'some-|thing'; '-|thing' *canceled;* 'subject' *interlined with a caret.*

Little Nelly Tells a Story Out of Her Own Head

Textual Commentary

"Little Nelly" was written as a literary sketch, but Mark Twain later had a typescript prepared in order to incorporate the piece in his Autobiographical Dictations. The typescript survives in a ribbon and a carbon copy; Mark Twain revised neither. Ordinarily, the absence of authorial revision in a typescript would lead one to disregard it entirely in establishing the text. But the typescript is not identical to the manuscript, and the variation is different in kind from the transcription errors usually encountered in direct copies. The title appears only in the typescript, for instance, and in two places (48.3–8 and 49.19–26) long breathless sentences are broken into shorter sentences quite different in tone. Mark Twain could have supplied the title orally or on a now-lost title page, and the typist could have introduced the other variants through the usual misreading and mechanical error; but external evidence read in conjunction with the variants points to two other possible hypotheses.

Like all the Autobiographical Dictations, the typescript bears the rubric "Dictated" and the date. This need not indicate that Mark Twain actually dictated the work, for he frequently turned manuscript destined for the autobiography over to the copyist, who typed the heading as a matter of convention, not fact. Nevertheless, he did at times read manuscript to his typist, altering passages as he did so. It may be that "Little Nelly" was dictated in this way; certainly the changes to shorter, more easily read sentences are consonant with oral transmission of the work.

It is also possible that a revised typescript, now lost, intervened between the manuscript and the surviving transcription. A note on the carbon, probably Paine's, reads "Copies Elsewhere." Paine also altered the first sentence of the work on the carbon (adding the words italicized here) to make it read "Twenty-two-or-three years ago, *when I was* in Cleveland, *on a reading tour* a thing happened which I still remember well." If this revision was made at the same time as the notation "Copies Elsewhere," the fact that Paine chose the carbon to edit may indicate that it was the ribbon copy which was elsewhere. But it is conceivable that Mark Twain initiated the revision on an earlier typescript, that—as frequently happens—the typist overlooked his interlineation, and that Paine, checking the new typescript against the old, corrected the error. In that case "Copies Elsewhere" (which appears to have been written with a harder or sharper pencil than the revision) would be Paine's recollection at some later time that he had compared two versions of the essay.

Attractive as these possibilities are, they remain speculation; the evidence is insufficient to fix the relationship between the manuscript and typescript. The present text, therefore, is based upon the manuscript, the only text which is certainly authorial. Only the title is taken from the typescript. Because of the typescript's uncertain authority, however, a special collation listing all typescript variants is provided in the textual apparatus. Even those variants which are unquestionably typing errors are included, so that the readings which may be authorial can be judged in context.

There are no textual notes.

Emendations of the Copy-Text

	MTP Reading	Copy-Text Reading
47.title	Little Nelly . . . Out of Her Own Head	Little Nellie . . . out of her own head TS; [*untitled*] MS
47.14	Grey	Gray
48.33	on:) TS	on):

Special Collation: Rejected Typescript Variants

	Manuscript Reading	Typescript Reading
47.2	suburbs,	suburbs;
47.8	City,"	City",
47.12	nevermindtherestofthe-name	never mind the rest of the name
48.4	centre	center
48.5–6	sexes, the	sexes. The

	Manuscript Reading	Typescript Reading
48.8	about ready to	about to
48.9	VI, . . . girl,	VI. . . . girl
49.17	good bye	good-bye
49.23–24	course, the	course. The

Word Division in the Copy-Text

47.16	drawing-room

Mark Twain's Revisions

47.1	Twenty-two-or-three] '-two-or-three' *interlined with a caret.*
47.2	well.] *followed by* '—and without difficulty.' *canceled in pencil; the period after* 'well' *added in pencil.*
47.6	a week,] *interlined with a caret in pencil above canceled* 'several days,'.
47.8	the . . . together] 'the' *and* 'we . . . together' *interlined with carets.*
47.9	Meantime, every day] 'every day' *interlined with a caret; the comma after* 'Meantime' *added.*
47.12	these] *originally* 'the'; *the* 'se' *added.*
47.13	serious and] *interlined with a caret above canceled* 'grave and'.
47.19	"out . . . head,"] *the quotation marks added in pencil.*
48.9	Edward . . . had] *follows canceled* 'Mi'; *originally* 'Edward VI had'; '(played by a girl,)' *interlined with a caret above canceled* 'VI', *the opening parenthesis canceled and* '(to be' *added to the interlineation;* 'VI' *squeezed in following* 'Edward'.

48.10   take] *followed by canceled* 'her'.

48.12   function,] *interlined with a caret.*

48.18   own] *interlined with a caret in pencil.*

48.36   then it] *follows canceled* 'and it'.

49.6   The] *the* 'T' *mended from* 't'.

49.8   a dear] 'a' *interlined with a caret.*

49.22   partner] *interlined with a caret in pencil.*

49.29   and everything.] 'and' *interlined with a caret in pencil following canceled* ', the tale,'; 'everything.' *followed by* 'Nelly knows' *canceled in pencil.*

The Second Advent

Textual Commentary

Copy-text for "The Second Advent" is the manuscript of eighty-four pages, twenty-two of which were originally part of "The Holy Children." Although Mark Twain revised as he went along while writing "The Second Advent," and the presence of alterations in pencil (p. 54.2) and in black ink (p. 58.3 and the canceled passage at 59.17) shows that he also checked his manuscript at other times, he apparently did not return to revise the work as a whole once he had completed it. Therefore, the story is essentially a first draft.

In addition to the pages adapted from the earlier tale, one other section, the description of the selection and packing of the jury (pp. 59.17–60.22), was written out of sequence. An examination of the inks used and of the watermarks and ragged edges of the torn half-sheets which make up the manuscript shows that this passage was written after Mark Twain had reached "and were not satisfied" (p. 61.4–5) and that the split between the clergymen and the editors was an afterthought. The same kind of evidence indicates that the title page of the manuscript, which matches the last page written for "The Second Advent," was supplied after the story was finished. A separate half-sheet of manuscript in the Mark Twain Papers, unnumbered and inscribed only "There was great stir and talk and wonder in Black Jack," was originally the first page of the story. It was probably a false start, discarded but not destroyed.

Of all the pronouns referring to God or Christ in "The Second Advent," Mark Twain capitalized only one ("He," p. 56.12). Although he often wrote these pronouns without capitals, ordinarily he expected his editors to provide conventional capitalization. In this text six pronouns referring to God have been so emended, since the tale would gain nothing from inconsistent capitalization or from an anomalous lack of capitals. However, pronouns referring to Christ and the new Savior have been left lower case, since Mark Twain makes the identity of the two, and the divinity of the latter, satirically ambiguous.

Following Mark Twain's revisions, a special collation records the changes he made in light blue ink to the penciled "Holy Children" manuscript when incorporating its pages into "The Second Advent." This list is cued to both pieces by page and line number ("The Holy Children" page and line numbers are in square brackets) and is arranged to show each change made for "The Second Advent" together with the reading in "The Holy Children" which it replaces.

Revisions made during the inscription of "The Holy Children" manuscript and incorporated in the text of both works are listed in the table of Mark Twain's revisions for "The Holy Children" where page and line numbers for both pieces are given.

Textual Notes

61.2   models of] In the top margin of the manuscript page above these words Mark Twain wrote and canceled the cue word "Talmage."

63.4   There was] The manuscript pages adapted from "The Holy Children" begin here.

63.35–64.7   now, that . . . desired him] One and a half new manuscript pages were added here to the pages adapted from "The Holy Children." Mark Twain had first changed "evidences were . . . and" to "evidence was" (p. 63.36) on the "Holy Children" page. He then enlarged the scope of the alteration by canceling the entire surrounding passage ("Holy Children" p. 73.7–13) and replacing it with the new pages. The first few lines of the canceled passage, including the revised phrase, were copied unchanged on the new pages ("now, that . . . dispute," p. 63.35–36).

64.11–22   of crops . . . consequence, he] One and a half new manuscript pages were added here to the pages adapted from "The Holy Children."

65.21–25   By this time . . . A rich] One new manuscript page was added here to the pages adapted from "The Holy Children."

Emendations of the Copy-Text

	MTP Reading	Copy-Text Reading
53.17	forerunners	forerunners,
54.4	abundance	abundace
55.1	Him	him *Also emended at* 64.6
56.4	accent?	accent.
58.10	Virgin	virgin
†60.23	no	no no
60.28	Himself	himself *Also emended at* 61.35
†61.11	the angel	The angel
62.4	He	he
64.9	although	Although
64.13	frostbitten	frosbitten
64.31	holy disciple	Holy disciple
65.5	holy Talmage	Holy Talmage
65.13	restored	rostored
66.10	transgressor.	transgressor *See Mark Twain's revisions for* "The Holy Children," 74.36
66.20	So the	So The
66.26	popularity	popularity,
67.5	raising	rasing
68.21	*Thy*	*thy*
68.23	holy disciples	Holy disciples

Word Division in the Copy-Text

58.11	newspapers
60.1	underhand
62.3	handmaid
62.36	hearth-stone
63.6	withheld
64.9	midsummer
65.8	undertakers
66.31	overflow

Mark Twain's Revisions

Written in light blue ink from beginning through 59.16

53.4   are rickety] 'are' *follows a wiped-out comma; written over wiped-out* 'out'.

53.18   Nancy] *follows canceled* 'M'.

54.2   and] *interlined with a caret in pencil.*

55.9   Barnes answered] *interlined with a caret and marked to begin a paragraph with a paragraph sign in dark blue ink.*

55.12   act] *originally* 'fact'; *the* 'f' *canceled.*

55.26   facts] *originally* 'fact'; *the* 's' *added.*

56.4   like] *written over wiped-out* 'wit'.

56.11   assured] *interlined with a caret above canceled* 'warned'.

56.33   Nancy] *follows canceled* 'her'.

56.36   world.] *followed by canceled quotation marks.*

57.2   it?"] *the question mark squeezed in.*

57.10   cheaper] *follows canceled* 'so'.

57.14   angel.] *followed by canceled quotation marks.*

57.18   is holy] *follows canceled* 'will'.

57.31   reinstituted] *follows canceled* 'decided'.

58.3   here] *interlined with a caret in black ink above canceled* 'her'.

58.17   presidents] *follows canceled* 'profes'.

58.22   move.] *the* 've' *written over a wiped-out unrecovered letter.*

58.36   editorial] *interlined with a caret.*

59.1   westward] *follows canceled* 'for the'.

59.1   praising God] *interlined with a caret.*

59.7–8   and resume] *follows canceled* 'and take'.

59.12   Arkansas] *follows canceled* 'ear'.

Written in dark blue ink from 59.17 through 60.12

59.17–60.22   After . . . follows:] *added on seven new MS pages, 34A-G, replacing a paragraph:* 'After breakfast the wise men went to see the Hopkinses; there they listened critically to the evidence offered by Nancy and Barnes, and watched narrowly for possible discrepancies, but the college presidents detected none. When the evidence was all in, the wise men examined it on all sides, but the college presidents were still unable to find any flaw in it. At last they said—'. *The first part of the paragraph,* 'After . . . watched nar-', *inadvertently not canceled at the bottom of MS page 34; the remainder canceled in light blue ink on page 35; in the original paragraph* 'detected' *follows canceled* 'foun'; 'the college presidents' *interlined with a caret in black ink both times it appears.*

59.19   and] *interlined with a caret.*

59.22   not by] *follows canceled* 'by'.

59.24   Greeley] *originally* 'Greely'; *the* 'y' *mended to* 'ey'.

59.27   The] *the 'T' mended from 'P'.*

59.32   eligible] *follows canceled 'qu'.*

59.35   Greeley] *originally 'Greely'; the 'y' mended to 'ey'.*

60.4   a] *interlined with a caret.*

60.11   could] *follows canceled 'had'.*

Written in light blue ink from 60.13 through 60.25 ('know')

60.16   and] *interlined with a caret.*

60.17   or] *written over a wiped-out 'b'.*

60.23   no whit.] *originally 'no longer.'; 'longer.' canceled and
                 'no whit.' interlined; the first 'no' inadvertently left
                 standing.*

60.23   We find . . . facts:] *interlined.*

60.24   Hopkins] *interlined with a caret.*

Written in dark blue ink from 60.25 ('this is') through
61.4–5 ('satisfied.')

60.29   Jackson] *interlined with a caret in light blue ink.*

60.29   verdict] *follows canceled 'tes'.*

60.32   Then] *follows canceled 'B'.*

60.32   the jury . . . faction] *originally 'they'; the 'y' canceled
                 and 'jury . . . faction' interlined with a caret in light
                 blue ink.*

61.4   murmured and] *interlined with a caret.*

Written in light blue ink from 61.5 ('Mr.') to end

61.9   none] *written over wiped-out 'and d'.*

61.10–11   We . . . that the] *'We . . . that' interlined with a caret;
                 the 'T' of 'The' not reduced to 't'.*

61.14	hearsay evidence] *followed by canceled* 'that'.
61.21	a young] *follows canceled* 'the'.
61.24	to it;] *the semicolon mended from a period.*
61.28	had] *follows canceled* 'would have'.
62.13	speaker] *followed by a canceled comma.*
62.20	they] *interlined with a caret.*
62.21	proclaiming] *follows canceled* 'ins'.
63.1	finally] *interlined with a caret above canceled* 'had'.
63.4–35	There was . . . shown,] *adapted from* "The Holy Children."
64.7–11	to pray . . . destruction] *adapted from* "The Holy Children."
64.19	praising God,] *interlined with a caret.*
64.22–65.20	changed . . . death.] *adapted from* "The Holy Children."
65.26–68.36	bachelor . . . 1881.] *adapted from* "The Holy Children."
66.30	twenty . . . twenty] *originally* 'twenty . . . twenty'; *both words canceled and* 'ten' *interlined above each in light blue ink; then each* 'ten' *canceled and* 'twenty' *interlined with a caret in light blue ink.*

Special Collation

	"THE SECOND ADVENT"	"THE HOLY CHILDREN"
53.1–63.4 [70.1–72.8–9]	Black Jack . . . morning.	These . . . triumph.
63.8 [72.12]	the saint	that pale slim child
63.10 [72.14]	he *Also at* 63.24 (*twice*) *and* 63.25	she *Also at* 72.28 (*twice*) *and* 72.30

	"The Second Advent"	"The Holy Children"
63.10 [72.14]	his *Also at* 63.10, 63.11, 63.23, *and* 63.25	her *Also at* 72.15 (*twice*), 72.28, *and* 72.30
63.13 [72.17–18]	thing . . . described.	matter . . . describe.
63.21 [72.26]	disciple's	child's
63.22 [72.27]	him *Also at* 63.23	her *Also at* 72.28
63.23 [72.28]	disciple	child
63.27–28 [72.31–36]	utterly. ¶ There was	utterly. ¶ It was . . . said. There was
63.34–35 [73.7]	holy disciple	Holy Children
63.36 [73.8–9]	evidence was	evidences were . . . and
64.1–7 [73.10–13]	But on . . . desired him	The calls . . . were asked
64.9 [73.14]	He consented; and although *See emendations.*	Although
64.11–22 [73.17–18]	complete; in . . . consequence, he	complete. . . . The children
64.23 [73.18–19]	day. These changes	day, . . . persons, and these changes
64.31 [73.27]	life	lives
64.31 [73.27]	holy disciple *See emendations.*	Holy Children.
64.32 [73.28]	saint was	children were

	"THE SECOND ADVENT"	"THE HOLY CHILDREN"
64.36–65.1 [73.33]	until now, when such	until such
65.5 [74.1]	holy Talmage was *See emendations.*	Holy Children were
65.6 [74.2]	He *Also at* 65.10	They *Also at* 74.6
65.8–9 [74.5]	nurses of . . . about rose	nurses rose
65.10 [74.5–6]	saint was	Holy Children were
65.13 [74.8–9]	saint	Holy Children
65.13 [74.9]	his	their
65.20–26 [74.16]	death. ¶ By this . . . A rich bachelor	death. A bachelor
65.29 [74.19–20]	to Black Jack . . . Savior	to our village . . . children
65.30 [74.20]	health. So . . . but	health. He
66.3 [74.29]	latter. Naturally . . . property.	latter. To return to my narrative.
66.12–13 [75.2–3]	previously giving . . . disturber.	previously warning . . . them.
66.14 [75.4]	Twelve Disciples	children
66.16–17 [75.6]	the several communities . . . labored	the community
66.20 [75.9]	next. So the *See emendations.*	next. The
66.20 [75.10]	Twelve wasted gradually	children began to waste

	"THE SECOND ADVENT"	"THE HOLY CHILDREN"
66.22 [75.12]	State	village
66.24 [75.14]	a hundred	five hundred
66.35 [75.25]	disciples *Also at* 67.9, 67.16, 67.27, *and* 67.33	children *Also at* 75.34, 76.5, 76.15, *and* 76.21
67.4 [75.29]	disciples'	children's
67.6–8 [75.31–32]	Yet at times . . . Savior.	Yet even . . . inconveniences.
67.8 [75.33]	man	bachelor
67.12 [75.36–76.1]	holy Twelve	Holy Children
67.20 [76.9]	region	village
67.24 [76.13]	disciples	Holy Children
67.24–25 [76.13]	moment, (for . . . him,) but	moment, but
68.16 [77.4]	any person in Arkansas	this village
68.18 [77.6]	one	man
68.20 [77.8]	Arkansas	this village
68.23 [77.11]	holy disciples *See emendations.*	Holy Children
68.26 [77.14]	Twelve	children

	"THE SECOND ADVENT"	"THE HOLY CHILDREN"
68.31–32 [77.20]	Savior and the disciples	children
68.34–36 [77.22]	crucified. . . . 1881.	shot.

The Holy Children

Textual Commentary

The manuscript of "The Holy Children," thirty-one pages long, was written and revised in pencil. Mark Twain further altered the last twenty-two pages in ink to adapt them for inclusion in "The Second Advent." (These changes are listed following Mark Twain's revisions to "The Second Advent.") It is possible that before doing so he started to revise the earlier tale in ink; certainly the ink revision from "half sister" to "step-sister" at 71.4 belongs only to "The Holy Children," and such an alteration as that discussed in the textual note at 76.13 would have been as appropriate in the earlier piece as in the later one. However, most of the ink changes are obviously intended for "The Second Advent," and no distinguishing characteristics of the inscription set these readings apart from those which might have been meant for "The Holy Children." Consequently, except for the ink change at 71.4, the penciled inscription is the copy-text for "The Holy Children."

In the table of Mark Twain's revisions, the entries for the pages of "The Holy Children" used in "The Second Advent" are cued to both pieces by page and line number. "The Second Advent" page and line numbers are in square brackets.

Textual Notes

71.4   step-sister] The change from "half sister" to "step-sister" is the only ink revision in the manuscript which clearly was made for "The Holy Children." The sisters do not appear in "The Second Advent," and the revisions for that tale start on manuscript page 10, while this alteration appears on page 4.

72.9   There was] Beginning here, the pages of "The Holy Children" manuscript were revised and incorporated into "The Second Advent."

74.16   death] In the top margin of the manuscript page above this word, Mark Twain wrote in pencil the cue word "disciple."

75.23   lost,] The comma, in ink, was probably added during the "Second Advent" revision. It is adopted here because it is a necessary correction for "The Holy Children" as well as for "The Second Advent."

76.13   moment,] After this word Mark Twain added in ink "(for they would be sure to raise him up in the hope of reforming him,)." Although the addition might have been intended to reiterate the sisters' efforts at redeeming sinners, in the absence of conclusive evidence that it was intended for "The Holy Children," it is omitted here but included in "The Second Advent" at 67.24–25.

Emendations of the Copy-Text

	MTP READING	COPY-TEXT READING
74.9	restored	rostored
†74.36	transgressor.	transgressor
75.16	popularity	popularity,
*75.23	lost,	lost
75.30	raising	rasing
77.9	*Thy*	*thy*

Word Division in the Copy-Text

70.9	overflowings
71.4	step-sister
71.25	midnight
73.14	midsummer

74.4   undertakers
75.21   overflow

Mark Twain's Revisions

Written in pencil

70.1–2   seventy] *follows canceled* 'sixty'.

70.3   can remember] *follows canceled* 'was twenty-one years old at the time'.

70.5   mother's] *interlined with a caret above canceled* 'father's'.

70.13   moved] *follows canceled* 'were beset all along by strangers and citizens'.

70.13   uncovered,] *interlined with a caret.*

70.14   bent] *followed by canceled* 'low'.

70.14   blessing;] *followed by canceled* 'also there were always people reaching reverently out to touch the hem of their garments;' *the semicolon following* 'blessing' *replaces a comma;* 'reach-' *at the end of a line followed by canceled* 'out'.

70.18   sweetest] *interlined with a caret to replace canceled* 'holiest'.

70.22   praise-meetings of] 'of' *written over* 'in'.

71.1   starved . . . to one] 'starved' *follows canceled* 'harsh and cold to one'; 'to one' *interlined with a caret.*

71.2   period.] *followed by canceled* 'The world was forgotten; its language was retained, but purified and elevated to the expression of higher and nobler meanings. Thus if one asked another how he was prospering, the answer would not refer to money affairs or physical health, but only to the progress of the soul. Thus I often heard the question "How are you?" answered with "Gaining in liberty"—meaning, gaining in ease and facility in prayer.'; 'prospering' *follows a canceled comma;* 'soul' *followed by an added period and canceled* 'toward spiritual'.

71.3–4   the one aged] *follows canceled* 'aged'.

71.4   step-] *interlined with a caret in blue ink above canceled* 'half'. *See textual note.*

71.8   matters.] *followed by canceled* 'They were never heard to laugh nor seen to smile; they cared nothing for toys, they never played, either together or with other children. Their sole occupation was the study of religious writings, their only recreation was prayer. They were exact and orderly far beyond their age.' *The cancellation originally ended with* 'prayer'; *the last sentence was deleted later.*

71.9   in turn.] *followed by canceled* 'twenty minutes.'; *the period following* 'turn' *mended from a comma.*

71.12   said] *follows canceled* 'follow'.

71.18   by and by,] *interlined with a caret above canceled* 'once,'.

71.20   until] *follows canceled* 'and'.

71.21   After] *follows canceled* 'But I'.

71.23   visiting] *follows canceled* 'cer'.

71.24   tracts, . . . food.] 'medicines, and food.' *interlined with a caret; the comma following* 'tracts' *mended from a period.*

71.25   From] *follows canceled* 'After their father's death'.

71.28   mustard seed] *follows canceled* 'grain of'; *followed by canceled* 'is'.

71.33   no] *written over an ampersand.*

71.35–36   bring . . . call.] *interlined above canceled* 'command the resources of heaven at will.'

71.37   and then,] *follows canceled* 'and then'.

72.23   turned] *followed by canceled unrecovered words; pos-*
[63.19]   *sibly* 'to and w'.

72.31   utterly.] *followed by canceled paragraph* 'The fame of
[63.27]   these things'.

72.33   answered,] *the comma mended from a period.*
[deleted]

73.3   was] *follows canceled* 'had'.
[63.30]

73.19   very] *interlined with a caret.*
[64.23]

73.23   wear muslin or] *interlined with a caret above canceled*
[64.27]   'carry a fan or clothe himself in'.

73.23   man] *follows canceled* 'most sad'.
[64.27]

73.25   found himself] 'found' *follows canceled* 'presently' *and
[64.28–29]   is followed by canceled* 'himself unable to predict'.

73.26–27   lost his reason] *interlined with a caret above canceled*
[64.30]   'went mad'.

73.28   Eventually] *followed by a canceled comma.*
[64.31]

73.32   they said,] *interlined with a caret.*
[64.35]

74.4   professional] *interlined with a caret.*
[65.8]

74.6–7   in behalf of] *follows canceled* 'for'.
[65.11]

74.11–12   His . . . altered.] *interlined with a caret.*
[65.15–16]

74.12   dying son] *follows canceled* 'son'.
[65.16]

74.14 [65.17]	strangely] *follows canceled* 'q'.
74.17–18 [65.27]	Encouragement of Missions.] *interlined above canceled* 'Propagation of Moral Purity.'
74.21–29 [65.31–66.3]	and legal . . . narrative.] *added on the verso of the MS* *page with instructions to turn over; replaces canceled* 'and would not give it up.' *on the recto.* [*For "Second* *Advent" see further revision in special collation.*]
74.21 [65.31]	legal] *follows canceled* 'their'.
74.22 [65.32]	they would] *follows canceled* 'the Society could'.
74.28 [66.2]	was any] 'any' *mended from* 'a'; 'was any' *follows can-* *celed* 'was a'.
74.30 [66.4]	the man] *originally* 'he'; *the* 't' *added and* 'man' *inter-* *lined with a caret.*
74.32 [66.6–7]	appealed;] *the semicolon mended from a comma.*
74.33 [66.8]	a suit] *follows canceled* 'a suit and thus disturb the'.
74.36 [66.10]	transgressor.] 'transgressor' *followed by a canceled com-* *ma, a canceled unrecovered letter, and canceled* 'Having gained this victory, the Society now became'. *The re-* *quired period was not added.*
75.1 [66.11]	the presiding . . . Society] 'the presiding officer' *inter-* *lined with a caret above canceled* 'such members'; 'So- ciety' *followed by canceled* 'as he could find,'.
75.9 [66.19]	likely] *interlined with a caret above canceled* 'going', *which follows canceled* 'likely'.
75.13 [66.23]	just] *interlined with a caret.*
75.14 [66.24]	enemies—] *the dash written over a period.*

75.14　　　　　natural] *follows canceled* 'perfectly'.
[66.25]

75.16　　　　　regained] *follows canceled* 'to'.
[66.26–27]

75.20　　　　　but] *written over* 'twe'.
[66.30]

76.18–19　　　attendance.] *the period mended from a comma; fol-*
[67.30–31]　　*lowed by a canceled ampersand.*

76.23　　　　　That the] *follows canceled* 'It is dangerous for any man
[67.35]　　　　or body of men'.

76.23　　　　　promise] *follows canceled* 'words'.
[67.35]

76.24　　　　　accepted] *follows canceled* 'regar'.
[67.36]

76.24　　　　　it shall] *follows canceled* 'whosoever'.
[67.36]

76.25　　　　　actually follow] *follows canceled* 'ask'.
[68.1]

76.28　　　　　were] *follows canceled* 'have'.
[68.4]

76.32　　　　　ordinary prayers] *follows canceled* 'prayers'.
[68.8]

77.3　　　　　　is able] *follows canceled* 'does not need' *which follows
[68.15]　　　　canceled* 'is'.

77.5　　　　　　venture to] *interlined with a caret.*
[68.17]

77.16　　　　　troublesome band] *follows canceled* 'band'.
[68.28]

77.16　　　　　tramps.] *the period follows a canceled comma.*
[68.28]

The International Lightning Trust

Textual Commentary

This work, recalled by Paine from Harper & Brothers after Mark Twain's death, survives in three copies: the manuscript, the typescript submitted to the publisher, and a carbon of the publisher's typescript. Mark Twain transferred the revisions on the ribbon copy to the carbon, apparently to preserve a record of the form in which it went to the publisher. Only the long cuts on the original typescript are not entered on the carbon (perhaps because he made them at the urging of F. A. Duneka, his editor at Harper & Brothers). Because it is otherwise identical to the ribbon copy, the carbon has been disregarded in establishing the text.

There are numerous ink revisions on the typescript; all are clearly Mark Twain's. Two penciled notations are ambiguous: question marks appear in the margin of three typescript pages (following 90.6), next to a passage which was eventually cut; and "religious" was substituted for "Catholics" at 94.13. The deletion of "Catholics" is in accord with Duneka's extreme sensitivity to even the hint of criticism of his church. (In his Autobiographical Dictation of 17 July 1906, Mark Twain complained that Duneka's piety had led him to tamper in a similar way with the "Chronicle of Young Satan" version of "The Mysterious Stranger.") Since it is likely that this change was Duneka's, and since Mark Twain used pencil nowhere else, the presumption must be that the question marks, too, are Duneka's. There is no subject for censorship in the deleted passage, however, and the query was almost certainly motivated by aesthetic considerations. "Catholics" has therefore been restored to the text, while, because Mark Twain responded to the queries by canceling the questioned passage in ink, the cut has been accepted.

The typescript is the authority for italics in the text. The typist did not reproduce the underscoring of the manuscript, and Mark Twain marked the typescript anew throughout.

Textual Notes

87.5   "It's a bill-sticker's establishment] In the upper left corner of the manuscript page beginning with these

words, Mark Twain wrote and canceled the cue word
"tariff." (See revisions, 90.6.)

88.27   prosperity!] Originally, the entrance of the landlady
              (90.7 in the present text) followed immediately. Mark
              Twain canceled the paragraph in which she enters and
              inserted eight newly-written manuscript pages expand-
              ing the discussion of the lightning trust scheme. (In the
              typescript he canceled a substantial portion of the added
              material.) The landlady's entrance is squeezed in at
              the foot of the last added manuscript page and is fol-
              lowed by the original pages restored and renumbered
              (90.9–92.8).

91.24   heaven. As] Someone changed this reading in pencil on
              the typescript to read "heaven, as." Since, on this type-
              script, Mark Twain traced his pencil revisions over in
              ink, the probability is that this change was Paine's or
              Duneka's. The original reading is therefore retained.
              (See note at 94.13.)

94.13   Catholics] Someone canceled this word on the type-
              script and wrote above it in blurred pencil "religious."
              Because of the blurring, the handwriting provides little
              clue to the authorship of the change. Since the penciled
              queries and alterations on the typescript seem not to be
              Clemens' work (see the textual commentary and note
              at 91.24), and since such revisions are more charac-
              teristic of F. A. Duneka than of Clemens, the original
              reading is preferred here.

99.8–26   Yes . . . name.] It was almost certainly from this passage
              that Mark Twain discarded the one known manuscript
              page from an earlier draft of "Lightning Trust." The
              page was enclosed in Clemens' copy of J. G. Frazer's
              *Passages of the Bible chosen for their Literary Beauty
              and Interest* and sold with the book after Clemens'
              death. As printed in "The Library and Manuscripts of
              Samuel L. Clemens" (Anderson Auction Company
              catalog no. 892—1911, p. 10), the page reads:

"Every vast commercial enterprise ought to have something theological about it somewhere—yes, sir, and right out in front. This is a Christian country and such a thing appeals to the sympathies and affections of the people, and they love to advertise it, they love to make it succeed. Our people are good and kind and earnest, and you can taffy them to tears if you know how to go about it. You'll see what that motto on our Great Seal will do for us."

"But, Jasper, didn't the government remove it from the coins?"

"For a while, yes, but it raised a storm and they had to put it back."

"I can't see why they ever took it off, Jasper. It was beautiful: 'In God We Trust.' What did they take it off for?"

A likely conjecture is that the page was replaced by the present manuscript page 60, which corresponds to 99.8–19 ("a splendid"), although it may of course have fitted elsewhere or be the remnant of a more complex revision.

100.15   suits] See note at 100.29.

100.29   suite] Although this spelling is not consistent with "suits" (100.15), neither is wrong. Under the definition of "suit," the 1857 and earlier editions of Webster's Dictionary comment, "This is sometimes pronounced as a French word, *sweet*; but in all its senses, this is the same word, and the affectation of making it French in one use and English in another, is improper, not to say ridiculous." For lack of evidence as to whether the inconsistency is intentional both spellings are preserved.

101.3   princes all the way down to] The manuscript reads, "princes down to." The typist omitted "down," and Mark Twain added the present reading on the typescript.

104.2   hosannahing] In the upper left corner of the manuscript page beginning with this word, Mark Twain wrote and canceled the cue word "Oskosh." (See revisions, 103.22.)

Emendations of the Copy-Text

	MTP READING	COPY-TEXT READING
80.title	Lightning Trust	Lightning-Trust
80.10	superannuated TS	superanuated
81.6	weeks' TS	weeks
83.27	dear-heart	dear heart
84.21	scheme? TS	scheme.
86.8	B	B,
†86.19	to TS	To
87.19	else? TS	else.
87.29	surely? TS	surely.
88.5	advantage? TS	advantage!
†88.34	so	So
89.13	others. TS	others?
†90.17	she	She
†90.29	each TS	Each
91.10–11	boarding house	boarding-house
91.19	mechanic's TS	mechanc's
96.1	thunder-storm	thunderstorm
98.12	Associated Press	associated press
99.2	Trust.' " TS	Trust.'
99.4	it? TS	it!
*101.3	all the way down TS	down
†101.35	increase TS	Increase
102.18	one." TS	one.
103.16	prophesying TS	prophecying

	MTP Reading	Copy-Text Reading
103.21	recognized	recognised
†104.7	wandering TS	wandering.
†104.11	twenty TS	twenty,

Word Division in the Copy-Text

88.18–19	lightning-rods
88.20	thunder-storms
93.11	fortnight
96.1	northward
97.14	greenbacks
101.31	understudies

Mark Twain's Revisions

Written in black ink through 102.18

80.title The . . . Story] *added to the MS in faded black ink; the original subtitle* 'A Love Story'; 'A Kind of a' *interlined with a caret in the TS preceding canceled* 'A'.

80.4 a . . . table;] *interlined with a caret.*

80.4 ditto] *interlined with a caret above canceled* 'pine'.

80.7 a scant outfit of] *interlined with a caret.*

81.7 impending to] *interlined with a caret above canceled* 'to'.

81.7 due] *interlined with a caret.*

81.8–10 I'm . . . work—] *added on the verso of the MS page with instructions to turn over replacing* 'Look at that shoe; do you see that toe sticking out? It's looking for work;' *canceled on the recto.*

81.10 Hunting] *interlined with a caret above canceled* 'Looking'.

81.11   'case'! . . .] *the exclamation point mended from a pe-*
             riod and the ellipsis added.

81.13   salaam aleikoom] *italic in MS.*

81.16   alone.] *followed by the passage below, canceled in the*
             TS after being revised in both MS and TS. The passage
             is reproduced from the TS with typing errors silently
             corrected. The superior numbers refer to Mark Twain's
             revisions which are listed following the passage.

'Like the wounded hart when forsaken by its fellows,
I can bleed my poor ruined life out in the solitude of the
forest, making no moan. . . . . Ah me, ah me, that *she*
should turn against me, that *she* should look cold upon
me! that[1] *she* should reproach me with my poverty!
She[2] whom I have so loved; she at whose feet I would
lay the ransom of a king if I possessed it. She said it
grieved her to sever the tender bond that bound us,
but she could not, *could not*[3] risk her fair young life
in the hands of a comp.[4] who couldn't even get subbing
to do. I begged her, I implored her, to give her poor
Steve a little longer time, but she repelled me, repelled
me[5] coldly, haughtily, and said please not call myself
her poor Steve any more. O, but[6] *that* cut! it cut deep,
it cut to the sacred deeps of my too-sensitive soul.
Think! it is *I* that am deserted for a plumber! O shame,
where is thy blush, O mortification, where is thy . . . .
why don't you say something!"
        'Jasper still sat wrapt and silent.[7]
    ' "Doesn't even hear me. Ah, I wish I could go off
dreaming, like that, and forget my sorrows in fulsome
fancies of a diseased mind. But'.

1. that] *originally* 'That'; *the* 't' *written over* 'T'.
2. She] *the* 'S' *mended from* 's'.
3. *not*] *roman in MS.*
4. comp.] *the period added to the TS.*
5. me] *followed by a canceled comma.*
6. but] *interlined with a caret in the TS.*
7. Jasper . . . silent.] *added following canceled* 'Silence.'

81.16   We] *the 'W' changed from 'w' in the TS.*

81.18   not . . . lion,] *interlined with a caret.*

81.19   breakfast] *interlined with a caret in faded black ink.*

81.19   cat's liver.] *interlined with a caret above canceled* 'spleen.'

81.26   *won't] roman in MS.*

81.28   by the] *originally* 'by that'; *the final 't' canceled and 'a' mended to 'e'.*

81.30   *you] roman in MS.*

81.31   phantasies] *follows canceled* 'fancies'.

81.37   what] *italic in MS.*

82.2   *can't] roman in MS.*

82.3   do] *italic in MS.*

82.9   away!"] *the exclamation point mended from a period in the TS.*

82.12–13   we've . . . have] *interlined with a caret above canceled* 'I've got'; 'got' *italic in MS.*

82.13   No—millions] 'No—millions' *in MS.*

82.13   submerged] *italic in MS.*

82.14–16   Buy . . . like!] *written on the verso of the MS page with instructions to turn over.*

82.21   per cent! tell] *the exclamation point mended from a semicolon in the TS;* 'tell' *italic in MS.*

82.29   We . . . Trust] *interlined with a caret above canceled* 'We the undersigned'.

82.30   feel has great] *follows canceled* 'feel will turn'.

83.1   No special] *follows canceled* 'Because of the comparative rarity of this form of death,'; *the 'N' mended from* 'n'.

83.2   furnished] *follows canceled* 'pr'.

83.4   to insurers] *interlined with a caret.*

83.4   exceedingly] *originally* 'exceeding'; 'ly' *interlined with
              a caret in the TS.*

83.8 $5 . . . $35,000.] *the* '5' *written over* '2'; '35' *written
              over* '10'.

83.10   covers] *the* 'c' *written over wiped-out* 'in'.

83.11   entire life] *italic in MS.*

83.13   special-stamp] *interlined with a caret above canceled*
              'registered'.

83.14   numbered ticket] *italic in MS; followed by a canceled
              period.*

83.15   in case . . . destruction] *interlined with a caret.*

83.18   Address] *italic in MS.*

83.18   International Lightning Trust,] *interlined with a caret
              preceding canceled* 'HACKETT & SPAULDING, Ltd.'

83.19   Court] *interlined with a caret above canceled* 'Square'.

83.20   jaunty] *the* 'y' *written over what appears to be wiped-
              out* 'ie'.

83.21   tossed a bulky] *interlined with carets above canceled*
              'handed out a'.

83.21   on the table,] *interlined with a caret above a canceled
              comma; originally* 'onto the table'; 'to' *canceled.*

83.24   hundred?"] *italics added then wiped out in the TS.*

83.26   astonishing!] *the exclamation point mended from a
              period in the TS.*

83.27   you invented] 'you' *italic in MS.*

83.32   I'd better] ' 'd better' *interlined with a caret above
              canceled* 'would do well and'.

83.35   he certainly is.] *interlined with a caret above canceled* 'you hear me.'

83.36   His . . . face.] *interlined with a caret.*

84.5   borrow] *italic in MS.*

84.13–14   one . . . five] *interlined with a caret above canceled* 'five or six'.

84.14   limit.] *interlined with a caret following canceled* 'ante.'

84.15   ten] *interlined with a caret above canceled* 'five'.

84.17   much,] *interlined with a caret above canceled* 'five,'.

84.19   Shake!] *originally* 'Shake hands!'; 'hands!' *canceled; the exclamation point added following* 'Shake'.

84.23   "My . . . daisy!"] *interlined with a caret above canceled* ' "Gr-eat Scott!" '.

84.25   what] *italic in MS.*

84.27   wild] *italic in MS.*

84.30   little . . .] *the ellipsis added.*

84.33   in] *roman in MS.*

84.34   trade] *italic in MS.*

85.10   business?"] *followed by canceled* 'Tell me'; *the quotation marks added.*

85.11   don't] *roman in MS.*

85.25   emperors] *followed by a canceled word, possibly* '—but'.

85.29–30   thirty-five thousand for five!] *interlined with a caret in the TS.*

85.32   Business?] *roman in MS.*

85.33   so,] *interlined with a caret above canceled* 'it,'.

86.4   a false address?] *originally* 'addresses and fictitious names?'; 'a' *interlined with a caret;* 'es and fictitious names?' *canceled; the question mark added.*

86.5   we want] 'we' *italic in MS.*

86.10   *see] roman in MS.*

86.12   Monday] *interlined above canceled* 'to-morrow'.

86.17   INTERNATIONAL . . . TRUST] *interlined above
              canceled* 'HACKETT & SPAULDING, Ltd'.

86.19   Series A] *interlined with a caret; the* 'T' *of MS* 'To'
              not reduced to 't'.

86.20   the . . . No. 21021.] *written on the verso of the MS
              page with instructions to turn over following squeezed-
              in* 'Begin'.

86.21   35,000,] *written over* '10,000'.

86.23   "Series C] *the quotation marks added in the TS.*

86.25   the numbers] *interlined with a caret.*

86.26   new] *originally* 'new'; *the italics canceled.*

86.28   better] 'be' *written over three wiped-out unrecovered
              letters.*

87.1   *There] roman in MS.*

87.1   done.] *followed by canceled quotation marks and can-
              celed paragraph* ' "Jasper, where is 102 Fordham
              Court?" '.

87.1–4   Another . . . Court?"] *squeezed in at the foot of the
              MS page.*

87.2   only] *italic in MS.*

87.5   bill-sticker's] ' 's establishment' *interlined with a caret
              in faded black ink above canceled* 'shed'.

87.7   good lot] *follows canceled* 'consi'.

87.8   here] *italic in MS.*

87.9   first.] *followed by canceled quotation marks.*

87.11   *proof] roman in MS.*

87.12	*There—now]* 'There—*now*' in the MS.
87.12	says] *followed by* 'that' *canceled in the TS.*
87.13	owner or bearer] *follows canceled* 'bearer' *and canceled* 'owner of the'.
87.15	hold] *italic in MS.*
87.19	*prove]* roman in MS.
87.22	says Owner] *follows canceled* 'says Bearer'.
87.22	or Bearer] 'or' *italic in MS.*
87.22	or somebody] 'or' *italic in MS.*
87.23	*anybody]* 'anybody' *in the MS.*
87.23	any] *italic in MS.*
87.23	lightning-victim] *interlined with a caret above canceled* 'corpse' *in the TS.*
87.24	money.] *followed by canceled quotation marks.*
87.25	did.] *the period replaces a question mark canceled in faded black ink.*
87.32	That] *italic in MS.*
87.32	foolishness?"] *the question mark mended from an exclamation point.*
87.33	deep;] *originally* 'deep." '; *the quotation marks canceled; the period mended to a semicolon.*
87.37	whole] *interlined with a caret above canceled* 'entire'.
88.2	person] *follows canceled* 'man'.
88.4	person's] *interlined with a caret above canceled* 'corpse's' *in the TS.*
88.5	"Gracious!] *interlined with a caret in faded black ink above canceled* ' "My land,'.
88.8	cadaver.] *interlined with a caret above canceled* 'corpse.'
88.10	why] *interlined with a caret above canceled* 'what'.

88.12   smashing] *interlined with a caret above canceled* 'splen-
               did'.

88.18   question.] *followed by canceled* 'You'll find'.

88.20   under high trees] *interlined with a caret.*

88.21–22   and in . . . thousand] *interlined above canceled* 'and in
               forty nine cases out of fifty,'.

88.24   *ever*] *the italics canceled in the MS and restored in the
               TS.*

88.25   not one person] *italic in MS.*

88.27   prosperity!] *followed by canceled* '. . . . *Come in!*" ¶ It
               was the landlady, Mrs. Maloney. Her face was dark and
               threatening. She stood a moment, accumulating gloom,
               then she began, austerely—'. *See textual notes.*

88.32   surface-transportation] 'surface-' *interlined with a caret.*

88.33   U. S.] *interlined with a caret.*

88.34   80,000] *the* '8' *written over* '6'.

88.34   wounded; so] *the semicolon mended from a period; the*
               'S' *of MS* 'So' *not reduced to* 's'.

89.6   "Oh . . . was] *interlined with a caret above canceled*
               ' "Now that is splendid! I was'.

89.6   discouraged,] *followed by canceled* 'Jasper,'.

89.8   "Twenty-eight.] *followed by canceled quotation marks.*

89.18   dollars] *interlined with a caret.*

89.22   like you.] *followed by canceled* 'Particularly the clergy.'

89.23   circular.] *followed by canceled* ', they're our meat.'; *the
               period added.*

89.23–25   Send circulars . . . universities.] *added on the verso of
               the MS page with instructions to turn over.*

89.28   and mechanics, and laborers,] *interlined with a caret
               in the TS.*

89.30   all] *italic in MS.*

89.33   them . . .] *the ellipsis added.*

89.36   idea] *follows canceled* 'grand'.

90.3   Distinctly a] *interlined with a caret above canceled* 'Mighty'.

90.4   the pews.] *followed by canceled* 'They'll like that, and they'll'.

90.5   Sabbath-breakers. . . .] *the ellipsis added.*

90.6   *Come in!"] follows* 'Steve!" ' *canceled in the TS and precedes the following passage which was revised in both MS and TS then canceled in the TS. The passage is reproduced from the TS with typing errors silently corrected. The superior numbers refer to Mark Twain's revisions which are listed following the passage.*

    ' "I'm listening."[1]
    ' "I've got another!"[2]
    ' "Well, fetch it out."
    ' "Another red-hot advertisement.[3] Listen:[4] we'll get a bill[5] through Congress putting a tariff on imported lightning."
    ' "Ah,[6] but will they do that, Jasper?[7] Why would they do it?"
    ' "To protect our infant[8] domestic product."
    ' "Sho, there isn't any domestic lightning, it's all foreign; we don't raise any."
    ' "Certainly—I know that. But Congress has to look ahead and protect infant industries that are as yet in the womb or somewhere. Like quinine, you know; and elephants, and radium, and angels, and—"
    ' "Angels? You don't mean that, Jasper. They wouldn't make an angel pay duty, it would be a scandal, and would make no end of talk. No, the[9] angel would get in free, I know it."
    ' "Let him try it, that's all. He would have to put up. Even Black-Handers have to do that, although they

have a vote in two weeks. And in four weeks they get a pension."

' "Pension for what?"

' "Fighting in the Revolution."[10]

' "But he didn't, Jasper."

' "Well then, they get it for the vote. It's what a pension is for. Now then, we'll get a tariff put on foreign lightning, then we'll privately get that tariff attacked in the newspapers; get them to[11] say it's done in the interest of a bloated trust that is insuring against[12] death by lightning, and finding millions of people foolish enough to chance a dollar bill on a death-risk because the Trust pays five thousand where an investor gets hit and draws a prize. It'll be a wonderful advertisement, Steve, if we can beguile the newspapers into doing that. My, the rages it will raise, and the talk it will make! Then we can reply back, and feel hurt, and unjustly and unfairly treated, and all that, and tell how but for the Trust the bereaved families of the twenty-eight thousand who died[13] by lightning[14] last year would now be suffering the pangs of penury instead of wallowing in sums ranging from five thousand dollars to a hundred thousand for each vacancy achieved in the hallowed home circle, and—"

' "Twenty-eight *thousand?* You said it was only twenty-eight[15] a while ago."

' "Yes, I know, but that is for private consumption; you've got to raise it to something impressive when you want to get the public to take notice."

' "But that is *such* a raise!"

' "Yes, it'll do for the present; we can give it another lift by and by if we need to . . . . . *Come in!*" '

1. listening."] *follows canceled* 'a'.
2. another!"] *interlined with a caret above canceled* 'a perfectly stunning idea!" '.
3. "Another red-hot advertisement] 'Another . . . adver-' *interlined with a caret above canceled* ' "It'll be such a grand adver-'.

4. Listen:] *interlined with a caret.*

5. a bill] *follows canceled 'the'.*

6. Ah,] *interlined with a caret.*

7. Jasper?] *followed by canceled quotation marks.*

8. infant] *interlined with a caret.*

9. the] *originally 'they'; the 'y' canceled.*

10. "Fighting . . . Revolution."] *interlined in the TS, replacing the MS reading* ' "Because their father served in the war." ' *omitted by the typist.*

11. get them to] *interlined with a caret above a canceled ampersand; the semicolon preceding added.*

12. against] *interlined with a caret above canceled* '280,000 persons per year against'.

13. died] *followed by 'in the Lord' canceled in faded black ink.*

14. lightning] *followed by canceled 'and went down'.*

15. twenty-eight] *interlined with a caret above canceled* '28'; *italic in MS.*

90.7–8   It was . . . austerely—] *squeezed in at the foot of the MS page. See textual note at 88.27.*

90.7   silent] *interlined with a caret in the TS.*

90.10   Ones and Twos] *'and' interlined with a caret above a canceled comma.*

90.17   But] *interlined with a caret in the TS; the 'S' of TS 'She' not reduced to 's'.*

90.18   when . . . money.] *interlined with a caret in faded black ink following a comma mended from a period.*

90.19   ring] *originally 'ring'; the italics canceled.*

90.24   otherwise . . . shout.] *interlined with a caret following a semicolon mended from a period.*

90.29   Privately,] *interlined with a caret; the 'E' of MS 'Each' not reduced to 'e'.*

91.2   pair of delinquents] *interlined with a caret in faded black ink; the preceding 'the' originally 'them'; the 'm' canceled.*

91.6   table] *written over wiped-out* 'lun' *or* 'ban'.

91.32   Steve!] *the exclamation point added following a canceled comma.*

92.2   silence. They] 'They' *written over wiped-out* 'th'; *the period mended from a comma.*

92.3   there] *written over wiped-out* 'they'.

92.5   The girls] *originally* 'They'; 'girls' *interlined with a caret; the* 'y' *canceled.*

92.5   nor yet] *interlined with a caret above canceled* 'neither the girls nor'.

92.12   back one.] *followed by canceled* 'A back one,'.

92.28   Nebraska.] *interlined with a caret in faded black ink above canceled* 'Montana.'

92.30   I thought] *follows canceled* 'If'.

92.30   Nebraska] *interlined with a caret in faded black ink above canceled* 'Montana'.

93.10   candidate] *interlined with a caret above canceled* 'couple'.

93.11   a couple,] *interlined with a caret above canceled* 'three,'.

93.23   they] *italic in MS.*

93.28–29   difficult for] *interlined with a caret in faded black ink above canceled* 'hard for'.

94.11   for us."] *written over a period and quotation marks.*

94.12   were a] *followed by* 'sad and' *canceled in faded black ink.*

94.14   divorce—] *the dash added above a canceled comma.*

94.14   desertion] *follows canceled* 'divorce'.

94.20   Kitty] *interlined with a caret in faded black ink above canceled* 'Molly'.

94.20–21   Molly in] *interlined with a caret in faded black ink above canceled* 'Kitty in'.

94.26   of moving down] 'down' *interlined with a caret above canceled* 'below' *in the TS; in the MS originally* 'to move on', *then* 'of moving on', *then* 'of moving below'; 'of' *interlined with a caret above canceled* 'to' *and* 'ing' *written over* 'e' *of* 'move'; 'below' *interlined with a caret in faded black ink above canceled* 'on'.

94.36   watches] *follows canceled* 'will'.

95.3   still,] *interlined with a caret following canceled* 'by'.

95.12   prosperity] *follows* 'the' *interlined with a caret in the TS then canceled.*

95.16–17   salvation, and he] *interlined with a caret above canceled* 'soul, and he'.

95.27   experts] *interlined with a caret in faded black ink above canceled* 'men'.

95.30   professionals] *interlined with a caret in faded black ink following canceled* 'experts'.

95.32   position.] *added in faded black ink following canceled* 'place.'

96.1   Next . . . city.] *interlined above canceled* 'The storm did its work, sure enough.'

96.2   evening] *follows canceled* 'latest'.

96.5   killed,] *interlined with a caret above canceled* 'slain,'.

96.10   wrings] *the* 'w' *interlined with a caret.*

96.10   hope] *follows canceled* 'hope somebody will'.

96.16   do] *roman in MS.*

96.18   I] *italic in MS.*

96.22   I'll] *follows canceled* 'it'll'.

96.30   with . . . feeling:] *added in faded black ink; the preceding comma replaces a colon.*

97.1	unfortunate] *follows canceled* 'unhapp'.
97.7	next] *interlined with a caret following canceled* 'same'.
97.18	never] *roman in MS.*
97.18	know] *italic in MS.*
97.20	It] *written over wiped-out* 'He'.
97.24–25	in his . . . struck.] *interlined with a caret above a canceled period.*
97.26	do] *roman in MS.*
97.27	at once] *interlined with a caret.*
97.31	I just knew it!] *interlined with a caret; the comma preceding mended from a period.*
97.32	a penny] *follows canceled* 'got'.
97.36	you—] *the dash written over a wiped-out ampersand.*
98.1	Active] *follows wiped-out quotation marks.*
98.4	unnecessary] 'ry' *written over wiped-out* 'rily'.
98.5	time,] *followed by a canceled dash.*
98.6	have] *italic in MS.*
98.6	careful] *follows canceled* 'very'.
98.7	deliberately] 'erately' *follows canceled* 'erately, after making some marks'.
98.9	one at a time,] *interlined with a caret.*
98.10	until a] 'a' *interlined with a caret above canceled* 'two' *in the TS.*
98.10	lay] *follows canceled* 'had'.
98.13	clerks;] *followed by canceled* 'It advertised for fifteen, and got thirty-five hundred applications.'; *the semicolon mended from a period.*
98.15	possession of] *interlined with a caret in faded black ink.*

98.15   on lease,] *interlined with a caret in faded black ink.*

98.16   the three] *follows* 'they took' *canceled in faded black ink.*

99.1   head,] *interlined with a caret preceding canceled* 'ear,'.

99.1   kneeling] *interlined with a caret.*

99.10   that one word] *italics added in the MS in faded black ink; roman in TS.*

99.13   ever] *interlined with a caret in faded black ink.*

99.13   had] *roman in MS.*

99.16   ancient, honored,] *interlined with a caret above canceled* 'old,' *in the TS.*

99.17   and look . . . result:] *interlined with a caret.*

99.22   Look at] *followed by canceled* 'Spiritualism; look at' *in the TS.*

99.23   exactly the] *interlined with a caret in faded black ink following canceled* 'the'.

99.24–25   and using . . . force—] *interlined with a caret in faded black ink following a canceled dash.*

99.30   or so] 'or' *added and* 'so' *interlined with a caret following a canceled comma.*

99.32   and pull . . . to do."] *added in faded black ink following a comma mended from a period and canceled quotation marks.*

99.33   with] *followed by a comma canceled in faded black ink.*

99.33–34   financed . . . 63?"] *originally* 'financeered us—the 63?" '; 'financeered' *mended to* 'financed' *and* 'us' *canceled then restored in faded black ink;* 'us . . . 63?" ' *interlined in faded black ink above canceled* 'us—the 63?" '.

100.9   vast new] *interlined with a caret in the TS.*

100.10   subways and all.] *interlined with a caret in the TS; the*
                preceding comma mended from a period.

100.12   letters,] *followed by canceled 'Asia'.*

100.17   others] *follows canceled 'and'.*

100.18   "Tariff Chamber,"] *interlined with a caret in faded*
                black ink.

100.19–20   with . . . added.] *added in faded black ink following*
                a comma mended from a period.

100.25–28   anything . . . nobility.] *added in three stages, each in*
                faded black ink, to replace the following passage:

                'Congress, they bought the Government, they bought
                legislatures, they bought the two great parties, the[y]
                bought municipal bosses here and there and yonder,
                all over the land, and they were deep in a plan to buy
                the army and navy and start a hereditary monarchy and
                nobility.' *First* 'Congress . . . land, and they' *canceled*
                and replaced by 'anything and everything that was for
                sale, except legislatures' *added on a new MS page; then*
                'anything . . . legislatures' *canceled and replaced by*
                'anything . . . whispered that they' *interlined with*
                carets; finally 'hereditary' *canceled;* 'whispered . . .
                nobility.' *canceled then recopied on the verso of the*
                MS page preceding.

100.29–101.4   In . . . there.] *added as part of a two-page insertion in*
                faded black ink on MS pages numbered 64A and 64B.
                The remainder of the insertion, reproduced below, was
                canceled in the TS. Only the MS was revised; the su-
                perior numbers refer to the revisions which are listed
                following the passage.

                'In the lady-parlors you could see our product, ranged
                around the walls, with their protecting mammas, wait-
                ing for custom, and sometimes looking pretty weary,
                poor girls. In the gentleman parlors the dukes and such
                were likewise ranged around the walls, awaiting inspec-
                tion, and often they looked weary, too. Now and then

a papa would enter, with the Count, and look the goods over, and dicker a little, and say he would think it over and come again. Now and then a nobleman would leave his base and visit the lady-parlors and inspect the crop and do a little dickering and say he would come again. An outsider might be deceived by these monotonies, and think there was nothing doing. A mistake: millions and millions changed hands there every day. Mainly the season's crop was sold to[1] minor nobilities, of course, but now and then, at happy intervals, a lucky papa got a duke for his money. And usually[2] a good husband for his daughter by the same trade; but not always. Sometimes an innocent papa who was satisfied with the price, went further and inquired about the gentleman's character. Count Alibi furnished him a prompt and frosty[3] answer:

' "Excuse me, sir, we trade in titles here, not the moralities. The entire value of our goods is in the title, the accessories are of no consequence. I offer you two dukes for choice: one is ripe, the other rotten; the price is the same, for the reason that in our market the rotten one is as saleable a property as the sound one." '

1. sold to] 'bought by' *interlined with a caret above canceled* 'sold to' *then canceled;* 'sold to' *restored in an interlineation.*

2. usually] *interlined with a caret above canceled* 'sometimes'.

3. and frosty] *interlined with a caret.*

100.31   capable] *follows canceled* 'experienced and'.

101.3   and Latin] *interlined with a caret.*

101.3   all the way down] *interlined with a caret in the TS. See textual notes.*

101.4   viscounts—] *interlined with a caret above canceled* 'baronets—'.

101.5   Molly had] *follows canceled paragraph* 'Molly and Kitty'.

101.8   cleared . . . and] *interlined with a caret in faded black ink.*

101.8   He did] *follows* 'There was no occasion for this, but' *interlined with a caret and canceled in faded black ink.*

101.14   Steve,] *interlined with a caret in faded black ink.*

101.16   in America; it] *interlined with a caret following canceled* '; it was'.

101.20   did that] *followed by a canceled comma.*

101.20   *say,* Jasper!] *originally* 'say!'; *the italics, comma and* 'Jasper!' *added in faded black ink over the original exclamation point.*

101.25   has] *written over wiped-out* 'so a'.

101.34   "Steve,] *interlined with a caret above canceled* ' "Jasper,' *in the TS.*

101.35   Due to] *interlined with a caret in faded black ink; the* 'I' *of MS* 'Increase' *not reduced to* 'i'.

101.36   you know."] *added in faded black ink following canceled quotation marks; the preceding comma mended from a period.*

102.3   winter, of course,] *italics added to* 'winter' *in faded black ink then canceled;* 'of course,' *interlined with a caret in faded black ink.*

102.4   that] *the italics added in faded black ink.*

102.5   keeps] *follows canceled* 'sets the newspapers to buzzing'.

102.7–8   to let . . . little,] *interlined with a caret in faded black ink above a canceled comma.*

102.10   poor] *interlined with a caret in faded black ink.*

102.14   down his back,] *interlined with a caret in faded black ink above canceled* 'on him,'.

102.15   including] *interlined with a caret in faded black ink above canceled* 'except'.

Written in faded black ink from 102.19 to the end

102.26   worshipped—] *the dash interlined with a caret.*

102.29   divine] *originally* 'divinel'; *the* 'l' *canceled.*

103.9   doubt] *follows canceled* 'lose heart'.

103.9   difficult and] 'and' *interlined with a caret above a canceled comma.*

103.11   no—] *interlined with a caret.*

103.12   faith,] *followed by canceled* 'in' *and canceled* 'and in a voice'; *the comma added.*

103.20   Far West.] *followed by* 'In the Far Far West—Idaho, in Montana.' *canceled in the TS; in the MS* 'in' *interlined with a caret before* 'Idaho' *then canceled.*

103.21   there,] *followed by canceled* 'and nothing'.

103.22   Arkansas Flats.] *interlined with a caret in the TS above canceled* 'Scranton.'; *in the MS* 'Oshkosh.' *interlined with a caret above canceled* 'Scranton.' *then canceled;* 'Scranton.' *again interlined with a caret.*

103.30   Sabbath.] *followed by* 'you understand.' *canceled in the TS; the period mended from a comma.*

104.2   happiness] *follows canceled* 'grati'.

104.4   And who] *follows canceled* 'The hand of Provid'.

104.4   It was . . . carpenter!] *roman in MS.*

104.6   I now recognized] *interlined with a caret above canceled* 'and'.

104.7   steps.] *added following a period inadvertently left standing.*

104.9   One] *interlined with a caret above canceled* 'Ten'.

104.11   tickets, Steve,] *interlined with a caret following a comma inadvertently left standing.*

104.19   us] *interlined with a caret in the TS.*

Colloquy Between a Slum Child and a Moral Mentor

Textual Commentary

The copy-text for this work is a typescript prepared by Dixon Wecter during his tenure as editor of the Mark Twain Papers. The manuscript, then in the possession of Samuel Charles Webster, is not currently available. That Wecter based his typescript on the manuscript is evident from the typescript's form—a diplomatic text which includes cancellations struck through and interlineations typed above the line. It is unlikely that Mark Twain ever had a typescript made.

The same principles of emendation have been applied to this text as to the other works in this volume, but in the absence of the manuscript it cannot be determined whether the oversights corrected were the author's or the typist's. Similarly, the list of Mark Twain's revisions may be defective and should be used with the caution reserved for a transcription that cannot be checked against its source.

No ambiguous compound is hyphenated at the end of a line.

Textual Notes

108.6	He] "He" is capitalized here and at 108.9 and 108.36 to conform to Mark Twain's usage elsewhere in the mentor's lines. The lower-case form is consistent in the child's lines and has been left unchanged.

Emendations of the Copy-Text

	MTP READING	COPY-TEXT READING
106.1	grass?"	grass?
*108.6	He	he *Also emended at* 108.9, 108.36
108.8	allowed.' "	allowed."
109.13	window-shutter	window shutter

Mark Twain's Revisions

106.10	God . . . grass] 'God' *followed by canceled* 'makes the grass and'; 'care of' *followed by canceled* 'it'.
106.14	tiny seeds.] *followed by canceled* 'You won't forget that'.
106.16	"Bet] *follows canceled* ' "You'.
106.19–20	shining's good . . . lush."] *interlined above canceled* 'I rope in shil'n from some of those flats. Oh, no, that cain't [*blank*] nor nothing, I don't reckon" '.
107.3	"No—but] ' "No—' *followed by canceled* 'they don't though,'; 'but' *interlined*.
107.5	ony] *interlined above canceled* ' 'cept'.
107.22	gov'ner] *follows canceled* 'gover'.
107.34	"Spare] *follows canceled* ' "More'; *originally* ' "Spares'; *the final 's' canceled*.
107.37	my element] 'my' *interlined above canceled* 'the'.
108.16	poverty!—yea,] *follows canceled* 'the'; *followed by canceled* 'even'.
108.27	That's bully] *follows canceled* 'Now'.
108.28	as he does] *followed by canceled* 'with'.
108.29–30	You ought . . . Him.] *interlined*.
108.31	"Gov'ner] *follows canceled* ' "Go slow,'.
108.32	above,] *interlined above canceled* 'God,'.
108.34–35	I had . . . 'em to me."] *interlined above canceled* 'he didn't notice that the bottom of 'em was out, maybe." '
109.1	cag] *interlined above canceled* 'bar'l'.
109.3	"Cellar] *follows canceled* ' "Shutter'.
109.6	how many] *follows canceled* 'of'.

Thoughts of God

Textual Commentary

The manuscript is copy-text; the author's unrevised typescript is also in the Mark Twain Papers. No ambiguous compound is hyphenated at the end of a line in the manuscript.

Textual Notes

113.28	and who humbly] In the upper right-hand corner of the manuscript page beginning here, Mark Twain wrote in pencil, and canceled in purplish-blue ink, the cue: "germ—microbe 18 colonies on a bank-bill."
114.6	animals] In the upper left-hand corner of the manuscript page beginning here, Mark Twain wrote in pencil, and canceled in purplish-blue ink, the cue: "snake, spider."
114.16	concreted] Mark Twain may have written the more usual "concrete"; the final "d" may actually be a long upstroke on the "e."
115.7–9	It . . . there.] The sentence is canceled in pencil in the typescript, apparently by Paine.

Emendations of the Copy-Text

	MTP READING	COPY-TEXT READING
†112.4	morals	Morals
112.13	long-felt	long felt
†112.21	let	Let

Mark Twain's Revisions

Written in faded black ink

112.title   Thoughts] *follows canceled* 'Some'.

112.3   instance.] *the period added preceding canceled* '; take the preacher.'

112.4   intelligence . . . concerned.] *originally* 'intelligence. Morals were not concerned.'; *the period following* 'intelligence' *mended to a comma;* 'were' *canceled;* 'being' *interlined with a caret; the* 'M' *of MS* 'Morals' *not reduced to* 'm'.

112.5   and] *interlined with a caret.*

112.6   have] *followed by canceled* 'been'.

112.12   but] *squeezed in at the end of the line.*

112.13   want] *mended from* 'was'.

112.14   contract] *follows canceled* 'job.'

112.19   Man] *the* 'M' *mended from* 'm'.

112.21   For . . . let] 'For . . . race' *interlined with a caret; the* 'L' *of MS* 'Let' *not reduced to* 'l'.

113.1   persons] *interlined with a caret above canceled* 'apologists'.

113.2   a scandal] *interlined above canceled* 'an excess'.

113.9–10   deliberation; . . . supply,] *following* 'deliberation' *the semicolon mended from a comma and* 'that' *interlined with a caret above a canceled ampersand;* 'was' *interlined with a caret; following* 'fore-ordered' *the comma added;* 'and that . . . supply,' *interlined with a caret above a canceled semicolon.*

113.11   was] *follows canceled* 'was'.

113.12   possible] *interlined with a caret.*

113.13   squalid] *substituted for* 'degraded' *interlined with a*
                caret and canceled above canceled 'nasty'; 'squalid'
                written and the cancellations made in purplish-blue ink.

113.14–15   Man . . . sort] 'Man' *written slightly below canceled*
                'man'; 'of a sort' *interlined with a caret; then in purplish-*
                blue ink 'Man' *canceled and added to the interlineation.*

113.20   lumbering] *originally interlined above uncanceled* 'un-
                desirable'; 'undesirable' *canceled and a caret added in*
                purplish-blue ink.

113.21–22   afflictions . . . discrimination.] *follows canceled* 'undis-
                criminated blessings and'; *followed by a canceled* 'or
                apology.'; *the period after* 'discrimination' *added.*

113.24–114.10   "Depart . . . fly."] *the quotation marks added later in*
                purplish-blue ink.

113.29   relief] *followed by a canceled comma.*

113.32   Fly,] *interlined with a caret in purplish-blue ink.*

113.33   praying] *interlined above canceled* 'asking' *in purplish-*
                blue ink.

113.34   forlorn and forsaken] 'forsaken' *canceled;* 'friendless'
                interlined with a caret then canceled; 'forsaken' *inter-*
                lined with a caret.

114.1   cunningly] *interlined with a caret.*

114.2–3   among . . . low, and] *interlined with a caret.*

114.7   here . . . hereafter;] 'here' *and* 'of it hereafter' *interlined*
                in pencil; then in ink 'here' *canceled then interlined*
                with a caret, a caret added canceling a semicolon fol-
                lowing 'hope', *and the semicolon after* 'hereafter' *added.*

114.9–10   Me . . . My glory Who] *the* 'M', 'M', *and* 'W' *mended*
                from 'm', 'm', *and* 'w' *in purplish-blue ink.*

114.11–13   His . . . His] 'H' *mended from* 'h' *(twice).*

114.14   Book and] 'and' *interlined with a caret.*

114.18   *due] the italics added in purplish-blue ink.*

114.19   without . . . risk] *interlined with a caret.*

114.22   work but confiscating] *originally* 'work and reserving'; *the* 'and' *canceled and* 'but confiscating' *interlined without a caret in pencil; then* 'reserving' *canceled and a caret added later in purplish-blue ink.*

114.24   dark] *interlined with a caret.*

114.33–34   *There . . . relieve.*] *the italics added in purplish-blue ink.*

114.34   *relieve.*] *interlined with a caret above canceled* 'heal.'

114.36   Source] *the* 'S' *mended from* 's'.

115.1   violate] *follows canceled* 'vi' *and canceled* 'logically'.

115.3   daily] *interlined with a caret.*

115.4   these] *followed by canceled* 'grotesque'.

115.6   trained] *interlined with a caret.*

115.9   superiority there.] *originally* 'superiority.'; 'there.' *added in pencil; later the period after* 'superiority' *canceled and* 'there.' *rewritten in purplish-blue ink.*

The Emperor-God Satire

Textual Commentary

The manuscript is copy-text. There are no textual notes, no emendations have been made, and no ambiguous compound is hyphenated at the end of a line in the manuscript.

Mark Twain's Revisions

118.3	a hundred] 'a' *interlined with a caret above canceled* 'two'.
118.6–7	(always . . . rank,)] *interlined with a caret.*
118.10	twelve] *interlined with a caret above canceled* 'six'.
118.11	varying] *interlined with a caret.*
118.11	eleven] *interlined with a caret above canceled* 'six'.
118.13	newest] *follows canceled* 'newest with any de'.
118.17–18	such comely] *follows canceled* 'a more'; 'comely' *interlined with a caret.*
118.22	called Unyumi,] *interlined with a caret.*
119.4	desires] *originally* 'desire'; *the* 's' *added.*
119.8	sore] *interlined with a caret above canceled* 'great'.
119.9–10	Prayers . . . petitions] *originally* 'Prayers, and peti'; 'and peti' *wiped out;* 'for spiritual help,' *interlined with a caret; then* 'spiritual' *canceled and* 'temporal and spiritual' *added.*
119.13	small per centage] *written over wiped-out* 'tolerable'.
119.15	Priests of] *follows canceled* 'A priest of'.
119.33	will] *follows canceled* 'wh'.

119.37   he] *interlined with a caret above canceled* 'but'.

120.3   baked,] *written over wiped-out* 'co'.

120.6   compacting] *follows canceled* 'sol'.

120.7   considered] *interlined with a caret.*

120.11   estate,] *originally* 'estate may be,'; 'may be,' *canceled; the comma after* 'estate' *added.*

120.16–17   importance, . . . famine;] *originally* 'importance;'; 'that . . . famine;' *interlined with a caret; the comma after* 'importance' *added and the original semicolon inadvertently left standing.*

120.19–30   momentary . . . disordered the] *on two inserted MS pages replacing canceled* 'momentary benefit of a single community. Yet at the same time an Unyumi chief whom he had sent to massacre some unsuspecting tribes over the border prayed to him for time and light to finish his work whereupon the Emperor caused the sun and moon to stand still in the sky during many hours, without moving. This so disordered the'. *Originally* 'border' *followed by a comma and* 'whose had'; 'had' *canceled; then* 'ancestors had been guilty of something in a former age,' *added; then the comma and* 'whose ancestors . . . age,' *canceled.*

120.19   community] *follows canceled* 'single'.

120.31–32   the turbulent . . . bounds and] *originally* 'they destroyed'; *the* 'y' *of* 'they' *canceled and* 'turbulent . . . bounds and' *interlined with a caret.*

120.33   yet these were] *interlined with a caret above canceled* 'these being'.

120.35   even] *interlined with a caret.*

120.37   theirs . . . Emperor.] *originally* 'their poor foolish wooden idols.'; 'poor foolish wooden idols.' *canceled in pencil and then the* 's' *of* 'theirs' *and* 'toward the Emperor.' *added in pencil.*

The Ten Commandments

Textual Commentary

The manuscript copy-text is headed "III"; the work may have been conceived as, or may once have been, a chapter of a longer piece. There are no textual notes, and no ambiguous compound is hyphenated at the end of a line in the manuscript.

Emendations of the Copy-Text

	MTP READING	COPY-TEXT READING
122.1	¶ The Ten	[*centered*] III ¶ The Ten
122.3	Thou	thou
123.11	inveigled	inviegled

Mark Twain's Revisions

122.2	animals.] *followed by canceled paragraph* 'Why should we think it strange?'.
123.3	deliberate] *followed by canceled* 'and'.
123.5	He did] *follows canceled* 'God gave'.
123.23	But] *follows canceled paragraph* 'But the *word* is the wrong'; '*word*' *canceled first with no substitution.*

The Private Secretary's Diary

Textual Commentary

The manuscript is copy-text.

Textual Notes

127.30   spoke] The manuscript may read "spake," but archaism seems out of place in a piece in which the "Cabinet" speaks the language of the board room rather than the Bible.

Emendations of the Copy-Text

	MTP READING	COPY-TEXT READING
126.title	Secretary's	Secy's
126.1	MONDAY.	*Monday.*
126.16	the Recording Angel	Recording Angel
127.13	His	his
127.20	Him	him
127.34	seized	siezed

Word Division in the Copy-Text

127.24	semi-deafness
128.2	re-performed

Mark Twain's Revisions

126.1	Cabinet] *follows canceled* 'Great'.
126.1	Present,] *followed by canceled* 'G., S.'
126.6–7	in . . . chamber,] *interlined with a caret.*
127.19	Lord] *the 'L' mended from* 'l'.
127.33	1890,] *the 'o' mended from* '7'.
127.37	afforded;] *followed by canceled* 'but the'.
128.10	Cabinet] *the 'C' mended from* 'c'.

In My Bitterness

Textual Commentary

The manuscript is copy-text. No ambiguous compound is hyphenated at the end of a line in the manuscript.

Textual Notes

131.2   years] Mark Twain left a blank space in the manuscript preceding "years," perhaps intending to return to it and fill in a number.

Emendations of the Copy-Text

	MTP Reading	Copy-Text Reading
131.10	He seems	he seems "he" *also emended at 131.12, 131.15, 131.18, and 132.1*
132.1	solace	solace/idol
132.2	His	his

Mark Twain's Revisions

131.1   I said] *an uncanceled caret written under 'I' with no interlineation.*

131.1   my darling] *interlined.*

131.3   lived;] *follows canceled* 'life'.

131.5   poor . . . set free] *follows canceled* 'set free'.

131.5   insult] *interlined above canceled* 'tyranny'.

131.9   He never] *the 'H' mended from* 'h'.

131.15   Him] *the 'H' mended from* 'h'.

The Victims

Textual Commentary

The manuscript is copy-text. No ambiguous compound is hyphenated at the end of a line in the manuscript. Because the work is little more than a rough set of notes, its texture has not been smoothed with emendations for consistency.

Textual Notes

137.2   his buttocks off] Canceled in pencil on the manuscript and "off his entire after deck" interlined above it. Although this change could have been by Mark Twain, the hand looks more like Albert Bigelow Paine's.

137.8   to the picnic] In the blank space above this phrase Paine scrawled four words in pencil. He may have written "near starvation from looks," or, thinking of the change he made at 137.2, he may have written "rear elevation" as an alternative to his earlier change, "after deck," and "forward works" as an alternative to "forequarters" more in keeping with his nautical imagery. The inscription is so nearly indecipherable that it admits either conjecture.

140.12–13   civilization . . . Went for More] The corner of the manuscript has been torn off; "civilization" and "Went for" are conjectures, first suggested on a DeVoto typescript.

Emendations of the Copy-Text

	MTP READING	COPY-TEXT READING
135.15	tenderly	lovingly/tenderly
*140.12–13	civilization . . . Went for	[*page torn*]

Mark Twain's Revisions

135.3   went] *follows canceled* 'then he'.

135.3   saying *Please*,] 'saying' *interlined with a caret.*

135.5   sundown, and] *followed by canceled* 'th'.

135.12   by her] *follows canceled* 'by she'.

135.14   giving] *interlined with a caret above canceled* 'and gave'.

136.4   his face] *follows canceled* 'a'.

137.3   Fanny] *follows canceled* 'Jimmy'.

137.7   Phoebe] *interlined above canceled* 'Jimmy'.

139.3   to] *interlined with a caret.*

139.9   west] *originally* 'western'; 'ern' *canceled.*

139.13   So little] 'So' *written over* 'L'.

139.16   rap] *interlined above canceled* 'punch'.

139.16   not] *interlined with a caret.*

140.5   —for—] *interlined with a caret above a canceled dash.*

140.9   captive] *interlined with a caret.*

140.12   "By] *follows canceled* ' "This'.

140.14   The sun] *follows canceled paragraph* 'At sundown mamma Molecule'.

140.16   deserted] *mended from* 'deter'.

The Synod of Praise

Textual Commentary

The manuscript is copy-text. Since the piece is essentially a set of working notes, neither Mark Twain's inconsistencies nor his occasionally telegraphic phrasing (like "It is word" at 143.6) have been emended. No ambiguous compound is hyphenated at the end of a line in the manuscript.

Textual Notes

143.10   Their] The manuscript reads "There." The sentence as it appears in the manuscript is grammatically correct, but Mark Twain can hardly have meant to say that in heaven brutes are punished for their sins on earth. With the substitution of the possessive pronoun the sentence expresses Mark Twain's frequently-reiterated complaint that animals are unfairly made to suffer on earth without men's hope of surcease in heaven. A slip of the pen seems to have distracted the author: he apparently wrote "Th" followed by a malformed letter, then wrote an "r" over the miswriting, and finally added "ere" over the "r." These handwriting difficulties may have contributed to the confusion in the manuscript.

Emendations of the Copy-Text

	MTP READING	COPY-TEXT READING
142.title	Synod	(Concert?)/Synod
142.6	GOD	God
142.6	Knocks	(Knocks
142.12	(sensation).	(sensation)

	MTP Reading	Copy-Text Reading
142.14	¶ Invites	Invites
*143.10	Their	There

Mark Twain's Revisions

142.title   The . . . Praise] *originally* 'The Concert of'; 'of' *wiped out and replaced with a question mark; parentheses added to enclose* 'Concert?'; 'Synod' *interlined and* 'of Praise' *added.*

142.2   the Cow,] 'Cow,' *added following canceled* 'the Giraffe,' *then* 'the' *interlined.*

142.7   always] *written over* 'all'.

142.11   lesson?] *the* 'l' *written over* 's'.

142.18   he owes] *follows canceled* 'and his dignity respected,'.

143.3   force] *follows canceled* 'usurpation'.

143.7   man's] *follows canceled* 'his'.

The Lost Ear-ring

Textual Commentary

The manuscript is copy-text.

Textual Notes

147.35   scanning] On the verso of the manuscript page beginning here, Mark Twain wrote "Schloss-Hotel" and below that "Heidelberg, June 5."

Emendations of the Copy-Text

	MTP READING	COPY-TEXT READING
†145.1	6, 1878.	6. 1878
145.6	stocking-knitter	stocking knitter
146.5	("Ah	(ah
146.12	to	too

Word Division in the Copy-Text

145.2   living-room
145.20   stocking-knitter

Mark Twain's Revisions

Written in black ink

145.1   June 6, 1878.] *originally* 'May 6.'; 'May' *canceled in pencil;* 'June' *interlined above* 'May' *and* '1878' *inter-*

*lined with a caret after '6.' in pencil. The period after
'6' inadvertently left standing.*

145.1–2   I reached . . . stepped] *originally* 'When I reached . . .
morning, and stepped'; 'When' *canceled*; 'about 11. As'
interlined with a caret; the ampersand mended to 'I'.

145.9   touched] *follows canceled* 'laid one hand upon one of
her ear-rings, and the other'; 'upon' *follows canceled*
'on'.

145.12   what . . . pays for] *interlined with a caret above canceled* 'the price of'.

145.15   consternation] *follows canceled* 'grief'.

145.16   the remnant] *follows canceled* 'the broken'.

145.19   thee] *follows canceled* 'us,'.

146.4   Fräulein] *follows canceled* 'Frau'.

146.6   jeweler] *follows canceled* 'gr'.

146.7   mate] *follows canceled* 'repr'.

146.13   ear-drop] *followed by canceled* 'with'.

146.16   start] *interlined with a caret above canceled* 'go'.

146.23   noon,] *follows canceled* 'afterno'.

146.25–29   again! . . . old] *added to the verso of the MS page with
instructions to turn over; follows* 'again; (for once the
tears' *added to the verso then canceled;* 'old' *followed
by a superfluous* 'stocking-knitter,' *canceled in purple
ink; the material on the verso replaces* 'again. So also said
the mother and the sisters; and so also did the kindly old'
canceled in pencil on the recto; 'again.' *on the recto
canceled, then interlined with a caret, then canceled
again;* 'and so also did' *interlined with a caret above canceled* 'and'.

146.25–27   This . . . lids.] *originally enclosed in parentheses; the
parentheses canceled; the* 'T' *of* 'This' *mended from* 't'.

146.29   interlarding . . . many] *interlined with a caret above canceled* 'with many'.

146.29–30   Ach Gott] *followed by a canceled caret.*

146.30   abide . . . sorrow!] *interlined with a caret above canceled* 'shiel' *and canceled* 'shield us!'.

146.30   so on.] *followed by a canceled dash; the period possibly added later.*

146.36   There] *follows canceled* 'The onl'.

147.2   the cause] *follows canceled* 'not'.

147.7   beech] *follows canceled* 'beach'.

147.8   The face] *follows canceled* 'As I approached,'.

147.10   looked] *interlined above canceled* 'glanced'.

147.28   bowlder—] *followed by a canceled ampersand.*

148.1–2   the side] *follows canceled* 'her'.

148.2   bough,] *interlined in purple ink above canceled* 'bow'.

148.5   with radiant face,] *interlined with a caret.*

148.9   followed] *follows canceled* 'cam'.

148.10   come] *follows canceled* 'ar'.

148.11   mastering,] *followed by canceled unrecovered word.*

148.20   is] *follows canceled* 'may'; *and canceled* 'has'.

148.20   for himself] *interlined with a caret.*

Goose Fable

Textual Commentary

The manuscript is copy-text. There are no textual notes, and no ambiguous compound is hyphenated at the end of a line in the manuscript.

Emendations of the Copy-Text

	MTP Reading	Copy-Text Reading
150.21	wrong?"	wrong?
151.23	you."	you.

Mark Twain's Revisions

150.4	gods] *the 'g' written over what appears to be 'G'.*
150.6	some solemn truths] *follows canceled* 'some matters of deep'.
151.19	oh] *follows an ampersand canceled in pencil.*

About Asa Hoover

Textual Commentary

The manuscript is copy-text. There are no textual notes, and no ambiguous compound is hyphenated at the end of a line in the manuscript.

Emendations of the Copy-Text

	MTP READING	COPY-TEXT READING
153.1	SEPTEMBER 6.	*September 6.*
153.3	Mississippi	Mississipi
153.4	juvenile	jevenile

Mark Twain's Revisions

153.1	Walters] *the 't' interlined with a caret.*
153.16	any] *follows canceled* 'Hoover'.
154.5	one] *follows canceled* 'person'.
154.11	Hoover] *follows canceled* 'The p'.

The Refuge of the Derelicts

Textual Commentary

"The Refuge of the Derelicts" is textually uncomplicated. The manuscript was typed through Chapter 10; the remainder of the work exists only in manuscript. Mark Twain made minor revisions and corrections on the typescript. There are indications, discussed in the textual notes to 238.32 and 244.4, that he discarded a chapter late in the work. He expanded Chapter 1 and reworked Chapter 2 by interleaving six new manuscript pages in two three-page groups, renumbering the original pages. The first two textual notes discuss this process of revision. With these exceptions, he appears to have made no major changes.

The establishment of the text is as straightforward as its course of composition. Only the policy regarding italics requires comment. In the first twenty-nine pages of typescript (through p. 175.4 of the present text), the typist reproduced the manuscript underscoring; she may have stopped at Mark Twain's request, for he often preferred to italicize a typescript anew, but in fact he paid little attention to the problem in this work. He underlined only twenty words in the typescript, eleven of them in the Admiral's comic catechism (192.30–193.14), where Mark Twain clearly labored to achieve just the right intonation. The other nine are sprinkled randomly through the remaining hundred pages of typescript. Sixteen of the twenty words italicized by Mark Twain in the typescript are italic in the manuscript as well. In two cases his typescript italics override the manuscript, but because the author made no concerted effort to replace the manuscript emphasis, it remains authoritative in the rest of the present text.

Textual Notes

163.1–24   "No . . . None but] This passage is on inserted manuscript pages 3–5. The pages originally numbered 3–18 were renumbered 6–21.

167.title–168.10 Chapter 2 . . . risk.] Mark Twain added the detailed description of the Admiral and his surroundings on three new manuscript pages numbered 22–24. The pages originally numbered 19–23 became pages 25–29. The renumbering indicates that the expansion of Chapters 1 and 2 was undertaken as a single revision. Mark Twain apparently went back to revise after writing part of the page now numbered 29, most probably just before writing Bagheera's entrance (169.26) which was added at the foot of the page.

170.7   legging] The typist read "begging," and it is possible that Mark Twain fused the final upstroke of a "b" with the "e." However, since "legging," a colloquialism meaning to bestir oneself for someone or something, fits the context, it has been chosen.

171.15   pride] The typist skipped over the manuscript reading "pride," and Mark Twain, copy-reading without reference to the manuscript, supplied "endorsement" as a correction. The manuscript reading has been restored.

173.37   from a tree] Mark Twain wrote and canceled three sets of marginal notes on the manuscript page which begins here. With one exception the notes look forward to the Admiral's encomium (175.11–17) three manuscript pages later. In the top left corner, Mark Twain wrote "hold arm out straight as stunsl boom" and "spanker-boom"; in the top right corner he wrote "garboard-strake, port side of keel"; and along the left margin he wrote "silvery" and "spanker-boom." In the text, "silvery" (174.4) is an interlineation.

176.28   don't it?] The manuscript reading "didn't it?" is interlined, making it likely that Mark Twain mistook the needed tense, either through carelessness or because of the proximity of three prior "didn'ts" in the paragraph. It is possible that he intended a dialect form, but the locution seems too bizarre even for the Admiral. His more usual colloquial form has therefore been adopted to correspond with his usage at 176.29 and elsewhere.

178.7   she's a Prisbyterian] On the manuscript page which
             begins here, Mark Twain wrote and canceled the cue
             "20 yrs."

178.16   about with your *which*] In the manuscript, Mark Twain
             canceled a question mark after "about" and interlined
             "with your." In converting two sentences into one, he
             left the "W" of "*Which*" upper-case. He may have in-
             tended the capital to stand for further emphasis, but his
             habit of failing to alter capital letters after altering his
             syntax makes it more likely that he simply overlooked
             the reading.

186.27   "Yes. Life's] At the top of the manuscript page be-
             ginning here, Mark Twain wrote and canceled "*Every*
             'reed' has been wrecked for an act of moral courage."

187.13–14   something shady] At the top of the manuscript page be-
             ginning here, Mark Twain wrote and canceled "Rat in
             man's pocket—went there for his lunch—escapes in
             'conference'—Bags gets him."

187.24   back; don't] A canceled note reading "Well, he's too
             incandescent for *me*" appears at the top of the manu-
             script page beginning here.

187.36   this. Away] Across the top of the manuscript page be-
             ginning here, Mark Twain wrote and canceled "needs
             transubstantiation—strangr would have thought hed
             had just become a mother." Above "needs" he wrote
             "fact," whether as part of the same note or a separate
             one is not clear.

188.11   "And he] A canceled note reading "X-Ray. Radium."
             appears in the top left corner of the manuscript page
             beginning here. In the top right corner Mark Twain
             wrote and canceled "Compound multiplex commuta-
             tion fracture—leg looked like basket of umbrellas."

188.23   land; he] Two notes are written and canceled at the top
             of the manuscript page beginning here—in the left
             corner "Cave Adullam." and in the right corner "They
             also serve who stand around."

190.22   one of his] At the top of the manuscript page beginning here, Mark Twain repeated, then canceled, his note at 188.23, "They also serve who stand around."

192.8   so. To] Mark Twain wrote and canceled "Adam" at the top of the manuscript page beginning here.

192.19   "Now then] Returning to the theme of his note at 188.11, Mark Twain wrote and canceled at the top of the manuscript page beginning here, "compound consti-pated fracture of every dam bone in his leg—*that* form makes the [originally "them"] bones spray out & stick up, you know—leg looked like sack of golf-clubs."

193.6–8   Well . . . that. . . . *holy*.] In the manuscript, "Well" and "that" are italicized, "holy" is not. The typist had stopped reproducing the manuscript emphasis, and Mark Twain here departed from his earlier markings although the subsequent italics in the paragraph dupli-cate those of the manuscript. Where, as here, con-flation of manuscript and typescript italics might distort Mark Twain's intention, the later typescript markings determine emphasis.

207.11   slave before] In the top left corner of the manuscript page beginning here, Mark Twain wrote and canceled "Put in XS. [Christian Science]"; in the top right corner, he wrote and canceled "Put in George?"

207.22   But, being black] Mark Twain wrote and canceled across the top of the manuscript page beginning here, "Many who read telegraphs are affected like Smith—modern & national—new disease—S. Islander." (The hand-writing is cramped; "national" may be "notional.")

207.31   are close] At the top of the manuscript page beginning here, Mark Twain wrote and canceled "The dipsomani-ac Beecher." In the typescript, a small penciled "x" appears above "are," and "is" is written in pencil in the margin, probably by Paine.

209.22   "Very well] The cue word "Phyllis" is written and can-

celed in the top left corner of the manuscript page beginning here.

213.title   George's Diary] In the top left corner of the manuscript
              page beginning here, Mark Twain wrote " 'This joint' "
              and below it "(ward-room)."

216.2   charge, and the] The typist omitted the "and," and
              Mark Twain simply mended the comma to a semicolon
              on the typescript. The manuscript reading has been
              restored.

216.11   away down down] Mark Twain interlined this phrase in
              the manuscript, and may have neglected to put a
              comma between the first "down" and the second. The
              typist either overlooked the second "down" or thought
              it an error, for she typed "away down." Since to emend
              would alter both rhythm and sense, however, the manu-
              script reading has not been changed.

217.24   lack . . . *lack*] In the manuscript the emphasis is reversed:
              the first "lack" is underlined, the second is not. The
              typist did not reproduce the original markings, and
              Mark Twain underlined the second "lack" in the type-
              script, supplanting the manuscript emphasis.

220.9–10   the rest about] The typescript reads "the rest of." Origi-
              nally, Jean Clemens typed "about the rest of"; in
              copyreading she canceled "about" in pencil. Mark Twain
              went over her cancellation in ink, but since he read the
              typescript without reference to the manuscript and
              made no independent contribution to the change, the
              original reading has been restored.

224.12   great] The typist incorrectly supplied "greatest" for
              the manuscript reading "great." Mark Twain, copy-
              reading without reference to the manuscript, changed
              it to "loftiest." The manuscript reading has been re-
              stored.

224.26   I was in it] A small penciled "x" appears above "was"
              in the typescript, and "were" is penciled in the margin

with a question mark above it. The hand is probably Paine's.

225.10 He made] In a note written and later canceled in the top left corner of the manuscript page beginning here, Mark Twain ordered himself to "find this d—d poet's name."

229.19 conquered] The cue word "loveless" is written and canceled to the right of the page number at the top of the manuscript page beginning here.

234.title Diary] In the top left corner of the manuscript page beginning here, Mark Twain wrote and canceled "Jimson Flinders."

234.3 inventor] In the manuscript, Mark Twain followed "ex-Senator, the" with a blank line. He may have planned to extend the list of derelicts when he revised the manuscript, but he did not return to the passage until it was typed, when he interlined only "inventor."

238.32 fashion?"] The typescript ends here. On the manuscript page beginning the next chapter Mark Twain wrote "Cancel preceding page?" The note may refer to an earlier beginning, subsequently destroyed.

244.4 hear.] Two manuscript pages, each numbered 290 and each opening with a chapter heading, follow the manuscript page ending here. Although it is possible that Mark Twain misnumbered the second page, it is more likely that the first is a discarded beginning that remained with the manuscript by chance. The brevity of the first chapter—a single page of 85 words—points to a false start, as does the weakness of the transition from the preceding chapter. Accordingly, the page has been deleted from the present text. The discarded page bears the note "Absent 2 years 'practising' (swearing)."

246.13 parts] Mark Twain may have written "ports"; the formation of the letter is ambiguous.

Emendations of the Copy-Text

	MTP READING	COPY-TEXT READING
163.25	seized TS	siezed *Also emended at* 184.25
164.30	Klondike	Klondyke
167.12	unpurchasable TS	unpurchaseable
†168.17	anemic	enemic
*171.15	pride MS	endorsement
172.14	Aunt	aunt *Also emended at* 178.4, 178.35, 179.27, 179.34, 180.1, 180.25, 181.11, 184.29, 185.23, 186.24, 190.2, 192.18, *and* 202.15
†173.20	Admiral	"Admiral
175.30	half-a-minute	half a minute
*176.28	don't	didn't
178.2	it's TS	its
178.5	it's	its
*178.16	*which* TS	*Which*
181.5	deal.	deal
181.36	uncertainty?	uncertainty.
183.13	spreading TS	spreding
†186.9	there's TS	There's
186.23	George.	George?
186.25	Protégés TS	Protegès *Also emended at* 186.26
187.13	recognized	recognised
187.14	Bags's TS	Baggs's

	MTP READING	COPY-TEXT READING
†187.24	mention TS	Mention
187.29	eruption	irruption *Also emended at* 201.25
188.29	secretary's TS	Secretary's
188.34	*black-balled.'*	*black-balled.'* "
189.9	bridegroom TS	bridegrom
189.10	recognize	recognise *Also emended at* 189.34–35
189.25	Derelict,' TS	Derelict,"
190.24	Bos'n TS	Bo'sn
191.22	were TS	was/were
*193.6–8	Well . . . that. . . . *holy* TS	*Well . . . that.* . . . holy
193.26	Uncle	uncle
†194.7	you	You
†196.2	father,	father,;
†196.12	show-off TS	Show-off
†197.19	tragedies! TS	tragedies,!
197.27	(ex-)letter-carrier	(ex-)letter carrier
199.20	like TS	liked
200.12	Smith's TS	Smiths
200.24	wits' TS	wit's
207.33	Aunty TS	aunty
209.16	paralysed	paralyzed
209.36	fa'rly	far'ly
210.33	dipsomaniac TS	dipsomanic
†212.30	he TS	He

	MTP Reading	Copy-Text Reading
213.2	bos'n TS	boso'n
*216.2	charge, and MS	charge;
*217.24	lack . . . *lack* TS	*lack* . . . lack
222.6	TEN DAYS LATER	*Ten days later*
†222.16	ago the TS	ago The
*224.12	great MS	loftiest
225.17	per cent	per cent. *Also emended at* 225.19
228.21	unforgettable	unforgetable
†231.33	welcome." TS	welcome"
†232.5	hard-a-port TS	hard a-port
234.16	two or three	two three
238.5	'caze	'case
239.4	territory	Territory
242.8	town	tow
†242.26	territories	Territories
†243.20	he had	He had
*244.4	hear.	hear. Diary—Continued The Governor does not believe in Adam—this week—but I have bought his approval of the monument by exhibiting a warm interest in his heart's latest religious pet, Christian Science. David's idea that every man has his price holds good thus far. The bos'n's idea that everybody is crazy holds good too—in the Governor's case, anyway.

	MTP READING	COPY-TEXT READING
		When he gets upon that C. S. subject his sorrows flit away, his face lights up with eager interest and his tongue begins to go at both ends.
244.17	casuals"	casuals
†245.28	read:	read
246.36	squirming	squrming
†248.2	vitals,	vitals

Word Division in the Copy-Text

166.24	worldly-wise
172.29	sealskin
173.7	something
176.36	danger-line
196.29	commonplace
198.14–15	good-hearted
201.13	earthquake
203.5	rearranging
204.9	himself
220.23	fig-leaf
231.10	fellow-feeling
238.15	ward-room
239.18	over-states
239.27	common-school
241.24–25	dressing-gown

Mark Twain's Revisions

162.2–3	from the Admiral!"] *interlined with a caret.*
162.4	the young poet-artist] *interlined with a caret; originally*

'the poet-artist'; 'the' *canceled and* 'the young' *added to the interlineation.*

162.5   poet-artist] *originally* 'poet'; *the hyphen added and* 'artist' *interlined with a caret.*

162.14   request . . . interview—] *interlined with a caret above canceled* 'card—'.

162.16   "invitation] *follows canceled* ' "an'.

163.1–24   "No," . . . None but] *replaces canceled paragraphs* 'George did it. He soon forgot his wound in the interest of his subject; his enthusiasm rose and grew, his eyes burned with a sacred fire, his words flowed from his heart and his mouth in an impassioned stream, Shipman sitting entranced and worshiping. At last—
               ' "I've got it, George!" cried Shipman, "I've got it! and it's a wonderful scheme, perfectly wonderful! Nobody but'; 'cried' *and* 'perfectly' *interlined with carets. See textual notes.*

163.2   tell you] *interlined with a caret above canceled* 'say'.

163.4   as] *interlined with a caret.*

163.11   "Adam."] *followed by canceled* 'That gracious light touched the deep eyes again:' *which originally preceded* ' "Adam." ', *was marked to follow it, and finally canceled.*

163.13   Gr-reat] 're' *written over what appears to be* 'ea'.

163.14   immediately] *interlined with a caret above canceled* 'promptly'.

163.15   give-away] *interlined with a caret beneath interlined and canceled* 'amazed'.

163.15   pure] *interlined with a caret.*

163.26   of . . . feel.] *interlined following canceled* 'of his admiration.'

163.27   pleasure.] *followed by canceled quotation marks.*

163.30   will] *follows canceled* 'can—and'.

163.31   George,] *interlined with a caret.*

163.32–33   Is . . . me."] *added following canceled* 'You will round-
                up those people, I know it. Give me the list." '; 'You'
                follows canceled quotation marks.

164.11   right one] 'one' *interlined above canceled* 'way'.

164.14   same] *followed by canceled* 'right'.

164.17   "David] *follows canceled* ' "Why,'.

164.19   the . . . way?"] *interlined with a caret above canceled*
                'it?" '.

164.30   gold] *interlined with a caret above canceled* 'money'.

164.35   goodness knows] *interlined with a caret above canceled*
                'good gracious,'.

165.4   Every] *follows canceled quotation marks.*

165.6   money; in] *originally* 'money. In'; *the period mended to
                a semicolon;* 'in' *interlined with a caret above canceled*
                'In'.

165.6   you beguile . . . that;] *interlined with a caret.*

165.8   instance—] *the dash interlined with a caret.*

165.16   is, no doubt . . . .] *interlined with a caret above canceled*
                'is, ...'

165.19   Even the] *originally* 'The'; 'Even' *interlined with a car-
                et; the* 'T' *of* 'The' *mended to* 't'; *followed by canceled*
                'grand'.

165.20   seas,] *followed by canceled* 'stern and grim with the
                daily drift through his mind of his crimson battle-
                memories, old, white-headed . . . . crutches, a leg gone,
                idol of the nation, the people baring their heads when
                he stumps by . . . . . what might *his* price be!" '; 'daily
                drift' *follows canceled* 're' *and* 're-living'; 'white-headed'
                followed by a canceled comma.

165.20–22   old . . . be!"] *added on the verso of the MS page with
               instructions to turn over;* 'old, white-headed,' *interlined
               with a caret;* 'beloved' *canceled following* 'Arthur was';
               'Launcelot,' *interlined above canceled* 'Arthur,'.

165.23   den] *followed by canceled* 'and'.

165.24   skeleton] *interlined with a caret.*

165.24   then] *interlined with a caret.*

165.24   moment.] *the period added; followed by canceled* '—
               and chuckling.'

165.27   denying] *interlined with a caret above canceled* 'getting
               around'.

165.28   it!] *interlined with a caret above canceled* 'it, I go bail
               for that!'.

165.28   over] *interlined with a caret above canceled* 'about'.

165.30   My,] *interlined with a caret above canceled* 'Dear-dear';
               'dear' *interlined above canceled* 'me'.

165.31   innocent!] *the exclamation point squeezed in.*

165.34   my] *interlined with a caret.*

165.34–35   —borrowed . . . Bacon—] *interlined.*

165.37   Take] *follows canceled* 'To'.

166.1   over] *followed by* 'to-night' *interlined with a caret and
               canceled.*

166.2   whenever you like, and] *interlined with a caret above
               canceled* 'to-morrow'.

166.6   —and right away—] *interlined with a caret.*

166.7   telephone] *follows canceled* 'tell him'.

166.9   shifted] *follows canceled* 'he'.

166.9   said] *follows canceled* 'he'.

166.13–14   (just . . . confidence,)] *interlined with a caret above
               canceled* 'knows it by heart,'.

166.16   dizzy,] *interlined with a caret above canceled* 'drunk'.

166.16   astronomically] *interlined with a caret to replace inter-*
                lined and canceled 'spaciously' *and* 'grossly' *above can-*
                celed 'grotesquely'.

166.23   is a composer . . . musician;] *interlined with a caret;*
                'believes' *squeezed in above canceled* 'thinks'.

166.28   "My word,] *interlined above canceled* ' "Goodness,'.

166.29   If he is, he] *interlined with a caret above canceled* 'He'.

166.30   to him] *interlined with a caret.*

166.35   when] *written over an ampersand.*

167.7   regained] *interlined with a caret above canceled* 'got'.

167.9   cat?"] *the question mark apparently squeezed in and*
                mended from a period.

167.12   driven] *interlined with a caret.*

167.14   way."] *originally followed by canceled chapter* 'II.', 'The
                Admiral.' *and by canceled paragraph* 'He was seated in
                an arm chair, when the poet entered. He reached for
                his crutches, but George begged him not to rise.' *See*
                textual note at 167.*title.*

167.15–16   Tall . . . resonant.] *interlined with a caret.*

167.17   Fairhaven] *follows canceled* 'New Bedford'.

167.22   not sound] *follows canceled* 'uns'.

167.24   retired.] *originally* ' "retired." '; *the quotation marks*
                canceled; followed by canceled 'That was his name for
                it.'

167.25   years.] *followed by canceled* 'and in the meantime had
                spent more time on shipboard, as passenger, than at
                home. He did not count those divergencies; he coldly
                ignored them, for he was proud of his retired condition.';
                the period after 'years' *mended from a comma.*

167.28   an] *interlined with a caret above canceled* 'a comfort-
              able'.

167.29   grog] *follows canceled* 'whisk'.

168.6–7   who . . . said—] *follows canceled* 'said—'.

168.12   a calm] *follows canceled* 'a critical'.

168.14   an effect which] *originally* 'this effect was not'; 'this'
              and 'not' *canceled;* 'an' *and* 'which' *interlined with*
              carets.

168.15   Admiral] *the* 'l' *written over* 'bly'.

168.17   slim . . . . anemic] '. . . . enaemic' *interlined with a caret*
              in the MS; mended to 'enemic' *on the TS. See emenda-*
              tions.

168.22   They . . . navy . . . . . .] *interlined with a caret.*

168.24   this one] 'tape-worm' *interlined and canceled above*
              'this one'.

168.27   Yes,] *followed by canceled* 'I reckon,'.

168.28   a pipe] 'a' *interlined with a caret above canceled* 'his'.

168.30   accident.] *followed by canceled* 'That's all right, it's
              their privilege . . . .'; *the ellipsis following* 'accident.'
              interlined with a caret.

168.35   start . . . conceited and] *interlined with a caret.*

169.7   muttered] *interlined with a caret above canceled* 'he
              said'.

169.10   do;] *followed by canceled* 'and you'.

169.16   here,] *followed by a canceled dash.*

169.26–27   The cat . . . Admiral,] *added at the foot of the MS*
              page. See textual note at 167.title.

169.29   of that species] *interlined with a caret.*

169.32   the] *interlined with a caret.*

169.36   across] *interlined with a caret above canceled* 'on'.

170.10   sudden?] *the question mark mended from an exclamation point.*

170.11   there,] *interlined with a caret above a canceled comma.*

170.11–12   the Admiral's latest] *interlined with a caret to replace canceled* 'his'; 'his' *interlined with a caret above canceled* 'the Admiral's latest'.

170.14   caressing] *originally* 'caressings'; *the* 's' *canceled.*

170.14   purring] *interlined with a caret.*

170.14   on,] *followed by canceled* 'the'.

170.25   off] *followed by canceled* 'the seat of'.

170.27–28   is dispersing a mob] *interlined above canceled* 'is quelling a riot'; 'riot' *interlined with a caret above canceled* 'mob'.

170.29   finally] *interlined with a caret above canceled* 'then'.

170.29   aside] *followed by a canceled comma.*

170.30   said, with . . . hand—] 'said, with' *interlined with a caret to replace canceled* 'with'; *the dash interlined above canceled* 'said—'.

171.2   has] *interlined with a caret.*

171.4   handed] *interlined with a caret above canceled* 'gave'.

171.4   gave] *followed by canceled* 'it'.

171.5   upon its under-half] *interlined with a caret.*

171.17   to this] *interlined with a caret.*

171.17   chatting] *followed by canceled* 'along'.

171.18   into . . . theme] *added following canceled* 'another apology' *and canceled* 'among its meshes'.

171.20–21   seated himself,] *interlined with a caret.*

171.22   then] *interlined with a caret above what may be a canceled ampersand.*

171.28   fallen] *interlined with a caret.*

171.37   sat up] *followed by canceled* 'and looked'.

171.37   lick] *follows canceled* 'make'.

171.37   use . . . forward] *interlined with a caret above canceled*
                'scrub'.

172.1   scrub his] *interlined with a caret.*

172.1   cheeks,] *originally* 'cheeks with them,'; 'with them,'
                canceled and the comma added after 'cheeks'.

172.5   lay down and] *interlined with a caret.*

172.14   or . . . Martha] *interlined with a caret following inter-
                lined and canceled* 'Fletcher,'.

172.15   most] *interlined with a caret.*

172.18   with his paw;] *interlined with a caret above a canceled
                semicolon.*

172.23   cutwater] *interlined with a caret above canceled* 'stem'.

172.24   spanker-boom.] *interlined with a caret above canceled*
                'his steering-oar.'

172.24   fringe] *followed by an uncanceled caret with no inter-
                lineation.*

172.30   sheen] *followed by a canceled dash.*

173.4   you] *interlined with a caret.*

173.5–6   comfortable . . . afternoon] *interlined with a caret
                above canceled* 'long'.

173.8   nor how] *followed by a canceled comma.*

173.9   . . . . Th—there] *interlined with a caret;* 'Th—there'
                interlined above canceled 'Tha' *which is interlined
                above canceled* 'Tha—there'.

173.10   there!] *the exclamation point squeezed in replacing a
                canceled exclamation point.*

173.11–12   like a fire-coal] *interlined with a caret.*

173.14   praise,] *followed by canceled* 'from'.

173.16   oh,] *interlined with a caret.*

173.20   "Bagheera!] *interlined with a caret; followed by inter-lined and canceled* 'Oh,'; *the original quotation marks preceding* 'Admiral' *inadvertently left standing.*

173.25–26   He took . . . back.] *interlined with a caret.*

173.26   is," he said.] *the quotation marks following* 'is,' *added on the line;* 'he said.' *and the following quotation marks interlined with a caret.*

173.27   Works] *the* 'W' *written over* 'w'.

173.27   Immortal] *follows canceled* 'Say'.

173.28   Admiral,] *interlined with a caret.*

173.29   It'll] *follows canceled* 'By God,'.

174.4   silvery] *interlined with a caret above canceled* 'soft'.

174.6   that] *interlined with a caret.*

174.7   was] *followed by* 'n't' *interlined with a caret and canceled.*

174.8   as . . . is.] *interlined with a caret following a comma mended from a period.*

174.14   "—sh] *originally* ' " 'sh'; *the quotation marks and apos-trophe canceled and new quotation marks and a dash added on the line.*

174.14   "Change] *follows canceled paragraph* ' "Chan' *and canceled run-on* ' "Ch'.

174.15   this . . . minute,] *interlined with a caret.*

174.22   some] *interlined with a caret.*

174.24   stepped . . . ear—] *interlined with a caret above canceled* 'broke in with a crash—'.

174.31   loud] *originally* 'loud'; *the italics canceled.*

174.33   damn] *interlined with a caret above canceled* 'dern'.

175.3   sure:] *interlined with a caret following a comma mended from a semicolon.*

175.5   duly] *interlined with a caret.*

175.10   ain't it?] *interlined with a caret following a comma mended from a period.*

175.11–12   of his keelson,] *interlined with a caret above a canceled comma.*

175.12   forrard] *follows canceled* 'aft the'; *followed by* 'of the mizzen' *interlined with a caret.*

175.13   When] *follows canceled* 'There—'; *the* 'W' *written over* 'w'.

175.16–17   . . . . Now . . . spinnaker."] *interlined following canceled quotation marks.*

175.18   fancy] *follows canceled* 'final'.

175.32   never] *interlined with a caret above canceled* 'not'.

175.34   whack!] *interlined with a caret above canceled* 'wipe!'.

175.35   resolute, ain't it] *interlined with a caret.*

175.36–176.1 He was . . . little. . . . .] *interlined with a caret.*

176.2   spat,] *interlined with a caret above canceled* 'whack,'.

176.2   it!] *added to replace canceled* 'the slap.'

176.2   about] *interlined with a caret.*

176.3   There!] *the exclamation point possibly mended from a comma.*

176.4   to a corner] *interlined with a caret.*

176.18   by gracious!—] *interlined with a caret above a canceled dash following a comma added on the line.*

176.20   have I, or] *interlined with a caret.*

176.26   would . . . and] *interlined with a caret.*

176.28   don't it?] 'didn't it?' *interlined with a caret following a comma mended from a period. See emendations.*

176.31   and unrelenting] *interlined with a caret.*

176.35–177.1   throw . . . wonderful] *interlined following canceled* 'do the/a judicious thing: he said it was perfectly wonderful'.

177.3   midriff,] *interlined with a caret above canceled* 'marrow,'.

177.17   patch-quilt] *follows* 'seamed and glowing' *interlined with a caret and canceled.*

177.17   remained calm] *follows canceled* 'was not affected'.

177.22   ventured] *follows canceled* 'm'.

177.22   lifted . . . gravely] *follows canceled* 'gravely'.

177.32   He] *follows canceled* 'A monu'.

178.11   twenty years; ten] 'twenty' *interlined with a caret above canceled* 'thirty'; 'ten' *interlined with a caret above canceled* 'twenty'.

178.11   here on land.] 'here' *followed by canceled* '—ten'; 'land.' *followed by canceled* ', that is. Ever since I retired.'; *the period added later.*

178.14–15   "Certainly . . . mean, *which* she?"] *added to the verso of the MS page with instructions to turn over.*

178.16   "*Which* she] *follows canceled paragraph* ' "She?'; *the* 'W' *of* 'Which' *mended from* 'w'.

178.16   with your *which*] 'with your' *interlined with a caret above a canceled question mark;* 'W' *of* 'Which' *not reduced to* 'w'.

178.19–20   storm-blue] *follows canceled* 'indig'.

178.26   gave] *follows canceled* 'no'.

178.26   falsely] *interlined with a caret.*

178.32   twenty-one,] '-one,' *interlined with a caret.*

178.34   although] *followed by canceled* 'she was'.

179.1   Sixty] *interlined with a caret above canceled* 'Fifty'.

179.12   twenty-one,] *the hyphen added on the line and* 'one,' *interlined with a caret.*

179.15   sixty] *interlined above canceled* 'fifty'.

179.16   sources] *follows canceled* 'an'.

179.17   twenty-one] *the hyphen added on the line and* 'one' *interlined with a caret.*

179.26   all's] *the* ' 's' *interlined with a caret.*

179.31   now,] *interlined with a caret.*

180.6   look at it] 'it' *interlined with a caret.*

180.8   anybody.] *followed by canceled* 'if he do'; *the period added.*

180.10   It] *originally* 'Its'; *the* 's' *canceled.*

180.13   always] *interlined with a caret.*

180.13–14   or a priest,] *interlined with a caret.*

180.27   glad] *followed by a canceled comma.*

181.3   told] *follows canceled* ' 'a'.

181.7   sixty,] *interlined with a caret above canceled* 'fifty,'.

181.7   twenty] *interlined with a caret to replace canceled* 'thirty' *interlined above canceled* 'forty'.

181.18–21   (Pause.) . . . (Pause.)] *the parentheses added on the TS.*

181.30   "How dreadful] *follows canceled paragraph* ' "Dre'.

182.22   and more.] *interlined with a caret above a canceled period.*

182.26   anyhow,] *originally* 'anyway,'; 'how,' *interlined above canceled* 'way,'.

183.14   with the] 'with' *written over an ampersand.*

183.19   never] *followed by canceled* 'g'.

183.22   ten years] *follows canceled* 'years'.

183.29   forty] *interlined above canceled* 'thirty'.

184.12   and whicker] *interlined with a caret.*

184.21   the cat] *follows canceled* 'that'.

184.23   launched] *follows canceled* 'made'.

184.23   missile] *follows canceled* 'catap'.

184.31   cordially] *written over what appears to be wiped-out* 'ef'.

184.32   mind,] *followed by canceled* 'old girl,'.

184.33   chief mate] *follows canceled* 'brains'.

184.34   there!] *originally* 'there, speaking!'; ', speaking!' *canceled; the exclamation point added.*

185.2   some day] *interlined with a caret.*

185.4–5   and wavy] *interlined with a caret.*

185.5   soft] *interlined with a caret above canceled* 'sweet'.

185.6   human] *follows a canceled ampersand.*

185.7   which] *interlined above canceled* 'that'.

185.11   temper] *follows* 'infirmities of' *canceled on the TS.*

185.16   no . . . money] *follows canceled* 'mon'.

185.24   anyhow,] *originally* 'anyway,'; 'how,' *interlined with a caret above canceled* 'way,'.

185.29   I am] *follows canceled quotation marks.*

185.32   her] *interlined with a caret above canceled* 'aunt Maria'.

185.33   know] *followed by canceled* 'the a'.

185.35   Go] *followed by canceled* 'and get y'.

186.1   George] *follows canceled paragraph* 'As soon as George'.

186.2–3   bos'n . . . another,] *interlined with a caret.*

186.4   in . . . house.] *follows a canceled period.*

186.9   And there's] 'And' *interlined with a caret; the* 'T' *of
                 MS* 'There's' *not reduced to* 't'.

186.14   When] *written over quotation marks.*

186.20   as I've said,] *interlined with a caret.*

186.24   Are] *follows canceled quotation marks.*

186.27   Derelicts,] *followed by canceled* 'that'.

186.28   forlorn.] *interlined with a caret above canceled* 'for-
                 saken.'

186.36   sort of spirit] *interlined with a caret.*

187.13   then,] *interlined with a caret following a comma added
                 on the line.*

187.16   —half . . . fact—] *interlined with a caret.*

187.18   that's] *the* ' 's' *interlined with a caret.*

187.19   lovely] *follows canceled* 'just'.

187.24   Because mention] 'Because' *interlined with a caret; the*
                 'M' *of MS* 'Mention' *not reduced to* 'm'.

187.27   the old mariner's] *interlined with a caret above canceled*
                 'his'.

188.2   in] *interlined with a caret above a canceled dash.*

188.9   cut] *interlined with a caret above canceled* 'froze'.

188.13–14   no one . . . them.] *interlined with a caret following a
                 comma mended from a period.*

188.15   name . . . at] *interlined with a caret above canceled* 'ap-
                 plication for membership in'.

188.16   Society's next meeting.] *originally* 'Society.'; ' 's' *written
                 over the period and* 'next meeting.' *interlined with a
                 caret.*

188.20–23   —with . . . sight of] *written on the verso of the MS page
                 with instructions to turn over, following a canceled pe-
                 riod and canceled* 'He began to repent of what he had
                 done before he was out of'.

188.24   most] *originally* 'mostly'; *the* 'ly' *canceled.*

188.29   secretary's] *interlined with a caret. See emendations.*

188.31–32   " 'Take . . . thirst!'] *originally* ' "Take . . . thirst!" '; *the opening single quotation mark interlined with a caret; the closing single quotation mark mended from a double.*

188.34   " 'Hasn't . . . black-balled.'] *the single quotation marks added.*

188.35–189.2   George." That . . . made. "You] *originally* 'George. You'; *the quotation marks added;* 'That . . . made.' *added to the verso of the MS page with instructions to turn over.*

188.35   David] *interlined with a caret above canceled* 'he'.

189.2   George,] *interlined with a caret; the preceding comma added.*

189.6   and] *follows canceled* 'and y'.

189.7   To] *follows canceled* 'The'.

189.8   bitter] *interlined with a caret.*

189.25   fallen;] *followed by canceled* 'It is the little seed from which has grown the sheltering tree of compassion and benevolence.'; 'little' *interlined with a caret; the semicolon after* 'fallen' *mended from a period.*

189.28   the] *interlined with a caret.*

189.29   The hand] *follows canceled* 'It was'; *the* 'T' *of* 'The' *mended from* 't'.

189.29   no] *follows canceled* 'the'.

189.31   impressively;] *interlined with a caret above canceled* 'reverently;'.

189.33   by Providence] *interlined with a caret on the TS.*

189.34   be patient] *follows canceled* 'be trustful and'.

190.title   From George's Diary] *added.*

190.1   I] *interlined with a caret above canceled* 'George'.

190.2   I] *interlined with a caret above canceled* 'George'.

190.2   the latter] *interlined with a caret.*

190.9   me] *interlined with a caret above canceled* 'George'.

190.13   we've] ' 've' *interlined with a caret above canceled* 'have'.

190.14   up] *interlined with a caret.*

190.15   (or . . . reproachfully,)] *interlined with a caret; originally* '(or . . . reproachfully, George thought),'; 'George thought),' *canceled and the new closing parenthesis added.*

190.20–21   he wore . . . side,] *interlined with a caret.*

190.21   gait] *interlined with a caret above canceled* 'motions'.

190.22   semi-circling] *interlined with a caret replacing canceled* 'striding' *interlined with a caret above canceled* 'stepping'.

190.22   one of his legs] *originally* 'one of his legs'; 'the game' *interlined with a caret above canceled* 'one of his' *and the* 's' *in* 'legs' *canceled; then* 'the game leg' *canceled and* 'one of his legs' *interlined with a caret.*

190.23   rigid] *interlined with a caret above canceled* 'stiff'.

190.24   called him] 'him' *interlined with a caret above canceled* 'Bo'son'.

191.1   mystic] *interlined with a caret above canceled* 'doubtful'.

191.3   that] *followed by canceled* 'it'.

191.17   did not] 'did' *interlined with a caret above canceled* 'could'.

191.24   realized] *follows canceled* 'seemed to'; *originally* 'realise'; *the* 'z' *mended from an* 's'; *the final* 'd' *added.*

191.29   cast] *follows canceled* 'throw'.

191.30   that] *originally 'that'; the italics canceled.*

191.35   alternating] *followed by canceled 'of'.*

192.3   If] *follows canceled 'It'.*

192.4   fiendishly] *interlined with a caret above canceled 'infamously'.*

192.9   discussion—] *the dash interlined with a caret.*

192.10   He was] *originally run-on; marked to begin a new paragraph with a paragraph sign.*

192.10   went] *follows canceled 'had'.*

192.13   of his own volition,] *interlined with a caret above canceled 'himself,'.*

192.15   then proceeded,] *follows canceled 'did not'; followed by 'without . . . comments:' added later.*

192.17   Adam—"] *followed by canceled paragraph 'Aunt Martha'.*

192.19   you] *italic in MS and TS.*

192.22   But] *follows canceled quotation marks.*

192.25   plan] *follows canceled 'scheme'.*

192.30   All] *italic in TS; roman in MS.*

192.36   Sacred] *italic in MS and TS.*

193.1   "Ye-s."] *added and marked to begin a new paragraph with a paragraph sign.*

193.2   "The, ain't it?"] *added and marked to begin a new paragraph with a paragraph sign.*

193.2   The] *italic in MS and TS.*

193.4   "What . . . it?"] *added and marked to begin a new paragraph with a paragraph sign; 'one' followed by canceled ' 's'.*

193.4   the] *italic in MS and TS.*

193.4   *only*] *italic in MS and TS.*

193.5   Aunt . . . silent.] *interlined and marked to begin a new paragraph with a paragraph sign.*

193.6   Well] *roman in TS; italic in MS.*

193.7   that] *roman in TS; italic in MS.*

193.8   Two, . . . Three,] *interlined with a caret above canceled* 'Two,'.

193.8   *holy*] *italic in TS; roman in MS.*

193.8   *all*] *italic in MS and TS.*

193.8   Four] *interlined with a caret above canceled* 'Three'.

193.9   *sacred*] *italic in MS and TS.*

193.9   Five,] *interlined with a caret above canceled* 'Four,'.

193.9   *the*] *italic in MS and TS.*

193.10   *the*] *italic in MS and TS.*

193.13   *ain't*] *italic in MS and TS.*

193.23   *Don't*] *italic in MS and TS.*

193.29   flitted] *interlined with a caret above canceled* 'vanished'.

193.30   just] *interlined with a caret above canceled* 'appreciative'.

193.35   of his middle] 'of' *interlined with a caret;* 'together' *interlined and canceled above* 'middle'.

194.7   Suppose you] 'Suppose' *interlined with a caret; the* 'Y' *of MS* 'You' *not reduced to* 'y'.

194.8   way just] 'just' *interlined with a caret.*

194.8   —only just once—] *interlined with a caret.*

194.13   dissent.] *follows a canceled period.*

194.16   didn't] *interlined with a caret above canceled* 'don't'.

194.19   Could he give] *follows canceled* 'Di'.

194.24   an opposition] *interlined with a caret above canceled* 'a dissenting'.

194.29   bishops] *the 'b' written over* 'B'.

194.35   Finally—] *the dash written above a canceled comma.*

194.36   to sin] *followed by canceled* '? Certainly.'

195.5   One] *italic in MS and TS.*

195.17–19   The soft . . . house—] *added on the verso of the MS page with instructions to turn over, to replace canceled paragraph* 'The bosn's deep voice pealed through the house—'.

195.22   some religious] *follows canceled* 'a'.

195.32   ever] *interlined with a caret.*

195.34–35   professionals puff] *interlined with a caret above canceled* 'folk praise'.

195.37–196.2 for the "anchor . . . salvation for his] *added on the verso of the MS page with instructions to turn over, to replace canceled* 'for "these." That was his word. He followed it by mentioning, name by name, his numerous derelicts; then his dead'; 'for the "anchor . . . brevity-title for' *interlined above canceled* 'for—I did not catch the word, but I perceived that it meant'.

196.2   dead a generation ago;] *interlined with a caret following a comma added on the line; the original semicolon after* 'father' *inadvertently left standing.*

196.2   then for the] 'for the' *interlined with a caret following canceled* 'the'.

196.3   for me] 'for' *interlined with a caret.*

196.6   O Lord,] *interlined with a caret following a comma added on the line.*

196.8   It startled] *follows canceled paragraph* 'It startled me—and not pleasantly.'

196.12   humility—show-off] *originally* 'humility. Show-off'; *a*

*dash written over the period; the 'S' of MS 'Show-off'
not reduced to 's'.*

196.14   moment!] *originally 'moment.'; the exclamation point
              added on the TS.*

196.15   I was] *follows canceled 'I was'.*

196.22   are] *italic in MS and TS.*

196.23   commonplace,] *followed by canceled 'but'.*

196.28–29   becoming] *interlined with a caret.*

197.6   Books?] *the question mark replaces a canceled exclama-
              tion point on the TS.*

197.6   So . . . He says] *interlined with a caret above canceled
              'For'.*

197.9   comedy,] *the comma added on the TS.*

197.9   The bos'n says there] *'The bos'n says' interlined with a
              caret; the 't' of 'there' mended from 'T'.*

197.14   derelicts] *follows canceled 'visiting'; followed by a can-
              celed period and 'and their intimates.' interlined with a
              caret.*

197.19   tragedies!] *the exclamation point written over what may
              be a colon following a comma inadvertently left stand-
              ing.*

197.21   Smith] *follows canceled 'H'.*

197.22   But] *follows canceled 'For'.*

197.24   mirror] *interlined above canceled 'measure'.*

197.29   am painting] *follows canceled 'I'.*

197.30   young] *interlined with a caret.*

197.32   thoughts,] *the comma apparently mended from a pe-
              riod.*

198.10   nearly] *interlined with a caret.*

198.10   some of the] *interlined with a caret above canceled 'the'.*

198.11   heart—] *the dash written over a period.*

198.11   the happinesses] *follows canceled* 'his'.

198.14   sane] *follows canceled* 'brave'.

198.15   and in the fifth] 'in' *written over* 'on'.

198.23   factors] *follows canceled* 'weapon the'.

198.24   The present] *interlined with a caret above canceled* 'Smith's'.

198.25   journeyman] *interlined with a caret.*

198.32   could have,] *followed by canceled* 'therefore'.

198.36   laborers.] *the period replaces a canceled semicolon followed by what appears to be canceled* 'wom'.

198.37   washing;] *followed by canceled* 'they looked'.

199.4–5   by . . . nights,] *interlined with a caret.*

199.16   Smith's] *the* ' 's' *interlined with a caret.*

199.27   Among] *follows canceled* 'To' *and* 'One'.

199.30   and more exacting] *interlined with a caret.*

199.30   before] *interlined with a caret.*

200.3   at this point,] *interlined with a caret.*

200.9   friends,] *followed by canceled* 'w'.

200.12   When] *follows canceled* 'Intercourse'.

200.13   Smiths and their] *interlined with a caret.*

200.14   were left] *interlined with a caret.*

200.15   people and] *followed by a canceled comma.*

200.15   and cheerless life.] *follows canceled* 'life.'

200.16   trifling,] *followed by canceled* 'as'.

200.29   him] *interlined with a caret above canceled* 'her'.

200.34   the machinists' union] *follows canceled* 'his union had'.

200.35–36   The words] *follows canceled* 'It is'.

201.1–2   when . . . at his] *follows canceled* 'at his'.

201.3   seven months] *interlined with a caret following canceled*
                 'two years and a half since he has seen Mary. She is
                 broken'.

201.3–4   last saw . . . A] *originally* 'has seen Mary. She had a';
                 'last saw' *interlined with a caret above* 'has seen'; *the
                 semicolon after* 'Mary' *mended from a period;* 'and . . .
                 him.' *interlined with a caret above canceled* 'She had';
                 'A' *written over* 'a'.

201.5   Her mind has failed.] *interlined with a caret.*

201.5–6   with . . . mother.] 'with' *interlined with a caret above a
                 canceled ampersand;* 'mother.' *followed by canceled*
                 'support her.'; *the period added.*

201.8–9   tried a reference to] *interlined with a caret above can-
                 celed* 'mentioned'.

201.10   At . . . name his] *interlined with a caret following can-
                 celed* 'His'.

201.13   earthquake,] *followed by canceled* 'thunder-burst,'.

201.15   hostility and] *interlined with a caret.*

201.17   One would] *follows canceled paragraph* 'The reason for
                 all this'.

201.18   last week, of] *interlined with a caret.*

201.21   should] *originally* 'would'; *the* 'sh' *written over* 'w'.

201.29–202.1   the healer] 'the' *interlined with a caret.*

202.3   The bos'n] *interlined with a caret above canceled* 'He'.

202.4   (emanating from David,)] *the parentheses added to re-
                 place canceled dashes; the comma squeezed in.*

202.5–6   the atmosphere] *follows canceled* 'his'.

202.10–11   that's private] *interlined with a caret.*

202.13   There ain't] *follows canceled* 'If a person'.

202.14   Miss] *interlined with a caret.*

202.20   only] *interlined with a caret above canceled* 'only'.

202.23   an ignorant] *interlined with a caret above canceled* 'a'.

202.25   myself] *interlined with a caret.*

202.33   and tall] *interlined with a caret.*

203.1   He is] 'is' *interlined with a caret above canceled* 'was'.

203.1   likeable] *the first* 'e' *interlined with a caret on the TS.*

203.14   Is—] *the dash interlined with a caret above a canceled comma on the TS.*

203.16   "What's] *follows canceled paragraph* ' "How old is he'.

203.23   and pet them] *interlined with a caret.*

203.27   you'll] *the* ' 'll' *interlined with a caret.*

203.27   too.] *interlined with a caret following a comma mended from a period.*

204.7–8   I winced a little.] *interlined with a caret.*

204.19   merely looked] *follows canceled* 'lo'.

204.32–37 I recognized . . . paper and said—] *added on the verso of the MS page with instructions to turn over replacing canceled paragraph* ' "Oh, stop! Don't go on, I can't stand it. I'm a dog!" '; 'Don't' *follows canceled quotation marks.*

205.1   you said] *follows canceled* 'I'.

205.1–2   I thought] *interlined with a caret.*

205.2   to—why] 'to—' *interlined with a caret.*

205.3   near to] *interlined with a caret.*

205.12   I'm down,] *interlined with a caret above canceled* 'you old rascal,'.

205.15   that's made] *followed by canceled* 'the way'.

205.17   it's . . . you!] *interlined with a caret above canceled* 'much! It makes me feel *very* good.'

205.25   you know] 'you' *followed by canceled* ' 'll'.

205.26   let up,] *interlined with a caret above canceled* 'go to hell'.

206.1   a feeling] *follows canceled* 'but alive'.

206.3   alive; alive] *followed by canceled* 'and a-quiver,'.

206.8   Incidentally,] *interlined with a caret above canceled* 'Without intending it,'.

206.10   the bos'n . . . care.] *interlined with a caret above canceled* '; indeed nothing could have prevented it, in the circumstances.'; *the comma preceding* 'the bos'n' *added on the line.*

206.11   I have not] *marked to begin a new paragraph with a paragraph sign.*

206.12   no . . . that—] *interlined with a caret above canceled* 'no question of it—'.

206.12   pushed] *follows what appears to be canceled* 'ju'.

206.15   spacious] *follows canceled* 'luxuriously' *interlined with a caret above canceled* 'very'.

206.18   smoke and read,] 'and' *interlined with a caret above a canceled comma;* 'read,' *followed by canceled* 'and tipple,'.

206.22   him from] 'him' *interlined with a caret.*

206.22   find] *interlined with a caret following canceled* 'discover'.

206.24   isn't;] *originally* 'isn't—'; *the dash canceled and the semicolon added.*

206.32–33   colored man;] *interlined with a caret above canceled* 'negro; large'.

206.34   broad-shouldered,] *the comma replaces a canceled semicolon.*

206.34 strong] *follows canceled* 'br'.

206.35 shrewd,] *interlined with a caret.*

207.5 ruin which slumps] *follows canceled* 'ruin which collapses like a child's toy ball'; 'slumps' *interlined with a caret above canceled* 'shrinks'.

207.7 rotting] *interlined with a caret.*

207.8 sorrowfully] *interlined with a caret.*

207.13 "goes] *interlined with a caret above canceled* ' "g' *and* ' "marches'.

207.17 Phyllis's] *mended from* 'Phillips's'.

207.19 Phyllis] *mended from* 'Phillips'. 'Phyllis' *is mended from* 'Phillips' *also at* 207.33, 207.36, 208.23, 208.27, 209.7, *and* 209.16.

207.19 born] *originally* 'borned'; *the* 'ed' *canceled.*

207.20 She was . . . War.] *interlined with a caret.*

207.20 toward seventy,] *interlined with a caret above canceled* 'well past sixty,'.

207.21 straight] *follows canceled* 'ere'.

207.27 her heart] *follows canceled* 'the deeps of'.

207.34 text:] *the colon replaces a canceled dash.*

208.5 glad] *follows canceled* 'natur'.

208.10 Adam, and] *followed by a canceled comma.*

208.11 *had* have had] 'have' *squeezed in with a caret.*

208.12 might] *follows canceled* 'w'.

208.17 minds,] *originally* 'mind,'; *the comma canceled and the* 's,' *added.*

208.22 orange] *interlined with a caret above canceled* 'hypothenuse'.

208.26 shall] *interlined with a caret above canceled* 'shall'.

208.30–32   Of course . . . applause.] *added and marked to begin a new paragraph with a paragraph sign.*

208.34   Stormfield.] *the period replaces a canceled exclamation point on the TS.*

208.36   ever] *originally* 'never'; *the* 'n' *canceled.*

208.36   befo'] *originally* 'before'; *the apostrophe added above canceled* 're'.

209.2   Die!] *italic in MS and TS; the exclamation point mended from a period in the TS.*

209.9   you] *originally* 'you's'; *the* ' 's' *canceled.*

209.9   nothin'] *originally* 'nothing'; *the apostrophe added above canceled* 'g'.

209.10   'rested] *follows canceled* ' 'e'.

209.13   didn't understand] *follows canceled* 'disobeyed'.

209.14   Why didn't he ask . . . meant?] *interlined with a caret.*

209.28   Henry:] *interlined with a caret above canceled* 'Johnny:'.

209.34   admitted] *follows canceled* 'frankly'.

209.36   warn't] *follows canceled* 'want'.

210.1   nowadays de'] 'de' ' *originally* 'dey'; *the apostrophe added above canceled* 'y'.

210.3   "Me . . . Phyllis.] *interlined above canceled paragraph* 'Converts Number 3. I was pros'; *the* '3' *written over* '2'.

210.4   Two new converts.] *originally* 'Three converts to date.'; 'Two new' *interlined with a caret above canceled* 'Three'; 'to date.' *canceled and the period added after* 'converts'.

210.6   he] *follows canceled* 'sh'.

210.9   insight and judacity,] *interlined with a caret above canceled* 'confidence,'.

210.10   all] *interlined with a caret.*

210.11   long] *interlined with a caret above canceled* 'strange'.

210.12   couldn't cash-in.] *interlined with a caret above canceled* 'lost confidence. Well, anybody would.'

210.12   for instance."] *follows a comma mended from a period and canceled quotation marks.*

210.13   Aunty] *originally* 'Aunt'; *the* 'y' *squeezed in.*

210.14–15   admiring astonishment.] *added following canceled* 'admiration.'

210.23   does] *interlined with a caret above canceled* 'do'.

210.24   mine] *originally* 'mined'; *the* 'd' *canceled.*

210.26   So dah] *follows canceled quotation marks.*

210.29–30   When . . . deserve it."] *originally interlined with a caret to follow* '(Thoughtful pause.)' *with quotation marks preceding* 'When'; *the caret canceled and a new caret inserted following* 'reasonable." '; *then the quotation marks following* 'reasonable.' *and preceding* 'When' *canceled.*

211.2   judgment] *followed by canceled* 'Adam'.

211.7   Jimson] *interlined with a caret above canceled* 'George'.

211.8–9   —stenographer . . . paper—] *interlined with a caret above canceled* 'in the butler line—'.

211.9   visitor] *followed by canceled* 'and fr'.

211.13   emphatic] *interlined with a caret above canceled* 'energetic'.

211.19–20   He . . . others.] *interlined with a caret.*

211.24   or a tadpole—anything] *interlined with a caret above canceled* '—anything'.

211.26   they would pass] *follows canceled* 'say pass'.

211.27   most] *follows canceled* 'som'.

211.27 pleased—such as] *interlined with a caret above canceled* 'pleased, some of them—like'.

211.28 such as buzzards] 'such as' *interlined with a caret above canceled* 'like'.

211.29 such as squids] 'such as' *interlined with a caret above canceled* 'like'.

211.30 reconnizing] *the first* 'n' *interlined with a caret above canceled* 'g'.

211.32 But] *originally began a new paragraph; marked to run on; the preceding quotation marks canceled.*

211.34–35 Nor . . . Christian—] *interlined with a caret following a period added on the line.*

211.35 from now,] *interlined with a caret above a canceled comma.*

212.2 orthography,] *interlined with a caret above canceled* 'spelling,'.

212.3 hastened] *originally* 'hasted'; *the* 'ned' *interlined with a caret above canceled* 'd'.

212.4 the alphabet] *interlined with a caret.*

212.4 even] *interlined with a caret.*

212.14 synagogues and things:] *interlined with a caret above canceled* 'trees.'

212.14–15 'Dinosauriumiguanodon] *the single quotation mark written above canceled double quotation marks.*

212.19 scoops] *follows canceled* 'picks'.

212.24 anyway.] *follows a comma mended from a period.*

212.27 I acknowledge] *interlined with a caret.*

212.28 he registered] *interlined with a caret above canceled* 'he named'.

212.30 Necessarily he] 'Necessarily' *interlined with a caret; the* 'H' *of MS* 'He' *not reduced to* 'h'.

213.2   the other] *follows canceled* 'down'.

213.3   —with a corky squeak—] *interlined with a caret.*

213.8–9   was not.] *originally* 'wasn't.'; 'not.' *interlined with a caret above canceled* 'n't.'

213.15   and give] *follows canceled* 'g'.

213.25   competent.] *followed by canceled* '—anybody knows that.'; *the period added.*

214.1   a gay and girly] 'a' *and* 'and girly' *interlined with carets.*

214.2   for her;] *the semicolon interlined above a canceled exclamation point on the TS.*

214.6   what the bos'n] *follows canceled* 'the Admiral in one way:'.

214.8   nothing by] *followed by canceled* 'starting it.'; *originally* 'starting it yourself.'; 'yourself.' *canceled and the period added after* 'it'.

214.8–13   trying . . . line.] 'trying . . . prays for' *interlined with a caret and* 'the salvation . . . line.' *added on the verso of the MS page with instructions to turn over;* 'again' *interlined with a caret.*

214.18   is what] *follows canceled* 'w'.

214.19   casual] *follows canceled* 'a'.

214.20   He is] 'is' *interlined with a caret above canceled* 'was'.

214.20   That is] 'is' *interlined with a caret above canceled* 'was'.

214.21   manages] *originally* 'managed'; *the* 's' *written over* 'd'.

214.21   likes] *originally* 'liked'; *the* 's' *written over* 'd'.

214.21–22   is disliked] 'is' *interlined with a caret above canceled* 'was'.

214.22   is championing] 'is' *interlined with a caret above canceled* 'was'.

214.24–25   him . . . all,] *interlined with a caret above canceled* 'Satan'.

214.28–29   As . . . difference!] *interlined with a caret.*

214.33   she] *originally 'she'; the italics canceled.*

214.34–35   not because] *'not' interlined with a caret.*

215.1   Creator] *the 'C' written over 'c'.*

215.6   lived] *follows canceled* 'subsisted'.

215.7   consequence,] *originally* 'consequences'; *the 's' canceled and the comma added.*

215.9   a thing] *follows canceled* 'it was'.

215.12   history] *follows canceled* 'youth'.

215.13   she] *interlined with a caret.*

215.14   call was] *followed by canceled* 'probably'.

215.16   she] *interlined with a caret.*

215.19   for the sky] *interlined with a caret above canceled* 'it'; *the comma preceding mended from a semicolon.*

215.19–20   a call . . . would have] *interlined with a caret above canceled* 'an echo has'.

215.20   something] *follows canceled* 'a'.

215.21–23   otherwise . . . not come] 'otherwise . . . call' *interlined and* 'was . . . come' *added on the verso of the MS page with instructions to turn over replacing canceled* 'it would sqwush into air and emptiness, and waste to nothing and be lost; hence the "call" did not come'; 'it' *follows canceled unrecovered word;* 'into' *followed by canceled* 'in'.

215.26   intended] *originally broken at the end of a line;* 'in-|' *followed by canceled* 'tended. Did you mean any harm, Tom Larkin?"
                 ' "No, sir," answered the bos'n respectfully, "I didn't mean any.';* and *canceled* 'tended. We will pass to the next charge."
                 'The marchesa, after denouncing the verdict as being rotten with nepotism furnished it:

' "He said I was so deaf I couldn't read fine print."
'Her face reddened with anger and the thought of it.';
'after . . . nepotism' *interlined with a caret following a*
comma added on the line.

215.28	as being] *follows canceled* 'in severe terms.'
215.30	the Admiral's] *interlined with a caret above canceled* 'his'.
215.30	called him] *follows canceled* 'said,'.
215.30	plainly and squarely] *interlined with a caret.*
215.36	cleared for action and] *interlined with a caret.*
216.4	Admiral's face . . . he] ' 's face . . . he' *interlined with a caret.*
216.7	The bos'n . . . tone—] *interlined.*
216.8–9	distorting my words.] 'distorting my' *interlined with a caret above canceled* 'putting'; 'words.' *followed by canceled* 'in my mouth that I never'; *the period added.*
216.11	away down down] *interlined with a caret. See textual notes.*
216.17	it falls] *follows canceled* 'if'.
216.26	properly recognizable as] *interlined with a caret following interlined and canceled* 'hence'.
216.27	therefore] *follows a canceled ampersand.*
216.28	these] *follows canceled* 'this'.
216.33	probable] *interlined with a caret.*
216.37	him.] *written over a period following* 'understand'.
217.14	here, marcheesa—"] *originally* 'here—" '; *the comma added;* 'marcheesa—" ' *added following canceled* '—" '.
217.15	fire] *followed by canceled* 'd'.
217.16	down] *interlined with a caret.*

217.19   loomed . . . platform] *interlined with a caret above canceled* 'sat there'.

217.21   wailing] *followed by canceled* 'and'.

217.24   lack] *roman in TS; italic in MS.*

217.24   *lack] italic in TS; roman in MS.*

217.30   Lord] *follows canceled* 'The'.

217.30   and there] *followed by a canceled comma.*

218.2   past—] *followed by canceled* 'the defeated, the derelicts!'.

218.2   brooding,] *interlined with a caret.*

218.2   hung,] *followed by canceled* 'brooding,'.

218.6–7   dead-in-hope] '-in-hope' *interlined with a caret.*

218.9   drooped,] *followed by canceled* 'toward the'; *the comma added.*

218.15   four] *interlined with a caret.*

218.18   his life] *follows canceled* 'all that was his is gone,'.

218.19   bankrupt;] *the semicolon mended from a comma.*

218.19   possessions] *follows what appears to be canceled* 'ri'.

218.19   accusing] *interlined with a caret.*

218.20   tear] *interlined with a caret above canceled* 'break'.

218.20   heart!] *followed by canceled* 'These, and one other—'.

218.22   time] *follows canceled* 'T'.

218.29   Aunty] *originally* 'Aunt'; *the* 'y' *squeezed in.*

218.29   humble] *interlined with a caret.*

218.32   investment,] *the comma added.*

218.33   each mistake] *originally* 'the mistakes'; 'each' *interlined with a caret above canceled* 'the'; *the final* 's' *canceled in* 'mistakes'.

218.35   "onlies"] *the quotation marks appear to have been added later.*

218.36–219.1   over it, . . . over it,] *'over it and over it and over it' in the MS; the commas added on the TS.*

219.6   until] *written over an ampersand.*

219.9   walking] *follows a canceled dash.*

219.9–10   to and fro . . . like] *the second and third 'to and fro' follow canceled ampersands.*

219.15   then, oh, then] *originally 'then' in the MS; the italics and a comma added and 'oh, then' interlined with a caret on the TS.*

219.19   was rising] *interlined with a caret.*

219.24   his heart out.] *follows canceled 'out'; 'out.' interlined with a caret above a canceled period.*

219.29   of how] *'of' interlined with a caret.*

220.1   air; drove] *originally 'air. Drove'; the semicolon mended from the period and the 'd' reduced from 'D' on the TS.*

220.7   It's] *the ' 's' interlined.*

220.9–10   the rest about] *originally 'the rest about' in the MS; the typist typed 'about the rest of'; 'about' canceled on the TS by both the typist and Mark Twain. See textual notes.*

220.15   Eve's, too.] *interlined with a caret above canceled 'It'.*

220.16   know] *followed by a canceled comma on the TS.*

220.18   like—] *follows a canceled dash.*

220.18–19   And . . . too.] *interlined with a caret; 'too.' added to the interlineation following a comma mended from a period.*

220.20   They are] *'are' follows canceled 'ha'.*

220.22   stand] *follows canceled 'we'.*

220.24   Nobody.] *followed by canceled* 'If a person naturally
                ain't modest he ain't going to learn it of *them*. Why,
                that's not modesty at all, when you come to look at it—
                it's ostentatiousness. Ostentatiousness of modesty. It's
                a contradiction. You can't be modest and ostentatious
                both at the same time. Modesty is only modesty when
                it ain't *thinking* about it. But if you go and advertise it
                with a fig-leaf, it shows you *are* thinking about it.'

220.25   didn't fuss . . . had it;] *interlined with a caret.*

220.26–27   whereas . . . around.] *added on the verso of the MS page
                with instructions to turn over following a semicolon
                mended from a period.*

220.31   There's] *the* ' 's' *interlined with a caret.*

220.34   fly] *follows canceled* 'louse, then a'.

220.34   cross these] *follows canceled* 'a'.

220.35   all kinds,] 'all' *squeezed in and* 'kinds,' *interlined with a
                caret.*

221.2   plant of amphibiums,] *follows canceled* 'plant of mam-
                mals,'.

221.2–3   which are] *follows canceled* 'such as'.

221.5–6   pterodactyl,] *originally* 'pterodactyle'; *the* 'e' *canceled
                and the comma added.*

221.8   animal life] *follows* 'the accumulated' *interlined with a
                caret; followed by* 'to date' *interlined with a caret.*

221.10   and monkeys] *interlined with a caret.*

221.11   and a mermaid they propagate] *interlined with a caret
                above canceled* 'they get'.

221.27   love] *follows what appears to be canceled* 'lea'.

221.34   who] *follows canceled* 'God bless him,'; *originally*
                'whose'; *the* 'se' *canceled.*

222.6   derelicts] *interlined with a caret above canceled*
                'troubled'.

222.6   by talking] *follows canceled* 'by tell'; *followed by* 'to me' *interlined with a caret.*

222.7   sorrows.] *followed by canceled* 'to me.'; *the period added after* 'sorrows'.

222.8   it is a part] 'it is' *interlined with a caret above a canceled ampersand.*

222.9   that I am] *interlined with a caret above canceled* 'because I am'.

222.10   for grief] *follows canceled* 'and this'.

222.11   a listener's] *follows canceled* 'th'.

222.12   teller,] *the comma replaces a canceled semicolon.*

222.16   About a week ago the] 'About . . . ago' *interlined with a caret; the* 'T' *of MS* 'The' *not reduced to* 't'.

223.9   behind] *interlined with a caret.*

223.12   its official name] *follows canceled* 'its baptismal name'.

223.13   Rev. . . . Wrought] *interlined with a caret above canceled* 'Poet'.

223.20   penitents] *interlined with a caret above canceled* 'repentants'.

223.23   teaching] *originally* 'teachings'; *the* 's' *canceled on the TS.*

223.25–26   Poet: the derelict] *interlined with a caret to replace canceled* 'the Poet; him'.

223.30   gray,] *the comma replaces a canceled semicolon; followed by* 'and that . . . is;' *interlined with a caret.*

223.32   lank and] *interlined with an arrow.*

223.33   Louis Stevenson.] *follows canceled* 'Savanarola looking out of his hood.'

223.35   unaware of it,] *the comma replaces a canceled semicolon.*

223.35   joy of life] *followed by a canceled comma.*

223.35   dance-music] *interlined with a caret above canceled* 'light'.

224.1–2   and distant goal] *follows canceled* 'goal'.

224.2   fixed] *interlined with a caret.*

224.3   it, determined] 'it,' *interlined with a caret.*

224.3   he did] 'he' *interlined with a caret.*

224.4   exultant,] *interlined with a caret above canceled* 'happy,'.

224.5   earth] *followed by canceled* ', there'.

224.7–8   dizzy . . . twenty-eight,] *interlined with a caret above canceled* 'snow-alp,'; 'eight,' *replaces canceled* 'five,' *in the interlineation;* 'snow-' *interlined with a caret.*

224.8   attained:] *the colon replaces a canceled dash.*

224.8   rising] *follows canceled* 're'.

224.10   wonderful] *followed by canceled* 'and gracious'.

224.11   in fancy] *interlined with a caret.*

224.12   great] 'loftiest' *interlined with a caret above canceled typist's error* 'greatest' *on the TS;* 'great' *in the MS. See textual notes.*

224.15   region round about] *interlined with a caret above canceled* 'land'.

224.16   and familiarly] *interlined with a caret above a canceled ampersand.*

224.17   large] *interlined with a caret above canceled* 'national'.

224.18   banquet . . . poem;] 'banquet,' *and* 'and his . . . poem;' *interlined with carets to replace canceled* 'distinguished banquet,'; *the comma following* 'distinguished banquet' *originally a semicolon.*

224.22   He was] *originally run-on; marked to begin a new paragraph with a paragraph sign.*

224.22–23	in the . . . memories,] *interlined with a caret.*
224.24	the mouldering derelict:] *interlined with a caret above canceled* 'he:'.
224.26	it . . . if] *interlined with a caret above canceled* 'I' *followed by* 'I' *squeezed in.*
224.26	and living] *interlined with a caret above canceled* 'body and soul, and lived'.
224.26	How real] *originally* 'Lord, how *real*'; 'Lord,' *canceled; the* 'H' *of* 'How' *mended from* 'h'; *the italics canceled.*
224.30	the faded] *follows canceled* 'my'.
224.32	air] *follows canceled* 'pleasant'.
224.34	Everything] *follows canceled* 'So'.
224.34	going] *interlined with a caret.*
224.35	fruit:] *the colon replaces a canceled dash.*
225.1	before;] *followed by a canceled ampersand; the semicolon squeezed in.*
225.2	even national fame,] *interlined with a caret.*
225.2	wouldn't] *follows canceled* 'didn't s'.
225.3	money,] *interlined with a caret above canceled* 'profit,'.
225.7	by and by] *interlined above canceled* 'presently'.
225.9	fell.] *followed by canceled paragraph* 'I have been concealing something—for a purpose—and will reveal it now, before proceeding. For I am not keeping this Diary for my own reading; I hope for other readers some day. It is from them that I have been concealing two or three details, and now I will put them in.'
225.13	might have] *follows canceled* 's' *and canceled* 'might stand in need of'; *followed by canceled* 'money'.
225.16	poorest] *followed by canceled* 'cardly'.

225.23–24   magazine!] *the exclamation point mended from a pe-*
               riod on the TS.

225.24   had happened] 'had' *interlined with a caret.*

225.26   hasten] *follows canceled* 'hurry'.

225.30   eye] *interlined above canceled* 'own'.

225.31   blandly] *interlined with a caret.*

226.1   is really] 'is' *interlined with a caret.*

226.12–13   the chief's . . . this.] *interlined with a caret to replace
               canceled* 'his cheek.'; 'and' *added to the interlineation
               with a caret above a canceled comma.*

226.17   am so] *follows canceled* 'was so'.

226.18   —and time] *follows a canceled exclamation point.*

226.23   If you will] *follows canceled quotation marks.*

226.23   old wrecked] *interlined with a caret.*

226.27   heavily] *interlined with a caret above canceled* 'greatly'.

226.29   Well,] *follows an ellipsis interlined with a caret; fol-
               lowed by* 'well,' *interlined with a caret.*

226.36   is] *italic in MS and TS.*

227.2–3   It pays . . . live.] *interlined with a caret.*

227.4–5   that this . . . head] *interlined with a caret above can-
               celed* 'this to come to me'.

227.5   life! . . . .] *the ellipsis interlined with a caret.*

227.10   oh, out of] *interlined with a caret above canceled* 'and
               with all'.

227.16   it was] 'it' *written over wiped-out* 'I'.

227.17   I have] *follows canceled* 'Henry,'.

227.17–18   He . . . directors.] *interlined with a caret.*

228.4   you.] *written over a period.*

228.6   He went . . . For] *interlined with a caret above canceled* 'For'.

228.7   at his non-success;] *interlined with a caret above a canceled semicolon.*

228.8   last] *interlined with a caret.*

228.9   money was all gone] *follows canceled* 'last penny was gone'.

228.14   from Australia] *interlined with a caret.*

228.15   Haskell] *interlined with a caret above canceled* 'Halsey, chief editor,'.

228.17   Haskell] *interlined with a caret above canceled* 'Halsey'.

228.29   influential] *follows a canceled ampersand.*

228.30   honored] *follows a canceled ampersand.*

228.30   other,] *followed by canceled* 'presides at the national conventions of the magazine people'; 'the' *preceding* 'national' *interlined with a caret above canceled* 'its'.

228.31   church] *follows canceled* 'pre'.

228.32–33   clasp his head] *interlined with a caret above canceled* 'dash the tears away'.

228.33   hands] *the 's' appears to have been added later.*

228.33   impotently] *interlined with a caret.*

229.2   again] *interlined with a caret.*

229.2   eager] *interlined with a caret above canceled* 'brave'.

229.5   aloft] *followed by a canceled comma.*

229.6   dwindled] *followed by canceled* 'so fa'.

229.7   fading] *interlined with a caret above canceled* 'mighty'.

229.7   I was] *interlined with a caret.*

229.10   that?] *the question mark written over a wiped-out* 'h'.

229.11   contained] *follows canceled* 'concerned'.

229.12   —that was all.] *interlined with a caret following a canceled period.*

229.17   seem to you] 'to you' *interlined with a caret.*

229.18   But] *interlined with a caret to replace canceled* 'to the reader. But' *which was interlined with a caret above a canceled period and canceled* 'But'.

229.19   who made . . . it,] *interlined with a caret above a canceled comma.*

229.19   conquered it] *follows canceled* 'climbed it'.

229.23–24   the average budding hero.] *interlined with a caret above canceled* 'everybody.'

229.25   Yet—toward] 'Yet—' *interlined with a caret; the* 't' *of* 'toward' *mended from* 'T'.

229.25   defeated] *interlined with a caret.*

229.28   loveless] *interlined with a caret.*

229.29   whose faces] 'whose' *mended from* 'whom'; 'faces' *interlined with a caret.*

230.2   members] *follows canceled* 'old Anchor Watch'.

230.5   stay-at-homes] *interlined with a caret above canceled* 'faces'.

230.7   thirty] *interlined with a caret above canceled* 'twenty'.

230.7   drift] *interlined with a caret above canceled* 'come'.

230.8   at . . . another] *interlined with a caret.*

230.10   loaf] *interlined with a caret above canceled* 'drift'.

230.13   two] *interlined with a caret.*

230.13   Members] *followed by a canceled comma.*

230.13–14   and the household,] *interlined with a caret.*

230.14   A . . . chance] *interlined with a caret above canceled* 'Chance'.

230.20   haven't any] *originally* 'have none'; 'n't any' *interlined with a caret above canceled* 'none'.

230.21   to . . . credit.] 'to' *interlined with a caret above canceled* 'for'; 'and . . . credit.' *interlined with a caret above a comma mended from a period.*

230.22   the strangers] *originally* 'them'; *the* 'm' *canceled;* 'strangers' *interlined with a caret.*

230.29   The] *originally* 'There'; *the* 're' *canceled.*

231.3   brisk] *interlined with a caret above canceled* 'lively'.

231.4   flesh-and-blood] *interlined with a caret.*

231.4   day] *interlined with a caret above canceled* 'one'.

231.5   part] *follows canceled* 'a'.

231.10   fellow-feeling—which is] 'feeling—which is' *replaces canceled* 'feeling—that is'.

231.16   She loves] *follows canceled quotation marks.*

231.18   Is that it?"] *added following canceled quotation marks.*

231.21   there's those that saw] *interlined with a caret above canceled* 'I've seen'.

231.23   on . . . floor,] *interlined with a caret.*

231.24   A] *interlined with a caret above canceled* 'The'.

231.25   fire-escape ladders,] *originally* 'fire-escapes, past windows'; 'ladders,' *interlined with a caret above canceled* 's, past windows'.

231.26–27   the crowd cheering; and] *interlined with a caret above a canceled ampersand.*

231.29   watermelon,] *the comma apparently mended from a semicolon.*

231.29–30   her over . . . again,] *interlined with a caret above a canceled comma.*

231.31   ever since,] *interlined with a caret.*

231.31   go] *interlined with a caret above canceled* 'walk'.

231.32   engine] *follows canceled* 'proces'.

231.32   —yes, sir,] 'yes, sir,' *interlined with a caret; the dash written over a period.*

231.33   welcome."] *originally* 'welcome, too." '; ', too." ' *canceled and the quotation marks added after* 'welcome'. *See emendations.*

232.5   a-port!] *interlined with a caret above canceled* 'down!'. *See emendations.*

232.9   though dern seldom] 'though dern' *interlined with a caret;* 'seldom' *followed by canceled* 'as'.

232.16   is fish.] *the period mended from a question mark.*

232.17   Now] *followed by a canceled comma.*

232.18   sunk in righteousness] *interlined with a caret above canceled* 'pious it will leave rat pie to go to Sunday school, and'.

232.21   real] *interlined with a caret.*

232.24   And . . . in] *interlined with a caret above canceled* 'In'.

232.25   he'll] *the* 'll' *written over* 'd'.

232.25   sermon.] *interlined with a caret above canceled* 'Bible.'

232.32   his last cigar] *follows canceled* 'cigars'.

232.32–33   blood—] *the dash appears to be written over a period.*

233.5   as busy] 'as' *interlined with a caret above canceled* 'as'.

233.17   along the road] *interlined with a caret; followed by canceled* 'I'.

233.20   ain't any] *follows canceled* 'any'.

233.25   am,] *followed by canceled* 'that,'; *the comma after* 'am' *added.*

233.29   pretty haughtily.] *follows a canceled period.*

234.1   was] *interlined with a caret above canceled* 'is'.

234.3   the General] *follows canceled* 'other derelicts, such as'.

234.3   inventor] *interlined with a caret on the TS; originally a space left blank on the MS.*

234.5   mere] *interlined with a caret.*

234.6   a matter] 'a' *interlined with a caret.*

234.10   Aunt Phyllis] *follows canceled* 'and became friend and comrade to'.

234.12–13   continued . . . opportunity.] *added following canceled* 'never ceased from debating it.'

234.16   two] *written over* 'a'.

234.18   as . . . decade,] *interlined with a caret above canceled* 'a good many years,'.

234.22   a pair of] *interlined with a caret above canceled* 'some'.

234.24   years.] *follows canceled* 'or three y'.

234.25   young and nervous,] *interlined with a caret above canceled* 'new,'.

234.29–30   a curtain of] *interlined with a caret.*

235.2   soon] *interlined with a caret.*

235.3   then the dust] 'then' *interlined with a caret.*

235.8   racing] *interlined with a caret above canceled* 'flying'.

235.10   sharp] *interlined with a caret.*

235.11   dim] *originally* 'dimly'; *the* 'ly' *canceled.*

235.12   its head] 'its' *interlined with a caret above canceled* 'his'.

235.14   yet] *interlined with a caret above canceled* 'but'.

235.21   flying] *interlined with a caret.*

235.25   matter, it] 'it' *interlined with a caret above canceled* 'the feat'.

235.28   the incredible thing] *interlined with a caret above canceled* 'the miracle'.

235.29   there was] *followed by canceled* 'w'.

235.29   nor] *originally* 'or'; *the* 'n' *interlined with a caret on the TS.*

235.29–30   in . . . about] *interlined with a caret.*

235.34   'Rastus had] ' 'Rastus' *interlined with a caret above canceled* 'he' *on the TS.*

236.2   idea] *originally* 'idear'; *the* 'r' *canceled.*

236.4   brains?] *interlined with a caret above canceled* 'mine?'.

236.6   brains,] *interlined above canceled* 'mine,'.

236.8   mind] *the* 'd' *written over an* 'e'.

236.12   eight] *interlined with a caret above canceled* 'two'.

236.19   han's?"] *interlined with a caret above canceled* 'hads?" ';
                  originally 'hands? Dat you done'; *the* 'n' *in* 'hands' *canceled;* 'Dat you done' *canceled and quotation marks added after* 'hads?'.

236.21–22   can't . . . can't] *originally* 'cain't . . . cain't'; *each* 'i' *canceled on the TS.*

236.21   git] *follows what appears to be a canceled* 'm' *or* 'w'.

236.24–25   thousan' dollars] *interlined above canceled* 'money'.

236.34   bawn] *the* 'aw' *appears to be written over* 'or'.

237.2   fifty] *interlined with a caret above canceled* 'sixty'.

237.14–15   lady's clo'es wuth] *originally* 'lady wuth'; *the* ' 's' *interlined;* 'clo'es wuth' *added following canceled* 'wuth'.

237.17   hund'd en] *originally* 'hund'd an'; *the* 'e' *written over* 'a'.

237.19   clo'es.] *the period replaces a canceled exclamation point on the TS.*

237.31   fo'git] *followed by a canceled comma.*

237.31   'bout it.] *the period replaces a canceled question mark.*

237.36   me o' gittin'] *follows an unrecovered canceled letter.*

238.10   pennies] *followed by canceled* ', he made'.

238.15   and has had] *interlined with a caret above canceled* 'with'.

238.16   here and] *interlined with a caret on the TS.*

238.18   thirty] *interlined with a caret above canceled* 'eighty'.

238.19–20   prosperous] *interlined with a caret.*

238.29   exackly at de] *originally* 'exactly at der'; *the* 'k' *mended from the* 't'; *the* 'r' *of* 'der' *canceled.*

238.30   kin!] *the exclamation point mended from a question mark.*

238.31   hoss] *italic in MS and TS.*

238.31   blame'] *interlined with a caret.*

238.32   fashion?] *the question mark appears to be mended from an exclamation point.*

239.1   of interest] *interlined with a caret.*

239.4   Secretary] *the* 'S' *written over* 's'.

239.12   anyway,] *interlined with a caret.*

239.12–13   and hear . . . us.] *follows a comma mended from a period;* 'utter . . . us.' *interlined.*

239.17   but as it is] *interlined with a caret.*

239.21–22   several years] *interlined with a caret above canceled* 'a year or two'.

240.2   all] *interlined with a caret.*

240.7   whereas] *interlined with a caret.*

240.7   many] *interlined with a caret above canceled* 'all'.

240.11   studied] *follows a canceled ampersand.*

240.26   for he] *follows canceled* 'he'.

241.11   them] *interlined with a caret above canceled* 'the maids'.

241.16   There's] *the* 'T' *appears to be mended from* 't'.

241.25–26   and sat] 'and' *interlined with a caret.*

241.31   fortnight] *written over* 'w'.

241.32   a speech] 'a' *interlined with a caret above what appears to be canceled* 'an'.

241.33   and meantime he] *interlined with a caret above a canceled ampersand.*

241.37   returned] *follows what may be canceled* 'look' *or* 'took'.

242.8   himself to her.] 'to' *followed by a canceled caret.*

242.9   new] *squeezed in with a caret.*

242.26   territories] *originally* 'territories'; *the* 't' *mended to* 'T' *Emended for consistency.*

242.32   other] *interlined with a caret.*

242.36–243.1   the convention.] *interlined with a caret above canceled* 'the place.'

243.8   the State assumed command,] *interlined with a caret above a canceled comma.*

243.11   recklessly] *interlined with a caret.*

243.12–14   Poor . . . prudence.] *added on the verso of the MS page with instructions to turn over.*

243.14–15   Garvey's] *interlined with a caret to replace canceled* 'his'.

243.20   After that, he] 'After that,' *interlined with a caret; the* 'H' *of MS* 'He' *not reduced to* 'h'.

243.20   care for,] *followed by canceled* 'then,'; *the comma added.*

243.22   he had had] *the first* 'had' *interlined with a caret.*

243.26   job] *originally* 'jobs'; *the* 's' *canceled.*

243.28   for . . . sympathisers,] *interlined with a caret following a*
                comma added on the line.

243.32–33   Secretaryship] *follows canceled* 'Sta'.

243.36   sorrow] *followed by a canceled comma.*

244.1   and faithful] 'and' *interlined with a caret.*

244.6   By] *the* 'B' *mended from* 'b' *following a canceled dash.*

244.10   Duff] *follows canceled* 'Plum'.

244.15   welcome] *mended from* 'well'.

244.21–22   "The . . . Nature."] *interlined with a caret above can-*
                celed ' "The Goodness of Providence." '

245.7–8   our . . . Nature's] *interlined with a caret above canceled*
                'the Creator's'.

245.8   her creatures] 'her' *mended from* 'his'.

245.8–9   from the highest] *interlined with a caret above canceled*
                'from man the majestic, the noble'.

245.10   dwelt at some length] *interlined with a caret above can-*
                celed 'remarked'.

245.10–11   her unfailing] 'her' *interlined with a caret above can-*
                celed 'the Creator's'.

245.11   her wards] 'her' *interlined with a caret above canceled*
                'His'.

245.11   wished] *the* 'd' *written over* 's'.

245.12   her intricate] 'her' *interlined to replace* 'His' *interlined*
                with a caret above canceled 'the Creator's'.

245.13   her selection] 'her' *interlined with a caret above can-*
                celed 'His'.

245.14   placing] *follows canceled* 'her' *interlined with a caret*
                above canceled 'His'.

245.15   Her tender] 'Her' *interlined with a caret following can-*
              celed 'Nothing was truer, he said, than the text which
              proclaimed that not even a sparrow could fall to the
              ground without the Creator's notice; no, His'; *the* 'H'
              of 'His' *mended from* 'h'.

245.15   he said,] *interlined with a caret following a comma*
              added on the line.

245.17   her watchful] 'her' *interlined with a caret above can-*
              celed 'His'.

245.17   her loving] 'her' *interlined with a caret above canceled*
              'His'.

245.28   to read] *interlined with a caret above canceled* 'the
              story:'. *See emendations.*

245.30   she] *interlined with a caret.*

245.31–33   dear . . . beautiful—] 'dear Mother Nature' *interlined*
              above canceled 'good Providence'; 'that . . . beautiful—'
              added on the verso of the MS page with instructions to
              turn over to replace canceled 'that protected her from
              harm, watched lovingly over her in the day and in the
              night, and made her little life sweet and beautiful—'.

246.2   hairy fat] *interlined with a caret above canceled* 'hairy
              fat'.

246.4   start,] *followed by canceled* 'slightly,'; *the comma added.*

246.7   lonely] *follows canceled* 'very'.

246.7–8   her young husband,] *interlined with a caret.*

246.8   fondly] *interlined with a caret.*

246.13   toward foreign parts.] *added following a canceled pe-*
              riod.

246.15–16   dropping] *interlined with a caret to replace canceled*
              'lifting'.

246.16   meekly,] *followed by canceled* 'aloft,'; *the comma added.*

246.16   "Our . . . will] *interlined with carets to replace canceled*
              ' "the Lord will'.

246.18   A . . . eyes.] *interlined with a caret.*

246.19   broke] *follows canceled* 'made'.

246.21   and began to suck] *interlined with a caret.*

246.21   a way] 'a' *originally* 'an'; *the* 'n' *canceled.*

246.23   sight] *interlined with a caret above canceled* 'horror'.

246.23–24   There . . . moment.] *added on the verso of the MS page
              with instructions to turn over;* 'lasted' *follows canceled*
              'bro'.

246.30   family.] *the period replaces a canceled dash.*

246.33   rapture] *originally* 'raptured'; *the* 'd' *canceled.*

246.35   frisky] *followed by canceled* 'and squirmy'.

246.35   horseflies—] *interlined with a caret above canceled*
              'houseflies—'.

247.2   and her body] *interlined with a caret.*

247.6   little darlings] *follows canceled* 'precious' *and canceled*
              'dear'.

247.6   "Nature] *interlined with a caret above canceled* ' "He'.

247.9   and imitate it] 'imitate it' *interlined with a caret;* 'and'
              added on the line.

247.10–11   and believe . . . ones.] *squeezed in following canceled*
              'and say with her, "He will provide" for our little ones,
              then wait in confidence for the result.'; 'provide' *fol-
              lowed by a canceled comma;* 'for our little ones,' *inter-
              lined with a caret; an instruction to turn over interlined
              with a caret and canceled above the cancellation.*

247.14–15   offspring.] *followed by canceled* 'Her heart was light,
              for she had placed her trust where trust never fails,
              where confidence is never betrayed.'

247.16   "Nature] *interlined with a caret above canceled* ' "He'.

247.19–20   struggling mother-spider] *follows canceled* 'mo'.

247.20   body.] *the period replaces a canceled dash.*

247.21   The audience] *originally began a new paragraph; marked to run on.*

247.22–23   and the spider . . . agony,] *added on the verso of the MS page with instructions to turn over.*

247.25   my friends,] *interlined with a caret.*

247.28   spider's] *follows canceled* 'was'.

247.28   her prey] *interlined with a caret above canceled* 'it'.

247.30   which] *written over an ampersand.*

247.31   at hand] *interlined with a caret.*

247.33   hymn] *interlined with a caret above canceled* 'prayer'.

247.33   kind and] *interlined with a caret above canceled* 'the'.

247.33   Nature, who] *interlined with carets to replace canceled* 'Providence that'.

247.34   her children] 'her' *interlined with a caret above canceled* 'its'.

247.35   wept—] *the dash written over a period.*

247.36   revolting] *interlined with a caret to replace canceled* 'terrible' *which was interlined with a caret above canceled* 'frightful'.

248.1   its way,] *interlined with a caret above a canceled ampersand.*

248.1–2   into the spider's vitals] *originally* 'in the'; 'the' *canceled*; 'into' *mended from* 'in'; 'the spider's vitals' *squeezed in; followed by canceled* 'through a ragged and slimy hole you could put your fist in,'; 'through' *interlined with a caret.*

248.2   legs] *followed by a canceled comma.*

248.3   sentiment] *interlined with a caret above canceled* 'prayer'.

248.6   she] *interlined with a caret to replace canceled* 'the sparrow that falls to the ground'.

248.8   faith,] *interlined with a caret above canceled* 'trust,'.

248.11   a contented . . . cheerfully] *interlined with a caret above canceled* 'the faith and'.

248.12   their sphere. I] *interlined with a caret above canceled* 'this our beautiful world. I'.

248.21   ways] *follows canceled* 'intelligent'.

248.26   of . . . Nature.] *interlined with a caret above canceled* 'of the goodness of Providence.'

"You've Been a Dam Fool, Mary. You Always Was!"

Textual Commentary

The manuscript is copy-text.

Textual Notes

251.3   smithy] The manuscript is torn, obliterating the "ithy."
                 Dixon Wecter's typescript conjecture has been followed
                 in supplying what must have been Mark Twain's in-
                 tention.

253.4–15   The men . . . tragedy.] This passage, corresponding to
                 manuscript p. 7, was apparently written out of sequence.
                 At the bottom of manuscript p. 6, after "pay up!" Mark
                 Twain wrote and canceled "(SKIP 2 pages—to p. 9)";
                 the present manuscript p. 8 is blank, and on its verso is
                 a canceled Mark Twain note, "7 & 8 (to be written)."

260.title   Chapter 3] In the top left corner of the manuscript page
                 beginning here, Mark Twain wrote "worry" and below
                 it "concerning," both in purplish-blue ink.

261.37–262.1   Carlina] Mark Twain may have left out the "o" of
                 "Carolina" by mistake, but since he may have intended
                 a dialect spelling the omission has been preserved.

269.6   There] In the top left corner of the manuscript page be-
                 ginning here, Mark Twain wrote a note in pencil: "Go
                 back & make it $8000 to Tom." He then wrote a "4"
                 over the "8."

Emendations of the Copy-Text

	MTP READING	COPY-TEXT READING
*251.3	smithy	sm[*page torn*]

	MTP Reading	Copy-Text Reading
251.5–6	storekeeper	store-keeper
252.23	considering	considing
252.29	allow	allow.
†253.28	he wasn't	He wasn't
254.19	'call	call
255.27	too	two
259.25	a-worshiping	a worshiping
†259.36	it'll	It'll
260.25	cost	caused
261.1	recognized	recognised
†261.8	parlor—	parlor,—
262.2	Great	great
262.29	Good-bye	Good bye
†265.21	worth	Worth
267.6	it's nobby	its nobby
272.3	was just a	was a just a
272.24	gentlemen?	gentlemen.
276.28	bet'—and I didn't.	bet—and I didn't.'
277.4	bottle'—	bottle—
277.12	of—	of
277.31	*Marsh,*	*Marsh*

Word Division in the Copy-Text

252.35–36	good-hearted
253.18	postmark
255.37	behind-hand
259.2	a-listening

262.33   window-shade
269.22   hand-shake

Mark Twain's Revisions

Written in dark blue ink through 262.32

251.2   houses] *follows 'dwelling' interlined with a caret then
                canceled.*

251.6   twenty-three] 'three' *interlined with a caret in purplish-
                blue ink replacing canceled* 'five' *here and at* 251.8.

251.9   a day] *interlined with a caret in purplish-blue ink above
                canceled* 'ten minutes'.

251.12–13   commands . . . around, and] *added on the verso of the
                MS page with instructions to turn over.*

251.14–15   of newly-inherited] *interlined with a caret in purplish-
                blue ink.*

251.18–19   sudden,] *follows canceled* 'sudden, considering'.

252.16   that] *interlined with a caret above canceled* 'who'.

252.18   was quiet] *follows a canceled comma.*

252.21   three] *interlined with a caret in purplish-blue ink above
                canceled* 'two'.

252.25   Tom. I] *interlined above canceled* 'Jimmy, I'.

252.29   reckon] *interlined with a caret in purplish-blue ink above
                canceled* 'guess'.

252.29   yourself—] *the dash written over a comma.*

252.35   old] *follows canceled* 'dear'.

253.3   now] *the italics added in purplish-blue ink.*

253.4–15   The men . . . tragedy.] *added on an inserted MS page.
                See textual notes.*

253.5   to] *written over a wiped-out* 'f'.

253.7   Marsh] *follows canceled* 'Hill'.

253.8   then] *interlined with a caret.*

253.10   start] *followed by a canceled comma.*

253.11   new.] *followed by* 'Or I'll send your half to you—which-
                    ever you'll think best at the time.' *added in purplish-
                    blue ink then canceled.*

253.12   t'morrer,] *interlined with a caret above canceled* 'in de
                    mawnin' '.

253.14   and more] *interlined with a caret.*

253.16   They ... last.] *interlined in purplish-blue ink above can-
                    celed* 'Several years went by.'

253.17–18   addressed ... and] *interlined with a caret.*

253.19   in Connecticut.] *interlined with a caret in purplish-blue
                    ink above a canceled period.*

253.19   Marsh, the] *interlined with a caret following canceled*
                    'the'.

253.22   Hill's] *the apostrophe and* 's' *added above a canceled
                    comma.*

253.27–28   When ... here he] 'When ... here' *interlined with a
                    caret in purplish-blue ink; the* 'H' *of MS* 'He' *not re-
                    duced to* 'h'.

254.9   money-account] 'account' *interlined with a caret in
                    purplish-blue ink above canceled* 'difference'.

254.9   my!] *followed by* 'land!' *canceled in purplish-blue ink;
                    the exclamation point added.*

255.4   and conscientiously—] *added in purplish-blue ink.*

255.33   *Say*] *the italics added in purplish-blue ink.*

256.13   though?] *followed by canceled quotation marks.*

256.16   *Jimmy?*] *the italics added in purplish-blue ink.*

256.19   it] *interlined with a caret in purplish-blue ink following canceled* 'they'.

256.26   a . . . excited] *originally* 'an excited'; 'a searching and' *interlined with a caret before* 'an'; *then* 'and' *canceled and* 'd' *added to* 'an'.

256.30   case.] 'case' *followed by canceled* ', with the manner of one'; *the period added.*

256.36   Sam] *interlined with a caret.*

257.10–11   arrived— . . . reckon—] *the dashes interlined with carets, the first above a canceled semicolon.*

257.12   in . . . little,] *added on the verso of the MS page with instructions to turn over; replaces* 'with a holy Christian lie' *interlined with a caret then canceled on the recto.*

257.12   actual facts] *follows canceled* 'fa'.

257.13   White] *the italics added in purplish-blue ink.*

257.13   hair] *follows canceled* 'shirt'.

257.20   the] *originally* 'them'; *the* 'm' *canceled.*

257.22   and talked about] 'and talked' *interlined with a caret.*

257.25   lawyer] *interlined with a caret above canceled* 'Presbyterian'.

257.25–27   so . . . I] *added on the verso of the MS page with instructions to turn over, replacing canceled* 'so they was full of reconcilement, being Campbellites, and I' *on the recto;* 'reconcilement,' *follows canceled* 'resi' *and is followed by canceled* 'sympathy,'.

257.32   best] 'handsomest' *interlined above* 'best' *then canceled.*

257.32   one] *followed by* ', which I reckon was old Mis' White's,' *interlined with a caret then canceled.*

257.37   debbuty, and] *interlined with a caret in purplish-blue ink above canceled* 'debuty, and'.

258.1   respected.] *followed by canceled quotation marks.*

258.1   *Say*] *the italics added in purplish-blue ink.*

258.3   envelops.] *followed by canceled* 'From one of'.

258.4   written] *followed by a canceled comma.*

258.5   roman capitals.] *interlined with a caret in purplish-blue ink above a canceled period.*

258.18   certainly] *follows canceled* 'ther'.

258.26   who read it.] *added following a comma written over a period.*

259.16   reverent] *originally* 'reverential'; 'ial' *canceled in black ink.*

259.18   Samson,] *interlined with a caret.*

259.24   trembled] *interlined with a caret above canceled* 'broke'.

259.30   it'll . . . circus!] *interlined with a caret above canceled* 'it's better'n a circus!'.

259.32   shirt—"] *the dash and quotation marks interlined with a caret in purplish-blue ink above canceled* 'or a last coat—" '.

259.35   vendue] *the first* 'e' *canceled and* 'a' *interlined above it in purplish-blue ink; then the* 'a' *canceled and the* 'e' *restored.*

259.36   My, it'll] 'My,' *interlined with a caret in purplish-blue ink; the* 'I' *of MS* 'It'll' *not reduced to* 'i'.

259.36   be] *follows* 'just' *canceled in purplish-blue ink.*

259.37   or three] *interlined with a caret.*

259.37   on the way,] *interlined with a caret in purplish-blue ink.*

260.1   Hill—] *the dash written over a comma.*

260.2   degree.] *followed by canceled* 'Samson'.

260.3   Marsh] *followed by canceled* 'had'.

260.7   by . . . his] *interlined with a caret in purplish-blue ink*
                 following canceled 'by his'.

260.9   was reported] 'was' *interlined with a caret in purplish-*
                 blue ink.

260.11   years] *interlined with a caret.*

260.14–15   underhand] *interlined with a caret in purplish-blue ink.*

260.17   now,] *interlined with a caret in purplish-blue ink.*

260.18–19   poor thing,] *interlined with a caret; the preceding com-*
                 ma added.

260.20   gilded] *interlined with a caret.*

260.26   wily strategist,] *interlined with a caret; the preceding*
                 comma added.

260.31   aspect] *interlined with a caret in purplish-blue ink above*
                 canceled 'look'.

261.8–9   —where . . . waiting—] *interlined with a caret in pur-*
                 plish-blue ink; the second dash written over a comma; a
                 comma after 'parlor' *inadvertently left standing.*

261.11–13   "Don't . . . Uncle . . . "Set] *marked to begin new para-*
                 graphs with paragraph signs in purplish-blue ink.

261.20   vandue] *originally* 'vendue'; 'a' *interlined above can-*
                 celed 'e' *in purplish-blue ink.*

261.21–22   without] *follows canceled* 'unless'.

261.31   do!"] *the exclamation point written over a comma.*

261.34–35   me and you] *follows canceled* 'you and'.

262.10–11   *The vandue . . . to-morrow.*] 'The . . . on.' *interlined*
                 with a caret in dark blue ink; ', to-morrow.' *added to the*
                 interlineation in purplish-blue ink; the comma written
                 over the period.

262.27   sobbing,] *followed by* 'a moment or two,' *canceled in*
                 black ink.

Written in purplish-blue ink from 262.33 through 277.26

262.33   him] *followed by a canceled comma.*

263.1   dear,] *interlined with a caret.*

263.9   know] *followed by canceled* 'that'.

263.11   came in presently and] *interlined with a caret.*

263.27   three hundred] *interlined with a caret above canceled* 'fortune'.

263.30   they . . . concert.] *interlined above canceled* 'she required it of him.'

263.31   help] *interlined with a caret.*

263.32   charmed] *interlined with a caret above canceled* 'delighted'.

264.1   During . . . afternoon] *originally* 'The afternoon of the day before the date appointed for the vendue'; 'of the . . . vendue' *canceled;* 'In' *added preceding* 'The'; *then* 'In The' *canceled and* 'During that same' *interlined with a caret.*

264.3   —gathering information.] *interlined with a caret above a canceled period.*

264.9   then] *squeezed in at the end of a line.*

264.15   look] *followed by canceled* 'my'.

264.16   me!"] *followed by canceled* 'old pal!" '; *the present exclamation point and quotation marks replace a canceled comma.*

264.18–19   this long time?] *originally* 'these years?'; 'i' *written over the first* 'e'; *the second* 'e' *canceled;* 'long time?' *interlined with a caret above canceled* 'years?'.

264.20   Jimmy?] *interlined with a caret above canceled* 'boys?'.

264.21–23   "I said . . . is] *added on the verso of the MS page with instructions to turn over; replaces canceled* ' "would you, Billy?" ' *and canceled paragraph* ' "Yes, and gilded to boot! Say—is' *on the MS page following.*

264.23   is] *follows a canceled dash.*

264.29   dispatched] *interlined with a caret above canceled* 'devoured'.

265.5   won't we?"] *follows canceled* 'lad." '

265.6   us.] *followed by canceled quotation marks.*

265.14   "No] *the* 'N' *written over a* 'Y'.

265.17   in] *interlined with a caret above canceled* 'in joy and'.

265.17   Samson] *interlined with a caret.*

265.17   immense—] *interlined with a caret above canceled* 'grand—it'.

265.19–20   splendidly . . . dramatic."] *interlined with a caret above canceled* 'perfectly splendid." '

265.21   Brer] *follows canceled* 'gay,'; *the comma preceding added.*

265.21   He's worth] 'He's' *interlined with a caret; the* 'W' *of MS* 'Worth' *not reduced to* 'w'.

265.21   upwards] *follows canceled* 'four'.

265.21   two] *interlined with a caret in pencil above canceled* 'four'.

265.23   hasn't] *followed by canceled* 'got a'.

265.25   do you sup—"] *added following canceled dash and quotation marks.*

265.29   night] *follows canceled* 'gaudy'.

265.30   Marsh] *follows canceled* 'Brer'.

265.31   "Indeed we do,] *interlined with a caret above canceled* ' "You bet your life,'.

266.1   disappeared,] *interlined with a caret above canceled* 'slipped out,'.

266.1–2   —hidden . . . place—] *interlined with a caret.*

266.6   blacksmithing] *follows canceled* 'an'.

266.7   boom] *followed by canceled* 'this'.

266.7   promising] *interlined with a caret above canceled* 'grand'.

266.8   the . . . now,] *interlined with a caret.*

266.9   dollars.] *followed by canceled paragraph* 'Then they finished the night and the whisky in repeatedly and joyously drinking success to the vendue.'

266.10   hilarity] *interlined with a caret above canceled* 'cheerfulness'.

266.12   there . . . hurry,] *interlined with a caret.*

266.35   Trust] *the* 'T' *written over a wiped-out* 'f'.

267.1   certainly,] *interlined with a caret.*

267.3   dim] *interlined with a caret above canceled* 'sickly'.

267.8   exclaimed] *follows canceled* 'said'.

267.14   it.] *followed by* 'Jimmy.' *interlined with a caret then canceled; the period mended to a comma, then mended back to a period.*

267.15   Jimmy,] *interlined with a caret in dark blue ink above* 'Jimmy,' *canceled in purplish-blue ink.*

268.1   "Billionaires?"] *squeezed in at the foot of the MS page in dark blue ink below canceled* ' "Missionaries?" '.

268.2   "Sho!"] *interlined in dark blue ink above* ' "Idiot!" ' *written in purplish-blue ink and canceled in dark blue ink;* ' "Idiot!" ' *had replaced* ' "Shucks!" ' *canceled in purplish-blue ink.*

268.5   "No—do] *follows canceled* ' "Do'.

268.11–12   but . . . Look] *canceled on the recto of the MS page in dark blue ink, then reinscribed on the verso in dark blue ink with instructions to turn over.*

268.16   "That] *follows canceled paragraph* ' "That in his turn he
           helps *them.* You know that'; *canceled quotation marks
           follow* 'them.'

268.22   "I . . . will."] *interlined with a caret above canceled*
           ' "Lord, but won't he!" '.

268.23   gaudiest] *interlined with a caret in dark blue ink above
           canceled* 'nobbiest'.

268.25   nobby.] *interlined with a caret in dark blue ink above
           canceled* 'bully.'

268.32   know,] *followed by canceled* '—but'.

268.34   of course—where] *interlined with a caret above can-
           celed* 'where'.

269.3   it] *followed by canceled* ', you'.

269.4   two] *interlined with a caret in pencil above canceled*
           'four'.

269.5   Get] *follows canceled quotation marks.*

269.6   There] *follows canceled paragraph* 'The response was
           the contented gurgle of a long-continued chuckle from
           the direction of Marsh's shake-down.'

269.8   Then] *interlined with a caret in dark blue ink.*

269.11   had] *interlined with a caret.*

269.16   and worried] *follows a canceled comma.*

269.20–21 At least . . . fervently.] *squeezed in following canceled
           quotation marks.*

269.27   bet] *originally* 'been'; *the* 't' *written over wiped-out* 'en'.

270.3   difficult] *interlined with a caret above canceled* 'giant'.

270.6   said . . . anxiously—] *interlined with a caret in dark blue
           ink above canceled* 'whispered in his ear—'.

270.8–9   our friends] *follows canceled* 'f'.

270.25   gently] *interlined with a caret.*

270.26	and poor] *follows canceled* 'and is'.
270.27	negro] *originally* 'nigro'; *the* 'e' *written over* 'i'.
271.2	were] *interlined with a caret above canceled* 'was'.
271.7	eagerly] *interlined with a caret.*
271.14	she'll] *follows canceled* 'where's your Standard'.
271.23	smithy.] *followed by canceled* 'and seated.'; *the present period written over a comma.*
271.25	Hall.] *followed by canceled* 'Mary'.
271.26	Mary] *interlined with a caret following canceled* 'her admiringly and expectantly at her'.
271.34	art . . . been] *interlined with a caret above canceled* 'art'.
271.35	which] *interlined with a caret.*
271.36–37	admire] *follows canceled* 'be sufficiently untranquillized by it to remember it.'
271.37	He] *followed by canceled* 'could'.
272.8	time,] *followed by canceled quotation marks; the comma mended from a period.*
272.21	came] *the* 'a' *interlined above canceled* 'o'.
272.22	pure] *interlined with a caret above canceled* 'sweet'.
272.25	"Five] *written over wiped-out* ' "Two'.
272.34	the rise] *interlined with a caret above canceled* 'it'.
273.19	In . . . out—] *added on the verso of the MS page with instructions to turn over.*
273.20	"Fifty!"] *added on the verso of the MS page in dark blue ink;* ' "Fif—" ' *and* ' "Fifty!" ' *canceled in dark blue ink on the recto.*
273.27	excited—] *follows a canceled dash.*
273.34	electrified] *interlined with a caret above canceled* 'ennobled'.

274.24   "and I] *interlined with a caret above canceled quotation
              marks.*

274.25   anvil,] *interlined with a caret above canceled* 'plant,'.

274.29   government] *interlined with a caret.*

274.36   I've] *interlined with a caret.*

274.37   just] *interlined with a caret.*

275.4   Nine] *interlined with a caret above canceled* 'Seven'.

275.4–5   nine, going at nine,] 'nine,' *interlined with a caret above
              canceled* 'seven,' *twice.*

275.11   "Three] *interlined in black ink above canceled* ' "Two'.

275.11   shouted Marsh.] *interlined with a caret in black ink; the
              preceding and following quotation marks added.*

275.15   auctioneer,] *followed by a canceled dash.*

275.25   "Yes!] *the exclamation point written over a comma in
              dark blue ink; followed by* 'I do!' *canceled in dark blue
              ink.*

275.28   great] *followed by canceled* 'high'.

275.32   Six] *the italics added in black ink.*

275.33   mud!"] *interlined with a caret in dark blue ink preced-
              ing canceled* 'money!" '.

276.2   provoked] *follows canceled* 'was'.

276.5   see] *followed by canceled* 'it is familiar'.

276.11   in,] *interlined with a caret.*

276.14   true,] *interlined with a caret.*

276.19   at last] *follows canceled* 'always'.

276.22   first] *the italics added in dark blue ink.*

276.24   (Laughter.)] *interlined with a caret.*

276.26   to myself,] *interlined with a caret.*

276.28   I didn't care] 'I didn't' *interlined with a caret in dark blue ink above canceled* 'I don't'.

276.29   square] *follows canceled* 'a'; *followed by canceled* 'game'.

276.34   A month] *follows canceled* 'The'.

276.37   found him.] *followed by canceled* 'I brought his half of the winnings along with me'.

277.2   for fun] *interlined with a caret.*

277.4   what] *follows canceled* 'just'.

277.7   half of the] *interlined with a caret.*

277.8   bonds,] *followed by a canceled dash.*

277.12   cries] *follows canceled* 'there'.

277.21   me;] *interlined above canceled* 'you;'.

Written in dark blue ink from 277.27 to the end

277.27   hardly contains a] *originally* 'contains no'; 'hardly' *interlined with a caret*; 'a' *interlined with a caret above canceled* 'no'.

277.29   persons] *interlined with a caret.*

277.29   for . . . known—] *interlined with a caret above a canceled dash.*

277.32   follow,] *interlined with a caret above canceled* 'use,'.

278.10   Mr. Hand] *interlined with a caret.*

278.11   the] *written over* 'an'.

278.13   his fund] *follows canceled* 'lived to see'.

Newhouse's Jew Story

Textual Commentary

The manuscript is copy-text. Page numbers, discussed in the headnote, indicate that the story was probably detached from a longer manuscript.

Textual Notes

280.title	Newhouse's Jew Story] "Newhouse's (Jew) Story" was added to the manuscript as a working title by Mark Twain.
280.1–2	There . . . nevertheless.] The first sentence was once canceled in pencil. Since both Mark Twain and Paine used pencil on the manuscript, it is impossible to tell who canceled the sentence or who erased the canceling line. The cancellation and two revisions in the sentence which are clearly Paine's may have been made because the story was extracted from a longer work. The sentence begins without a paragraph indentation and presumably continued a paragraph on the lost page which preceded it. Paine changed "was" to "is" to smooth the abruptness of the beginning and altered "had value" to "seems worthwhile."

Emendations of the Copy-Text

	MTP READING	COPY-TEXT READING
*280.title	Jew	(Jew)
281.8	bowie-knives	bowie knives
†281.11	at	At
281.34	toothpick	tooth-pick

Word Division in the Copy-Text

281.13	mud-clerk
281.23	maid-servant

Mark Twain's Revisions

Written in faded black ink

280.2   1860.] '60' *mended from* '58' *in black ink.*

280.3   *Child] followed by a canceled comma.*

280.4   George] *follows* 'Mr.' *canceled in black ink.*

280.6   pleasure trip] 'trip' *interlined with a caret in black ink above canceled* 'excursion'.

280.7   and practice] *interlined with a caret in black ink.*

280.10   Newhouse . . . place.] 'house . . . place.' *added in black ink replacing canceled* 'house was a kindly and amiable old gentleman, but he turned straight on the man and ordered him out of the pilot house. That was a surprising thing, and so'.

280.12   he was.] *follows canceled* 'he was—and all for the sake'.

280.12   This, he said,] *the comma added after* 'This'; 'he said,' *interlined with a caret.*

280.13   in memory] *follows canceled* 'he said'.

280.13   then his] *interlined with a caret above canceled* 'presently his' *in black ink.*

280.21   their] *originally* 'there'; *the* 'i' *added and* 'e' *canceled in black ink.*

280.22   the] *originally* 'they'; *the* 'y' *canceled.*

280.22   and his] *follows canceled* 'and his officers were afraid of them'.

281.4   not] *originally* 'no'; *the* 't' *added in black ink.*

281.8   As a] *follows canceled* 'That'.

281.9   it] *interlined with a caret.*

281.11   Now and then at] 'Now and then' *interlined with a caret;
             the* 'A' *of MS* 'At' *not reduced to* 'a'.

281.11   terms.] 'terms' *followed by canceled* '; these men'; *the
             period added.*

281.15   the rich . . . planter,] *interlined with a caret.*

281.18   out of] *interlined with a caret above canceled* 'upon'.

281.20   and the] 'the' *originally* 'then' *or possibly* 'they'; *the final
             letter wiped out.*

281.32   at] *the* 'a' *written over the beginning of an ampersand.*

281.34   went on] *follows canceled* 'merely'.

282.1   she swept] *follows canceled* 'she swept thr'.

282.4   part with] *interlined with a caret above canceled* 'see'
             in black ink.

282.8   said, rudely—] 'rudely—' *interlined with a caret above
             canceled* '—rudely—' *in black ink; the comma after*
             'said' *added in black ink.*

282.13   "I can't] 'I' *written over* 'C'.

282.16   shook] *interlined with a caret above canceled* 'trem-
             bled' *in black ink.*

282.20–21   the weapons,] *follows wiped-out and canceled* 'the
             wome'.

282.21   or] *interlined with a caret above a canceled ampersand.*

282.23   about it] *interlined with a caret.*

282.27–28   The . . . apiece] *originally* 'They chose seconds'; *the*
             'y' *of* 'They' *and the* 's' *of* 'seconds' *canceled;* 'duellists',
             'a', *and* 'apiece' *interlined with carets.*

282.32   tune] *followed by* 'softly' *canceled in black ink.*

282.35   satisfied wink,] *interlined with a caret in black ink above canceled* 'slow and pleasant wink'; 'pleasant wink' *canceled in black ink;* 'slow and' *canceled earlier.*

282.36   "Well] *follows canceled paragraph* ' "B' god, it wasn't the Jew." '

282.36   it] *follows a canceled dash.*

Randall's Jew Story

Textual Commentary

The manuscript is copy-text. No ambiguous compound is hyphenated at the end of a line in the manuscript.

Textual Notes

285.22 Luck] Following this word someone has interlined "(and science)" with a caret in pencil. Although the writing may be Mark Twain's, no other pencil additions on the manuscript are his; Paine, however, added quotation marks to the last paragraph and made a few pencil notes on the manuscript. He is presumably the author of this addition as well.

Emendations of the Copy-Text

	MTP Reading	Copy-Text Reading
284.1	Hath not	Hath not not
284.11	Bank,	Bank
288.28	slave girl	slave-girl
†289.6	So he	So He

Mark Twain's Revisions

284.10 one—] *the dash mended from a period.*

284.13 word] *follows canceled* 'thin'.

284.17   he did.] *interlined with a caret above canceled* 'I saw him do.'

284.18   the Jews] *originally* 'a Jew'; '*the*' *interlined with a caret above canceled* 'a'; *the* '*s*' *added.*

285.3   self-complacencies] *follows canceled* 'vanities'.

285.9   in . . . when] *interlined with a caret following canceled* 'when'.

285.10   course.] 'course' *followed by canceled* ', no southern gentleman could associate with a nigger-trader.'; *the period added.*

285.15   daughter,] *followed by* 'a' *and* '—Miss Sarah—', *both canceled.*

285.15   winning.] 'winning' *followed by canceled* '; just a darling, in fact.'; *the period added.*

285.16   —Judith—] *follows canceled* 'who'.

285.16   and] *interlined with a caret above canceled* 'a'.

285.21   one night,] *interlined with a caret above a canceled comma.*

285.21   surprise and distress] *interlined with a caret following canceled* 'vast astonishment and disgust of the other passengers. This was about'.

286.3   mockingly:] *interlined with a caret above canceled* 'ironically:'.

286.10   ventured a] *interlined with a caret above canceled* 'laughed a'.

286.12   half past three] *interlined with a caret above canceled* 'two'.

286.25   victoriously,] *interlined with a caret above canceled* 'joyously,'.

286.31   What] *follows canceled quotation marks.*

287.4   as] *follows what appears to be* 'af' *mended to* 'as', *then canceled.*

287.6   trader] *interlined with a caret above canceled* 'planter'.

287.8   The Jew] *follows canceled quotation marks.*

287.15   *not* be torn] *follows canceled* 'not be anybody's chattel'.

287.20   heart—] *followed by canceled* 'yes'.

287.27   words, but] *follows canceled* 'words and her heart along with'.

287.28   young man,] *interlined with a caret.*

287.31   Jew was] *the* 'w' *of* 'was' *mended from* 'p'.

287.33   me.] *originally* 'me, not'; 'not' *canceled; the comma mended to a period.*

288.7   fifteen hundred."] *follows canceled* 'two tho'.

288.15   "I've started . . . fail.] *interlined with a caret above canceled quotation marks.*

288.17   —this!"] *follows wiped-out and canceled* 'that' *and canceled* '—that!" '.

288.23   it] *follows canceled* 'we'.

288.23–24   and we] *follows canceled* 'in'.

288.28   again—] *the dash interlined with a caret above a canceled dash.*

288.29   safe;] *originally* 'safe.' *followed by paragraph* 'There, that is the whole story—said [blank] —and ever since then I've held that there is good in a Jew.' *and by Mark Twain's signature indicating an intent to end the manuscript here; the space following* 'said' *left blank by Mark Twain; then the period following* 'safe' *mended to a semicolon and* 'There . . . Jew.' *and the signature canceled.*

288.29   dead] *interlined with a caret.*

288.30   there were] *originally* 'he had'; 'he' *mended to* 'there'; 'were' *interlined with a caret above canceled* 'had'.

288.36–289.1   left . . . girl,] *interlined with a caret written over a comma.*

289.6   So he] 'So' *interlined with a caret; the 'H' of MS 'He' not reduced to 'h'.*

289.6   you see] *interlined with a caret.*

289.9   in his] *follows canceled* 'at him'.

289.11   on] *written over* 'in'.

Mock Marriage

Textual Commentary

The manuscript is copy-text; the author's unrevised typescript is also in the Mark Twain Papers. There are no textual notes, and no ambiguous compound is hyphenated at the end of a line in the manuscript.

Emendations of the Copy-Text

	MTP READING	COPY-TEXT READING
293.10–11	mock marriages	mock-marriages
299.13	ring,	ring
300.27–28	mother-like	mother like
†301.8	endurable—	endurable.—

Mark Twain's Revisions

291.3	office] *the 'of' written over a wiped-out unrecovered letter.*
291.11	had an attractive] *follows canceled* 'was'.
291.13–14	palace. . . . domino.] *added on the verso of the MS page with instructions to turn over to replace canceled* 'palace. There were to be 26 grooms and 26 brides.'
291.15	Out of these,] *followed by canceled* 'woul'.
291.20	drawing N] *the 'N' written over* 'D'.
291.21	gold rings] *follows canceled* 'plain'.
292.4	After the first] *follows canceled* 'After marriage they would immediately separate and mingle with the

crowd.' *and canceled* 'After the completion of the 13 weddings the dancing would begin.'

292.4   the fun would begin.] *originally* 'then the fun.'; 'then' *and the period canceled and* 'would begin.' *interlined with a caret.*

292.5   his bride] *interlined with a caret above canceled* 'the lady'.

292.6–7 and be . . . crowd.] *interlined with a caret above a canceled period;* 'they would' *interlined with a caret within the interlineation;* 'and be . . . crowd.' *replaces canceled* 'A pause of two minutes for bets, by the house, as to who's who. Then, at the word, the mock-married couple must unmask.'

292.8–10 the thirteen lots . . . masks.] *added on a separate MS page to replace canceled* 'the 13 lots were all wedded and tallied off.'; 'wedded and' *interlined with a caret above canceled* 'revealed and'.

292.11   grotesque] *originally* 'grotesques'; *the 's' wiped out and canceled.*

292.12   revealed] *interlined with a caret.*

292.20   under] *follows canceled* 'was'.

292.22   through] *follows canceled* 'among'.

293.3   B] *followed by a wiped-out period.*

293.7   in line] *interlined with a caret.*

293.24   Brevoort] *originally* 'Breevoort'; *the first 'e' canceled.*

294.1   pronounced air] 'air' *appears to have been mended from* 'aur'.

294.7   Schuyler] *follows canceled* 'Van'.

294.17   religion and] *interlined with a caret.*

294.32–33 Is not . . . poverty—"] *squeezed in following canceled quotation marks.*

295.2	said—] *follows canceled* 'he'.
295.8	laying] *the* 'l' *written over a dash.*
295.19–20	any words] 'any' *interlined with a caret above canceled* 'the'.
295.22	Edith was] 'was' *interlined with a caret above canceled* 'stood'.
295.23	dazed;] *follows canceled* 'dizzy,'.
295.23–24	with a . . . two she] *interlined with a caret.*
295.25	in her mother's] *follows canceled* 'upon her'.
295.28	mother,] *followed by canceled* 'dear,'.
295.28	let me] 'let' *written over wiped-out* 'cl'.
296.13	widow!] *the exclamation point mended from a semi-colon.*
296.16	upon] *interlined with a caret above canceled* 'in'.
296.18	pain:] *followed by a canceled dash.*
297.6	training of our] 'our' *interlined with a caret.*
297.30	frankly] 'fr' *written over wiped-out* 'in'.
297.37	"That poor] *the* 'T' *written over a wiped-out* 'D'.
298.23	"Thank you for] *originally* 'Thank you, L'; *the comma canceled and* 'for' *written over the* 'L'.
300.3	saying] *follows canceled* 'cry'.
300.8	"What, mother!"] *follows canceled paragraph* ' "Well, mother'.
300.10	yesterday] *written over wiped-out* 'this'.
301.8	endurable—] *originally* 'endurable.'; *the dash added; the period inadvertently left standing.*
301.9	rising] *followed by canceled* 'up'.

Concerning "Martyrs' Day"

Textual Commentary

The manuscript is copy-text. A typescript with two revisions in black ink ("Ought" italicized at 305.9 and "or so" interlined at 306.1) also survives. Although handwriting does not entirely rule Mark Twain out as the author of these revisions, a series of minute tracings-over of defectively typed letters in the same ink suggests Paine, who made a number of changes on the manuscript, or a Harper's editor as the reviser. Mark Twain almost never troubled himself about such details.

There are no textual notes, and no ambiguous compound is hyphenated at the end of a line in the manuscript.

Emendations of the Copy-Text

	MTP READING	COPY-TEXT READING
304.27	voluntary-subscription-paper	voluntary-subscription paper
†306.12	$700,000,000,000-worth	$700,000,000,000,-worth
306.15	Monument	monument

Mark Twain's Revisions

303.1   I . . . suggestion] *originally* 'I have read the proposition of Cardinal Gibbon and' *followed by one and a half blank lines;* 'supplication of' *and* 'appeal' *interlined with a caret then canceled above canceled* 'the proposition of'; 'his Eminence' *interlined then canceled above canceled* 'Cardinal Gibbon and'; 'in . . . suggestion' *added in the blank space.*

303.3   the President] *follows canceled* 'the Congress'.

303.5   promptness] *follows canceled* 'the unselfish enthusiasm'.

303.5–6   any avoidable] *follows canceled* 'unnecessary' *and canceled* 'discreditable'.

303.10   slightly.] *originally followed by* 'Instead of giving the Martyrs' Day a particular date'; 'the' *canceled;* 'giving . . . date' *canceled and* 'having a Martyrs' Day' *added; then* 'Instead of having a Martyrs' Day' *canceled.*

303.11   limiting] *follows canceled* 'ca'.

303.17   52,264,534] *follows canceled* '61'.

303.20   daily] *interlined with a caret.*

303.21 $70,000,000,] *the final* 'ooo,' *interlined with a caret.*

304.2–3   per day; and . . . day.] *originally* 'per year. Thirty years later we shall have multiplied our population three times, and the daily earnings of our workers will aggregate the splendid sum of $300,000,000 per day.'; 'daily' *canceled;* 'year.' *canceled and* 'day;' *interlined with a caret;* 'Thirty . . . day.' *canceled and* 'and . . . hence.' *interlined; the period after* 'hence' *mended to a dash and* 'that is . . . day.' *added to the interlineation.*

304.6   voluntarily] *interlined with a caret.*

304.7   will] *interlined above canceled* 'would'.

304.15   if] *written over wiped-out* 'exce'.

304.22   a proffered . . . volunteer.] *squeezed in following canceled* 'the overwhelming bulk of it.'; 'overwhelming' *interlined with a caret above canceled* 'mighty'.

304.24   by . . . contribution] 'by voluntary' *interlined above canceled* 'with volunteer'; *the* 's' *of original* 'contributions' *canceled.*

304.27   paper; and] *originally* 'paper. And'; 'And' *canceled; the period mended to a semicolon; an ampersand squeezed in.*

304.30   monuments] *the 'm' written over wiped-out 'af'.*

304.33   or] *interlined with a caret.*

304.35   built.] *originally* 'built, the'; 'the' *canceled; the comma mended to a period.*

305.2   subscription-] *canceled then restored with the instruction* 'stet'.

305.5   liberal and] *interlined with a caret preceding canceled* 'whole and'.

305.6   nobody's] *originally* 'nobody feels it'; 'feels it' *canceled; the ' 's' squeezed in.*

305.8   You get it?] *squeezed in at the end of the line.*

305.9   Ought . . . escape] *originally* 'Should the poor escape'; 'Should' *canceled;* 'Ought' *and* 'to' *interlined with carets.*

305.10–11   No . . . conceded] *originally* 'Upon reflection—I must concede'; 'Upon . . . I' *canceled;* 'No, it' *and* 'be' *interlined with carets; a final* 'd' *added to* 'concede'.

305.11–12   they . . . nation:] *interlined with a caret above a canceled colon; the comma preceding added.*

305.16–17   cash-levy] 'cash-' *squeezed in at the end of the line.*

305.32   I would] *follows canceled* 'the ans'.

305.36   mark out] *interlined with a caret following canceled* 'lay'.

306.7   from] *interlined with a caret above canceled* 'in'.

306.8–17   they would . . . sky-scraper.] *added on inserted MS page 9A replacing* 'they would be celebrating Alfred's second millennial then—and on a sufficiently small scale by comparison.' *canceled at top of MS page* 10.

306.9   Centuries] *follows canceled* 'By that time'.

306.10   a billion dollars,] *interlined with a caret above canceled* '$1,000,000,000,'.

306.12   Seven Hundred Billions] *originally* 'a Billion Million
                Dollars'; *first* 'Dollars' *canceled; then* 'a' *and* 'Million'
                canceled; finally 'Seven Hundred' *interlined with a caret;
                the* 's' *of* 'Billions' *added.*

306.12 $700,000,000,000] *originally* '$700,000,000,000,000,-
                000'; '000,000' *canceled; the comma inadvertently left
                standing.*

306.12–13   of good commercial] *interlined with a caret above can-
                celed* 'of'.

306.13–15   Ten . . . Monument.] *interlined with a caret.*

306.16   contrasted . . . snow-capped] 'contrasted with snow-
                capped' *interlined with a caret above canceled* 'along-
                side it'; 'it' *then interlined with a caret after* 'with'.

306.17   sky-scraper.] *followed by canceled* 'Many of us will not
                live to see that day, but in spirit we can look forward to
                it with pride and satisfaction.'

306.18–19   that . . . Monument] 'that' *followed by canceled* 'Wash-
                ington and'; 'city and the' *followed by canceled* 'nation'.

306.26   Widows] 'id' *written over wiped-out* 'om'.

306.28–30   a week . . . Labor Day] *originally* 'a week to get over
                Labor Day'; *a comma added after* 'week' *and* 'five times
                a year,' *interlined with a caret;* 'five' *canceled and re-
                placed by* 'seven'; *a caret added and canceled after* 'over';
                'over' *canceled and* 'over the famine of Lincoln's Day,
                and Washington's Day, and' *interlined with a caret;
                the* 'n' *of* 'famine' *mended from* 's'.

306.31   hard-pressed Jews] *follows canceled* '1200,000 J'.

306.32   their own] *followed by canceled* 'and 52 contributed by'.

306.33   111] *originally* '109'; '11' *written over* '09'.

306.34   seven—] *interlined with a caret above canceled* 'five—'.

306.34   that] *interlined with a caret.*

306.36   thing] *mended from* 'their'.

307.2   in Italy] *interlined with a caret.*

307.4–7   Even . . . credit.] 'Even in' *added on the line;* 'those . . .
               credit.' *added on the verso of the MS page with instruc-
               tions to turn over.*

307.14   Monument.] *originally followed by* 'It is an elegant idea,
               and will warm every patriot heart—bake it, maybe.' *and
               the signature* 'Mark Twain', *indicating that the MS was
               to end here; a period added after* 'heart', *the dash can-
               celed, and the* 'b' *of* 'bake' *mended to* 'B'; *then* 'It is . . .
               Twain' *canceled.*

307.17   would not] *follows canceled* 'is not safe,'.

307.20   should] *follows canceled* 'coul'.

Abner L. Jackson (About to Be) Deceased

Textual Commentary

The manuscript is copy-text. No ambiguous compound is hyphenated at the end of a line in the manuscript.

Textual Notes

311.32	dollars' worth] The discarded ending to the story, reproduced in the headnote, begins here with the second syllable of "dollars'."

Emendations of the Copy-Text

	MTP READING	COPY-TEXT READING
310.1	Esq.	Esq
311.25	too	two
311.35	$25	$25,
311.35	$150.00	$150.00.
311.36	45.00	45.00.
311.37	20.00	20.00.
312.1	half-brother,	half-brother
312.1	150.00	150.00.
312.2	relatives,	relatives
312.7	Missions	Missions,
312.8	Union	Union,
312.9	Cats	Cats,

MTP Reading	Copy-Text Reading

312.20	748.00	748.00.
312.25	States	States,

Mark Twain's Revisions

310.7	his capacity,] 'his' *interlined with a caret.*
310.15	but was] *follows canceled* 'and was graduated with honor in 1829.'
310.20	change] *the* 'g' *written over* 'c'.
311.1–2	company] *follows canceled* 'cop'.
311.6	necessary, and] *followed by canceled* 'in'.
311.9	experience] *follows canceled* 'his'.
311.9	government;] *the semicolon mended from a comma.*
311.11	headquarters . . . signed,] *interlined with a caret above canceled* 'the railroad depot with the troops'.
311.12	passing] *interlined with a caret.*
311.17	employed] *follows canceled* 'has'.
311.21	be] *interlined with a caret.*
311.23	hopelessly] *follows canceled* 'in'.
311.24	and had] *follows canceled* 'and was'.
311.33	$90,000] *originally* '$95,000'; 'o' *written over the* '5'.
312.4–5	Inhabitants . . . Found] *the initial letters of* 'Inhabitants', 'Lands', 'Within', 'When', *and* 'Found' *mended from lower case to capital letters;* 'Lands' *followed by canceled* '—if any such—'.
312.10	American] *follows canceled* 'Association for the Protection of the Sanctity of the Lord's Day . . . . . 13.00'.
312.10	Tract] *interlined with a caret above canceled* 'Bible'.
312.21	Society] *the* 'S' *written over* 'F'.

The Secret History of Eddypus, the World-Empire

Textual Commentary

The manuscript of "Eddypus" is copy-text. Jean Clemens prepared a typescript which includes all but the last three chapters of the piece. However, since the author did not revise the typescript, it has no authority.

The manuscript of "Eddypus" consists of sheets from "Par Value" tablets. The pages vary slightly in size; presumably the pages of a given pad were all the same size, but the pads themselves were not absolutely uniform from one to the next. A consideration of page sizes and ink colors reveals many details of the order of composition.

Mark Twain began "Eddypus" by writing sixty-one manuscript pages which he numbered consecutively, apparently regarding them as a unit. The first fifty-two pages, constituting all of Book 1 (except its last two paragraphs, which were added later), remain in the order in which they were written; the last nine pages subsequently evolved in the course of revision into Chapter 3 of Book 2. This first stint of writing is in a black ink which on the last few pages gradually blends to brown. Before writing any more new pages the author went back and in brown ink began to revise what he had written. On manuscript page 11 (322.title–13), which was apparently written at this time to replace an earlier version, the brown ink changes gradually to blue. Still using blue ink, Mark Twain finished revising what he had written and then added twenty-one new pages, which eventually would become Chapter 4 and part of Chapter 5 of Book 2.

At this point Mark Twain started Book 2 by writing in blue ink fifteen pages of Chapter 1 (presently 336.6–337.18 and 341.12–345.10). Shifting to black ink he added eight more pages (345.title–348.5) to Chapter 1 of Book 2. Then he reduced Book 1 to its present size by moving its last thirty pages (the nine in black and brown ink, and the twenty-one in blue ink) to Book 2 where he designated them Chapter 2. Presumably it was at this time that he replaced these pages with the two short paragraphs which now conclude Book 1.

Having finished Book 1 as it now stands, Mark Twain completed Chapter 1 of Book 2 by inserting ten new pages (337.19–341.12). He further expanded Book 2 by adding a new Chapter 2, the phrenology sketch. This episode, originally paginated 1–8, had been written as a separate piece in a greenish-black ink not used elsewhere in "Eddypus." Using black ink, Mark Twain added five new pages to adapt the sketch to "Eddypus" and to identify its protagonist as "The Bishop of New Jersey" (348.title–25, 350.9–19, and 352.8–26). Then in brown ink he added a brief conclusion to the new Chapter 2 (352.26–353.10).

The insertion of the phrenology sketch as Chapter 2 caused a second displacement of the thirty pages originally shifted from Book 1. Mark Twain moved them to the position they now occupy (353.11–364.25) and changed the chapter designation on the first page of the group from 2 to 3. He then added twelve more pages (364.26–369.3), carrying the work to the end of Chapter 5. Nine months later he added a final thirty-four pages during his last stint of work on "Eddypus." (Headings for Chapters 3 and 4 of Book 1 and Chapters 4 through 8 of Book 2 have been inserted where Mark Twain indicated breaks but did not supply numbers.)

Textual Notes

318.title   A.M.] Although internally inconsistent and often arithmetically wrong, "A.M." dates have not been emended. Whether deliberately, as a way of poking fun at his narrator, or inadvertently, Mark Twain used two dating systems. In the first, here and at 324.15, A.M. 1 is A.D. 1901; at 319.2–3 and 331.22, A.M. 1 is A.D. 1865. Although based on A.M. 1 = 1865, A.M. 47 at 319.2, 327.n and Book 2, 337.8, and A.M. 70 at Book 2, 337.9, are mistakes in calculation. Apparently Mark Twain made a one-year dating error by simply subtracting 1865 from 1912 to get 47, and 1865 from 1935 to get 70. At 318.17 the author initially made the same mistake in "A.D. 1898 = A.M. 33," then compounded the error by inexplicably changing "33" to "30." In Book 2 at 341.28 he repeated the first mistake but not the second when he dated the Bishop's book A.M. 33.

320.17   Anno Matris] Mark Twain originally wrote "Anno Mater" and later interlined "rice" above the "er" of "Mater" as an alternative ending, without indicating a choice between readings. At 331.12–13 he wrote "*Anno*

Mater" and interlined *"Matris"* above *"Mater,"* again without indicating a choice. Since he was not satisfied with "Mater" in either case, and "Matris" is grammatically correct, while "Matrice" would be nonsense without purpose, "Matris" is the chosen reading.

322.title   History of Holy Eddypus] In the top margin of the manuscript page Mark Twain wrote in the same black ink as the text, "Golden Rule"; below this he later wrote in blue ink, "set it right." The author discusses the Golden Rule at 326.32–327.2.

324.1   At the time] In the top margin of the manuscript page above this phrase Mark Twain wrote "Carnegie."

324.12   "Old Comradeships,"] In all subsequent references, the title is given as "Old Comrades." Because there is no indication of what the change might have been intended to mean, the reading is not emended.

324.21   Bostonflats] On the manuscript a pencil mark which could be an incomplete "E" interlined above this word, and a mark through "Bos" which could have been intended as a cancellation, suggest that Mark Twain may have thought of changing this to "Eddyflats" as he did at 319.5. "Bostonflats" is unchanged, however, at 332.14 and 335.2.

325.17   "Old Comrades."] See note at 324.12.

328.26   could not be] In the top margin of the manuscript page above these words Mark Twain wrote the cue word "Parcelsius."

329.1   Charles the Bald] Mark Twain's "a" and "o" often look identical, and he may have meant "Charles the Bold" here, as the typist rendered it. However, his original intention to play on the idea of hair color (see 326.12 and revisions at 327.18–19, 329.1–2, and 329.36–37) and his failure to alter this reading when he abandoned the running joke suggest that "Bald" is the correct reading.

331.12–13   *Anno Matris*] See note at 320.17.

332.20   early historians] In the top margin of the manuscript page beginning with these words, Mark Twain wrote in pencil, "We have discarded punitive laws—the Bible has not. Are we better than our God?"

332.33   Twain] At the top left of the manuscript page beginning here, Mark Twain wrote in pencil, "Great Monopolies. Silly nature of all punitive laws, human and divine." At the top right he wrote, "Tunnel disaster, murder for money."

341.29   Eddyburg] Mark Twain apparently forgot that in Book 1 he had already used Eddyburg as the new name for Rome.

347.31   waltz!] On the left side of the top margin above this word Mark Twain wrote, then canceled, "Tom and Huck."

349.1–20   THE PARTING . . . Gilder.] The poem, printed on a slip of paper which is pinned to the manuscript page, is surrounded by a decorative border below which is printed its source: "*Harper's Weekly* 17 *March* 1900." This citation is canceled in ink.

357.11–12   Wells . . . others] Mark Twain left space for about two lines of writing after "Wells," to permit the addition of other names.

360.2   do it] At the bottom left corner of the manuscript page ending here, Mark Twain wrote, then canceled, "Free-thinking."

360.30   to their] At the bottom left corner of the manuscript page ending here, Mark Twain wrote, then canceled, "Free thought."

364.26   supposed, up to] In the top margin above these words Mark Twain wrote "Asteroids."

365.10   Izaac] Mark Twain may have been trying to compound the comic confusion of Izaac Walton and Sir Isaac Newton by spelling the first name in two different ways.

However, it seems more likely that he simply forgot which form he had used previously, and therefore the name is emended here and at 378.31 to conform to the dominant earlier usage.

366.9   citizen of] In the bottom margin below these words Mark Twain wrote, then canceled, "Daguerre."

368.15   look pleasant] In the top margin above these words Mark Twain wrote, then canceled, "living photo."

368.28   up as do . . . who is] In the top margin above these words Mark Twain wrote on the left "printing (see figures made at the farm." On the right he wrote "steam—boat —rail—ship" and on a second line "bycicle—mobile." At the bottom of the page he wrote the note "Watt— Whitney—Arkwright. H. Beecher Stowe, John Brown (Reb) and other anti-slavery." later lightly canceled in pencil.

371.19–22   models—a procedure . . . now.] Mark Twain added "— a procedure . . . now." on the verso of the manuscript page without indicating where it was to be incorporated in the text. The manuscript page, beginning with "stood 600 to 1" (371.15) and ending with "Man, with the" (371.32), seems to offer no other place for interpolation.

376.4   on a matter] In the top margin of the manuscript page beginning here Mark Twain wrote in pencil, "The Great Civili & how Xn S. destroyed it."

380.1   The vast] In the top margin of the manuscript page beginning here, Mark Twain wrote in the same black ink as the text, "Print" and below that, "steam."

382.11   irresistible] Mark Twain interlined "irresistible" without a caret above "long." Although he may have meant both adjectives to stand, so that the phrase would read "long irresistible tidal-waves," the absence of a caret, which Mark Twain seldom fails to provide when revising, makes it more likely that he regarded "irresistible" as an alternative to "long."

Emendations of the Copy-Text

	MTP READING	COPY-TEXT READING
318.1	DEAR X	*Dear X*
318.16	To-wit	To wit
319.22	stood,)	stood),
320.6	Eddy III; TS	Eddy III.;
320.12	Her	her
*320.17	Matris.	Mater./rice.
323.6	Papal	papal *Also emended at* 324.2 *and* 332.14
†323.10	the Only	The Only
323.15	Papacy	papacy
324.5	ancient one,	ancient one
325.15–16	first century	First Century 'Century' *Also emended at* 356.26 *and* 381.34
†328.2	Peter TS	Peter's
328.17	up-to-date	up to date
330.6	Admiral TS	Amiral
330.17	prosperity TS	properity
*331.13	*Matris*	*Mater/Matris*
331.13	A.M. TS	A.M
331.16	A.D.;	A.D.,
331.18	A.M.; TS	A.M ;
331.20	B.M.B.G. TS	B.M.B.G
331.21	Baker G.).	Baker G.)
332.34	ch. 7, vol. II	ch. VII, vol. 2

	MTP READING	COPY-TEXT READING
334.32	Croker TS	Crocker
335.31	worshiping	worshipping
338.5	history	History
340.1	"The . . . it."	The . . . it.
340.19	to-morrows	tomorrows *Also emended at* 340.20
341.27	"The Gospel	the "Gospel
341.29	Comrades," TS	Comrades,
342.9	every TS	evry
344.6	*Morte*	*Mort*
344.33	disappeared TS	diappeared
345.20	candles TS	candes
†349.10	Downward TS	downward
†349.10	the TS	The
350.11	diagnosis TS	dignosis
351.15	3 . . . moderate	3, . . . moderate,
352.1	Amativeness,	Amativeness
355.11	burden	burthen
357.5	Priestley	Priestly *Also emended at* 361.4, 361.15, 361.23, 362.1–2, 362.3, 362.5, 362.13, 362.16, 362.25, 363.1, *and* 378.31
357.9	Kirchhoff	Kirschoff
357.19	authenticity	authencity
357.21–22	Attraction of Gravitation	attraction of gravitation
357.22	Gravitation of Attraction	gravitation of attraction

	MTP READING	COPY-TEXT READING
358.14	Cross TS	cross
360.8	its	it
360.16	potato	potatoe
364.15	undiminished,	undiminished
364.31	law	Law *Also emended at* 378.8 *and* 379.7
*365.10	Izaac	Isaac *Also emended at* 378.31
366.6	Kirchhoff	Kirschhoff *Also emended at* 378.35
366.11	revolutionizer	reovolutionizer
366.30	cause . . . to stand	make . . . stand/cause . . . to stand
366.31	eruptions	irruptions
†367.22	refuge	refuge.
368.12	soldier clothes	soldier-clothes
369.16	Huguenots	Hugenots
369.17	emigrés	emigrès
*371.19	models—	models.—
377.26	Man	man
378.1	into a rat	into rat
379.25	suspect	supect
380.15	Evolution	evolution
380.20–21	prophesying	prophecying
380.24	States,	States
382.4	its drapery	it drapery
*382.11	irresistible	long/irresistible

Word Division in the Copy-Text

319.33	falsehoods
324.9	trustworthy
328.10	pains-takingly
334.5	border-line
340.25	To-morrows
344.32	misspelling
346.29	swallow-tail
351.31	low-downest
360.14	mustard-seed
371.35	paper-weight

Mark Twain's Revisions

Written in black ink from 318.title through 336.5

318.title   A Private Letter] *originally* 'Some Private Letters.'; 'Some' *and the* 's' *of* 'Letters' *canceled in pencil;* 'A' *interlined with a caret in black ink.*

318.title   Date, A.M. 1001*] *originally* 'A.D. 2906.'; 'N.E. 1001.' *squeezed in above canceled* 'A.D. 2906.'; 'O.M. 1001.' *interlined with a caret above canceled* 'N.E. 1001.'; *the* 'A' *written over* 'O'; 'Date,' *added in brown ink; the asterisk and footnote added in pencil.*

318.1–3   conveyance. . . . ours.] *originally* 'conveyance. I believe you are right in thinking there . . . one form.'; 'I . . . thinking' *canceled; the* 'T' *of* 'There' *written over* 't'; *the period after* 'form' *canceled and* 'of . . . ours.' *added, all in brown ink.*

318.9   There is a] *followed by* 'good deal of' *canceled in brown ink.*

318.14   Rank] *followed by canceled quotation marks.*

318.14   and odd] *interlined with a caret in brown ink.*

318.15   Bull] *interlined with a caret above canceled* 'Encyclical'.

318.17   (A.D. 1898 = A.M. 30)] *interlined with a caret above canceled* '1898'; *the original interlineation was* '(A.D. 1898 = N.E. 33) apparently'; 'O.M.' *written over* 'N.E.', *then* 'A' *written over* 'O' *and* '30' *mended from* '33'; 'apparently' *canceled in brown ink.*

319.1–2   A.D. 1912 = A.M. 47.] *interlined with a caret above canceled* '1912.'; 'N.E.' *changed to* 'A.M.' *as at* 318.17.

319.2–3   (A.D. 1865 = A.M. 1)] *written above canceled* '1865'; 'N.E.' *changed to* 'A.M.' *as at* 318.17 *and* 319.1–2.

319.3   Science and Health.] *the period replaces a canceled comma followed by canceled* 'with Key to the Scriptures.'

319.5   Eddyflats . . . Boston,)] *originally* 'Boston,'; 'Eddyville, (anciently called' *interlined with a caret preceding* 'Boston,'; *the closing parenthesis added;* 'Bostonflats,' *interlined with a caret to replace canceled* 'Eddyville,' *in brown ink;* 'Boston' *of* 'Bostonflats' *canceled and* 'Eddy' *added in pencil.*

319.7   many] *interlined with a caret above canceled* 'three'.

319.9   away] *interlined with a caret above canceled* 'off' *in brown ink.*

319.12–13   a philologist] *interlined with a caret in brown ink.*

319.18   Bull] *interlined with a caret above canceled* 'Encyclical'.

319.19   Our Mother] *originally* ' "Our Mother" '; *the quotation marks canceled in brown ink here and at* 319.31.

319.19   usual and natural way] *originally* 'usual old way'; 'old' *canceled and* 'commonplace' *interlined with a caret;* 'commonplace' *canceled and* 'and natural' *interlined with a caret, both in brown ink.*

319.19–20   in safe hiding] *interlined with a caret in brown ink.*

319.20   paper] *followed by* '—I know where—' *canceled in brown ink.*

319.20   which . . . us] *interlined with a caret.*

319.21   at Eddyburg,] *interlined with a caret.*

319.21–22   (where . . . stood,)] *the parentheses added.*

319.22   Her . . . Her] *originally* 'her . . . her'; *the italics canceled; the* 'H' *written over* 'h' *in brown ink (twice).* 'Her' *altered from* 'her' *in brown ink here and at* 319.32 *and* 319.33 *(twice). See revision at* 320.5–6.

319.24   Ages of Light] *originally* 'Light Ages'; 'Light' *canceled and* 'of Light' *interlined with a caret in brown ink.*

319.24   a daring] *follows canceled* 'an'.

319.30   Bull *Jubus*] 'Bull' *interlined with a caret above canceled* 'Encyclical'; '*Jubus*' *followed by canceled* 'etc.'

319.32   She] *the* 'S' *written over* 's' *in brown ink.* 'She' *altered from* 'she' *in brown ink also at* 320.11 *and* 320.12.

320.1   *a.* "Every] *originally run on; marked to begin a new paragraph with a paragraph sign;* '*a.*' *interlined with a caret.*

320.2   My Name] *mended from* 'my name'.

320.5–6   II; Her . . . Her] *mended from* 'II; her . . . her'. *See revision at* 319.22.

320.7   My Name] *the* 'M' *of* 'My' *written over* 'm'.

320.8   Last Day] *follows canceled* 'end o'.

320.9   from] *originally* 'for'; 'rom' *written over wiped-out* 'or'.

320.13   august] *interlined with a caret above canceled* 'great'.

320.14   None] *followed by* 'but an idiot' *canceled in brown ink.*

320.16–17   Christian Science] *interlined with a caret in brown ink.*

320.17   Anno Matris.] *follows canceled* 'A.M.'; *the* 'A' *of* 'A.M.' *written over* 'O'; *the MS reads* 'Anno Mater.' *with the alternate ending* 'rice.' *interlined above the* 'er' *of* 'Mater' *in brown ink. See emendations and textual notes.*

320.19   Indeed] *interlined with a caret above canceled* 'Privately in your ear—', *in brown ink.*

320.21   That is] *originally* 'Well, that is'; 'Well,' *canceled and the 'T' of 'That' mended from 't' in brown ink.*

320.22   that and] *follows canceled* 'just'.—

320.24   Christian Science] *interlined with a caret in brown ink.*

320.25   A.M.] *the 'A' written over 'O'.*

320.25–26   of Rome,] *interlined with a caret above a canceled comma followed by* 'His Holiness' *squeezed in.*

320.26   Pius] *follows canceled* 'Pope'.

320.27   Roman] *followed by canceled* 'Catholic'.

320.30   perish.] *interlined with a caret in brown ink above* 'go.'

320.32   diminished powers at] *interlined with a caret in brown ink above canceled* 'damaged assets at'.

320.35   time,—] *the dash squeezed in.*

320.35–36   a safe . . . win.] 'a safe' *interlined with a caret in brown ink to replace canceled* 'a'; 'tranquilly . . . win.' *interlined with a caret in brown ink above canceled* 'play a waiting and a winning game.'

320.36–37   over-anxious] *originally* 'anxious'; 'over-' *interlined with a caret in brown ink.*

320.37   to end . . . Churches,] *interlined with a caret in brown ink above canceled* 'to settle and have things peaceful and pleasant,'.

321.1   merger. Her] *interlined with a caret in brown ink above canceled* 'trade. Her'.

321.3   she] *originally* 'she'; *the italics canceled in brown ink.*

321.3   command] *the italics added in brown ink.*

321.10   Bones—] *interlined with a caret above a canceled dash.*

321.14   offered] *interlined with a caret in brown ink.*

321.14   of half-and-half;] *interlined with a caret in brown ink above canceled* 'just as they stood—'.

321.15–17   her to pare . . . whole.] *interlined with a caret in brown ink to replace canceled* 'her to knock off half.'

321.18–19   their properties] *follows canceled* 'under the'; 'properties' *interlined with a caret above canceled* 'assets' *in brown ink.*

321.23   abolished] *follows canceled* 'extingu'.

321.24   and his . . . clothes,] *interlined with a caret above a canceled comma.*

321.25   Mistress] *interlined with a caret to replace canceled* 'Lord'.

321.25   under the name] *follows canceled* 'under the' *and* 'put on the'.

321.27   (that is, he)] *interlined with a caret in brown ink, here and at 321.29.*

321.28   and in his] *follows canceled* 'and wh'.

321.28   Atkins.] *followed by* 'These are impressive events.' *canceled in brown ink.*

321.31   eight hundred] *follows what appears to be canceled* 'all of'.

321.32   and since] *interlined with a caret above canceled* 'but from'.

321.32   that day] *followed by canceled* 'to this,'.

321.34   Christian.] *interlined with a caret above canceled* 'Roman Catholic.'

321.36   authentic.] *followed by* 'In truth it *was* a conquest, if you turn it the other way about.' *canceled in brown ink.*

322.title–13   Another . . . more or less] *written on one MS page apparently replacing an earlier page no longer part of the MS; written in brown ink blending to blue by 322.9; written in blue ink from 322.9 ('and hungers') through 322.13 ('more or less').*

322.13   danger] *follows* 'I dare empty it into for my relief and joy. You are safe enough, but I will make you safer. There is a trifle of' *canceled in blue ink.*

322.14   kind] *interlined with a caret above canceled* 'one'.

322.15–16   bargain-counter] *interlined with a caret above canceled* 'pharmacy'.

322.21   of Holy Eddypus] *interlined with a caret.*

322.25–323.1   —if . . . right—] *interlined with a caret.*

323.1   personages] *follows canceled* 'things'.

323.2   The . . . caution.] *interlined with a caret above canceled* 'and goes through the motions of doing it still.' *following a period added to replace a canceled comma.*

323.3   family] *interlined with a caret.*

323.7   an Eddymanian priest] *originally* 'a priest'; 'Eddymanian' *interlined with a caret; the* 'n' *of* 'an' *added.*

323.9   other words] 'other' *interlined with a caret;* 'words' *written over wiped-out* 'our'.

323.10   name. In . . . era the] *originally* 'name. The'; 'In the second (or first?) century' *interlined with a caret and* 'of our era' *added on the verso of the MS page with instructions to turn over, in black ink;* 'In . . . century' *then canceled and replaced by* 'In the third century' *interlined on the verso in blue ink. The* 'T' *of original* 'The' *not reduced to* 't'.

323.11   and abolished a religion] *originally* 'and abolished a superstition'; 'and abolished' *interlined with a caret in black ink; then* 'a superstition' *canceled and* 'a religion' *added to the interlineation in blue ink.*

323.13   Eddymania.] *followed by* '(sometimes Eddyolatry.)' *added in black ink and canceled in blue; the period following* 'Eddymania' *appears to have been mended to a comma and then restored.*

323.22   clergy . . . altar] *originally* 'clergy, . . . altar,'; *the com-
             mas canceled.*

323.25   such of the] *follows canceled* 'the'.

323.27   Sermons,] *followed by canceled* 'and'.

323.27   Letters,] *followed by canceled* 'and'.

323.29   such of the] *follows canceled* 'those'.

323.30   in verse-form] *follows canceled* 'in vers'.

324.1   secret] *interlined with a caret.*

324.1–2   libraries, in the beginning] *originally* 'libraries, museums
             and seats of learning, in the beginning'; 'museums . . .
             in' *canceled and* 'in' *added following* 'libraries,'.

324.2   sixth century] *originally* 'second (?) cen'; '(?) cen' *can-
             celed and* '(or third?)' *added;* 'second (or third?)' *then
             canceled and* 'fourth (or fifth?)' *interlined with a caret;
             finally* 'fourth (or fifth?)' *canceled and* 'sixth' *interlined
             with a caret.*

324.2–3   books and] *interlined with a caret.*

324.4   also hurtful.] *interlined with a caret following a comma
             mended from a period.*

324.5   and one ancient one] *interlined with a caret following
             an added comma.*

324.7   precious, it being] 'it being' *follows canceled* 'It is the
             one'; *the comma after* 'precious' *mended from a period.*

324.11   ten centuries] *interlined with a caret above canceled*
             'eight hundred years' *in blue ink.*

324.11   twenty years ago.] *interlined with a caret above canceled*
             'two centuries ago.' *in blue ink.*

324.14   revered] *mended from* 'reverend'.

324.14   Mark Twain] *the* 'M' *written over a wiped-out* 'P' *or*
             'B'.

324.15   A.M. 12.] *followed by canceled* '(or 36?)'.

324.21   Bostonflats] 'Bos' *canceled and an incomplete* 'E' *written above it, both in pencil. See textual notes.*

324.26   times of] *followed by a canceled caret.*

324.31   special] *interlined with a caret in blue ink.*

325.2   Scientific] *follows canceled quotation marks.*

325.5–6   nearly complete.] *followed by canceled* 'almost utterly complete.'; *the period after* 'complete' *mended from a comma; both revisions in blue ink.*

325.7   the most of] *interlined with a caret in blue ink.*

325.8–9   —shortly . . . Consolidation—] *interlined with a caret in blue ink.*

325.10   also . . . museums.] *interlined with a caret following a semicolon expanded from a period.*

325.13   made,] *followed by an uncanceled caret with no interlineation.*

325.13   —histories] *interlined with a caret.*

325.14   tradition.] *followed by* 'no doubt.' *interlined with a caret then canceled; the period after* 'tradition' *mended to a comma and then restored.*

325.15–17   noted. . . . . raid] 'noted.' *followed by canceled* 'Up to that time it is possible that some books that had escaped the second raid were still in existence, but there is no actual proof of it.'; 'No . . . veracity' *interlined above canceled* 'Certainly no books of early date'; 'that final raid' *interlined with a caret; all revisions in blue ink.*

325.17   This great work] *interlined with a caret above canceled* 'It'.

325.18   twenty] *interlined with a caret in blue ink above canceled* 'three'.

325.19   hundred years;] *interlined with a caret in blue ink above canceled* 'centuries;'.

325.20   absolutely] *interlined with a caret in blue ink.*

325.21   (So . . . better.)] *squeezed in at the end of the line in blue ink.*

325.22   Of the] *follows canceled* 'The'.

325.23   infallibly] *originally* 'very'; 'very' *canceled and* 'closely' *interlined with a caret in black ink;* 'closely' *canceled and followed by* 'infallibly' *in blue ink.*

325.24   many instances] *interlined with a caret in blue ink above canceled* 'the main degree'.

325.25   is] *interlined with a caret above canceled* 'seems to be'.

325.27   history] *follows canceled* 'early his'.

325.28   even] *interlined with a caret.*

325.29   make] *follows canceled* 'attem'.

325.31   earliest times] 'earliest' *interlined with a caret in blue ink above canceled* 'beginning of'; *the* 's' *of* 'times' *added in blue ink.*

326.1   Uncle] *interlined with a caret in blue ink.*

326.2   discovered] *follows canceled* 'overthrew it and'.

326.2   Livingston.] *followed by canceled* '(supposed to have been one of the Filipinos.)'; *the period after* 'Livingston' *changed from a comma.*

326.7   sufficient.] *followed by* 'for the time being.' *canceled in blue ink; the period added after* 'sufficient'.

326.10   Bunker Hill.] *written in blue ink following canceled* 'the Pass of Thermopylie.'

326.16   refrain from] *interlined with a caret in blue ink above canceled* 'eschew'.

326.18   exalted] *interlined with a caret above canceled* 'encouraged'.

326.19   codified the laws,] *interlined with a caret above canceled* 'wrote philosophies,'.

326.24–26   He . . . Forest.] *originally* 'He had many and fruitful wives, and after a career of unexampled posterity he was drowned by accident in a butt of Malmsey by Wat Tyrell while hunting in the New Forest. He was called the Father of his Country, on account of the color of his hair.'; 'romantic . . . after' *interlined with a caret above canceled* 'and fruitful . . . after'; 'of' *canceled after* 'career'; 'for brilliant . . . escapes,' *interlined with a caret after canceled* 'posterity he'; 'while' *interlined with a caret above canceled* 'by . . . while'; 'He was . . . hair.' *canceled; all revisions in blue ink.*

326.33   Crusades,] *interlined with a caret in blue ink above a canceled comma.*

326.34   Flinders] *follows* 'Of the nature and character of the Golden Rule we cannot now be sure, but' *canceled in blue ink.*

326.36   the Golden Rule] *interlined with a caret in blue ink following canceled* 'it'.

327.1   he states] *interlined with a caret in blue ink.*

327.1   Rule] *the* 'R' *written over* 'r' *in blue ink.*

327.1–2   was identical . . . Brazen Rule] 'was . . . that of' *interlined with a caret in blue ink above canceled* 'as indicated by the circumstances, was, Do unto others as shall seem best to you to do unto them, not using compulsion except when necessary. That is the spirit of'; 'so-called' *interlined with a caret in black ink.*

327.7–8   an elusive . . . precise meaning] 'an elusive . . . not easy' *interlined with carets above canceled* 'a difficult term. It is not possible'; 'precise' *interlined with a caret; all revisions in blue ink.*

327.9–10   godliness] *follows what appears to be canceled* 'kind'.

327.10   we gather] *interlined with a caret in blue ink.*

327.18   his grandson,] *interlined with a caret.*

327.18–19　　called . . . He was] 'called' *follows canceled* 'so'; 'the Black Prince' *interlined with a caret*; 'armor.' *interlined with a caret above canceled* 'hair. He was not related to his father by marriage, but'; 'He' *interlined with a caret; all revisions in blue ink.*

327.26　　　numerous] *interlined with a caret above canceled* 'several'.

327.29　　　armed] *interlined with a caret in blue ink.*

327.33　　　his] *follows canceled* 'the'.

327.35　　　when . . . purchaser.] *added in blue ink following a comma mended from a period.*

328.1　　　with] *followed by canceled* 'this'.

328.2　　　the Hermit's] *interlined with a caret in blue ink.*

328.5　　　next] *interlined with a caret in blue ink.*

328.6–7　　and in . . . Christians] *interlined with a caret; the preceding comma mended from a period.*

328.8　　　Old] *the* 'O' *written over* 'N'.

328.8　　　other] *followed by canceled* 'part'.

328.12　　　day] *interlined with a caret above canceled* 'time'.

328.13　　　that] *followed by canceled* 'it was'.

328.22　　　a revelation] 'a' *interlined with a caret.*

328.22　　　Eddyphone,] *followed by canceled* 'and written down by his secretaries,'.

328.22　　　he being] 'he' *originally* 'she'; *the* 's' *canceled in blue ink.*

328.24　　　he, in turn] *originally* 'she'; *the* 's' *canceled in blue ink.*

328.24　　　his secretaries] *originally* 'her'; *altered to* 'his' *in blue ink.*

328.25　　　of the Christians] *interlined with a caret in blue ink.*

328.32　　　we infer] *follows canceled* 'we are'.

328.33   Bible] *followed by canceled* 'by the Christian'.

328.35   Roman] *interlined with a caret.*

328.37   read it."] *the quotation marks added in blue ink; followed by* 'Also they took their Christmas Day away from suppressed heathendom, just as our Church has taken it away from Christendom and made it the natal day of Our Mother. Also the Christians took over many other assets of heathendom and renamed them; in doing the same with the assets of Christianity our Church has but followed custom and usage." ' *canceled in blue ink. The semicolon following* 'them' *mended from a period and* 'in' *squeezed in to replace canceled* 'In'; 'but followed' *follows canceled* 'not'.

329.1   of] *interlined with a caret.*

329.1–2   called the Unready. His] *originally* 'so called from the color of his hair. His conduct'; 'conduct' *follows canceled* 'treatm'; *then in blue ink* 'so' *canceled and* 'the Unready. His' *interlined with a caret above canceled* 'from . . . His'.

329.3   Wishington] *originally* 'Washlington'; *the* 'i' *written over* 'a' *and the* 'l' *canceled in blue ink.* 'Wishington' *altered from* 'Washlington' *in blue ink also at 329.18–19, 329.27–28, 329.35, and 330.12.*

329.3   hewed] *interlined with a caret above canceled* 'chopped'.

329.3–4   the emblem . . . tyranny,] *interlined with a caret following an added comma, all in blue ink.*

329.5   originally] *follows canceled* 'further than that he was'.

329.9   as some] *follows canceled* 'himself,'.

329.9   excused] *follows* 'distinctly' *canceled in blue ink.*

329.14   crush] *follows canceled* 'steal'.

329.16   sympathy. The Americans] *originally* 'sympathies. They'; 'y' *written over* 'ies' *of* 'sympathies'; *the* 'y' *of* 'They' *canceled;* 'Americans' *interlined with a caret.*

329.25   could get.] *followed by* 'And he used these memorable
            words: that he "would not give a damn for such a Dec-
            laration." ' *canceled in blue ink.*

329.26   put forth] *interlined with a caret in blue ink above can-
            celed* 'coopered up'.

329.27–28   did really . . . Wishington] 'did . . . Wish-' *interlined
            with a caret in blue ink above canceled* 'actually went
            into business on that lofty but yet fanciful basis. Wash-';
            see revision at 329.3.

329.28   in time it] *follows canceled* 'it'.

329.29   the government thenceforth] *interlined with a caret.*

329.33   It lost its] 'It' *originally* 'Its'; *the* 's' *canceled.*

329.36–37   England,] *followed by* 'and was called the Father of
            American Veracity on account of the color of his hair.
            He won the battle of Traffleger on the Plains of Abra-
            ham under the walls of Mosco,' *canceled in blue ink;*
            'battle' *follows canceled* 'decisive' *and* 'Plains' *follows
            canceled* 'Pain'.

330.1   or lowness (shallowness?)] *interlined with a caret.*

330.1   exact] *interlined with a caret.*

330.4   wilds] *follows canceled* 'Wi'.

330.7   wherefor] *originally* 'whereforwhich'; 'which' *canceled
            in blue ink.*

330.17   Nineteenth] *follows canceled* 'Eigh'.

330.21   stood still.] *followed by canceled* 'And its mightiest half
            was its last half.'

330.22   mechanical and scientific] *interlined with a caret.*

330.30   panorama] *interlined with a caret above canceled* 'view'.

331.6   days, time was] *follows canceled* 'times, dates were';
            'dates' *follows a short unrecovered cancellation.*

331.12–13   *Anno Matris,*] 'Anno Mater/Matris,' *follows canceled* 'M'. *See emendations and textual notes.*

331.15   or four] *interlined with a caret.*

331.17–21   A.D. in America . . . Baker G.).] *originally* 'A.D. and replaced it with our A.M ; within a single century after we began work.'; *the semicolon after* 'A.M' *mended from a period;* 'and' *and* 'within a' *canceled in blue ink and* 'single . . . work.' *canceled in pencil;* 'in America in 1960 and' *interlined following* 'in 70 A.M ;' *which was interlined with a caret then canceled, all in blue ink;* 'in England . . . Baker G.)' *interlined in blue ink. See emendations.*

331.22   When] *originally* 'Just where'; 'where' *mended to* 'when' *first in pencil, then in ink;* 'Just' *canceled and* 'W' *written over* 'w' *of* 'when'.

331.22   we know.] *follows canceled* 'I am not able to say.'

331.22   1865.] *followed by canceled* 'O.S.'; *the period mended from a comma.*

331.23   Our Mother] *the* 'O' *of* 'Our' *mended from* 'o' *in pencil here and at* 331.31, 331.34, 332.5, *and* 332.10.

331.23   She] *the* 'S' *of* 'She' *mended from* 's' *in pencil here and at* 331.26, 332.5, 332.6, 332.11, 332.12, 332.15 (twice), 332.20, 332.21, *and* 332.23.

331.24   Her] *the* 'H' *of* 'Her' *mended from* 'h' *in pencil here and at* 331.31, 331.33, 331.34, 332.16, 332.19, 332.21, *and* 332.23.

331.25   were early] *originally* 'were'; *the italics canceled and* 'early' *interlined with a caret in blue ink.*

331.25–26   (discredited . . . who] *interlined with a caret in blue ink above canceled* '(they died mysteriously), who'.

331.30   ravished.] *interlined with a caret in blue ink above canceled* 'gobbled.'

331.30   (similarly discredited)] *interlined with a caret above
              canceled '*(they also died mysteriously)'.

331.31   Herself] *the 'H' of 'Herself' mended from 'h' in pencil
              here and at 332.23.*

331.31   put] *interlined with a caret in blue ink above canceled
              '*shovel'.

331.31–32   —albeit . . . form—] *interlined with a caret.*

331.32   labored] *interlined with a caret in blue ink to replace
              canceled '*battered'.

331.33   shape] *interlined with a caret in blue ink above canceled
              '*form'.

331.33   examples of] *interlined with a caret in blue ink above
              canceled '*some'.

331.33–34   discredited] *interlined with a caret in blue ink above
              canceled '*early'.

331.34   asserted] *originally '*(there was a graveyard of these)
              asserted'; 'was . . . asserted' *canceled, an 's' written over
              the 'r' of 'there', and '*were retired to rest and peace
              with those others), asserted' *interlined; '*(these . . . as-
              serted' *canceled in blue ink and '*asserted' *interlined with
              a caret in blue ink.*

332.1   suppressed] *interlined with a caret in blue ink above
              canceled '*earlier'.

332.3   about.] *followed by '*(These also were accumulated in
              that prosperous graveyard.)' *canceled in blue ink; '*pros-
              perous' *interlined with a caret.*

332.7   That . . . heaven] 'That She flew alive to heaven' *inter-
              lined with a caret in pencil above canceled '*This detail
              of sacred history'; 'passed' *written over '*flew' *in blue ink.*

332.8   that . . . since] *interlined with a caret above canceled
              '*that'.

332.13   ancient] *interlined with a caret.*

332.13–14   also . . . Masters,] *interlined with a caret.*

332.22   pictures] *originally* 'picture'; *the* 's' *added; followed by canceled* 'of'.

332.24   Those . . . Index.] *originally* '(Those historians have congenial company in that accumulation where they lie.)'; *the opening parenthesis and* 'congenial . . . lie.)' *canceled in blue ink and* 'been . . . Index.' *interlined with a caret in blue ink.*

332.24   an] *interlined with a caret.*

332.27   sparkling] *follows canceled* 'gay'.

332.29   —differently . . . significance—] *interlined with a caret.*

332.31   determinable,] *interlined with a caret in pencil above canceled* 'discoverable'.

332.32   represent] *follows canceled* 'have had a'.

332.35   two] *interlined with a caret in blue ink above canceled* 'four'.

333.1   Scroll and Key] *interlined with a caret in pencil.*

333.3   a university . . . seat] *follows* 'there had been' *canceled in pencil;* 'had its seat' *interlined with a caret in pencil.*

333.5   ecclesiastics.] *interlined with a caret in blue ink above canceled* 'of the clergy.'

333.9   inherited] *follows canceled* 'born'.

333.12   truthful] *interlined with a caret in blue ink above canceled* 'veracious'.

333.13   to picture] *follows canceled* 'this'.

333.14   political] *followed by canceled* 'and religious'.

333.18   shining] *interlined with a caret.*

333.24   the sun's . . . ink-black,] 'the sun's face is blotted out,' *interlined with a caret;* 'blotted out,' *canceled and* 'ink-black,' *added.*

333.28   Civilization] *the 'C' mended from 'c'.*

334.10   athwart the sombre] *'athwart the' interlined with a caret
                above canceled* 'across the'; *'sombre' interlined with a
                caret.*

334.11   fair] *interlined with a caret.*

334.11   saw on the] *follows canceled* 'saw the'.

334.17   of our . . . globe] *interlined with a caret.*

334.17–18   Republic . . . America.] *'and was . . . America.' inter-
                lined with a caret; the comma following* 'Republic'
                mended from a period.

334.20   own] *followed by canceled* '—government, law-making
                body'.

334.21   provincial] *interlined with a caret.*

334.22   sometimes] *follows canceled* 'called'.

334.30   preserved] *follows canceled* 'a curious old document'.

334.33   hills and hillocks] *'hills' originally* 'hillocks'; *'ocks' can-
                celed and the 's' added; 'and hillocks' interlined with a
                caret; all in blue ink.*

335.11   or Fromton,] *interlined with a caret in blue ink.*

335.12   of] *interlined with a caret above canceled* 'with'.

335.13   and another . . . Built,"] *interlined with a caret.*

335.15   tells . . . about] *'tells us a world about' interlined with a
                caret to replace canceled* 'lights up'; *'much' interlined
                with a caret in blue ink above canceled* 'a world' *in the
                interlineation.*

335.16   relatives,] *the 's' added; followed by canceled* 'with a
                dazzling glare'; *the comma added in blue ink.*

335.17   That stately] *follows canceled* 'A statue'.

335.17   meaning:] *the colon replaces a canceled dash.*

335.22   the lights] *'the' interlined with a caret.*

335.35   now,] *interlined with a caret following an added comma, all in blue ink.*

Written in blue ink from 336.title through 337.18

336.7   Bishop] *follows canceled* 'sometime'.

336.9   witness] *interlined with a caret.*

336.11   the first] *follows canceled* 'its first'.

336.16   us] *interlined with a caret above canceled* 'our hands'.

336.25   great] *interlined with a caret.*

336.25   several] *follows canceled* 'a num'.

336.27   "The Gospel] *follows canceled* 'the'.

337.6   extinguished] *interlined with a caret above canceled* 'punished'.

337.10   even, than] 'even,' *interlined with a caret;* 'than' *followed by canceled* 'even'.

337.15   lineage.] *followed by canceled* 'being descended in the direct line from Adamandeve. We have now no means of ascertaining who Adamandeve was.'; *the period mended from a comma.*

337.18   his counsel] *follows canceled* 'him'.

Written in purplish-black ink from 337.19 through 341.12 ('and')

337.19–341.12   He had . . . learning and] *added on 10 inserted MS pages numbered 4A to 4J following canceled paragraph* 'He was a man of great learning and'.

337.19   indeed] *follows canceled* 'indeed, slips of his pen'.

337.19–20   random . . . gossipy] *interlined with a caret above canceled* 'slips of his'.

337.21   often] *interlined with a caret.*

337.24   literally] *interlined with a caret above canceled* 'almost'.

337.27	clergy] *follows a canceled caret.*
337.30	consecrated official] *interlined with a caret.*
338.3	as much] *interlined with a caret above canceled* 'more'.
338.5	aver . . . that] *interlined with a caret above canceled* 'say,'.
338.6	half] *follows canceled* 'is'.
338.8	unwritten] *follows canceled* 'invisible'.
338.10	flashed and flamed] *interlined with a caret above canceled* 'burned'.
338.23	deeply] *interlined above canceled* 'fervently'.
338.32	these] *follows canceled* 'them we'.
338.33	do] *interlined with a caret.*
338.35	varied] *follows canceled* 'efforts'.
339.1	lack] *follows canceled* 'destitution'.
339.6	often] *interlined with a caret.*
339.23	meant] *follows canceled* 'should'.
339.35	What] *the 'W' written over* 'w'.
340.10	when] *follows canceled* 'these'.
340.21–22	could . . . down,] *interlined with a caret.*
340.31	ill-considered] 'ill-' *interlined with a caret following canceled* 'un'.
341.1	this] *follows canceled* 'that'.
341.3	several] *interlined with a caret above canceled* 'two'.
341.4	irrelevancies] *the 'irr' mended from* 'in'.
341.6	conceived,] *interlined with a caret above canceled* 'granted,'.
341.9	relieving that] *follows canceled* 'stripping that'.

341.10   cloud] *follows canceled* 'accumu'.

341.10   were worth] *follows canceled* 'was wo'.

Written in blue ink from 341.12 through 345.10

341.12–13   activities] *written over a wiped-out and unrecovered word.*

341.19   French] *interlined with a caret.*

341.19   Golden] *follows canceled* 'Vi'.

341.32   interesting] *interlined with a caret.*

341.33   all sorts] *follows canceled* 'no distinction'.

342.1   illustrate] *interlined with a caret above canceled* 'make'.

342.4   but] *interlined with a caret above a canceled ampersand.*

342.14   write] *followed by interlined and canceled* 'and print'.

342.15   this] *followed by canceled* 'mans'.

342.15   that the publishing] *interlined with a caret above canceled* 'the printing'.

342.15–16   be securely] *follows canceled* 'to'.

342.16   friend's] *interlined with a caret above canceled* 'man's'.

342.23   have arrived.] *originally* 'should arrive.'; 'have' *interlined with a caret;* 'd.' *written over a period.*

342.26   deformity] *follows canceled* 'moral'.

342.27   yet] *interlined with a caret.*

343.3   histories] *interlined with a caret above canceled* 'history'.

343.4   then] *interlined with a caret.*

343.12   things—] *the dash interlined with a caret above a canceled comma.*

343.19   necessity of] *interlined with a caret.*

343.19   translation.] *the period added above a canceled comma.*

343.22   that the] 'the' *written over* 'a'.

343.24   Since] *follows canceled* 'It'.

343.29   this] *mended from* 'these'.

343.29   book] *interlined with a caret above canceled* 'pages'.

343.31   perishable] *follows canceled* 'is'.

343.34–35   Ah . . . immortality!] *squeezed in.*

343.36   *Morte d'Arthur*] *originally* 'Mort d'Arthur'; *the* 'e' *squeezed in.*

344.9   Beowulf] *follows interlined and canceled* 'a case of'.

344.15   constructed] *interlined with a caret above canceled* 'made'.

344.15   especially] *originally* 'specially'; *the* 'e' *added.*

344.19   out] *interlined with a caret.*

344.19   current] *followed by canceled* 'for'.

344.19   remote] *interlined with a caret.*

344.21   in . . . time] *interlined with a caret.*

344.25   thenceforth] *followed by canceled* 'while'.

344.28   result.] *followed by canceled paragraph* 'Here following I'.

344.30   spelling] *interlined with a caret.*

344.31   early] *interlined with a caret.*

345.4   eddyplunks] *follows canceled* 'Ed'.

Written in black ink from 345.title through 348.25

345.title   To . . . Book] *follows canceled title* 'A Friendly Word.'

345.11   for the last time;] *interlined with a caret above a canceled comma.*

345.15   this] *follows canceled* 'these'.

345.22–23	our goblets.] *interlined with a caret preceding canceled* 'glasses. For'.
345.29	us dissipate] *follows canceled* 'us be'.
346.10	handsome] *follows canceled* 'pr'.
346.27	projecting] *interlined with a caret above canceled* 'striking'.
346.27	used to] *follows canceled* 'used to'.
346.32	national] *interlined with a caret above canceled* 'chosen'.
346.35	greatly] *interlined with a caret.*
346.37	quite] *interlined with a caret.*
347.9	rain] *the* 'r' *written over* 'a'.
347.10	But] *follows canceled* 'Clink again.'
347.12	both] *the* 'b' *written over a wiped-out unrecovered letter.*
347.18	these talons?] *interlined with a caret.*
347.33	oil! . . . .] *the ellipsis interlined with a caret.*
348.title	A Character . . . Incomplete] *follows canceled title* 'His Character.'
348.7–8	The first . . . breaks] *interlined with a caret above canceled* 'It breaks'.
348.8	no ending.] *followed by canceled* 'Evidently it once had a beginning, but it lacks it now; doubtless his type-writer skipped a page without being aware of it.'
348.9	One perceives . . . poet] *interlined with a caret following canceled paragraph* 'One perceives that a poet' *which was written above canceled paragraph* 'It is inferable from the opening sentence of the fragment, that a poet'; 'a poet' *in this last instance interlined with a caret above canceled* 'someone'.
348.9	majestic] *originally* 'quite extraordinary'; 'quite extra-

ordinary' *canceled and* 'most noble' *interlined with a caret then canceled;* 'majestic' *interlined with a caret.*

348.11   might] *follows canceled* 'would'.

348.17   the beginning . . . third] *interlined with a caret following canceled* 'his first'.

348.18   speaks of] *interlined with a caret above canceled* 'refers to'.

Written in greenish-black ink from 348.26 through 350.8

348.28   fenced around] *interlined with a caret above canceled* 'marked'.

348.28   broad] *interlined with a caret.*

349.10   Downward] *the poem as printed read* 'The other downward'; 'downward' *marked for transposition; the* 'd' *of* 'downward' *not changed to* 'D'; *the* 'T' *of* 'The' *not reduced to* 't'.

349.21–22   But I resolved . . . might.] *interlined with a caret in black ink.*

349.28   forehead] *interlined with a caret in black ink above canceled* 'foreward'.

350.5   Piccadilly] *the* 'P' *mended from* 'p'.

Written in black ink from 350.9 through 350.19

350.10–11   might . . . might] *interlined with a caret above canceled* 'would' *(twice).*

350.12   seemed] *follows canceled* 'w'.

350.14   character?] *the question mark mended from a semicolon.*

350.16–17   resolved to] *interlined with a caret following canceled* 'would'.

350.18   these] *follows canceled* 'them'.

Written in greenish-black ink from 350.20 through 352.7

350.29   Briggs] *interlined with a caret in black ink above canceled* 'He'; *follows* 'Briggs went on' *canceled in greenish-black ink.*

350.31   street—] *the dash interlined with a caret.*

350.31–33   Five . . . business?] *added on the verso of the MS page with instructions to turn over; written in black ink.*

350.34   I was . . . get] *interlined with a caret in black ink above canceled* 'What I wanted was'.

351.3   anything] *follows two wiped-out and canceled unrecovered letters.*

351.7   flatulent] *interlined with a caret.*

351.14   called] *written over wiped-out* 'av'.

351.21–22   Firmness o] *the zero written over the figure seven.*

351.23   first glance] 'first g' *written over wiped-out* 'once w'.

351.28   then] *interlined with a caret.*

351.29   quits] *follows canceled* 'stops'.

351.35   if he had one,] *interlined with a caret above canceled* 'who had done me no harm'.

351.36   in case . . . one.] *interlined with a caret in black ink; the preceding semicolon mended from a period.*

352.1   6.] *interlined with a caret above canceled* '7.'

352.3   mother dear!] *interlined with a caret in black ink above canceled* 'pray!'.

Written in black ink from 352.8 through 352.26 ('before')

352.13   have swept] *follows canceled* 'have overturned thr'.

352.14   made] *follows canceled* 'and buried them under it'.

352.15   not] *interlined with a caret.*

352.22   with] *follows canceled* 'and'.

352.22   chaplain] *originally* 'chaplains'; *the* 's' *canceled.*

352.23   preceding] *follows canceled* 'in his train.'

Written in brown ink from 352.26 ('This') through 353.10
Written in black ink from 353.11 through 353.31

353.13   the Great] *follows canceled* 'Civi'.

353.16   centuries] *interlined with a caret in blue ink above canceled* 'hundred years'.

353.18   The driver . . . slave.] *interlined with a caret.*

353.31   supplanted] *follows canceled* 'repla'.

Written in brown ink from 354.1 through 356.24

354.17   this] *follows canceled* 'it'.

354.18   for] *interlined with a caret in blue ink.*

354.18   gin] *follows canceled* 'pick'.

354.19   profit] *originally* 'profita'; *the* 'a' *canceled.*

354.20   The drink] *follows canceled* 'In'.

354.22–23   It is] *follows canceled* 'They are still still'.

354.26–27   the projectiles] *follows canceled* 'our'.

354.30   was a] *follows canceled* 'was an auction block'.

354.31   and vagrants] 'and' *added in blue ink following* 'and' *canceled in blue ink and* 'for' *added then canceled in blue ink.*

354.32–33   They . . . only.] *interlined with a caret in blue ink.*

355.4   Now . . . unfamiliar.] *interlined.*

355.7   advertisements] *follows canceled* 'poli'.

355.11   100] *follows canceled* '50'.

355.13   All . . . wood.] *interlined with a caret.*

355.15   and destructive] *interlined with a caret.*

355.20   5,000] *the '5,' interlined above canceled '10'; follows a canceled unrecovered figure or letter.*

355.21   15,000] *the '15' written over '30'.*

355.21   four-fifths] *follows a canceled unrecovered figure or letter.*

355.23   famine] *follows canceled 'disease,'.*

355.27   *domestic] 'domestic' interlined with a caret in blue ink above canceled 'home'; the italics added in pencil.*

355.31   the people] *follows canceled 'the American'.*

356.13   strength] *follows canceled 'power'.*

356.13–14   and influence] *interlined with a caret in blue ink.*

356.16   and contentment] *'and' interlined with a caret above a canceled comma; 'contentment' followed by a canceled comma.*

356.19   patriotism] *follows canceled 'lofty'.*

356.22   about] *interlined with a caret above canceled 'ready'.*

356.23   is matter] *follows canceled 'only'.*

Written in blue ink from 356.25 through 364.25

356.25   months of the] *followed by 'twenty' interlined then canceled.*

356.26   born] *followed by 'scientists, inventors, financiers, etc., —' interlined with a caret then canceled.*

357.2–3   another . . . later;] *interlined with a caret following canceled 'and'.*

357.3–4   and beyond, these relays] *interlined with a caret above canceled 'these two bands'.*

357.5 In the] *follows canceled paragraph* 'To us, at this distance, they'.

357.5 Lyell] *follows canceled* 'Franklin,'.

357.6–7 Lavoisier] *follows canceled* 'Pasteur,'.

357.7 a number] *follows canceled* 'and' *and* 'Field,' *interlined then canceled.*

357.8 and third] *interlined with a caret.*

357.9 Field,] *interlined with a caret.*

357.10 Carnegie] *follows canceled* 'Vanderbilt,'.

357.15 I shall] 'I' *interlined with a caret above canceled* 'We'.

357.17 later] *follows a canceled caret.*

357.18 I . . . I] *interlined with a caret above canceled* 'we' *(twice).*

357.18 closely] *follows canceled* 'sub'.

357.21 Sir] *interlined with a caret in pencil.*

357.27 a rule] *follows canceled* 'that'.

357.30 the ancient] *follows canceled* 'the days of antiquity'.

358.10 of a magnet,] *interlined with a caret above canceled* 'of the earth'.

358.22 presently] *interlined with a caret.*

358.25 Izaac] *follows canceled* 'gravi'.

358.25–26 attracting it,] *followed by canceled* 'His grandson'; *the comma mended from a period.*

358.26 great-great-] *interlined with a caret.*

358.31 that since] *follows canceled* 'that perhaps the'.

359.3 He noticed that the] 'He noticed that' *interlined with a caret; the* 't' *of* 'the' *mended from* 'T'.

359.3 looked] *interlined with a caret above canceled* 'was'.

359.5	constructed] *the 'c' written over 'n' or 'w'.*
359.8	and Saturn,] *interlined with a caret in pencil.*
359.9	at any] *follows canceled* 'that one,'.
359.10–13	These . . . earth.] *written on the verso of the MS page with instructions to turn over.*
359.11	floating] *follows canceled* 'that had'.
359.12	since] *follows a canceled comma.*
359.14	Leverrier,] *interlined with a caret in pencil above canceled* 'Laplace,'.
359.22	than itself] *follows canceled* 'than himself.'
359.23	uneasy] *interlined with a caret above canceled* 'annoyed'.
359.30	turned] *follows canceled* 'happened'.
359.35	peculiar] *originally* 'peculiarly'; 'ly' *canceled.*
360.2	had always] *follows canceled* 'was'.
360.6	flight] *interlined with a caret above canceled* 'way'.
360.11	and dignified and stationary] *interlined with a caret.*
360.12	beyond] *follows canceled* 'a'.
360.13	a moon] *the 'a' written over an ampersand.*
360.14	stars—] *the dash interlined with a caret above a canceled comma.*
360.16	proud] *the 'p' written over 'g'.*
360.19	had happened] 'had' *interlined with a caret.*
360.22	a bewildered little] *interlined with a caret above canceled* 'and an'.
360.22	left . . . cold,] *interlined with a caret.*
360.24–25	should you say] *interlined with a caret.*
360.29	haze,—a] '—a' *interlined with a caret above canceled* 'a'.

360.30–31   a paradise whose] *interlined with a caret above canceled* 'whose'.

361.6   of pretty] 'of' *interlined with a caret.*

361.12   was] *interlined with a caret above canceled* 'is'.

361.16   finally] *written over a wiped-out unrecovered word.*

361.18   world] *follows canceled* 'scientific'.

361.20   Institute] *originally* 'Institution'; 'on' *canceled; the* 'i' *mended to* 'e'.

361.26   oxygen.] *interlined in pencil above canceled* 'established.'

361.29   park] *follows canceled* 'squar'.

361.31–32   together] *follows a canceled caret.*

362.4   costly] *interlined with a caret above canceled* 'co'.

362.14–15   and would] *follows canceled* 'and his serv'.

362.15   out] *follows canceled* 'to the limbo of the forgotten deeds of men'.

362.20   This] *follows canceled* 'The reason that'; *the* 'T' *of* 'This' *mended from* 't'.

362.24   the air] *follows canceled* 'the animals,'.

362.29   on, and had] *originally* 'on, has'; 'and' *interlined with a caret; the* 'd' *of* 'had' *written over* 's'.

362.34   shrink] *interlined with a caret above canceled* 'reduce'.

363.3   the enraged people] *interlined with a caret above canceled* 'it was'.

363.25   can he] *follows canceled* 'will he'.

363.27   and big . . . results!] *interlined with a caret.*

364.1   difference] *originally* 'different'; *the* 'ce' *written over* 't'.

364.1   between] *interlined with a caret above canceled* 'in'.

364.1   it] *originally* 'its'; *the* 's' *canceled.*

364.2   exactly] *follows canceled* 'rep'.

364.6   when] *follows canceled* 'if'.

364.9   localities] *follows canceled* 'towns'.

364.12   the fogs,] *follows canceled* 'and'.

364.12   the hail, the snow,] *interlined with a caret.*

Written in brown ink from 364.26 to the end

364.27   golden] *interlined with a caret.*

364.33   kinsmen,] *interlined with a caret above canceled* 'blood-
               kindred,'.

365.4   appeared] *follows canceled* 'Kir'.

365.8   blood-kinship] *follows* 'physical' *interlined with a caret
               then canceled.*

365.13   colors] *follows canceled* 'o'.

365.15   from whence] 'from' *interlined with a caret.*

365.22–23   called . . . Trust,] *interlined with a caret.*

365.28–29   personally] *follows canceled* 'its'.

365.29   sublet] *follows canceled* 'sub-let'.

365.30   ten] *the* 't' *written over wiped-out* 'f'.

366.6   great] *interlined with a caret.*

366.30   cause] *interlined above* 'make'. *See emendations.*

366.30   to stand] 'to' *interlined above* 'Europe'.

366.33   by] *follows canceled* 'for'.

367.19   curses] *follows canceled* 'black'.

367.21   fatal] *follows canceled* 'evil'.

367.22   there] *follows canceled* 'there, to the number of nine-
               teen'.

367.36   whom] *follows canceled* 'who was a super'.

368.13–14   with . . . other;] *interlined with a caret.*

368.14   also] *follows what appears to be a canceled* 'i'.

368.17   groups] *follows a canceled comma.*

368.18   waists,—] *the dash interlined with a caret.*

368.34   fathomless] *follows canceled* 'measureless'.

369.1   yet] *interlined with a caret.*

369.1   other] *interlined with a caret above canceled* 'more'.

369.1   jurisdiction of] *originally* 'jurisdictional'; 'of' *written over wiped-out* 'al'.

369.9   enthusing] *follows canceled* 'generous'.

369.11   land] *follows canceled* 'dark'.

369.18   written down] *interlined with a caret.*

369.19   experienced] *follows canceled* 'daily endured'.

369.20   Henri] *follows canceled* 'Henry'.

369.30   had] *interlined with a caret.*

370.3   which] *follows canceled* 'that'.

370.9   ignorant of] *replaces canceled* 'without'.

370.17   Luther] *interlined with a caret above canceled* 'He'.

370.21   stored] *follows canceled* 'to'.

370.21   patterns] 'pat-|terns' *in MS;* 'terns' *follows canceled* 'terns for the'.

370.22   The] *follows canceled* 'His theory'.

370.24   With] *follows what may be canceled* 'Within', 'With-ou', *or* 'With n'.

370.30   animal] *follows canceled* 'com-|'.

371.5   them] *interlined with a caret preceding canceled* 'them too far, and'.

371.6   mistake.] *followed by canceled* 'They discovered Man. This was not itself the mistake, yet it' *and canceled* 'They'.

371.7   was] *follows a canceled caret.*

371.7   had] *interlined with a caret.*

371.10   A damp] *follows* 'Out of 600 models registered, this was the first female one.' *interlined then canceled.*

371.14   figured] *interlined with a caret above canceled* 'stood'.

371.14   but] *interlined with a caret above canceled* 'they'.

371.16   at all] *interlined with a caret above a canceled semicolon.*

371.18   special] *interlined with a caret.*

371.19–22   —a procedure . . . until now.] *added on the verso of the MS page with instructions to turn over. See textual notes.*

371.19   eminently] *interlined with a caret.*

371.20   strange and multifarious] *interlined with a caret.*

371.21   but] *interlined with a caret above canceled* 'and'; *follows canceled* 'but which had defeated all'.

371.23–24   not . . . inferior] *interlined with a caret following canceled* 'inferior'.

371.27   was] *follows canceled* 'was not'.

371.28   presumptive] *interlined with a caret above canceled* 'nega' *and preceding canceled* 'assumptive'.

371.29   the Man] *follows a canceled dash.*

371.29–30   a model of baked clay,] *interlined with a caret.*

371.31   exist] *followed by a canceled comma.*

372.5–6   daughtered . . . desiring] 'daughtered . . . de-|' *interlined with a caret above canceled* 'fathers of daughters de-|'.

372.6   then] *interlined with a caret above canceled* 'finally,'.

372.7   with] *interlined with a caret.*

372.7   and insult] 'and' *interlined above a canceled comma.*

372.8   at last] *interlined with a caret.*

372.10   know] *follows canceled* 'be'.

372.13   months] *interlined with a caret following* 'ago' *which was interlined with a caret then canceled.*

372.17   Profane] *interlined with a caret above canceled* 'Criminal'.

372.18   extenuating] *interlined with a caret above canceled* 'mitigating'.

372.21   In the] *marked to begin a new paragraph with a paragraph sign.*

372.21   innocently] *follows canceled* 'thought'.

372.23   concerning] 'co' *written over wiped-out* 'as'.

372.24   were eager] *follows canceled* 'were y'.

372.30   and intoxicated] 'and' *interlined with a caret.*

372.31   and regard] *follows a canceled period.*

372.34   might] *interlined with a caret above canceled* 'would'.

372.35   with] *interlined with a caret.*

373.1   despondent.] *the period mended from a comma; followed by canceled* 'for *his* bones also had given out.'

373.4   came upon] *interlined with a caret.*

373.5   black-spotted] 'black-' *interlined with a caret above canceled* 'blue-'.

373.7   one ear . . . cocked,] *interlined with a caret.*

373.22   considered.] *followed by canceled* 'it.'; *the period added.*

373.28   race in and] *interlined with a caret.*

373.31   was] *interlined with a caret above canceled* 'and those others were'.

373.33   Paint] *interlined with a caret above canceled* 'It'.

373.34   as] *interlined with a caret.*

374.2   traveled] *interlined with a caret above canceled* 'made'.

374.3   sparing] *follows canceled* 'gladly'.

374.5   grief] *follows canceled* 'dis'.

374.7   hole] *interlined with a caret above canceled* 'place'.

374.8   it in] *follows canceled* 'the'.

374.9   their] *originally* 'their'; 'ir' *canceled to make* 'the'; 'their' *interlined with a caret above canceled* 'the'.

374.16   before,] *interlined with a caret.*

374.18   he said] *originally* 'he said'; 't' *added to* 'he' *and* 'professor' *interlined with a caret;* 'the professor' *canceled and* 'he' *restored.*

374.23   built] *follows two or three unrecovered canceled letters.*

374.25   that] *interlined with a caret.*

374.27   talks] *follows canceled* 'random'.

374.29   high] *interlined with a caret above canceled* 'great'.

374.31   always] *interlined with a caret.*

374.31   him] *followed by a canceled comma.*

374.34   and hideous monsters] *interlined with a caret.*

374.35   were] *interlined with a caret.*

374.35   by report] *follows canceled* 'only'.

375.4   and ambitions] *interlined with a caret.*

375.5   fiendish] *interlined with a caret.*

375.7   patron, who] *interlined with a caret above canceled* 'professor, who'.

375.9   In the] *follows canceled* 'The'.

375.10   gone dry,] *interlined with a caret above canceled* 'struck bedrock,'.

375.11   a-hunger] *follows canceled* 'a h'.

375.20   in that] *follows a canceled comma.*

375.21–22   prodigal and] *interlined with a caret.*

375.23   forsaken] *follows canceled* 'sad.'

375.23   Judge] *follows canceled* 'the'.

375.24   had gloomed] *follows canceled* 'had appointed death'; *the* 'g' *of* 'gloomed' *written over an* 's'.

375.25   Assize . . . among] *squeezed in to replace canceled* 'Assize, appointing death to'.

375.25   ragged] *interlined with a caret.*

375.26   erring] *interlined with a caret above canceled* 'erroring'.

375.30   through] *follows a canceled comma.*

375.31   family] *interlined with a caret.*

375.34–376.1 What . . . knew."] *added on the verso of the MS page with instructions to turn over.*

376.1   at Rome,] *interlined with a caret.*

376.2   wanton charge of nonconformity,] *interlined to replace canceled* 'wanton charge' *which was interlined with a caret above canceled* 'deadly charge of witchcraft and intemperance at Rome'.

376.5   an] *follows what appears to be canceled* 'his'.

376.8   names] *follows canceled* 'families.'

376.11   Geology] *the* 'G' *written over* 'g'.

376.18   rocks?] *followed by a canceled caret.*

376.19–20   And not . . . day?] *squeezed in.*

376.29   reason;] *the semicolon replaces a canceled question mark.*

377.4   after] *follows canceled* 'the matter'.

377.11   Deluge] *the 'D' written over 'd'.*

377.13   claimed] *interlined above canceled* 'suggested'.

377.13   while] *interlined with a caret.*

377.15   observed] *follows canceled* 'sugges'.

377.18   distinct] *interlined with a caret.*

377.19   bottom] *interlined above canceled* 'early'.

377.20   the fossils of] *interlined with a caret.*

377.21   succeeding] *interlined with a caret above canceled* 'next'.

377.21   these] *follows canceled* 'above'.

377.23   and leaving] *follows a canceled comma.*

377.24   the pterodactyl and the mastodon;] *interlined with a caret following what appears to be a canceled ampersand.*

377.26   then,] *interlined with a caret.*

377.29   not] *interlined with a caret.*

377.30   that was] *follows canceled* 'that'.

377.31   doctrine] *followed by canceled* 'that'.

377.32   Darwin] *followed by canceled* 'and Wallace and Herbert Spencer studied'.

378.5   business,] *interlined with a caret above canceled* 'matter,'.

378.8   all-clarifying] *interlined with a caret.*

378.9   claimed] *followed by* 'and proved' *interlined with a caret then canceled.*

378.9–10   universe] *follows canceled* 'universe and was obey'.

378.10   proved that] *interlined with a caret.*

378.10   of its] *interlined with a caret above canceled* 'of whose'.

378.12   constellations,] *the comma mended from a semicolon.*

378.12   and] *interlined with a caret above canceled* ', the'.

378.12   of systems] *follows* 'and extinction' *interlined with a caret then canceled, following canceled* 'and decay'.

378.13   government] *originally* 'governments'; *the* 's' *canceled.*

378.14–15   slow . . . persistent,] *interlined with a caret.*

378.16   form] *followed by canceled* 'and'.

378.18   in] *written over* 'm'.

378.25   and wonder] 'and' *interlined with a caret above canceled* 'they'.

378.26   out] *follows canceled* 'of.'

378.27   the ball] 'the' *written over wiped-out* 'al'.

378.30   and flake . . . majesty.] *interlined with a caret; the preceding semicolon mended from a period.*

378.34   deeps] *interlined above canceled* 'vacancies'.

378.34   dim-flecked] *follows canceled* 'with'.

378.36   Buffon] *follows canceled* 'Darwin'.

378.36   Cuvier] *follows canceled* 'and'.

379.9–10   and the History . . . revealed!] *interlined above canceled* 'and the History of', *canceled* 'and the Genesis of Things', *canceled* 'and the History of Things stood revealed, and the puzzles of their apparently capricious and methodless propagation unriddled', *and canceled* 'the manner of their propagation laid bare'; 'apparently' *follows canceled* 'seem'.

379.14   breeds] *follows canceled* 'to'.

379.15   on] *mended from* 'out'.

379.18   contributor] *originally* 'contributors'; *the* 's' *canceled.*

379.29   Individuals] *follows canceled* 'Men do'.

379.34   ridden] *interlined with a caret following canceled* 'rode'.

380.15   law] *originally* 'laws'; *the* 's' *canceled.*

380.15   automatically] *interlined with a caret.*

380.15   directed] *followed by canceled* 'over its course'.

380.16   forces] *follows canceled* 'automatic'.

380.23   logically] *follows canceled* 'sound, and ma'.

380.28   circumstances,] *followed by a canceled caret.*

380.31   American] *interlined with a caret.*

381.12   price] *follows canceled* 'profit'.

381.14   America] *originally* 'American'; *the* 'n' *wiped out.*

381.17   long] *follows canceled* 'everywhere' *and* 'ceased'.

381.18   But] *originally a new paragraph; marked to run on.*

381.20–21   because . . . day.] *replaces canceled paragraph* 'Then the'; *the preceding comma mended from a period.*

381.24   then a . . . that,] *interlined with a caret.*

382.6   and blind] *interlined following canceled* 'Evolution carried' *and canceled* 'developed'.

382.9   the work] *interlined with a caret.*

382.10   unintelligent] *follows canceled* 'and'.

382.11   irresistible] *interlined above* 'long'. *See emendations and textual notes.*

Eddypus Fragment

Textual Commentary

The manuscript is copy-text; there are no textual notes.

Emendations of the Copy-Text

	MTP READING	COPY-TEXT READING
384.14	ambushed	abushed

Word Division in the Copy-Text

384.17   common-sense

Mark Twain's Revisions

384.6   the sole] 'the' *interlined with a caret above canceled* 'a'.

384.6–7   function . . . earth] *originally* 'function—to furnish light'; 'of' *interlined with a caret above canceled* '—to'; *the* 'ing' *of* 'furnishing' *squeezed in;* 'light' *followed by canceled* 'to the earth at night.'

384.10   the unbusiness-like] *follows canceled* 'in'.

384.17   'If] *the single quotation mark mended from double quotation marks.*

384.17   gas] *interlined with a caret.*

384.18   cities] *follows one or two wiped-out unrecovered letters.*

384.20   built?'] *the question mark added.*

385.1-2   never . . . ruins.] *originally* 'never to rise from its ruins more'; 'more' *canceled then interlined with a caret to follow* 'never'; *a period and quotation marks added after* 'ruins'; *the quotation marks canceled.*

History 1,000 Years from Now

Textual Commentary

The manuscript is copy-text; no ambiguous compound is hyphenated at the end of a line in the manuscript.

Textual Notes

387.7   2899] Mark Twain wrote "2999," apparently equating the 2900's with the 29th century. His error has been corrected.

Emendations of the Copy-Text

	MTP READING	COPY-TEXT READING
*387.7	2899	2999
388.8	seizure	siezure
†388.27	existence.	existence,

Mark Twain's Revisions

387.2   no doubt] *interlined with a caret.*

387.6   couple of] *interlined with a caret.*

387.7   2899,] *follows canceled* '2900, or'.

388.7   less] *interlined with a caret above canceled* 'no'.

388.9   now] *interlined with a caret.*

388.21   grandeur] *follows canceled* 'importance'.

388.27   existence.] *originally* 'existence, except our own.'; 'except our own.' *canceled; the comma after* 'existence' *inadvertently left standing.*

Passage from "Glances at History" (suppressed.)

Textual Commentary

The manuscript is copy-text; the author's unrevised typescript is also in the Mark Twain Papers. The letter "x" follows the page numbers in both manuscript and typescript, presumably because Mark Twain once intended to integrate the piece in his sequence of biblical writings. He used a numeral plus initial formula in numbering most of the works in the sequence. For a full discussion of the work's relation to the Adam and Eve writings, see the headnote to "Passage from a Lecture." There are no textual notes, and no ambiguous compound is hyphenated at the end of a line in the manuscript.

Emendations of the Copy-Text

	MTP READING	COPY-TEXT READING
†391.20	Merely a	Merely A
392.10	republic	Republic

Mark Twain's Revisions

391.title	Passage . . . century] *follows canceled title* 'First Fall of the Great Republic.'
391.2	and which . . . intact,] *interlined with a caret.*
391.6	malicious] *interlined with a caret.*
391.15	I . . . consider.] *interlined with a caret following canceled paragraph* 'We are now en'.
391.16	trivial . . . against] *originally* 'trivial war, against'; 'war' *interlined with a caret preceding* 'against' *and* 'a' *added at the end of the line above.*

391.17   our citizens] *interlined with a caret above canceled* 'the
                people'.

391.20   Merely a] 'Merely' *interlined with a caret; the MS* 'A'
                not reduced to 'a'.

391.20   a blood-stirring] *follows canceled* '—a'.

392.1   *Country] the* 'C' *mended from* 'c'.

392.4   school-house in the] *interlined with a caret.*

392.5–9   And . . . nation?] *added on the verso of MS page with in-
                structions to turn over following canceled* 'That insult
                to the nation!'; *the comma after* 'wrong' *mended from a
                period;* 'and urge on' *interlined with a caret following
                canceled* 'and support the little war.' *and canceled* 'and
                support'.

392.11   the Government] *interlined with a caret above canceled*
                'it'.

392.14   Its . . . them.] *interlined with a caret.*

392.20   isn't.] *followed by a canceled question mark; the period
                added.*

392.28   which course] *follows canceled* 'who is a patriot and who
                isn't.'

392.29–30   to be . . . inexcusable] 'an' *interlined with a caret;* 'in-
                excusable' *follows canceled* 'shameless'.

392.31   men] *interlined with a caret above canceled* 'us'.

392.34   hold . . . head!] *originally* 'hold your head up!'; 'up!' *can-
                celed and* 'up' *interlined with a caret following* 'hold';
                the exclamation mark after 'head' *added.*

392.35–393.1   republic's . . . republic's] 'republic's' *follows canceled*
                'nation's' (*twice*).

393.4   one:] *interlined with a caret above a canceled colon.*

Passage from "Outlines of History" (suppressed.)

Textual Commentary

The manuscript is copy-text; the author's unrevised typescript is also in the Mark Twain Papers. A double "x" follows the page numbers in both manuscript and typescript, in accordance with the numbering system Mark Twain developed for the works in his Adam and Eve sequence. Presumably he once intended to integrate "Outlines" and its companion pieces, "Glances at History" and "Passage from a Lecture," in his sequence of biblical writings. The relationship of the three works to the Adam and Eve writings is discussed more fully in the headnote to "Passage from a Lecture."

Textual Notes

396.21   conquests—] Followed on the manuscript by a caret, above which Mark Twain wrote in ink in the top right margin, "under a Presid[e]nt coward & hypocrite & windbag & weather-cock." The addition may have been written originally either as a marginal note or as a revision. The caret follows another caret which had been canceled in the ink used throughout this manuscript. The addition has been canceled in pencil; there are no other penciled revisions on the manuscript. Although the cancellation cannot be assigned to Mark Twain with certainty, the phrase has been omitted from the text because its mood is inconsistent with that of "The sleeping republic awoke at last . . . and put the government into clean hands" (395.18–20).

Emendations of the Copy-Text

	MTP READING	COPY-TEXT READING
395.10	aristocracies TS	aristocrasies

	MTP READING	COPY-TEXT READING
395.16	South	south
396.4–5	irremovable	irremoval
396.22	to do	do

Word Division in the Copy-Text

395.19   money-changers *Also at* 396.15, 396.26, 396.27

Mark Twain's Revisions

395.4   endure . . . like] *interlined above canceled* 'trample upon
                the weak'.

395.7   rich] *interlined with a caret.*

395.8–9   There . . . pocket.] *interlined with a caret.*

395.11–12   the plutocrats . . . time] *originally* 'they in time came';
                the 'y' *of* 'they' *and* 'in time came' *canceled;* 'plutocrats
                . . . time' *interlined with a caret.*

395.13   toward] *follows canceled* 'toward eventual monarchy
                was'.

395.16   went down] *follows canceled* 'succumbed'.

396.1   before] *interlined with a caret above canceled* 'ago'.

396.4   a machine . . . time] *interlined with a caret above a
                canceled ampersand.*

396.7   pensions] *originally* 'pensioners'; 'rs' *canceled and the*
                'e' *mended to* 's'.

396.8   who . . . came] *follows canceled* 'came'; 'in their lives'
                interlined with a caret.

396.20   A . . . answer.] *interlined with a caret.*

396.21   conquests—] 'under a President coward and hypocrite
                and windbag and weather-cock.' *interlined with a caret*
                above the dash then apparently canceled in pencil; the
                caret is canceled then rewritten in ink; the dash may or
                may not have been added. See textual notes.

396.24   rushed] *follows canceled* 'pr'.

396.26   privately sold] *follows canceled* 'sold'.

396.31   still] *interlined with a caret.*

Passage from a Lecture

Textual Commentary

The manuscript is copy-text; the author's unrevised typescript is also in the Mark Twain Papers. The second through fourth pages of manuscript were originally numbered 94–96. They were apparently written as part of another work which cannot now be identified. When Mark Twain added the present first page and the concluding four pages to the manuscript, he numbered them 1Cc and 5Cc through 8Cc, respectively, and renumbered the original pages to conform to the new system. This numbering system, carried on into the typescript as well, indicates that he probably once intended to integrate the piece into his sequence of Adam and Eve writings. Mark Twain wrote "Eve" in block capitals on the verso of the last manuscript page. See the headnote to the work for a full discussion of its relationship to the biblical sequence.

Textual Notes

399.5	Angina Pectoris] Someone, probably Paine, canceled these words in pencil on the manuscript and wrote above them "Reginald Selkirk."
401.35	It is even] The last paragraph is canceled in pencil on the manuscript, but "stet" is written in the margin. Probably Paine canceled and restored the paragraph.

Emendations of the Copy-Text

	MTP READING	COPY-TEXT READING
†400.12	etc.	etc
†401.36	rise, in the old time,	rise, in the rise, old time,
402.9	Repetition	Repetitions

Word Division in the Copy-Text

400.8   head-tops

Mark Twain's Revisions

399.1   monthly] *interlined with a caret above canceled* 'anual'.

399.1   Imperial] *interlined with a caret.*

399.9   terms of the] *interlined with a caret.*

399.10   Repetition] *followed by canceled passage* 'what the deso-
               late world will look like when we see it again; and tell
               me, oh, tell me that there will be no more floods."
                  "Ah, madam, I would I could, but I cannot. By the
               Law of Periodical Repetitions—"
                  "Oh, go on—why do you stop?"
                  "I thought you were in pain."
                  "Never mind it; it was nothing; it has passed. I
               brought it upon myself."
                  "The pain?"
                  "The *cause* of it. Pray go on."
                  "Well, then, as I was about to say, by that Law,'.

399.10   happen . . . only;] *originally* 'happen but a single time;';
               'but' *canceled;* 'only;' *interlined with a caret written over
               the semicolon.*

399.14   superb] *follows canceled* 'most'.

399.21   If you ask—] *added following canceled quotation marks.*

400.2   the *average*] 'the' *originally* 'they'; *the* 'y' *canceled.*

400.5   Yes,] *follows canceled opening quotation marks.*

400.5   I answer,] *interlined with a caret.*

400.6   If I may] *interlined with a caret following canceled* 'To'.

400.7   the race . . . feet] 'the race' *followed by a comma added*

and canceled and by 'say,' *interlined with a caret and
canceled; then* 'say,' *interlined with a caret again following* 'at'.

400.9–10   That floor . . . changes.] *interlined with a caret;* 'and'
             interlined with a caret following 'masses'.

400.10–11   Here . . . above it] *originally* 'Above it here and there,
             miles and miles apart, will project a head'; 'Above it'
             canceled, the 'h' *of* 'here' *mended to* 'H', *and* 'above
             it' *interlined with a caret following* 'project'; 'miles and'
             canceled; then 'a' *canceled and* 'and be noticeable a'
             interlined with a caret preceding 'head'; *finally that inter-
             lineation and* 'head' *canceled and* 'a head' *interlined
             with a caret following* 'apart,'.

400.11   one . . . inch,] *originally* 'three intellectual inches,'; 'one'
             interlined with a caret above canceled 'three'; *the* 'es' *of*
             'inches' *and the comma canceled; the comma following*
             'inch' *added.*

400.11–12   speak . . . spread] *originally* 'speak, and in a spread';
             'and' *canceled;* '—men . . . etc;' *interlined with a caret
             written over the comma. See emendations.*

400.12–13   of five thousand] *interlined with a caret above canceled*
             'of a hundred'.

400.13   three] *originally* 'three'; *the italics canceled.*

400.13   still] *interlined with a caret written over an unrecovered
             wiped-out word.*

400.13–14   —men . . . fame—] *interlined with a caret.*

400.15–23   three—a man . . . dominion.] *originally* 'three.'; *the
             period canceled;* '—a man of world-wide renown, a man'
             interlined with a caret then canceled; '—a man . . .
             dominion.' *added on the verso of the MS page with in-
             structions to turn over.*

400.15   (temporarily)] *interlined with a caret.*

400.16   finally,] *followed by canceled* 'above even this'.

400.19   fame] *originally* 'name'; 'fame' *written over* 'name' *then canceled;* 'fame' *interlined with a caret above the cancellation.*

400.20   name] *originally* 'fame'; *the* 'n' *written over* 'f'; *the* 'f' *then partially canceled in pencil.*

400.20   colossus] *interlined following canceled* 'genius'; 'genius' *interlined above canceled* 'prodigy'.

400.22   like him who,] *follows wiped-out and canceled* 'wh'.

400.23   shoe-hammer] *follows canceled* 'shoemaker-h'.

400.25   distinguished;] *followed by canceled* 'and in the isolated highest head you have the poet or the general or the orator or the statesman who appears in the earth once in an age'.

400.26   of . . . distinction;] 'of' *interlined with a caret above a canceled ampersand;* 'and more lasting' *interlined with a caret.*

400.27   final] *follows canceled* 'isolated'.

400.31   and always] 'and' *interlined with a caret.*

400.32   In each] 'each' *interlined with a caret above canceled* 'a given'.

401.2   then] *interlined with a caret.*

401.11   thing] *interlined with a caret.*

401.12   law.] *the period mended from a colon.*

401.27   more] *the* 'm' *written over one or two wiped-out unrecovered letters.*

401.36   Did . . . and did] *originally* 'Did not Christian Science rise, a century after the coming of the Savior? and did'; 'the' *interlined with a caret above canceled* 'Christian'; 'a century . . . Savior?' *canceled;* 'of Health rise, in the' *and* 'old time,' *interlined with carets; the original* 'rise' *following* 'Science' *inadvertently left standing.*

401.36　　　　　pass] *followed by canceled* 'away'.

402.3　　　　　and again.] *followed by canceled* 'Will Christ Himself come again'.

402.6　　　　　yet] *interlined with a caret.*

The Stupendous Procession

Textual Commentary

"The Stupendous Procession" survives in manuscript and in a typescript sketchily revised by the author. Copy-text is the author's inscription in the manuscript or in the typescript when a holograph change there supersedes the manuscript reading.

The manuscript consists of torn half-sheets and is written in black ink and faded black ink; it is revised in faded black ink and pencil. When Mark Twain reached about 416.17 he refilled his pen with an ink slightly lighter than he had been using. From that point on, the ink becomes lighter with a faint brownish cast, and the faded black of the last pages is the same as that used for revision of the earlier pages. The pencil revisions on the manuscript appear to have been made later than those in faded black ink everywhere but at 408.9–14, where the faded black ink is the latest marking.

Only ten words, all italic in the manuscript, were italicized in the typescript: *"their"* (410.24), *"there"* (411.5), *"now"* (411.13), *"Will"* (411.15), *"got"* (411.34), *"No"* (411.36), *"had"* (415.2), and *"He"* (418.17) were underscored on the typewriter; *"seem"* (409.10) and *"they"* (409.23) were underscored in pencil. Since Mark Twain made no systematic effort to add italics to the typescript, and nowhere supplanted the italics of the manuscript, the manuscript markings remain authoritative.

Because the work was left unfinished, it is inconsistent in spelling, hyphenation, the placement of items on the page, and marking for such typographical devices as capitals and italics. These inconsistencies have not been emended.

Textual Notes

405.title   The Stupendous Procession] Above the title on the typescript, Mark Twain wrote in pencil, "Motto—Indemnity, & 'one-third extra—to be used in propagating the Gospel.' As per unrepudiated statement of Rev. Dr.

Ament, Dec. 24, 1900." He later changed "propagating the Gospel" to "church expenses," and canceled "unrepudiated." Above this note, Paine, or perhaps Mark Twain, added an unrecoverable word and "1901" in black ink.

406.1   *Supporters.*] At the top of the manuscript page beginning here, Mark Twain wrote "Queen."

406.6–7   MUSIC . . . Influence.)] Circled in the manuscript.

406.8   Purchases] The word is typed lower-case, and Mark Twain added quotation marks on the typescript instead of restoring the manuscript capital. An initial capital is consistent with the author's usage elsewhere in this work, and since the revision was occasioned by a typing error, the manuscript reading is preferred here.

407.19   *Mutilated* . . . "Madagascar;"] At the top of the type-script page beginning here, Mark Twain wrote in pencil "I also said, Shake off the dust (almost illegible)," then canceled "Shake off the dust" and substituted "Go into all the world."

407.21   bearing] In the right margin of the typescript near this word, Mark Twain wrote in pencil, "report of Ament," a note which was expanded in the next sentence, also added in pencil.

408.21–409.8   *Fat Spanish Friar* . . . carrion!"] Mark Twain added this passage on new manuscript pages 7 and 7A. The original page 7 was renumbered 7B, and its first sentence, which had been copied as the first sentence of the new page 7, was canceled (see revision at 409.9). A comparison of the edges of the torn half-sheets on which the manuscript is written reveals that the two inserted pages were originally the other halves of the last two pages of the manuscript and therefore were almost certainly written after completion of the first draft of the piece.

408.24   again."] Originally followed by a superscript "1," the first of eleven such numbers written in faded black ink and referring, perhaps, to working notes or a source. Mark Twain deleted most of the numbers from the typescript. He overlooked "4," "10," and "11"; "9" was deleted, then reinscribed, perhaps by another hand. The proximity of the paragraph numbers which were added to the typescript beginning at 408.25 and continuing through 409.31 may indicate a relationship between them and the canceled numbers. All paragraph numbers except 3 and 4 directly follow or precede canceled superscripts. The superscript numbers originally appeared at:

408.24 again."[1]	412.16 pollution."[7]
408.26 return."[2]	415.25 *him*."[8]
409.2 Manila."[3]	415.27 Man's?"[9]
409.22 negroes—"[4]	415.32 *killed*."[10]
409.27 *Volunteers*[5]	416.25 hells.[11]
409.31 Roll call:[6]	

409.22   negroes—"] A superscript "4" appears in the typescript. See note at 408.24.

410.9   lot."] Manuscript page 9 ends with "lot" followed by a comma, here emended to a period. Since neither "Another," which begins the inserted new page 9A, nor "A Float," which begins page 10, can appropriately follow a comma, it is possible that Mark Twain may have discarded one or more pages of manuscript here.

410.10–412.7   *Another Stranger* . . . sufficient, sir."] Mark Twain added this passage on new manuscript pages 9A–9E, probably after inserting the new pages at 408.21–409.8. The original conclusion to the new passage, canceled on the typescript, is listed at 412.7 in Mark Twain's revisions.

411.24–26   6,600 . . . 21,000] Mark Twain added up the recruiting figures on the verso of the previous manuscript page.

411.36   draft."] Added to the manuscript in pencil in a space originally left blank. In the top right corner of the manuscript page Mark Twain wrote the cue word "conscription" in pencil.

414.13   discreetly] Mark Twain wrote "sorrowfully" above "discreetly" in pencil on the typescript. Although still legible, the penciled word is smeared, and since Mark Twain normally erased words by rubbing them out, the first reading has been retained.

415.27   Man's?"] A superscript "9" appears in the typescript. See note at 408.24.

415.32   *McGugie*] Mark Twain at first misspelled the name "*McGugle.*" His revision restores the name as it appeared in the newspapers.

415.32   *killed.*"] A superscript "10" appears on the typescript. See note at 408.24.

416.2   Disposed] In the left margin of the typescript Mark Twain wrote "The new hero." in pencil. Although there is a caret, apparently added later, underneath the phrase, there is no appropriate place for it in the passage, and it appears to be a marginal note, not an interlineation.

416.17   *8th Group.*] At about this point the ink color begins to change from black to faded black, and it becomes impossible to distinguish between earlier and later revisions.

416.22–417.8   *9th . . . 17th*] Mark Twain canceled the original "ninth group" on the typescript but neglected to renumber the following groups.

416.25   hells.] A superscript "11" appears on the typescript. See note at 408.24.

418.2–3   *But . . . polluted?*"] Mark Twain added this sentence to the typescript without italics. Since manuscript italics have been restored throughout the work, italics have also been added here to conform with the first part of the motto.

418.4–6   THE PIRATE FLAG. . . . myself."] In the manuscript as in the present text, "THE PIRATE FLAG." is centered as a heading and "Inscribed" begins a new line.

However, the typist indented both "THE PIRATE FLAG." and "Inscribed . . . myself.'" as paragraphs. Presumably without checking the manuscript, the author made the passage into a single paragraph by marking "Inscribed" to run on after "FLAG." Since this revision was occasioned by a typist's error, and since similar headings elsewhere in the piece follow the manuscript rather than the revised typescript form, the manuscript reading has been restored.

419.3   pageant.] At the foot of the last typescript page Mark Twain wrote in pencil, "The new Siamese twins—Gen. Funston & Judas Iscariot." Below this note he wrote and canceled "The latest idea of a hero."

Emendations of the Copy-Text

	MTP READING	COPY-TEXT READING
405.12	Filipinos	Filippinos
*406.8	Purchases MS	"purchases"
†408.15	Independence, TS	Independence.
†409.3	¶ 5. On	5. ¶ On
*409.22	negroes—"	negroes—"4
†410.9	lot."	lot,"
412.5	you you TS	you
412.8	Philippine	Phillipine
412.23–24	Ladrones	ladrones
†413.18	*Filipinos*	*Philippinos*
413.24	*Filipinos*	*Phillipinos*
415.11	seize	sieze
*415.27	Man's?"	Man's?"9

	MTP Reading	Copy-Text Reading
*415.32	*killed."*	*killed."*[10]
†416.19	passenger TS	Passenger
*416.22	*9th*	*10th*
416.24	*10th*	*11th*
*416.25	hells.	hells.[11]
416.26	*11th*	*12th*
416.27	*12th*	*13th*
416.29	*13th*	*14th*
416.33	*14th*	*15th*
417.1	*15th*	*16th*
417.5	*16th*	*17th*
417.8	*17th*	*18th*
417.16	"IN TS	IN
*418.2–3	*But am I polluted?*	But am I polluted?
*418.4–5	[*centered*] THE PIRATE FLAG. [*flush with left margin*] Inscribed	¶ THE PIRATE FLAG. Inscribed
†418.22	extinguished	extinguished.
†419.2	pained	indignant/pained

Word Division in the Copy-Text

413.5	shirt-tail

Mark Twain's Revisions

Written in black ink

405.title	Stupendous] *interlined with a caret in faded black ink.*

405.1   At] *follows paragraph canceled in faded black ink* 'The arrangements being now complete, it will move'; *the 'A' mended from 'a'.*

405.1   it . . . world] *interlined with a caret in faded black ink.*

405.3   THE TWENTIETH CENTURY,] *originally the heading* '1st Section.' *followed by a line beginning* 'The Nineteenth Century, a fair young'; 'First' *interlined above canceled* '1st', 'Twentieth' *interlined above canceled* 'Nineteenth', *and* 'Twentieth Century' *italicized, all in black ink.* 'Division.' *interlined above canceled* 'Section.', 'First Division' *italicized,* 'The *Twentieth* Century' *changed to full capitals, and* 'First Division.' *and* 'THE TWENTIETH CENTURY,' *canceled; finally,* 'THE TWENTIETH CENTURY,' *interlined as a heading, all in faded black ink.*

405.4   creature] *follows canceled* 'maiden'.

405.6   Tammany Bosses,] *interlined with a caret in faded black ink.*

405.7   Convicts,] *interlined with a caret in faded black ink.*

405.9   CHRISTENDOM,] *added in faded black ink above canceled heading* 'Second Section' *and canceled paragraph* 'Christendom,'.

405.10   On her] *followed by* 'breast the crucified Christ reversed; on her' *canceled in faded black ink.*

405.11   golden] *interlined with a caret.*

405.12   Filipinos] *the 'F' interlined in pencil above canceled* 'Ph'.

405.14   Protruding] *follows canceled* 'Necklace'.

406.1   *Slaughter,] interlined above* 'Humbug,'; 'Humbug,' *canceled and a caret added in faded black ink.*

406.1   *Hypocrisy.] followed by* 'The one singing "The White Man's Burden," the other "The Missionary Hymn." ' *canceled on the TS.*

406.2   with motto] *originally 'with motto'; the italics canceled.*

406.4   Missionaries, and] *interlined with a caret on the TS.*

406.5   soldiers] *followed by a canceled ampersand interlined with a caret on the TS.*

406.5   with loot.] *followed by paragraph 'Poet Laureate, attended—Kipling.' canceled in faded black ink.*

406.6–7   MUSIC . . . Influence.)] *added in faded black ink above canceled heading 'Third Section.'*

406.8   Children—] *the dash written over a colon.*

406.8   Purchases] 'purchases' *in the TS; altered to* ' "purchases" ' *by Mark Twain; the MS reading has been restored. See textual notes.*

406.10   ENGLAND.] *originally began the paragraph; marked as a heading in faded black ink.*

406.11   *Supporters,*] *originally* 'Supporters,' *run on; the italics added in pencil; marked to begin a new paragraph with a paragraph sign.*

406.11   Rhodes. Followed] *originally* 'Rhodes, followed'; *the period written over the wiped-out comma and the 'F' mended from 'f' all in faded black ink.*

406.15   THE GOOD QUEEN,] *originally began the paragraph; marked as a heading in faded black ink.*

406.17   broke] *follows 'shames' interlined with a caret in black ink, then canceled in faded black ink.*

406.19   A haughty . . . sceptred.] *interlined with a caret in faded black ink.*

407.1–4   RUSSIA, . . . Followed by] 'RUSSIA,' *marked as a heading, and* 'A crowned Polar Bear, head piously a-droop, paws clasped in prayer. Followed by' *added in faded black ink on the verso of the MS page with instructions to turn over; the addition replaces the heading* 'RUSSIA.' *and paragraph* 'Followed by' *canceled in faded black ink on the recto. On the TS,* 'and mitred' *and* 'Sacred and Supreme Pontiff of the Great Church," *interlined with carets.*

407.12–17   FRANCE, . . . On foot—] *added in faded black ink on the verso of the MS page with instructions to turn over; the addition replaces the heading* 'FRANCE.' *and paragraph* 'Followed by' *canceled in faded black ink on the recto;* 'worn-out' *interlined with a caret above canceled* 'battered'; '—gagged' *follows a canceled caret.*

407.15   beloved—] *interlined above* 'gang—' *on the MS; typed as* 'rest of the beloved-gang—laureled'; '-gang' *canceled on the TS.*

407.21   *Guard of Honor—] interlined with a caret in faded black ink.*

407.21   Detachment . . . Army] *originally in italics; the italics canceled in faded black ink.*

407.21   Chinese] *interlined with a caret in faded black ink.*

407.25   GERMANIA,] 'GERMANNIA,' *interlined to replace canceled* 'GERMANY.' *in faded black ink; the second* 'N' *canceled on the TS.*

407.26   A Helmeted] 'A' *added in faded black ink.*

407.26   Mailed . . . aloft—] *originally* 'mailed Fist,'; *the* 'M' *mended from* 'm'; *the comma canceled and* 'holding . . . aloft' *interlined with a caret, both in faded black ink.*

408.2   a Monument] *originally* 'and Monument'; *a caret added following* 'and'; *then* 'and' *and the caret canceled and* 'a' *squeezed in, all in faded black ink.*

408.6   As per . . . Mr. Ament.] *added on the TS;* 'unrepudiated' *interlined with a caret.*

408.9–14   Standing . . . Followed by] *added in faded black ink on the verso of the MS page with instructions to turn over to replace heading* 'AMERICA.' *and paragraph* 'Supporters —Greed and Falsehood. Followed by' *canceled on the recto;* 'Treason', *written in pencil in the margin above* 'Falsehood', *also canceled in faded black ink.*

408.11   a noble] 'a' *interlined with a caret above canceled* 'A'.

408.11   crying] *follows canceled* 'her'.

408.12   Cap of Liberty] *originally* 'cap of liberty'; *the* 'C' *and* 'L' *mended from* 'c' *and* 'l'.

408.15–16   Independence . . . Administration] *originally* 'Independence." The Administration'; 'An allegorical Figure of' *interlined with a caret and the* 'T' *of* 'The' *mended to* 't' *in faded black ink; an ampersand added to the interlineation and the* 'A' *of* 'An' *mended to* 'a' *in pencil; the period following* 'Independence' *inadvertently left standing.*

408.21–409.8 *Fat Spanish . . . over this carrion!*"] *written in faded black ink on two inserted MS pages.*

408.22   wet-nurses.] *followed by a canceled superscript* '1' *in the MS.*

408.24   again."] *followed by superscript* '1' *in the MS;* '1' *typed on the line in the TS and then canceled in pencil. See textual note at 408.24.*

408.25   1. Banner] *the* '1.' *added on the TS.*

408.26   return."] *followed by superscript* '2' *in the MS;* '2' *typed on the line in the TS and then canceled in pencil. See textual note at 408.24.*

408.27   2. Banner] *the* '2.' *added on the TS.*

408.29–31   3. . . . 4.] '3.' *and* '4.' *added on the TS.*

409.2–3   Manila." 5. On the] *originally* 'Manila." ' *followed by superscript* '3' *and* 'On the' *run on;* '3' *typed on the line in the TS and then canceled in pencil;* '5.' *added, followed by a paragraph sign interlined with a caret. See emendation at 409.3 and textual note at 408.24.*

409.7   caressed] *originally* 'has caressed'; 'has' *canceled on the TS.*

409.9   *The Immortals] follows paragraph 'Fat Spanish Friar* wrapped in the Treaty of Paris—labeled "This is Nuts for Us." ' *canceled in faded black ink.*

409.10   *seem] the italics added in faded black ink.*

409.12   *Adjutant General—] interlined with a caret above canceled 'Secretary of War,—' all in faded black ink.*

409.14   serfs,] *originally* 'patriots'; *the 's' canceled and '-serfs,' interlined with a caret in the MS;* 'patriot-serfs,' *canceled in the TS;* 'subjects,' *added, then canceled, and* 'serfs,' *interlined with a caret.*

409.15   brothers and neighbors] *originally* 'brothers, and neighbors'; *the comma canceled and* 'old' *interlined with a caret following* 'and'; 'old' *canceled. The caret canceled in faded black ink.*

409.15   humble] *interlined with a caret.*

409.16   which] *interlined with a caret in faded black ink above canceled* 'that'.

409.18–19   'You . . . milk.'] *the italics added in faded black ink.*

409.20   China;] *the semicolon squeezed in before a canceled dash in faded black ink.*

409.20–21   —as usual—imitate?] *interlined with a caret in faded black ink above canceled* 'do?'.

409.22   negroes—"] *followed by superscript* '4' *on the MS;* '4' *typed on the line in the TS and inadvertently left standing. See textual note at 408.24.*

409.23   *Frivolous] interlined with a caret in faded black ink.*

409.23   didn't] *originally* 'did not'; 'not' *canceled and* 'n't' *interlined with a caret in faded black ink.*

409.24   only] *interlined with a caret.*

409.25   *Adjutant General.] interlined in pencil above* 'Secretary of War.' *canceled in faded black ink.*

409.27   6. *Body . . . Volunteers*] *'Volunteers' followed by super-*
          script '5' in the MS; '5' typed on the line in the TS and
          then canceled in pencil; '6.' added in pencil on the TS
          preceding 'Body'. See textual note at 408.24.

409.27   three] *interlined with a caret above canceled* 'twelve'.

409.28   patriotic product] *originally* 'products'; *the 's' of* 'prod-
          ucts' *canceled and* 'patriotic' *interlined with a caret.*

409.28   a week's] *interlined with a caret in faded black ink above*
          canceled '8 days' '.

409.28   recruiting] *follows canceled* 'recruiting in 600 recruiting
          stations'.

409.31   7. Roll call:] *'Roll call:' originally run on following*
          'bayonet.' and followed by superscript '6' interlined
          with a caret; '6' typed on the line in the TS and then
          canceled in pencil; a paragraph sign and '7.' interlined
          with a caret preceding 'Roll'. See textual note at 408.24.

410.2   Allerheiligenpotstausenddonnerwetter] *originally* 'Alle-
          heiligekaiserpotstausenddonnerwetter'; *the 'ts' of* 'pots'
          written over two wiped-out unrecovered letters on the
          MS. On the TS, 'kaiser' *canceled and* 'r' *and* 'n' *inter-*
          lined with carets in pencil following 'Alle' *and* 'heilige'.

410.3   *Adjutant General—*] *interlined in faded black ink above*
          canceled 'Secretary of War—'.

410.4   enthusiasm] *follows canceled* 'of'.

410.7   a scant] *interlined with a caret.*

410.8   *Frivolous*] *interlined with a caret in faded black ink.*

410.8–9   "Thank . . . lot."] *originally* 'Thank . . . lot,'; *the quota-*
          tion marks added in pencil; the comma after 'lot' *inad-*
          vertently left standing.

410.10–412.7 *Another . . . sufficient, sir."*] *written in faded black ink*
          on five inserted MS pages, the last portion of which was
          canceled on the TS. See revision at 412.7.

410.22   thinking of how] 'of' *interlined with a caret.*

410.30   and foreigners] *interlined with a caret above canceled* 'and men'.

410.31   long] *follows canceled* 'tough job'.

411.1   sir:] *originally* 'sir—'; *the dash canceled and the colon added.*

411.12   That . . . expensive.] *interlined with a caret above canceled* 'But we can't do that, sir.'

411.17   12 months] *the* '12' *interlined with a caret above canceled* '6'.

411.18   5000] *originally* '2,500'; '2,' *canceled and the third zero added.*

411.18   End of 1902.] *interlined with a caret above canceled* 'Next 12 months, 50 a'; *the* '12' *interlined with a caret above canceled* '6'.

411.18–19   For 1903 . . . 1200.] *interlined with a caret; the caret in pencil.*

411.33   full-up] *the hyphen interlined with a caret on the TS.*

411.36   draft."] *added in pencil.*

412.1–2   —now . . . game—and] *interlined with a caret following a canceled ampersand.*

412.3   asking,] *followed by canceled* 'now that they have found out the Government's game' *interlined with a caret.*

412.4   your countrymen,] *interlined with a caret above canceled* 'them,'.

412.5   They] *the* 'y' *written over wiped-out* 're'.

412.5   a minute.] *follows a canceled dash.*

412.7   sufficient, sir."] *originally followed by* '(To West Point Cadet: "Take this person and exercise him. When finished, report here with the remains." '; *the parenthesis canceled on the MS;* 'To West . . . remains." ' *canceled on the TS.*

412.10   one year] *originally* 'ten months'; 'two years' *interlined*
                with a caret in faded black ink above canceled 'ten
                months'; *then* 'two' *canceled,* 'one' *interlined above*
                and the 's' *of* 'years' *canceled, all in pencil.*

412.11   America, this year,] 'this year,' *interlined with a caret*
                and the comma following 'America' *added, both in faded*
                black ink.

412.11 $1,] *originally* '$7,'; '6' *written over* '7', *then canceled*
                and '1' *interlined, all in pencil.*

412.12   gradually] *interlined with a caret in pencil.*

412.15–16   A *Large* . . . "pollution."] 'A *Large* . . . "pollution." ',
                followed by superscript '7', *added in faded black ink on*
                the verso of the MS page with instructions to turn over;
                '7' *typed on the line in the TS and canceled in pencil.*
                See textual note at 408.24.

412.17   Brewer] *the* 'rewer' *of* 'Brewer' *written over wiped-out*
                'rewer'.

412.20   Civil War] *originally* 'war'; 'Civil' *interlined in pencil;*
                a caret below 'Civil' *added and the* 'W' *of* 'War' *mended*
                from 'w' *in faded black ink.*

412.20   man] *follows canceled* 'life'.

412.23   *Frivolous*] *interlined with a caret in faded black ink.*

412.25–28   "Excuse . . . Administration."] *the quotation marks*
                added in pencil on the TS.

412.29   *Filipino*] *the* 'F' *of* 'Filipino' *written over a* 'P'.

412.30   Report:] *the colon mended from a period on the TS.*

412.34–35   *We have . . . deportation."] the italics added in faded*
                black ink.

412.36   *Spanish*] *interlined with a caret in faded black ink.*

413.4   full] *follows a canceled comma; the* 'f' *of* 'full' *written*
                over an unrecovered letter.

413.7   CONGRESS] 'Congress' *originally run on after* 'Amend-
               ment." '; *altered to full capitals and marked to begin a
               new paragraph with a paragraph sign in pencil.*

413.8   noble] *carelessly written without an* 'l' *on the MS and
               typed* 'robe'; 'robe' *canceled and* 'noble' *interlined with
               a caret on the TS.*

413.11   equal. . . . .] *originally* 'equal." . . . .'; *the quotation
               marks canceled on the TS.*

413.11   Now we are . . . . .] *follows canceled* 'We here highly
               resolve . . . . th'; *an ellipsis interlined with a caret then
               canceled preceding* 'Now'; *the ellipsis following* 'are'
               interlined with a caret above canceled 'engaged in a
               great civil war,'.

413.13   endure."] *originally* 'endure." '; *the quotation marks
               canceled and* '. . . . . We here highly resolve that this
               nation, under God, shall have a new birth of freedom." '
               added, both in black ink; then '. . . . . We here . . . free-
               dom." ' *canceled and the quotation marks following*
               'endure' *restored, both in faded black ink.*

413.18   *Filipinos,* marked] *originally* 'Philippinoes'; *the* 's' *wiped
               out, the* 'e' *canceled with a dash and* 's' *written over the
               dash before* 'marked' *was written; typed* 'Philippino-
               marked'; *the hyphen canceled and* 's,' *interlined with a
               caret following* 'Philippino'. *See emendations.*

413.18–23   "Rebels." . . . it is."] *originally* ' "Rebels" because they
               resisted an authority to which they had not sworn al-
               legiance.'; *the period added after* 'Rebels', 'because . . .
               allegiance.' *canceled and* 'Shade . . . allegiance.' *added
               on the verso of the MS page with instructions to turn
               over, all in faded black ink;* 'pro' *of* 'promised' *written
               over wiped-out* 'swo'; *following* 'allegiance' *on verso, the
               instruction to turn over canceled in pencil and* ' "Is it
               not . . . it is." ' *added in faded black ink.*

413.25   *Band of Porto Ricans] the italics added in faded black
               ink.*

413.25   "Subjects."] *follows canceled ' "Unclassifiable." '*

413.26   the Frivolous Stranger] *originally* 'that Stranger' *pre-
              ceded by an unrecovered canceled word; a caret added
              preceding* 'that', *the caret and* 'that' *canceled,* 'the
              Frivolous' *interlined with a caret, and the italics can-
              celed, all in black ink.*

413.27   'Unclassifiable?' "] *the first single quotation mark
              mended from a double quotation mark and the last inter-
              lined with a caret, both in pencil.*

413.28   "They do not] *follows* ' "Because they have sworn al-
              legiance to the United States,' *canceled both in black
              and in faded black ink.*

413.36   Frivolous] *interlined with a caret in faded black ink.*

414.6   CUBA,] *originally began the subsequent paragraph; can-
              celed and rewritten as a heading in faded black ink.*

414.13   business,] *originally* 'busy,'; *the* 'y' *and the comma can-
              celed and* 'iness,' *added in faded black ink.*

414.13   discreetly] 'sorrowfully' *interlined in pencil above* 'dis-
              creetly' *on the TS, then wiped out. See textual notes.*

414.14   Each . . . banner.] *added in faded black ink.*

414.15   1. Banner] 'Ban' *written over wiped-out* 'Mott'; '1.'
              added in faded black ink.

414.17   2.] *added in faded black ink.*

414.18   speak."] *originally* 'speak." '; *the quotation marks can-
              celed and* 'Don't *think, at all." ' added in faded black
              ink; then* 'Don't . . . all." ' *canceled and quotation marks
              following* 'speak.' *restored in pencil.*

414.20   majestic] *interlined above canceled* 'great' *on the TS.*

414.25   with Spain] *follows canceled* 'buying air castles from
              Spain for Twenty Million Dollars.'; *within the cancella-
              tion* 'Spain' *followed by a canceled period.*

414.25   a pair of] *interlined with a caret above canceled* 'two'.

414.28   lot.] *follows 'jo' interlined with a caret, then canceled,*
                in faded black ink.

415.1   inscribed—] *interlined in pencil above canceled* 'with
                motto—'.

415.2   *had*] *the italics added in faded black ink.*

415.3   obtrusive] *interlined with a caret in faded black ink.*

415.8   Upon] *follows canceled dash; the 'U' of 'Upon' mended*
                from 'u' in faded black ink.

415.8   them are] *follows canceled* 'them 10 ships bringing'; *the*
                '10' *written over* '16'.

415.10   inscribed—] *interlined with a caret in pencil above can-*
                celed 'with motto—'.

415.15   victorious] *interlined with a caret.*

415.16   Filipinos] *the 'F' written over a 'P'.*

415.18   bearing] *interlined with a caret.*

415.19–20   *three . . . 694] added in faded black ink in a space origi-*
                nally left blank.

415.20   wounded."] *followed by superscript '8' written and can-*
                celed in faded black ink. See revision at 415.24.

415.21   *Star Spangled*] *interlined with a caret above canceled*
                'Black'.

415.22   *Float*] *originally followed paragraph* 'General's Pennon,
                with motto—"Educated at West Point." '; ' "Educated
                at' *canceled and* ' "Graduated from the Hazing Depart-
                ment of' *interlined with a caret in faded black ink;* 'Gen-
                eral's . . . Point" ' *canceled on the TS.*

415.22   Waving over it—] *added in faded black ink.*

415.23   *Star Spangled*] *interlined with a caret above canceled*
                'Black'.

415.24–25   mother . . . him."] *originally* 'mother—' *followed by a*
                blank line; the colon added and ' "We never . . . him." '

followed by superscript '8' squeezed in in faded black ink; '8' typed on the line in the TS and canceled in pencil. See revision at 415.20 and textual note at 408.24.

415.26–27   *Banner . . .* Brown Man's?"] *'Banner . . .* Brown Man's." ', *followed by a superscript '9', added in faded black ink on the verso of the MS page with instructions to turn over; the 'h' of 'has' mended from 'H'; '9' typed on the line in the TS and canceled in pencil; then superscript '9.' added and the question mark mended from the period, both in pencil. See textual note at 408.24.*

415.29   *Star-Spangled Banner,] interlined with a caret above canceled* 'Placard,'.

415.30   seven] *originally 'seven'; the italics canceled in pencil,* 'seven' *canceled and* 'seven' *interlined with a caret in faded black ink.*

415.32   McGugie] *originally 'McGugle'; the 'l' canceled and 'i' interlined with a caret in pencil. See textual notes.*

415.32   killed."] *followed by superscript '10' and canceled instructions to turn over; '10' typed on the line in the TS. See textual note at 408.24.*

415.33   *Star-Spangled] interlined with a caret above canceled* 'Black'.

415.35   persuade] *interlined with a caret above canceled* 'teach'.

415.36   neighbors—. . . 'patriotism.' "] *originally* 'neighbors." '; *the quotation marks canceled, the period mended to a dash, and* 'and to add the last possible infamy to the act by naming it 'patriotism.' " ' *added in faded black ink;* 'to add . . . by naming' *canceled and* 'call' *interlined with a caret in pencil.*

416.8   clergyman.] *followed by squeezed-in* 'Court moss-grown with age since trial of the case began.' *in pencil on the MS; the addition canceled in pencil on the TS.*

416.13   1800] *the '8' written over '7'.*

416.14   and all hands] *follows wiped-out and canceled* 'and nobo'.

416.14   without complaint] *originally* 'without thought of complaint'; 'thought of' *canceled on the TS in pencil.*

416.14   *Banner,] interlined with a caret in faded black ink to replace canceled* 'Banner,'; *an unrecovered word added beneath the line in faded black ink and canceled in pencil.*

416.15–16   "When . . . other."] *added in faded black ink on the verso of the MS page with instructions to turn over to replace* ' "America the Land of the Meek." ' *canceled in faded black ink on the recto.*

Written in faded black ink from 416.17 to end

416.18–19   Roasting passenger] *originally* 'Passenger'; 'Roasting' *interlined with a caret, wiped out, and then retraced; the* 'P' *of* 'Passenger' *not reduced to* 'p'.

416.19   piously] *follows a canceled comma.*

416.20   in fortifying] *interlined with a caret above canceled* 'in preparing'.

416.21   public."] *originally followed by paragraph* '9th Group. The mayor fishing for Irish votes; the flag at full mast and the kindly Queen dead.' *canceled on the TS.*

416.22–23   *9th Group . . . patients.]* '*10th Group . . . patients*' *added on the verso of the MS page with instructions to turn over. See textual notes.*

416.24   *10th Group.]* '*11th Group*' *in MS; originally* '*10th Group*.'; *a* '1' *written over the zero. See textual note at 416.22.*

416.25   hells.] *followed by superscript* '11' *in the MS;* '11' *typed on the line in the TS. See textual note at 408.24.*

416.33–34   owned . . . leader,] *interlined with a caret.*

416.34   print.] *followed by canceled* 'Leader's name—'.

417.3 $50] *followed by* 'apiece' *canceled on the TS.*

417.9–10   *undergoing treatment]* *interlined with a caret in pencil*
                above canceled 'being treated'.

417.10   *unnameable]* *interlined with a caret in pencil above can-*
                celed 'sexual'.

417.11   sarcastic] *interlined with a caret.*

417.16   IN OUR] *originally* 'IT IS'; 'IN' *mended from* 'IT'; 'IS'
                canceled.

417.18   *Frivolous]* *interlined with a caret.*

417.19   *the]* *interlined with a caret.*

417.19   *Ceremonies.]* *originally followed by* 'To the Stranger.';
                'Frivolous' *interlined with a caret before* 'Stranger' *on*
                the MS; 'To . . . Stranger' *canceled in pencil on the TS.*

417.22   property—] *followed by canceled* 'to-wit:'.

417.29–418.1   A Crowned . . . concubines—joint property of the Firm.]
                added on the verso of the MS page with instructions to
                turn over; 'Crowned', 'joint' *and* 'joint' *interlined with*
                carets; on the TS, 'Sultan' *interlined with a caret above*
                canceled 'Monarch'.

418.2–3   *last. But . . . polluted?"]* *originally* 'last." '; *on the TS,*
                the quotation marks canceled and 'But . . . polluted?" '
                added. See textual note.

418.10–11   *Declaration of Independence.]* *added in pencil.*

418.13   *Ibid.]* *added in pencil.*

418.20   *Declaration of Independence.]* *added in pencil.*

418.22   World] *originally* 'world'; *the* 'W' *of* 'World' *mended*
                from 'w' *in pencil.*

418.22   extinguished and reversed.] *originally* 'extinguished.';
                'and reversed.' *added; the period following* 'extinguished'
                inadvertently left standing.

418.22–25   Followed by . . . crêpe.] *interlined to replace canceled heading* 'THE PRESIDENT' *and canceled* 'Bearing the American Flag—furled, draped with crêpe, and reversed.'; *in the canceled paragraph* 'THE' *follows canceled* 'A' *and an unfinished letter,* 'furled,' *interlined with a caret above canceled* 'folded,' *and* 'draped . . . crêpe,' *interlined with a caret.*

419.2   pained] *interlined above* 'indignant' *in pencil on the TS.*

419.3   pageant.] *originally followed by paragraph* ' "These pigmy traitors will pass and perish, and be forgotten—they and their treasons. And I will say again, with the hope and conviction of that other day of darkness and peril, 'This nation, under God, shall have a new birth of freedom.' " '; 'they' *follows canceled* 'I say it again'; 'pigmy . . . treasons.' *canceled and* 'dark days, with their treasons, will pass, and be forgotten.' *interlined with a caret in pencil above the cancellation; then* ' "These . . . freedom.' " ' *canceled in pencil.*

Flies and Russians

Textual Commentary

The manuscript is copy-text. As the headnote indicates, page numbers show that "Flies and Russians" was originally part of a longer work, probably "The Czar's Soliloquy." No ambiguous compound is hyphenated at the end of a line in the copy-text.

Textual Notes

423.15–16   absolutely] Mark Twain canceled "absolutely," inter-
                 lined "quite" above it, and wrote "stet" in the margin.
                 It is possible that the "stet" was written before "quite"
                 was interlined. If so, he intended "quite" to be the
                 final reading, but forgot to cancel "stet" when he made
                 the addition. However, since it is impossible to deter-
                 mine a time sequence for the changes, "stet" has been
                 regarded as a direction to restore the original wording.

Emendations of the Copy-Text

	MTP READING	COPY-TEXT READING
421.1	A PAUSE	A *pause*
422.36	long-felt	long felt

Mark Twain's Revisions

Written in black ink

421.1   (A *pause*] *follows canceled original title* 'A Difficult
                 Conundrum'; *canceled paragraph* 'The basis of it is the

following cablegram, which I have been studying for two months; (the italics are mine):'; *and canceled instructions to insert cablegram;* '(the italics are mine):' *added following a semicolon mended from a colon;* 'A pause . . . read.)' *interlined with a caret in dark blue ink; then closing parenthesis canceled and* 'Takes . . . fascinated.)' *added in faded black ink;* 'and stands . . . fascinated' *written on the verso of the MS page with instructions to turn over.*

421.5–6   approximately plausible] *interlined with a caret.*

421.7   discontinued] *followed by canceled* 'and transferred to the cemetery'.

421.8   these . . . may] *originally* 'these, Russia may'; *the comma canceled;* 'the' *and* 'nation' *interlined with carets;* 'n' *added to* 'Russia'.

421.8   as an] *interlined with a caret above canceled* 'as a conspicuous'.

421.12   were] *follows canceled* 'were'.

421.13   opinion,—] *the dash interlined with a caret.*

421.13   months of] *followed by canceled* 'patient'.

422.5   and add the bee,] *interlined with a caret above a canceled comma.*

422.12   to live on.] *squeezed in at the end of the line following a canceled period.*

422.15–16   a single family . . . oppressors,] 'a' *added at the end of the line;* 'single family of heartless brutes and assassins,' *interlined with a caret at the beginning of the line below;* 'bloody and' *interlined with a caret and* 'oppressors,' *interlined with a caret above canceled* 'brutes and assassins,'.

422.22   ever going] *follows canceled* 'g'.

422.24   time] *followed by canceled* 'of'.

422.25   grotesque] *interlined with a caret above canceled* 'flab-by'.

422.29   fully] *interlined with a caret.*

422.30   have] *followed by canceled* 'every'.

422.34   idea] *follows canceled* 'ori'.

422.36   We all know] *interlined with a caret following canceled* 'You know and I know, that'; *canceled* 'that' *follows* 'know' *within the interlineation.*

423.7   moan] *interlined with a caret above canceled* 'wail'.

423.10   mistake] *followed by a canceled comma.*

423.13   to be] *follows canceled* 'be'.

423.13–14   persuasions, . . . intellect.] *the comma mended from a period;* 'nor . . . intellect.' *interlined with a caret; originally* 'gay intellect'; *then* 'and frivolous' *interlined with a caret; finally* 'gay and' *canceled.*

423.15–16   It . . . useless.] *interlined with a caret;* 'quite' *interlined with a caret above canceled* 'absolutely' *within the interlineation; the instruction* 'stet' *written in the margin. See textual note.*

423.17   By and by] *interlined with a caret above canceled* 'Then'.

423.19   want] *follows canceled* 'want in the market'.

423.22   Next] *interlined with a caret above canceled* 'Then'.

423.24   pterodactyl] *originally* 'pterodactyle'; *the final* 'e' *wiped out.*

423.24   better.] *interlined with a caret above canceled* 'politer.'

423.25   alligator, a sarcasm] *originally* 'alligator, a Countess Massiglia: a sarcasm'; 'kind of' *interlined with a caret preceding* 'Countess'; 'Ribaudi-' *interlined preceding* 'Massiglia:'; *the colon following* 'Massiglia' *mended to a semicolon; then* 'kind . . . Massiglia; a' *canceled and* 'a' *interlined with a caret preceding* 'sarcasm'.

423.32   now extinct] *interlined with a caret.*

423.35–36   a museum . . . her.] *interlined with a caret above canceled* 'she never thought of a museum.'

424.3   achieved by her] *interlined with a caret above canceled* 'she has made'.

424.3   fifteen hundred] *originally* 'a hundred and fifty'; 'a' *and* 'and fifty' *canceled;* 'fifteen' *interlined with a caret.*

424.15   and worry and cussing] *interlined with a caret.*

424.19–20   become? ¶ And] *instructions to leave space squeezed in between the two paragraphs.*

424.22   How] 'ow' *mended from what appears to be* 'ard'.

424.25   would] 'w' *mended from* 'c'.

424.29   applied.] *followed by Mark Twain's signature and* 'November 29' *written above canceled* 'October 10'; 'November 29' *canceled. Below the date, written and canceled in faded black ink, is* 'Postscript.' *[centered] and the paragraph* 'I grumbled it out as above, at that date. Not for publication, but only to get the fret of it out of my mind. But I see, now, how mistaken I was'; 'grumbled it out' *interlined with a caret above canceled* 'wrote it'; 'only' *followed by canceled* 'merely'; 'fret of it' *interlined with a caret to replace canceled* 'irritating subject'; 'mind' *followed by canceled* 'so that I could do some work which I needed to do.'; *the period following* 'mind' *mended from a comma.*

The Fable of the Yellow Terror

Textual Commentary

The manuscript is the copy-text; the author's unrevised typescript is also in the Mark Twain Papers. There are no textual notes, and no ambiguous compound is hyphenated at the end of a line in the manuscript.

Emendations of the Copy-Text

	MTP READING	COPY-TEXT READING
429.7	Grasshopper	grasshopper

Mark Twain's Revisions

426.4	etiquette] *follows canceled* 'the'.
426.9	spread it] *follows canceled* 'cram it.'
426.13	pagan insects] *originally* 'pagans'; *the 's' canceled and* 'insects' *interlined with a caret.*
426.15	trader-bugs] *originally* 'traders'; *the 's' canceled and* '-bugs' *interlined with a caret here and at 426.16.*
426.16	diplomat-bugs] *originally* 'diplomats'; *the 's' canceled and* '-bugs' *interlined with a caret.*
426.16	undertaker-bugs] *interlined with a caret above canceled* 'soldiers and gunboats'; *originally* 'undertakers'; *the 's' canceled and* '-bugs' *added.*
426.18	deathbed,] *the comma mended from a period.*
426.18–19	Butterfly] 'B' *mended from* 'b'.
427.6	a weak] *follows canceled* 'an'.

427.8   nothing at all.] *followed by canceled* 'he despised them.'; *the period mended from a comma.*

427.8   he went] *follows canceled* 'he sent a missionary'.

427.13   shoving] *originally* 'shovel'; 'ing' *written over wiped-out* 'el'.

427.22   persuasions.] *followed by canceled paragraph* 'At l'.

427.26   were tired] 'were' *interlined with a caret above canceled* 'got'.

427.28–29   yearning] *interlined with a caret above canceled* 'affectionate'.

427.30   moral-plated] *interlined with a caret above canceled* 'pious'.

427.32   contented] *followed by canceled* 'and ignorant'.

428.3–4   by themselves] 'by' *interlined with a caret above canceled* 'to'.

428.8   each of] *interlined with a caret.*

428.10   damages on] 'on' *written over an ampersand.*

428.25   clever] *interlined with a caret.*

428.36–429.1   while working this specialty] *interlined with a caret; the comma preceding added.*

429.2   likewise] *interlined with a caret.*

429.3   prompt and] *interlined with a caret.*

429.5   the weapons] *originally* 'them'; *the* 'm' *canceled and* 'weapons' *interlined with a caret.*

429.7   supplied] *interlined above canceled* 'furnished'.

429.25   conferring] *interlined with a caret.*

429.25–26   annexing] *interlined with a caret.*

429.29   lose your stings] *follows canceled* 'be merely'.

429.30   and remain] *interlined with a caret.*

The Recurrent Major and Minor Compliment

Textual Commentary

The manuscript is copy-text; the author's unrevised typescript is also in the Mark Twain Papers. There are no textual notes, and no ambiguous compound is hyphenated at the end of a line in the manuscript.

Emendations of the Copy-Text

	MTP READING	COPY-TEXT READING
431.6	strength TS	strenth

Mark Twain's Revisions

431.title   Major and Minor] *interlined with a caret.*

431.1   A beautiful girl] *originally* 'I suppose that a beautiful girls'; 'I suppose that' *canceled,* 'a' *mended to* 'A', *and the apparently inadvertent* 's' *of* 'girls' *canceled.*

431.2   major] *interlined with a caret.*

431.5   it is paid] *interlined with a caret.*

431.6   splendid] *interlined with a caret.*

431.8   it is] *interlined with a caret.*

431.11   great,] *followed by canceled* 'and the sound of it is such music to your spirit'.

432.3   detects and compliments] *follows canceled* 'co'.

432.4   ten of] *interlined with a caret.*

432.5   —hardly a response, indeed.] *interlined with a caret above a canceled period.*

432.17–18   takes . . . him.] *follows canceled* 'has no'.

432.20   imagining] *followed by canceled* 'that'.

432.27   "I believe] *originally run-on; marked to begin a new paragraph with a paragraph sign.*

432.34   reflect] *followed by canceled* 'up'.

432.37   large and] 'and' *interlined with a caret.*

433.13   dread,] *follows canceled* 'the'.

433.13   sleepless nights,] *interlined with a caret.*

Ancients in Modern Dress

Textual Commentary

The manuscript is copy-text. There are no textual notes, and no ambiguous compound is hyphenated at the end of a line in the manuscript.

Emendations of the Copy-Text

	MTP READING	COPY-TEXT READING
436.9	to see	too see

Mark Twain's Revisions

435.3	a revelation which] *follows canceled* 'one'.
435.8	her friends] *interlined with a caret.*
435.8	think] *originally* 'thinks'; *the* 's' *canceled.*
435.20	We] *follows canceled* 'Shaks'.
436.31	of his Holiness] *follows canceled* 'of the'.

A Letter from the Comet

Textual Commentary

The manuscript is copy-text. There are no emendations and no textual notes.

Word Division in the Copy-Text

439.2   overlook

Mark Twain's Revisions

438.6   annoying.] *followed by canceled* 'What goes with those people? And w'.

438.8   fellow] *follows canceled* 'youn'.

438.14   forward] *followed by canceled* 'to'.

439.4   thirty million years.] *follows canceled* 'eight hundred thousand years.'

439.12   him] *interlined with a caret above canceled* 'them'.

Old Age

Textual Commentary

The manuscript is copy-text. There are no textual notes, and no ambiguous compound is hyphenated at the end of a line in the manuscript.

Emendations of the Copy-Text

	MTP READING	COPY-TEXT READING
441.1	here	there/here
441.21	into indefinite	into bearded/indefinite
442.1	aggressive	large/aggressive

Mark Twain's Revisions

441.3	care-free] *the hyphen interlined with a caret.*
441.4	novel] *interlined with a caret above canceled* 'new'.
441.4	striking,] *the comma mended from a period.*
441.6	perfectly] *a hyphen interlined with a caret and canceled between* 'per' *and* 'fectly'.
441.7	this?] *followed by canceled quotation marks.*
441.7	this talk] 'this' *mended from what appears to be* 'the'.
441.10	natural;] *followed by canceled* 'when you reflect;'; *the semicolon following* 'natural' *mended from a comma.*
441.11	world's] *interlined with a caret.*
441.12	behind oxen;] *follows canceled* 'in the'.

441.12   when . . . pace] *interlined with a caret above a canceled ampersand.*

441.14   69; 69 looked like] *follows canceled* '69; 69 looks like'.

441.14–15   back . . . beginning.] *interlined with a caret above a comma mended from a period.*

442.3   foreboding Age,] *the comma added to replace a canceled semicolon.*

442.5–6   of a foolish dream] *follows canceled* 'of a dream'.

442.7   You] *the* 'Y' *mended from* 'y'.

Word Division in This Volume

To facilitate quotation, ambiguous compounds hyphenated in the copy-text which happen to be hyphenated at the end of a line in this volume are listed here. Ambiguous compounds hyphenated at the end of a line in this volume are written as single unhyphenated words in the copy-text unless they appear here.

70.5	farm-fence	240.8	helter-skelter
80.5	pie-slice	261.15	dry-swallowing
80.7	much-worn	262.10	*to-morrow*
92.18	thunder-blast	277.1	to-day
95.28	such-like	300.27	mother-like
113.7	far-reaching	300.31	re-change
113.9	fore-ordered	300.34	fore-front
127.1	after-effects	304.18	hard-working
142.8	over-adequately	320.36	over-anxious
168.4	dome-like	322.15	bargain-counter
170.25	arm-chair	334.22	law-making
173.12	sub-cellars	341.33	door-yards
178.19	storm-blue	346.27	snow-white
190.2	baby-chair	353.16	stage-coach
199.24	old-time	353.18	Ox-wagons
202.28	looking-glass	354.30	slave-pen
203.5	sailor-knot	366.26	wide-spread
217.16	far-away	368.28	candle-flame
219.27	fellow-feeling	375.5	spike-tailed
230.25	man-o'-warsman	427.20	hard-working
235.16	dust-cloud	442.3	white-headed

The text of this book is set in Electra, a type face designed by W. A. Dwiggins (1880–1956) for the Mergenthaler Linotype Company and first made available in 1935. Electra avoids the extreme contrast between "thick" and "thin" elements that marks most modern faces, and is without eccentricities which catch the eye and interfere with reading. It is a simple, readable type face which immediately conveys a feeling of ease, vigor, and speed, characteristics that were much prized by Dwiggins. Headings are set in Michelangelo and Palatino, two display faces designed by Hermann Zapf for Stempel Type Founders in 1950. These graceful types blend admirably with the text face.

The book was composed and printed by Heritage Printers, Inc., Charlotte, North Carolina, and bound by Mountain States Bindery, Salt Lake City, Utah. Paper was manufactured by P. H. Glatfelter Company, Spring Grove, Pennsylvania.